A Dance of Mist & Fury

R.A.Morley

Table of Contents

This is a work of fiction. Names, characters, places, and incidents either are the product of the author's imagination or are used fictitiously. Any resemblance to actual persons, living or dead, events, or locales is entirely coincidental.

Dedications

Thank you to all the friends who encouraged my imagination and made this book possible. And to those who lied to me about what the inspiration-based books were about. I hated it. Honestly, why would you do that? There was no need for that. But we had fun trying to figure it out and coming up with these concepts.

Thank you to my artist Jubalina, who always manages to capture the beauty and grit of my stories and characters.

Thank you to Sappha, Anne, and Ian for enduring the prior with me, and the hype for reimagining that became this book.

Dedications Continued

Chase Rahilly	Franchesca Caram
Kayla Ann	Emma Laeser
Shanon S.D. Huston	Steven Byrd
Egao Chan	Alexandra Corrsin
mrgiddykitty	Ashley Dougan
Tetiana Kocherhan	Helen Ellison
John "AcesofDeath" Mullens	

And in loving memory of
John Hoddy

There is the great lesson of

"Beauty & the Beast" that

a thing must be loved before

it is loveable

-Dupuis

Chapter 1
One Summer's Day

Summer, and the rainfall passed through gently this year. It seemed like, ever since my mother passed away, our village had been subjected to misfortune. She'd died the year of a drought, when harvests were poor and taxes high, and no amount of bucketing water from the river could compensate. The fish must've known, because there were so few that year as well. We managed to mend the fields in the following year, and the tea trees stubbornly held to hope and refused to die just like we did.

Two years after, the monsoons made up for their missed time, and were merciless. The river swelled so high, more than half the fishing boats were stolen by the rushing water, and anything that was normally a safe distance was swept away with them. That included poor Renzo's hut. Thankfully, everyone in that family was wise enough to seek higher ground, and asked for shelter. The fields were another matter. Everything flooded so badly or got washed away. Worst were the landslides that buried so much.

A terrible earthquake took away any comfort we had in the following year. Any part of the tea field, unlucky enough to be in the softest soil, was swallowed up. Other houses suffered, and only by the grace of heaven did none of them collapse.

After that, hardly anyone had time to do anything else but pick up the pieces and try to make do. Instead of getting rid of us, the droughts and floods and earthquakes brought us closer together. We all worked to help fix houses and unbury the fields. We shared our tools and clothes, patiently waiting for the merchants to pass through and try to replace anything that was lost. Though, sometimes, it was too costly, and we'd have to wait for the following year.

It wasn't a miserable life. My mother would take my twin brother and I out into the forests, showing us how to find fruit trees and animal tracks. I learned where all the peach and plum and tangerine trees were; but my favorites were the round pears and the apricot trees. I also learned to be mindful of the ground as well, and to respect distance between myself and snakes going about their business.

When we were small, mother would draw the butterflies while the two of us stuffed our faces with tasty fruits and berries. Two of a kind, she'd say. We were like the hare, so similar that it was hard to tell us apart, especially as newborns. So, she gave us the same names. Hisa and Hisato. And we never resented it. Our older brothers were always too busy for us in the beginning, working to appear grown up. We'd always rush to share our delicious finds when we saw them coming home, and they would shower us with praise.

It was never an easy life, but it was also not an unhappy one. Not all the time at least.

When our mother died of fever, I clung to the rabbit doll she'd sewn for me, and Hisato to his. They were soft, made from the most expensive material we could afford at the time—when times were good and plenty. At nine years old, I was suddenly the woman of our home, with three brothers and a father to look after.

I cooked what I knew how to make, which wasn't very much, and did all the cleaning. My father took care of any repairs around the house, and helped me to tend to the ducks and the garden. When there was nothing to be done at the house, he'd set to fishing. Hisato and our second eldest brother, Raeden, would go out hunting every day. They'd learned how to cure the hides so they could be sold or made into something from a more experienced member of the village; in exchange, they always shared some of the meat from whatever they caught on Mount Tora. Only our eldest brother, Kenta, worked in the fields.

On my twelfth year, a pox ravaged the village. I tried to look after my family, but I didn't know what to do and was ill with it myself. I prayed and prayed, often crying myself to sleep in frustration. My prayers were answered though. In my dreams, I saw one of the Juneun, a heavenly spirit, heal us with hands that were cool and soothing. Though, we were speckled with teeny scars all over our bodies. They were easily overlooked, however, and I thought nothing of it for a long time.

I was simply thankful that I wouldn't have to mourn my father or one of my brothers, and said so in every prayer thereafter. If I had an extra coin, I made sure to give it to the shrine just before the red gate further up the mountain.

My brothers would try to save up all year, and would surprise me with a gift when they could afford it. I loved trying to draw like our mother did; and she would give me praise for my attempt, even though they weren't very good at all. After she passed, it was my favorite way to spend any free time. Drawing reminded me of her, and felt special, so I kept practicing. And my brothers would surprise me with canvas and paint and brushes. The brushes were often old, and the canvas would have a hole or scuffs, but I loved them all the same. On a very good year, after selling the pelts, they afforded a brand-new brush and canvas; but couldn't afford paints after it. I smiled so wide that day, admiring the taught perfection of one and the soft, splendid bristles of the other.

Before my fifteenth year, I used to help the other young girls in the tea fields every spring. A good harvest often paid the taxes and made for fine offerings to the spirits of the mountain. We'd ask for their protection, and to bless our homes in dire times. When we tried to recover some of the swallowed-up trees from a massive mud slide the previous rain, a wicked branch swatted my face and left a large, ugly scar. I was fourteen. That same spring, Hisato climbed higher on the mountain to ask for medicines. My wound was so bad that it'd made me sick. He found a medicine woman, and hastily come down the mountain, spraining his ankle in the process. Father tended to us the best he could.

When I was well again, I tried to continue on. A year later, as the youngest girl in the village that reached her womanhood, I took the children into the woods—the same as my mother had done—to teach all that I knew. One day, after it'd rained, one of the children slipped. I hurried to catch them, losing my own balance in the process and hit my head against a boulder. This time, the wound didn't get infected and make me sick, but left an unshapely scar over my eyebrow opposite my scarred cheek.

I knew I would never be beautiful. I was barely fifteen, and would always be ugly from there on. There was a hope in me that, if I was clever enough, perhaps I could hide those ugly things behind my hair. That hope was stolen midspring with an outbreak of lice, and we all had to shave our heads. I allowed Kenta to take off my long hair, crying as he did. It was that or risk falling ill and spreading them again to my brothers.

So, I spent my days weaving together straw sandals for us all, and extras to trade for winter shoes since I didn't know how to make those. Kenta brought in more rice hay, and I stayed vigilant in my work, stopping only when our father returned home with freshly caught perch and a fat eel. I revived the cooking fire and measured out the rice. A part of me greedily hoped that Raeden and Hisato would be home soon with apricots or wild radish and onion. They'd brought home ginger a few days before, and I'd added small amounts to flavor up our food.

Summer was going by so quickly, already half gone, and I started to think about the upcoming autumn. Perhaps this year, I should save every piece of bronze coin rather than give it in prayer, or become fiercer in my bartering, so I could get another ceramic pot for pickling. The winter had cracked the smallest one. I'd overstuffed it and wasn't careful in storing it from the biting cold. I decided then to dry out or pickle half of whatever my brothers brought home to better last us through the next winter. We had a little left over in the spring, but we'd acted very carefully.

Renzo's wife pickled quite a lot of cabbage every year. Perhaps she'd trade a bit of it for sandals for each of their children, or tightly woven mats and blankets. A house of nine probably wore through them quickly. I'd go there myself as long as Kyu wasn't there.

As children, I would daydream about becoming his wife. He was a tall boy, and brave. On especially hot days, when we took a break from working outside, he'd show off, jumping from the highest rocks into the river. I would share the wild strawberries I'd found, and watch how happy it made him. But I knew better than to hope for that. Without all my scars, I still wasn't very shapely—I was small in every way. It was no secret these days that most of the boys looked at Fumei; she was beautiful and kind and never complained about the hard work in the tea fields. We'd even become close friends.

I wanted to be angry, knowing that the boy I liked probably only had eyes for Fumei. But I couldn't find it in myself to be hateful as much as I was envious. She was three years older than myself, and almost of marrying age. Of course every young man would have their eye on her. The best I could do was hope, and sometimes my jealousy drove me to pray, that some rich man would get lost on his way to his new fancy manor and happen by. He'd see Fumei and whisk her away to a life of luxury that befitted her beauty. Even if that did happen, there were other girls who would make for a lovelier wife.

I couldn't be angry at my friend. Only myself for how clumsy and careless I'd let myself be. Even so, I was afraid to run into Kyu. Afraid of what he'd think of me with my hair barely starting to grow back, and no way to hide the scars on my face or hands. I'd crudely sewn an addition to my pants to better cover my legs, but half my shin was still showing. No, he'd think too much that I look like a boy. And my heart wouldn't be able to handle that, even if he didn't say a word.

A gentle rain began as I cooked and planned out my days, fast becoming a heavy deluge. Thunder clapped in the distance and rumbled overhead. There was no flash of lightning, which I felt grateful for. Not because I was afraid of it, I wasn't. I was more afraid if a cruel bolt struck our house, or any of the other houses in the village. Our rooves were reeds, tightly tied together, and thick layered, and I worried they might still catch fire despite all the rain.

I'd been so distracted with all these things, that I hadn't noticed Raeden and Hisato weren't home yet. Not until I began to set the table and get our bowls ready.

"I should go and look for them," argued Kenta. "I'm younger. If they're hurt, I can carry them home one at a time."

"And if you get hurt doing that?" countered father. "We need one strong man, at least. I will go."

"Baba, you're too old," said Kenta. "I'll be careful. I won't take any unneeded risks. And I'm less likely to catch a cold in the rain."

"Couldn't we ask anyone in the village to help search for them?" I asked.

Kenta and father both hesitated.

"I don't want a big fuss," said Kenta. "And I don't want to risk others getting hurt or sick." He placed a hand on father's shoulder, standing proud and seeming like the most respectable of men in the village. "I'll take the straw cloak. And I'll bring a bit of supplies, just in case. But I promise I will be home before sunrise, with both of them."

I never understood how Kenta could make such impossible promises. But every time he did, he always came through. I didn't have any reason to doubt him, and ate up my supper beside father. But as the hours went by, my stomach tightened.

To keep from pacing around, we busied ourselves with some menial task, waiting. I found myself stopping often as I wove more sandals, and looked at the door a long while. For the first time, doubts crept into my mind. What if they'd all fallen somewhere? Or bitten by some creature, or became prey to a leopard? There were stories like that. Of vengeful beasts that turned men into meat.

I told myself that if they didn't walk through that door the next time I looked up, then I'd go to every house in the village and beg for help. And I didn't care if Kyu saw me then. Not if it meant getting my brothers back.

I set aside another sandal, and made to start weaving together its twin. Father put another log into the cooking pit, our source of light and warmth in the room. Thunder rolled overhead, and I couldn't help wonder if some wicked Kurai spirit was responsible and now laughing.

The door flung open. Kenta walked in with Raeden partially sheltered under the straw cloak. Both were soaked to the bone. Relieved, I hurried to fetch dry clothes for them, and stopped when I didn't see Hisato.

"Where is—?" I began to ask. My heart dropped, seeing the sorry looks on each of them.

"He's been arrested," said Kenta.

"What?" I gasped. So did father. Both of us fumbling with a flood of questions.

"He shot down a deer on the spirits' grounds," said Raeden. "A sacred deer. It was a mistake, he didn't know, but they..."

Kenta shed off the straw cover, hanging it to drip dry near the entrance of our home. "I'll ask to borrow Lan's horse at dawn. Hopefully I can make it up the mountain and try to fix things."

"The horse is old," said father, a weep in his voice.

Kenta shook his head slowly. "It's the best we have to get there quickly. They won't answer this late into the night." He looked at father with sorrow, having broken his promise.

I felt my eyes swell with tears. I didn't know what to do, but morning felt too far away. Though, what else was there?

Chapter 2
In the Rain

We all tried to get some rest. I lay in my bed, holding that stuffed rabbit close to me as I tossed and turned. Heavy raindrops sounded more like applause for our misfortune. And it didn't get better when everything went still and quiet. I couldn't fall asleep.

I thought about all the stories. The ones the merchants told when they passed through. That people who committed terrible crimes against their lords or the divine spirits were executed as the sun emerged in the morning. Would that be my brother's fate? Even though it was an accident?

Hisato and I were two of a kind, and I couldn't imagine a world without him. He'd been by my side before we were even born. It was always the two of us, grown up or not.

My stomach soured, forcing me up.

I clung to that toy, remembering how Hisato traded his for a stack of paper and fine charcoal for me. I'd been the selfish one, unable to let go of one of the last things I had of our mother. I parted first with the only fine dress our mother owned—the one she took out on special days. That dress gained us ample supplies, and bought me time to adjust to my new role as the woman of the house.

I couldn't stand it. I pulled on my day's clothes, and dug out my deel from its drawer to slip on for added warmth. Just in case. It had tears and snags all over, and I'd nearly outgrown it, but it still kept me warm. My sandals tied on, I crept out the door, my stuffed bunny in hand, and lit the lantern. I knew it was childish, but holding it gave me comfort. And if I grew tired, wanting to head back, looking at it would remind me of the important mission I set myself to.

I would beg for his freedom. Do whatever this lord of the mountain wanted if it meant keeping my family safe and together. I'd weave a thousand sandals and mats without rest, or light a thousand fires day and night. Whatever it took!

So, I ran. As fast as my skinny legs would carry me, I ran.

Angry barking stopped me in my tracks. "Shh! Chocho," I scolded in a whisper. The black dog hushed, but didn't stop. I held the lantern up, showing my face to him. "It's me. Hisa. Now go back. Go on, go! Be a good boy, and be quiet."

I tip toed onwards, my fingers digging into the plushness that toy rabbit. Chocho still growled, uncertain, and gave a whining bark.

I whipped my head back for a last scolding. "Shh!" And ran.

The red gate was always visible from the mountain shrine. That's where I went. Every day I'd given to the shrine, and said my thanks—if ever there was a time I needed prayers to be answered, it was now. Wet grass tried to catch me, slow me, stop me. Several blades clung on, ripped from their stem. Rather than take the conventional route, which was probably coated in mud anyway, I took a shortcut, one I'd taken several times in the past. Like the grass, low hanging branches tried to grab me and keep me from going to the spirits.

If they were the Juneun, the benevolent sort of spirits, like the kind that came and healed us, surely they'd hear me out. Hisato wasn't a vicious person. He wouldn't have hunted on their lands, or wounded a sacred animal, much less kill it, not if he'd known. It was all an accident. They would understand, wouldn't they? They would know that humans are flawed, that we make mistakes. The Juneun would release him if I could make them understand. Not like the cruel Kurai spirits who reveled in causing bad things to happen.

In my frantic pace, my shortcut somehow felt so much longer, though I knew I was going in the right direction. It seemed like my legs weren't moving fast enough, and that the sun was in a greater hurry than I was. I heard the rip of a new tear in my deel, though I didn't dare stop to look.

When the shrine came into view, I smiled. Maybe I wasn't that slow after all. I wiped the sweat from my face, the muggy air heavy and gluing every bit of moisture to my skin.

I'd never been further than this point, and the villa was nowhere in sight. But how much further beyond the red gate could it possibly be? Maintaining my pace, I climbed the slick, mossy, and uneven stone steps towards the gate. In the shadow of a cloudy night, the gate looked black and ominous, rather than the red, regal archway that stood out from the green of everything else around it. Closer and closer, the gate stood tall and wide, empty and imposing. It drank in the light of my lantern, hardly allowing the lacquered red color to show. At the thresh of it, my heart quivered. The air felt somehow cold. There was an instinct of fear deep within me. Without realizing it, I'd come to a complete stop, staring upward at its top and then beyond to the endless stone stairs and darkness.

My legs weighed like lead. My feet wanted to turn back. It felt like the gateway was breathing, cold and unfeeling breaths. The breath of a merciless predator. Testing me.

I looked to my toy rabbit, one of its sewn eyes frayed and halfway gone, an ear hanging on by its last threads. My hand squeezed, afraid for a moment that anything less would result in losing it. And I pressed it into my chest.

We were two of a kind. Me and Hisato. Like the hares.

I couldn't stop here.

The flame in my lantern shuddered as I walked on. A single step beyond the red gate, and the air felt the same as it always had. I looked behind me, at the shadows that lead to my village, and said a quiet prayer for strength. I would need it if I was going to be able to climb to the top before sunrise.

Not long into my climb, I slipped. My shin scraped against the sharp edge of the stony stairs. Beads of red quickly grew, gliding down in lazy streaks towards my ankle. I wasn't deterred. Picking myself up, I straightened my lantern, and kept a protective hold on my bunny, ignoring the blood snaking down my leg.

It dawned on me then, how careless I'd really been. Not once did I think about if I stepped near a snake, as my mother had warned me of so many years ago. No. I wouldn't allow that. I wouldn't turn back, or die from snake bite.

I had to free Hisato.

Slowing my stride just enough for caution, I didn't look up to see how terribly far I had to go. I fixed my eyes on the few steps ahead, making sure my worn sandals would keep me sure footed, and that I didn't step on or near something dangerous.

I climbed higher, and the forest thinned for a moment. Flashes of lightning far away illuminated the space around me for less than a second. Thunder lazily rumbled behind it. I felt an unease suddenly. The same kind as though something was watching me, stalking me. A leopard? A tiger? I held out my lantern as far as my arm would stretch, slowing my pace further as I looked around but never stopping. Another flash of lightning showed me the shadow of some large and lumbering thing. A bear? Or maybe a boar? It seemed too big to be a boar, yet too small to be a bear. I didn't dwell on it. I couldn't. Instead, I muttered my prayers, asking for courage and strength, and pressed that toy flat against my chest.

The more afraid I grew, the louder I prayed. But I never stopped. Not until I was parched and found a stream, clean, and cool, and fast flowing. I set down my lantern, and my bunny near to it, since I needed both hands to scoop up a drink of water. Greedily, from thirst, I scooped up four more times to sate myself.

I hadn't realized how much I was panting until then. My body felt heavy, and my lungs burned. Shedding off my deel, the air felt immediately crisper, and helped to cool me and speed my recovery. Though, it wasn't long before I began to shiver, and put it back on.

I couldn't see the red gate anymore, nor could I see the top of the mountain. How long had I been running, walking, climbing? I needed to rest. Only for a minute. Just until I caught my breath. I felt so tired. How much farther did I have to go? Would I make it in time? Before anything horrible could happen to my brother?

I was tired, and in pain. But I didn't let myself cry. Hisato once went to the spirits to ask for medicine for me. He didn't cry. He hurried back for me. Now it was my turn to do the same for him.

Perhaps that would move the Juneun, enough to grieve their hearts if we should forever be separated. It sounded like the sort of beautiful thing to make a story about. The twins who risked themselves to protect one another. Surely, it was a tale worthy of his release.

I felt my confidence return, reigniting my courage. Before setting out again, I cleaned away the blood from my shin and foot, and took a last drink. Distant applause of rain echoed up to me. I had to hurry, or I'd be slowed even more.

I tried to think of how I would best explain things, something to impress the spirits that arrested my brother. And I didn't feel quite so tired in my continued climb. Not until I tripped again. My sandals were beginning to fall apart.

Just a little longer, I begged.

Though, my begging was for not when I came across a river that divided the stairway of the mountain. Large, flat stones created a stepping path, but I would still need to jump to reach from one to the next, and I didn't trust my sandals to hold. Not with how fast the water rushed between each boulder. I unfastened them each in one swift pull, and set them aside to collect on my way back. Even though I wouldn't wear them again, I could dry them out and use them for tinder in the cooking pit.

Perhaps I could weave this detail into my plea. That I ran up in reckless abandon, so much that my shoes fell apart and I had to continue bare footed. The story certainly moved my own heart. Surely it wouldn't go ignored.

I steadied myself at the water's edge, trying to gauge how far I needed to hop, and how quickly I could manage without slipping. I decided not to focus on that last part. This time, I would go as slow as needed. It didn't do any good to save Hisato if I fell in and was swept away to drown.

Unwilling to risk it, I tucked my bunny into my shirt, fastening everything to stay snug. After each successful short jump from one stone to the next, I checked to make sure it was still in place and that everything was still snug.

I knew it was childish of me to put so much importance on a toy. But it gave me hope and courage, fueling my determination.

My mind began to play tricks on me, making me more afraid of this strange river. What if there were alligators, or leeches, or some terrible Kurai stalking just beneath the surface? I knew the water was rushing too quickly for any of that to come true, but the very idea made me fearful all the same, and I found myself reaching over my heart for comfort.

When I made it to the other side, I was glad to put that river behind me. Then I remembered Kenta's plan. Even on a young horse, that current was too swift, and the rocks too slippery. He probably didn't know, and would either have to turn back or tie up the horse and hope nothing decided it looked tasty.

Lan's favorite ox had been subjected to a bullying boar two years back. Its tusks had cut so deep, the poor animal was bleeding out. By the time enough of us had gathered to shoo it away and our hunters shot it down, it was too late. There was no helping that poor ox. She'd lost too much blood, and left a calf not yet weaned. I remember how the calf would cry, and I would abandon some of my work to try and comfort it, to let it know I understood; it continued to cry for a week.

I wondered if my brothers would also sneak away to comfort the calf. In my heart, I think perhaps they did. They'd lost mother too, and knew the pain of it.

We weren't about to lose another family member. Not without a fight.

I made myself fast march up the stairs. They'd evened out and stayed well kempt. Care went into them on this side of that strange river. Crickets and frogs sang out, and fireflies enjoyed the break in the summer rain. In this part of the mountain, it seemed like nothing terrible had happened at all. It made me an odd sort of angry, and pushed me to keep my pace—determined to make it to the end long before the sun could show itself.

That drive wavered when my lantern burned out. I'd been too focused on looking just a few steps ahead to notice it dimming, warning me it was about to extinguish. My stride slowed in the new darkness. There wasn't any point in carrying it along. So, I set it down to collect on my return.

If it was tragic that I should make so much of the journey on naked feet, perhaps this too would bolster my plight. Having to trek the last stretch under a moonless, starless night to rescue my brother. It was a story the Juneun could tell to others, and embellish it to be more dramatic.

That was, if I could get there first. I had no way of knowing how close I was, or any means of measuring how much farther I had to go. All I knew was the sweat pouring off my body and the burning of my lungs and the heaviness of my legs, and the ache of my spine. Still, I pressed on without slowing.

To my great relief and equal dread, it wasn't too long before I could see pristine white walls, and a heavy wooded moon gate. Behind it, the tiled rooftops of buildings. The villa.

Chapter 3
Goodbye Brother

I ran the last hundred yards, where cobble stone plateaus divided small sets of stairs, guided by the lantern light of the standing guards. I must have looked dreadful, because their faces took alarm to my approach.

"Please," I said, panting. "Please, let me speak with the lord of this place. He arrested my brother over a big misunderstanding. Please, you have to let me explain!"

"Lord Kwan is asleep," said one guard, sounding irritated with me already. "Do you even know what hour it is, boy?"

"I'm sorry," I said. "But I knew I had to be here before sunrise. Please."

"Go home," said the other, who seemed a little more patient. "The sun will be up in a few hours. You can come back in the morning."

I shook my head. "I came from the village below the mountain. And I've already walked through my shoes and all of my lamp oil just to get here now."

"The village?" repeated the second guard. "But that would mean you're..."

I gulped air, trying to keep my knees from shaking.

"You're a human," said the first, sounding both astonished and annoyed. "That must mean you're here for—"

"Let the boy speak," said the second guard. "It's not an easy trek for humans as it is."

It didn't bother me that they kept calling me a boy. What mattered was trying to get Hisato out of there. "My brother accidentally crossed the boundary while hunting. He didn't know. He's not a cruel person, or a greedy one."

"Hunting?" said the first guard. "Yes, I know who you're speaking about. But he killed the sacred deer. A white doe."

I clasped my hands over my chest, clinging to the bunny hidden beneath. "He didn't mean to. Hisato wouldn't do something like that on purpose. A lot of the villagers have a hunter in their family. It's how we're able to get by, you see."

"Silence!" scolded the first guard.

"Hang on," cooed the second, tempering his companion. "If that's true, it should be brought to the master. It might interest Lord Kwan to know this about his neighbors, in case something like this does happen again. Better he know the circumstances than to believe the humans are deliberately trespassing."

The first guard scoffed. "I'm not waking him at this hour. He'll bite my head off! He's been in a foul mood these last fifty years at least."

A foul mood? For fifty years? I began to lose hope that my story would be moving at all. Still, I held back my desire to cry. I had to stay strong.

"I'll wake him then," said the second. "Just as soon as we're relieved from this post. And you can keep an eye on the boy. If the master is going to be cranky, then it's best to not make him walk all this way."

"You want me to watch the child?" complained the first.

"Unless you want to be the one to wake the master," said the second.

The first guard grumbled, fixing his eyes directly on me. "Alright then, boy. I'll escort you in. But you had better stay by my side, or I'll have to cut you down."

Fearful, I nodded.

"We can't have strange folk running around. Even if you are just a half-starved human whelp."

"How old are you, anyway?" asked the second guard, a spark of realization in his voice.

"My brother and I are fifteen," I answered, a little too fast. It was all I can do to not tremble too violently—I couldn't focus on steadying my words. In truth, I was glad I had the strength to say anything at all in that moment.

"Still a child," said the second guard, more to himself than to his friend.

The first guard sighed, grumbling.

It was all I could do to keep myself standing as I waited. My eyes kept glancing eastward, dreading that they might see a hint of morning light. What felt like ages came to an end when a pair of new guards, similarly dressed in red and gray, stepped out from the moon gate. The large, wooded doors were easily three times my height, yet these men pulled them open with ease; they glided without a creak in their design or a sharp squeak from their hinges.

The guards I'd waited with gave some brief explanation, though I was too focused on trying to get my tale straight to hear what was said. The first one motioned to me to stay beside him, and I obeyed. When he walked, I walked. When he stopped, I stopped. He went left, and so did I. Whatever direction, whatever pace, I matched it. I couldn't risk irritating them with a question or complaint, or by any distraction that would slow me down.

Behind the moon gate was another long flight of stairs, guiding through a pleasant bamboo forest and towards a new white wall and gate. The rooftops from before were outposts. The wall here was shorter by compare at only twice my own height. For privacy? I'd never been in a city or a palace or anything like that, so it was hard to say. Nor had I ever spoken to a lord or heavenly spirit before. Unless the guards counted, though I hadn't thought about that in my desperation to make it here.

Past the smaller moon gate, a pretty courtyard greeted us. A wide space with a small fountain tucked into one far corner and babbling away pleasantly. The greenery was kept simple, and flat sones placed close together made for a walkway towards the magnificent house. That wasn't the direction we headed to, however. The guard escorting me motioned for me to go towards a storage shed, and to sit on the veranda there to wait. The second, kindlier guard set down his spear and other effects, and took a measured pace towards the house.

I stared after him, anxious and waiting. Again, I rehearsed what to say in my head, worried I would forget pieces, or get them mixed up.

"Here," said my escorting guard.

Looking up, he handed me a pretty cup. Green ceramic with a pronounced floral design at its base. "Thank you," I said, hoarse.

Water. I didn't realize how parched I was until then, and drank it down in heavy gulps. He took back the cup and filled it again for me. I repeated my thanks, and drank only a little slower. He didn't offer me a third.

I looked at the twigs and thorns and leaves that clung to my deel, picking them off hesitantly. I looked so shabby that it probably wouldn't make a difference. At the same time, I remember my parents telling me and my brothers to always look our best for guests and strangers. It would be shameful and embarrassing to appear wild. But I might gain more pity and better secure Hisato's release if I looked so pathetic. Which one was best?

A bit of red caught my attention. My leg had bled a little more since I cleaned it by that stream, and already it began to bruise. My pants weren't long enough to conceal that. Pitiful as it was.

Light began to appear in the cloudy sky. My nerves wracked at my body. I'd made it. Surely. I couldn't see Hisato anywhere, but I'd made it to the villa before sunrise. Wasn't that enough?

I fidgeted with the cuffs of my sleeves, my eyes fixed on the house. I almost didn't believe when I saw the kindlier guard and a handsome man come around the corner and into view. They'd said their master had a foul mood for fifty years—I didn't think a youthful lord would come to meet me. In remembering where I stood, I realized how silly it was to expect an old man to appear. The lord of this place was a Juneun, a heavenly spirit. Of course he wouldn't be old, not unless he wanted to appear that way. He was timeless, like all his kind were; whether they were Juneun or Kurai, they were eternal compared to humans.

His long silken robes of black, white, and gray flowed so seamlessly as he walked. His face pale like snow, while his long, black hair shined. He hadn't bothered to tie it up, perhaps thinking

I wasn't worth the effort; and I couldn't blame him for that, considering how I arrived. His eyes were a mixture of brown and orange, something predatory and tiger-like, and seemed in conflict against his stony expression. I found I couldn't read him at all, and it worried me. Perhaps all lords were taught to present themselves like this, since they were so different from us villagers.

I stood, trembling. A part of me wanted to flee, while another part of me wanted to throw myself at his feet and beg for my brother's release. What would I say? I'd been so shocked by the lord of this villa that I'd forgotten everything I practiced in my head. His every stride seemed deliberate and powerful and all authority, and I couldn't look away.

My hands went to my chest, pressing hard on the stuffed rabbit beneath my clothes. It was enough to remind me of the important things to say.

He stopped a few feet away, looking down at me, and I felt so exposed and pathetic in that moment. What right did I have to ask him anything? Hisato. I had the right as a sister to try and save her brother.

"This is the village boy?" asked Lord Kwan.

"I..." my voice felt stuck, and I swallowed hard on the sticky spit that coated my mouth.

"Gi tells me you came up on behalf of a brother. The one who killed the sacred doe of the mountain."

"He didn't mean to," I said, a bit too loudly.

Lord Kwan raised a brow, but otherwise stayed unmoving.

I reined my voice in, holding tight to my bunny and fighting the urge to fall shaking on my knees. "I'm sure he'd tell you. Many villagers go into the mountain to hunt. And I know he wouldn't deliberately hunt on your lands, or kill an animal that was sacred. He wouldn't do that if he knew. He, he must have thought it was an ordinary deer, or maybe didn't see how special it was—"

I paused, catching Gi, the kindly guard from before, mouthing something. *My lord*. He was cuing me to use manners I wasn't used to. My face paled when I realized. He stopped, abrupt, as his master turned his head slightly.

"I'm... I'm sorry, my lord." I tore away my gaze, looking at the gravel between myself and Lord Kwan. "When I heard, I came up in desperation. My shoes shredded and my lantern ran out of light long before I even made it to your walls. We're twins, you see. And I can't bring myself to know a life without him, my lord."

A long silence.

"You don't look anything alike," said Lord Kwan, pondering.

I faced him again, blinking. "We did as babies, my lord. And he's the kindest brother in the world. When I fell sick because of this," I placed my fingertips on the large bulbus scar on my cheek, "He climbed up here himself to ask for medicine. And he was in such a hurry to bring it to me, he got hurt coming down."

"He's been here before?" asked Lord Kwan.

I nodded.

"And yet, he didn't know he was hunting on my lands."

I gasped, realizing my mistake. "He took the stairs to get here that time, my lord. Hunting in the forests... there aren't any markers to tell us where your lands begin. He wouldn't have known!"

I caught a glimpse of Gi, motioning for me to calm and flashing a look of concern.

"So, it is my fault?"

I shook my head, feeling cornered. "N-no, I didn't say that."

He brushed back some of his smooth, black hair with a flick of his hand, his expression still stone. "Explain it to me, then."

I did my best, recounting in a more organized fashion and looking to Gi often for cues. I explained our age and the series of misfortunes that befell the village, putting us into a greater poverty as a community. And I made sure to mention the pox that plagued us, and my gratitude for the mysterious Juneun who healed us, and how I gave back in prayer as often as I could. I said it all in the hope of making a better appeal. Though, Lord Kwan didn't seem impressed in the least.

Instead, he looked me up and down, stoic.

Displeased? Annoyed? Sympathetic? I couldn't tell.

"What do you want me to do?" asked Lord Kwan, cold in his tone.

I tried to meet his eye without shaking, then bowed low, the best I knew how to do. "Let him go home, my lord. And forgive his mistake. Please." It was all I could do not to cry in that moment. Hisato's life was still on the line.

He grunted at my request, and I didn't know if I should take it as a good sign, or a bad one. "The killing of sacred things cannot go unpunished. Even if I forgave the trespassing."

I fell to my knees then, begging. "Then let me be punished, my lord!"

He stopped in his words, and I couldn't hold back my tears anymore. I was about to lose my brother.

"My brother hunts because I can't work like he can. I'm not so strong. So, his crime was because of me. I should be the one punished."

I wept, afraid of what might happen next. It was still early in the dawn, and I had no one to rescue me. Even if Kenta rode in a gallop the entire way and leapt over the river, he wouldn't make it in time.

Finally, I was able to reel myself in a bit. Lord Kwan waited until that moment before giving me a command.

"Stand up, boy. And stop your crying."

I obeyed, my legs wobbly, and wiped my face with my sleeves. But I dared not meet his eye again.

"I will take your offer. Under the condition that you say not a word when he leaves. I won't have this back and forth begging for each other."

I nodded.

"If you speak, I will take him back and send you away. And it will be as though you never arrived. Do you understand?"

Again, I nodded at his cold instruction.

"Look at me, and answer."

I breathed in, holding tight to my chest to muster courage, and forced myself to look into his eyes. "Yes, my lord. I understand." My voice was a whisper, but it was the best I could do.

He stared at me, watching me shake, but I wouldn't look away.

"Fetch the boy," said Lord Kwan with a sigh. "And escort him to the river. He can make his way from there."

Both Gi and my escort guard obeyed, answering and giving a slight and swift bow before leaving. It was the two of us then. I stayed trembling and staring at the cold features of this lordly spirit's face. Wordlessly, I said my goodbyes to my family and friends, to the hopes and dreams I had for my future, to the perfect canvas and brush I would never use, the drawings I would never see again, the fields and animals and river that I grew up with. I resigned myself, or tried to.

I held onto that bunny hidden beneath my shirt, telling myself it would be alright. I would be with my mother again. And Hisato would be freed and live a good and long life. My brothers would marry kind and beautiful girls, and have families of their own. Perhaps one of their children would like drawing and painting, and would put my abandoned things to use.

Maybe Fumei would marry Kenta or Raeden, and would cook all sorts of things and be a gentle force in their life. She was kind enough that she might do that for my family anyway, and maybe that's how she would fall in love. It sounded terribly romantic, and I found a comfort in thinking my dear friend would be there for my family.

The sound of iron and heavy footfall broke my thoughts. My eyes pulled away from Lord Kwan, who'd stayed perfectly still in studying me, and to my brother. Hisato seemed resigned to a gruesome fate, his wrists and ankles in chains. When he looked up, he blinked at me, like he was looking at a ghost. His face paled then, and shouts of protest left him, though the guards shoved to keep him moving forward.

I wanted to say so many things then. To tell him to use any savings he had to hire one of Renzo's daughters to cook and clean. To sell the sandals I'd woven, and all of my things to be sure they had enough. To replace the ceramic pot and to help father with pickling for winter. I wanted to say that I loved him, and that I wanted him to live the happiest of life for me. To tell Kenta and Raeden and father that I loved them with all my heart. I wanted to say so much, and put my hands tight over my mouth to keep from any of it.

I'd promised to not say a word. My sobs were muffled, and my tears flowed freely.

"Hisa!" called Hisato. "Hisa! What did you do? Hisa, no! Hisa!" He called for me, for some explanation, and I couldn't say anything—not even to comfort him.

The wood doors of the moon gate closed, but I could still hear my brother calling my name. I fell back on my knees, squeezing my hands over my mouth so hard I thought my teeth might bend. And I stayed there shaking for a long while. Long enough that I didn't notice when another Juneun walked up. Lord Kwan instructed him to take me somewhere, and he obliged with a soft voice.

"Hey."

I looked up, seeing the ginger-brown hair and fox ears of this spirit. Whereas the guards looked like fit men in peak health, and their lord ethereal, this spirit looked so strange. I'd never seen such color of hair, except on animals, nor had I ever seen someone with animal ears. And there was only ever one spirit I knew who had anything to do with foxes. A Kurai called Gumiho. But the spirit in front of me was a young man, and smiled gently. He sounded kind, and softened his voice to a coo for me.

"Can you stand?"

I nodded, trying to clean up my face as I did. He helped me to my feet anyway, and held my hand the first few steps as he guided me somewhere. And, though I knew it was rude, I couldn't help but stare at his ears as I obediently followed.

"Are you Gumiho?" I asked in a whisper.

He stopped, turning to look at me with an embarrassed expression. "No, I'm not. My name is Syaoran. I'm a fox spirit, but I'm not with Gumiho. I'm a servant to Lord Kwan."

"Oh," I said, feeling ashamed for having asked. "I'm sorry."

He shook his head. "Most people who don't know have their suspicion. Spirit or human."

He continued on, and I followed. I didn't want to give any reason to upset him or anyone in these walls.

"I saw what you did for your brother," said Syaoran. "It was brave of you."

I shook my head. "All I did was beg and cry." Looking around, I admired the beauty of the house and the other buildings, and of the garden and decorative things that seemed perfectly placed.

"That leg of yours says otherwise. Climbing up here from the lower river is difficult enough in fair weather. But on a rainy night, without even a lantern? I'd say that's brave."

"He's my brother," I whispered.

Syaoran chuckled. "I wish I had brothers like you."

"I'm his sister," I said absently, and nearly walked into him as he came to an abrupt stop.

He looked at me then, wide eyes blinking and fox ears pointed high. "Sister?"

I gave a single nod, and pressed my arms defensively against my chest. Did I make a mistake in revealing that?

He stared at me, taking it in. And then relaxed with a sorry expression. "I think that makes you even braver."

I stared back at him, unsure what to make of it. There was a comfort in how he spoke, and his handsome features coupled with his strange hair and fox ears didn't make me feel as afraid as I did before.

We walked on.

"Are you a Juneun?"

He laughed. "Sort of. There's different kinds. I'd say I'm closer to it than the guards and staff here, but not the same as Lord Kwan."

I didn't quite understand, but decided not to pester with any more questions.

I was brought to the kennels. Empty as they were. Syaoran ushered me to one with a thick bed of hay, saying how they didn't have a place for prisoners and that I would stay here until tomorrow. Then he asked what my favorite foods were, so that I could have them for today. It was a kind gesture, and I tried to take it with dignity. When he left, and the finality of my fate set in, I curled up in the hay and wept.

Fishing out my beloved stuffed bunny, I stroked its soft ears and stared at it like a child. My sole consolation.

Chapter 4
Lord Kwan

The boy in front of him appeared half-starved, a raspy and shrill voice begging and weeping. Always, humans and the lower spirits came only to ask something. He couldn't recall how long it'd been since a human did actually come to beg something in person. However, he found it no more amusing or moving as the last time. It'd been the lesser spirits with their own agendas for the last century, hoping to play the games of court and elevate themselves.

He was tired. Too much to pay attention to the child's rambling explanation. A lengthy tale, undoubtedly rehearsed.

His energy spent in preserving the doe's soul, before it was too late, took its toll on him. Could he weep for the loss, in the privacy of his room, he would. Things were different now. For over fifty years, he hadn't the will to smile for courtesy, let alone to mourn a loss.

He'd given his judgement, lacking the conviction to entertain anything more.

Syaoran walked to his side, taking instruction and making some question about what ought to be done.

"I'll deal with this tomorrow morning," said Kwan before leaving. He shut out the sobbing of one child, and the impetuous cries of the twin, walking back to his room. He shouldn't have even entertained a hearing. There were more pressing matters.

In the last twelve years, more Kurai trespassed with impunity. Not only on Mount Tora, but in other parts of the land as well. It was a constant test to see if they had the strength to hold back the surmounting evil. If he had the strength. Gumiho had a fragment of his soul in her claws. Naturally, the others would press their luck, assume him too weak.

The trouble was: they might soon be right. It'd been getting harder to banish and fell wicked creatures without his soul. But he wouldn't risk letting another part of it be taken.

For twelve years, more brazen Kurai used the humans near Mount Tora to lure him out. Using innocents as pawns and play things to get at him. Droughts, floods, pestilence... anything to force his hand and cause him to spend too much of his energy.

He leaned against the north facing wall of his room, opposite the door, and looked out the window beside him. His breakfast went largely ignored. Events so early in the day souring his stomach. Staring out, he watched the birds as they chirped and went about their way, and the breaking of the clouds to allow the sun to shine. Insects sang loudly in the balmy summer day, and the wind sighed pleasantly, bringing the smell of jasmine and tea trees with it.

He was tired. Tired enough to slumber for a century, but unable to sate the desire.

A butterfly landed on the window's ledge, flexing its wings to drink in the warmth of the sun.

He watched it, wondering if it was alone in the garden. Not likely. Why would it tolerate loneliness? What was the most beautiful of gardens to a butterfly if it was alone? He no longer had the time to compose poems to capture the idea, nor the drive to ponder the musings deeply.

Gumiho was out there. Waiting. With so many of the most powerful Juneun busy against forces elsewhere, who was left to stop her if he fell?

He should've sent away the boy, rather than allow himself to indulge the tale and offer a trade. It already took so much of his strength to spare the spirit of the doe. And now its mate, the sacred stag of the mountain, would be without her. There was no fawn between them. Not that he knew. And he pitied the thing, knowing it'd search for its mate to no avail. Until the next life.

The butterfly left as the door opened.

"Lord Kwan." Syaoran made his polite greetings, waiting for an invitation in. Only after an acknowledgement did he go on.

"Any news on the Kurai?"

"I," hesitated Syaoran. "I'm not sure."

Kwan grunted, returning his gaze out the window.

"My lord, about the prisoner."

"I will carry out the sentence myself in the morning."

His servant stumbled. "Yes. But, my lord, don't you think it's a bit cruel? The child has already—"

Kwan whipped his face to look at his servant, a sever expression marring his features. "Then carry it out yourself. It's of little interest to me."

"If that's the case, why not—?"

Kwan slammed his palm to the floor, a loud thud reminding Syaoran of his place and his overstep. "We are finished discussing it. You can carry out the execution today, or I can carry it out tomorrow."

Sadness filled Syaoran's expression. "Yes, lord."

Kwan relaxed himself, leaning against the wall again, and letting the back of his head thump softly with him on the cool wood. "I'm so tired."

The young fox spirit said nothing, watching his master with a curiousness.

"Truth be told, I'm glad of the delay. I didn't know if I'd have the strength to bear such a thing today."

Silence.

"A tiger's legs are strong. The strongest part of it." A smile tried to form on his face, failing completely. "When it dies, it's legs will continue to hold it upright, while the rest of it falls limp." It wasn't the first time he'd said this, and swam in the romantic tragedy of the words.

"The tiger's fur is orange and black," said Syaoran, "Against a forest of green. It walks through, proud, yet remains unseen."

Kwan managed the smallest smile, returning his gaze to his friend. "That's a good one."

Before further conversation, a reprieve from recent events, could continue, frantic footfalls echoed. A scout, still half-coated in mud and leaves, slid into view.

"Lord Kwan," called the scout, making a quick bow. "There was a sighting of the fox clan."

Kwan's voice went cold, and his eyes steely. "Gumiho?"

He shook his head. "We're not sure. But several from her clan were confirmed."

Before the scout finished his words, Kwan stood and grabbed his sword in swift movements. He rushed past the others in a blur, a bolt of lightning without thunder. He put aside any further thoughts of the prisoner boy, hurrying to stop whatever calamity his quarry planned.

Chapter 5
Thistles & Sorrow

I found I had no appetite, even with all my favorite things right in front of me. And I sobbed all through the night. My eyes were swollen, puffy and pink, by morning. When a guard came in, I waited for the gate to open and the command to follow him. I told myself I'd look towards the sun one last time, and hope that I'd led a good enough life to be granted peace. Mother would be waiting for me. I wouldn't be alone. And I could watch over my brothers, and over father, beside her.

The gate opened, and I tried to steel myself—prevent myself from shaking, which was harder than I could've anticipated. He left a bowl of rice for me instead, and gave no command. Looking up, it was Gi.

"They said you weren't eating. So, I thought, maybe something easier to digest would help."

I blinked at him as he bent to meet my eye. "Thank you. That's very kind of you." I tried to control my voice. In order to keep from trembling, it stayed hushed. "But I don't need food if I'm going to die."

Gi bent his brow at me. "Well, not today. The master left in a rush. Kurai were seen coming this way. He hasn't said what the sentence should be. Given time, after he's rested, he might decide against death."

I breathed in, not daring to hope no matter how much I wanted to.

"I heard Syaoran already tried to talk to him, right before he got this news. He might mull it over while he's resting."

I looked down at the rice, white and brown and red, and some of it shining black. Lord Kwan might let me go? Then again, he might not.

"It was a noble thing you did, taking your brother's place. How often does that happen for one brother to sacrifice himself for another? Most would stay quiet so they could inherit more."

I shook my head. "Even if there was something like that, I'd still have made my decision."

"Heaven smiles on that kind of brotherly love," said Gi, sounding so sure. "Lord Kwan couldn't go against that. It's the principle of the matter. And if he's set on carrying out a strict punishment, maybe just holding a prisoner or laboring off the debt would equal it out."

Against my better judgement, I began to hope. "How long would that be? Wasn't it the sacred doe that was killed? How much time would pay off a debt like that?"

Gi scratched at his cheek, smiling. "I'm not sure. Maybe only twenty or twenty-five years."

I paled again. An entire lifetime. Though, perhaps the spirits didn't understand mortal lifespans. "If..." I hesitated, looking for a way to explain. "If that becomes the case, would someone tell my family? Tell them that I'm working off the debt and not dead?"

"I imagine someone would," said Gi, about to stand up.

I shook my head. "I want to know you'll tell them."

"Me?"

"You treated me with so much kindness and patience. I don't know that I could believe if anyone else said they did it."

He chuckled. "I can't promise that. But I can make inquiries to be sure they did get the message. But none of that matters if you starve yourself first."

Taking the hint, I grabbed the bowl of rice and thanked him again.

"Try to have patience. At fifteen, you're almost a man. You don't want to be acting like a scared girl. Have courage."

The words stung. I knew he meant to bolster my confidence, to be kind, but it quietly hurt.

I ate slowly after he left, and looked around the empty kennels. What was the point of them if there were no dogs? Maybe there were once, and something happened. I started to think of Chocho and how unhappy he would be stuck in one of these day in and day out. I'd feel the same way if I had to stay in one for twenty years. Maybe death was better.

I shook away the thought and scolded myself. If I were only a prisoner, Hisato wouldn't blame himself too much, and we could all hold the hope of seeing each other again. I knew I would likely never be married as it was, so coming home too old to wed anyway wouldn't make a difference. No, if I had to sit in the kennels for twenty years, it was better than death. I knew it.

I worked to keep my mind in a happy state. Maybe Lord Kwan would understand that years are more precious to humans than to spirits. And if I didn't cry anymore, if I never complained, maybe I wouldn't have to be here quite so long. I didn't let myself think of the alternative.

I felt in a much better mood the following day, and ate breakfast heartily. Though, with nothing else to do but wait around, I looked at the unique colors hidden in the stones that made up my prison cell; in some, I found impressions of plants and tiny creatures from long ago. The heat of summer was a great deal more tolerable in the kennels, with one open wall, plenty of windows, and thick stone to shield me. But the muggy air was everywhere. This wouldn't be such a comfortable place come winter, and I was glad then that I brought my deel. Perhaps I could make something from the straw that made my bed, and ask for more if it was going to get thrown out anyway.

I set to work, combing through it all and organizing the strands by length. If they did allow me more straw to make things, I could weave plenty of mats and blankets to stave off the cold. With nothing better to do, I got started. I could make one thick mat with what I had, and use that for a bed.

At sunset, supper was brought to me, and I convinced myself that it was a wonderful thing to have someone else cooking for a change. I was only halfway complete on my work when the sun had gone and I had no more light.

But that wasn't strictly true.

There was a glow of something under a floor stone. Something I didn't notice until everything else was completely dark. Curiosity drove me to look. My fingers were skinny enough that I could get the loose stone up myself. Beneath it was a deep hole, and a small box at the bottom, where a soothing light bled from.

I knew better than to take it. It wasn't mine. And if someone went through the trouble of hiding it here, it was probably important. But why hide it in an empty dog kennel? I knew I shouldn't, but I grabbed the box anyway. I stayed quiet, trying not to grunt as I stretched my arm down and reeled back up.

A puzzle box of some kind. I'd seen one as a little girl when a merchant passed through. Whatever was in there would stay locked unless the combination was made. He'd said the one he had was a picture, while others were sometimes riddles. We didn't need anything like that in the village. Who would be stealing that we'd need to put something important into a box like that? We weren't a large village, and everyone shared what they had if it could be spared. Often, we traded things with each other, a fair exchange.

My nerves got to my senses, and I put it back where I found it, covering up the hole and making to get some sleep.

I finished my mat the following day, just before sun down, and happily ate my supper on it. But I wasn't tired. And with nothing else to do, I brought out that puzzle box again and slid the pieces around to pass the time. I knew I wouldn't solve it. There was writing on it, and I couldn't read. No one in the village could. Though many families often dreamed of being able to send one of their sons to the city for a better life, where he could learn reading and numbers and a great deal else.

They were only dreams, but it lit up my imagination. What if Raeden went to school and became a wealthy man? Out of all of us, he was the smartest and would come up with unconventional solutions to problems, helping to make life just a little easier. And he wasn't shy about asking to learn how to do something. If anyone could learn to read, to do so many things, it'd be him. And perhaps he'd find good jobs for Kenta and Hisato too. And they would be so wealthy, they'd invite father and I to live with them. I could help with raising the children when they were married and had babies. I knew a rich man wouldn't want to marry me, not unless he was blind. But I thought of how I could still be in my brothers' lives in this wonderful fantasy.

It was my favorite thing to daydream about at home. Sometimes I'd think: and then if I found a rich man with a kind heart who would need a wife, I would ask Fumei to come visit, and arrange to have them meet. Or maybe a prince would pass by when she visited and fall instantly in love, and she would be so grateful that she'd invite us to her palace often. Sometimes, I would imagine that Kyu was the one to go to school, and come back to confess how he'd loved me all along too, and we'd live in a big house where we never had to work hard.

Now, though. Now things were different. In twenty years, I would be too old to get married and have a family, even if I were beautiful like Fumei. Kyu would marry someone else. If he did secretly love me, twenty years was too long to wait. A part of me tried to imagine he waited anyway, though I couldn't quite picture how he would look as almost forty years old. It would be the most romantic thing, to have waited and loved no other.

But I knew that was asking too much.

I would instead resigne myself to taking children into the forests and teaching them like I'd done before. And I would spend more time in the mountain learning where every fruit tree was, and planting seeds to see if they grew. In my daydreaming, they always grew, and the village never went hungry after that. They would say: *Hisa grew the trees! And we are so happy! Her hard work has paid off and benefitted everyone. All young girls should work hard and make kindness their priority, just like Hisa.* I found I would smile as I imagined that.

On the night of the third day, I woke with a fright. Ferocious growls echoed through the night, howling pierced my ears, and a mighty roar shook the house and kennels. I curled up in my corner, hiding under my deel and clinging to my bunny. Voices, urgent and shouting over each other made me more afraid. I could hear people running above, in the room of the house that acted as the ceiling for the kennels. The growling grew louder, chants and shouts competed with one another, though I couldn't hear what any of it was.

I curled up tighter, shaking. Was I going to be eaten by a Kurai? Did one of them get into the villa and now had everyone fighting it off? What was happening?

A soft glow, barely visible, peered through my woven mat. I don't know what possessed me, but I pulled back my mat and took off the loose stone. Before I realized it, I had the puzzle box with me, hiding under the fleece of my deel. The glow poured out from the tiniest slits on the box, and provided a comfort to me while roaring and snarling and other terrible sounds shook the room above.

I didn't wake early the following day. In fact, it wasn't until the gate to my cell closed and was locked again that I opened my eyes. It was already late into the morning, and the guard who had brought me my breakfast walked away tired. But I stayed still, waiting to be sure no one would come around so I could put away the puzzle box.

I ate quietly that day, still uncertain of what to make of the fuss the night before. Where did those horrible sounds come from? Would it happen again? What should I do if it did happen again? What *could* I do?

Making things worse, my blood had come. I hadn't planned on staying here at all, much less prepare. There were no guards to check on me, or a soul in sight until my supper was brought. I asked if I could speak to a staff woman on a private matter, and he blinked at me, quizzical. I tried to hide my blood and my embarrassment, asking with fervor and saying it was urgent. It wasn't until the following morning that a woman came to my cell, and I worked hard not to cry as I explained myself, asking for a cloth and a water bucket so I could clean it.

She looked at me with shock. I suppose they all thought I was a boy, unshapely as I was with my hair barely growing back.

"Syaoran was right to send me," said the woman, composing herself again. "The guard from last night made light of it this morning, and had his head nearly chewed off for delaying. Apparently, he's the only one who knew you're a girl. Or, a young woman."

"I'm sorry," I said. "I didn't say anything at first because I was desperate to free my brother. And after, I thought I would die, so there wouldn't be any point." I had to focus to steel myself and keep my voice from cracking or my tears from falling.

She sighed. "Leave it to him and his soft spot for downtrodden folk. You must have looked terrified that he learned you're a girl for him to keep it secret. Rest assured, the menfolk here aren't so barbaric. I'll fetch you a cloth." She turned swift on her heel, her beautiful silken dress flowing with her movement.

I was trembling. She sounded perturbed with me. I'd made a plan to not cry, not cause trouble or complain, and already I'd done the opposite. It wasn't my fault, but still...

I thanked her repeatedly when she returned, though she looked at me with suspicion and demanded I explain myself. My appearance, she meant. And I answered every question, doing my best to be polite and truthful. I'd even explained how my first blood terrified me. That I thought I was dying, and one of the neighboring women had to come to explain things to me. My mother had died when I was too young to have that talk.

Through it all, she twisted her face this way and that, judging my words and deciding if she believed me or not.

"There aren't many women attending to Lord Kwan or the house as it is. I head seven others, and that is all."

I blinked, not understanding.

"And getting a man to come and take your wash bin every day is near impossible. For the warrior sort, they're squeamish around a woman's blood."

I apologized to her again, barely audible though I tried to sound firm. What else was there for me to say?

She sighed again, pensive. "I'll speak with Lord Kwan when he's a little recovered."

At that, I blinked, wondering when he'd returned. Perhaps to battle back whatever horrible creature had come the night before.

"We can't have you like this, no matter how long."

I didn't know what that meant exactly, and I worried that I'd jeopardized any chance of leniency to my punishment. For the moment, all I could do was clean myself up.

It was days later, and Yua—the woman who'd brought me a cloth—was right. Whatever guard was in charge of me was now more eager to be in and out as quickly as possible. I felt even more isolated and alone. But I wouldn't cry over it. At least, not enough to sob. Tears fell from me one night, and my breathing in that moment took the occasional shake. Though, I was determined to not make a fuss of it. I wouldn't let them hear or see how upset I was.

Five days, and my blood over, Gi came to my cell with Yua. The kind look of him replaced with an anxious uncertainty and fidgeting.

"They said you're actually a girl," said Gi. "Is that, is that true?"

I retreated my arms to myself, tucking down my neck as I nodded.

"I already told you that, you fool," said Yua, unlocking my cell.

Gi fumbled, seeming awkward and not at all the put-together guardsman I'd met. "About all the things I said before—I never meant to..." he seemed as much a loss for words as I was.

I tried to repay his kindness, with a small gesture of my own. A single shake of my head, and an answer. "It's alright."

That was enough to cause him to relax a little. "If you do need something, I've been restationed to the house wall. The master thinks I'm too trusting to be at the outer one anymore."

"You are," said Yua. "Are you coming, girl?"

"Coming?" I repeated.

"To start your chores. Your cell will remain unlocked, and you can return here to rest when you've completed the day's work. Unless you'd rather stay locked in here."

I didn't let myself hesitate. At the very least I could be in the sun again, and I wouldn't be so bored. Better, if I had chores, it meant that Lord Kwan decided not to execute me after all.

Chapter 6
Lord Kwan II

Five days since his return. He'd pushed himself too far when fighting with the fox demons, and lost control again. But he needed to call on that power, lest they harm more people. In the aftermath, he'd regained some of himself—enough to sprint back here and be put under chains until he was too worn to be dangerous.

On the fifth day, he felt he finally had the strength to get out of bed. The incents in every corner and on every surface of his room left a feint haze. He opened his window, wincing at the sunlight and cacophony of birds. His lungs took in the fresh air, helping to ease him from the sudden shock of the environment. He breathed in more deeply, staring out the window and looking over the gardens.

A young woman in his staff fed the koi in the pond, graceful in her movements—contrasted by the thrashing of the frenzied fish. A male servant worked a net, cleaning any leaves or other debris from the water. Other young men worked to keep the area neat, perfect looking.

The butterfly from before returned. It's long and pointed black wings fluttering to keep it airborne until it decided to land. Again, it was alone.

He took his meals, replaying as much of the battle as he could remember in his mind. It'd been a trap. Somehow, word slipped about his spent energy for the doe's spirit. Gumiho was there, somewhere in the shadows. He'd felt it. Still, he couldn't pin-point it, no matter how slow or how often he recounted the events. The moment he assumed his more powerful form, darkness clouded his memory. Streaks of red. Dead Kurai. But not their queen.

He stayed shut in. He wasn't ready yet to be himself. To plan, to issue orders, to do anything. His relief was in knowing he didn't hurt a member of his household when he returned. In his haze, he retained enough control of himself to do that much.

With or without a soul to help control that power, the gods didn't forgive senseless killing, especially in one's own house.

They'd come close, closer than he'd anticipated. There wasn't any question about it now. The Kurai were becoming bolder. A thought Kwan mulled over for a long time.

Every drop of the bamboo fountain, and its strangely therapeutic clank, measured the quarter hour. More than ten had passed before Syaoran came, inquiring about the duties he was to perform as acting master. The conversation was kept brief, with Kwan too exhausted to indulge in banter or anything more. It was mid-afternoon before his next visitor came.

Yua announced herself, asking for entry. He said nothing. Rather than leave, she waited. And when she grew tired of waiting for her master's response, she announced that she was coming in anyway. From the small antechamber to his apartment in the house, she stepped delicately and with dignity. She was his servant, but a lady in her own respect.

It was the way of things. The least prominent daughters of noteworthy families served the greater lords, elevating their family's status in that way. Often, the hope was that the daughter would be favored enough to become a consort, or a second wife after the first died (if she was lucky).

Not that there was a passion between them. She'd been in love with the lesser son of a different Juneun, and waited for him still. Kwan, knowing how volatile he might become, didn't want to involve another who might get used to hurt him. Rather, they were a practical pair, treating each other as equals and more familiar than they ought to be, respectably. She had a way of tempering his choices, the hard choices. And he ensured there was no unwanted attention to her or her ladies.

Were it anyone else, he'd see the intrusion as a slight on him.

"My lord," greeted Yua, direct and with only a slight bow of her head, "About the prisoner in the kennel."

"Prisoner?" He looked from the window to her, cold. "Yes. What about the prisoner?"

"What do you plan to do with her?"

"Her?"

"The young girl who took her brother's place, my lord."

He narrowed his eyes, reading her expression. She returned his stony gaze, unrelenting in her stillness. When he gleamed her meaning, he looked back out the window, embracing the sun on his face.

"What does it matter?"

"It matters because she's a fifteen-year-old girl in the kennels," said Yua, taking a sharpness to her tone. "She didn't even have a cloth for her blood, and she's outgrown what she arrived in. If you plan to carry out an execution, it is cruel to make her wait and give false hope. If you plan to keep her, some arrangements must be made."

Kwan sat there, chin in his palm, thinking it over.

"She fully expected to die the morning following her arrival. From what I gathered, she accepted the fate. Then you took off so suddenly."

"I had no choice."

"It has been near a week since your return, my lord. The child needs an answer."

He stayed silent, stoic, thinking. "What was the crime?"

Yua, caught off guard, hurried to answer. "The doe. Her brother was hunting on your lands and shot it down. He mistook it for an ordinary beast."

"That's right," said Kwan, cool in his tone. "I remember now."

"Syaoran knew she was not a boy, but elected to withhold that information from us."

"From you," said Kwan, now more absent in his voice.

The butterfly took flight, gliding away to the shade of trees further into the garden.

"If I recall, he wanted to speak on the matter that same day. Until we were interrupted with urgent news."

Yua scoffed, irritated by the revelation. "What is to be done with her?"

He thought on it longer, more to make Yua wait than anything else. He was her lord, and spoke on his terms, not hers. "I suppose it's late for an execution. Therefore, the punishment is for poaching."

"And that is?"

He made her wait. "Five years."

"She's to sit there like a dog in all that time?"

"Since we don't have anywhere else to keep her."

"And what about when her blood is in? Or baths? And winter is—"

"The villagers have endured worse, thanks to brazen enough Kurai."

Yua sneered, her temper fast getting out her control. "I never knew you could be so callus. Did you lock away your heart as well as your soul? Or did Gumiho take that?"

Kwan whipped his head back to face her and stood. Bearing a sever scowl, he took deliberate steps towards her.

Yua clasped her hands over her mouth. She'd been too liberal and spoken out of turn to her master. As he came near, she stepped back, past the antechamber and onto the veranda, eyes wide the entire time.

He stopped at the edge of the antechamber, a hand to each of the paper doors. In a swift movement, he shut them together with a slam. He repeated the motion with the inner doors as well, sucking in a deep breath through his nose to hold for a second longer than usual. After a slow release, her heated words resounded in his mind.

Had he become so cold?

He was no longer able to laugh, and scarce could muster a smile. He rested his forehead on the wood frame of the paper-paned doors. It seemed like all happiness and warmth was fleeing his heart. A soulless heart. Was it really so?

He had to find Gumiho, and end things once and for all. Only then would it be safe.

Chapter 7
It's Hard Work

"The tea house was damaged in the last earthquake," said Yua. "The men have taken apart the flooring, and repairs are needed for the heating. Today, they'll finish dismantling the inner workings of it. And they'll need wet clay to begin making it anew."

"A lot of the houses in the village had the same problem," I said, happy to know I could do the task asked of me. "We've been repairing them one by one. Ours didn't seem too badly damaged, so we were going to take care of it last."

"So, you're familiar with the clay mixing process?"

I nodded, eager to prove myself.

"Then you'll know quality clay from contaminated clay. The tea house is just over there, and the pit is this way."

I followed behind, glancing to where she gestured so I could memorize what it looked like.

"Tomorrow, you'll mop the veranda of the main house. You'll find everything you need in the shed there."

Again, I looked to where she pointed, working to remember where everything was.

"If you haven't finished by sundown, continue in the following morning. Most of all, stay out of the way as much as you can."

"Yes, ma'am," I said, committing as much as I could to memory.

"If you do finish, we'll find some other task to keep you occupied."

The clay pit was outside the first wall, though I didn't dare dream of running. I'd taken my brother's place. Running might undo all the pleading that freed him. Aside from that, I couldn't hope to make it back to the village. There was still another, bigger, more splendid wall between me and home.

Gi stopped outside the gate, giving me a word of encouragement. I wanted to stop to ask if he would tell my family about my new arrangement, but Yua didn't slow her pace and I didn't want to risk getting lost before I'd started. It'd have to wait until I made the route a few times and wouldn't forget.

Syaoran overlooked the clay pit, his fox ears picking up the sound of our approach and turning before he faced us. He greeted with a warm smile, and I was happy to see him. Hearing that the guard brushed off my request and he'd sent Yua to me, I felt grateful. Aside from Gi, he seemed like the only friend I had—if I could call him a friend, as a prisoner.

"You're looking much better," said Syaoran. "How's your courage holding up?"

"She's here to work off her debt," said Yua.

"Her brother's debt," corrected Syaoran, keeping a lightness in his voice. "But I see your point. Does Lord Kwan know about this?"

"He left the matter to me," said Yua, direct. "Until I can think of something better, this will have to do."

Syaoran chuckled. "Well, this is better than staying locked up like a dog, if you ask me."

"She said she's familiar with what needs doing. So, there shouldn't be any reason to hoover over her. Let her work."

I took that as a cue, and gave a deep bow with the pledge to work hard.

Syaoran laughed. "Courage is intact. I'm glad. But there's no need to bow to anyone other than the master. And any guests he has. I appreciate it though."

"You're going to spoil the girl out of good manners, aren't you?" said Yua, sharp.

Syaoran only smiled.

When he motioned for me to come, I did. Yua helped me, and I think she meant to be kind, but there was a coldness about her that put me on edge.

I worked tirelessly, despite the thick, muggy air. At some point, wiping me face with my sleeve became pointless, and only smeared streaks of dirt and clay on my skin. The sun was hot that day, and I sighed with every reprieve the clouds gave in blocking its brightness for a time. My bucket would become heavy with clay, and I hurried to bring it to the tea house where the men softened it with water and mixed it to make it workable.

Bucket after bucket, I was determined to show my worth. I wouldn't be thought of as lazy or lowly.

The clouds thickened overhead. We were all glad of it, as well as the cool breeze blowing through. All our working came to a sudden halt when the rain pounded down without warning. I'd accidentally shrieked in surprise. Everyone hurried out of the clay, taking a moment to enjoy the feel of the water rinsing away sweat and grime once we were in the grass.

Syaoran dictated that work for the day was done, and would resume only after the rain had completely stopped. Everyone walked back to their rooms, and I headed for my cell. I hadn't worked the entire day, but felt tired enough to not worry. At the very least, I didn't need to wash now. Inside the wall again, Syaoran spotted me and came to walk me back. He held a palm upward, an invisible force keeping himself, and now me, from being pelted by water.

I'd told him what Yua had said, asking him to point out where I might find the supply shed again. In all my running around, I'd forgotten. He didn't scold me for it. With a warm smile, he pointed it out. When I asked if news of my arrangement would go to my family, he assured me that he'd send someone personally. I knew I had no right to ask any favors, but I couldn't help myself. I asked if Gi could be the one to take the message. He chuckled, saying couldn't guarantee that particular detail.

Regardless, I was relieved.

At the kennels, Syaoran and I parted ways. He didn't come in, complaining that it still smelled of dogs and made him uncomfortable. I couldn't smell a thing, but I didn't have the nose of a fox spirit. Still, I thought it was for the better. Alone, I could take off my soaking clothes and slip into my deel. My bunny waited in the corner for me. Thoughtless, I sat with it in my lap, stroking its soft ears as I looked outside.

The rain continued into the following day. I set to work without Yua telling me, and fetched a bucket and rags to mop up the veranda, careful not to leave it scuffed or streaked. A fine polish to each floorboard. It took me hours for one length, from corner to corner. The job would take days, and I'd probably need to start again once I finished. It didn't seem fair. Though, it was better than being trapped in a cell. At least I could take short breaks and admire the house and the gardens.

I was nearly done with another section, putting all of my lean weight into polishing with a thick folded rag, when I accidentally collided with someone's toes as they came around the corner. I scooted back, making a series of apologies. When I looked up, I paled. The toes belonged to Lord Kwan. Not knowing what else to do, I kept on my trembling knees and bowed with another set of apologies.

He said nothing for a while. Was he furious?

"You're the prisoner girl?"

I looked up at his stony expression and studying eyes. My voice wouldn't come, so I nodded.

He looked me over. "You're thin."

I nodded again, confused. Was I supposed to continue on? Or wait for a command? What cue was I supposed to be looking for?

"What are you doing?"

"I was," my voice came out as a squeak. "I was mopping the floors, my lord. I was told to."

"All of them?"

"The veranda at least. I don't know what I'm supposed to do afterwards."

He stared at me, taking in a deep breath before looking away. "Ridiculous."

I held myself from shaking. What did that mean? Was he going to send me back to my cell, to sit and wait for the years to pass?

"Don't you have something better to do with your time?"

I didn't know what to say. I was a prisoner, and I didn't have anything with me for a hobby.

"Answer me, girl."

"I'll work harder," I whispered.

He looked at me then, still with that cold expression. I felt then that I'd said the wrong thing. Rather than chastise me or scold me, he said nothing, and walked away.

I sat there a long while, unsure of what I ought to do. But knowing nothing else, I tried to put aside the uncomfortable meeting and press on.

For three days it rained. And we still had to wait an extra day before we could gather more clay without getting stuck. When enough had been brought, and the restoration well underway, the men bid me to fetch other things.

"Salt?"

"It's in the storage shed in the furthest part of the yard," said one worker. "The one by the old back well."

"Shed in the back yard, by the old well," I repeated, partly for myself, and partly to let him know I understood.

He nodded. "We'll need four sacks. But they're heavy."

"I can do it," I said. Anything so I wouldn't look so useless.

"Go on then."

I sprinted, as fast as my legs would take me. My bruises had gone, allowing me to run without any soreness.

The farthest part of the yard, behind the main house, looked half wild. Hedges and trees grew long, shading and sheltering the area. It looked forgotten and mysterious, as though there was magic in its wake. I decided that I liked it back here where it felt so quiet and hidden. Even the old wind chime stayed silent, with algae and moss taking over it.

I knew I should hurry, panting as I was, but I felt drawn to the old well. The wood planks that covered its opening had a layer of dust and leaves and growing things on it. Gentle, I brushed off as much as I could with my bare arm. The wood looked in good enough condition, leaving me confident that it would crumble or break if I lifted it. Still, I was careful.

The board I'd chosen was stuck. Undeterred, my fingers wiggled under to pry it up. It came free, and I slowly lifted it away to set aside. Peering in, in went far down, into a dark pool of water. So dark, it looked black. I was curious now, and started to drop in the bucket to bring out a sample for a closer look.

"Lose something?"

I jumped with a shriek, turning around to see Syaoran stepping into the shade. In my fright, I'd dropped the bucket, the rope going with it faster than I could think to grab. Looking back at him, I felt myself shrinking with embarrassment.

"It's alright," said Syaoran, a laugh in his kind voice. He trotted up, waving a hand over the well, his fingers dipped down, and he raised his arm in a lifting motion, like he was pulling up something that wasn't there. Magic, I realized. And the rope obediently came up, snake-like, with the bucket in tow. At his gesture, they neatly set themselves aside.

I gawked, having never seen magic up close. Or ever, really. I supposed there was that first rainy day, though I was tired and didn't give it any thought in the moment.

"What were you doing?" asked Syaoran. "Hiding something?"

"No," I said quickly, shaking my head and pulling my arms into my stomach.

"I'm only teasing," said Syaoran. "Really, now. What were you doing?"

"I just," I could feel my tongue wanting to stutter, and slowed down my words. "I wanted to see what was down there."

"Aha. So, you *were* looking for something." He leaned over me, smiling.

"N-no."

He laughed. "I don't think you're trying to cause trouble. But it's best to not let others see you acting suspicious."

"I, I wasn't. I was just curious." I pulled my hands higher on my torso, hiding behind them.

"They might not see it that way." He straightened himself, standing proud. "Think about it: a prisoner wandering around and rifling through things so secretively. It doesn't look good."

I wanted to repeat myself, but it would only sound silly. He was right.

I started to get used to his odd colored hair and fox ears. He no longer seemed so strange to me. Now, I could see he did have a handsome face, one that was always smiling with a kind expression. In that brief moment, I wished that I wasn't so ugly—that I had a clear face or long and shiny hair, or a more womanly body, something that would be called pretty.

It was a selfish and shallow thought. He was a Juneun, after all, and I was a poor, mortal, village girl.

"Why are you back here, anyway?" asked Syaoran, sounding a little serious. "Keeping cool in the shade?"

"No, I was—" I gasped when I remembered. "I was told to get the salt from the storage shed back here."

"From back here?" He quirked a brow as he spoke, a look of intrigue on his face.

I hurried to the shed, finding the lock open but the door unwilling to move. It hadn't been opened in a long time, by my guess. Syaoran's magic opened it for me, and I gave a quick word of thanks before going in to look for the sacks of salt. They waited in sloppy stacks. To make up for lost time, I picked up two. They were heavy, but I thought I could manage well enough. Syaoran said nothing, giving an amused look as I shuffled quickly past.

Chapter 8
The Secret Door

On my way back, I thought I could make up more time by crossing the corners of the veranda on the main house. In doing so, one of the salt sacks slipped from my grip. It hit the wooden floor with a dull thud, spilling some of its contents. I couldn't just leave it there. Setting the other down, I positioned them better and lifted them more comfortably. They didn't spill too much, and I could hurry back to sweep away the mess.

As I muttered it to myself, turning to run to the tea house, I collided with someone. I made my apologies, stepping back and out of the way, only to see it was Lord Kwan. Worse, there was clay and dirt and salt on his robes, right where I'd bumped into him.

He looked from his clothes to me, annoyed. For a long while, he stared. "What are you doing?"

"I," it was difficult to keep my voice from breaking. I swallowed and tried again. "I was told to bring the salt from the back shed, m-my lord."

He studied me. Ferocious eyes looking at every inch of his prisoner. "The salt is no good."

I blinked.

"Everything in that storage shed is spoiled. After the last earthquake, it was badly damaged and the rain fell in."

A fool's errand. The men working to repair the tea house sent me away on a task they didn't expect me to complete. I dropped my head, shifting my weight from one foot to the other.

"Get yourself cleaned up," said Lord Kwan, dismissive. "You're done for the day." He walked off, regal in every step.

I stood there a while, holding off tears. It made no sense to play such a cruel joke. I felt like a complete fool. Regaining my will, I walked back to the forgotten shed to put back the salt. Rather than going back to my cell, I stayed in the shade, finding a bench that was overtaken by vines and other plants to sit on. I couldn't understand why I was sent to here in the first place.

I looked down at myself, my legs coated in dirt, clumps of clay sticking to my clothes, and my hands dry and wrecked from it all.

"Back already?" teased Syaoran.

I swallowed my sorrow and self-pity before looking up at him.

"Hm? What's wrong?"

"I just..." I paused. I said I would never complain. I would be on my best behavior, and I wouldn't cry. Even if they were cruel to me, I wouldn't let them see me cry. "Could I go to the river?"

"The river? Why?" He tucked his arms into the opposite sleeves, looking more elegant.

"Lord Kwan told me to clean up."

"And you want to go to the river for that?" The way he asked, it was as if I'd made an absurd request.

I nodded.

He sighed, brow furrowed. "I probably shouldn't do this, but I'll show you a secret way there so you can have some privacy. But, only if you promise you won't run away. Because if you do, we'll both be in trouble."

"I won't," I said. I already wouldn't, in case it meant resulting in the death of Hisato and myself.

"Good. Follow me."

I didn't have to follow. He grabbed my wrist, leading the way quickly through the dense growth of the back garden. His hand felt warm, and soft. Not the sweaty sort of warm, but a tender and comforting sort. My own hands were rough and callused. A part of my wondered if it felt odd to him, uncomfortable perhaps. Though, he didn't say a word about it.

"Even when this place was well kept, this door stayed hidden. I like to use it sometimes to get away and be alone without someone following me."

I began to worry with how ominous that sounded.

Sure enough, a small door at the base of the white wall stayed tucked away from view until we were in front of it. There was writing on it. A word of some kind. I didn't ask.

He let go of my wrist. "After you," he said, opening the door.

It wasn't so small that I needed to crawl. I crouched low and made it through easily enough. To my surprise, there wasn't a forest on the other side. It stayed kempt, with the lowest branches of the trees pruned back.

"Let's go," said Syaoran, taking my wrist again.

We passed under the trees and through the beams of sunlight that filtered through. It was a pleasant place, though I felt somehow exposed. I began to look around as he pulled me along, my eyes taking in the pretty scenery and the butterflies fluttering through the air.

When we came closer to the outer wall, taller than I remembered, I noticed a part of it had crumbled. The land beside it too, looked as if it'd been split and shoved down.

"What's that?"

"Hm?" Syaoran stopped to look. "Oh. That happened after the earthquake. Don't tell anyone. Lord Kwan has enough to worry about. As long as our enemies don't know about it, we can fix it quietly. It'll take a while though."

I blinked at him. "Why? Can't you use magic?"

"Some, yes. But water likes to pool there so the ground isn't stable anymore."

I stared a moment, thinking how tragic it sounded. When he tugged on my wrist again, I complied, and picked up pace.

Another small door with another word on it, hidden by shrubs and treetops. Outside the wall, thick forestry. I began to worry I might get lost in the trees. There were no well-worn paths for me to follow. Syaoran didn't share the feeling, leading at a more manageable pace. He pointed out the markers he'd made, though some were hard to see.

I kept looking back towards the wall, hoping to remember what the path looked like that way.

Most prominent of the markers were the stone tigers that sat like guardians. They weren't large, and might be easy to miss if I didn't know they were there. I felt more secure in being able to pick them out to help retrace my steps.

Finally, we came to the river. Though, here it looked more gentle, wider yet somehow shallower.

"If you do get lost," said Syaoran, "just follow the river and it'll take you to the stairs. And try not to be seen. You can follow the wall easily enough, I think."

"Thank you," I said, smiling shyly. "You've been so kind to me."

A sly look came on him, making him appear more fox-like than ever. "Usually, when a nobleman does great kindnesses for a maiden, they reward him with a kiss."

I gasped, blushing. Not that I didn't want to, but because of the implication. Did *he* want me to kiss him? I remembered Yua saying that the menfolk serving Lord Kwan weren't so brutish, even if I didn't really understand what that meant. The other men had played a prank, sending me away. Was this another joke? Did Syaoran mean to take advantage of me somehow? What if I refused?

He laughed. "I'm only kidding. In the stories, it's because the two become lovers."

Lovers.

"But a fifteen-year-old girl is too young for me."

His smile stayed warm, though I couldn't help but wonder if he'd change his mind when I was a little older. I broke free of that fantasy a second later. A Juneun would fall in love with another heavenly spirit, surely, or a very beautiful mortal. And I wasn't either of those.

He waved me off.

"Are there," I stumbled in my words. "Are there leeches in the river?"

His smile faded, replaced by a puzzled expression. "Not that I've encountered."

"And... alligators?"

His smile returned with a chuckle. "No. You're perfectly safe from them. Snakes and other things, I can't promise."

"I know to look out for those," I said, feeling relieved.

He nodded. "Don't take too long then." He left in a flash, faster than my eyes could see and leaving a wind in his wake.

Alone, I stripped down and washed my clothes first. Finding a bit of sunlight, I laid them out to dry. Then, carefully, I waded into the river. I didn't dare go deeper than my knees, fearing I would slip and be swept into a watery grave. Instead, I sat in the water and worked furiously to scrape off as much as I could. Admittedly though, I did linger a while, enjoying the cold of the river after the hot summer day. I would've stayed all afternoon, except that I didn't want Syaoran to get in trouble if I was gone too long.

My clothes were still wet when I put them back on. I didn't mind. They'd probably dry by the time I got back to my cell.

Through the first small door, I took a moment of pride. I didn't get lost. It would be easy from here to get to the other hidden door. I didn't go as fast as Syaoran did when showing me the way. Hands behind my waist, I looked up to admire the trees and the way the leaves played in the sunlight. The birds flew from one place to another, singing their beautiful melodies. Though, sometimes it sounded like a squabble more than it did a song. I smiled anyway, happy to listen and walk at my own pace. For the moment, I imagined I was a guest and not a prisoner, an important friend of a proud lord and this was his private garden—a tamed forest between mighty walls.

Butterflies, too many to count and of all shapes and colors, made me stop to admire their beauty. I saw a few that I remembered mother drawing when I was small. My smile widened when I saw a few I'd tried to draw. They seemed to like the area beside the crumbling walls. I would've stayed for an hour or more, just watching them, pretending that mother was beside me, drawing.

But it was getting late.

I stopped before I really started. A sharp chirping, distressed, caught my ear. It sounded like a hurt frog. My eyes scanned, ears honing in to find the source. Not a frog, but a baby bird with hardly any feathers on it; what feathers it had were still in shafts and useless for the moment. It'd fallen from its nest, and my heart pitied it. I cooed as I scooped it up, and craned my neck as far back as I could to find the nest. If it was near enough and on a strong branch, maybe I could return it.

No such luck. Either it'd fallen quite some distance, or unwittingly crawled to a different tree. So, I stood there, looking between the trees and the tiny creature in my hands, listening to its exhausted cry. Maybe I should've left it, but my heart wouldn't let me. It was more helpless than I was.

"Don't worry," I whispered to it. "I'll take care of you until you're ready to fly. I'll keep you safe." I knew it didn't understand, but I said it all the same and gently tucked it into my shirt to better comfort it and keep it quiet.

Before leaving the forgotten part of the yard inside the walls, I ripped up some long grass and thin vines. If someone watched me, I probably looked suspicious, sneaking back to my cell. When I'd made it, I sighed in relief.

I brought out my new friend, who calmed and looked at me with perplexed, black eyes. I sat him on my mat, and went right to making a nest for him. I needed to hurry, before supper, figuring I could use my stuffed bunny to better conceal him in the corner of my cell.

When my supper was brought, I waited patiently to make sure no one else would come by, and took tiny pinches to feed my new friend. He ate it up greedily, always asking for more, despite the fact that I could see he was full. It was instinct I suppose, to always ask for more and grow faster.

I did the same in the morning, waiting to be alone and then feeding the chick before hiding it behind my bunny. Straightening up, I went right to work to clean the veranda and the mess I'd left the day before.

Before I could move on to a new section, however, I noticed the tea house flooring was full of clay and mud. If left there too long, it would damage the wood. With renewed supplies, I went to work. The men from before might have been unkind, but I wouldn't let one incident prevent me from doing what I knew was the right thing. It was Lord Kwan's tea house, not theirs. Syaoran spoke highly of his master, and, if nothing else, it'd make him happy to see it complete and polished.

I didn't realize the extent of it, but pushed on anyway. The sun began to hang low in the sky, letting me know that I'd spent the entire day cleaning one place. My back began to ache, and I stretched up to soothe it with a groan for good measure.

With the water in my bucket too murky to use, I slid it to the edge by the shrubs, and flung out the water as I had each time before. Though, if I wasn't so eager, I would've noticed Lord Kwan and not accidentally splashed the bottom hem of his beautiful robes.

He looked down with a raised brow, keeping that same stony expression. Then his gaze went wherever it was wet, before moving to look at me.

I bowed deep, making an apology. This was the third time I'd made some offense. My gut turned over, waiting for him to yell or command me to go back to my cell.

He stepped forward, and I feared he might beat me first. I'd heard tales of servants receiving that kind of punishment for being clumsy in the presence of their master. When he walked by, I couldn't help but look up and watch. His eyes inspected the floor, the finished and polished sections and the bit that still had a layer of clay in need of scrubbing.

"Who told you to do this?"

"No one," I said. "I saw that it was dirty, so I cleaned it, my lord."

He stayed still, looking it over again. I didn't know if I was meant to carry on or not, and fidgeted with the hems of my sleeves.

"You were missing yesterday," said Lord Kwan. "Where did you go?"

I flinched, thinking quickly how to say things without getting Syaoran in trouble. "You ordered me to clean myself up. So, I went to the river to bathe."

"The river."

I became rigid.

"Who said you should go to the river?"

"No one, my lord. I was so heavily caked in clay and dirt that... I'm more used to cleaning in a river than with a bucket, my lord."

He looked at me then, with that stoic expression. "I'm surprised you didn't run back to your village. None of my gate guards saw you leave. Either they're blind, or you have some magic to you. A witch maybe."

I shook my head. "It's only as I've said, my lord. I promise." It took all the strength I had to keep my voice under control, and not cave into my panic. "I said I would take my brother's place, and I'll work the debt owed. I stayed on this side of the river. I swear. Twenty years is not too long a time."

"Twenty?"

I started to crumple into myself.

"I commanded five."

We stared at each other. Only five years. My heart swelled with hope.

That night, I ate heartily and slept deep. For the first time since I'd come here, I slept well. Well, and happy.

Chapter 9
Lord Kwan III

Kwan looked at his clothes, and the red dust threatening to stain it. Not that the stains mattered. He didn't go to courts, nor did he hold any unless made to. It wasn't like his youthful years, when everything seemed so simple and happy. He didn't have the strength to attend or host. Not while Gumiho was still out there. Holding court would only lead to spent energy, enticing her to attack. Some days, it was all he could do to safe guard this mountain from Kurai. Other days, it wasn't enough. And now that the doe...

Better that all the Juneun though he'd become a shut in than to know the truth. Afterall, Gumiho wasn't the only threat. Given the chance, however, he feared she'd trick others into a trap and torment them. As she'd done before. He'd never forgive her, from that day onward. So he set his home on Mount Tora, keeping her backed to the edge of the world and as far away from all else as possible.

He couldn't allow distractions.

Shedding his clothes to change, he reminded himself of that. He was still weak from the last confrontation; his only solace knowing that he'd dealt a heavy enough blow to keep her at bay. He needed to pretend he had more strength to him than he felt. If he gave even the slightest hint that it was taking longer for him to recover, Kurai from all over would swarm. They'd start with the mortals and the forests first. If he was to protect them, he needed to appear just as strong, if not stronger.

No distractions.

He looked at his discarded robe, at the red clay spattered on it. The scene replaying in his mind. Then Yua's words haunting him after.

The girl looked frightened every time he laid eyes on her. Shaking and pathetic. In spite of it, she labored without complaint. He'd first thought her a puppet, or perhaps her brother as one. But the parting of them didn't appear as much. He wouldn't put it past a Kurai to ensnare a desperate mortal and use them to get close. Though, if that was the case, she would have acted while he was in recovery.

Unable to stand it, he left his room freshly dressed, sword at his side. They kept her in the kennels, if he remembered right. He mused at the irony. A kennel without hounds, and a prisoner without a prison. Walking past the tea house, the men hastened to look busy.

"I want the job completed before sunset."

One man complained, saying it was delicate work that required more time.

Kwan stopped, turning on his heel. "Then you should have used the girl for an actual task to speed things along, rather than send her to fetch worthless things from a leaky shed in the farthest part of the estate."

To that, they went rigid and quickened themselves. He'd struck at them before for drunken insolence, and again when they sobered. His reputation might imply a hermit-like behavior, but his family line demanded a disciplined household. If only they knew, understood, that every laxed action could potentially spell their doom. He had to act as the master, regretting his allowances as it was.

When he reached the kennel, he found it empty, except for a woven mat, a tattered deel, and a child's toy. He stared a while, at how tidy it was kept. What an odd prisoner. Then again, what an odd place to hold one.

He walked out, crossing the path of a guardsman back from his post.

"Gi."

The guard halted, standing in attention.

"Where is the prisoner girl?"

Gi twisted his face at the question, bewildered. "I haven't seen her since this morning when she was bringing in clay, my lord."

It was an odd thing to imagine, though it explained a lot. "How often does she do that?"

Gi shrugged as he thought. "About as often as the men. She's a hard worker for a mortal girl."

Kwan grunted. It seemed lax behavior was rampant in his home. "Thank you, Gi." He walked on.

A new inspection of his estate began, walking the grounds and mulling over the new bit of information. In all his meandering, he hadn't crossed paths with his prisoner. Regardless, he needed to record his findings, and made to return to his room.

On the veranda, Syaoran walked by, stretching his arms with a wide yawn.

"Have you seen the prisoner girl?" asked Kwan.

"I haven't seen her all day. She's most likely gathering clay as Yua instructed, or in her cell."

Kwan grunted, continuing his path.

In his room, he set up his ink and paper. But it bothered him. She couldn't just vanish into thin air. He stared at the blank page, unable to collect his thoughts—Yua's words echoing in his head. He set aside his things, and concentrated. As long as she was on the mountain, he'd be able to find her.

His sight magnified, piercing through wood and stone and metal as he searched. It was a frivolous thing to waste energy on. And if it didn't put his mind at ease? Either way, he'd already used the spell.

He spotted her by the river that cut through his lands. So, she was running away; looking for a place to cross without being spotted. Then, something unexpected happened. She began to undress. Did she think that would help her crossing? She didn't cross though. It was to give her clothes a wash.

He let go of the spell, crinkling his nose as he tried to make sense of it. Of course, he'd told her to go and clean up. If she hadn't come into the house, she wouldn't know about... His eyes shut, helping to free him of the distraction so he could write down what needed attending and label them by order of importance.

When he completed it, some hours had passed. He heard no news of her.

Ridiculous.

As much as he resisted, his curiosity got the better of him. Again, he cast his sight to find her. She wasn't beside the river anymore. In his search, he found her inside the outer wall, smiling as she watched something intently. He fixed his gaze more. Butterflies. In great abundance. She was smiling at them. It was the first time he'd seen her unafraid, at peace. Curious.

Ending the spell, he leaned back where he sat, turning his head over his shoulder to look at the paper-paned window.

Curious.

After sunset, he walked the veranda of the house, with every member bidding him a good night as they retired to their rooms or went to take their post. In passing the tea house, he frowned at the mess. Lax behavior indeed.

Holding his palm upward, a small light formed to illuminate his path in a gentle glow. At the kennels, the girl didn't stir. She stayed blissfully asleep. He watched her a moment, trying to figure out how this same trembling mortal could be so still. There was the curiosity of that toy rabbit. What was the significance that she kept her cell tidy for it?

What a strange mortal.

He left without a word. Whatever way she'd found in and out of the walls, she chose to return. Why? Was her prisoner life preferable to her village? If so, why had he only seen her smile once, when there was not another around?

A strange prisoner.

Chapter 10
Summer's End

Yua collected me in the morning. Two weeks since Lord Kwan told me I would only stay a prisoner for five years and not twenty. I was to clear out the stables and stock the pens fresh with straw. I'd only ever known Lan's old mare, patting her when he stopped to let me. But I knew a few bits of caution: to never be close behind a horse, what it meant when they swished their tails, how the position of their ears told you their mood, and that they could kick just as hard to the side if they felt threatened. That was the extent of my knowledge, which was better than nothing, and let me feel like I shouldn't fear them.

The horses here were bigger. Tall with proud muscles and thick legs, I felt some intimidation being so close. Though, there were not too many. Only six.

When it came time to lead one out, they seemed to already know, and bent their head down to accept the lead rope. They kept a slow step behind me, patient with my pace. I patted them as I tied them off, exactly the way I was shown, giving them praise for their good manners. They didn't acknowledge it much. Perhaps as they grew used to me, they would. We could become good friends in time.

I cleared out the old bedding straw, hoisting it onto a cart that would take it away, and replaced it just as quickly with fresh stock. Something that reminded me to ask if any could be spared for my own cell. I resolved then to do the job perfectly. If the stable master found it pleasing, he wouldn't deny my request, would he?

When I came to the last horse, the sun was hanging low. It was a stallion fit for a lord. His dark brown fur gleamed in the soft rays of sunlight, looking like fire lurked just below. His yellow mane seemed to glow as well. He was nothing at all like Lan's mare, and I adored him from our first meeting. The stallion seemed curious about me as well, putting his nose close and taking in deep breaths of my scent. His lip played with my shirt for further investigation, though I pulled away in case a curious bite would follow. He didn't give me a reason to suspect that, but better to stay cautious. I didn't want to look incompetent before asking my favor.

Despite being the biggest horse, he was also the gentlest, keeping a keen look out for my bare feet. In his paddock again, he inspected my work, pawing at the straw before laying in it and rolling with a grunt of approval.

I chuckled, watching him; a magnificent creature behaving in the silliest way. He got back to his feet with little grace, shaking out with more sounding approval.

"He likes you," said the stable master. An older looking man with white hair neatly tied up, and a long, matching beard that looked finely combed. I thought it odd, since all the other spirits looked youthful and strong and graceful. Perhaps he was a much more ancient spirit.

"He does?" I asked, thoughtlessly swatting at my ear to shoo bugs. I remembered then that it was my hair, having grown and tickling.

"He doesn't see many ladies come through. The women of the house complaint it's too dirty."

I laughed. "I'm not afraid of a little dirt."

"No, you most certainly are not afraid of a little dirt." There was a pleasantness to his old voice as he spoke, patting my head.

"None of the girls in my village are," I went on. "We all help in the fields when there's a lot to do. There's no avoiding getting dirty at that point."

A smile, something like mischief came over his face. "Maybe they could learn from the human village girls. Sometimes I think Lord Kwan spoils them—but don't tell him I said that."

I shook my head, smiling.

"I'm sorry about the prank the others played you for." He straightened himself, looking back at the lordly stallion. "Lord Kwan was most upset by it. Said they were undisciplined and becoming lazy. Started whipping them into shape the next morning."

I paled a little. "Because of me?"

He gave a single, slow shake of his head. "It's true, we've become too relaxed under Lord Kwan's protection. Having one of the strongest Juneun as your master will do that. And since he decided to stop hosting court and festivities, there wasn't a need to keep things so pristine. You saw the neglect to the yard farthest in the back, correct?"

"He's one of the strongest?" I asked, curious. While we'd known a Juneun lived on the mountain, no one ever dared to come this far unless they were desperate, and so we knew very little about which one specifically lived here.

"His family's crest is the tiger. You can't just pick out a crest, you know, it has to be earned. Every heir of that family has a different colored one from their great deeds to the world."

I stared a while, taking in the story, and looked back to the stallion. "What great deed did Lord Kwan do?"

"He's the only one who can match Gumiho's power. That's why he chose here to live. He pushed her as far back from good lands as he could, to the edge of the world."

I placed my arms atop the paddock door, resting my head on them as I listened.

"I don't think he has the heart to destroy her. He's not that kind of man. That's why he took in Syaoran. The fox queen cast him out for some slight against her. Anyone else would have seen him as just another devil, and killed him. Lord Kwan took pity on the boy. You won't find a more faithful servant to any lord."

That surprised me. I'd wondered about Syaoran, but thought I would be seen as rude if I asked.

"Lord Kwan loved walking the woods. He was also quite the poet, and many ladies sought him out, dreaming he might choose them as a bride. It all changed a little over fifty years ago."

"Why?" I asked, looking back to the stable master. "What happened fifty years ago?"

He twisted his face in thought. "If you don't know, then it's probably for the best."

I didn't understand, but decided not to pry. If Lord Kwan was angry enough at his servants for a slight on his prisoner, I didn't want to know how he'd respond if he thought I was causing trouble. "If it's alright," I said. "Could I take any of the extra straw back to my cell?"

"Hm?" He looked me over. "I suppose so, though there's not much left. And Saburo likes you. I'm sure he won't mind."

"That's the stallion's name?"

He nodded at me, pointing. "It's here on his door."

I looked at the lines, trying to understand. It must've been a while, because I felt the stable master staring at me. I ignored it the best I could, wanting to remember what the name looked like.

At my cell, my face went pale. Tori, the bird I'd found, was missing. He'd been starting to fly short distances, but always stayed in the cell before. In a frantic whisper, I began to call for him. What if a snake had come in? Or one of the staff saw him and tossed him out? He wasn't strong enough just yet.

I called, my whispers quickening.

A set of demanding chirps caught my attention, calming me. I called again. Demanding chirps answered. I followed, calling again and listening. He'd gone to the back of the kennels, showing off that he could fly while demanding his supper.

I'd caught him easily enough, much to his displeasure, and hurried back to my cell to sit him in the nest I'd made.

"You can't just take off and explore on your own," I scolded, hushed in my tone. "You're not strong enough yet. What if something had happened to you?"

He stared at me with black eyes, as if he weren't the least bit naughty.

"I know you want to go out. But you have to wait for me to come back first."

He blinked, turning his head in what I knew was his way of being impatient.

"I promised I would keep you safe. So, you need to stay here while I work off my debt. I promise I'll try to be quicker so I can come back here earlier for you. Have patience."

"Who are you talking to?"

I jumped at the sound of Lord Kwan, getting to my feet awkwardly and bowing. I didn't hear him walk up, and now he stood in my cell with me.

He kept silent, waiting for an answer.

"I was..." I hesitated. Would he tell me to get rid of Tori? My mind searched for some lie I could tell, something that would protect my little friend, but he'd already caught me. "I found a baby bird, my lord, and I've been raising it you see."

He cocked a brow, a question on his stone face. "A bird?"

"I couldn't find his nest to return him, so I..." my fingers began to fidget with each other. "I couldn't just leave him there on the ground. He'd die, my lord. So, I thought maybe I could raise him and have him for company in my cell."

Lord Kwan blinked, slow. I remembered what the stable master had said. His crest was a tiger, and his eyes reflected that so clearly now. "It sounded like you were bargaining with it. Are you sure you're not a little witch?"

I shook my head, wanting to curl up and retreat into myself. "I'm not. I just," again, I hesitated, trying to figure out how to say things in a way that made sense. "I wanted a friend, my lord. Please don't make me put him out. He's not ready just yet."

He looked from me to the straw I'd brought in. "You were going to make it a cage?"

"N-no, my lord. I don't know how to make one. The straw is to make blankets for winter. I was told I could have a bit."

His eyes slowly made their way back to me. "Resourceful."

I blinked, not knowing if that was good or bad.

"I won't make you throw away your friend. You can keep him if you wish."

I felt relieved, and tried to smile as I said my thanks. He left without another word.

After supper, I kept my smile as I worked to weave a blanket together and started to think of how much I would need to secure myself from winter.

Out of new habit since my happy news, I brought out the puzzle box. The soft glow from within was a comfort to the aches I collected in the day, and there was something soothing in sliding around the pieces. Tonight, by chance, two of them clicked together. I found it difficult to separate them, and left them to slide around the others aimlessly until I grew tired.

At the end of the following day, I found a bird cage in my cell with Tori happily in it, jumping from place to place to strengthen his wings. A note was attached. I stared at it, not knowing what it meant or who did this. Still, I smiled, admiring the bamboo cage as my tiny friend showed off inside it.

Chapter 11
Autumn Harvest

Autumn was here, with a great deal less to do. I'd snuck through the secret door, taking Tori to the place where I'd found him. He'd grown to a fully matured bird. Selfishly, I'd kept him a bit longer. But I'd promised to give him back. It wasn't right to keep him locked away, in my heart I knew that. Even though I'd raised him, he was still wild. He didn't belong with me. Not if he didn't want to.

Leaves had fallen, leaving so many of the trees half naked.

Holding him, I recounted how I'd found him, explaining that this was that very spot. I told him how fond I'd grown of his company and how much I would miss him. He probably didn't understand a word, but it was a comfort to me.

The butterflies had gone for the season, and the grass was drying out and becoming brittle.

I told my friend he could visit me any time he wanted. Opening my hands, he stayed a moment. I thought perhaps he didn't want to leave. Then he gave me a last, loud, set of demanding chirps and flew off.

I stood there a while, my fingers fussing with my tattered deel. A part of me regretted the decision, wanting the company. It was too late now.

Walking back, I felt lonely.

Lord Kwan had a visitor, and the whole of the staff tried to make a show of themselves. I was to stay out of the way, which I didn't mind. Whoever this guest was, if they put everyone else on edge, I didn't want to meet them. They'd likely be in the tea house; or, that's what everyone said. Horses were brought into the stable, having carried the visitor and their entourage, preventing me from going to see Saburo.

I tried to stay where no one else was, and move out when I heard people coming.

A mess of mud was on the veranda near Lord Kwan's room where I next tried to keep out of sight. The servants told me never to disturb Lord Kwan, or enter his room. If I had some urgent message, I was instructed to give it to one of them to tell him. I didn't mind that rule either, strange as it was. But if his visitor was really someone important, the mess would be unsightly.

The rest of the staff was busy, and probably hadn't seen it yet. With nothing else to do myself, I fetched what I needed and started to clean it up. As I did, I noticed it spread farther than I first thought, and I went over it several times to make sure.

I could hear voices coming from Lord Kwan's room, and hurried so I could leave.

Somehow, the mud and mess seemed to reappear just as quickly as I'd cleaned it away. I couldn't have missed so much, I was sure of it. Putting in more of my strength, I worked as diligently as I did quickly, building sweat on my face.

Then the paper-paned doors slid open.

I froze. In the moment of wordlessness, I looked up. A toad-faced man with bulbous eyes stared at me. More than that, he seemed half toad and half man all in one. I knew it was rude, but I stared. I'd never seen someone who looked like that.

He breathed in deep, sniffing. "A human? Ah, you must be Lord Kwan's human prisoner." He leaned in, and I instinctively went rigid and scooted back. "You must be a gentle human because you smell sweet. The tastiest kind!"

"Now, Juro," said Lord Kwan, "Don't torment the girl."

"Girl?" said Juro in a start, looking from me to Lord Kwan and back.

"She's the hardest worker I have. I'd appreciate if you didn't tease."

An awkward smile stretched on Juro's face. "Old Kurai habits. I was only joking, of course. A human that small wouldn't make for a full meal anyway."

I pulled my arms in, using all my strength to keep from trembling.

"Juro," scolded Lord Kwan, keeping his voice leveled and polite.

The former Kurai laughed.

Lord Kwan placed a hand on Juro's shoulder, stealing his full attention. "If too many old habits slip back, we can finish what we started the day we met."

Juro's jaw became tight and his body rigid.

"You see she's trying to clear away your mud essence. When I tell you she's a hard worker, did you think I exaggerated?"

Juro relaxed, snickering.

When I looked around, I saw why. It was as though I'd never started to clean at all.

"Don't laugh," cooed Lord Kwan. "A human wouldn't know. Yet she tried. I don't doubt she stayed vigilant in an impossible task."

"It's a shame she's not a beauty. It'd make for a better story."

"Story?"

I stayed there, uncomfortable as they talked about me.

Rethinking himself, Juro let go of the conversation. "I should be getting back. Who else is going to make sure those damned leech demons are going to stay dead if I'm not there?"

Lord Kwan let his hand drop. "It was good to see you, my friend."

"Just make sure you give Gumiho what's coming to her," said Juro. "After what she did to the toad clan, I'd wring her neck myself if I could." He marched off to the stables, holding himself proud. "And don't forget what I told you. I'll come swift as the rain if you need me, my friend."

"I thank you for the offer, but you've done more than enough for me."

Juro looked satisfied and smug and disappointed all at once, his face contorting strangely as the range of feelings passed through him.

Lord Kwan stayed on the veranda, servants gathering one by one on cue to see off his visitor. In a weird way, I felt happy that he stayed there with me. Safe. Lord Kwan was one of the most powerful Juneun, enough to turn a Kurai good. He'd praised my efforts, odd as it was, but it made me happy.

"You shouldn't have any trouble with cleaning, now that Lord Juro is gone."

I looked at him, but he stayed staring across the courtyard and the gardens as the servants dispersed to take care of their own tasks. He turned to retreat to his room, and I'd realized then that I hadn't retained my manners. I gave a slight bow of my head, hoping to make up for it.

He hadn't closed the doors when a man, lightly armored, rushed to him.

"Lord Kwan," called the man, bowing quickly as he panted. "It's the west province. Lord Kwang is holding them off, but—"

Without further explanation, Lord Kwan grabbed his sword and took off, faster than Syaoran had, leaving a violent wind in his wake.

The messenger continued to pant, led away by a servant with the offer of rest and refreshment.

I stood there, confused. What was wrong with the west province, wherever that was? Who was Lord Kwang? Why did the name send Lord Kwan into a mad dash with his sword?

I remembered that I was told not to, but no one was around and my curiosity was too great. His doors were still open. I peered in from the edge of the veranda, glimpsing the fine table and tea set in such a spacious room, and the lovely green ceramics.

"Yua will tidy it," said Syaoran.

I pulled myself straight and look at him, bashful.

"Lord Juro doesn't usually come so early into autumn. He was curious about you."

"Me?"

Syaoran smiled. "Word has gotten out that Lord Kwan has a human prisoner. It's quite the curiosity. He lingered as long as he did hoping to catch you. But by the time he finally saw you, he was already leaving."

"But why?"

Syaoran shrugged. "Lord Kwan isn't one to keep prisoners. As you can tell. He usually leaves that to some other lord to sort out. Naturally, others would be curious why you're here."

I looked from the room to the courtyard, contemplating what I understood to make sense of what I didn't.

"And I wouldn't take Juro's teasing to heart. He's uncouth at best, and the title of lord is more honorary than anything. He brings the ginseng tea to Lord Kwan and blesses the ground to help with harvests."

"The harvests in the villages?"

He nodded. "He can't do anything about the rain. Floods and droughts are another matter. But he puts a blessing in the soil to help keep the crops and trees going."

I must have seemed in awe, judging by Syaoran's snickering. I never knew what forces kept us going in the hard times, much less that it would be a former Kurai.

"Why don't you join me in the tea house?" offered Syaoran. "I lit the furnace when Juro first arrived, so it should be warm in there."

"Thank you," I said. "But isn't that only for important guests?"

"Juro came here just to get a look at you. I'd say that makes for an exception. At least for today. Besides, Lord Kwan isn't here and I'm acting master while he's away."

"I still have to clean though," I said, a warm smile taking me. "But afterwards, I'd be glad to. If that's alright."

"What? That?" Syaoran waved his hand and snapped his fingers. The mess was gone in an instant.

I blinked, jaw dropped.

"Yua used it more as an excuse to get you access to the grounds. No one actually thought you'd try to work yourself to death."

My head was spinning, even as I followed Syaoran to the tea house, trying to understand the past weeks I'd been here and what it amounted to. Another joke at my expense? Or to keep me out of trouble?

It became less important with a hot cup of red tea and Syaoran's company. The floor was warm, heating the entire space comfortably.

In our conversation, he asked what I enjoyed in my free time, implying I'd have more of it. I told him about my mother, and how I'd been trying to draw as well as she could. He asked about my brothers next, and their hobbies. When I asked in turn, he told me how he liked to race through the forests on horseback. I learned he once had a sister as well, and that my shyness reminded him of her. I wanted to ask where she was, what she thought of his serving Lord Kwan. At the same time, I was afraid of the answer.

Over the next few days, I'd learned that the spells Syaoran performed were easy enough for him as a more powerful spirit, and that there were spirits who couldn't perform any magic at all. It brought me some comfort, thinking that my chores weren't there to make me look foolish. I'd been given some paper and charcoal to with as I pleased, and often sat on the veranda near Lord Kwan's room, where there was usually no one, after I'd completed my day's work. On warmer days, I would go between the walls to draw.

I could never get anything just right. It always looked slanted and odd, but I kept at it. Sometimes I'd imagine myself creating precise imagery, beautiful gardens and landscapes, after five years of practice.

On my walk back one day, I'd decided to detour to the house rather than straight back to my cell. If I kept close to the walls, I could feel the warmth of the interior floor on my feet. I wasn't allowed into the house. I was still a prisoner after all.

On this particular afternoon, a horrible roar shattered the very air. I dropped to my knees and held my palms tight against my ears. My drawing book fell with me, its pages flapping and threatening to break free of their twine binding. They stilled only after the roar ended. I shook, confused as I saw every staff member rush in one direction.

Growls rattled the house. Calls between all the spirits clapped back and forth, an organized panic ensued.

I was afraid, and ran to go to my cell. Syaoran was thrown down the adjoining veranda, a river of blood across his face and a pool of it at his torso. I slid to a halt, petrified by the sight. I wanted to run, but couldn't pick a direction. I stood there, stupidly, shaking, unable to tear my gaze away from him.

He groaned, rolling to his side and slow to get up. Propped on his elbow, he saw me and his face slackened and paled. "Hisa! Get out of here! Hide!"

Another roar sounded, and I fled. The most direct path to my cell cut off, I thought to run around to get back. But where was there to hide? Terrified, I ran into the first open door to the house. I didn't know what room I entered—it didn't matter. My eyes looked for some corner or pile of things I could tuck myself into. The growls didn't relent. I could feel every hair on me stand sharp, and dashed further in the house.

Stairs. For whatever reason, I thought I could hide from the danger on the ground if I were on the second floor. The growling didn't quiet, pressing me to find anywhere to hide. A heavy, lacquered, wood door at the far end of the house. It seemed the most secure in my panic, driving me to hurry inside. It was opened a little, and proved very heavy. I couldn't budge it. In my terror, I squeezed myself in.

A storage. I recognized the landscape beyond the widow. This was the room that acted as the ceiling for the kennels. I could hear the cacophony below, and looked for somewhere I could tuck myself away.

Incents and barrels of persimmon wine. Strong smells that would mask my own human scent. I hurried to find something to crouch behind. The growling grew louder. Desperate, I climbed over to wiggle in a hollow spot and pulled a lid to conceal myself.

The growls grew louder and more frequent. I could hear shouting. All of it sounded like it was getting closer. The dragging of chains joined in the noise. Chanting, footfall, dragging. I curled tighter, trying to shrink myself if possible.

The sound of those heavy doors flinging open shocked me. Whatever was going on, it was being brought into the same room I'd taken shelter in. I shut my eyes and pressed my hands over my ears. Don't shriek. Don't cry. Don't even breathe.

I failed in that last one, but tried to make it so shallow and quiet that I wouldn't be heard.

It felt like ages. Silent, hot tears rolled down my face. Then, it stopped. Most of it anyway. The shouts, the chanting. Only a resounding, low growl and snorting breath, interrupted with the scrape of chains against each other.

The monster had won. That's what it sounded like. Whatever Kurai this might be, I hoped the smell of the incents and the wine would mask my own scent. I didn't want to be eaten. I didn't want to die.

Another loud growl and a stifled roar. I flinched, staying hidden. There was something odd in that moment, when things quieted again. It sounded like, whatever it was, it was in pain. I stayed still a long while, summoning the courage to open my eyes to the darkness.

I still winced at the growls as they grew more menacing. But there wasn't a thrashing to indicate rage.

I steeled myself, braving to peer out of my hiding place.

Lord Kwan.

Only, he didn't look like the stony, elegant lord I knew. He seemed half beastly, his eyes feral. Chains, pulled taut, held his arms outstretched and gaged him. His clothes were shredded, his arms and most of his chest bare.

What happened to him?

His hands flexed, trying to break free of his restraint. Another roar left him, vibrating in my bones. I ducked down, afraid. Afraid of him, of what he'd become.

Afraid.

Did he feel that way too? It was happening to him. And he was alone to endure it.

I remembered the night I heard such horrible sounds. Did it happen often? Was he always alone? I began to pity him, calming myself. He was my jailer, but he was also the protector of this mountain. Of my village.

I summoned my courage, holding fast to it with a prayer, and slowly climbed out of my hiding place. Lord Kwan didn't notice. I took an uneasy step, needing a deep breath to steady myself and try again. Walking around, in slow, soft steps, I attempted to meet his eye.

"Lord Kwan?" I whispered. I didn't mean for it to sound so quiet, and swallowed hard.

His eyes fast found me, and he thrashed in his bindings, growling louder.

I tried to speak more clearly, but all I could muster was a hushed voice. "I thought... are you scared too?"

He snarled, looking at me with a heated intensity.

"I was scared from when I first met you. Who was I to ask anything of a mighty Juneun? It wasn't that you looked monstrous—just the opposite. It was that, when I saw you, I realized my place in the world. How lowly I am. Yet I climbed up to make demands of you."

His growls ceased, but the snorting breaths and deep snarl remained.

"I thought, first that you were the one taking my brother away. Then, that you were my death. Then, my warden. I thought maybe you were deliberately cold. But I realized that wasn't it. You spoke directly, and I didn't understand the way of things here. Just because you didn't speak to me with a bright smile didn't mean you didn't care."

A low, rumbling growl left him, interrupting his panting.

I sat down, arms wrapping around my legs, and thought of some way I might help. So, I spoke about my village. Something to distract. I described how the fields probably looked, and the gentle current of our river. I smiled as I talked about the pickling of fruits, and which ones were my favorite. I talked about what I'd be doing if I was at home this time of year, what I'd be cooking or crafting, and the excitement of waiting for the merchants to pass through. I told him about the gifts my brothers would save up for, about my friends in the village and the crush I'd had. I went at length on every happy thought I could remember.

I didn't know if it helped at all. I fell asleep in that position, no longer troubled by the glare or the growls.

In the morning, the chirping of birds and soft rays of light woke me. Everything else was silent. Opening my eyes and looking up, I saw Lord Kwan—still tied up but himself once more.

The chain had fallen from his mouth, his breathing controlled. His eyes lifted, slow to look at me, though he seemed exhausted.

"What is your name?" asked Lord Kwan in a whisper.

"Hisa," I said, shrinking into myself. The sun behind him, he looked more ethereal and handsome.

He repeated my name, keeping his stony expression.

Chapter 12
Lord Kwan IV

Kwan met the young lord over a field of flame, dashing through the wreckage that'd once been thriving towns. Bodies of humans, demons and spirits lay strewn among the debris.

"What happened?" demanded Kwan.

The young lord, armored and tiring, furrowed his brow and tensed his jaw. "It's Borsi."

"Borsi?" Kwan cast his greater sight, piercing through the destruction to find the Kurai.

The pig-headed warrior held his halberd high, with each maneuver, fire leapt from the metal. He squealed out a blood curdling war-cry, rallying his clan warriors.

"I can't explain it," said the young lord. "One day he was fine, stopping for a visit before heading out to pay homage to the Cat Clan. The next day, he went berserk!"

Kwan released his spell. "I don't think he made it to that Cat Clan. This is fox magic. It's got him in a blind rage."

"Fox?" gasped the lord. "Are you sure? This far away?"

"I can feel it," said Kwan. Without another word, he took off, sword drawn.

The young lord stayed close, joining the charge. "What do we do?"

"There's only one thing we *can* do."

Boar warriors made to intercept, struck down by the pair. A distraction. Allowing the shadows of the fox clan to spring up. Kwan cut them from hitting the young lord, taking the brunt of attacks aimed for him.

"Kwan!"

"Don't let your guard down! Stay vigilant!"

The young lord obeyed, battling back boar warriors and fox shadows.

Again, Kwan used his magic to sift out where the fox Kurai were hiding, finding them with ease. He launched, sword in both hands. When they realized he headed their way, it was too late. He'd jumped into the middle of them, bringing down one and narrowly missing another. One of his quarry took a chance, slashing at his back with their claws. Kwan cried out, quickly recovering his stance and bringing his sword around to kill.

They tried to attack as one, harrying and chancing their luck. What a fine prize he'd make. Kwan could see the very thought in their eyes. He attacked with more ferocity, taking one, then another and another. He was bloodied, but victorious.

The battle wasn't over.

Panting, he ran to aid the young lord, intercepting a strike from Borsi that would've killed him. Kwan put all his strength to throw aside the attack.

Borsi was powerful, and had been a valued ally for over a hundred years. Now, he acted as an enemy.

Kwan roared out, calling lightning to his blade and swinging to unleash its fury. Borsi withstood it. The young lord charge in next, thrusting his palm forward to send wind like a hurricane. Borsi struggled against it, using his sheer strength to keep his feet planted and stay balanced. Kwan issued a quick chant, calling a bursting bolt of lightning from the heavens.

Borsi cried out, falling to his knees.

Kwan charge in, sword ready, riding on the wind of the young lord. Borsi parried with his own weapon, refusing defeat.

"Borsi," cried Kwan. "You have to fight her! Whatever she's put into your mind, fight it! We're friends, Borsi. You served as general to my father's army. Remember!"

Borsi said nothing, leering at Kwan with pure malice in his eyes, empty eyes, as he pushed back in a great show of strength.

Kwan retreated ground, holding his sword in a defensive stance. "I can't get through to him."

The young lord became aghast. His hands tightened on his sword hilt, jaw set. "Let me try."

"No—"

"If anyone can get through, it'll be me! We've fought side by side for forty years. Please!"

Kwan paused, giving a quick look between Borsi and the young lord. Then, he nodded.

The lord rushed in, Kwan breaking away to harry and distract. Borsi, however, didn't take the bait, staying fixed on his quarry. The halberd swung. The young lord blocked. Borsi kicked at his ankle, putting his foe off balance. Kwan cast a spell, threads of white wrapped fast onto the halberd, bringing it to a halt mid swing. Borsi's gaze followed the threads, and cast a spell of his own. His weapon flew at Kwan, and his fists freely swung at his opponent.

Kwan leapt out of the way, an uncalculated move in the short second he had to act. He stepped among bodies, a splintered bone sticking into his calf. He grunted his pain, sucking in air between clenched teeth. Forceful, he reclaimed his leg. He placed weight on it, feeling the searing pain shoot upwards through him. Wincing, he pushed through, rushing back to aid the young lord.

Fox Kurai came running in, acting separately from their queen and taking the risk for an attack. Kwan stood firm, parrying and countering to maintain distance. Surrounded, he changed his stance, straightening himself and holding his sword upright. A single word of a spell as they charged in. A bolt struck down on him, splitting to lash out at the surrounding foes. Free of them, and his sword sparking with held power, he resumed his charge.

The young lord scooted away, face bloody, hand searching for anything to defend himself with.

Kwan leapt, bringing his sword down.

Borsi turned, his halberd returning to its master's call to intercept. He held off the tip of Kwan's blade, needing his full attention and strength to keep it at bay as the Juneun pressed down on him.

Then, sudden release.

The young lord's sword plunged deep into Borsi's back.

Enraged, Borsi roared out his war-cry, fire expelling from him. Hot enough to force a retreat of ground from his foes, and he didn't yield. He swung his halberd in a wide circle.

Kwan pushed the young lord out of range, taking a cut across his stomach. Falling back, he knelt on one knee, his leg giving way with the new pain surging through him. He breathed in heavy gulps. From his peripheral, he spotted something ominous.

The shadow of a familiar foe crawling forward in the distance. A wide, glistening grin of sharp teeth.

With no other choice, he unlocked his primordial power. His roar shook the air, and his vision went dark.

A lucid moment came to him. The flames burning away, and the young lord, bloodied, in prayer. Kwan aimed himself south, for home. If he could just get there, seal himself until he was no longer a danger to anyone—

Darkness.

He regained a moment of himself, amid the bones of an animal, the meat nearly stripped off completely. Again, he pressed to get to his shelter. He tried not to think about the circumstance of the lucid moment, praying he'd not crossed paths with anyone, human or spirit, to cause harm.

Darkness.

The smell of a fox spirit. He felt himself in a rage. He'd made it home, though it didn't bring the peace he'd hoped. A weight to one arm. Then the other. On his chest and neck. He wouldn't be a danger. For now.

Darkness.

The incents and smell of wine clouded his senses. Mixed in was an unusual scent, earthy and wet. It was faint, but it was there. And a sound. Not the chants to spellbind him or the clamor of shouts. Not the clanging of chains or the sharp cut of a blade through the air. A soft sound. A voice.

His sight remained blurred, requiring him to focus it. The prisoner girl. No. Couldn't she see he wasn't himself? The fear compelled a jolt to run through his body, and attempt to get free. Still, she stood there, speaking softly to him.

His sights went in and out, lucidity gained and lost. But she remained, speaking gently about idle things. Things that had nothing to do with their current state. She sat unafraid, a partial smile on her face. Sliding back into the darkness, the rawness of his emotions simmered into something more manageable.

In the late hours of the night, he remembered himself whole. He lifted his heavy eyelids, the chain falling from his teeth. She was still sitting there, curled up and asleep. In that moment, he thought of their every interaction before now.

A strange thing.

A gentle thing.

She could have banged on the door and cried out for release. And if no one answered, he wouldn't blame her weeping. Staying hidden would've been the most optimal choice.

Always, she presented as such a meek creature. And tonight, she braved his company.

He looked her over in her tattered clothing and bare feet. It was only then that he recalled that detail of her initial story. Her sandals had torn in her race up the mountain. She loved her brother that much.

Meanwhile, he didn't know if he'd caused the death of his own brother. He couldn't recall any action taken once he succumbed to that power.

This human girl had compassion. Not the usual envy and greed he'd known in the courts. Compassion. Enough to give to the most helpless of creatures when she had nothing of her own. And he didn't even know her name. It didn't seem important before. She was a prisoner girl who would wait the five years owed, and that was all.

No. He couldn't treat her like that. She'd freeze in her first winter. She'd done a kindness to him. He didn't expect to remember himself until dawn at the earliest. Now, he owed her a debt. Whether or not she knew it.

Chapter 13
A New Arrangement

I was ushered out that morning when Syaoran came to check in on Lord Kwan. He seemed horrified to find me in there. Lord Kwan said nothing about it. Though, I thought I saw a kindness in his eyes. They didn't seem as cold or predator-like. But I was tired, having spent the night reminiscing on happier times. My eyes didn't see things quite as they were yet.

Yua, baring a stunned expression at the news, inspected me. She appeared more alarmed to find not even the smallest scratch on me. It didn't prevent her from scolding me though. I was told the seriousness of the event, and the danger that could've happened. I remembered Syaoran, bloodied because Lord Kwan didn't recognize his own friend. When he was in that state, Lord Kwan was no longer in control of himself.

It should've made me more afraid. Instead, it made me pity him. My heart hurt at the idea of it. I wouldn't be able to forgive myself if I'd hurt my brothers, or any of the villagers at home. If I'd hurt Fumei or Kyu or Chocho. I couldn't live with the guilt.

Yet, it was something he endured in order to keep Gumiho's cruel influence at bay. To protect us. Not only the spirits here, but every settlement near the mountain. The animals too, I was certain. I began to realize the immense pressure he must feel.

"Are you listening?" asked Yua, pointed.

My face snapped up to meet her eye. "Yes, ma'am. I'm sorry."

"There's nothing to be done about it now," said Yua. She inhaled, long and sharp, before releasing it in a resigned sigh. "Go to the tea house and bring a sample of the ginseng that Lord Juro brought. Lord Kwan will be wanting it."

I obeyed, hurrying slowly. The ground was cold, and my legs were tired.

After I'd completed that task, I set to light the furnaces that would heat the floors of the main house, as I'd done the last several days. Today, I moved more slowly, and set my feet near the fire to warm before tending to the next one.

At the last furnace, I kept my feet and hands close until they started to turn red and burn. I knew any breakfast waiting for me would already be cold by the time I got there, so I didn't rush.

Instead, I let myself drink in as much warmth until I couldn't stand it, and hoped I could hold onto it through the day.

I remembered my drawing book then, and tried to look for it without getting in the way as everyone cleaned up from the ordeal of last night. My heart became heavy in thinking it'd gotten thrown out when I couldn't find it. Downtrodden, I returned to my cell.

There, my heart broke completely.

My bunny was gone. I didn't care that there was no breakfast waiting, or that the bird cage was also gone. The last thing I had of my mother, the only bit of comfort I had with me through the night—the thing that reminded me to stay brave, reminded me of Hisato—was taken away.

I was being punished. One mistake too many.

Tears swelled in my eyes. My hands turned into fists. The whole of my body shook with anger. It took a conscious effort to steady my breathing, to not break down. I swore I wouldn't let anyone see me crying. I wouldn't let them know they broke me. Not for one second. No matter what, I had to stay strong.

"There you are," said Yua.

I didn't turn to face her.

She didn't care, and uttered a command. "Come with me."

I waited to hear her start to walk away, then quickly wiped up my face before following. She led me through the main house, a shortcut, to the farthest part from the kennels. There, she opened the doors to a room and stepped aside, gesturing for me to go in.

I was hesitant. Was there an additional punishment awaiting? Her face looked tired and severe, annoyed with me. I steeled myself, taking in a slow gulp of air, and walked inside.

It was just a room. A very nice room. Not quite like Lord Kwan's, not even close, but grander than my family's house. It was warm and spacious and cozy.

At the far end, beside the bed, my bunny sat waiting. I didn't notice my drawing book and the birdcage were also there as I ran in to take it into my arms. I must've seemed like a child in that moment, but I didn't care. My most precious possession was here.

"Lord Kwan ordered that you stay here from now on," said Yua. "You should thank him when he is well again."

"This room is for me?" I asked, turning back to face her. I was sure I misheard. Afterall, I was a prisoner and this was a fine room.

"That's what I said. Be sure to remember your manners when you next see Lord Kwan and thank him."

I jumped to my feet. "I'll thank him now."

She refused me with a slow shake of her head. "The master is tired and won't be receiving visitors other than Syaoran and myself."

I blinked, not understanding but not brave enough to argue or ask.

"Get yourself settled in. Your meals will be brought here and left on the table."

I clung to my bunny, watching her look me up and down, and gave her a hushed thank you.

She responded with a long, low grunt, and closed the doors with grace.

Alone, I looked around. This was my room now. Still, I was afraid to touch anything. None of it belonged to me. I was a prisoner given a more comfortable place to sleep so I wouldn't freeze in winter. Nonetheless, I appreciated it. Though, I couldn't ignore everything provided in the room.

I had a layer of dirt on me, and the river was too cold. Even if the river was boiling, my feet and legs would pick up a new layer of dirt on the walk back. So, carefully, I took the wash bin and cloth that were in the room and undressed.

The water was cool, but not cold, made bearable by the warmth of the room and heated floor. I felt renewed after cleaning, and took out the used water myself so I could put it all away quickly. On my return, I noticed a beautifully wrapped present on the vanity with a note attached. I didn't dare try to peek in. It was wrapped so delicately that I was sure I'd never be able to put it exactly back. That assumed I opened it without tearing any piece of it by accident. I stared a long while at the paper, sitting down to admire the faint print designs on it. With nothing else to do, I took my drawing book and charcoal, fixing the pages as best I could, and tried to copy the design.

It wasn't remotely alike.

But I now had something to practice if the snows became too deep this high on the mountain and kept me inside. With that thought, I was more relieved Lord Kwan gave me this room to stay in.

I lay warm and comfortable in bed that night, holding my stuffed rabbit close. And slept deeply and happily; so much that pleasant dreams came.

In the morning, my breakfast was more bountiful. Rice and thin sliced beef and pickled vegetables, and a persimmon to the side. I ate it all heartily, and hurried to start lighting the furnaces again. I took on the chores no one really wanted to do, and felt I had the energy today to do them three times or more.

The furnaces were lit, the chickens fed, eggs collected and brought to the kitchen. Then I went about sweeping off the stones that made the walk ways through the yards and gardens. The stables didn't need cleaning again just yet, but I did it anyway, and patted Saburo.

I told the magnificent stallion about my new room, and about how happy I was that I wouldn't need to worry so much about winter. He stared at me as I spoke, watching me brush out his fur as I babbled on. He felt so warm, with a long and slow rhythmic rise and fall of his sides that comforted me. He wasn't my horse, but I loved him like a friend.

Going back that evening, I started for the kennels out of habit. When I realized, I smiled and laughed at myself. It was a little hard to remember where my new room was, but I found it.

Alarm came in finding Syaoran inside. He sat beside the table, his injuries concealed by white cloth, and looked over with an amused smile when I entered. I probably looked like a startled fawn in my shock.

"Yua told me you're staying in here now," said Syaoran. His warm voice settled me. "I thought I'd bring some red tea here to celebrate." He motioned for me to come in and sit with him.

I did so, shy as I was in that moment. "Celebrate what?"

"Everyone is talking about how you stayed the night with Lord Kwan," said Syaoran, as though it were obvious. "Even I'm not brave enough to do that." He pointed to his bandages, but kept a kind smile all the same.

"I was accidentally stuck inside," I said. "You know that."

He poured the tea, having brought in a pot and cups for the occasion. "But you stayed."

I felt my cheeks and ears warm. "When you told me to hide, I ran into the house. I looked for anywhere to go and found that room with the heavy doors. I didn't know it had a purpose."

He chuckled. "Any other girl would probably run out the moment they realized what was going on."

I tucked my neck into my shoulder. Of course I wanted to bolt out of there. "I was too much of a coward. And I couldn't move from where I wedged myself for a long time."

He laughed. "I like the story better that you braved it from the start. My sister would have stayed hidden all night and part of the next day."

"Where is your sister?" I asked without thinking.

For the first time, his kindly expression faltered. A sadness replaced it, slowly consuming him, and he looked to be battling it off. "She's in a faraway place."

I wanted to ask so many questions then. Where exactly, and for how long? Was it because of Gumiho? Or because his sister was also a fox spirit but didn't find the luck in gaining the protection of a Juneun like Lord Kwan? I wanted to ask so much. But I didn't want my friend to become sad or annoyed with me. I couldn't pry, not after all he'd done for me.

"The tea is delicious," I said, trying to change the subject and distract from the feeling.

He regained some of his previous expression. "I'm glad you like it."

"It's not made from the tea trees in the village, is it?"

He shook his head. "This one came from the northeast. But I can show you what the tea from your village is like here. We put it through a long fermenting process. It's my second favorite."

I smiled, beaming. "I used to pick the leaves every spring with my friend Fumei."

"Did you now?"

I nodded. Even if he wasn't really interested, I wanted to get away from sad thoughts.

I didn't tire much in the following days. Cleaning became second nature by then. I'd even offered to chop the wood to make tinder, though the men at the task didn't think I was strong enough. Instead, I was sent away with my arms full of small pieces to restock beside the furnaces. I stacked them neatly, fitting as much as possible for good measure.

I looked forward to cleaning off my legs and face at the end of every day. It helped me to feel refreshed, coaxing me into a deep sleep afterwards when I had a fully belly. It was barely midday, and I smiled at the thought of drawing all afternoon.

Climbing back onto the veranda, I stopped after only a few steps. Lord Kwan walked in my direction, again himself. I waited patiently, nervous. My fingers fussed with my tattered deel, and my eyes kept wanting to look down rather than face him. I tried not to shift my weight from one side to the next so often. What should I say? A simple thank you didn't seem sufficient. But he'd likely get annoyed if I rambled.

When he came near, I bowed deeply, the best I could for respect. "Lord Kwan."

He stopped.

I straightened, keeping my hands folded in front of me. "Thank you, my lord. F-for the room you let me stay in. Winter is almost here, and it was very kind of you to consider allowing me a warm and comfortable stay."

He said nothing, looking me over for a long time. Perhaps it only felt like a long time because of the silence between us. Either way, my smile began to wane. Did I say something out of turn? I could never read him, or guess at his thoughts.

"You're still in those rags?"

I looked down at myself, slow to understand him. "I have nothing else, my lord."

He blinked, slow. Taking another step to me, he grabbed my wrist to lead me along. I gasped in surprise, dreading what might happen. He said nothing, walking at his own pace. His hand was cool to the touch; not icy, but not warm.

"Are you sending me back to the kennels?" I asked in a whimper.

"No," replied Lord Kwan, abrupt.

We walked down familiar paths and through the house. At the door to my room, he stopped only to open it, and towed me inside. We stopped in front of the vanity. Our reflection captured perfectly in the mirror, I saw just how shabby I looked next to him.

He looked down at something, silent and studying. "You didn't like it?"

"Like what?" My voice came out as a trembling whisper.

"The dress I gave you." His eyes made their way from that wrapped package over to me.

"Dress?"

He held it up, the tiniest hint of a smile on his face. "It's your name on the note."

I blinked, slow to piece it all together. "I... I can't read, my lord."

He raised a brow, that hint of a smile fading away.

"I did see the package. But it wasn't mine, so I didn't touch it. I just admired it."

He set it back down and took my hand again, holding out one of my fingers to trace the lines. Even in here, where it was so warm, his touch remained cool. "This is the character that means receiver. And this one is your name."

I looked away from his face and down to the note as he guided my finger to trace out my name. I'd never seen what my name looked like. It seemed like such a simple set of lines, but I gawked anyway.

"Now you know," said Lord Kwan, in a gentle tone I wasn't used to from him.

I looked back up, not realizing he'd leaned in to speak, and met his eyes immediately. They were more fierce and handsome up close, though not as intense as I remembered. "Did you send the bird cage as well?"

That hint of a smile was back. He nodded. "You couldn't read the note to know." He stepped away to fetch the note, bringing it back to have me trace out what it said, his hand guiding me the whole way. "For Tori."

I felt his breath beside my ear as he spoke, and my skin prickled with a strange excitement.

"It looks like he escaped somehow," said Lord Kwan.

I shook my head. "I let him go."

He looked back at me, studying, but that hint of a smile remained. "Weren't you keeping him as a pet?"

"Not as a pet, my lord," I said. "He wanted to be wild. I just raised him. I, I didn't want him to die before he'd ever really lived."

"That was kind of you," said Lord Kwan.

I felt a warmth in my cheeks, and a sense of pride filling my gut.

"Everything in this room is yours. Do with any of it what you like."

"All of it?"

He said nothing, leaving with controlled and regal steps, and closed my doors behind himself, gentle.

Chapter 14
One Winter's Night

It was already midwinter. My birthday had been three days before. It was the first one where I didn't have Hisato beside me to share it. I didn't have any of my family with me. Nor did I have a friend to stop and say a blessing, or tangerines with heavy cream and a heavy, honey bread.

Selfishly, I chose to stay in my warm room that entire day.

Yua had shown me how to put on the fine dress that Lord Kwan gave me. I'd never worn anything so beautiful, or in so many layers. Thankfully, there was a trick to it, and I didn't need to tie too many things. I especially adored how it flowed and trailed behind me as I walked. And, not wanting to be stared at, I would go between the walls to run and watch how prettily the layers flew behind me.

I'd also been given a night gown that was easy enough to put on and figure out on my own. Crisp, white silk. It felt good against my skin. Often, I brushed my fingers down the length as I wore it, admiring the texture.

A pair of wood sandal were given to me as well, to keep my feet out of the mud. I wore them when I changed into my old clothes to work. I didn't want to ruin such a fine gift. But always, I would hurry to get the few chores done so I could clean up and wear my dress.

There were tiny, delicate patterns embroidered in. Flowers. All different kinds, most prominently displayed along the hems of any piece. It looked like something a princess would wear. And for the first time, since I was a little girl, I felt beautiful. I never looked at myself in the mirror though, fearful that it'd break my illusion.

Syaoran made the comment once, the first time that he saw me in it.

"You look like a real lady, now." And though I knew he meant to compliment me, and his expression and voice were the kindliness I'd grown used to from him, I felt so exposed.

I shied, retreating into myself. "I'm not..." I became more aware of how unsightly my hair was in its slow growth back, of the scars on my face, my rough hands and small figure. The only womanly thing about me being a curved waist that was concealed by the beautiful clothing.

He'd come back that following eve with a pair of black slippers, embroidered at the seams the same as my dress, saying that the only thing missing from me bring a lady was the right shoes. He was the kindest of friends, mentioning that he guessed his sister's size would match my own. He was right. They were a little loose, like the dress, but I was still growing.

This deep into winter, the snow had piled too high for me to go out the secret door. Most of my time outside my room was spent walking anywhere it was clear. Some days I spent hours in the stable, brushing out Saburo's coat or sitting in his paddock with him. On several occasions, the stable master took him out for exercise, and I'd watched from the sidelines. But now the snow was too deep for him to flex his proud muscles.

Lord Kwan had gone off again. A part of me worried he might return changed like before. If that did happen, what should I do? Yua warned about the danger of staying with him like I'd done. Syaoran seemed impressed by it.

As I thought about it, remembering, I couldn't help but feel staying was the right choice that time. Maybe not always though. I didn't feel brave in the moment, and I wasn't sure I could summon up the courage to be there on purpose.

I walked the veranda in thought, past rooms where several spirits gathered to share drinks and supper. The winter solstice already passed; I'd wondered before if the spirits honored it the same way as humans, all coming into the same house and sharing in the dried and smoked fruits, and treats the women made? Did they tie strips of red ribbons on bamboo ropes that stretched from one roof to the next? Were there any songs or dances? Did they make snow art and place lanterns into patterns to bring light until morning? Did they try to stay up so they could see the sunrise?

But it'd been such a quiet event.

I stopped when I noticed how full and bright the moon was that night. It bathed the slumbering, snow filled gardens in a ghostly light. Everything looked haunted and still and beautiful. I stared, about to sit down when I remembered my drawing book. It was almost completely filled, but I knew I had two or three pages that were blank. I wanted to try and draw it. The way the shadows looked.

With my book and charcoal in hand, I searched for what felt like the perfect spot for an imperfect artist. I found it. Not too far from Lord Kwan's room, on a corner spot of the veranda. I sat there, keeping a light touch of the charcoal against the page. Careful as I was, it barely looked anything like what my eyes saw right in front of me.

That was alright. After five years, I'd have it to remind me of how beautiful a sight this was. It didn't have to look perfect to make me remember.

I started again, trying different strokes, smaller, to see if it helped improve at all.

"It's beautiful, isn't it?" said Lord Kwan.

I gasped, going rigid and pulling my drawing close to my chest to hide it. The initial surprise lasted only a second, then my muscles freed enough for me to look over my shoulder and up. He wasn't raging or feral or tiger-like at all. His face was his own, that hint of a smile softening his stony expression, rather than a snarl and the start of a snout. His hands were like a man's, not clawed and red. There were no stripes or texture of fur. He was himself and only himself; if not a bit more tired and dirty.

The sight brought relief.

"Aren't you cold?"

I folded back my drawing book to close, holding it tight against me as a stood. "A little. But it was so pretty in the moonlight that I wanted to look at it longer."

He grunted, leaving me unsure of whether or not he approved.

"You're not hurt?" I asked. It sounded weird, though I didn't know how to phrase my asking after him.

"Not badly," said Lord Kwan. "Fetch me some barely tea."

"Oh," I looked from him, to the route, to my book and back in quick succession. "Yes, my lord."

He offered out his hand. I blinked, needed a moment to understand the silent ask of my book. From instinct, I held it more tightly and shook my head.

"Let me see that."

Again, I shook my head, shutting my eyes.

"I could command you to."

I sucked in a deep gasp, bringing my head back up slowly to meet his eyes. "It's just a drawing book, my lord. And none of them are particularly good."

He studied me a moment. "You don't want me to see them?"

I shook my head. "They're not any good, my lord."

"Shouldn't I be the judge of the quality?"

I looked away, trying to come up with some excuse.

"Then, I will give my word not to glance at them. Until you're ready." He kept his palm up.

I was reluctant. He'd given his word, and I had no reason not to trust that he'd keep to it. He was strange that way. Over time, it seemed like he'd made more lenient decisions, lessening the harshness I was originally met with. If he said he wouldn't look, then I believed him.

Slow, I released my drawings to his care.

"Bring the tea ready to my room," said Lord Kwan, an ease in his voice. With the instruction given, he walked to the entry of his quarters.

"Yes, my lord," I said, bowing my head slightly and hurrying off to take care of the task.

I did exactly as I was bid, finding the barely tea in the stores of the tea house and brewing it to bring back. A bronze kettle to boil it up, I took it with a clothed hand when it was ready. Hasty, with care, I went to Lord Kwan's room.

I called, announcing myself.

He made no answer.

A part of me worried he played down any injury he brought home, and lay collapsed on the ground in need of help. I set down the kettle and slid the paper paned door to peer inside. A small antechamber and second set of doors. Perhaps he simply didn't hear me.

I went in, bringing the kettle and setting it down to close the doors once more. I thought better than to take my wooden sandals in, and slipped them off before repeating my previous motions. When he didn't answer this time, my fear for him intensified.

"Lord Kwan?" I set down the kettle again, sliding open the doors enough to look inside.

He wasn't on the ground, but in the midst of redressing. His long, silken, black hair pulled forward, I saw the toned muscles of his back. My cheeks flared in a rosy heat, my eyes went wide and my spine stiff. I closed the doors right away, hoping he hadn't noticed.

I waited, touching at my face and making a silent plea that I wouldn't look so pink when he asked me in. I didn't want to confess I'd seen him in such a state. Not only for my own embarrassment, but so that I didn't irritate him and ruin the good graces he'd bestowed to me.

When at last he called me, I tried to empty my head of the image and rein myself in. I opened the doors with a bit more grace, fully this time.

"Close it behind you," said Lord Kwan. He waited at his table, a teapot and two cups set.

I obeyed, trying to seem dignified like the women who served the house. Bringing the kettle to him, he opened the lid of the teapot. On his cue, I poured in. It was only a small teapot, and I was sure I would stop soon after I started. Careful, so as to not spill the hot contents, I tipped it to pour. And pour. And pour. Until it was emptied. I didn't understand how, though this time I didn't bother to ask. This was a house of a Juneun. Was it so surprising that a teapot would have some kind of magic to it?

That hint of a smile remained on his face. I set aside the kettle, about to serve when he'd already done it. One of the tea cups was placed in front of me, and he poured in the hot beverage.

Taking mine, I noticed our hands side by side rather than my own hidden under his grasp, how dark my skin still was compared to him. I spent my life outdoors, helping in the fields and playing when I had the time. Even here I toiled in the sun to pay off the debt owed. I would never be like the porcelain ladies painted on the vases and hanging scrolls. The servant women here were just as fair, and I hadn't thought much about it until I was alone with him.

After he set the pot back down, he finally spoke.

"I want you in my company any time I return from elsewhere."

"Me, my lord?"

He sipped, and I took it as my cue to do the same.

"That will be your only chore from now on."

My only chore? No more cleaning or laboring or fetching of things? But, why? Was there some trick? Something I wasn't aware of?

"I feel calm around you. So, when I return from anywhere, I want you to be beside me. Like we are now."

I furrowed my brow, staring at him while my fingers drank in the warmth of the cup. "Why? Wouldn't Yua or Syaoran make for better company? I'm only a human prisoner."

He grunted, taking his time to meet my eye. "You don't ask anything of me. Not since we first met. That's what I want." He sighed, almost silent. "Syaoran and Yua mean well. But the last thing I want is a barrage of questions and recounting of things. I want my return to be like this. The company, and nothing more."

I looked away as I considered it. "I'm grateful for the kindness you've shown me, my lord. But I *am* still just a prisoner. I have no right to ask anything of you."

He stayed silent a long while, likely mulling over the logic. We took our drinks in the wordlessness. After refilling, he spoke again.

"When you stayed with me that night. What did you speak about?"

I stopped mid sip, blinking at him.

"I wasn't aware of much that went on." His voice lost some of its initial softness. "In the moments I started to remember myself, I saw you there. Just sitting there. Speaking to me calmly. What did you say in all that time?"

I sipped, thinking how best to answer. "I talked about my village, my lord. About life there. And my family and friends."

He stared at me. A long and silent stare.

Uncomfortable, I looked to my drink, sipping at leisure and basking in the heat that went down my throat to my stomach.

"Will you tell me now?"

"Tell what, my lord?"

"About your village."

A fluttering feeling coursed through my gut. "I don't think it would interest you, my lord. I only went on about it then because I didn't know what else to do."

He placed an elbow on the table, resting the side of his chin in his hand and put the full of his attention on me. "Tell me anyway."

I smiled.

Less frightened than I was that night, I talked about winter in my village, how my brothers would lay traps for birds and small animals to bring home to cook. I admitted to how lackluster my skill was, and my determination to improve as more things were brought home.

When I began to tire, Lord Kwan didn't pry for more. He dismissed our company, allowing me to go to my room.

"The winters can be long this high into the mountain," said Lord Kwan.

I stopped in the doorway, looking back to him.

"If it's of interest to you, I will teach you to read and write."

My face lit up.

That hint of a smile flexed before I could answer. "I take it the idea is exciting."

"It's been a dream for so many of us, my lord, to learn to read and go to a school."

He watched me, never eager to respond. "Come here midday tomorrow. We can start then."

I felt like I could leap to the moon in that moment, and thanked him before leaving.

Though, as I lay in bed, I found I was too excited to sleep. I would learn to read and to write. And if I could master it while I was here, then I could teach it to my brothers when I returned home. I could teach it to the entire village maybe. A merchant wouldn't try to cheat any of us, or make us believe the value of something being less or greater than it was if we could understand it all. Perhaps one of the younger men would become bold with the skill, and go to the city for school. How changed our lives would be.

Chapter 15
Less Than Ordinary

I worked hard to be a diligent student. My sleeve tied back to prevent it from touching the wet ink as I practiced, it was different from drawing with a charcoal but not too difficult. I caught myself sticking my tongue out and up as I focused, trying to make each brush stroke perfect. Lord Kwan said not a thing about it. He was a patient teacher, encouraging my efforts.

"Why do you keep that toy in your room?" asked Lord Kwan.

In our few hours a day of tutelage, it wasn't uncommon for him to ask something from seemingly nowhere.

I looked up from my sloppy penmanship. "My rabbit?"

He nodded.

"My mother made it for me when I was a baby, and starting to walk. She made one for my brother Hisato as well."

"And your other brothers?"

"No. When they were babies, she made them something different. A ram for Kenta, and a panda for Raeden."

"And they still have those toys?"

I shook my head. "Kenta accidentally dropped his in the river when he was little, and it was swept away before Baba could catch it. And Chocho, the village dog got a hold of Raeden's when he was still a puppy and didn't know any better."

He took in the story, relaxed in his posture, and moved to cut an odd-looking fruit. His small knife sliced into it expertly in his palm. Then he offered me a piece. I looked at the red and yellow skin and the white interior of it.

"It's called an apple," said Lord Kwan. "It grows in a faraway land, and harvested in autumn. The weather is cold enough here to keep them fresh a little while longer. I don't have many left from this year."

I accepted the offer, taking the smallest bite to test it. A little crisp, but fast crumbling in my mouth, it tasted sweet and a little tart. Curious, I took a bigger bite.

"Do you like it?"

"Very much," I said. "Thank you, my lord."

"Not many in my house feel the same. They're suspicious of foreign things."

"But, why?"

"Often, something different means change will follow. It is never certain if change will bring prosperity, or devastation. It takes time for new to become accepted. Like the bathhouse I had built."

"Bathhouse?"

He paused his cutting to look at me. "You haven't seen it?"

I gave one shake of my head, intrigued.

"Ask Yua to show you. A hot soak does wonders."

The following afternoon, my curiosity became too much. I asked Yua about using the bathhouse. With great reluctance, she led me to it. A small building, I'd passed it a thousand times before but never knew what it was or what was inside. She had me light the furnace first, and we came back to it a short while after. Inside, a large, stone tub sat at the far end, wide enough to fit an entire family. She showed me the lever beside it, and pulled. A steady stream of water spilled into the tub, slowly filling it.

"The lever sticks sometimes if it's too cold," said Yua. "The water comes from a line that leads from the river higher up, down to here. And the fire heats it. When the tub is full, put the lever back to its original position."

I watched the working of it, awestruck. "Does the lever get stuck going back?"

"Not often," said Yua with a shrug.

She might not have found this impressive, but I certainly did. In the village, we didn't have time to heat up a large tub and soak in it leisurely. It wasn't something any of us considered. And in winter, it would drain away precious supplies we'd stocked up in autumn.

"When you're finished, pull out that stopper from the bottom."

"Stopper?"

She pointed. "Pull that out and the water will drain into another line that leads back into the river further down."

"Amazing," I said.

"Yes, well, I think it's a waste. But it's become in fashion for the high lords among the Juneun to have them."

"Why don't you like it?" I asked, absentminded.

"It's too large and time consuming. I prefer the privacy of my room."

"In the village, all the women would go to the river together to bathe, and the men further down the way."

Yua scoffed, disinterested. "I'll leave you to it." She left, and the bathhouse fell silent except for the flow of water to the tub.

It was half full when I put the lever back. Reaching down, it was warm, and felt like it'd grow warmer still. I straightened, hesitating at first, and undressed. My skin prickled in the air. Oddly, it felt satisfying. I folded my things and set them neatly aside, then went to step in. Hot. A little too hot.

Putting my strength into it, I pulled the lever down, waiting as long as I dared before trying again. Not quite full, I couldn't stand it anymore and stopped the waterflow. Stepping in, it felt warm. I submerged, sitting quiet as the temperature slowly climbed and turned the water a relaxing kind of hot.

It was strange. All I did was sit there in the warmth. But it felt good to do so. I held my breath, sinking below the surface. The heat soothed me, coaxing me to stay as long as my lungs would allow. Coming up again, my hair clung to the top of my neck and forehead, and uncomfortably behind my ears.

My body absorbed the warmth. My lungs took in the steam. My eyes began to relax, almost to the point of sleep. And I hummed quiet songs in the cozy solitude. I couldn't make myself completely free of anxious thoughts. Some part of me scrutinized, a dozen suggestions of things I ought to be doing. But Lord Kwan had ordered only one task of me. A task that wasn't needed today.

I should be practicing, I thought. Improve my writing to look neat and tidy, clean like Lord Kwan's. And I ought to work on my drawing skill. A good enough drawing might get a small exchange with the merchants. I wondered if there was a place to learn to make pottery here. If I knew how to do that, I could make jars to preserve stock for winter, in such abundance that it could be shared out—we'd all be fat come the following spring.

So many things competing in my mind, but I didn't have the will to leave the bath. Not yet.

My fingers and toes became pruney, prompting me to get out. I waded to the other side of the tub, looking for the stopper that Yua indicated to me earlier. I couldn't reach it without dunking my head beneath the water. It slipped from me in my first try. In my second try, it was sucked back in. I had to come up for air. In my third try, I held tight and brought it out of the water as the bath drained.

Slowly, my body came in contact with the air, prickling as it breathed again. My short hair dripped dry as I waited. With the water completely gone, I replaced the stopper and stepped out. A stretch of folded cloth sat on a shelf near where I'd set my dress. Silk, though not nearly as soft as the clothing I'd been gifted; still, I enjoyed the feel of it around me. Droplets leapt into the fabric from my skin, leaving me comfortably dry.

I put on my silk shirt first, and the accompanying jacket over it. My under trousers next, tying it to sit atop my hips without it feeling too snug. Next came the trickiest part: My sheer skirt raised to just an inch beneath my armpits and tied to keep it in place while I adjusted my bouses—now half hidden beneath it—for comfort and an even look, then I retied the sheer skirt to better secure it. Last came the over skirt and its beautiful pastel layers and embroidered hem. It needed to sit just barely over the sheer skirt, then I could bring around the soft twine to tie off at the front. My knot making wasn't as perfect looking as the women of the house, though I was still relatively new to it and hoped I'd improve with time.

Not that it mattered. After my five years, I'd likely never wear anything so fine again. It wasn't the type of thing I could farm or clean in, never mind walking through the mountains to gather fruit. I would probably put it away until special days, like my mother.

Remembering how I'd sold the only fine dress she'd ever owned, a selfish worry came into my head. If we went into another dire year, I might be forced to sell this one as well. I didn't want to—I didn't want to even think about it! Lord Kwan gave me this dress, and it was the only pretty possession I ever had.

Catching my thoughts, I scolded myself. I'd have no choice if hard times came again. It was selfish of me to be so attached.

Several more times, and into the spring, Lord Kwan went away. Without him, I continued to work on my writing, practicing over and over. The first thing I wanted to master was my name, and Hisato's since it wasn't too dissimilar. The second thing I wanted to master was Lord Kwan's name. I wanted it to be perfect, so that I could thank him in writing.

During the time he was gone, I would try and stay up as long as I could, busying myself as I waited for him. I had one task that he commanded me, and I would see it through promptly.

Sometimes we said nothing for long periods. Mostly, he would ask about my life. On occasion, he would share something of his own experiences. I learned not to be so meek around him, gradually getting used to his way of things, and always looking for that hint of a smile on his face. Actually, I began to enjoy and even look forward to when I could carry out the task of taking his company. Perhaps we would grow into friends over these five years.

I daydreamed about it sometimes. About helping to care for my future nieces and nephews, and telling them stories about my Juneun friend in the mountain. I imagined coming up again once in a while, just to be in his company, even as I grew old. He wouldn't grow old though. He was a divine spirit and would look timeless for centuries to come.

In midspring, the abandoned part of the farthest yard was cleaned up. The shed taken down to rebuild later, when supplies arrived, it looked more spacious and inviting. The bench was reclaimed and restored, making it the perfect place to be when the sun shone too brightly. A little further back, a small shrine was uncovered. I didn't know for what reason a shrine would be there, but it was beautiful to simply look at.

On a pleasant day, I took my new drawing book with me between the walls, to the place that sank and butterflies gathered. Few at first, but more came every day. I sat in the shade, trying to capture their likeness with my charcoal.

Once in a while, my hand reflexively stopped to swat behind my neck. At pestering insects, but also from my hair tickling back there. I wasn't used to the feeling. It seemed like it started to grow faster in the second half of winter. I noticed I was a little more filled out myself.

A quick something whizzed by in the distance, causing me to jump and squint in that direction. I didn't see anything, about to resume my sketching when I heard it again from a different direction. Looking that way, I still didn't see anything. Then I heard it again elsewhere.

On my feet, I held the book close and whipped my head around to search out the source of the noise. I kept hearing it, but from where I didn't know. Making to bolt I stopped before I could take my first step, my scream caught in my throat and my eyes wide.

A beautiful girl with pale skin, long, shiny, black hair, and snake's eyes was right there, staring at me. Dressed in beautiful silks, the lower half of her body was that of a serpent that stretched far into the grass behind her.

"You're a human," said the girl. "What is a human doing here?"

"I'm," I swallowed hard, my saliva thick, as I tried to steady my voice and prevent it from cracking. "I'm Lord Kwan's prisoner."

"You don't look like a prisoner to me," said the girl, leaning this way and that, and using her snake body to stand taller over me. "Are you sure?"

"For another four and a half years, yes," I said.

"I guess that'd be a silly thing to lie about. Does he keep other prisoner between the walls now as well?"

I shook my head, clinging to my book.

"What happened to your hair?" asked the girl, leaning in close. "Where did you get those scars? And what's wrong with your teeth? Why is that one crooked?"

In my panic, and feeling cornered, I tried anything to distract. "Are you a Kurai?"

She brough herself back down, leaning away with her hands clutching her arms as her face soured. She stuck out her tongue, grimacing and making a disgusted sound. "Never! I'm Feng of the Sho family."

I calmed, watching her animated reaction. "Then, you're a Juneun?"

She nodded. "And Lord Kwan's future bride."

I repeated the title, and smiled. "That's wonderful! Lord Kwan is a kind and powerful spirit. I'm sure you must be the same way if he picked you for his bride. When will you marry?"

A look of discomfort consumed her. "Well, he hasn't said yet. But I'm sure he'll make all the announcements soon."

I nodded. I didn't know how nobles carried out wedding planning, though something told me it was probably far more complicated than how we did in the village.

She composed herself again. "So, what were you doing out here, human prisoner girl?"

I suddenly felt uncomfortable. I technically wasn't supposed to be here at all. "I..."

"Yes?" she leaned in slightly.

"I came to look at the butterflies. They like to gather around this spot."

A bright smile came over her face. "They do. That's why I like to stay under these trees. I was asleep, and when I woke up, I saw you looking suspicious."

"Suspicious?"

"But if all you're doing is watching the butterflies, I think that's okay."

I stared, transfixed by how friendly this spirit was from the start of our meeting, and how beautiful she looked. In the swaying sunlight, as the breeze shifted the younger branches above, she was more beautiful than Fumei, more than Yua, more than anyone else I'd ever met. And she was not cruel.

I held to my smile, thinking how she'd make a good wife to Lord Kwan. She had so much expression to her, while he stayed stoic. But both were kind at heart.

"What's that you're holding?"

"Oh," I broke from my thoughts. "It's the drawing book Syaoran gave me. The new one at least."

"Let me see," she said, a laugh in her voice as she snatched it.

On instinct, I tried to take it back. She rose on her snake body, too high for me to reach.

"No! Please, give it back!"

She flipped through them, ignoring me. "They're not very good. But you did say you were a prisoner and not an artist."

Perhaps I was wrong to assume she wasn't cruel.

Lowering herself again, she handed back my book, gentle.

I snatched it to hold close.

"But I had a teacher to show me how to do things properly. I suppose most humans aren't as fortunate."

I said nothing, retreating into myself. My mother taught me to always be aware of snakes on the ground or in the trees when I went into the mountains, but I was woefully unprepared for what to do with a snake Juneun.

"Aren't you going to answer any of my other questions, prisoner girl?"

I shook my head, taking a step back.

She frowned. "Why not?"

I didn't answer. Instead, I ran for the secret door, wanting to hide. I knew I probably shouldn't have. It was rude, and this was Lord Kwan's intended. My emotions got the better of me, continuing to do so as I crouched behind the shrubs inside the wall and against the little door. Tears rolled off my cheeks, and sobs escaped me. I knew I wasn't beautiful, or skilled at my art, but it still hurt to hear someone point out every imperfection.

I stayed in place, trying to bring myself under control. It took a while. The words cut deeper than I ever expected. I had to remind myself that I swore never to let anyone see me cry while I was a prisoner—to never let them know they hurt me. I needed to hurry in calming down. I didn't want to look so pathetic if Lord Kwan returned today. Not after he explained why he wanted me to go to him on every return, and made it my only task.

Chapter 16
It's My Duty

A week passed since I met Lord Kwan's bride-to-be, and he still hadn't returned. I started to get worried until Syaoran laughed, saying he'd gone to meet with his family, and sent word he would be away for the Mokryon celebration. He laughed again when I asked what that was. Juneun seemed to have special days of their own. Festivities were quiet during the solstice, but perhaps that was simply the way of things for a Juneun. Whatever Mokryon was, it must've been important.

Syaoran made a quiet complaint on the matter, saying how it was a shame Lord Kwan didn't host such an event himself. And, stupidly, I asked why his future bride didn't just host it in his stead. The look of pure confusion marred Syaoran's face. I explained. He laughed.

"So, Feng is back. She's persistent, I'll give her that," said Syaoran, relaxed as he leaned back into the shade of the veranda. "But, no, she's not the master's intended."

"But, she said—"

"She dreams of it, sure. But she runs away with a broken heart every time she tries to persuade him to make a proposal and speak to her father. She's been infatuated with him ever since he came south. More than a century, certainly, but I don't think it's been two just yet."

Two hundred years of unrequited love. I started to think on it. And here I was, a human at sixteen who cried over a barrage of naïve questions that shouldn't have bothered me to begin with.

"She probably heard about Lord Kwan actually joining a celebration and figured he might be in a good mood again."

Good mood again? It reminded me. "The night I came here, Gi said that Lord Kwan was in a foul mood for the last fifty years."

That bit of information surprised Syaoran; or, at least, his face reflected it before bunching his brow in a silent apology. "Well, he's not wrong. But it's more of a private matter."

I nodded, even though I didn't quite understand.

Into the afternoon, as I walked the grounds, I pondered on the strange things I'd learned. What was so personal about Lord Kwan that everyone knew but kept from me? Maybe it was the fact that I was human, and still somehow untrustworthy. The idea bothered me as I walked the farthest garden. What would justify the prejudice? I was human, but surely that didn't make me dishonest by default.

I didn't have time to be angry about it for long. A hand came over my mouth and an arm across my torso. I struggled in my moment of panic, becoming still when I recognized the voice whispering my name. I looked up, slowly freed from my restraint.

Raeden.

"It's really you, isn't it? You're alive." He pulled me into an embrace.

I hugged my brother back, burying my face in his shirt and whispering. "What are you doing here?"

"I had to come," said Raeden, slow to let go again. "I couldn't stand it."

"How did you get in? Did the guards let you pass?"

He shook his head. "I walked the outer wall and found a place I could climb over first. And did the same to get in here."

I went pale. I didn't want to know what might happen if we were spotted. I knew he worried, but I had to protect him. I had to protect my brother. "It's not safe to talk here." I took his hand, dragging him behind the shrubs and keeping low until we got to the secret door.

Safe on the other side, I exhaled my relief.

"How did you know that door was there, and not sealed?"

"A friend showed me." I didn't stop to explain, fearful someone would hear us. I took my brother's hand again, leading him further from the inner wall.

When at last we were far enough away, hidden under the protective boughs of the trees between the walls, I gave him another hug.

"Hisa," cooed Raeden, squeezing me close. "Are you hurt? Are you okay?"

I pushed off gently, shaking my head to stop his rapid questions. "I'm fine. I'm working off the five years I have to stay. And I'll be allowed to go home when the time is up. He's, he's really not a bad person. He protects the mountain and all the surrounding villages. And he—"

Raeden looked me up and down as I rambled on, quirking a brow and twisting his face. "Has he touched you?"

"What?" I blinked. Then I looked to my clothes, searching for some clue to what my brother meant.

"The way..." He hesitated, eyes darting down and teeth gnawing at the corner of his lower lip. "The way a man touches a woman. A husband and wife."

When I understood, my I felt my face flush with a deep heat. I shook my head, quick, tucking into my shoulders. "It's not like that."

"Then come with me. I can show you where I climbed over."

He took my hand, but I pulled away. Confusion consumed his face.

"I made a promise," I said. "To take Hisato's place. If I leave…"

An understanding, and sadness, claimed his expression.

We sat there in the shade, talking. Raeden was the better hunter among my brothers. And the skills worked for him to come so far to see me. A brave and noble effort, I thought.

I told him of my time here, about Syaoran and Gi, about learning to write. I didn't mention the night Lord Kwan returned in a blind fury, or his request my attending him on every return. I didn't want to trouble my brother with any potential fears.

Then he told me about the heartbreak of our family. The day a letter arrived, with none of them able to understand and under the assumption it was a notice of my death. And the mention by one of the women in the village who'd climbed up in search of more fruits finding me by the river. He said she'd run home claiming to have seen my ghost—*They drowned her! They drowned her! And she's haunting the very spot of her death!* It was terrible of me, but I laughed at the retelling.

Life at the village had gone on, trying to move through the mourning. Fumei came every other day at least to stand in for me, often walking to our house with Kenta. Kyu had made a proposal to her, but she refused him. It warmed my heart to know I was right about my friend, that she had taken the initiative to look after my family. And, though I knew I was selfish for it, I was happy to hear she refused the boy I secretly loved.

More boar had come into the village this past year, trying to break into people's homes and storerooms during the winter. Raeden sounded proud as he recounted how he'd only missed once in all the arrows he let fly. Nine boars. In our worst year with the beasts before, it was five. But they made for good meat, enough to smoke and preserve to last everyone through winter.

"I was following the trail of another one when I found the upper river," said Raeden. "Then all I could think about was Nami terrified that she'd seen your ghost. One of the younger girls said she saw someone that looked like you walking up from the river, but no one believed her. Some of the children talked about the rumor that you were still alive. But when we asked where they'd heard it, they just said *the nice man told us*."

"It might've been Gi," I said. "I asked him to make sure the message was brought to our home. He said he would try."

"Maybe. But I never saw anyone."

That gave me cause to wonder.

"Either way, I'm glad the rumor is true. We miss you, Hisa. Home isn't the same. But at least now, we know you'll come back."

I nodded, smiling to assure my brother. "I swore to work hard so they don't have any reason to keep me longer."

He smiled back, letting it fall as he seemed to realize something. "Wait a minute. Is your hair growing back faster than mine?"

"Huh?" I slid my fingers through my short length of hair, trying to gauge the length and compare.

He pointed, his eyes wide for a second. "It is! That's hardly fair."

I chuckled. "Maybe. I've been eating well."

He took a moment, pretending to consider. "Maybe I should get arrested by the Juneun too."

"Don't you dare," I scolded. "Father relies on all of you, and so does the village. Did you forget how many boars came through this year alone?"

He snickered. "I was the one that told you."

I softened my voice, letting my fingers fuss with the skirt of my dress. "You shouldn't joke like that."

"Okay." He reclined, showing me a smile that meant he was quietly sorry.

"I know you're one of the best hunters in the village. But I still would get worried every time you went into the mountain—even just to set or check traps."

"I know."

We shared a sigh, looking at the golden shine on the grass in the afternoon sun.

"Hisa," said Raeden, his voice taking a melancholic tone. "It's my fault you're here."

"What do you mean?" I shifted my gaze to him, seeing a serious expression on his face.

"That day." He put his arms around his knees. "Hisato and I had been getting on each other. I made the decision to separate. I went to check on the traps, and sent him on a false trail. We both knew the tracks weren't fresh, but I pushed him to go anyway."

I placed my hand to his arm. "You couldn't have predicted things. When I made my plea to the spirits here, I accepted it. Then I was told I'd work twenty years. Then only five. They'll get tired of me quick and probably send me away before then." I brightened my smile, coaxing him to copy.

His own smile was soft, filled with quiet apology. "You work as a maid here. His servant and his—" he stopped himself, looking again at my dress and furrowing his brow. "Hisa, you can tell me. If he has touched you."

Puzzled, it took me a second to understand the desperate anger in his voice. "He hasn't. Besides, there's a beautiful Juneun who's in love with him and has been for centuries. If he was going to do that to anyone—"

"But, Hisa, it's different with lords and servants. I've heard the tales from the merchants. How they take their servant girls into their bed and won't marry them."

I gave a stern look to my brother. "That won't happen. He's never done that to any of the servant girls here, and they're more pretty and have been here for years."

He gave me a sorry look, and pulled me into a hug. "Come home."

My hands held onto him, like we were children all over again. "I will. The moment I'm released, I'll dash straight home."

I saw he wanted to argue.

"I don't want to risk any of you getting in trouble if I run away."

We lingered a little while longer, a part of us not wanting to be separated again. I'd told him everything I wanted to say, and led him to the next secret door to get out. We hugged one last time, saying I love you. He crawled through, being much taller than me, and I closed the door behind him.

My heart felt light.

I returned to my room, wanting a private space to replay the time shared with my brother that day, over and over. However, I came back to an odd sight. Syaoran was in my room, caught searching around.

He gave an apologetic expression. "It looks bad, but I promise it's not."

"What are you doing?" I asked, meek. I didn't want to reveal anything with a guilty tone. More than that, I didn't want to make accusations and get myself in any trouble.

"I... lost something. Something important to me," his fox ears flopped down, and his eyes looked away from me. "I was retracing my steps, but... I don't think it's here."

"What is it you lost?" I set my things down, tying up my sleeves to help in the search.

He shook his head, holding up a palm. "It's not something a human should touch. In any case, it's not here."

"Couldn't we ask Yua or anyone else to help?"

He went rigid for a second, his fox ears pointing up. "I don't want to get anyone involved. It's—" his eyes darted away, and his jaw locked on itself in the same instant. "It's something that might help me get to my sister."

"If it's that kind of important, shouldn't we get the others to help look for it? Or at least tell Lord Kwan?" I folded my hands over my chest.

"No! No, no," alarm hung heavy in his voice. "With the others. My sister is a fox spirit. They wouldn't understand."

"Lord Kwan would—"

He shook his head. "It's my sister. I need to keep her safe. Protect her however I can. I'd do anything. And Lord Kwan would try to talk me out of it if he knew. You understand, right?"

I did understand. Of course I did! And it was why I wanted to help him all the more. With a nod, I tried some other way to see if I could be useful to my friend. "Humans shouldn't touch it. But then tell me what it looks like. If I do see it, I can—"

He gave a forced chuckle, massaging his sinus. "I appreciate the thought. Really, I do." A sad smile, and my heart was pained for him. "But I—"

A thunderous roar shook the house. We both lost our balance. Syaoran falling into a kneel, and me to all fours. Lord Kwan was back, and not himself.

Syaoran got to his feet, quick to take action. "Stay here, where it's safe."

"But Lord Kwan said—"

"I think this makes for an exception, Hisa," scolded Syaoran. He didn't stop in his stride, hurrying to contain his master's fury.

I twisted to sit on my thigh, listening to the ongoing chaos. That terrifying roar recurred, shaking the delicate things placed on the vanity and table of my little room. Even my bunny trembled and fell over.

My bunny. The only companion I had in those first weeks here, and who hid away Tori to keep him safe while I was away.

No. I gave my word to Lord Kwan's request. Even in this state, I wouldn't let him be alone on his return. I would be his faithful companion for the years I had to be here.

I gathered my courage, taking in a breath to fasten my resolve with a prayer, and got to my feet. I could feel the unsteadiness in my bones with every small step, taking all my will to walk to the room with the heavy doors and not run to hide in some corner.

Out to the veranda. To the other side of the house. Up the stairs. My steps were heavy, begging me to reconsider. It felt harder to move my legs as the heavy doors came into view. But I walked on, keeping a silent prayer in my heart.

They were pulling his chains taught when I arrived, about to close the doors. Syaoran noticed my approach, calling for me to go back, that it was dangerous.

I held on to my courage, muttering my prayer before answering him. "Lord Kwan commanded that I stay in his company on his return."

There were objections by the men, some of them having faced a strike of blind fury.

"I know he said that," said Syaoran. "But he's not himself. Whatever arrangement—"

"He is my master and I am his servant," I said, firming my voice and raising it to a shout. "He bid I do this task, no matter, and that is what I will do." In that moment, I hardly recognized myself. I was shouting at the spirits, at a Juneun. "If this is my labor to get me home, then I will complete it the best that I can. And I won't be delayed from what will free me to go home." I spoke with as much eloquence as I could imitate. I wasn't a lady, but maybe presenting like one would garner some level of authority in this circumstance.

Syaoran frowned, protesting again. I ignored, taking a step forward. One of the men made to grab me and I pulled away.

"I'm not staying any longer than I have to. So I will do as the master commands me to." I gave my most severe scowl. Though, I probably didn't look at all threatening, never mind enough to be taken seriously.

"Hisa," cooed Syaoran, reaching for my hand.

I resisted. He was my friend here in the house, but I resisted all the same. "He won't hurt me. And if he does... I'm only a prisoner. It's sheer luck that I wasn't executed that following morning as planned."

He still argued. I shook my head.

"I can handle it. I did once before."

He hesitated, reluctant to leave until I leered at him enough to show I wouldn't move. It hurt to do so. I knew he was only trying to protect me. I was trying to do the same, though I hadn't the words to explain it.

When the doors closed, I looked back to Lord Kwan. He thrashed in place, snarling. Those stripes returned on his face, his arms. His hair unbound and wild, he didn't resemble the ethereal lord I met the year before. Hands clawed again, and that feral look in his eyes, I saw it all far more clearly in the daylight. He really did look like a tiger that'd been cornered; or, how I imagine it'd look. He was still mostly a man, fighting against an inner beast for control of his senses, for his body.

I smiled softly. Feet planted, I gave a polite bow, exactly as I'd practiced over the months. "Welcome home, Lord Kwan." Then I sat myself down comfortably and spoke to him.

I talked about the spring. What trees I thought might still be blossoming, which ones might already start bearing fruit. About the planting in the fields and the harvesting of the tea. I talked at length how we prepared the leaves to send out as offerings and for the taxes. I explained that every girl would have a walking stick with her to poke ahead in case of snakes. Then I reminisced on Fumei, how she would sing the first days of picking tea leaves.

I quietly sang, though I knew it wasn't as pretty as when my friend did it. In the fields, we'd sing together. One of the older girls, Yi, was the best singer in our village. Though, I supposed she should be called a woman since she was married last summer. I talked about the wedding we all put together for them, how her sisters made her a beautiful dress for the day. I remember my hands were red from staining chicken feathers with berry juice. We hung them up around their houses to keep away any malevolent spirits, and set citrus leaves to smolder by the doors and windows for the same reason.

His snorting breath slowed as midnight crept closer. I'd talked from the late afternoon and into the night, pacing myself. He thrashed now and again, growls and roars stifled by the chain that gaged him. Those grew fewer as well.

I don't know when I dozed off, or for how long. I woke to the raspy call of my name.

"Hisa."

I sat myself up, prompt, rubbing my eyes free of sleep. "Yes, my lord?"

"Unbind me."

My brain failed to understand, to obey. "My lord?"

"I am myself. And I am tired." He kept his eyes shut, but everything about him appeared subdued compared to his arrival.

I got to my feet, pinching my cheeks to better wake me. If I wasn't half-dazed, I would have thought to ask a guardsman to help. A small part of my mind that was awake and rallying, the rest of me began to hope this would reduce my time here. If staying by accident earned me a room and clothes that better fit me, staying deliberately surely brought me closer to going home.

I went to where the chains were anchored, loosening them. He slumped forward with the new slack. I couldn't quite figure out how to undo them from that end in the dark. Frustrated, I shuffled over to untether his arms at the source. As I worked the binding, I could see him straining to stand, and hurried my effort.

One wrist freed, and the other after—though it was more stubborn to pull loose. I reached to guide him as he took his first step, though his strength gave out in that moment. My reflex was to catch him, as though he were a child that'd slipped. I went down with a sharp shriek, Lord Kwan collapsed on top of me. He was heavy. Crushing me.

A pained breath, and a groan, he raised himself enough to free me. Were I thinking properly, I should have gone to the door for help. Instead, I stupidly tried to help him to his feet on my own.

My shriek didn't go unnoticed. The doors opened, with six guardsmen at the ready. It must've been a ridiculous sight, since they stopped to raise a brow and stare.

Slow, my mind formed the words needed. "He needs help to his room."

No further direction was necessary. Two of the guardsmen placed down their weaponry to assist their lord, shouldering his weight and carrying him out of the room. I stepped out last, not wanting to impede.

Syaoran came running in that moment, dressed in his night clothes. "I heard a scream." He panted, slowing his dash to a halt as we locked eyes. Then his gaze moved Lord Kwan. "Already?"

I was too tired to make inquiries, heading for the tea house as I typically did when Lord Kwan returned from elsewhere. Syaoran stopped me.

"Get some rest." A look of approval shined, and his tone as warm as the hand on my shoulder.

"I can stay with him a bit longer," I said. "He didn't dismiss me."

"I'll dismiss you and fetch the tea," said Syaoran, coaxing. "You need to sleep."

It was kind of him to consider me, I thought. But I shook my head with a yawn. "I'll stay with him. Like I swore to do."

"Did you swear, or were you commanded?" teased Syaoran, still trying to persuade me into better judgement.

I simply smiled, unable to think of anything clever to say in return. I'd grown fond of him, and didn't think of him as quite so strange anymore.

Chapter 17
Lord Kwan V

He left the mountain at the summons of his father. Undoubtedly, this had to do with Borsi and Lord Kwang. Another excuse to chastise.

She smiled when she saw him off. Not polite or sly or to stand on ceremony. She was uncouth. There wasn't a hidden agenda to it. It was simply a smile.

In the hall of his ancestral home, where his brothers sat down perfectly lined in attention, backs straight, he found the entire thing tedious and dull. When someone talked, there were meanings in what was said and unsaid. Most important was how much the silence spoke. Twice, a low cunning hint went into his marital status and shut-in lifestyle. He kept the reason hidden from them, making no response then or now. However, the inevitable happened: each of them got in a sly remark on why he hadn't slain Gumiho yet. He didn't know for sure if the knowledge of her theft of his soul, part of it, remained secret from them.

In silence, he watched, looking for signs that any of them knew of that bit.

The only part he allowed them to be aware of was that she attempted the theft, and that he'd sealed it away to prevent such a case. The second half, only his youngest brother was told. From previous experience, he couldn't trust his older brothers with sensitive information. Now, he tested his youngest brother.

Thus far, that much remained unknown to the rest of them.

They droned on about their own skirmishes. The Kurai clans they locked horns with, the toll they claimed to have lost. The state of their houses and ongoing of court. What tactic ought to be used to stave off what clan. Repetitive.

Every one of them had perfect manners and a double-edged smile.

His mind began to wander. Back to that sincere smile. The one that didn't ask anything of him, or try to make some small quip at his expense. She was a strange thing. Careful, though sometimes clumsy, and completely unaware of herself. He found it irritating at first. Then amusing. And now, surrounded by his kin with their perfected façades, he missed it.

He lingered on the thought of how her face twisted, and her tongue stuck out as she practiced her brush strokes. There wasn't a Juneun or noble spirit who would allow their expression to be anything but serene, alone or in company.

She couldn't conceal her feelings, much as she might try. Fearfulness, sadness, joy... as obvious as a red streak of paint on a white canvas. The musing Syaoran said came back to him.

The tiger's fur is orange and black, against a forest of green. It walks through proud, yet remains unseen.

Not quite a poem.

Too much like courtly life. Nothing like her.

She was a magpie in the summer gardens. Surrounded by all the colors of the world, and standing out in both sight and sound. The other birds tuck themselves in the thick of the bush, or hide among the boughs of the trees. But she is obvious wherever there is sunlight.

"What say you to that, Lord Kwan?" his father put an emphasis on his title, implying he noticed a complete lack of attention.

"I think discussions are better held when speaking plainly and not on ceremony," said Kwan, unbothered.

"You had the chance to slay Gumiho when Borsi betrayed us," said his brother Beom. He'd taken to be direct without much prompting, and tried to mask a smugness in his statement.

"I did," said Kwan.

"What delayed you?" pressed Beom.

"Borsi," replied Kwan, keeping a tone of disinterest.

Before Kwang could speak up, their father interrupted. "You lost control."

"I had distractions."

"Borsi should've been easy to deal with," said his father, pointed as he narrowed his eyes. "It serves us right, trusting that a Kurai could change their ways. Change their own nature."

"Borsi didn't willingly betray us," said Kwang, sounding fed up at last with being overruled and ignored. "My lord father, it was fox magic. And our brother snuffed out the source."

"Snuffed it too late," said Seong. His face worked hard to keep off a grin, though some of it still shone through. "What was this great fox magic that you couldn't free Borsi, and had to slay him—?"

"They stole his soul," said Kwan, if for nothing more than to silence his battle-hungry brother. Of all of them, Seong reveled most in the thrill of fighting. And he hated his brother for it. There was nothing noble or glorious about warfare. Always, it was a tragedy. So much life lost while those in power were infatuated with the idea, and treated it like a game to be continued until all the pieces were gone.

"And how do you know this?" asked Beom, a hint of interest.

Kwan took his time to answer, making them wait only to irritate. "Because I saw it in his eyes."

Objections took place, growing into an uproar. Kwan stayed silent, watching the masks, the perfectly curated image of each of them, slip out of their control for an extended moment.

"So now we have proof of our suspicion," said Kwan, just as the men of his family began to compose themselves again. "When a powerful Kurai has a soul in their clutch, they become the puppet master."

"It's one of a few suspicions," said Kwang, agreeing but resigned to want to deny it.

"The stories had to come from somewhere," said Kwan.

Discussion resumed, with the elder brothers set on not hearing more from firsthand accounts. For the best. Being ignored gave him time to contemplate.

How would he bring an end to Gumiho's reign of terror?

He remembered that smile, from when they were children. It'd looked so genuine then. Long ago, he truly believed there was no difference between them. That it was a choice.

He was disturbed from his thoughts again when Kwang insisted on his accepting of an invitation, and the rest of the family dispersed. The youngest brother would host the Mokryon.

"I know you dislike to host, but consider joining. Get out of your house for leisure. Not just for Kurai or because father summons us. And there will be the biggest assortment of lovely girls. It would make one less thing for any of them to say about either of us."

"I can't," said Kwan.

His brother, undeterred, pestered him on the matter.

It brought an idea to the forefront of his mind. Word of his coming to an event after fifty years shut-in would spread faster than fire across dried grass. Among Juneun, yes. And among Kurai also. He could lure her out.

He agreed, but didn't smile. He continued to appear reluctant, disguising his plan in a façade of his own.

Word did spread. Exactly as anticipated.

Kwan had no intention of actually attending, even as he sent a letter back to his house stating otherwise. Walking the grounds of his family home, he found it difficult the dig up the happier memories. It now felt unwelcoming, as though he were a stranger.

"You don't smile anymore."

He tore his gaze from the courtyard and pond garden beyond. His sister Sara walked up, poised, refined—a proper lady. At her approach, he said nothing, keeping his watch on her. When she stopped beside him, expectant, he answered her. "I have a lot to consider."

"No, it's different from that."

Kwan stared at her a moment, reading her perfect composure, hunting for wordless clues. A small grunt leaving him, he slowly pulled his eyes back to the scenery.

"Ever since that confrontation with Gumiho. You started to smile less. Now, you don't smile at all." She pressed her brow together, mimicking concern. What she wanted, he knew, was some slip of information to play with. "It changed you."

He let the statement linger, choosing what words to sharpen for this battle. "You changed too."

Her imitated expression went slack, reforming a second later.

"Jiana died. And you no longer had someone to mirror. You had the chance to be yourself. Instead, you deny all truth, and became this."

She gave up on looking sympathetic, her face taking to stone. "I don't expect you to understand what it is to be a woman in this world. Let alone the last daughter in this family."

"And yet, you pester me with your woes as if I *could* understand it."

"Pester?" snapped Sara. "You lost one sister. I lost three. Jiana was all I had!"

He kept silent, refusing to acknowledge.

"Every day you let Gumiho live, I'm kept a prisoner here. I paint because that's what I'm supposed to do, and smile because it's expected. I compose poetry, because there's not an acceptable way for a lady to express herself otherwise, and even then I have to conceal some things. I play whatever instrument on whatever day because father commanded it for his guests. And when they speak it makes my skin crawl and I'm expected to never notice they said a thing."

"Dreadful," said Kwan, disinterested.

"It's a beautiful cage," said Sara. "But it's still a cage."

"Maybe you should smile," said Kwan, finally looking at his sister again.

Her face turned ugly, showing her true feeling for the first time in over half a century. It surprised him, yet he stayed still in his posture, staring.

She leered at him, giving up when he remained unchanged—opposite to what she'd grown used to with servants. She inhaled deep, composing herself again. "I wonder if you even remember how to smile. You may want to practice for Mokryon. That cold face of yours will scare away every prospect." She pushed back her long hair with a flick of her wrist.

He said nothing, not caring to indulge her quips.

"Remember me when you're dancing with a beauty, brother. For I will be in my prison and unable to witness." She walked back the way she came, confirming that her purpose was to pry at him, and not a stop along her route.

He watched her leave, every step smooth to make her appear weightless. His mind reclaimed the image of her scowl, the first piece of honesty from his sister in many years. Then the memory of a twisted face with a tongue sticking out came up to compare. A true opposite. He thought about the perfect pace of Sara's walk, and the stumbling jog of a human carrying salt. The genteel and the boorish.

He waited days and nights. If she didn't come, he would go home. On the chance that she did, he'd take the chance to end things once and for all.

Keeping unseen and silent, he lurked in the wilds. If the hope was to lay an assault on his return, that worked just as well. The assumption of spent energy would be her downfall.

When she finally made her move, that seemed the case. She planned on giving him no reprieve on his return. The smell of fox hung thick in the air.

Kwan kept to the shadows, moving expertly, sword drawn. He saw her, red painted on her lips and eyes and pinking her cheeks. A lovely visage. That's what he would've thought so long ago. She'd painted her nails black, likely lacing them with venom. Her ears and tails highlighted her power, a warning to onlookers, giving no doubt as to who their queen was.

He could do it. He was so close to her now. His sword raised. Pointed. Silent. She hadn't spotted him. One fell strike. That's all it would take.

He set his feet.

Fast as lightning, he launched himself into a sprint. Gumiho turned, a look of horror, seeing it was too late. His blade thrust, plunging deep into her chest.

Then, laughter. Echoing around him.

"I didn't think you had it in you, Kwan."

He looked around, seeing a sea of copies. Gumiho, an ocean of rouge pained faces, red dressings, and smokey, dark, ginger hair. An illusion. All of it. He folded a hand, arcing his arm to dispel the images.

"How like you to go straight for my heart," taunted Gumiho, voice coming from every direction.

His eyes searched, sword held to parry.

"But I'm afraid you're losing your touch!"

A shadow, and arm—a claw—leapt at him; violet eyes behind it. He swung. She yelped. His feet moved, closing the distance between him and those violet eyes.

Teeth snapped. He swung again. Fire flew at him, and he turned on his heel, dodging, sword defending. He charged her again. She blocked with a knife, the claws of her free hand swiping at him. His spell of white threads holding her off, buying a breath of time for him to swing at her again. She broke free.

Other Kurai gathered, hastily put together and rushing towards the sound of combat. One pressed in, his neck met with the slash of Kwan's blade.

He twisted himself back, holding off Gumiho from an opportunistic stab. A cut made it to his foot from elsewhere. He pushed off, casting his spell of lighting to give himself space, a barrier to buy precious seconds. Mind reeling, eyes counting, and breath held steady.

Muttering his spell, he poured magic into his sword.

An ambush attack.

He swung, slicing the very air and cutting them down. Hot blood sprayed, forcing him blind as he raised a sleeve to shield himself. Gumiho struck, her knife going deep into his gut. His magic failing to shield him from her own, steeling his mind from her illusions, he needed to act. Grabbing fast to her, fighting the shock and the pain, he brought around his sword. She slipped from him, escaping a fatal blow, but not before taking a deep wound herself.

The others closed in.

He couldn't hold them off. Not like this. And the darkness took his senses once more.

In the dark, he remembered a voice: *are you scared too?*

He regained himself for a moment, realizing where he was on his mountain. The upper river. Darkness.

His senses freed another second, enough to see he'd jumped the walls.

Darkness.

That voice. His senses returned a moment, his arms pulled taut and his mouth gaged. She sat down, a soft smile, and went on to speak gently. This time, she didn't tremble. Rather, she appeared perfectly at ease, as if he were himself and sharing tea.

Darkness.

He could hear humming, but his sight didn't return to find the source. They were odd songs, and off key, but sincerely bittersweet.

When he awoke, the night had not ended. He'd managed to come directly home, and already calmed enough to regain himself.

The girl lay on the floor, asleep. Even in slumber, she wasn't a graceful thing. Drool pooled beside her mouth, snores leaving her due to a crooked neck.

What was it about the humans—about this human—that dispersed his reckless fury? They were strange things. Ordinary things. Humans. No culture to them compared to a Juneun. Even the noble society of them was poor imitation.

He called to her, giving his command. It was safe. He wasn't a danger to his household. She worked prompt at her task, without question or hesitation. His eyes struggled to stay open, and his legs strained in trying to stay up. In his first step free, he fell. The floor wasn't hard. A warm breath caressed his neck.

He quickly made sense of it, angry with himself, and tried to stand. She scrambled out from under him, a hare running from the bite of a tiger.

Someone carried him, though he didn't recognize who in his bleary state. His eyes closed.

When he woke again, he was in his bed. The room well lit, and the smell of persimmon wine gone, and the haze of incents beginning. Looking over, his sore muscles urged him to stay still. The girl was there, asleep against the wall. Steam rose from the spout of the teapot.

She'd stayed beside him, performing her duty. He hadn't dismissed her, though she could've assumed it. But she didn't. A kindness?

He thought of the bird she fostered. Promising to look after it until it was well to fly.

Loyalty.

No, that wasn't the right word.

She had nothing to gain from continuing on. She had nothing to lose in going to her bed. The choice was an easy one for a lady. For a servant. Yet, she stayed to the end.

Dutiful.

Compassionate.

Chapter 18
New Friends

Lord Kwan required rest. When he took tea, Syaoran arrived, and I was allowed to leave. I'd slept late into the day and retired early into the night.

Still, I couldn't help but wonder about my Juneun friend. What had he been searching for? And what did he mean when he said *already* about Lord Kwan's condition? I remembered the puzzle box in the kennels. Perhaps that was it. Though, if not, I would've given false hope. He said it was something a human couldn't touch, allowing my mind to let go of the idea.

In the following day, I walked the grounds. Lord Kwan was still in recovery. Everyone else seemed in a rush of preparation for something, similar to how they'd been when Juro visited. A shudder went up my spine in thinking he would make another visit. He wasn't a terrible person, or evil by any means, but he unsettled me.

Walking alone through the court yard, I found the moon gate of the inner wall open and unattended. Curious, I wandered over and stuck my head out. The guardsmen had completely abandoned their posts. I looked for Gi, wondering if something brought him away. It still left the mystery of why the gate was open. But I never came to this part between the walls, and decided it made for a good excuse to do so.

Before, my leaving the interior was done more secretively, so as not to invite trouble. Now, I could say that the gate was open and I'd gone looking for the men in charge.

In my aimless meandering, a question crossed my mind: what caused Lord Kwan to become such a monster? He always seemed so in control of himself otherwise, I couldn't imagine the source. Perhaps it had something to do with the thing about him that everyone kept quiet from me. Something that happened fifty years ago that made him go into a foul mood. In remembering how fearful I felt with that information, I wondered if it was exaggerated. He was cold, but not cruel.

Though, I didn't know him half a century before and had nothing to compare.

In the time I spent with him, serving his teas on his return or practicing my writing, he showed a curiousness about the villages surrounding his mountain. I could only speak on mine, since I'd only ever traveled to one other when mother was still alive; I was little, and we weren't there for long. Sometimes people from one of the nearest neighboring villages would come by for one matter or another—Lan's wife had grown up in a different village—but seldom to socialize.

I wondered why no one had given warning about Lord Kwan, should he rush through in that state. Perhaps they thought humans would retaliate against the spirits out of fear.

In my walking, I came to the clay mining pit. It looked freshly worked, though I didn't know for what reason. I remembered this being my first chore, and how I toiled to prove my worth under a hot sun amid the muggy air. The water barrel was still half full, reminding me to take a drink in the warm, spring weather.

I grabbed the ceramic cup, making sure it was clean, and scooped out some of the water without letting my finger touch the surface. That was the way of things, so that clay and dirt didn't contaminate it. I savored the cool of it running down my throat, looking over the pit.

Something struggled at its base, writhing around in desperation. Squinting, I recognized it for a snake. A small part of me instinctually urged running. I'd screamed and taken off more than once when I found a snake in the tea fields. I was afraid of their bite, afraid of their venom. The men of my village would cut the heads of snakes when they made an unwanted appearance. But looking at it now, from a safe distance, I pitied the poor thing.

It didn't ask to be born a snake. To have no arms or legs that would help it to climb out of a sheer spot in a clay pit. It struggled to get out against the smooth chiseled sides of a newly dug out section. When the men in service to Lord Kwan came back, they'd likely treat it the same as those in my village. And I felt sorry for it. My own situation was originally not so different.

Against my fear, I hiked up the skirt of my dress and tied it off. The full of my shins and knees were showing, skinny as they were, but there was no one around to see me. The cup refilled, I kicked off my shoes and made my way carefully down.

I came as close as I dared, gaining its attention and freezing as it flicked a black tongue at me. Not taking my eyes off it, I set down the cup, watching it open its mouth to hiss. Then I stepped away.

It stared, flicking its tongue and closing its maw. Its fangs sheathed again, it came to investigate.

"It's water," I said, more to secure my courage than anything else. I knew it didn't understand me. "For you."

It slithered forward, inch by inch, never taking its unblinking eyes off me. Its forked tongue came out, more slow and cautious, tasting the water. Feeling safe, it dipped its jaw in and began to drink. Though, it never looked away from me, even after it had its fill.

I searched for something to help, climbing out to open more options. There was bamboo not too far away, gathered thick. I ran over, looking for any younger shoots I could break off and use.

I managed it with a struggle, and hurried back to find the creature trying again to climb out on its own with no success.

Careful, I slid the far end of the shaft under it. Immediately, it tried to use the leverage, falling off in the attempt. I repeated my effort, trying to move with it so as to keep it balanced. Once high enough, it took off.

Relieved, I dropped the bamboo and fetched the cup, cleaning it with my sleeve before exiting. Half way out, I noticed the reptile waiting, watching. It stared with a keen interest, then took off the rest of the way and into the grass.

Still a little fearful, I retrieved the bamboo and got out.

On my walk back, bamboo tapping the grass ahead, I found the gates still open, with new furnishings being brought in. Before I could ask, Yua took me aside, a severe look on her face.

"Listen carefully," said Yua, on edge. "Several members of the master's family will be coming to stay a while. Keep out of their way, out of sight if you can manage that much. If, by chance you do come across them, say nothing and keep your head bowed in their presence. They likely won't ask you much, but if one of them does try to pry anything out of you, say nothing about Lord Kwan's states of return. Do you understand me, girl?"

She spoke quick, and sharp, her fingers digging into my arm. I nodded, not quite understanding it all but repeating it in my mind to memorize the instruction.

"Do not speak to Lord Kwan while they are here. We're all given a level of freedom and leniency under our master, but his relatives dislike that sort of mingling entirely. For heaven's sake, I wouldn't be surprised if they're still under the same assumption of my own being here as it is. Say nothing of Syaoran either. After this last incident, they'll be looking for reasons to rip this house apart."

"Last incident?"

"The less you know, the better."

Why was that always the case with the Juneun? In the village, it was just the opposite. We were more useful to each other if we knew as much as possible so we could lend the best of our skills to the problem.

"Say nothing of Feng either. If they do ask questions, you're obligated to answer. It's best that you appear as ignorant as possible."

"When will they be here? How many?" I began to worry. How long did I have to prepare? What if I couldn't hide away in time, and crossed paths? Would I need to stay locked in my room?

"In about a week," said Yua, sensing how seriously I took her warnings. "And four of them, we think. They'll only be here a few days. That family has never been patient, and if they can't find reasons to stay, they'll go back."

I nodded, showing I understood. "Is Lord Kwan still resting?"

She sighed. "We're concerned about that as well. He needs to appear strong. Whatever the reason for this visit, he can't be seen as anything less. It'll only lead to questions."

The day came when we expected the arrival of the guests. I'd put on my old clothes, making sure everything was polished, and kept a watch for the fastest route to the secret door. When I heard horses, I put away my things and bolted to go between the walls. I was told to stay out of sight, and that seemed the best way to achieve it. I could bathe in the river, and forage for things to eat, and it was warm enough now that sleeping outside wouldn't be horrible. The fireflies might even keep me company and scare away the dark from becoming too much.

Though, I went in so much of a rush that I didn't think to grab my drawing paper and charcoal. I'd need to come up with other ways to pass the time until Lord Kwan's guests left.

On the other side of the small door, I made to hide myself beneath the trees, running across the open space in an effort to remain unseen. Once in the shade of their branches, I no longer heard anything going on at the house.

A good thing of it since I looked away from the wall and shrieked. Feng stood directly in front of me with a wide grin.

"I know your secret," said Feng, leaning in closer.

I gulped. By secret, did she mean Raeden? He wasn't supposed to be here, sure, but he didn't break in exactly or do anything wrong. Right?

I wanted to run away, stopped in place as she encircled me. The slick, smoothness of her snake tail rubbed against my ankle, sending a shiver up my body and paralyzing my legs in fright.

"Secret?" I repeated. Taking Yua's advice, I tried to appear naïve.

"Did you think *I*, of all people, wouldn't know?" She continued to circle, broadening her grin.

"Know what?"

"*You're* afraid of snakes."

That was enough to bewilder me. I never considered that a secret, since everyone in my village knew.

"Do you recognize her?" Feng held out an open palm, allowing a serpent to slither out from under her sleeve.

I covered my mouth to keep from screaming. It was so close to my face! And I stared unblinking.

It returned the stare, expressionless.

"I knew it! You do remember her," said Feng. "She says thank you."

"What?" I braved looking away, to Feng.

"Most humans cut off a snake's head simply for being in the wrong place at the wrong time. They're cruel and evil, taking delight in killing."

"That's not, humans aren't evil," I tried to argue. In the moment I understood the perspective. I just didn't have all the words to try and explain. "It's just... snakes have venom, and if they bite—"

"Bite some giant, clumsy, evil human? Good riddance!"

I shook my head, getting angry with Feng for her callousness and frustrated with myself for my lacking. "Snakes bite humans because they're afraid. And humans kill snakes for the same reason. We're both afraid of each other."

"Then why didn't you?" She leaned in, her nose almost touching mine.

I had the answer to that. What I didn't have were the words. Worthy words to explain and make her understand. "I just... thought..."

"You're different from other humans," said Feng.

With that, I didn't know how to argue. I didn't think of myself as spectacular at anything. Ordinary. Unremarkable compared to the other girls of my village. Underwhelming against any of the spirits in Lord Kwan's house. But I wouldn't have said I was *different* in that sort of way.

"So, what are you doing out here today?" asked Feng, uncoiling and smiling bright as she gave me back much needed space. "More butterfly watching? But you don't have your drawings."

"Oh. No, everyone at the house is in an uproar and I was—"

"You'll be looking for Syaoran, then." She took my hand, piecing things together for assumptions rather than listen to another poorly worded ramble. "He's over this way. The upper lords don't like him much either."

I was yanked by her, with my eyes on the ground so as to not step on her tail by accident.

Syaoran lay in the grass under the shade near the sunken part of the wall, fast asleep. He didn't look as noble or regal as I remembered. His face looked like an ordinary young man, peaceful.

"He came out early this morning," whispered Feng. "Probably right after breakfast." She slithered to him, poking at his side.

He groaned, muttering something.

"Get up," complained Feng. "Human prisoner girl is looking for you."

He rolled off his side to sit up, looking me up and down with incredulity. "You got the same plan as I did, didn't you?"

"To stay out of the inner wall?" I asked.

He nodded, slowly bringing up a pleasant smile. "Well, now I suppose we both have half a truth for an excuse. You came looking for me, and I had to keep an eye on you."

That didn't make a lot of sense to me. But Yua made so much secrecy that I didn't want to ask. I was happy enough to know I wouldn't be alone for the next few days. And I had so many other questions anyway.

"Why do we need to be kept secret from Lord Kwan's family?" I sat myself down beside him. "We're only his servants."

Feng hissed, indignant.

"And," I corrected with hesitance, "his potential fiancée."

"Potential?" repeated Feng, insult heavy in her tone.

Syanoran laughed, loud and unabashed.

She glared at him.

"Well, whatever we call ourselves," said Syaoran, ignoring Feng's look, "his brothers aren't the most understanding."

"Do they not get along with Lord Kwan?"

Feng shook her head, softening her expression as she provided a wordless answer.

"Not at all," said Syaoran.

"Why?" I scrunched in my face, thinking to every family in my village. None went without squabbles, but they loved each other—we loved each other. More or less, we all got along.

"Most noble families have infighting," said Syaoran. "A climb for power."

"What do you mean *a climb for power*? They're all nobles in the same family. Wouldn't that make them equal?"

Both he and Feng gave me crooked looks, as though I'd said something outlandish.

We spoke at length after that. I did my best to keep up with the conversation, realizing then how little I knew of the spirits I stayed with. How little I knew of Lord Kwan. My present company hesitated or otherwise avoided any questions I had on him. It wasn't their place to tell, they said. Thinking about it, I respected the decision. I wouldn't have wanted someone divulging my life's story to a stranger.

Were we still strangers?

When my stomach complained, I walked towards the secret door in the outer wall.

"Where are you going?" asked Syaoran.

"To forage for something to eat."

"Most of the fruit trees don't have much to give yet. I can show you." He got up to follow.

"There could still be mushrooms or wild turnips," I said, smiling. For once I felt confident in my ability to do something useful. "And there should be young bamboo shoots."

"Bamboo?" said Feng in disgust.

"They're not so bad. But you have to cook them first so you don't get sick."

"How do you even know that?" asked Feng.

I blinked at her, mirroring her bewildered expression. This was common knowledge, or so I thought. Everyone in my village knew these things. Surely sprits, Juneun or otherwise, knew this too. But, looking at them, that didn't appear the case.

My smile returned, broadening. "I can show you. It's easy."

We spent the afternoon gathering an assortment of things. I'd found some radishes, showing my friends the shape of the leaves. Syaoran brought out a knife, cutting away the leaves and dropping them. I gave a confused look. He mirrored once he noticed. They didn't know that part was also eatable.

Nightshade was mistaken for another berry, which I swatted away and scolded Feng for. It made me happy to see them take to trying to forage, though the natural consequence was plucking up something toxic. The same when we found wild choy plants; the lower stem and roots were fine, and the leaves poisonous. The children of the village would wait until I directed, or come up immediately to show a find and ask if it was okay to eat. Seeing it now, with grown individuals, felt odd.

We washed what we gathered, and I set to find a suitable flat stone to cook on. Syaoran prepared tinder, and started a fire to cook by the river, where we were confident we'd remain unnoticed. Cut, cleaned, and cooked, we ate our supper. It wasn't flavorful, especially not compared to what they were used to in Lord Kwan's house, but it kept us full.

"All the humans know how to do this?" asked Feng.

I shrugged, feeling put on the spot in that moment. "Everyone in the villages. We have to. Sometimes we don't get a good harvest, and the tax that year still needs to be paid in what yield we did manage."

"Makes sense," said Syaoran. "Goes to show how resourceful humans are without magic."

"My mother taught me these things when I was little. And I would take the children of my village into the mountain to teach them."

"I don't think even the servants know this," said Feng. "And here it all is, just outside the walls."

"It is the sort of thing that seems useful to know," said Syaoran. "We built walls around ourselves and our homes. So much is cut off. If our castles fell tomorrow, how helpless would we be?"

"There's a lot about your life I don't know about," I said, more to comfort than any admittance. It was painfully obvious how little I knew away from my home. "I have no idea what it's like to be a lady. And I'm not so great a servant as it is."

"I could teach you that," said Feng. "It's easy. Even a mouse could learn it. How much do you know right now?"

I slackened my expression, feeling suddenly exposed. "Um..."

"Aside from the bows and glide stepping and all that, I mean."

"Glide stepping?"

She gave me a quizzical look then.

"Any dancing?" asked Syaoran. "Lord Kwan is teaching you to write, but is there the chance you can recite poems?"

"I've heard poems from the merchants as they pass through. I have a few memorized."

"You've never composed one?" asked Feng.

I shook my head.

She sighed, nose crinkled and brow pressed. "So, the only think you know is your bowing."

"Actually," said Syaoran. "I've seen her try, and..."

"No even that?" whined Feng.

"It's not something we did very often in the village," I said, trying to defend myself.

Without warning, Feng got up and grabbed hold of me, yanking me to my feet. "We'll start at the very beginning then. My husband can't have a servant who lacks etiquette."

"Who's your husband?" teased Syaoran.

Feng shot him a cold look. "You too. Get up so we can practice."

"Ahh, so that's your plan." A sly grin crawled across his face, and he looked fox-like for a spell of time. "If you can teach a human from scratch, you can keep and coordinate an entire household. Is that it?"

Her face went pink, and her frown deepened. "Do as I say."

"You're not my mistress yet, and already giving me commands." He laughed at his teasing, but got to his feet nonetheless.

I'd always assumed that a girl would keep her hands folded in front of her with a bow. And the deeper anyone bowed, the more respect it showed.

This was not the case.

There were ones for greeting important guests, for addressing one's master, one's spouse, and ones which one lord or lady might give to another lord or lady. There was a bow for a guest to a host, and it differed depending on the status of each. And there was a bow for deep humility and apology. She showed more than twenty different kinds, each for a specific scenario. I mimicked well enough, but often forgot which one was meant for what circumstance.

Syaoran played the part of whomever I was meant to address, annoying Feng by behaving dramatically. It made me smile that he did, and eased some of the tension I'd worked myself into.

There were moments he and I laughed, unable to contain ourselves with his theatrics and Feng's serious responses and scolding. I thought about Fumei and the other girls of my village. So often we teased that the most beautiful girls would be swept away to a better life by a rich man. Though, a rich man, a noble or someone equally as important wouldn't bother with a pretty girl if she didn't have manners to match. This was another skill I could bring home when my time was up.

In the night, as we lay in the grass under stars and firefly light, I imagined a prince coming through and being very impressed; enough that he'd have to fall in love with one of the girls and take her to his castle to wed. In my daydreaming, the girl would send gifts as a thank you, and the village would be richer for it.

Chapter 19
I'm Learning to

I woke up in Syaoran's arms, held close to him. The feel of his shirt against my face had me confused. It wasn't until he wished me good morning with a gentle coo in his voice that I realized. Startled, I pushed away and sat up.

He laughed. "You were shivering in your sleep."

I fumbled with my words, stuttering an incoherent babble. Pausing with a quirked brow as I saw Feng cuddled up against his back.

"I have a warmer body heat." He spoke so matter-of-fact that it caused me to ponder. "Nothing happened, I promise."

"Do you mind?" moaned Feng, yawning wide. She pulled Syaoran closer to her, with her tail lain over his legs to steal more warmth. "It's too early."

He gestured a thumb at her. A clue to how comfortable the situation was, innocently made. Still, I couldn't help but remember what Raeden said. Had I been touched in that way, he asked. I felt a discomfort, shifting where I sat.

"What's wrong?" asked Syaoran.

I shook my head. "I've just... never woken up in someone's arms. It feels strange. Even if we didn't..." I rolled my bottom lip between my teeth, failing to stop my cheeks from heating up. "If we didn't touch."

He chuckled. "You don't have a sweetheart at home that you've snuck over to?"

I felt my face flare and form a scowl. "No! That's not—we don't do that!"

"So much yelling," complained Feng, sitting up to stretch.

"Really? Never?" asked Syaoran. "You can be honest. I've had the occasional girl sneak over to me. Then again, you're still just... how old are you?"

"S-sixteen." I stared at him, at how casually he confessed such a thing.

He turned to Feng. "What does that mean in human years?"

She shrugged. "I'd heard they marry off the girls at fourteen. So, I can't imagine she's still too much of a child at all."

"Fourteen?" I gaped.

They looked at me with my jaw wide open.

"In the noble houses, yes," said Feng. "That's what I've heard, at least."

"That's far too young," I said, louder than I intended. "I'm not of age yet."

"Really?" said Syaoran. "I know humans often don't make it past eighty. Fourteen or fifteen seems like a reasonable age to get married at that rate."

I shook my head. "It's not."

"In any case, you can't be too far away from that age. And sometimes young men and women simply can't wait, or they get curious."

I knew he was teasing me now, but I shot up onto my feet in a huff. "I'm going to look for some breakfast."

"I think I'll come with you," said Feng, newly uncomfortable.

Syaoran smirked at her then. "You mean to say that in the last century you never once tried to go to Lord Kwan somewhere in the night?"

"Absolutely not!" Feng glared at him. "That will wait until our wedding night. My sisters will be jealous. They lay with their beloved and still haven't gotten a proposal."

"And in other parts of the world, proposals do happen after laying together. It's entirely possible. Several girls starting as servants are now the ladies of the house. Sometimes it seals the love."

"Not a chance," said Feng, ignoring any semblance of evidence Syaoran might present.

We discovered an apricot tree, its fruit just ripe, and walked to enjoy our collection at the edge of the sunlight and the forest. More conversation, pleasant conversation, took place as we savored the sweet find.

"You've never been to the top of the mountain?" asked Syaoran in disbelief.

"We're usually too busy to even get as far as the upper river," I explained. "Why? What's there?"

"The top of the mountain is a crater, and water pools in there to form a giant lake," said Syaoran. "Lord Kwan and I liked to race up to there on horseback. I won twice."

"Typical," said Feng. "Of course, my fiancée would be the better horseman."

"Have you been to the lake, Feng?" I asked.

"It's where we fell in love."

"You mean, where you fell in love," teased Syaoran. "And I don't recall that being the story."

"This is why no one will want to marry you, fox," snapped Feng.

"Speaking of which," he pulled a gourd from his belt, bearing a catty grin. "Rice wine."

Feng stuck out her tongue.

"You don't like it?"

"The very smell makes me sick."

"And that's why you'll never get married. It's a staple of every wedding."

She grimaced.

"What about you, Hisa?"

"I've never had it," I said. "The last wedding that happened, I was still too young."

"Don't bother," said Feng. "It's a vile thing, wine. Too much of it makes men into beasts and ladies into fish ripe for the catch."

I didn't understand a word of that, though I knew it couldn't be literal. At least, not with humans.

Syaoran laughed. "Lord Kwan likes pomegranate wine. What are you going to do if you've married and he drinks it?"

She crossed her arms, turning her head away. "I will refrain from kissing him. At least until the smell is off his breath."

"And if he drinks it regularly? You might not kiss him for a very long time. Much less anything more." He put on another fox-like grin. When she looked about to argue, he cut her off. "That's okay. If you get so lonely and need some to kiss, I supposed I can fill in for him."

"I wouldn't kiss you if you were the last Juneun in the world. I'd rather kiss a human before you," said Feng, sharp, and stuck out her tongue at him.

"That's harsh," said Syaoran, smiling bright and carrying a laugh in his voice as he reclined on the grass. "What about Hisa? Would you kiss me if I was the last Juneun in the world?"

"I," my mouth went suddenly dry. I did like Syaoran. I liked that he was kind and always smiling, but I never thought I'd even be considered for a kiss from someone like him. "Um. I just, I think—"

"You have kissed someone before, haven't you?"

"Of course I have." I hadn't. But I didn't want him to know that. I didn't want to seem so very unwanted.

"See? Even a human wouldn't kiss you," said Feng, an air of superiority in her tone. "I'm starting to doubt there was ever one girl sneaking over to sleep with you."

Syaoran pretended to be wounded, struck in the heart, dramatic. "Am I so ugly?"

"N-no, you're not," I said, realizing the implication afterwards. "But I—I only want to kiss someone I'm in love with." It was partially true. I often daydreamed about being so in love with someone that I was the only person they'd ever or would ever kiss. Though, it'd be a lie to say I'd deny someone like Syaoran a kiss if they liked me in return and asked to. I just didn't want a kiss, my first kiss, to be meaningless.

"See? Like that," said Syaoran, looking right at Feng. "You can say no without being nasty about it."

She scoffed. "I would, if you were good for more than being a warm pillow."

"Be sure to remember that on those cold and lonely nights in the house," teased Syaoran. "I'll be waiting."

"You're disgusting."

I felt like an outsider. The two had centuries of knowing each other; how to act friendly and annoy each other without overstepping. It looked that way. To me, they seemed already an old married couple playing to get a rise out of the other.

We learned dancing that day. Two different dances.

One for a group with a collective effort for coordination—to which Syaoran created illusions of himself and me to act as other couples in the dance. I couldn't help but get distracted, watching our copies dancing, moving with grace. He'd given the illusions fine clothing, and I squinted at my own, wondering if I really did look so put together or if it was a generous overstatement.

It took the better part of the day, stopping to look for something to eat for lunch and continuing on a short while after.

The other dance was a more intimate one, meant for having one partner to coordinate with rather than a group. It made me a little nervous in the first step-by-step instructions, and after. In this dance, I'd be close to Syaoran with our hands touching for nearly the entirety of it, and in several steps his hand would go to my waist or my back.

In the village, dancing was divided between boys and girls, and any mingling of the two consisted of more skipping and clapping, timing the turn of a heel in sync with the others before starting from the beginning again. It was never complicated.

"And when he asks you to dance, which bow do you use?" Feng quizzed, watching me with a hungry eagerness.

I put my arms out and forward to make the shape of a circle, my fingertips touching. My chin dipped down and my back slightly with it.

"No, no," scolded Feng. "It's like this."

As she demonstrated, I again noticed how fair her complexion was to mine. I had the skin tone of a farmer, and she a noble lady. My hands still had a roughness to them, while her own were soft and flawless.

"And bend your knees only slightly, keep your back a little bit straighter."

I did my best to follow the instruction exactly.

"Much better."

I smiled, relieved for a moment. Syaoran offered his hand, and I took it. His own had a roughness as well. Not the sort of someone who labored in the fields, but the hands that were used every day. Warm hands. Strong hands.

"You're blushing," said Syaoran.

"What?" I looked up, realizing what he'd said.

"Nervous?"

I was, but I shook my head in denial.

He smiled. "It's alright. It's just us. No one is watching, and you don't have to get it perfect."

A part of me felt better at that notion: I didn't need to be perfect. But my heart still fluttered. As we went through the motions at Feng's instruction, I pulled away my thoughts to concentrate on the next step and the next one.

"Stop sticking your tongue out," scolded Feng.

I suddenly became aware of the face I was making. Syaoran chuckled.

"I don't mind it," whispered Syaoran. "When you know the dance by heart, it'll be fine."

I felt a little embarrassed, and tried to mind both my dancing and keeping my tongue behind my teeth without making some other face. It allowed me to forget that I was dancing with a Juneun. In the moment, he was just my friend.

We stopped before the sun began to set, going back into the forest to forage. Kumquats, the last of the season, hid in high branches. The wood too thin to climb and the leaves too thick to navigate. Feng used magic of her own, causing the tree to shiver and drop its fruit.

After eating, with my reminiscing on making sweet paste from boiling and straining them in the village beside the other girls, we practiced our dance again. And once more after.

Syaoran complimented my improvement, remarking how Feng intervened less that time. He brought up his gourd taking a celebratory drink. I took one as well, feeling I'd earned it. It didn't have much of a scent to it, and the initial flavor was sweet with an aftertaste that was hard to describe. It felt like it left a thin film in my mouth that quickly disappeared. It was odd, making my jaw lock for a second, but not at all unpleasant.

My body became warm with a bit more, and I fell asleep easily.

After two more days, I became confident in my slow mastery of things. I could carry myself in genuine politeness rather than a clumsy hope.

However, both Syaoran and Feng grew anxious. I couldn't blame them. They weren't accustomed to sleeping away from comfortable beds and private rooms. We went back between the walls, to the familiarity of things where butterflies gathered.

"You can go in and take a look," said Syaoran.

"Why me?" I protested.

"You're smaller than us."

"You're faster," I argued.

"Only with magic," said Syaoran.

"They'll sense magic," added Feng, fussing with her hair.

"Just go around quietly and see if they're gone yet," said Syaoran, warm yet distracted.

"You want me to leave the two of you alone?" I started, giving a sly look of my own. "Is it because you want to ask Feng to kiss you, and don't want me around? You seem really eager to get rid of me."

He smiled, though there was a rigidness to it.

She grimaced, scooting away.

"I didn't hear denial," I said. After four days alone together, I felt comfortable enough to give small teases.

"Just go," groaned Syaoran.

I chuckled. It felt like so long since I could behave this way, to simply be *Hisa*. Not a human, or a prisoner, or a servant. Myself.

As I came to the hidden door of the inner wall, I felt disquiet. What would my relationship with Syaoran and Feng look like once Lord Kwan's family left? Would I be allowed to continue behaving so familiarly with them, and carry on banter as I had away from the house? Or would I be expected to act only as a servant, my emotions kept at arm's length from them? A part of me wanted to go back, to lie and say all of them were still there and looked like they'd stay for quite some time. But what sort of friend would that make me? I would be forfeiting all trust.

So, I went in.

Peeking around every corner and through every shrub, I moved quick and quiet. More than once I startled and hid behind something at the sight of a guardsman, mistaking him for a relative of Lord Kwan.

I didn't hear unfamiliar voices. Nor did I count more horses than originally were in the stable.

I breathed relief, hurrying to go tell Syaoran and Feng the happy news. Coming around one corner of the veranda, I slid to a stop. Lord Kwan, in conversation with someone I didn't recognize. I turned on my heel, dashing back flush faced. Maybe they didn't notice me.

"Hisa," said Lord Kwan. A low and gentle call, judging by the tone. It didn't sound like a demand, or angry. More like he was taking note as he passed by.

Now, I needed to make a choice. I didn't think I'd be able to hold myself together if a series of questions were asked. At the same time, I would humiliate Lord Kwan if I didn't return and answer his call. And I had only seconds to decide.

I walked back. Humiliating him was the greater offense. I'd just need to keep my wits and avoid answering directly as much as I could.

Standing before them in my rough-spun clothes, I bowed the way Feng instructed, and kept my head low. "My lord."

"Your bow improved. More refined than I remember," said Lord Kwan.

"I've been practicing, my lord," I said, biting at my tongue when I realized that I'd volunteered information. Information that would surely invite questions. "I was told you were expecting important guests. I didn't want to embarrass your household."

"Only my household?"

"Or you, my lord," I stuttered, correcting myself.

"Look at me, Hisa."

I breathed in deep, praying for courage, for strength. Looking up, Lord Kwan's brother was almost a mirror image. His jaw slightly more squared, eyes silver, and a thin scar through his left brow differentiated him from Lord Kwan; things easily missed until closer inspection was made.

"A human," said his brother.

"My brother, Kwang, will be staying with us an additional day. Let Syaoran know he can come home."

"Syaoran?"

He gave me a knowing look with that hint of a smile. "You've been hiding out together, have you not?"

I went rigid.

"I don't blame her," said Kwang. "Our brothers aren't known for patience. I'm surprised not all the servants hid themselves away."

Lord Kwan ignored the comment. "Invite Feng in as well. Best not to annoy her or lead her to feel jilted."

"Is she still looking for a proposal from you?" teased Kwang.

"It would appear so," said Lord Kwan. "When you return, Hisa, rinse off and bring in the tea from your village. My brother has been curious to try it."

I obeyed, swift as my legs would take me—remembering, once at the hidden door, that I'd forgotten to bow before leaving.

My message delivered, I hurried to my room to clean and dress to present myself better. I fetched the tea my village gave as offerings, brewing it as I'd done every time before. And, as I'd done every time before, I waited for Lord Kwan's invitation into his room after I announced myself. So, I was surprised to see the doors open and Syaoran gesturing for me to enter.

Like me, he'd cleaned himself up and changed into fresh clothing. I felt strange in that moment. I'd never seen him behave so much like a servant. He stood, impressive and with every movement under full control.

Unlike all my previous times in Lord Kwan's room, I wasn't invited to sit with him. Instead, I stood beside Syaoran while the lords enjoyed seasonal fruits and tea. I stole glances to Syaoran, looking for cues on what to do. Twice, I saw him stealing a glance to me. Concern?

"So, you're from one of the villages under my brother's protection."

I was slow to realize Kwang spoke to me. Another stolen glance, Syaoran gave a slight point of his chin.

"Yes, my lord."

"He never speaks about the humans," said Kwang. "Tell me, is he feared or revered?"

I didn't know how to answer, looking to Syaoran and he tried to subtly mouth the word *loved*.

"We," I hesitated, "don't know him well enough for either."

Kwang went into a fit of laughs. Lord Kwan, on the other hand, didn't appear bothered by it. He remained placid, peeling an orange with ease; the skin of it in one piece.

"We're grateful," I tried to correct, "for all his protection. Sometimes the years are hard. Without him, I think they might be impossible. He makes sure the earth is blessed, and fends off the Kurai from plaguing us. All without seeking reward."

"That sounds about right," said Kwang, musing.

"I don't require acknowledgement to perform my duties to the world."

I looked to Lord Kwan, wondering if I'd said something out of place.

"Other Juneun could learn from you," said his brother. "But it's not such a bad thing to receive due praise and gifts once in a while from the humans. Most are so struck by our mere presence, they grovel."

"It is not necessary," said Lord Kwan. Dismissive, but I respected it.

"Our sister would argue that the accolades bring clout and raises one's station."

"Our sister knows nothing of the troubles in the world. She only thinks she does. Status means nothing against the Kurai. Not the smart ones."

"It scares off the weaker ones. Saves us a lot of trouble."

Upon their cue, I stepped over to them, refilling their cups with their chosen drink.

"How do you like being in the service of a Juneun?" asked Kwang.

Caught off guard, I nearly spilled. My mind raced to form a suitable answer—one that sounded elegant enough. "Lord Kwan doesn't say much. When he does, he's precise with his words. He's not unkind, and I think he is a good master."

Kwang snorted in his laugh. "It's a safe answer."

"Speak freely, Hisa," commanded Lord Kwan. He didn't look up from his drink, which somehow made me feel more watched.

I looked to Syaoran for cues. He stood perfectly still.

"I," my throat grew dry and tight. "When I first arrived, I was afraid. I thought he was cold. But I've learned it is just the way of nobles, and I wasn't used to it."

"And are you used to it now?" Kwang stared at me, the same as Lord Kwan had, studying the slightest movements consciously and unconsciously done. Like his brother, his eyes held an intensity. Unlike his brother, a smile accompanied his gaze, seeming amused.

"I think," I said. "Or, I'm learning to be."

He shifted his gaze to Lord Kwan, waving me off to dismiss.

I wasted no time retreating back to Syaoran's side. Again, I stole glances, trying to measure if I'd done anything wrong and looking for cues on what to do next.

He kept still, regal.

"She cleans up okay," said Kwang. "Not very pretty though."

Again, the words stung. I knew the truth, but it still hurt to hear.

"Beauty is not necessary to be a good servant," said Lord Kwan, setting down his tea.

"I helps," said Kwang with a shrug.

"In what way?" Much like a tiger, he cut his brother from any cheeky response. "Does beauty allow them to brew the tea faster? Clean more efficiently? Does it command the fruits to ferment into wine and sooner?"

Kwang grumbled. "If this is how you treat me, I'd hate to see how you treat someone you hate."

"Usually with the tip of my blade," said Lord Kwan.

His brother snickered. "Sara tells everyone you've lost all humor."

Chapter 20
A Breath of Fresh Air

I was relieved when Lord Kwan's brother left. It felt like everyone breathed out a held sigh, sharing the same sentiment. In the shuffling about, returning the house to its state prior to receiving visitors, a newly planted sapling snapped. It'd gone ignored, and, not wanting it to die, I tried to mend it. I didn't have so many chores now, and was in the way otherwise.

With sap from a clipped branch of a bigger tree, I glued the strained wood back together. Fast as my fingers would allow, I fashioned some twine from straw. I used a stiff bamboo stick to act as an anchor, and the twine to wrap around the two pieces. Hopefully, that'd keep the small tree upright and help it to heal.

In trying to remember how an elder assisted in the recovery of several tea trees, I gathered ash and fallen leaves, tilling it gently into the soil. At the very least, I did something rather than watch it wither. All that was left was to wait, checking in on it every morning and eve.

For a long time, it stayed as it was. Neither growing nor dying.

Summer came, ushering in seasonal rains. Worried, I checked the sapling more often. It held.

On a clear day, when I headed back to it, Lord Kwan stood there. He looked at my handywork in trying to mend the tree, staring with the same quiet intensity as he did with everything.

"Hisa." I stiffened at his soft call. "Can you explain this to me?"

I approached, unsure if he was displeased or testing me in some way. "It accidentally broke, my lord. When the house was getting back in order. So I—"

His gaze moved to me, reading me.

"I've been trying to mend it, my lord. With sap and twine and the bamboo for support."

He blinked, slow, mulling over what was said. That's what it felt like, anyway. He answered things in his own time, while all else answered right away. I learned after nearly a year spent here that he never hurried to speak, and considered what to say when he spoke to anyone at all. The exception being his brother.

"I have a lazy gardener, who only today informed me about this and asked what ought to be done."

"My lord?"

He looked back at the sapling, his hand reaching slightly for his fingers to brush against the leaves. "If this happened that long ago, it should have been pulled out and replaced. You've been tending it instead?"

I nodded. "Every day."

"Devoted to it, I see."

It surprised me how quickly he responded, letting only a few seconds hang. More, his eyes somehow appeared softer when he looked at me again. That hint of a smile there as well. He approved. For whatever reason, that made me glad.

"Your brother came for you not long ago," said Lord Kwan, looking back to the leaves of the young tree, and that small happiness vanished from me. "What did you talk about?"

I wanted to deny it, deny I'd even seen anyone from my village since coming here. It was my instinct to protect my family in whatever meager way I could. But... if he already knew. Whether a guardsman spotted us, spotted Raeden, or if Lord Kwan himself saw us, he'd know it was a lie. I wanted to protect my brother. And I didn't know how.

"He," I had to swallow hard and clear my voice. "He wanted to know that I was alright, my lord. A message was sent, I know, but no one in my village knows how to read. I told you that." I tried to keep my voice steady, watching as he kept his attention fixed on the sapling.

"You were gone some time."

"I didn't leave the estate, my lord. I promise. He didn't come to steal me back. It was only to see that I could bear myself. And... I did have questions about our village as well. To know that my family was looked after, and to tell him how best to sort through some things until I get home. I only wanted my father and brothers to be well off while I'm here. Wouldn't you do that same for your brothers?"

A slight wince marred his face. If I wasn't looking at him so intently and unblinking in my scramble to explain, I might've missed it. Seeing it, however, I thought I'd said the wrong things. But they were the honest things. Now I worried perhaps I'd lose all my privileges; that I'd be back in the kennels and would have no more writing lessons or drawing paper or any comfort I'd earned.

"My lord?"

"Get an ewer and come to my room at the end of lunch. My guest wants you there." He turned quick on his heel, walking back to the house.

"Guest?"

He didn't answer.

I did as commanded, attempting to appear dignified like the rest of the household staff. The bronze ewer weighed heavy, filled with water, causing me to hold it close while I walked with caution, trying not to spill. To my surprise, Lord Kwan's doors were open. I stepped into the antechamber, taking off my sandals. In his room, Syaoran stood ready again. The guest however, confused me.

Feng.

A small luncheon was set on the table, breads and rice and sliced fruits and steamed vegetable. Soft conversation was held; more from Feng than from Lord Kwan. It shouldn't have surprised me. She'd said herself that she fell in love with him, and made up her mind to become his wife.

I remembered my manners, making a polite entrance and bringing in refreshment for them before standing beside Syaoran. Still, I couldn't keep a smile from my face. I wanted to see love triumph, wanted to see my friend be with the man of her dreams. And I did believe we were friends.

I'd not been paying attention, daydreaming as I waited for cues to attend. When she turned her head sharp, a grin painted on her face, I forgot myself.

"You agree, don't you?"

"Agree?"

She turned back to Lord Kwan, who'd said hardly a thing and looked off with wordless disinterest often. "Since I've already taught her, I may as well keep her as my servant. She can stay in the same room, of course, it's the smallest one anyway."

I blinked, stealing a glance to Syaoran for some clue as to what I should do or say. He stayed still, glancing back with a hint of worry.

"Maybe I'll claim another from the villages when she's getting too old to serve," said Feng, unbothered. "Humans are like that. She can help to select my next servant. Won't that be novel? That this house always retains a human servant? Though, I'd have preferred if she was a bit taller."

"I'm," I started, baffled by the conversation and trying to understand. I remembered that a servant wasn't supposed to speak first, let alone interrupt, but both of them were already looking at me, expectantly. "I'm only here for four more years."

Feng blinked. "But you would stay if Lord Kwan and I said to."

I gave a slow shake of my head, sure that I was somehow overstepping. "I want to be with my family after my service is up."

"In that run down little village?" asked Feng, brow quirked and tone in alarm. "Wouldn't you rather be here as a servant where you have a nicer room and better food? You wouldn't need to forage ever again if you were the servant to Lord Kwan's bride."

"It's not—" I wanted to argue with heated words, tempered by the quiet watch of Lord Kwan and the soft grunt from Syaoran. "It's my home. Where my friends and family live."

She frowned. "Are you saying that living among Juneun is beneath you?"

I shook my head with a gasp, trying to make myself small enough to hide behind the ewer I held.

Lord Kwan raised his cup, looking off into some part of the room rather than to anyone there. Syaoran answered, replenishing the pomegranate wine. Feng winced at the smell, working hard to hide the expression and keep herself composed.

"If it's the company you want, we'll have a full staff once we're married. I can claim other village girls, and you can instruct them like I taught you. That should suffice. Now, you will stay."

"That's not what I meant," I said, looking between Lord Kwan and Syaoran in a silent plea for help.

"How can you stand there and refuse your master's bride?" scolded Feng.

"You forget," said Lord Kwan after a long while. His eyes returned to her, that quiet intensity staring from his stony face. "I've made no offer of marriage. Nor will I."

Feng gave a look of shock.

I heard an odd sound by my side. Syaoran's face was crinkled, locked tight as he held in laughter.

She stared at him a while in disbelief. "But, my lord—"

"I will make no bride of someone whose goal is to achieve status in marrying into a higher family. I have no use for a greedy woman that would become a demanding wife." He looked away, slow and unconcerned, towards the door and the sunlight beyond.

"How can you say these things?" demanded Feng, face scowled and at the brink of tears. "I've loved you since I was only a girl. You would treat me so cold? With such contempt? Do centuries of love mean nothing?"

His gaze went back to her, a predator about to lash at a rival. "And the length of time makes you entitled to my heart?"

"At this moment, I wonder if you even still have a heart." She'd spoken out of anger, and a look of horror—realizing her words and her tone—came in the next second.

Lord Kwan's expression remained unchanged. In that moment I wanted to run to her, hug and comfort her. I knew she loved Lord Kwan, speaking of little else than her dreams of what life would be like with him. I didn't think she pursued him for status or wealth or anything like that. Then again, those few days outside the walls taught me that I didn't know much at all about the way things are done with noble families. Was it not at all sincere? It couldn't be.

She stayed in stunned silence; silence that Lord Kwan allowed to hang over at his leisure.

"Leave," said Lord Kwan, in as close of a growl as I'd ever heard since the morning I arrived.

Feng fled, crying, whipping by impossibly fast.

I felt for her, and my feet started to chase after. Syaoran stopped me, quick to take my arm and shake his head. I studied his pitying expression, slow to move my watch away to Lord Kwan, who sat still and breathed in deep. There was something more to this strange event. Something that no one wanted to speak on or tell me.

"Sit," commanded Lord Kwan.

I stepped in line with Syaoran, following his example. Though, in taking a place at the table, he flicked my thigh, reminding me that the way a man sat was different from how I (as a woman) was expected to sit. I disliked it for how uncomfortable and unnatural it felt, dreading that I'd be made to stay that way for long; I didn't want my leg to fall asleep and pain me when I was allowed to stand and walk again. Despite that, I obliged. Our ewers set aside, hands placed politely, I felt a strange pressure to be better than my very best behavior.

"When she leaves," said Lord Kwan at long last, though he didn't look at either of us, "I want the gates closed."

Syaoran dipped his head slightly in a show of understanding. I copied.

"I will not be holding court this year."

"Understood," said Syaoran.

"Let us hope this is the last of foolhardy pursuits," said Lord Kwan, glancing between us. "I refuse to entertain these games." He held out his cup for water, and I acted on the cue.

"But, don't you think that that was harsh—" I spoke without thinking, my mind a mess of confusion.

Syaoran's hand, hidden beneath the table, grabbed my thigh, the nearest hidden part of me, to stop me. I held fast to the ewer, a shiver of surprise surging through me. Warm and strong fingers begging me to hold myself while his eyes stayed on Lord Kwan. A heat entered my gut, my heartbeat out of rhythm as his hand lingered there.

Lord Kwan watched me, stoic. He waited until I'd set aside the drink and resumed my seat. "It will always appear harsh from an outsider's perspective. They're not the ones being emotionally manipulated."

I stayed still. It felt like I was being scolded, but not quite so cold.

"Lengthy talk on what might be, the allure of a perfect life by her standards and lofty to the standards of onlookers. Accusations of unrequited love. And the summoning of insincere tears. Every lady of breeding has these weapons at her disposal, an attempt to try and shame any refusal to her."

Weapons? He implied that this entire thing was set up. An act on Feng's behalf. And that I was victim to her manipulation of the truth.

"Do you owe a man in your village your heart, even if you have never loved him, purely because of spectacle or expectation?"

"No, my lord," I answered quietly.

"Even if he declared you beautiful? And brilliant beyond your peers?"

My voice became quieter as I understood. I was not a beauty, nor was I particularly skilled in a great many things, and barely learning to read. If someone came to me and said this was true, contradicting what I otherwise knew, I would see he was shamelessly lying. And if I'd said so, I would seem ungrateful, unreasonable. "No, my lord."

Syaoran loosened his grip, fingers relaxed and feeling like they would dip further against my inner thigh. Out of reflex, my own hand moved to halt his, hidden on this side of the table.

Lord Kwan sipped from his cup, in complete control of every smooth movement. He looked away, over his shoulder at the window, eyes fixed on something. "What would it take to convince either of you to marry?"

"Each other, my lord?" said Syaoran in a tone of confusion. His hand flexed, palm pressing down only just.

I felt my neck, face, and ears starting to warm, and tried to think of anything else to help keep it from showing.

"In general," said Lord Kwan.

"I confess I hadn't thought about it. I'm not quite four hundred yet." With his free hand, he massaged at his neck and through his hair. "I suppose, a woman who is beautiful and loves to race on horseback. And who can laugh with me. And with an appetite for rice wine."

I loosened my grip on his hand, reasserting it as he moved up my thigh only slightly. My heart slowed in sadness. I was not beautiful, nor had I ever ridden a horse, and I didn't like the rice wine enough to say that I had an appetite for it.

"Hisa," commanded Lord Kwan.

I realized then that he'd been expecting an answer, and I'd been absent minded. "For me, my lord?"

Syaoran's fingers slid a little more on my inner thigh, and I reflexively tightened my grip.

"I," I stuttered, distracted. "Someone who is honest, my lord. And kind. Most of all, kind."

"Not handsome or wealthy?"

I put both my hands on Syaoran's, trying to keep from further distraction. "I wouldn't care how he looked, my lord. Or if he was as poor as I am. Not if he loved and treated me so well."

That hint of a smile returned. For almost a full moment, I thought I could see he was planning at something. "I'll inform Lord Juro, and make arrangements. He was quite taken with you."

"Lord Juro?" I said, more panic-stricken than I realized. My shoulders rose up, and my head tucked down at the memory of the former Kurai.

"You said yourself that appearances don't matter. And he is a Juneun attracted by smell more than he is by beauty."

I shook my head, vigorous and fearful. My hands held tight to Syaoran, and I looked to him with a wordless plea. Again, his face crinkled, holding in a laugh.

"You wouldn't want him for a husband?" said Lord Kwan. "Then appearances do matter."

"It's not his appearance, my lord," I said, louder than I meant to in my defensiveness. "It's... when he spoke to me. I felt uncomfortable. It was as if I was being looked at like thick, sweet cream and ripe fruit, rather than as a person."

Lord Kwan rested his head in his palm, leaning over the table. His expression went unchanged, but I thought I could tell there was a level of amusement in his eyes. "So, there is more to your willing to love and be married, then."

"I suppose," I said, calming. "It's a complicated feeling."

"In fairness," said Syaoran, reclaiming his hand, "Juro has a reputation of gluttony and womanizing. I don't doubt he would be good the woman he marries, but I wouldn't go so far as to say he would always be faithful to her. And we might say that behavior is *not* kind."

His amused gaze moved to Syaoran. "We might agree on that. But it is common for a higher lord to have consorts as well as a wife. The humans imitate this as well with their kings."

"I believe that is your way of saying you desire a harem," teased Syaoran. All previous tension was broken at my expense.

I was glad at the ease from it, if not annoyed by the method.

"One often speaks his own desires as someone else's," said Lord Kwan, placing a cup to each of us.

I chanced it, to be even a little bold. "What about you, my lord? What would entice you to marry?"

Syaoran didn't waste his opportunity. "Hisa is planning to court the master directly."

Flustered, I snapped at him. "That's not what I said! I only meant, since we were asked..."

His fox ears went flat, but his smile remained as he poured the wine for me. I wanted to say a dozen things. Something to taunt him back with. But I didn't know how far I could allow myself abandon in the presence of Lord Kwan.

"Something different," said Lord Kwan at last, diverting our attention. "The courts are filled with women who paint their faces to hide how they really look, and carry a practiced demeanor to conceal how they really behave. I think I should agree with you both. Someone who is honest, and who also enjoys a race across my lands."

"Do we speak literally of your lands, my lord? Or metaphorically?"

I didn't quite catch what Syaoran meant. Judging by the sly grin, it was probably best that I didn't.

Lord Kwan elected to ignore it. "And someone who chooses to be patient. Working through tough times and hard decisions, rather than give up or want to start over. A breath of fresh air. Something away from castle walls and paved roads."

"Sounds like you might fall into conflict more often than fall in love with that sort of person, knowing you," said Syaoran.

"Because I am set in my ways?"

"And because everyone you can bear to tolerate already lives here," said Syaoran, ears still flat as he teased.

Chapter 21
Only Knowing Half

Midsummer, balmy and quiet. The rains came and went, sometime in a torrent, sometimes only enough to water the gardens over hours on end. My blood had come in, merciless in the pain it dealt. Because if it, I kept to my room, curled up in bed as I tried to wait it out without complaint. Yua had come to check in, giving little sympathy but refrained from any lecturing.

I stayed in my night gown, trying to make myself sleep until it was all over.

I heard my door slide open. Likely Yua with something to help. As cold as she presented, she didn't let things go ignored. I wouldn't have called us friends, but I also wouldn't have called her unkind.

A cool hand rested against my forehead. Not Yua. I turned over in alarm, wide eyed.

"Lord Kwan?"

He recoiled his hand, slow. "Yua said you were feeling unwell."

I blinked, calming. "Not in that way, my lord. It's... a woman's ailment."

He tilted his head, taking his time to decide what to do. Standing, he walked away. "Regardless, the herbal tea will help with pain." He gestured to a teapot, its spout steaming, and a cup beside it.

The door closed, quiet.

When I summoned the strength, I followed his advice and poured myself some of the tea. A strange scent to its yellow-green color caused my nose to crinkle. But he'd said it would help with pain. And mine was so bad that I lost most of my appetite.

The taste made me shudder and want nothing to do with it. Determined, I swallowed in fast, large gulps. The warmth of it raced to my stomach, which growled its complaint like my tongue had.

Of everyone at the estate, I didn't think he'd be the one to come with concerns about my health.

In the following week, Syaoran delivered a package to my room. I hadn't finished with breakfast, listening to everyone else shuffle around with some unusual whim. He bore his usual warm smile, fox ears pointed high. With a hint of mischief in his voice, he instructed that I go to the stables in an hour.

A note came with the paper-wrapped parcel. *For Hisa.* The same as it'd been on the note for my dress.

Opening it, it wasn't exactly a new dress. There were more pieces than previously. A pair of pants, I realized, with several layers of billowing silk to replicate the look of the skirt part of my dress. Two more blouses and a jacket piece, and another overlay bit of silk that confused me. It stood to reason that they all belonged together for some purpose or specific event. I couldn't fathom what or why, but I had just under an hour to figure it all out.

It took nearly the full of the hour.

I layered the bouses and jacket, the same as I would with my dress, but didn't quite know what to do with several tie off ribbons on the jacket. In fastening the pants, it became a bit more clear that they were meant to go over the blouses but under the jacket, and the odd, extra ribbons were meant to anchor to the pants piece. Except, that wasn't entirely correct. The final piece was meant to be anchored to one part of the jacket and sit over the pants, looking more like a complete dress.

I rushed out as quick as I dared, not wanting to dirty myself before I even arrived. Whatever guest or reason I was expected to show up in this particular outfit, I wanted to make a good impression.

The horses were out and saddled. All of them.

"What's going on?" I asked, not really expecting anyone to answer.

Yua stood beside a dappled mare, dressed similarly. My mind raced to piece it together, and I became horrified. Did they expect me to ride? I'd never even sat on a horse—and these were larger than Lan's old nag.

"Hisa."

I jumped at the voice. Gi, beaming with excitement. "Why are the horses saddled?"

He laughed. The answer was obvious, but my mind denied it. "Lord Kwan wants to take a ride. And he appointed me as an accompanying guard."

"He's taking guards?"

"It's more a formality than anything. But I'm not arguing against it—it'll be the first time in seventy years that I've taken a ride."

"Seventy years," I repeated. Sometimes I forgot that the spirits were eternal. Seventy years might seem like less than a decade, less than a single year perhaps.

"Normally, three of us would be appointed. But he sent for you to come, and there's not a seventh horse."

I shook my head, my dread coming into fruition. "I've never ridden. I don't know how!"

"Hisa," called Lord Kwan. He stared in my direction, expectant.

Timid, I approached to answer his summon. My throat tightening, and any voice I had was reduced to a whispering squeak. "Lord Kwan, I—"

"You'll be taking Susa," he gestured to a black mare. "Gi will assist you getting in the saddle."

I shook my head in terror. The horse was enormous. "I can't! I don't know how!" I retreated into myself, wanting to curl up right then and there to cry.

Lord Kwan stopped, blinking at me while I trembled horribly. "Susa will do most of the work."

I shook my head again, defiant in my fear. "I'm scared... If she bucks and throws me, or I fall..." I remembered Raeden in that moment, and how he'd been thrown after a wasp stung the belly of Lan's horse in the midst of teaching my brother. He'd broken his arm and dislocated his shoulder. He screamed so horribly that it made me afraid to even ask to learn to ride.

Lord Kwan studied me, releasing a quiet, pensive sigh before mounting on Saburo. "Gi. Help her up here."

"What?" I didn't have the time to understand what he meant, let alone object. Gi came swift to obey, placing his hands on my waist and hoisting me up.

"Get your leg over," directed Lord Kwan as he took hold of me.

I was all awkward and fidgeting, seated right in front of him—between his thighs—and holding fast to the pommel of the saddle. Yua came up beside us, already on her horse, and motioned for me to fix my garment to cover my exposed leg.

"Inform Kazuo that we will need his company as well," said Lord Kwan. "It wouldn't be right to leave Susa behind."

Gi bowed his head in a smooth, quick motion, hurrying to carry out his command.

I watched, pressing my brow together and unable to sit comfortably. My legs were spread farther than they'd ever been, and I tried not to touch any part of Lord Kwan. Were the rise of the pommel not in the way, I'd scoot up further.

He put a hand on my belly, sliding me back in place, though my own hands refused to relinquish their grip. "You will fall that far up." He placed his hand on my shoulder next, correcting my posture. "Keep your back straight for balance." And then to my hip. "Don't make yourself rigid. We won't be riding fast. Feel the way he moves and allow yourself to move with him. You'll hurt yourself otherwise."

I tried to follow his instruction, ignore his breath brushing past my ear, and overcome my fear. My fingers refused to budge.

"I won't let you fall," said Lord Kwan. "Syaoran suggested bringing you to overlook the lake."

"The lake?" I repeated shakily. It took a few seconds to remember one of the conversations we'd had outside the walls.

"He was adamant that you should come," said Lord Kwan. "The two of you have grown close."

I tried to look at him, over my shoulder, only able to catch sight of his chin, silk shirt, and locks of black hair like ribbons on his chest.

"When you get used to it," said Sayoran, his own stallion pawing at the ground with anticipation, "that's when you'll want a horse of your own. The feeling is freeing. Just you and him." He patted his mount, keeping that smile to comfort me.

"It's been forty-seven years since we last rode out," said Yua. "They're excited to get out as well."

"How long do horses live for?" an odd question, I knew. Lan's horse was more than twenty. But to reach almost fifty was something else. They all looked relatively young.

"They're spirits too," said Syaoran with a laugh.

I felt foolish in that moment. Of course they wouldn't be normal horses. Not for a Juneun.

Once our escort guards mounted up, we left the estate in a soft trot, picking up the pace only a little once we left the outer wall. Even so, I still went rigid and felt it was too fast. I teetered this way and that, my fingers a vice-grip in their chosen spot.

Lord Kwan scooted me back again, correcting my posture with a touch. "Relax. Keep your muscles loose so you can feel the way he moves under you."

That was easier said than done.

"You won't fall. Saburo tells me you're quite fond of him."

"He told you? How?"

"The same as when he suggested to have you in the saddle with me."

"But, he didn't say anything." Try as I might, I couldn't relax, or look over my shoulder to see Lord Kwan's eyes. He said nothing more, leaving me to replay the scene and look for what I missed. My conclusion being that it was a special way a spirit like Saburo communicated with Juneun and other spirits. A silent understanding.

The mountain was dotted with shade and sunlight. We went where no path existed, yet Saburo behaved as though there were one, however treacherous it might be. I found myself leaning back at times, pressed into Lord Kwan's torso. He said nothing about it.

We reached the top just past midday, though it may as well have been the next day for how tired I felt. Lord Kwan dismounted first, helping me down—and I needed the help. My legs had become too stiff and sore to do what I wanted, and it pained me to even move them. When my fingers released the pommel of the saddle, they left indents in the leather, and grew small blisters on my skin.

When I finally touched ground again, my legs gave way. Lord Kwan caught me, staying placid in his manner.

It was Gi who came over and asked what was wrong.

"My legs hurt," I said, trying not to cry with the pulsing pain. "Everything hurts."

"It's to be expected if you've never ridden," said Syaoran. "And we've gone a few hours at that. Not to mention you stayed rigid, and made your who body tense the entire way. There's a lot of fatigue."

Lord Kwan said nothing, looking from Syaoran to myself with his usual stone expression. To my surprise, he acted patiently. Taking my hands in his own, using his other to keep me standing, he raised my blistered skin closer to his face and blew gently. The dry tenderness subsided. Letting go, I pulled them back to inspect. Hardly a show that they were ever there.

His cool hand then brushed down the length of my body, passing over my thighs and shins twice. It wasn't a rapid disappearance, but I noticed the pain ebbing away. He held me a few seconds more before finally saying anything. "Now?"

"It's still hurts a lot," I kept my eyes down, fascinated, until some small part of me reminded myself that I'd forgotten all manners. "But it's a lot more tolerable now, my lord. Thank you."

He stared, as he always did when measuring what someone said, and brushed his hand from my belly to my ankles once more. "Can you walk?"

I tested a step. "I think so. Enough to keep up."

He said nothing more, letting me go and leading Saburo by the reins to wherever he delighted.

"A lot of us forget how delicate humans are," said Gi. "We never really worry about fatigue or injuries thanks to Lord Kwan."

"To Lord Kwan only?"

"It takes a powerful Juneun to use healing magic."

That much puzzled me. When I think of what it meant to be *powerful*, I thought of a warrior's strength. I never considered the ability to heal others as being a pinnacle of power. It was a strange concept, how the spirits revered healing magic while humans valued physical capability. Stranger still was thinking how effortlessly Lord Kwan performed healing magic, after I'd seen him in a state where he couldn't recognize his own friends.

Following, I awed at the scenery. Lord Kwan selected the most marvelous spot to view the crater of the mountain and the lake within it.

"This place used to be a volcano," said Syaoran. "Almost four hundred years ago, now. Maybe a little over."

Again, I was surprised. I never knew Mount Tora was a volcano. A swell of questions flooded my mind. Had it erupted before? Was it safe to live at the base of it now? Would it erupt again? My concern must've been obvious, because he smiled with a chuckle at me.

"It's perfectly safe. The mountain responds to Lord Kwan's presence. It respects the rest of us being here, but it will slumber while his soul resides somewhere on the mountain. No matter what tremors a Kurai might cause, it'll stay asleep." He stretched up and outward, basking in the soft sunlight.

It wasn't quite as hot here, I noticed. This time of year would be sweltering in my village; and while it was as balmy, the heat wasn't nearly so unbearable. I'd helped to set up for a luncheon, unable to stop looking over at Lord Kwan as he stood a short distance away staring at the lake. That same, intense stare he gave so often, studying the scenery.

I realized then that I'd met him almost a year complete, yet I knew very little about him at all. He was a quiet person. So often, our conversations revolved around village life and how humans perceived things and carried on in their roles. A few times, it'd been more personable questions directed at me, but I scarce knew anything about my jailer. The day Feng left was the only time I'd seen him so relaxed, and divulged a fragment about himself and his thoughts.

I may have thought him a heartless person on first meeting, naïve as I was to not understand the ceremony of everything. But he'd not proven himself a terrible monster of a man. He tried to be compassionate in his own way, and he was hard to understand, but I wouldn't say he was a bad person. Someone weighed with troubles and responsibility sounded more accurate. And maybe it made him lonely.

If we did grow to be friends, I'd make the promise to visit him, simply to keep him company for a short while. The worst that could happen at that point was him getting annoyed and commanding that I make no more visits.

But maybe that was more cruel. As I watched his easy posture around Yua and Syaoran—relationships that spanned across centuries—my visiting to keep his company in a mortal life might cause more pain than comfort.

After eating, I helped the guardsmen put things away. Or, I tried to. I was more in the way than anything, interrupting practiced movements. Syaoran and Yua had walked on with Lord Kwan, leaving the guards to mind the horses as they grazed, and myself to wander a little bit away.

If the trek to get here wasn't so far and so rough of terrain, I'd come here again once I was free. But I knew a host of animals wouldn't care for my trespassing, and I'd likely get lost in trying to find my way back. For the moment, I pretended otherwise. I pretended that I was free, and made the trek safely up on my own.

"Hisa," called Syaoran. "Come here, and grab a basket!"

I looked from my friend to the shimmering lake, taking in the cool wind. Clouds were slowly ushered in, and more rain with it. I didn't want to leave my spot, but my curiosity coupled with my obligation pulled me away.

We walked under the shade of a copse of trees, navigating to a small peach grove. Large, firm, and beautifully colored to show their ripeness, I wanted to bite into them greedily. We'd come up this way for the scenery, and to collect the fruit of this grove. It was special, I somehow knew. The peaches bigger and more fragrant than whatever wild ones I'd find near my village. Eventually, I'd filled my basket and couldn't pick it up again with how heavy it was. Gi took it. The accompanying guards carried a basket in each arm, as though it hardly weighed a thing.

Lord Kwan continued to pick, examining the peach in his hand with something I thought resembled admiration in his stoic gaze. With only Syaoran, Yua, and myself left in the grove with him, he bit into it.

"What do you think?" asked Syaoran, a lightness to his tone.

Lord Kwan, in the most inelegant fashion I'd seen from him yet, licked up the droplets of juice running down his hand. After some consideration, he answered. "They'll make a fine wine."

He seemed ordinary in that moment, even with his silken clothes and stony expression. Somehow, he appeared completely comfortable. I was glad of it, and wasted no time to follow his example in plucking up a peach of my own to eat. Like Lord Kwan, juice ran down my hand and arm, and I didn't care about anyone watching as I slurped it up. It was one of the sweetest peaches I'd ever tasted, making me determined not to let even a drop of it go to waste.

Yua looked about to scold me, quickly giving up in favor of having a peach of her own to eat more delicately.

I enjoyed the quiet company, and the conversations that meant little of anything. There was a kind of comfort in it, of being allowed to be myself, and not a human servant. As I sat there, taking ambitious bites of my peach, and watching Syaoran and Lord Kwan behave similarly (if not mildly more restrained), the day replayed in my mind.

A memory sprung up. Cool hands. Healing hands. And the Juneun I didn't know from years ago, curing the pox. I made to ask when some of the peach's juice slid to the back of my tongue. I coughed, embarrassed, trying not to choke on the rest in my mouth.

My suspicion would need to wait. They'd given a fast concern, refraining when I quickly explained the problem in a strained voice. After I recovered myself, the guardsmen returned.

We didn't head back, however, not right away. Instead, we detoured further down the opposite side of the mountain. While Yua carried herself competently, I struggled in my sandals. Noticing, Syaoran offered his hand to help me keep balance. I still slipped now and again, crashing into him. After the third time, he teased that I must want to be closer to him.

A part of me did, though not so publicly or clumsily.

The ground evened out, and he let go of my hand to walk on ahead. My feet started picking up pace for a few steps, not wanting to be parted from him.

A blanket of kudzu lay in our path, coating every boulder and tree and open space. Syaoran cast a spell, some form of fire magic that looked cold and ghastly. The woody, vining plant shriveled up and recoiled, only for the untouched parts to reclaim the space instantly.

Syaoran's ears flopped down. "Feng really left a mess for us."

Yua huffed, stepping forward. She held up three fingers, touching the ends of her thumb and pinky to form a spell casting sign. Muttering a chant, the vines shivered. Rather than move out of the way, or whatever she was trying to do, they grew thicker. She scoffed, her face marred by a deep scowl. "It's eating magic."

"So, we'll have to wade through it," said Syaoran, though he didn't sound excited by the idea.

Neither was I. My mother had warned me never to walk through kudzu. All sorts of things hid under its dense leaves, and its woody lower stems made it difficult to trek.

He offered a hand to Yua. "I think I can keep it at bay long enough to take the next step."

She sighed, reluctant, but accepted the gesture. They walked close, hand in hand, as the vines gave way for only a second.

I marveled at the magic. While it didn't fix anything, I felt I understood a bit more about it. My brain tried to put things to scale. Feng must've been a powerful Juneun as well if Syaoran's magic couldn't do much about it. Though that hardly seemed to impress Lord Kwan as he studied the plants and observed Syaoran's tact.

He looked to me, offering his hand.

From deep seeded instinct, I shook my head with fierce denial. "I'll wait here for you, my lord."

"I will keep you steadied," said Lord Kwan after a thoughtful moment.

"It's not that, my lord. It's—what if there's snakes or spiders? Or a hornet's nest?"

He cocked a brow, measuring my fear. It seemed silly to him, perhaps, to worry about these things when I'd be beside him. He stepped over, looking down at me. Not with his usual intensity, but something of an understanding in his eyes. "I will keep you from danger."

I expected he'd offer his hand again. Instead, he scooped me up, as though I were light as a sparrow. I gasped at the unexpected, reflexively clinging to his shirt.

"I won't let you fall," cooed Lord Kwan.

I looked back to his face, placid, and then to my hands, convincing my fingers to let go. His every stride was smooth, that I hardly felt us moving at all. His feet didn't sink to the bottom of the thick blanket of vines either; no more than if he were walking the supple grass of the courtyard.

"You are a puzzle," said Lord Kwan. "Afraid of snakes, but befriending Feng. Appearing on my door as a presumed boy, and not the slightest insult enough to correct. An admiration of Saburo, yet afraid to ride. The willingness to duck behind my shrubs, but not to cross wild kudzu. Taking a pet, only to set it free. A young woman, but keeping a child's toy."

I shied at the last contradiction.

"What kind of human are you?"

I looked up, blinking and bewildered. "Only myself, my lord. I never thought of what sort of human I ought to be." When he gave no reply, I tried to think how to better explain myself. "I only know how to be myself. It never occurred to me that I could try to become like someone else."

He stayed silent a while, with Syaoran and Yua a short distance ahead. Before I could try again at my explanation, he finally spoke, keeping his eyes forward.

"I understand."

On the other side of the kudzu, stone tiles surrounded a painted statue atop its dais. Magic or not, the plants respected this sacred place. Light filtered through the branches that kept high on their ancient trees. The statue was a tiger, painted red and black, white and gray, orange and gold, and regal in its pose. It wasn't life-like at all, but that didn't detract from its majesty. It seemed as timeless—eternal—as a Juneun. It had been there forever, and would be there forever.

Lord Kwan stepped forward, placing a hand on the large, bronze bell at the foot of the statue. An echoing ring came from it. Not terrifyingly loud, or the sort that vibrated through my bones. Rather, it felt like it was waking something. A moment passed, and another, Lord Kwan resumed his place beside us.

A fierce roar, quickly shifting into a growling complaint. I swore I saw the statue shift, and stepped in front of the others out of instinct. As though my small, powerless body could deter a tiger, magic or ordinary. I'd put myself in front of Juneun spirits, with magic I could never fully fathom; they weren't children that I needed to keep together in the forest.

The sound of chuffing, and a low, moaning growl.

"As soon as Gumiho is felled, I will," said Lord Kwan, answering without waiting.

There was a conversation I wasn't privy to. While I shouldn't have minded it, I felt annoyed. Syaoran placed a hand around my arm, coaxing me back.

Chuffing.

"It is in my charge, Dareun."

Growls.

"I would invite your blessing all the same."

I looked to Syaoran for cues, seeing that he stood still and proper. When I looked to Yua, it was more of the same. I felt out of place, and unaware.

"It is my decision what to do," said Lord Kwan, sounding as though he were negotiating something. "You know the particulars if you watch these lands so closely."

A threatening sound emitted from the statue. Lord Kwan's stony expression crinkled, just for a second. A wince.

"I keep nothing in my house so vile."

Syaoran's fox ears twitched, a look of dread on his face. Until I'd come to rescue my brother, I'd assumed, like everyone else, that all fox spirits were Kurai. The sort that delighted in chaos and misery. A burning feeling started in my gut. Since I'd arrived, Syaoran had been kind—a friend. If the tiger, spirit or something else, accused him of anything terrible, it was wrong. In my heart, I knew it was wrong.

"Everything is kept safe from Gumiho's reach," said Lord Kwan, a tone of finality in response to the other half of a conversation.

Another low, whining growl.

"Do I have your blessing or not?" asked Lord Kwan, irritated.

Silence. Then a resounding roar. Lord Kwan appeared to accept whatever transpired, with Syaoran and Yua looking both troubled and relieved.

Chapter 22
Where Friendship Blooms

In the following day, I'd left to go to the river. My riding clothes had collected dirt and sweat, hoarding the worst of it the last few inches of each pant leg. And my dress was in need of a gentle rinse itself. I worked at it delicately, not wanting to ruin any piece by accident. They were lovely gifts, but I couldn't expect more to come my way.

I'd grown since my arrival, and filled out from abundance in my meals, making my tattered rough-spun clothes snug on me. Not so much as to not be able to move, but enough for some discomfort as I worked. And, often, my hair tried to tangle itself in the collar of my shirt, or hide beneath it.

The snap of a twig over the gentle flow of the river caused me to jump. My eyes scanned quickly for the source, spotting it right away.

Fumei stood on the opposite bank of the river.

"It really is you," said Fumei. "You're not a ghost."

"What are you doing here?"

She ignored my questing, looking for the shallowest route and wading in. I put my things aside, worried she might get swept off if she slipped in her hurry, and went in. Taking her hand, we went to my side of the river, soaked to the bone, and embraced.

Fumei hugged so tight I didn't think she'd ever let go again. When she did, she looked me over, like an older sister making sure of my health. "You're not hurt?"

I shook my head, pulling my friend back into another hug. "How did you know to find me here?"

She kept her arms wrapped around me. "When Raeden told us you were alright, and laboring as a servant, I remembered how everyone said you were a ghost by the river. So, I looked for where a stable part might be. Where the current is gentle. I kept coming back, hoping I'd find you."

I pulled back, letting our foreheads touch. Fumei was the sort of girl I could never be. And she was my dearest friend. I started to cry. My most devoted friend braved the forest time and time again to look for me. My heart felt ready to burst with happiness.

We let go of each other, sitting at the edge of the water with so much to say and not knowing where to begin.

"They have you doing laundry?" asked Fumei.

I followed her gaze, nodding. "It's not so bad."

"They're so beautiful," said Fumei. "I'd be afraid I'd accidentally rip a piece, they look so delicate and perfect."

"The silk is a little stronger than you'd think," I said.

She looked at me then, twisting her face into a question. I blinked, looking down at myself to realize she'd noticed how I'd outgrown my clothes again. "I can bring you one of mine."

"You don't have to," I said. "I don't want you to get in trouble."

"After what you did to save Hisato, I can handle a stern scolding," said Fumei. "If my mother is mad enough to smack me, I won't care."

I shook my head, dreading such a thing.

"None of my sisters would've run up the mountain for me. To be completely honest, it made me a little jealous."

"Jealous?" I tried to read her face.

Her expression turned sad as she looked away, to the other side of the river. "Not just that you loved your brother enough to take his place. But that you were brave enough to try. I would have stayed home and cried, rather than face the spirits and demand anything."

I smiled for her, taking her hand. "It wasn't a demand so much as it was begging. And I was terrified the entire time."

"You can't be brave unless you're afraid first, right?" She firmed her hold on my fingers, putting a smile on for my sake.

"Maybe," I said, shy. I wasn't sure if I believed that; believed what I did was anything astounding.

"What are the spirits like? Are they frightening or monstrous? Hisato said they looked like people. But Raeden said he'd seen some that looked part animal."

I told her everything then. About how they mostly looked human, and how some Kurai changed their hearts and swore allegiance to the Juneun. I told her about Lord Kwan, and his power and protection over Mount Tora and the lands around it.

"I've been practicing my manners too," I said at the end. "And learning to read and write. So I can teach you and my family and everyone in the village."

"All of us?" repeated Fumei in disbelief.

I nodded. "You could master them easily. And we could put together a beautiful dress and find a way to go to the city. A noble lord or a rich man will want to marry you. Maybe a prince."

She looked horrified by the prospect. "I wouldn't make for a good princess. Or a rich man's wife. It would be too different, too strange. I wouldn't fit in."

I blinked, never expecting my friend to doubt herself. "I always imagined you'd end up with a rich man. And live a life of beauty and comfort."

She shook her head. "I want to marry someone who's kind and gentle. Someone who understands what a pain it is to be cleaning and cooking after a long day in the tea fields."

I chuckled. "I think you just described every girl in the village."

"Did I?"

"And if you have children... I don't know that the men could ever fully understand."

"I'm not sure I want children."

That surprised me more. "Why?"

"I'd be too afraid." She pulled her knees against her chest. "Bringing a child into the world is painful. And something could go wrong. Even after a baby is born, I'd be too scared that something would happen. They'd get hurt, or sick, or worse. Yi lost a baby this past winter. It had a slight cough, nothing anyone worried about, and died in the night. What if that happened?"

I hadn't thought about all that. It seemed the most natural thing to fall in love, marry, and raise a family. But I never imagined all the terrible bits that could happen. I wanted so much to be a lovely enough girl, where nothing bad happened.

"The village women, and the men now too, they say things," said Fumei.

"Say things? Like what?" I looked from the water, breaking my thoughts to read her troubled face.

"They say that, because you're alone and a servant to a lord, surely he's..." She bit at her lip, cheeks turning pink at the mere idea. "That he's taken you into his bed."

"That's not true!" I admit that I even scared myself in the moment, yelling as I did.

"I know it's not," said Fumei. "You would never. But that's what they've been saying, and it doesn't matter how much me, or your brothers, say differently. They say that if you are a servant, you would have no choice if he commanded it. And even if a servant girl refused, the lord might take them by force."

I shivered while a rage broiled inside me. How could such a horrible lie start and be allowed to spread? "He hasn't!" I shouted. "The other servant girls don't go to his bed, and they're far more beautiful. He hasn't touched any of us. He wouldn't do that!"

Though I raised my voice and balled my fingers into fists, I wasn't angry with Fumei. I was angry with the rumor, the lie. I was angry that I couldn't defend myself against the accusation. And any small hope I had that someone might still love me and want me for a wife vanished. Without all my shortcomings and underwhelming appearance, no one would want a ruined woman. Even if I were beautiful, the damage of my reputation would stave off any good and sensible man.

Whatever thread of hope I had was now gone. Only a desperate man would have me, and I'd be forever locked in a loveless and miserable life if I accepted.

Fumei must've read my thoughts, or known what my tears meant. She'd been the one to offer me optimism in my woe and insecurity. "Then that's settled. I won't marry either. Not until you have a good husband first." She took my hand as she made her vow, a serious expression on her face, looking me in the eye.

I wiped the tears from my hot cheeks. "You can't. What if you fall in love?"

She shook her head and pulled me close. "I won't ever abandon my friend to rumors. And if someone does love me, really love me like that, then they'll understand."

I hugged tight, burying my face in her shoulder.

We couldn't linger there for long. Only enough to gather ourselves again. I finished the rinsing of my clothes, putting them to dry. Fumei made a promise to return the day after tomorrow with clothes from home.

As much as I liked the things I was gifted, they weren't the best for doing any chores or walking beyond the gardens.

It was late by the time I'd come back, and started to rain again. I'd put my things away, hurrying to help turn down the house and spare others from getting soaked. Though, with how heavy the deluge became, I decided to light the furnaces that would heat the floors. I did so in a hurry, making a silent note to myself that I'd restoke and do a better job in the morning if the rain continued.

After I completed my task, I rushed to my room to dry off and change. Dressed in my night robe, and pulling my deel over, snug as it'd become, I went to clean up the mess I'd brought in my wake. It was dark already, and I didn't want anyone to slip if they walked through for any reason.

The rain clapped on the ground and the roof, so noisy that I could barely hear myself think. Walking back to my room, I heard something else. Groans and grunts, two separate voices. Were I not the only one still up and all else outside of the rain quiet, it would've gone unnoticed.

Syaoran's door was opened slightly. No more than an inch. The smell of spilled peach wine was strong. For a moment, I feared he was in trouble. Until my eye caught the scene in side. Quite the opposite of my assumption.

One of the servant girls, bare, lay on his bed. Syaoran, half undressed, between her legs in a rhythmic motion. Words were exchanged, taunting from Syaoran and moans from the girl.

I wasn't so naïve. I knew what they were doing, and turned away only a second after I'd seen. I felt my insides churn over. My hand hid my jaw-dropped face, questions running through my mind. I'd been so adamant in my denial to Fumei. Was it a servant at the behest of someone with higher status, a master? Did he love her?

In my bed, I kept wondering which version was true. And my heart saddened at both. I told myself it was silly, having a crush on a Juneun, handsome or not. I was a human village girl, and shouldn't have thought of his kindness as more than that. More than pity, friendship at the highest. Of course he would pick a spirit, or someone beautiful. He'd said so himself.

I dwelled on it the next few days, putting a front as I met with Fumei again.

Sitting on the veranda, well into summer, Lord Kwan took tea outside of his room. It'd been a year complete since I first showed up. I drew the pond garden to distract myself. In another four years, I would go home. A part of me rejected the fact, wanting to hide here forever. I didn't know how to handle people whispering about me, gossiping about a lie as though it were indisputable truth.

"Do you enjoy drawing?" asked Lord Kwan.

I stopped, looking over in bewilderment. Nothing had probed or led into the question. We'd been quiet for some time, simply in the company of one another. "My mother used to draw. I guess I do like it. It reminds me of her, and, in a way, makes me feel close to her, even though she's gone." My voice cracked slightly. Even now, after so many years, it still pained me to remember her, to miss her.

He moved from his reclined spot, walking to look over my shoulder at my work. Reflexively, I tucked it closer to my chest, slow, to hide it.

"Let me see it."

I hesitated. He'd commanded it, and I was obliged to obey, though it left me feeling somehow exposed. My nerves wracked every inch of me the moment my book left my hand, watching him as he studied one page. In unhurried, fluid moments, he flipped to another page, staring over with his usual intensity. Then another.

"Your mother taught you?"

"She started to, my lord. But I never got a good enough handle on how to..." my voice trailed as I watched him sit beside me. His hand open in a silent command for my charcoal. I gave it over without question.

"Hold it delicately," said Lord Kwan, demonstrating. "Begin with the lightest touch. Like a butterfly, not a tiger."

I watched, eyes fixed to take in every detail of how he conducted the charcoal.

"What were you trying to draw?"

I straightened, looking up and into his eyes. A patience stared back from them. "The flowers, my lord. Right in front of the pond."

He nodded, looking back to the paper to give his instruction. "Start with a line to follow for shape. Then a circle for where you want the edges to be."

He handed back my things, leaving generous space for me to try and copy. I did the best I could, and he took it back when I was finished to give the next demonstration. In the end, I saw improvement, but nothing near to his skill. At least I now had a better grasp on how to work things out. It seemed like such an obvious approach now.

"Do you paint?" asked Lord Kwan.

I kept a smile on, happy to know I could better my skill more effectively and eager to keep trying. "When I can. But paint is expensive, so I rarely get the chance. But I like it. Putting color to a picture, bringing it a little more to life. Maybe not life-like, but not as distant as it is with only charcoal."

A quiet fell over us.

"Do you like to, my lord?" I looked at him.

He quirked a brow, breaking the stone expression I'd grown used to, a question splayed on him. "Paint?"

I nodded.

He looked away, stony again, to the garden ahead, and said nothing.

I thought I'd upset him. I didn't know how; it wasn't a personal or deep question. But I felt like a barrier had been put up. "I'm sorry," I said, even though it sounded silly to do so. "I just, I wanted to know a little more about you, my lord. In the past month alone, I thought about how little we know of each other. It felt weird to think I'd spend five years serving someone and know nothing much about them."

He stayed silent, keeping his gaze to something distant. For a long time, he said nothing, leaving me to sheepishly resume my practice. "Not as much as you seem to."

I stopped, looking at him again, though he stayed as he was.

"It's something to pass the time. I hadn't much use to indulge far enough to say I enjoy it."

It struck me as odd, *something to pass the time*. In the village, we didn't have that sort of concept. There was always something to do. And if, by rare chance, every task was complete, we took to things that brought us a moment of pleasure or play. Just as I enjoyed drawing, my brothers would play a sport with friends, or we'd go to swim if it was too hot a day to do anything else. There wasn't a day where we just wasted time.

We sat in quiet company a long while more. Me with my drawing practice, and Lord Kwan with his thoughts.

"You may ask me one thing per day," said Lord Kwan. "But I'm not obligated to always answer."

It took me a minute to realize the context. When I did, a flood of questions fought to be the first. Now it was me who was staring at him with intensity as I tried to decide something. Why did he sometimes come back in a blind rage? What were the rest of his brother like? Did he get along with them? What was it like growing up as a Juneun lord? Did he always want to be a lord? How did he meet Feng? Syaoran? Yua? Why did he choose Mount Tora to live?

"What's your favorite thing to eat?" There were a thousand more important questions. Yet, none of them felt like they'd let me know who he was right now. It was a silly question, maybe, but it was all I could think that would bring some kind of familiarity.

He didn't look at me, and took his time to reply. For a brief second, I thought he meant not to answer at all. "Apricots."

I smiled wide. Finally. "That's something we have in common."

He faced me, slow and deliberate in his movements. But I didn't care. I finally knew something about him that I understood.

Chapter 23
Lord Kwan VI

Of all the things she could've asked. Every exploitative question he braced himself for. Yet, the simplicity of it felt somehow personal. That irritated him. Something so trivial. So why did he need to think on it?

Were she someone of noble birth, he was sure the question was only leading into some game of politics. But this was different. Sincere. Something Kwan wasn't accustomed to. Sometimes not even from his own household.

When he answered, she beamed.

That wide smile stayed in his thoughts, long after the sun had set. When did he last give time to something that pleased him to that degree? In something so simple?

Another rain began, echoing into his open window. He stared at the ceiling, unable to fathom that her question was at face-value. No trick. No agenda. Just a question.

A butterfly fluttered in, seeking shelter.

Kwan stared. A different one, but still alone. Short, black wings spotted with yellow, damp and velvety.

A shadow of something in the far corner of his room stole his gaze. A second butterfly. Wings of yellow, spotted with black. It'd flexed its wings only when the other came in. They were not alone.

A calm came over him.

Though, his restless mind refused to let it stay. There was the threat and warning Dareun made, as though Kwan were blind to the goings on of his own home. He'd been lenient. To those whose crimes were not their own, he'd shown a mercy, and a respect. Hadn't he?

The loyalty earned wasn't from a show of force. He didn't see it that way. It was unlike his father and eldest brothers, who confused submission with fealty. Even his younger brother started to succumb to the idea, slowed only by love. Though, was taking in a desperate soul, grasping for any respite truly different? In all this time, surely, a resentment would've sprung up. An active search for his downfall rather than to come to his aide. Kept from the one they wanted so much to see safe, holding to the promises he'd made.

He sighed, shoving the thoughts away. Looking back to the ceiling, the butterflies were gone. They'd met on his table without his notice. Wings flexing, they shared a single spilled drop of peach wine.

They were not alone. And they were happy for it.

The memory of Kwang came next. Their other brothers found disappointment, having brought a small force and enough dogs to fill the kennels. When it became clear that Kwan had no intention of an active pursuit on Gumiho, they left. Chastising as they were, it made little difference. A Juneun's eagerness was his downfall when it came to her.

You know more than a hundred ladies came to Mokryon for you.

He wasn't enticed by his brother's news. One hundred girls clawing for status, willing to pretend to be whatever they thought he wanted. If he'd promised them marriage should they lay bare with the pigs for a night and a day, they'd compete to see who could stand it longest. If he brought them to serve in his home and in his bed, they'd happily oblige and pretend to be thrilled with every touch. And if he'd said he would only wed a bald woman, they'd all shave off their hair in court—anything to win status.

He considered attending court only to announce he would marry the best farmer. How prosperous a time that'd make. Or perhaps every family would be so insulted they'd refrain from further pursuit. The scandal it would cause in his house.

He wasn't blind to the games played behind closed doors. It was a poor secret that his parents tried to make strategic arrangements for all of their children. That was the way of things. That was the way for his two eldest brothers, and his eldest late sister. After the tragedy, the game seemed less important. But perhaps enough time had passed.

Kwang was agreeable enough to be fooled by a well performing girl. Beom, on the other hand, would frighten off all but the most determined, and likely would accept an arrangement.

A sinister piece of him wanted to make the declaration—perhaps make it from the least likely of spirits, the lowliest daughter of the lowliest family. It'd certainly spite his family, his society. But what of the girl? Could she bear a loveless marriage—knowing she was only a pawn, even if it brought her and her family up from the gutters? He couldn't do that. Not to an innocent being dragged along by the high lords and their games of society. Heaven's sake, he'd allowed the belief of Yua as his consort, which most decidedly didn't help her own plight. What he thought would protect her, damaged her. And he'd yet to tell her of it.

No. The best decided form of spite was to remain as he was.

That smile made its way back to his mind. A youthful memory, when everything seemed so simple. Was it once sincere as well? Or always painted on, pretending to be what he'd desired?

He turned over, shutting his eyes and ridding himself of further intrusive thoughts.

Kwan watched Hisa's penmanship. She still dipped the brush too far, and held it like an amateur painter rather than delicately, further up the shaft. Unrefined. But genuine in her delight to try. Her face crinkled and twisted as she concentrated, her tongue fighting not to make its ungraceful appearance.

Nothing at all like his sisters. Straight backed and poised, rather than leaning forward and hovering just above the paper.

As inelegant as she was, Kwan liked it. Something real, pacifying his cynicism. A smudged line of ink appeared on her cheek. How, he had no idea. Reaching over, he stopped her hand and lifted her chin to better see. "How did you manage to get ink on your face?"

"Huh?" she blinked at him, the terror she'd had upon arrival gone from her eyes. "I do?" She wiped with her palm, leaving a second smudge.

Taking her wrist, warm, and thick in her bones, he turned it over. A dab of ink from her clumsiness peeking up at them. "You're holding too close to the brush."

Her cheeks pinked up. A part of him braced for lashing out, or to play it off coyly. Instead, she stayed quiet, tucking her head into her shoulders. No excuses, no games.

A pass of his thumb ridded her of the ink. "If you keep hovering over, eventually your hair will fall in the ink."

"It's not that long," said Hisa. "It barely touches the edge of my cheek."

He watched as her free hand went to measure, making sure that was indeed the case. "You keep brushing it back with your hand. It'll stay better if you sit properly."

She straightened, though hunched again over time. She wasn't the same as a lady in the courts. That was something she could never be. And it comforted him to think that.

Looking at her now, the more he reflected on earlier thoughts, the more he realized how impossible it would be. He wouldn't be able to stand it, the ineptitude of it all.

Though, he recalled the praise Syaoran and Feng gave her. The skill she had from a young age, and was lacking in higher bred families. Not inept. Just different.

"Do you have a favorite animal?"

He broke from his thoughts, looking at her and that waiting smile. Perhaps she expected some obvious answer: a tiger. And would otherwise tease that it was not. No matter his answer, it invited games. "No."

She stayed wordless. Confusion on her face. Then a softer smile returned to her. "I like hummingbirds the best."

He stared, puzzled. Was it not a trick? His mind mulled it over, sure that the question was somehow insincere. He repeated her answer in his head. No. It was genuine.

Then he remembered that he did have a passion once. For something that was more than to pass the time. "Put on your riding clothes tomorrow."

When Hisa arrived, nervous, Kwan couldn't help but compare. She'd cleaned up in appearance, her hair a bit grown, and she didn't tremble in sheer terror at the verge of tears. Though, she couldn't conceal her fear. There was no pretense to how she felt, which both annoyed and fascinated him.

Saburo breathed out deep, posing the question.

"You like her well enough," said Kwan, avoiding it.

Saburo nickered, repeating his question.

Kwan didn't answer.

Once she was in the saddle, alone, he gave instruction. She'd been a quick learner with writing. However, she also wasn't terrified of writing. A scared fawn. A little doe.

"Keep your heels down, and back straight," said Kwan, correcting the angle of her ankle. "Put your weight into your heel for balance. If you try to stand on your toes, you'll fall. Everything else should stay loose. Let yourself feel how he moves."

"What if I..."

He looked up, slow, seeing her arms already pulled to her chest. "You won't fall." He took her hands, far from that of a delicate lady, and placed them properly. "Have a little faith in Saburo."

"It's not him that I doubt, my lord," said Hisa with a sigh.

Kwan watched, taking the words to think over. "You doubt me?"

"That's not what I said, my lord," her tone became defensive.

He allowed a moment to pass, putting a hand to her spine. "Back straight."

It went about as well as expected. At a walk, she still curled in fear. By the end, she gained a slight confidence, and let her body assumed the proper position a little more.

She'd run up the mountain, he remembered. And the scrape of her leg. The villages around the mountain had oxen and horses, and surely there were those who rode them adeptly. Even if she'd owned a horse, she'd still have run.

Helping her down, he watched for signs of fear. They were there, but to a lesser degree. "Can you walk?"

She nodded, her hands releasing his arms.

"You will do this twice a week."

She looked at him, brow pressed and face twisted. "Why?"

"So I can show you what I enjoy. The way you enjoy your art."

They'd started into the soft trot on the fifth lesson. The change of speed, motion, caused her to revert to how she'd been in their initial session. At first. Before half their practice was up, she'd corrected herself. He smiled, a little.

Until a sealed letter was handed to him.

Yua stood, formal, addressing him by his full title. Which typically meant there was some dispute he was getting dragged into. He allowed his frown to speak for him, taking the letter and opening it with little grace.

Worse awaited him than some petty argument over slights. It was a formal summons, in which his father anointed him as a representative. To take court with the Mireu family. The crown family of all Juneun. Why him and not one of his, likely more favored, brothers? Who could say? There was something not right. Regardless, he couldn't ignore it. The best he could do is decipher any clue lain in the letter, and prepare himself.

He counted through the family names and tribes he recognized, which would make for the easiest way of guessing. The Sho family, the Cat Clan, the Fire Dogs Tribe, the Lion Clan, the Samjo family, and the Bear Clan. There were others, though he wasn't familiar. Not that it mattered.

The summer had passed too quietly. He hadn't a sense or report of Gumiho since their last encounter. Though, if she'd slipped through his boarders and into another, there wouldn't be any notice. It was too late to discuss Borsi again. If a new antic, a new puppet plagued the crown's lands, the summons was necessary.

The assembly could be a war council. Though, perhaps sparce if the crown family indeed intended it to be that. Prominent families assembled, though particularly selected, left questions.

"See to the lessons in my stead," said Kwan, giving only a glance to Yua as he stood. He'd need his sword. Whatever sharp words might be exchanged were worthless without means to back them up.

He said no farewells, nor gave an estimate to his time away. His eye, however, peeked over his shoulder, to a small, sweating face marred with scars and confusion.

Kwan's race to the palace didn't go unnoticed. Taiga of the Lion Clan. In the final stretch, the last ten miles, their steps became nearly identical. Kwan didn't care for the show of it, the feat meaningless if all it did was bolster pride. He'd willingly slow his own pace if it wouldn't have been seen as an insult and caused problems before they arrived.

At the palace gate, they came to a swift end. Both standing straight and awaiting entry.

Taiga grinned. A mane of yellow hair and squared features that hinted at the muscular body hidden beneath silk and armor. "I believe I won by half a centimeter."

He didn't.

"I believe you did," said Kwan without looking in his direction. He wouldn't bother acknowledging the claim any further, or encourage bragging.

Instead, he kept his eyes on the red lacquered doors, standing tall as a giant. They opened, slow and with an initial creak from the weight, but smooth in their glide to welcome the two in.

Urekkato of the Cat Clan already stood in the vast courtyard. The white of his hair, ears, and tails caught the sunlight and broadened his Juneun etherealness. Unlike the boastful colors of Taiga's silks, Urekkato kept a more subtle coloring; something that distinguished him as a part of the head family, yet allowed for him to go unnoticed in deep shadows. He was more slender built, even compared to Kwan, but no less deadly with his swords. While there was never a need to say so aloud, the Cat Clan princeling was superior at combat than most others of his station. Including Taiga.

"Who got here first?" asked Urekkato, a slight grin to him.

"I did," announced Taiga.

"Which means I owe Zhen a hefty sum," said Urekkato. His voice held a complaint, though his expression only deepened, knowing. "I placed my bet on Kwan."

"Everyone is here, then?" asked Kwan, walking towards the palace and dismissing all else.

"We're still waiting on Haru," said Urekkato, stretching out and assuming a relaxed posture. "The Bear Clan isn't known for punctuality."

"You're well informed on who ought to be here," said Kwan, making no attempt to hide his annoyance.

"I'm just lucky," said Urekkato, though they all knew that wasn't true. The luck was fabricated, waging war on the psyche while his real methods were subtle and unshared.

"Can your luck tell us why Dae Jum summoned us here?" continued Kwan.

Urekkato shrugged. "At the behest of his wife."

That narrowed down a number of reasons. Likely, this wasn't a meeting of war. And all associated possibilities as well. It would be a more personal matter. A courtly matter.

He walked on, not waiting for the company before entry.

Inside, Zhen, in his black, iridescent armor and silk, stood waiting. He smiled, a scoff leaving him. "And now I owe Urekkato an even greater sum. I bet that Taiga would be at the gate first. But he placed a second bet that you would be in the palace first." He pushed back his raven hair, watching Kwan with mindful, gray eyes. "Did he stall the lion? Or was it his luck playing a factor?"

"Neither," said Kwan. He walked by, giving no notice and not wanting to engage in the frivolity. Kept away too long, Gumiho would take her advantage. And he'd spent much of himself in his dash here. Though, had he taken Saburo, a question might have occurred. He needed to appear strong, lest some foolish gambit overstep and play into a Kurai trap.

He remembered clearly the promise he'd made. They were practically children then, playing at being grown up.

I will keep you safe from all of them.

Oaths ran deep. He was bound to it. How stupid he was. A child making the promises of a man. And any trespass on this oath would need to be met with steel.

Sixteen young lords assembled, two rows of eight, with Dae Jum and his queen at the head of the chamber. They sat in silence for a near half hour, straight backed with perfect discipline. Until the king spoke.

"Borsi is dead."

It wasn't shocking news. Most of them knew. All of them waited. Waited for the relevance of it. The reason for the summons.

Dae Jum shifted his golden eyes across the selection of representatives. His crown of antlers, decorated in fine jewels, stood as the reminder of his authority in his complete stillness. "The betrothed of my youngest great granddaughter is dead."

No one spoke.

Now, it made sense. Every representative was unmarried; of a reputation in their family that might best secure stronger ties to the Mireu name. Pawns of their parents, willing and unwilling.

"It grieves us all to hear of your loss, excellence," said Zhen.

Dae Jum said nothing.

The queen, however, shifted her eyes to measure each man there, weighing a promise unspoken.

"How is the young princess?" attempted Taiga. He'd realized the reason for his being there, and wasted no time in testing.

"She was fond of Borsi," said Dae Jum. "I'd spoiled her as my favorite, and allowed her to choose for herself. I see now the decision was folly. She will be just as happy with a husband of her own rank."

A different tension fell over them.

"Every family covets tying their name to ours. Undoubtedly, you understand the part you were sent to play. What to speak on, in regards to your merit. Your family's merit is already known. And they've sent you to convince me of a choice."

Unease spread. Eagerness entwined with careful consideration. Speaking up first seeming too bold, but not doing so meaning the loss of opportunity.

"Well?" said Dae Jum. "Or am I to select from your silence?"

"Select from what the stars say, or the bones, excellence," said Kwan. "Since the queen has been assessing this past half hour, I would ask her."

She smiled, red painted on her lips, gold painted on her eyes. "Sharp tongues. Would you speak so direct to your bride?"

"I speak as freely as I desire in my own house," said Kwan.

"I seem to recall Lord Kwan has already met our great granddaughter."

A new haste came with the queen's words.

"But has she seen his lands, my queen?" asked Bul Gae. "The Fire Dog Tribe has happily occupied territory where tribute is plenty. East and west. The princess would find Lord Kwan's house dull and lackluster by compare."

"I see," said the queen, feigning intrigue.

"If the princess desires decadence right away," said Zhen, "I doubt she will wait patiently for imports. The lands of my family are abundant in farming and flora."

"That is impressive," said the queen.

"Do you accept this insult to your name and your house, Lord Kwan?" asked Dae Jum.

"I have not yet heard any insult, excellence," said Kwan. "Merely comparison."

"He is well tempered," said the queen.

"But, my queen," said Shion of the Sho family. "Lord Kwan is already engaged to my sweet cousin Feng. His appearance is surely only a formality or because his other brothers are indisposed."

"Indisposed?" said the queen. "It is quite the insult to send a man who is already betrothed. How is the king to make a decision without seeing who asks for the princess's hand?"

"Are you already matched?" asked Dae Jum, ignoring the queen's implications.

Now, he was trapped. To say he was would mean his consent to the Sho. To deny it, meant he might be commanded to a marriage by the crown family. He couldn't use his usual silence, and buy time to think. This was the king.

"I have made no formal proposals," said Kwan.

The queen laughed. "A sharp tongue, a steeled temperament, and a solid mind. I begin to understand how he earned his reputation."

Dae Jum shifted his gaze to his wife with a slight turn of his head, taking her amusement into consideration. "The queen favors Lord Kwan, then? Who may or may not already be betrothed."

"Excellence," said Urekkato. "Yours is a word that cannot be defied. Though I have concerns about selecting a lord who must break his own word to another family, if that is the case."

Dae Jum returned his watch to the men before him. "Meaning?" He'd understood. That much was obvious. The question didn't imply ignorance; merely it was to see if the princeling could be made a fool.

"If Lord Kwan, who may or may not be engaged, is to make a declaration of his love, let it be made in earnest. That it was his decision alone, and not the noblest intention on match making by the crown."

"And the Cat Clan would allow such a prize to slip their claws?" asked the queen.

"I can't speak for my father, Lord Cha Kla, or the rest of my family," said Urekkato. "Only myself."

"That is a sensible thing," said the queen.

Kwan, seeing opportunity, spoke up right away. "I would vouch for Urekkato's good reputation. Sensibility, as you say, is rare when pride is the modern currency. The Cat Clan has always been loyal to your house. And it is said that luck forever follows Urekkato. Perhaps enough that the two might find love in one another should a meeting between them be arranged."

Taiga threw a fierce leer at Kwan. "The princess will not be charmed by the promise of luck. Luck cannot stop the Kurai should they plot to cause her misery again."

Dae Jum looked at Taiga, his eyes narrowed. "Explain."

"It is strength that will ensure the princess's safety, excellence," said Taiga, finally able to get himself noticed.

"Would the princess agree?" said Urekkato. "Perhaps she might not feel so safe in marital company that included so much strength."

Zhen held in a laugh, ruining his composed face and tightening his shoulders.

It was decided that the princess would choose from among them, being told only what the king and queen though of each, and the reputations of their families. Which bode better for a few, whose individual reputation might come across as unsavory. What woman was there, human or spirit, who was not enchanted by Urekkato's words and handsomeness? And there were rumors of Zhen having taken pretty and youthful men behind closed doors. Bul Gae had too much love of imported wines and was unhappily sober. Taiga's gluttony spread into his hunger for battle, something to prove his power that would go unchallenged in the courts. And no one had forgotten the joke Shion made, in bad taste, on how wealthy he would find himself if he became a widower, if only to find a woman to match.

They were not cruel men, not that Kwan considered. They were flawed. And there was not a living thing that went without flaw. Not even the dragon king of the Juneun.

The princess couldn't decide. With sixteen men staring at her, awaiting her choice, she broke into tears and fled. There was a brief moment when her trembling reminded him. Though she wore the finest of silks, dyed in so much color, and embroidered with the tiniest of jewels woven in. There was also the paleness of her face, pinkness of her cheeks, and long, shining, black hair that reached for the ground. The eyes were different too. A deep gray rather than a dark brown.

They were hosted, unable to leave without the king's dismissal, for several days. In which time, the princess moved to meet each suitor one at a time.

Haru of the Bear Clan seemed especially tender with her, showering his affection in awkward gestures. He seemed genuinely taken with her, though her own feelings remained closed from the others. She'd been taught to not reveal herself; perhaps she was also punished for her previous public display. Though, if she loved Borsi, truly loved him, perhaps she was not yet ready to move on.

When she managed to catch Kwan alone, in spite of his avoidance, she invited him to sit with her under the willow and observe the lake beside it. An invite, from royalty, he couldn't refuse. No matter his wanting otherwise.

"I've made my decision," said the princess.

Kwan looked at her, rosy cheeked and delicate. Still, he pretended not to know. "Which of them will it be?"

"Not them."

He looked away, facing the lake to watch the dragonflies dance over the water with their reflections. "I would ask you to reconsider, princess."

"I've made my choice."

He kept quiet, trying to think. "And if your choice refuses you?"

She let her own silence fall, allowing for thought. "Even after coming all this way?"

He said nothing, carefully selecting the words that wouldn't lean towards insult.

She took his hand. "I would make you a good wife. You've known me since I was a child. And never did you ask a thing of me. Except if there was something you could do—"

"You would be wedding the man who killed Borsi."

Wordlessness. Minutes stretching as long as hours without a thing said between them. She kept her hand on his, though its grip lacked all conviction.

"I did love him," said the princess. "Or, I thought I did. Now, I'm told that I shouldn't have felt that way at all. That it was not love."

Kwan contemplated the words. What it all meant from her perspective as quiet tears left her. "Do you want to marry another?"

She hesitated. "I do not know. But I must. For the family."

He couldn't tell if she spoke with sincerity, or if it was indeed another part of the game. Exposing this to garner sympathy and play to his resentment at familial duty. Surrendering your choice for the good of your clan.

"You would not have me?"

He looked at her again. "Were it my choice alone, I would only have the person who I can be myself with, and share in a happiness."

"You make it sound ideal."

"There is a burden on me beyond court and family. Whomever I choose, if it is my decision alone, must be willing to accept that as well."

She removed her hand. A hand that was small and slender, thin, dainty fingers, and a wrist too delicate. Things he'd seen of every woman in the courts his entire life, never considering the wealth of things the features said about the girl.

"I hope she is worthy of you."

"It must be her choice as well."

"Then I hope you are also worthy of her." She stood, taking small and graceful steps away.

Chapter 24
Forthcoming

It was autumn when Lord Kwan returned. He looked tired, though was himself at least. I took to my task, but didn't ask any question that day. He seemed, to me, sad in some way. His face still stone, it was something in his eyes. And while he'd always been few of words, I thought he was particularly quiet.

He kept me in his company the following day as we walked between the walls. To my surprise, he seemed fully aware of the part of the outer wall that had sunk halfway, and the marsh in its wake. Holding a palm up, his magic pulled the wall back to its original state.

"Will that cause the butterflies to leave?" I asked. I didn't realize how naïve it sounded until after I'd said it.

He stayed wordless, looking at me. Something about his placid expression hinted at how the spell took its toll. I couldn't place what exactly lent me that notion; a gut feeling or some intuition told me. Still, he waited for further explanation.

"The marshy spot there is where loads of butterflies like to gather."

He looked from me, back to the spot he'd corrected.

"It's one of my favorite places for that reason. I liked to sit under the shade of these trees and try to draw them."

He studied the spot with his usual intensity, keeping me from guessing his thoughts. "This is where they've been?"

"It's more vibrant in late spring, my lord. And most of summer. Everything is drying and bracing for winter now."

He looked up to the trees, some losing their leaves in a fanfare of color, others stubbornly holding to their green. "How often do you come here?"

A shiver sparked through my spine. I'd caused trouble for myself, I was sure of it. "When," I hesitated. "When you are away mostly, my lord. So that I'll stay out of the way when any chores I'm required to do have been taken care of."

"I've given you a single chore." He kept his eyes on the branches, slow to move his watch towards me. "Did I not?"

I wanted to stuff rocks in my mouth at that moment. Something that would prevent me from saying anything more that would get me in trouble. But I didn't have a pebble, let alone anything substantial. "You did, my lord," I stuttered. "It's only that, well, I don't like staying idle." I looked away, my gaze pulled back in knowing his hadn't shifted. "I'm not used to it. And I feel useless seeing everyone attending something of their own."

His attention went back to the trees.

"And I don't think of this as a chore, my lord," I said, hoping to smooth over whatever irritation I'd caused. "I thought it was a strange thing to want me to do, at first. But I've started to like it. And, I wanted to think that, maybe over time, we'd be friends."

"With your jailor?"

"I guess that does sound weird," I said, trying to follow whatever he'd fixed his sight on. "But it's also a little weird that a jailor would give his prisoner a comfortable room and a fine change of clothes."

In his own time, as always, he came up with an answer. "Humans are not as resilient. You would have frozen to death."

"That's true," I said. "And it is odd to think of a jailor teaching their prisoner to read and write and draw and ride. I think that's more akin to a friend than a jailor."

"What if the jailor despises stupid prisoners?"

I laughed. I didn't mean to—or make him think I was laughing at him—and cupped my hands tight over my mouth. "If a prisoner were already smart, they wouldn't be imprisoned, right?"

He looked at me then, quizzical.

"I... I only meant to say that—"

"I understood," said Lord Kwan. His eyes moved back to the where the wall once sunk in, and the muddiness before it. "I've never heard you laugh."

I blinked at him. It seemed like an odd thing to find fascinating. Had I been so meek and quiet around him? I supposed it was only recently that I felt comfortable in his presence. At least, enough not to worry so much about formality, not when it was the two of us and I already made myself look ridiculous so often in front of him.

Quiet came over us again.

"I was made an offer of marriage," said Lord Kwan. "The reason I was called away."

I blinked at him. It was unusual for him to volunteer information about himself in general, let alone something that seemed so personal. Something that invited an invasion of privacy. Something vulnerable. But why share it with me, and not Syaoran or Yua? It felt like he'd revealed it deliberately, though I couldn't comprehend why.

"Did you accept?"

He inhaled deep, letting it out with resignation and closed his eyes. "I may have to."

I didn't know what to do with that. Was marriage so different for nobles and Juneun? I'd only ever seen it as a union of love. But I fast realized in my short time here that I knew little of the world beyond our villages and mountain.

"Do you love her?"

He opened his eyes, turning to look at me with a hint of a smile. "That's two questions."

It took me a few seconds to realize. I felt my face twist and loosen as my mind raced to figure things out. "Oh."

He walked on, and I followed. I supposed that might be the end of our conversation. Assuming he probably had more to contemplate, he wouldn't reveal much more to me.

"No. I don't."

His answer surprised me, and a storm of questions came. I still didn't understand why he chose to tell me this. I wasn't a permanent part of his house or a Juneun or anyone important.

"What do you think about it?"

Again, I was astonished. "I don't know, my lord. I only know that you have told me the offer was made and you don't love her. It doesn't seem like enough for me to think anything of it."

We went on a while.

"So, what *do* you think?"

I was thinking why my opinion mattered at all. But, since I didn't know, the best I could do was answer honestly. "I don't know that I could bear being wed without love, my lord. Any time I imagined my future, love was at the center of it. As impossible as that might be now, I still imagine it that way. I never knew you could be married against your will. Any stories brought into the village would say that the lord and lady, or prince, or princess, would get married, but it always sounded like both agreed to it."

Quiet. For minutes on end.

"Why would it be impossible?"

My brow pressed, bending in humiliation, and I looked down. Even though he walked ahead of me, I didn't have the courage to look at him when trying to explain. "I know I'm not pretty, my lord. And now there's talk in the village about..." I didn't want to say it. It hurt my heart too much to repeat those rumors. And I hurried to come up with anything passable. "That I'm now like a criminal. There's no knowing the full story of things, and it's gotten all confused somehow."

He stopped in his stride, and I'd nearly bumped into him, looking at something in the distance. "You know this how?"

I hesitated. Surely, I was about to get myself and Fumei in trouble.

"The same person who brought you rough-spun clothes," said Lord Kwan.

I was jaw dropped.

"The ones you started to wear recently aren't as tattered or small on you."

I stayed quiet. What could I say?

"Why do you feel the need to hide that from me?"

"I just," I stopped, stopped myself from crying in the moment. "I didn't want to get anyone in trouble. It was when I washed my riding clothes the first time. I went to the river, my lord. But I never went to the other bank, I swear it!"

He looked to the ground, as if preoccupied with something else.

When I opened my mouth to say more, to try and soothe whatever irritation I'd caused, he spoke again.

"If you were going to run, you would have done so long ago." His eyes shifted to me. "What I value is your forthcoming nature. You're a terrible liar."

I gulped. "Yes, my lord. I'm sorry."

"Surely, any tales about your criminality are corrected. I'd be more surprised if not a single accusation came up about ruining you. That's the usual rumor in regards to a girl, unmarried, away from home, and serving a lord or greater."

I understood then why he'd said I was a terrible liar. It might've been obvious to him, but I was shocked when I first heard it.

"You are a strange thing," said Lord Kwan. "You say to me that it matters not what your future husband looks like, yet you're ashamed of your own lack of beauty."

It did seem strange. At the same time, it was a natural thing. Beauty was always in the list of reasons why any particular man chose a girl to marry. He might like her singing or that she weaves masterfully—and, of course, he thought she was very pretty.

"Your forthcoming is why I asked your opinion," said Lord Kwan, stealing me from my thoughts. "Of everyone, you're the only one who stands nothing to lose or gain. Some might insist I marry the princess for a variety of opportunities for themselves. Not least of all is an elevation of their status, that they now also serve a direct royal member. Others might want to convince me otherwise, in the fear that their position is jeopardized should she bring her own staff. But if you cannot be honest, I see no reason to confide in you again."

I felt more ashamed. Of course I should've stayed honest. How long could I hold even a small lie when I served him and lived in his house for another four years? "I understand." I didn't beg or apologize more. It seemed like a rude and greedy thing to do. Better that I accept he'd again be closed off to me, rather than hope to be more than master and servant.

"Knowing that," said Lord Kwan, which astounded me more, "what do you think?"

I took the question in. A warmth flowed through me, knowing I hadn't lost his trust. "I think, unless it is for a very good reason, no one should wed without love."

He walked on again, and, again, I followed.

"What would make a good enough reason to you?"

"I..." I was stumped. It seemed like the right thing to say, but I didn't have any examples of what that might be. "I don't know. Maybe there isn't a greater reason than love for why two people ought to be together."

He stopped again, and looked back at me. A hint of a smile on his face, he appeared more kindly than I'd ever known him to. "I said the same thing to her. Though, in a different way."

I smiled.

He'd confided in me afterwards that he'd been appointed to host court for garden patrons come summer. We had until then to prepare, and create an area where the event would take place between the walls. Somewhere prettily set, where displays could be erected and easily looked after. Since they were not personal guests, only a select few would be allowed past the inner gate. Though, he wasn't pleased in the least to host. It invited trouble, he'd said.

I remembered what Syaoran had said, what so many said in regards to Lord Kwan, and how he'd pushed Gumiho to the edge of the good lands to keep her at bay. If she was so sly, it stood to reason he'd worry that she'd take advantage of the distraction if she knew of it. I had to stay vigilant for him when the time came. Though, summer seemed so far away with autumn newly arrived.

Yua had come in not two weeks after Lord Kwan and I walked between the walls. "Stand up, and hold still." She had a bit of measuring twine with her.

"What for?"

"We all need to look our best when Lord Kwan hosts court. So, something will be sewn up to distinguish us as members of the house. And, the rank of each, of course."

"I can make something," I said with a smile.

She gave me a horrified look.

"I learned to make clothes in the village. One of the women taught me—"

"Which is why you will not be involved."

I blinked, looking from her to the folded set Fumei had brought me beside my bed. I wasn't fantastic at sewing together clothes. But I made do with what I'd learned. In the village, clothes didn't need to be pretty or complicated. They just needed to be functional. A house with a lot of daughters might spend their time improving the skill, making nicer things and practicing for the day they'd sew a dress for one another for a wedding. All I had were brothers.

"I could learn to do it," I said.

"Absolutely not."

"But, why?"

"The process will take most of winter as it is. First, we dye the patterns on the lengths of silk, which in of itself is time consuming when done properly. Then to be sewn and cut carefully, wasting as little as possible and making it appear seamless—"

"I can learn," I insisted. "It feels weird to wait around for someone to make me clothes. Couldn't I at least try?"

"You have other tasks."

"So do the other women servants. And I'll work just as hard. The ground will be too cold to ride soon, and I can continue my penmanship in between each section like you were saying."

She sighed, pensive as she looked for some way to convince me otherwise. "If you can get Lord Kwan's approval. These things are not cheap. I doubt he'd allow a novice to dabble in it."

I didn't waste a moment once Yua left, and went to find Lord Kwan to explain myself and ask his permission. As usual, he watched me, making me wait, with a stony expression. The audacity, he might've thought, that I should ask something like this. Or, maybe he thought I was odd, excited to begin a task that I was warned was extensive and tedious. After waiting so long, it felt like he'd tell me no. But he gave his approval.

I was delighted. Another skill I could bring back to my village. If I could remember them all, ours might stop being so poor and flourish in new wealth. We wouldn't have to save, and hope to afford a new pickling jar, if we had more to bargain with. We'd be able to buy the biggest one, and a new one every year, without a second thought.

As I lit up with his answer, that hint of a smile came back to his face. Though, I couldn't help thinking it looked slightly stronger.

The women weren't as pleased. Teaching me, they said, would slow them down. I stayed determined. A stencil was given to me, something I'd never seen and surely would've made drawing easier to learn if I'd known they existed. Yua instructed, direct with her words, placing the selected dyes and short haired brushes beside me. I smiled. The brushes reminded me of one my brothers had gifted to me. I'd used it as a paintbrush, not knowing it had a specific purpose. I was to hold it upright, pressing lightly and coloring in using small, circular motions.

As I focused, my tongue poke out and stretched up my lip. Yua scolded me for making such a face, and the other women snickered. I didn't bother with it too much, even though I felt a little embarrassed, and tried to go on while being mindful. After the fourth time, Yua gave up on telling me I'd made the same face. I stayed fixated on my work, trying to make everything as exact as possible and not mess it up.

I didn't notice the conversations between the other girls. Not that it mattered, since I wasn't a permanent part of the house. What little I did catch was in regards to whether or not Lord Kwan would marry that girl. Giddy talk, jealous talk.

Likewise, I didn't notice my back getting stiff until I'd decided to straighten myself and shift in my seat to reset my comfort. Despite that, I kept at it, determined to show I could work just as hard, as diligently, as the rest.

When they'd leave to take a break and have lunch, I kept working. I wouldn't let myself fall behind. Mastering this, bringing the skill to the girls in the village, that's what mattered. Maybe I could learn to make a stencil, and use my own drawing to make new patterns. Merchants would come from all over to get it, I was sure. It'd be a rough start, costly, but might pay off over time.

I'd continued on after the sun went down, and everyone else attended to chores before going to bed. I stayed outside, working. My hands started to get cold, and my feet as well, but I wanted to keep going.

Lord Kwan walked the veranda, coming over. I kept working. So, I didn't notice he'd brough me a bowl of broth and noodles.

"You're planning to skip every meal and work through the night?"

I looked up, noting the lantern light of the house as my sole source to see. It'd become later than I thought. And the moment my nose smelled food, my stomach growled loudly. I reached for the bowl, noticing my hands and fingers were spotted with the dyes. In a hurry, I tried to wipe it off on my clothes. It didn't do much to help.

"Come to the veranda," said Lord Kwan. "It's warmer."

"Yes, my lord," I said, and hurried to put everything away. Careful as I could manage, giving the stretch of silk a wide berth with the left-over dyes.

On the veranda, backs against a wall, my skin soaked in the warmth. Someone had gone ahead and lit the furnaces to heat the floors. Likewise, my hands drank in the warmth of the cup, and my tongue the broth as I sipped.

"It won't be finished in a day," said Lord Kwan.

I stopped, looking up at him.

"Nothing worth making ever is."

I smiled, looking into my bowl. "I know. But I want to prove myself."

He waited until after I'd slurped in some of the noodles. "Prove to who?"

It was a question that sounded obvious, though I couldn't conjure a suitable answer right away. "I'm not very skilled in a lot of things, my lord. I took on an important role when I was nine, and I never got the chance. I think, as much as I want to show I can keep up here, I want to make up for lost time."

Lord Kwan sighed, grunting.

"I'm just a human. So, time feels... It feels like it goes by so quickly, too quickly. I can't imagine how it would be otherwise. It's all I've known."

He said nothing more about it, leaving me to my supper and my thoughts. After a time of relaxing, I realized just how tired I was, from head to toe. It didn't seem like too difficult of work, though I'd never stayed on one task from morning well into the night. Always, I'd have to stop to tend to something else and move about. It was a new kind of fatigue. One that caused me to sleep deep as soon as I lay in my bed. Regardless, I was up promptly the following morning to continue.

Chapter 25
First Kiss, Second Prayer

Lord Kwan left several times during autumn, returning with heavy fatigue but always himself. I was thankful for it. Less because I was afraid—and I was still afraid—and more that I hated seeing anyone chained up like a monster.

When he did arrive home, I put aside all other things to tend to him. In one instance, his arm was bloodied, cut deep, as was his side, and a slash cut across his face. I wasn't completely useless on that return. I'd learned how to help clean and mend wounds after that boar tore up Lan's poor ox. And Lord Kwan's house was stocked with medicinal herbs to turn into salves. Yua, however, took care of the stitching needed to his arm, convinced I was still too clumsy. I didn't argue it. Nor did I ask Lord Kwan what'd happened, or why he didn't use his magic to close the wounds.

If he'd come back in such a state, it surely wasn't the business of a human to know. A part of me didn't want to know, didn't want to think that there really could be something out there more powerful than Lord Kwan. I only wanted his recovery, and stayed beside him for as long as he let me.

Even though I knew he would be fine, being a powerful Juneun with healing magic, my human brain was still fearful for him at the sight of his injuries. For anyone in the village, wounds like that would need constant monitoring and care for a week or more, and still the man would need to take rest to fully recover.

Winter.

And I spent a great deal of my time in my room, sewing together the dress I would wear when Lord Kwan hosted court. The other women went between making their own, and sewing up the uniforms of the male servants. I was far slower, trying to make things as near to perfect as I could. Even though I knew I would be so slow, a novice at the craft, it frustrated me. I wanted so badly to become adept enough to be useful.

There was also the realization that I wouldn't have more practice if this wasn't a regular occurrence. I'd need to look for other ways to practice any part of it.

The season was a balance of opposites. A quiet that allowed Lord Kwan to stay, yet everyone was abuzz with anticipation for spring. The dread of waiting until the deep snows were gone, yet thankful they were there to give rest. Cold air and warm floors.

I'd lost track of the days until I heard a passing mention of the winter solstice. Counting from there, it was almost my birthday. In two days.

Again, I would be away from Hisato and the rest of my family. I wondered if they were alright. Did enough get preserved for winter? Was there wood to keep the house warm? Did they manage to trade enough to get winter shoes? Were all the blankets in good shape, or in need of reweaving to hold in warmth?

Saddened, I took more breaks over the next few days. Mostly, I walked the veranda, with everything else covered in thick snow. The white landscape lonely without the colors of spring and summer. It didn't look dead, per say. Rather, it slumbered deeply, patiently waiting.

I needed to be patient too.

The day I turned seventeen, I lay in bed, thinking; my bunny staring back at me, reminding me of every intrusive thought that bid me to go back to sleep. Even as my body told me to get up, to do something with myself, I tried to make myself still. I did eventually give in, and not too long after. Rather than put any work into my usual task, I walked aimlessly wherever I could, sorely missing my family.

"Hisa?" Syaoran took my shoulder to turn me around. "You're not your usual self. You've walked by here twice already."

"Did I?" I blinked, my mind slow to regroup.

"Is something wrong? You're usually busy about something or another, and not walking circles around the house."

I tried to smile, the biggest one I could muster. "I'm just feeling homesick. It's my birthday, mine and my brother's. I just really miss them. And, I'm worried about them. If they're okay."

"I didn't know it was your birthday," said Syaoran, seeming to ignore the rest. He held out a palm, furling his fingers into a gentle fist. When they opened again, a silver coin was in his hand.

I admit, I was impressed by it. I'd only ever seen a silver coin half a dozen times in my life, and my family only ever held one twice. "Magic?"

He smiled. "It's an easy spell." He took my hand, placing the coin in it. A small thing that I feared would get lost in the snow if I dropped it. "For children, it's a bronze coin. For you, a silver. And gold is for when a girl or boy reaches marrying age. It's usually the last one they get."

"For what?" I asked.

"It's a gift. For your birthday," he flashed a toothy smile, and the same warmth he'd shown from the day I arrived. "You don't need it now, of course. But when you go back, you'll have a couple in hand. So no more pacing around worried. It's making me nervous."

"I make *you* nervous?" I said with a cocked brow.

His ears drooped. "Force of habit. People walking by frequently for seemingly no reason make me feel like I'm being watched. Like they think I'm up to no good."

Which reminded me. "Did you use this spell to find what you were looking for?"

His ears pointed straight, as though I'd blurted out his most humiliating secret in the midst of a crowd. "It's, well, that's a little more complicated. The spell summons small and ordinary things. But if something has magic attached to it, it usually won't come when it's called by a spell. That's why I've been looking for it without magic."

"You still haven't found it?" I asked in a whisper, my brow now pleading to let me help him. "If you told me what it looks like, at least—"

He shook his head, raising a palm to stop me from finishing my words. "I appreciate the thought. It's kind of you. But, I don't want to get you in the middle of things."

"*That* sounds like you're up to no good."

His ears drooped again, and his hands combed nervously through his ginger hair. "I guess it does. But, I'm not. I swear."

I nodded, bowing afterwards the way I'd practiced to allow him to leave. He did the same, and walked opposite my direction. When he turned the corner, I sighed and looked at the little coin. I didn't need it right now, that was true. At the same time, it was so small that I worried I'd lose it before a year complete. Were it a simple bronze coin, it'd be something I'd give in prayer without hesitation.

I remembered then what most of my recent prayers had been. For the health of my family, and the safe returns of Lord Kwan. And any time I'd given thanks in the past year, when Fumei brought me news about the village, or the day following Lord Kwan's recovery. But I could scarce remember when I gave back in prayer for the good things that happened. Two years, I think, or three.

As much as I wanted to keep the coin, to take it home, it seemed like such a selfish thing to do. But the shrine was below the mountain. Well, the shrine I'd always prayed at. In remembering, there was another shrine kept in the villa, tucked in the farthest back garden. Though, the path was likely blocked with snow.

No. I'd made up my mind.

Changing into my rough-spun clothes, laying my small ones under what Fumei brought for me, and pulling my deel over it, I clutched that coin tight in my fist. The snow reached my knee as I worked to break a path, my feet freezing instantly. It caused so much pain that I stopped to go back and stand on the heated floor until I recovered. Back and forth like a lunatic, until I'd made it to the shrine in the late afternoon.

I was panting, sweating, but my toes were numb and swollen and cold. In my attempt to recover, I kicked off my shoes and wedged myself to fit inside my deel. My hands reached under, rubbing back and forth to heat up my feet.

Now that I was here, however, I started to doubt. All my prayers and thanks were because of the unfortunate events that kept me on this side of the river. Did I actually owe anything? Or was it my optimism, defending my mind from fully understanding that I was still a prisoner—that my fate hung on the whims of a single person? He enjoyed my company on his terms, but that wouldn't spare me the rod or being placed back in the kennels if he decided so.

I don't know how long I stayed there, cocooned in myself. I'd never hesitated before. And I couldn't tell if it was because the coin was silver, or if I had genuine resentment and only now realized it. My frustration and solitude led me to cry, freely. I couldn't hold back anymore after all my confusion and loneliness. So, I stayed curled up, sobbing.

The air bit at the tips of my ears, driving my hands to bring my hair forward to cover them. It wasn't very long, but enough to make it less likely that someone would mistake me for a boy again. Brushing my shoulders and still horribly uneven, though it felt thicker and full of life. After five long years, would my brothers recognize me? Would I recognize them? They'd also shaved off their hair to rid themselves of lice.

The silver coin still in hand, I got to my feet and started to walk back to the house. Of the thousand things I could ask for in prayer, I knew in my heart that the things I desired most were impossible things. Things for a life I'd never be able to lead.

The sun hid itself away, painting the sky in deep, vivid colors as the first stars shown against the darkest of blues. And though the temperature grew colder still, I stopped to watch it. Was there ever a more beautiful thing than the heavens?

A twig snapped, sounding as if it'd been pulled from a bush. Twisting my neck to look over, I saw a white doe looking at me. Though there were hints of the ordinary deer coloring to her rump and shoulder. Her eyes perfectly brown, and her nose perfectly black, she looked surprised to see me and that I'd seen her. A few curious steps closer, and to my left, her ears went on alert. Everything about her gave her an air of grace and shyness. I was transfixed.

In shifting my weight, I'd slipped. My arms shot out, sinking into the snow but stopping the rest of me from doing so. Whipping my head back up, the doe was gone. Not even a break in the crisp, white of winter to indicate she was ever there to begin with. I got up, dusting myself free of clinging cold, and realizing I'd dropped the silver coin.

It served me right, I supposed, being selfish. And I wished I'd never gone to the shrine at all. There was nothing to be done about it now, except to continue to the house.

Halfway back, I spotted Lord Kwan walking up the path I'd made. There wasn't room for us to pass each other, and I'd stood still in trying to decide if I should turn around and let him be on his way, or if it looked like he came this direction to inspect some other part of the yard.

His eyes looked from my sloppy work, studying, to me. He tilted his head, taking in my shabby appearance as he came closer.

"Eager to get to the shrine?"

I started to nod, fast remembering my manners and straightening my posture. "I went to pray, my lord."

"Did you now?" His voice took a gentle curiosity. "What was so important that you broke this path?"

I kept my hands in front of me, red and bitterly hurting as they were. "It's my birthday, my lord. And I wanted to make a wish. But I don't think any of my wishing will come true."

He stayed silent, unmoving. "What did you wish for?"

"My lord?" I blinked up at him, not quite understanding what he wanted.

"If it is your birthday, it shouldn't be such a sad event. Name what you wished for. I will present it to you."

I gave a look of apology. Of course I wanted so many things. It just didn't feel right to ask it of my jailor. So, I thought of which one sounded most impossible. "The same wish I've made since I was fifteen."

He quirked a brow, that hint of a smile waiting on me.

"For my first kiss."

He grunted, soft and quick in his reaction.

"So, you see, it's impossible of me to ask it of anyone. A kiss should be freely given, not coerced."

"Indeed," said Lord Kwan. "It's a waste of a first kiss if one or both feel obligated to it."

"Right," I said with the best smile I could conjure.

"Close your eyes," said Lord Kwan.

My smile faded, brow pressing as I tried to understand his tone and read his placid expression. "Huh?"

"You don't trust me?"

I tried to bring my smile back. "As you trust me, my lord, yes."

He waited, weighing what I'd said, and repeated his command. "Close your eyes."

I was confused, but obliged. Perhaps he meant to do the same fanciful trick as Syaoran, and place some trinket in my hand. My fingers fidgeted, readying to be plucked up. What I didn't expect was the brush of his lips against mine, cool to the touch, or his hand cupping my chin to lift my face. A tender press against my lips. I felt his fingers glide across my cheek, over that ugly scar, and under the back of my jaw so softly. Through it all, I kept my eyes closed.

It was gentle, and short lived. And I liked it. That's what surprised me the most.

When he lifted his lips from mine, and his hand fell away, the bite of winter's wind didn't feel quite so cruel. I opened my eyes, my heart light and racing.

That hint of a smile seemed somehow stronger on him. "It was not such an impossible wish after all."

I stood there, blinking, stupefied. I felt my face flush a slow and rosy color, my breath caught in my throat. I stared, wordless.

"Shall we go back inside?" He turned, walking on without bothering to see if I followed.

All I could do is replay what happened in my head, over and over to try and make sense of it. His cool hands—not cold—and the gentleness of his touch. "Lord Kwan!" I called, well, shouted.

He stopped, looking back at me in a casual pace.

"I haven't asked you my question today."

His eyes gave a slow blink, reminding me how much like a tiger I first imagined him to be.

"Did—" No, that wasn't how I wanted to say it. Why was it so hard every time to ask this particular thing? "Are you the one who cured the village of the pox all those years ago?"

He watched me, saying nothing and keeping that soft smile on his face. His eyes closed, and he turned to continue for the house.

Snow began to fall, soft and silent.

I couldn't fall asleep easily that night, tossing and turning and confused as I was.

He'd kissed me. One of the most power Juneun, a handsome spirit, a noble lord, kissed me. It was not a violent sort of kiss, where a man might grab a girl and pull her against him. Nor was it a passion of mutual embrace, clinging to one another. It was something more innocent, and yet with just as much feeling.

But why? Why did it feel that way? Why did I think it felt that way?

My face grew hot the more vividly I remembered, or if I tried to picture what it might've looked like. If his eyes were opened or closed.

It had to be my imagination. That part of me always secretly running wild with wishes. He was engaged to a princess. Wasn't that the whole reason for the fuss around the house, preparing to host court in the summer? Of course I was imagining things that weren't there. And my imaginings held me hostage from any rest.

When I did finally fall asleep, I was glad to not have a single dream of it. Instead, my dreams were of a white stag, trudging through the snow, searching for something. A modest crown of brown antlers, and the steam of his breath, distinguished him from the tundra. He called out, a haunting echo of a cry, and waited in the silence for a response. When none came, he pressed on.

I didn't understand why, but it made me sad.

I woke late that following morning, finding a set of gifts on my table. Notes accompanied each, though not all from the same person. Some seemed as though they tried to compliment. Previous assumptions somewhat waved away. I didn't think anyone genuinely took notice or cared at all for my efforts. Some characters were harder to decipher, reading around them to help me guess at what the whole of the note said. Although there were no names to any of them, I treasured it all the same. Happier tears silently rolled from my face.

I didn't feel quite so alone now. Even though I didn't know who'd written any of them, I somehow felt valued by the acknowledgement. Hugging them close, I put the small collection of notes safely away, so that I could keep them.

One present was a new deel, lined with soft fur and lengthened a few inches shy of my ankle. Another was a brightly colored sash to keep the deel snug against me. A pair of thick boots, also lined with fur, and another containing heavy socks to help my feet fit in the boots better. The final one being a boar-hair brush.

They were not the very finest things, but I felt rich in that moment. So much joy swelling that guilt ensued for my having abandoned the shrine so selfishly.

I ate my breakfast, barely warm at that point, and hurried to put on my warm things. In doing so, I admired the comfort of the socks, the forested green of the boots, deep maroon of the deel, and brilliant cerulean of the sash. A quick brush of my hair, and I rushed out my door. I had to find that silver coin and give it to the shrine in thanks.

To my relief, the snowfall during the night didn't undo too much of my previous day's work. I wasted no time stomping through it, looking for where I'd dropped the coin. When I'd found the two holes my arms made, I squatted down and carefully filtered through the fresh ice. My hands were fast numb, forcing me to stop several times to spew hot breath into them and rub them together fiercely before continuing on.

I wasn't sure how long I'd been at it, but I eventually found the coin and held fast to it. My legs had stiffened from staying in the same position so long in the cold, but I commanded them onward. At the shrine, I didn't hesitate, tossing in the piece of silver and steepling my hands to give my sincerest apology and show of gratitude.

Chapter 26
The Way Things are Done

I worked tirelessly from there on, all winter, my soul renewed and happy.

When I completed my own dress, after having to redo a section more than once to Yua's standard, I did my best to lighten the burden of the other women by picking up extra chores for them. One commenting happily on my warmer wear, and another informing me that Lord Kwan sent the men to clear the garden pathways after they'd complained that they'd also wanted to go to the shrine and never could. After what I'd done, the men didn't have much of an excuse to ignore it. The human girl made a path. Lord Kwan was seen walking to the shrine as well in the path.

It wasn't my intent to make that the case, but I returned the smiles they offered. I didn't feel so much like an outsider anymore, or beneath them.

With the paths clear, I'd taken it upon myself to restock the tinder and wood beside each furnace that would heat the floors of the house. Morning and eve. When I found a shortage of tinder, I looked for a small hatchet I could use to make more. It was tedious work, and I had to concentrate so as to not let the cold numb me enough to slip and cut myself. Kenta had done so once, when mother was still alive, and seeing so much blood spill from his hand made me afraid to go near an ax of any kind for a long time. I couldn't avoid it forever though, and always stayed cautious.

Little by little, I made smaller pieces out of larger split wood and piled it. It was midday when I stopped, and return the hatchet. Placed back in its shed, I closed the door, checking to make sure it was secure against winter's touch.

Two men walked up, carrying shovels and other snow clearing tools. One appearing to need repairs as the metal head jostled on the end of the wood shaft. The two stretched and rolled their tired shoulders. I stepped aside, bowing politely; not the sort for a lord or an honored guest, but one slightly deeper than if I'd meant to say goodbye, as I thought that would best show my gratitude.

"Thank you for clearing the paths," I said.

They both looked at me then, seeming to only just notice I was standing there. One, who I recognized as the man who sent me for the salt my first summer here, gave me a deeply annoyed look.

"It's always to do with you," said the man. "Every time the master is on my ass, it's to do with you."

"Sen, stop," said the other, more quietly to better coax.

I retreated into myself, unsure of what it was I'd done.

"Had to speed up our work with the chimneys, work the farthest yard—no one went back there for decades!"

I felt cornered, not knowing what to do. Out of instinct, I tried to run.

He grabbed my arm, holding tight. "You sucked him off and got a cozy room and pretty dress out of it. Then you give him your ass regularly and suddenly you no longer have to do anything. His ugly, human whore."

"Let me go!" I shouted. His grip tightened, painfully so, and I couldn't break free.

"Sen, that's enough," said the other man, grabbing at Sen's shoulder to pull him off.

Sen swatted him off. "You go into his room regularly, alone. You sit in the saddle with him, galloping somewhere secluded. Now suddenly you think you own the place. We never had to labor in winter, it's the season of rest! Now we're out here for hours every day because Kwan's whore wanted to walk the gardens."

I slapped him. Terrified and unable to escape, my anger boiled over. I felt my heart pound, my ears burning, and my breath growing heavy. A few seconds after, I realized I slapped a spirit. A new horror took me, deepening when he turned back to me with a hateful glare.

"I might forgive you if you sucked me off. Maybe then I'd see if the fuss over you is worth it." He started to drag me back to the shed.

"Sen, stop. Let her go," argued the other man.

"Why? She's supposed to be a prisoner, right? So, she'll oblige us with a little ass after we've worked so hard to clear the snow for her. She might like a little snow in her."

I thrashed more fiercely, shouting at him to release me. Now, I wished I still had that hatchet, or anything I could use as a threat for my freeing, even if he was a spirit.

The other grabbed him. "You're going to get us in trouble. Just let her go before you do something stupid."

"Coming from a spirit who's about as powerful as Kurai piss. Don't forget that I outrank you still."

My eyes went to the other man, pleading for help. But he looked away.

"She's a little slut. She wanted it. Do you think Kwan is going to believe her over us? He's known us for more than half a century."

He shook, face crinkling and a frown forming. "You're that desperate to play with your cock, then go to one of the villages and claim you're a Juneun."

"Why do I need to leave when there's a village girl right here?"

Desperate, I slapped him again, hard and deliberate. I went to strike him a third time, only for him to catch my wrist. Before he could make his next threat, a hand ripped his from mine.

Lord Kwan, stony faced, stood there.

Sen's expression paled, and he fumbled for an excuse.

"You can leave Sen," said Lord Kwan. "You're no longer welcome on my lands, or that of any member of my family."

"You're not saying..." the words fled from Sen. "But, my lord."

With every excuse Sen made, Lord Kwan stayed silent, letting his wordless stare reign. He said nothing, making us wait. "I cannot trust you with the women who serve my house, then I have no use for you. You will not be serving me. Or my future bride. I do not want a reckless and lazy servant."

Sen opened his mouth, about to argue, until Kwan's face formed a scowl.

A strange feeling took the air, a kind of magic, one that made me feel frail and uncomfortable.

Sen swallowed his words, giving a bow and marching off. The other also bowed, setting down the tools and awaiting his judgment. Replacing his superior, I expected.

"You may also leave," said Lord Kwan. It surprised us both. "I have no need for a weak and cowardly servant either." He pushed his long hair behind his should with the flick of his wrist, dismissive of all else.

The man, wide eyed with shock, bowed and left in a more somber pace.

I stayed where I was, holding the tender spot on my arm. Confusion wrapped around my brain. When both men were out of sight, Lord Kwan looked to me, irritated and with ample disapproval.

"Put these things away, Hisa," said Lord Kwan, low. "And bring me a white tea." He left, headed for the house.

What did he think of me? Or the scene as a whole? I didn't get the chance to collect myself and explain, to ask questions.

My hands shook as I collected the dropped tools, my fingers slipping from the door twice as I pulled it open. In the shed, I felt sick. Sen's words ringing in my ears. I'd been so happy to think I was finally accepted in a small way, never realizing that my effort to prove my worth put others on edge. It felt like, no matter what I did, I was causing some sort of trouble.

What hurt the most was the repeated phrase against me. Something that churned up the memory of the rumors about me in the village. Was that all anyone thought of me? I didn't know why Lord Kwan brought me anywhere or asked me to do anything. All I knew was that I was here to serve out a sentence, temporarily forfeiting my freedom to save my brother.

Lord Kwan's sharp words came back, and the image of Syaoran with one of the other women. Again, I had so many questions. As I waited for the tea to brew, my mind was a tempest, inquiries loud in my ears, frustration pounding my head, while the rest of me tried to rid myself of trembling.

Taking the kettle to his room, going through the expected motions, neither of us said anything. I'd poured the whole of the kettle into the teapot and served him. No offer was given to me. He sat, silent, sipping from his cup. When it emptied, I refilled, waiting in the uncomfortable stillness. In all the times I'd come and served his tea, I'd never felt as alienated as I did in that moment. I shifted where I sat, my leg threatening to fall asleep, while my eyes looked to anywhere in search of words to break this quiet discontent.

In a way, it felt like I'd done something wrong. I knew I didn't, but the continued wordlessness whispered it.

At last, after he'd finished his second cup and refilled it, he offered a share to me. "Juro came mid-autumn."

I stopped, startled by his words and casual tone.

"He was quite crestfallen to find you were unable to greet him or see him off."

I stiffened. "I didn't know he'd even come, my lord."

He met my eye then, a gentleness to them, and that hint of a smile with it. Though, there was something that seemed like he was planning. "He commanded that I provide you with whatever you desire in his stead."

"What?" I whispered, confused by it all.

"He said it's the payment owed for all the years of bringing ginseng tea, blessing the land, and now for closing the clay pit."

"Closed the clay pit? So, it's flat earth now, like the rest?"

He ignored my puzzlement. "What will he think if I say to him that your deepest desire was for a first kiss? I suppose he'll insist that it ought to have been him to deliver such a gift."

A shiver shot up my spine. "Lord Kwan, please—" I stopped when he tilted his head and I realized: he was teasing me.

"I suppose I should keep it secret this time. Lest he feel slighted by a trusted friend. Even if he has no right to command anything of me to begin with."

I felt my cheeks pinking, and sighed in an attempt to push down my feelings.

He looked away, to a distant something that I couldn't see. "I don't know how to apologize to you. For Sen's actions."

I looked away from the distant nothing, back to him. "You don't owe me that, my lord. It was his behavior, not yours. If anything, I should apologize for not thanking you for coming when you did."

"You don't owe me any thanks or apology for it. I'm ashamed. This is my house, and I allowed this kind of behavior to fester."

I didn't know what to say. I could see the guilt on his shoulders, and I wanted to do something to help, but I didn't know how. With all my courage, I did something I knew I shouldn't, and took his hand in mine. I wasn't supposed to. We weren't equals, or close enough friends, for me to take the initiative. He was a lord, and I was only a village girl and servant.

His head turned, quick, bewilderment painted across his face.

"You can't blame yourself for what other people do. It's Sen who should be ashamed, not you. You put things right. And you can't know what everyone is doing at all times, no one can."

He stared, jaw slack and slow blinking.

I kept my gentle hold on his hand, cool to the touch.

He reclaimed his expression. "Did you not arrive to take responsibility for your brother's actions?"

Now it was my turn to reflect his bewildered look.

He turned his hand over, gently putting his fingers around mine. "Thank you, for your comfort. It's rare that I find myself in the company of a friend."

I started to smile, sliding back into my confusion. "But, Yua and Syaoran… aren't they friends, my lord?"

"In a way," said Lord Kwan, cocking his head in reading my expression. "But each has their own unspoken agenda as well. You speak on what your objectives are, making it easy to predict what you're up to."

"When you say it like that, it doesn't sound very nice."

He stayed silent, though I swore I saw something like laughter in his eyes. It was strange—like a part of him was sealed off, wanting to come out.

"It's why I enjoy your company. Someone who's there, simply to be in the company of another, brings a comfort and pleasantness with them."

I smiled, leaving my hand right where it was.

"Do you have a question for me today?"

A chuckle escaped me. I'd been so caught up in an ever-changing storm of emotions, that I'd forgotten about that. "When I'm free to go home again, can I come back to visit my friend?"

His eyes took me in, as though he needed time to understand. Or, perhaps it was his usual pause and I'd wanted there to be something more. "Of course."

My smile brightened.

Lord Kwan left a week later, kept away for nearly a month. As spring arrived, and the snows began to melt, the house was newly abuzz to prepare for hosting court. Three young men came back with Lord Kwan, newly in his service, each giving me a curious stare. They'd never met a human before.

While there were questions to be sure, they stayed devoted to their task. The women, meanwhile, hurried to get courtly clothing made for the new arrivals. I helped where I could, doing my best to alleviate some of the burden.

Days fluctuated in their climate, often starting cold, only to warm enough by midday to take off my deel, and then need it again before evening. A heavy mist might start the day, only for the sun to show by midmorning and be covered by clouds before sunset; sometimes the clouds came early and the sun never touched the ground.

One hazy morning, as I lit the furnaces and went to feed the koi so that more attention could go to the making of clothes, I spotted a peculiar thing at the edge of the water. A young rabbit had fallen in, looking as though it'd drowned. With pity, I hurried to toss in the koi food and get it out of the water. It kicked, weak as it was, showing that it still had life left; though it was cold and exhausted. My heart hurt for it. It'd somehow gotten itself separate from its family and into trouble.

Like with a stray kitten, I tried to revive it by tucking the poor thing into my deel and tightening the sash to prevent it from sliding out. It felt so cold and weak against my stomach that I worried I'd come too late.

It was one thing to trap a rabbit for eating later, but another thing entirely to just let something die. I kept a quiet prayer going for it while I continued with the chores no one wanted to do, or which took too much time. Every so often, I would peek down my deel to see its nose going, breathing, still alive.

When every task was finished, I set to finding where it could have come from. Lord Kwan likely wouldn't approve of rabbits burrowing in his gardens. But if it was hidden enough and out of the way, maybe he wouldn't find out. Pesky as they might be to such an immaculate landscape, they were just little creatures, living things, that didn't know better.

Its fur was a dark brown, thick to stave off winter's cold, and coarse, making it slow to dry. I remembered Syaoran saying about my mindless wandering and looking suspicious. Though, I didn't know how to look for a rabbit hole casually, without drawing attention and raising brows.

"Hisa?"

I jumped at the sound of Lord Kwan's voice. I'd been so engrossed in my search, I didn't notice him walk across the newly emerging grass towards me. I acknowledged and bowed, trying not to shift too much and disturb my hidden animal. My mind flooded with worry, wondering if I'd looked like I was up so something or if a different matter caused him to seek me out.

"Still taking on an abundance of chores?" said Lord Kwan, his hint of a smile showing. "Even after I'd dictated otherwise?"

"I'm not one for staying idle, my lord."

"I see that," said Lord Kwan, a curiousness in his eyes. "What do you have hidden there?"

I looked down, not seeing any sign of how he could know I was hiding anything, and back. Over and over as I tried to come up with some compelling explanation.

"Hisa?"

Guilt washed over me. I couldn't bear to break his trust, and carefully produced the small rabbit from the warmth and safety of my deel. It squirmed in protest, though still too weak to do much else. "I found it in the pond," I said. Whispered, really. And tried to strengthen my voice. "It was soaked, and so cold and exhausted, I thought—if I could just get it warmed and rested and find…" My words failed when he reached to pick up the rabbit in a slow, deliberate motion.

He stared at it, watching as it curled into itself with a shiver. "You might have saved me a bit of trouble."

"What do you mean, my lord?"

His gaze moved back to me, that hint of a smile broadening. "I have several nieces and young cousins who are not yet old enough to come to court. Now, I have an idea how to make it up to them."

I repeated his conclusion, puzzled by the lack of context.

"I'll have Syaoran find the burrow," said Lord Kwan. "Catch them, clean them up and tame them. Then I can send them to live a life of luxury as a pet."

"So, you won't chase them out?"

"Did you want me to?"

I shook my head.

He cocked a brow at me. "Were you intending to keep it."

"No, my lord," I said, hurriedly. "I only wanted to make sure it would be okay, and put it back to the wild with its family."

For a long time, we held each other's gaze, measuring intentions.

"They'll be well looked after then?" I asked, not knowing what else to do or say and wanting to break the stillness. "The parents too?"

He gave me a knowing look and walked away, rabbit gently in hand.

The equinox had passed. Spring came into its full. Grass grew thick, in need of taming, which the new men saw to. Flowers budded and bloomed. Gravel and flat stones were meticulously lain into new walkways and spaces where court would take place. Stands were thoughtfully erected, each reserved for some thing that would be viewed once guests arrived.

It didn't make much sense to me, since it seemed like it'd be a far easier task to adjust the courtyard and gardens around the house rather than to lay out new foundations. But only the most important of guests would be allowed to wander the house grounds, and fewer allowed to stay. It was all so divided, as if to say that some spirits were less worthy than others. Even if some could perform godly feats of magic and others none at all.

It wasn't quite that way in the village, where we all had to rely on each other to pull through, especially in hard times. There were those more skilled or more experienced or wiser that we might look to in some circumstances. Other villages might be better with their harvests, or produce more livestock, and we bartered with them. But I never thought of one being superior to the other. Perhaps I was naïve.

"I'm telling you, there's been a weird smell lately," said Syaoran. His fox ears pinned back, and his posture looked unnerved by something.

"That nose of yours is overreacting," said Yua, dismissively. "Unless there's evidence of some wry thing, don't bother the master. Things are stressful enough as it is." She went about the work being done, taking notes as she paused to study the progress.

"It'll be more stressful when whatever it is disrupts the viewing and upcoming announcements," said Syaoran, sour in his tone.

I could be remised for forgetting that the purpose of Lord Kwan holding court, despite his dislike of it, was to announce his engagement to a princess of the Juneun. Over the time spent here, where I'd formed a friendship with my jailor (odd as that sounded), all else fell away from my concerns at times. Lord Kwan wasn't in love with her, he'd said, and spoke little of her at all. It was an arranged marriage, as I understood it; something tragic in my mind. I didn't understand how anyone could make two people marry when they didn't love or even like each other. Perhaps, if one were in love and the other in desperate state—though it still sounded like a tragedy.

I wasn't ignorant of my own state, my lack of beauty and wealth. Even so, I didn't think I could be compelled to marry for money. Listening to how the other women spoke, sometimes, about what brought them into Lord Kwan's house, I wondered if I'd be seen as selfish or stupid if I refused a rich man too blind to see what I was. Considering the rumors now, that may be the case. My brothers, and my father, might be understanding; but someone from another village might twist it into something cold.

In trying to avoid a weighted pain in my heart, I began to busy myself with imagining what the princess was like as I brought things to and from the site. My imagination painted her to have the silkiest black hair, so long that it trailed behind her. Porcelain skin, since she wouldn't have to ever work outside, and could stay comfortably in the shade every summer. She probably wore the most beautiful dress, an array of colors and patterns. She must have a voice that was perfect for singing. And she smiled a lot, having lived a life without having to labor or go hungry.

I spent so much time thinking what the future would look like, imagining that I'd stay to have tea and my usual lessons in their company, of showing the improvement to my drawing, that I missed Yua calling me.

When I did snap from my daydreams to notice her, she held a severe look on her face and bid me to go to her. I did, embarrassed by my lack of awareness.

"Come along," said Yua, impatient. "The water is already running."

I repeated her statement as I followed behind.

"For the tub. Looking our best does take time, otherwise we'd stall until the night before. And there's still the fittings to be had, to make sure no adjustments will be necessary."

"You mean for the clothes we sewed?"

"Obviously," said Yua, a little annoyed that I fumbled in trying to keep up with her agenda. "It's not something that can be put on alone, so we're to be divided into two groups the morning court opens. Someone will be sent to wake you an hour before dawn. You'll go to Lin's room, since it's the second biggest and assist where you can."

"Yes, ma'am," I said. It was already confusing, but I didn't want to provoke her any further.

In the bath house, the small assembly of women waited, undressing only after Yua and I entered and closed the door behind us. The tub was near full, and oils had already been added. I wasn't shy about a group bath; we did similar in my village at the river, our river.

There was talk almost instantly about what will happen after court. If a bigger household will be brought in, and if that meant any of their own positions hung in the balance. Defensive points were made, justifying their necessity to the estate. One of the girls was teased for her indiscretion in visiting Syaoran on occasion.

"Of course, you won't have to worry, Hisa," said Lin. "Lord Kwan likes you well enough, and you're stuck here anyway."

I allowed my brow to bend and plead my case. "If he did want me away, though, I wouldn't argue it. I miss my family."

"That's something we can all relate to," said Lin, a heavy laugh in her tone. "I haven't seen my family in over a century."

"It's ninety-six years for me."

"Seventy-one for me."

"About forty for me."

"Lord Kwan doesn't allow you to visit them?" I asked.

"It's not the way things are done," said Yua. "It's not merely to work for a lord, it's the adoption of a lifestyle."

"They don't do that in the human world?"

I shook my head. "At least, not in the villages. Everyone goes home to their families at the end of the day."

"That sounds weird."

"So how do you bring yourself and your family up if you always return home like an ordinary laborer?"

I twisted my face, not understanding.

"You know, to gain more titles and wealth, your status with the ruling families and how much consideration your given."

"And if you're lucky enough to be picked as a mistress. The more a lord or a prince or king likes you, the better your treated and pampered."

"If I were a prince's mistress," said Lin, "My father would be gifted lands and a lesser title."

"It's the best we ladies can do for our families, since we're not noble and stand little chance of marrying well."

"Sometimes at all."

I felt barraged by the information, the revelation of it all making my head to pound. I had a hundred questions, and was too meek to ask any. They seemed like they'd be personal and cause offense.

"But Lord Kwan is fond of Hisa, he might command her to stay anyway."

I broke from my thoughts and idle scrubbing in that moment.

"But I just realized, if Hisa leaves, that means we won't be able to skip out on chores now and again. It's work, work, work all the time."

"And the men get lazy after a while. Can you believe they have the nerve to say we have it easy?"

"Maybe we should all pretend to be sick when Lord Kwan is away and make them pick up the slack," said Lin. "That'd show them just how much work we do."

"You'll do no such thing," said Yua. "Slight the master like that over your pride, and you'll be out the gate in an instant."

The quiet from her scolding didn't last for long.

"If the village girls are all that hard working, maybe Lord Kwan could be convinced to adopt one every few years."

Yua shot her a look.

"Humans are short lived," said Lin. "It's different for them. I don't think many live to see their first century. A mere decade is probably a lifetime."

"It is a long time," I said, shy, if only to get expecting gazes off of me.

"The only one who'd really know is Gi. He's been fascinated with humans forever."

"Probably because he started off collecting the offerings and saw them more often."

"I heard he used to get Syaoran to disguise him as a villager or something, and would sneak off to be with the village girls he especially liked."

"That would make sense why Lord Kwan keeps changing his station. Keeping him out of trouble. But trouble just seems to follow that poor fool no matter what."

"He is a little handsome, though, when he's not armored." That garnered teasing from all the other women. Even Yua's strict features softened into an amused smile.

I felt more at ease among them than I'd had in almost two years. For the time, we were just girls around each other. Though, I was still perplexed and a little uncomfortable with their more strategic talk.

"Are you men getting a good view?" announced Syaoran from beyond the paper-paned doors.

At once, we all sank ourselves a little deeper into the water and covered with our arms. A slew of accusations, demands to leave, and names were shouted.

Syaoran laughed. "I'm only kidding. There's no one here. But I can have a look, can't I?"

More of the same came from the women.

He snickered, his shadow walking away.

"Of course, the real prize for us would be if Lord Kwan decided to take a mistress, but Syaoran is a good enough second pick with his standing in the house."

"If he picks you and makes it official."

"Maybe one of us will be lucky and catch the eye of a visiting lord during court," said Lin.

"You'll get nowhere with any of the lords, behaving as you are now," said Yua.

I thought it all strange. I wouldn't want to be someone's mistress, there on the whim of some lord who could easily cast me out. There wasn't a security in that—there wasn't a love in that. While the chance was likely impossible, I made myself a wordless promise to refuse any offer of becoming a mistress to anyone.

Chapter 27
A New Proposal

The day finally arrived. We'd all prepared the best we could in the previous day, staying up as late as we dared to make sure it was all perfect. Lord Kwan had called for me to serve his tea, though we held no conversation that eve. I supposed he was nervous, and wanted the company a while. Something I was happy to provide for my friend. In that quiet, however, my mind kept going back to how he'd kissed me the previous winter. It was all I could do to keep my face from pinking up, or fidget with the discomfort I'd caused myself.

When I woke up, I was too tired to think of anything except to collect every piece I would need and walk to Lin's room. My hair had already been cut to even out its unruly growth. A bit shorter now, though I could hide most of my scarred cheek beneath the remaining length. It was the best I could do. We'd been told to present ourselves to impress. And I couldn't compare to the natural beauty of a spirit as it was. In my walk to Lin's room, I kept thinking about what I would give to have Fumei's beauty just for a day.

The dressing really was an ordeal.

Starting with what I normally knew, with some exception on how the blouses ought to be set. Help was needed with the additional pieces, each one color coded to show where we ranked in the house. Mine were earthen tones rather than any deep or vibrant hue of Lord Kwan's colors.

The first wrapped around me from my mid-hip to just an inch below the top hem of my dress. The second piece wrapped around that stayed in line, though allowed the top and bottom of the first to show by two inches. The third wrapped around that, allowing only half an inch of the previous to show at either end. Then the sash, dark red, was carefully wrapped around and around to keep everything comfortably (though I still felt rigid and suffocated by it) in place; Yua explained that the purpose was to keep my posture correct and prevent too much fatigue at the end of the day. Finally, the red and gray braided ropes, as thick as my thumb, to hang decoratively in line with the sash and dangle free. Something to identify which member of Lord Kwan's clan we belonged to.

A hurried breakfast, and we were set to work. Except that an angry scream disturbed the quiet. A trail of mud was found on one stretch of the veranda. Whatever tracks were there were smudged and unidentifiable. A few suggested that whatever it was had claws.

Syaoran cast his spell after an investigation, clearing away the mess. "I told Yua I smelled something."

"Lord Juro is supposed to attend court," said Lin. "Are you sure it wasn't him? The mess was right outside the room we readied for him."

"As far as I'm aware, Lord Juro hasn't arrived yet," said Syaoran, annoyed. "Keep an eye for anything out of the ordinary. Anything. And report it to me."

I started to worry, and kept looking over my shoulder. Nothing dangerous would dare come to Lord Kwan's home, right? But if it was powerful enough to get past the walls and guards without being noticed, maybe it was just as malevolent. What could I do against something like that? I probably wouldn't even be capable of outrunning it, especially not in my court wear.

I shuffled back and forth, bringing things as quickly as I could from the house to the event space, wary of some horrible thing as well as a possible, uncomfortable, run in with Lord Juro. In my to-and-fro, I noticed something odd in the corner of the west garden, as though the earth had been turned over. Setting down my tray of sweets, I took a closer look. Something had been there, tearing up the roots of the bushes, and the extent of the mess went further than I initially thought.

Coming back to my tray, in a new rush to deliver it and find Syaoran, I almost missed it. There was a sweet milk-bread missing, and a smudge of mut at the lip of the silver carrier.

I handed it off quickly, lifting a part of my dress to give me greater reach with my legs as I scoured for any sight of Syaoran. It wasn't quite midmorning yet, but I could hear the distant murmur of guests arriving. Running the veranda and peeking in doors, I finally saw the tips of animal ears and the owner basking in the warm sun just off the veranda.

"Syaoran, I found—" I stopped, in both words and strides. They weren't fox ears.

The cat-eared man with white hair peeked up, turning his head to see me. A stranger. My feet carried me back the way I came, but halted at his command.

"Come here, girl."

Though I was afraid, my legs slowed to a stop, turning me gradually. I looked at him, now standing, dressed finely—finer than I'd ever seen Lord Kwan—though my eyes kept going between his white ears, yellow cat eyes, and white tails. I took leaden steps towards him while trying to hide behind my scrawny arms.

He stepped up, meeting me at the edge of the veranda, giving me a studying look as his nose twitched. When I stopped, he leaned forward and inhaled deep. "Human? You're a human—You're Kwan's human. I heard about you."

I said nothing, holding perfectly still.

He cocked a brow, his face twisting into a question. "Most servants bow to a lord."

I sucked in a gasp, and made to bow the best my dress would allow. His hand took my chin less than a second later, white, claw-like fingernails brushing against my skin, and lifted my head to meet his eye.

"You're about as tall as I figured. I just thought you'd be more..." he tilted my face from one side to the next. "Well, I thought you'd be more." He let go, straightening himself. "Are all humans like you?"

I didn't know what he meant, let alone how to answer. My hand went to the scar on my cheek.

"No, not that." He crossed his arms, his ears swiveling to some distant sound. "Your hands are thicker, and skin darker."

"I'm from a farming village, my lord," I finally answered, though wished I had spoken with a steadfast voice rather than a quick one.

He looked me over again. "You don't know who I am, do you?"

I shook my head.

He grinned. "I imagine you must be looking for Lord Juro's room, weren't you?"

"N-no, I wasn't—"

He pulled me close to point. "It's right there."

It wasn't.

"No, wait. I believe that's your room. His is on the opposite end. And I'm right on top of you."

"What?" My skin prickled and my heart picked up pace. A warm shiver ran through me from where his hot breath grazed my ear.

"My room. It's on the upper floor." His smile turned playful, as though the conversation was innocent. "Syaoran is trying to hide in the tea house. Your master's brothers will be here soon."

I stepped back, testing if I could freely leave. With a departing bow to make up for my manners, I bolted away. I could feel how hot my face became in the short interaction, a part of me almost forgetting why I was looking for Syaoran in the first place.

I was kept more out of sight than anything, sent to take care of things or fetch from the house. It didn't bother me. The Juneun lords and ladies made me nervous. They kept looking over at me, perplexed; though I suppose if few or any humans were in service, I was a novelty.

The set up was beautiful. The bonsai displays gracefully placed for leisurely viewing. Though, it fell short in a few ways when compared to the lavishly dressed guests as they walked by.

Just past noon, as I sweated and tried to not show my discomfort and tiredness, Lord Kwan made his appearance with four of his brothers. They were all brilliantly dressed in robes of their clan colors, and holding themselves regal above all else. One of few differences between them being the ornament which tied up their hair, indicating which was the eldest to the youngest.

An announcement was in the making, though I missed a great deal as I refilled wine cups.

"So, I present the Princess Eumeh."

Soft applause erupted, approving awes in tandem with it as I stood straight and formal.

Eumeh walked from her entourage in a dress layered in spring colors of silk, appearing to float with every step. She was prettier than my imagination. Though her hair had been styled to keep it from dragging on the ground, and I couldn't have pictured the elaborate jewelry that adorned her ears, neck, wrists, and even the top of her head. Everything about her was elegant as she accepted Lord Kwan's offered hand. A petite set of antlers crowned her head, a Juneun princess.

"And her intended, Lord Urekkato."

The cat Juneuen from before walked up, handsome and dignified, making a polite bow as he took Eumeh's hand. He placed a tender kiss on her knuckles, righting himself and facing the crowd with a content expression.

"As promised, the princess will marry the man who brought Gumiho's head to our king. So, the honor goes to the Cat Clan prince."

The applause resumed at much the same volume, though slight puzzlement marred their expressions and muttering between several of the guests took place.

I was just as confused, looking from Lord Kwan, to the betrothed couple, to his unhappy brothers, and the crowd around me. I'd been told that Lord Kwan, alone, was the only one powerful enough to keep Gumiho at bay, and that he was arranged to wed the princess. My eyes found Syaoran across the newly made plaza, looking distressed as he tried to keep his formality. Needing answers for what to do, I turned my gaze to Yua and the other women, noting that a distance was given to the brothers of Lord Kwan.

Another man, older somehow, stood among the guests with deep displeasure.

When my pitcher emptied of wine, I left to dutifully replenish. A reprieve was given when Lin informed me that servants of the Cat prince would take over the tasks. I didn't ask anything further, leaving the jug and assuming it'd be found.

My feet throbbed, my shoulders ached, my midsection felt like something planned to slice me in half over the course of a year. I was tired too. So much so that I wanted nothing more than to have something to eat and get to bed. It wasn't proper, but I couldn't stand it anymore and removed my wood sandals and cotton socks to let my feet touch the earth. I sighed in relief, enjoying the soft, cool feel of the summer grass.

I lingered a while. Too long I supposed, since I could hear the start of raised voices in a heated conversation between men. Not wanting to get tangled in it, or to know a word of it that might get me into trouble, I went as quickly as my legs would allow, away from the storehouse and to the veranda. Whatever the reason, I was sure I could wait it out in the shade of the trees beside the shrine.

I climbed the veranda, checking that my feet wouldn't be trailing mud over my chosen short cut. Though, with a second of consideration, I decided to head to my room first to change. I didn't want to get my ear chewed out if I'd gotten the dress or any of its pieces dirty or damaged—not a thread out of place.

"Hisa," called Juro.

My spine went rigid, but I couldn't ignore a guest to Lord Kwan's house. I slowed to a stop, taking in a breath and a prayer to keep my composure, and turned to greet him.

He walked up, an odd, sheepish smile on his toad-like face. "I was near heartbroken not to have spoken with you on my last visit. Hard at work in service to my friend."

"Lord Kwan did relay your disappointment, my lord," I said, trying to sound as distant and formal as I could. After a year and a half, I'd picked up on how the servants spoke, particularly towards a superior, and did my best to imitate it now.

"Disappointment is an understatement," said Juro, taking a lengthy breath through his nostrils. "Naturally sweet. So many have a slight sourness or bitterness to them."

"I wouldn't know, my lord."

He waved aside the polite statement. "They think I don't know what they say about me, and that's fine. At the end of any given day or night I'm still a titled lord."

"As you say, Lord Juro."

There was a hint of annoyance at my addressing him. I put on a smile, not wanting to provoke.

He retrieved his expression, and gave a playful undertone to his next set of words. "You needn't address me as *Lord* Juro."

"I am only a servant," I said.

"For now, yes. But, the happiness of today has prompted me." He stepped forward, mud building in his wake and causing me to break my posture as I stepped away.

"My lord, calm yourself, please!" My words came out fast in alarm.

He looked down. "Oh, you will be used to that, I'm sure, coming from a poor village."

I blinked, trying to piece together what he alluded to.

"You do look more like a lady with proper clothes now. And your hair will grow to be more feminine with time."

He snatched my hand. I admit that I expected his skin to feel slimy or sticky, though it looked like the hands of any ordinary man, if not discolored to a more gray and yellow tone. It did not.

They were like any others and lacking in dirt. I stared at his gentle hold, blinking as what my eyes told me didn't match what my skin told me.

"I know you've undoubtedly heard about my habits. But I promise, I will make you a good husband."

"Husband?" I repeated. The hair on my neck stood.

"I want your smell all around my house, and in my bed."

"You can't be saying this to me, my lord." I tried to pull away.

His fingers tightened only enough to prevent me, and his eyes gave a plea. "My house and lands are not nearly as vast. But if it pleases you, I will build it grander than Lord Kwan's estate. I'm told you're fond of walks between the walls, and take refuge in the shade. And that you have a love for apricots. You know that I can bless the lands to be the most fertile, and so I will install an entire grove for you."

"You're planning when I haven't said—"

"I may still keep a mistress. Maybe two. But I will always return to your sweet smell, knowing you will patiently wait for me."

More mud accumulated around him, spilling over my toes. I looked down with worry, my other hand dropping my sandals to try and keep the dress from touching any of it.

"And we might be blessed and fertile as well that you will produce fine children, fragrant and divine."

My head whipped back to him. "Children?"

"Eight or nine," said Juro. "I don't want to be too greedy."

"Nine?"

"Do you prefer the higher number?"

I pulled my hand free. "Lord Juro, I plan to serve out my sentence and go home to my father and my brothers—"

"Yes, of course. And I will ask your father's permission, though I expect he'd approve of our love. I am a lord and can provide well for his daughter, more than a villager could hope to dream."

I felt my face start to heat. From humiliation, from shock, but mostly from anger. He wasn't listening to me, assuming I'd already agreed—that I was willing, happy. I wanted to shout, wanted to smack him! But I knew if it came to that, I couldn't put up a fight. Nor could I expect someone to rescue me. Juro wasn't a servant over stepping his place in the house; he was an honored guest, a lord among the Juneun.

"I believe you are blushing," said Juro.

"I'm—"

He reached for my hand again. I pulled away and stepped back, wincing.

"Is it my face?" asked Juro, a touch of sadness to his voice.

It took me by surprise, the bravado vanishing from him before I looked at him again. "What? N-no, of course not. It's just—"

"I know I'm not a naturally handsome man. I didn't think that would matter to a human, but I can change my face if it'll make you happy."

"That's not what I—"

My shoulders went up and my neck tucked in on instinct as I saw his face twist and contort. It went from something resembling a frog to a normal man, though his skin was still dark gray with a brown and yellow tint. My eyes went wide and I squirmed, uncomfortable with what I'd witnessed.

"Not this one either, my love?"

I couldn't stand it. As he came closer, reaching for my hand, I bolted away. Lifting my dress to my knees, I ran around the corner and down to hide in my room. In my rage, I took off the damned thing as quick as I could without tearing it. When one of the knots wouldn't come loose, I gave up, leaning my back on the nearest wall and sliding down to curl into a ball. I couldn't take it. All the teasing at my expense from these high lords, the stares from strangers, and how I was talked about as though I weren't right there beside the other women. I was frustrated by it all, and tired of being compared to standards that were impossible for me to reach.

Was that what prompted this?

That I was so far beneath any prettiness that I ought to rejoice at Juro's proposal—my only prospect? My fingers left their place on my knees, touching my scars, the lumpy texture that distinguished them from the rest of my skin. And my arms and chest too, were speckled with tiny pox scars.

It was a running joke, I thought, to make me feel like some handsome, high lord Juneun found me desirable with insinuating comments. That Juro assumed I'd leap at the chance to marry him, grovel at his muddy feet in gratitude.

I felt the tears roll down my face, and sobbed a long while.

Hunger eventually drove me to leave my room. I hadn't eaten since dawn, and couldn't have much with how tight everything was tied on me. Now calm, I undid the knots, and changed into my rough-spun clothes.

I caught a glimpse of myself in the vanity mirror, something I usually avoided. Looking at myself, I did appear pathetic. Lowborn. A pretty dress and decent manners didn't change that. And it made me angry all over again. Though, rather than cry, I took the disassembled pieces of my court dress and used them to cover up the mirror.

Clutching my door, I prayed for strength. Sliding them open, I steadied myself with a deep inhale. Immediately I accidentally kicked something. Looking down, my wood sandals and cotton socks sat there neatly, or had been before my foot collided with them. Not a spec of mud on them.

A part of me regretted having run. The rest of me reminded that part why I'd run.

Yua had told us that after breakfast, it'd be left to us to find means of eating. The cooks would be busy with catering to Lord Kwan's guests. A larger household staff might handle it better, though we'd all assumed he was engaged and his betrothed would bring in her own staff to join. It seemed now that he'd no intention of bringing in extra workers, or to ever hold court again.

Walking to the kitchens, I heard Syaoran's laughter. I was hungry, but my curiosity triumphed. He'd looked woefully uncomfortable the last time I saw him. Now he was standing beside the koi pond, and Urekkato with him.

"She ran away from him?" asked Syaoran.

"In tears, I heard," said Urekkato.

"What could Juro have said to make her cry?"

"I think it was that he changed his face and it frightened her. Humans have a low tolerance for magic. They scare at anything they don't understand."

I frowned. My blood began to boil and my brow turned sharp as my fingers furled into fists.

"He's consoling himself with one of my maids, now," said Urekkato, as casual in his tone as it might be over small talk about the weather. "I told you it'd be easy to make a fool out of him. The whole court will be talking about how even a human won't have him."

"And your maid?" asked Syaoran, equally casual.

"She's low enough that being his mistress would be an elevation. Shame, considering how pretty she is. I guess she gave up on sneaking into my room, she figured she may as well try and win over another lord."

I marched over, my ears ringing. I didn't know what I'd do, what I'd say, but I'd put an end to it somehow. Syaoran caught sight of me, plastering on a pleasant expression that quickly became quizzical.

"Hisa?"

I shoved him. I wasn't strong enough to actually do anything, and he stepped back out of shock more than from whatever force I could deliver. Still, it felt good. I shoved him again.

"Hisa, what are you doing?"

I didn't answer. A plan started to form in my mind. With every inch I could make him step back, I'd push him right into the pond. I shoved again, hard.

"Hisa, calm down."

I ignored him, and shoved again. On my final effort, he disappeared. I fell, catching myself on my palms. It wasn't enough to humiliate me this time. I was too upset to be embarrassed by a stumble. Instead, I glared over my shoulder at his dumbfounded face, and got to my feet.

Urekkato laughed. I ignored it.

"You think it's funny to toy with people's feelings?" I yelled. The rational part of me pleaded to stop, warning me about consequences. And yet, my outrage overruled my sensibility. "How could you be so soulless? There's nothing funny about getting someone's hopes up, for their dreams, and putting them in a position to get hurt. It's not a game!"

"We were just encouraging our friend," said Urekkato, a feigning of ignorance. "He's not the most confident, so a few words of affirmation wasn't supposed to hurt."

I glared at him next. "You knew exactly what you were doing. It was cruel. And you'll stand there pretending to be his friend while quietly waiting for him to fall."

"Hisa—"

"You're speaking to a prince, little girl," said Urekkato, annoyance plain in both tone and expression.

"Then act like one," I said, still yelling.

"Watch it," warrened the Cat princeling.

"If you were my prince, I wouldn't fight for you, not after seeing how you treat someone you *say* is a friend and who trusted you." My head screamed at me to shut up, to stop, to apologize and beg forgiveness, but my anger wasn't yet done with my tongue.

"Hisa, listen," said Syaoran.

But I had no intention of listening to anything he had to say in that moment. "And I'm ashamed I ever called you my friend if you were willing to do something like this so easily, just for your own entertainment. Your skin might run hot, but your heart runs colder than ice." With that, I stormed off, shaking with rage and breath gone from me.

"I think that's almost enough syllables to make a poem," said Urekkato, a false cheer to his voice.

I marched on without so much as a glance behind me.

A part of me felt relief, exhilaration. Another part weighed with dread and guilt. I'd yelled at Syaoran. I'd yelled at a Juneun prince. All the stories from merchants about the punishments dealt by a lord towards a servant or a stranger with the audacity to insult them came flooding back. Lord Kwan was an understanding person, and forgave my mistakes and accidental trespasses. But I'd never done something so deliberately brazen as this, and to a personal guest staying in his house.

Chapter 28
Lord Kwan VII

"This is an insult to the family!"

Kwan ignored his father's roaring.

"Are you listening to me? For centuries, everyone believed you, alone, held some power against Gumiho. And that soft-faced princeling is the one to bring her head to the royal court! Do you know what position you've put us in?"

"I'm sure the clan will recover," said Kwan, disinterested.

"I'm to suffer my youngest sons allying themselves with Kurai—former or not, they're still devils among us. And now to lose this connection to the crown. Have you lost all sense, boy?"

Kwan said nothing, maintaining a distant stare.

"Father, please," said Kwang. "You know Borsi and the others swore their fealty to our family. The betrayal was not done willingly. And you forget that sixteen clan lords snuffed out Gumiho, with Kwan taking the lead. For the first time in centuries, a unified force came down on a single foe. Even so, two of the lords lost their lives."

"Do not make excuses for your brother!"

Kwang went rigid, shoulders stiff, jaw set, and brow somewhere between a scowl and a plea.

"The princess was undecided," said Kwan. "So, the king demanded a trial to decide who to pick. Urekkato brought Gumiho's head back. That was the condition."

"But, surely you cut the bitch's head from her shoulders. Not a small lord still wet behind the ears," said Beom, goading.

"Shut up," demanded their father. "I have it on good authority Eumeh already decided on Kwan, and he refused it. His arrogance knows no bounds."

"I have other brothers you could have sent."

"I sent you specifically," growled their father. "You had one job in the royal court, and you still managed to fail the family."

Kwan shifted his gaze. "As I said. I have other unmarried brothers. It is not my fault you chose poorly among us."

A threat now loomed in his voice, "If we were not surrounded by guests, I would whip sense into you."

Kwan held eye contact; stone faced an unimpressed.

With a pensive sigh, the Tiger Clan patriarch reeled in his tone. "I will not stay. I've suffered enough insult to last centuries." He stood, looking down at his sons—his surviving sons. "I suspect you never meant to avenge your sisters. It should have been you to walk into the grave."

"Father, you don't mean that," said Seong. The first to want for a fight, but had boundaries of his own, even when it came to their father.

"You are upset," said Yuz. "These are the heated words of anger."

"What's worse," said their father, his tone bordering defeat, "is that you let that fox trounce around your house like he's one of us. We should kill them all, if we know what's good for us. After what they did."

"You are tired, father," said Yuz. "And it is a long way to home. I will ride with you."

"And I," said Seong.

Kwan shifted his gaze to his elder brothers, the only thanks he could offer under the watch of their father.

He wandered the walk ways of his estate, aimless as he thought back to the events that transpired. It'd been Urekkato to suggest the condition that would win the engagement, with Taiga and Haru fast to agree. He'd made a promise, so long ago that he wondered if it'd all been a dream. A promise to protect her from all of them. But to argue would only lend suspicion. He was bound by this oath, having made it in a passion of youth. At the same time, he couldn't ignore the decree of his king. His only hope, to save face, was to make it to her first and do the deed himself.

So, he did. The race to get to her past the hoard of Kurai in her guard, and the fear of what should happen if he didn't make it first—would he be forced to turn his blade on a fellow Juneun? He couldn't risk it. He couldn't risk the slight chance that he'd be forced to turn on his kin, and leave himself open to Gumiho.

Bloodied and exhausted, but still himself, he hatched the plan with Urekkato to hand over the credit. The Cat Clan princeling displayed skill and grace, speed fluid and in full control. He'd kept on his feet, and the Kurai slain were beyond counting. If Dae Jum wanted a champion, Urekkato would suffice better than himself, and with a charm that was infectious in the courts.

His thoughts faded as he noted Juro placing a pair of wood sandals in front of a room that was not his own. His friend struggled to maintain a face that was also not his own, and carried himself with heavy shoulders. A strange sight.

He brushed it off, continuing his walk.

The carefully curated smiles of his guests bothered him. As they gossiped, and as ladies ran their eyes over to weigh their chances, it bothered him. They had no grasp of the tragedy it took to achieve this moment. Blissful ignorance with total disregard to the cost of war. Better if it'd stayed his burden alone. It wasn't simply two lords lost in pursuit of a princess. Men from each clan, loyal and brave to their last, were lost as well. The delay in this announcement was not simply to wait out the winter.

In his careless stroll, his foot knocked the edge of something. Looking down, he saw the sandals Juro had placed earlier, and now noted the door before them was Hisa's room.

The human had stayed beside him on his return, never asking with words what'd happened. It was the concern in her eyes that asked while her mouth refrained from making them real. There was no chastising or exaggeration either. The simple want of his recovery, and to be of use. He closed his eyes, shutting out the memory. Even so, he could remember humming—pleasant, though not very prettily—in short spells.

It seemed she knew a kind of loneliness, and refused him that experience. No matter how he returned, he couldn't scare her off. From that first night, she'd decided there would be no more loneliness, and stayed.

Whatever transpired, leading to this moment, he wouldn't get answers staring down.

Urekkato and Syaoran held each other's company beside the koi pond, seeming in good humor over something. One of few that the fox spirit felt comfortable around.

"Where is Juro?" asked Kwan.

Urekkato looked up. "I believe he went up river, grieving a broken heart."

Kwan stared, tired and in no mood to guess at the implication.

"He proposed to Hisa," explained Syaoran. "And she refused him."

"Ran from him is more like it," said Urekkato. "Or, that's what the serfs who claimed to have seen it say."

"I see," said Kwan, not wanting to indulge their gossip. He moved on, now having a heading. Though, he was in no great hurry.

Despite his attire, Kwan walked through with unmatched silence.

Unlike Juro, whose love making was noisy and easy to follow. Hence the reason for straying so far from the walls of his estate. They were still his lands, however, and right of way was given to him, regardless of desired privacy.

The girl was bent over a fallen trunk, and her dress tossed above her hips.

His approach was well timed, judging by the relief of both that it was over. "Juro."

Juro jumped, assembling himself. "Lord Kwan, yes. I was in the midst of vigorous discussion."

The girl too, in service to Urekkato, tried to appear properly put, and seated herself out of the way.

"Of course," said Kwan. "I've already heard minor details about the topic."

Juro sighed.

"You know that she cannot accept any offers of marriage or mistress while she's serving out a sentence, do you not?"

His face screwed itself up, twisting back to its original form. A moment of contemplation, and a false smile grew on him. "Yes. Of course. I suppose I was caught up with the happiness with the announcement of the princess's engagement, I forgot the circumstances."

Kwan watched, seeing the inner workings of Juro's mind written across his face and spreading to the rest of his body language. A slow rebuild of himself.

"Her retreat was not rejection, but in honoring her service first."

"A wonderful virtue," said Kwan.

Juro scrunched his face. "There are rumors that your bed has seen the virtue of every lady in your house."

Kwan folded his arms, scoffing. "I have taken none of the women in my service to my bed. I find myself more preoccupied with too much else."

The response seemed to satisfy the former Kurai. A relief from the thought of comparison.

"Still, I must send her a token of my affections now and again, lest she forget me in my absence. Tell me, what are the things she adores most in this world? I would have them sent to her frequently if possible."

"You'd fare better to ask her yourself," said Kwan, taking his time with his words. "It doesn't suit to let a woman think you can read her mind. Best she knows an active effort is made for her affection. Do you agree?"

"It is true. Though I will save it for tomorrow when we have both recovered."

"Before you ride off, then. It'll stay fresh in your mind."

"That is a fact to consider."

Kwan looked from the former Kurai to the woman shifting in her spot. "Are you quite done with your vigorous discussion?"

"We need a little more time, I think," said Juro, looking to her and waiting for agreement.

A reluctant nod.

"If you're certain," said Kwan, giving a last chance. She didn't accept, allowing him to dismiss himself and head home.

"Come here," cooed Juro when more secure of no further interruption. "You may help me to practice for my wedding night. I did inform that I would still have a mistress, and I do enjoy the crisp and wooded smell of you. Should your lord allow it."

Kwan continued his pace, remembering a conversation. *We might say that is unkind.* Though, if she had a change of heart, he wouldn't dissuade her from her choice. It would be a leap in her station. One any family would likely accept with reverence and waste no time bragging to their neighbors.

If she had such a motive, then she was simply a variant of what he knew in the whole of his life.

He bid his farewells to guests as they left. Going through the motions practiced and perfected in his earliest years. Comments on the beautiful displays, the wines, and the weather went among other small notes covering what they'd really wanted to say. Insincere smiles and a double meaning to words, hinting at an insult.

It didn't matter. In a decade, the event will have been forgotten.

Syaoran walked the courtyard, deep in thought.

"You look as though you mean to tell me bad news," said Kwan. "To do with Beom or Kwang, undoubtedly."

His fox ears flattened, and he gave an apologetic face. "No, lord. It's... One of your house gave insult to Urekkato. A few heated words. And he's soured."

"Then take a bamboo stick and deliver forty swats," said Kwan, dismissive and walking on. It irritated him, expecting better of his staff in how they treated a high-ranking guest in his home. Something that, surely, all of them knew.

"It's Hisa, my lord," said Syaoran.

Kwan stopped in his step. Timid Hisa? His mind recalled every time he'd seen her trembling and meek, as recently as this past winter. So he kept still, contemplating.

"I provoked it, my lord," said Syaoran, with an undertone of urgency. "The lashings should go to me."

Kwan turned. "Explain."

"I'd accidentally exposed Lord Juro's excitement to Lord Urekkato. And I allowed myself to be convinced of encouraging an encounter I knew wouldn't end happily."

"It sounds as though the slight was against Juro, and not Urekkato."

Syaoran averted his gaze. "Hisa confronted us. She'd overheard our reveling."

"I see."

Syaoran gave a deep bow, straight backed and humbled. "I accept full responsibility."

Kwan observed, weighing his options. "Where is Hisa now?"

"I'm not sure," said Syaoran, staying in place, head low.

"Urekkato?"

"I believe he planned a bath and then to retire to his room."

Knowing the Cat Clan princeling, he was unlikely to be alone for either. Which made for a good enough distraction for him, and a simple enough excuse to delay action on Kwan's behalf.

"Have Hisa sent to me first thing in the morning," said Kwan. Hopefully, he could think of some suitable outlet by then. Forty strikes to someone ignorant, reacting to a provocation, seemed overly excessive. She was also human, and likely wouldn't withstand it at the hand of a Juneun.

Lying in bed, Kwan's mind refused him rest. Even as the night grew ever late, sleep evaded him.

Gumiho was dead. He could replace his soul. But there was something still in his gut, warning him. He felt, somehow, still bound to his promise. Maybe the rowdiness within his house put him on edge. No, the feeling was before then. It'd been there through winter.

The distant moans didn't bother him. Nor the pleading of one to another, whispering their desire. It was different, from within. Today burning a fiercer warning, telling him not to drop his guard.

He looked to his newest scar, running the length of his arm, finely visible, and touched at his face where he'd been cut. A thread of a mark left from nose to ear, though it rightly should've taken his eye.

No announcement of Gumiho's death was made until today. Kwan wanted to be sure, even in spite of the evidence. Yet, he still wasn't.

The door slid open, hardly making a sound. His head swiveled over, seeing Eumeh in her night gown. Sitting up, he tried to read her expression for clues. She kept her face down.

"Princess? What is the matter?"

She walked to him. As he started to stand, her hand went to rest atop his shoulder and stopped him. "Nothing is the matter."

He stared, trying to see through her coy demeanor.

She pressed herself on him, lips touching, he pushed back only just. "You are engaged to another."

"And my future husband doesn't take fidelity seriously. Why should I?" strands of silken, black hair slid forward as she looked down at him.

"Because you are a woman."

She frowned. "He's with two of my maids right now. More interested in seducing servants than to seduce his own fiancée."

Kwan lifted her hands from him, placing them to her sides.

"I wanted my first to be with the man who loves me. Not a man who appears to only love my title and assets. Now, I refuse him being first."

"I cannot," said Kwan, looking away. "Whatever kindred feeling, that is all there is. I will not insult the crown, or my friend. And not while both are a guest in my house."

"If we were not in your house?"

He leered at her.

"If I command you of it?"

Kwan's jaw locked, holding heated terms.

"I am a princess. And you are a vassal of the royal family. You refused me once already."

"I will refuse again, rather than tarnish honor."

Her frown deepened. "I know it was you who suggested a trial. Even if Urekkato named it, I know it was you who initiated it. Do you find me so repulsive?"

Kwan sighed and looked away. "I did not say that, princess."

"Then do me this kindness. At the very least so that I am prepared for whatever mockery I'm to endure with him."

He said nothing, and kept his gaze down.

She advanced, raising her knee to straddle him. His hand reacted, stopping her. They matched each other's glowering.

"Then I will say you stole me into your room," said Eumeh. "And that you robbed Urekkato of his wedding rite. How many enemies can you afford, now that Gumiho is dead?"

Kwan's nose crinkled. "Whether I do or do not, you could claim the same."

"Then you may as well."

His lungs drew in a slow inhale, tempering his muscles. This wasn't a foe he could cut down.

She climbed on him, unfastening the ties of his own night gown and sliding them off his shoulders. Pulling him to her lips, she disrobed herself. Her eyes shut, his lingered open. Regardless of what transpired, she was a princess and held the final word. One that could ruin him, yes, imprison him, of course, and which robbed his personal dignity. His hand took the small of her back as he came up with a plan; something to remind her that he wasn't a pet or personal toy.

He shut his eyes, bracing her against him and swallowing in her giggling moan.

She pushed off him for breath. "That's more like it."

Kwan said nothing, taking his free hand to hook behind her head, fingers combing through her hair and bringing her down for a more passionate kiss—providing the illusion she wanted. He felt her lips smile, her arms wrapping around him. The hand on her back sliding down, guiding her hips into a repeating motion against him. When she got the idea, going on her own initiative and at her own pace, his hand fell a little lower to grasp at her.

He pretended to explore her, a playful aggression. She slowed, perhaps understanding he wouldn't deliver what she wanted any time soon. So, he took a lover's role, pulling her to her back while he loomed over giving only a brief moment to seem as though he needed to catch his breath in a pant. Kisses were planted down her neck and between her breasts, pretending he'd submitted to the role and biding time for her to trust his next move.

He lifted her up on him again, thumbs brushing up and down her inner thighs. She looked down into his eyes, bringing herself closer to him. Seizing his chance, he turned her around, pinning her to his table.

"What are you doing?" demanded Eumeh in a whisper.

Kwan placed his torso against her back, allowing his weight to hold her. "I have no security that you'll make me free of this. So, I will perform in the way that gratifies me most."

Her face twisted, indignant. He ignored it, and did as she originally commanded. If the private humiliation was enough, she wouldn't come to him again, or command that he come to her. So, he didn't put on the pretense, and was not the tender lover she wanted out of him. The sooner they were through, the sooner he'd know his fate.

Chapter 29
The Prince

I couldn't sleep. My face flushed hot, not from the confrontation, though it didn't help.

It was the moaning and the giggling that sounded from the floor above my room. And through my walls. A number of women from the staying households wasted no time in seducing one of the lords with the hope of becoming his wife or mistress; a life that would be of comfort rather than service, of sleeping in and receiving priceless gifts while he remembered them.

Still, I dreamed of a family in the village. The rules of nobles were suffocating. While the other women wished for court to be held regularly, and increase their chance of escape, I prayed Lord Kwan wouldn't take up any more events while I stayed.

I tossed and turned, hiding under my covers, pressing my bunny against my ear to muffle the sounds. It worked for a while. Then there was the sound like one woman was enduring unimaginable pain in a similar rhythmic pattern to previous moans. I was so tired, yet unable to fall asleep.

Until finally I did.

It didn't feel like a long enough rest when I was woken up to go to Lin's room again. Four more days of this. I wasn't sure I could handle it.

In the midst of dressing, Syaoran tapped Lin's door with a message. Lord Kwan wanted to see me. The women helped me to hurry and be out, carrying my wood sandals and cotton socks. I wanted my trek to go unnoticed, and to not wake anyone that might still be asleep.

He was only half dressed when I arrived. While I didn't see any bare parts of his chest or below, it was improper. So many rules for a servant. Like so many layers of clothing before you were deemed decent. He bid I come in anyway.

When I did, I stayed at the threshold of the door, now closed behind me.

He was in the midst of writing something. The brush in his hand held perfectly, and each movement graceful. His eyes stayed fixed on his work, letting silence hang over us. In waiting, my own eyes began to wander, noticing how parts of his room looked out of place.

"I was told you insulted one of my guests in my own home," said Lord Kwan.

He didn't sound angry or even a little upset. His tone was more matter-of-fact than any hint of threat. Still, my spine went stiff and my gut went cold. "Yes, my lord," I whispered, hoarse as it was.

He said nothing for a while, finishing the last strokes with his ink brush before setting it delicately aside. "For what reason?" Finally, his eyes looked up at me past his unkept hair.

I dropped my gaze, hoping beyond hope that my feet might somehow provide me with useful words.

"Look at me," commanded Lord Kwan, still tempered in tone.

I obeyed, slowly, needing courage. "I was angry, my lord. And I yelled at Lord Urekkato. It was wrong of me, I know, but I couldn't stop myself. I'm sorry."

"What was it you said?"

My thumbs moved closer to each other, fidgeting. "I'd said," I swallowed hard. Thick and sticky spit moved down my throat, landing hard in my stomach. "That it wasn't a joke to play with the feelings of others. And that it was especially cruel to do so to someone who thought of them as a trusted friend."

"Reasonable," said Lord Kwan, resting his cheek atop folded fingers. "Was it necessary to yell and be so direct with Lord Urekkato?"

I shook my head and looked down.

"Hisa, look at me."

I did, needing to call back some of my bravery. "I was scolding Syaoran, my lord. And Lord Urekkato—I couldn't stop myself from snapping at him. I'm sorry, my lord."

He stared at me, deciding what to do. "It is not me you need to apologize to. Urekkato has always been prideful. And his pride in himself has only increased with his betrothal now official." He rolled up the paper he'd written on, tying a finely braided piece of twine around it expertly.

I nodded my understanding, already thinking of how I should make my apology.

"I've already sent for him to come here after his breakfast. In the meantime, you will attend me, so that we have an excuse for your being here."

"Excuse?"

"I will tell him that I have dealt with the matter. That Yua has whipped you and that you were made to sleep in the stables last night. You must allow that to be the truth. And you must then bow on your knees to make your apology. It has to appear as though I have broken you, and you made the initiative to avoid further punishment."

It sounded horrifying. So much over a short, angry burst. It scarce came to blows in the village, though it did sometimes happen between the men. And I'd seen frustrated women, irritated over months or longer, lash out at each other and needing to be separated. A few seconds of only words seemed nothing, and was usually buried behind by morning.

Regardless, I nodded my understanding, and repeated the story in my head to make myself believe that'd been the case.

"Come," said Lord Kwan.

My feet complied. When he bid I fetch this robe or that, I did, and helped to place it neatly on him. In spite of the fastenings, it seemed fairly obvious where something ought to go; certainly, it was less complicated than what I was made to wear, but elegant all the same. When he changed his mind about one and asked for another, I folded the first and brought what he indicated to. When he said to tie tighter, I did so gradually.

Then came the point where he stopped me, raising my chin to face him.

"You must act as though this is not your first time attending."

I blinked, not understanding. I'd thought I was doing well in figuring things out during my first try. It was when he placed the backs of his fingers against my cheek, cool to the touch, that I realized. Despite my every distraction, I was blushing. I closed my eyes and took in a deep breath, though I wasn't sure if that actually fixed anything.

"It doesn't make sense to you, I know," said Lord Kwan. "And you're nervous."

I met his eye again, seeing concern within them. Again, it felt like there was some part of him locked away, only able to be seen through his eyes, and only if you were looking closely enough.

"I will be with you."

I nodded, though I didn't really get what he meant. Even so, it made me feel calmer, and I continued on.

When he'd changed his mind about something a second time, it dawned on me that he was stalling. He wanted it to look like Urekkato's arrival interrupted us.

There was little to do to buy out more time, and I was bid to comb his hair. In that, I needed more direction. Five combs, and not just any one would do. They each had a specific purpose. This ritual of preparation for the day felt just as tedious as my own for court. I'd never thought of Lord Kwan as being vain, but these were odd circumstances today, and in need of a show. Presentation, no matter how trivial, somehow became necessary for court.

We were interrupted then, as I'd begun to tie up his hair into his preferred style. Urekkato announced himself and came in. As instructed, I stopped what I was doing on sight and fell into a groveling bow to deliver my apology. I didn't dare to look up or move from that pathetic position, not even to see if there was a wordless acceptance of what I'd said.

Quiet lingered over me. I stayed perfectly still.

Only when Lord Kwan bid I resume did I stand, and did so hesitantly.

Urekkato bore a perplexed expression, assessing what'd transpired. Lord Kwan gave his assurance that I'd been dealt with, and that no future insult would arise. I kept out of their conversation, even as topics changed.

Syaoran brought rice wine, and I was bid to serve.

As I stood, pitcher in hand and waiting to refill, I wondered about why Lord Kwan went through the effort of a lie for me. From friendship? And would it cause trouble with the others?

"I say that I'm surprised," said Urekkato. "Your lowest ranked girl is your preferred attendant. But you're like that, I suppose."

That drew my attention. My eyes glanced to my court wear, colored to show my status among the household staff. Looking up, I'd missed exactly when Urekkato held up his cup to refill, and went on so as to not make him wait.

Lord Kwan said nothing in response.

"There's rumor that Yua is your mistress at last. Is it finally true?"

As he always did, Lord Kwan took his time to respond, setting down his drink first. "I have no mistress."

"It's been how long?" asked Urekkato with a smirk. "Ninety years? Ninety-one? Though I make up for the both of us."

Lord Kwan stared ahead at him, saying nothing.

"You were a lot more sporting when you were younger. Maybe your tastes have changed and you prefer human concubines now." His expression grew more devilish as he teased. "Makes more sense. There's only so long that they live. And it allows for variety and the thrill of a new love all over again."

"That is not my reason," said Lord Kwan, conservative in his words and inflection.

"It would explain a few things," said Urekkato, turning his gaze to me.

I tried not to wince, making myself keep still as though I hadn't heard a thing he said.

"Tell me, my friend," he shifted his eyes back to Lord Kwan. "Have you told Yua about her beloved yet?"

Lord Kwan's expression darkened. "I did not want to distress her before court."

"Compassion? Or selfishness?" teased Urekkato.

"That depends," said Lord Kwan. "If allowing grief to take its course on her own terms is compassionate or selfish."

"Lord Kwan has a heart," said Urekkato, putting on a pleasant smile. "It makes up for what he's locked away."

No response. He raised up his cup, allowing wordlessness to fill the space between himself and his guest as I replenished it.

The door opened again, without announcement. Two of Lord Kwan's brothers walked in. A cup was given to each, and I acted. The younger giving me a look of recognition, and the elder seemed not to notice my presence at all.

"Perhaps that compassionate heart extends to punishments as well. I don't believe you'd deliver forty strikes."

"You are free to believe whatever you like."

"Forty strikes for what?" asked Kwang.

"A ravenous set of insults from his servant to a Juneun lord, of course."

"Forty is soft," said Beom. "Fifty is the threshold."

"Ah, but the threshold was lowered, since the offender was human."

Both Beom and Kwang looked at me then, and I tried not to squirm or sweat under their gaze. Beom shifted his eyes to Lord Kwan, narrowing them into a scowl.

"They are a fragile thing," said Kwang. "I'm impressed she'd withstand ten."

From his tone, I understood the young lord meant to diffuse tension.

"It is indeed impressive," said Urekkato, his finger pushing his cup closer to the table's edge.

"Likely because my brother delivered nothing of the sort," said Beom.

"To whom was the offense," said Kwang, hoping to distract.

"Among your present company," said Urekkato, casual in his tone.

They looked between him, to their brother, and to me.

"The matter has been dealt with," said Lord Kwan, his watch on his brothers holding a finality to it. "It will not happen again."

"It is insult after insult with you," grumbled Beom. "Were it my house, I'd hand the rod to the offended lord."

"It is not your house," reminded Lord Kwan. "And your input is not desired."

I was relieved to finally be dismissed, and took whatever task meant being away from court guests. Mostly, that meant fetching water for the kitchen. I didn't mind it. The nearest well was the restored one in the back, and I was happy for the lack of people so I didn't have to look proper just to carry a bucket.

It was tiring work, climbing up and down stairs with a heavy pale while dressed so restrictively. Past midday, I took a break, sitting on the bench and enjoying the shade of the trees. Light filtered through new leaves, making a mesmerizing scene above whenever a breeze passed through. It felt good to be off my feet and out of my wood sandals for a while. A part of me missed the straw sandals I would weave, even if they didn't last for too long and were more time consuming to put on.

I knew I couldn't stay idle, sighing as I got my shoes back on and walked to bring up more water. My initial steps away from the well, my foot slid, making me stop to balance and try to fix it in the next step. Before I could take it, I was pulled off my feet, losing the sandal entirely and dropping the pale. An arm restrained me, and a hand over my mouth.

"I know you didn't sleep in the stables last night," whispered Urekkato. "I was there, more than once."

I struggled to get free, made still when he tightened his restraint on me.

"I just want to talk. So, I'm letting go. Don't scream. I hate the sound of screaming, regardless of why."

My breath became shallow, rapid. My legs begged me to run, while the rest of me wanted to collapse in a terrified puddle. He was slow to release, testing to see if I'd do something in contradiction with his plan. When I felt free enough, I pushed away, stumbling a few steps to put distance between us.

"Kwan keeps surprising me," said Urekkato in a pleasant voice.

I glared, my face turning hot. Though, there wasn't much that I could do against a Juneun.

"Out of all the things to surprise me most, I would never have guessed it would be his match making me to a princess, or that he would lie to me over a human."

I froze. Every part of me screamed to run, but I couldn't.

"What is your relation to my dear friend Kwan? It's not just anyone he's put so much effort into a charade for, that much is certain."

I drew an unsteady breath, reining my voice to my control. "He is my master. And I am his servant—"

"Yes, yes. A well-rehearsed answer. What is your relationship really? Why does he care so much?"

I retreated my arms to my chest trying to think, trying to hide. "Wouldn't it be better to ask him?"

He took a step closer.

I took a step back.

A wry smirk spread over his lips. "I figured it'd be better to ask you directly. You're not exactly elegant with your words, village girl. It could be an entire day of circling around with conversation before I finally get an answer from my kind. You'll stay here until I get an answer."

I turned my eyes down. "I'm just a servant."

"I seriously doubt it," said Urekkato, from behind me.

My head shot up, looking over my shoulder as the rest of me stumbled forward. I fell. He caught me, preventing me from hitting the ground, and standing me straight. Whatever the reason, I didn't like it.

"Is there really nothing? I find it hard to believe."

I shook my head. "He's my master. But I, I do think of him as my friend as well."

"A friend?" He scoffed, as if the idea was invalid. "Just a friend?"

I nodded.

"Kwan. Friends with his human prisoner?"

I stared, not knowing what else to say.

He studied me in turn. "What did you do?"

"My lord?"

"Kwan hasn't made an effort of attachment in a long time. And a long time to a Juneun is unfathomable to a human."

"What do you mean?" I knew it was a stupid question, but the words spilled out of my mouth before I considered as much. The same way I backed up until I was against the lip of the well.

He gave me a quizzical look, twisting his face into a question before relaxing into a knowing expression. "They haven't told you, have they?"

"Told me? Told me what?"

He grinned. "Not since Syaoran. And that relationship is more on the fox's effort than on Kwan's. A bit of boot licking to save his own skin."

"I don't understand."

Urekkato vanished, reappearing right in front of me. One hand on my shoulder, the other holding the edge of the well, he leaned in close to whisper. His hot, uncomfortable breath tickling my ear, I winced. "He doesn't have his soul."

I stood, stunned and blinking.

"Gumiho ripped it out of him," continued the Cat lord. "Some say he locked it away and hid it where no one would find it." He leaned back, meeting my eye and measuring how shaken I was. "And some say she outright ate his soul. Regardless of what version of the story is true, that's when he changed and closed himself off."

"But he's not closed off," I argued, as pathetic as my voice sounded. "He's, well, he can be hard to understand. And maybe he doesn't smile often. But I think—"

His hand left the rim of the well, lifting my chin to better lock eyes. "Is that so? I was thinking you had an effect on Kwan. But maybe it's the other way around and he has quite the profound effect on you."

My eyes blinked in rapid succession, clearing my sight though unhelpful in deciphering the full meaning of Urekkato's words.

"To think he refused a beauty like Eumeh, but went out of his way for you."

I frowned, turning my head to pull away from his touch.

"But really, what do you hope to gain from someone willing to lock away his soul?"

I glared, my face fast becoming hot. "He's my friend. And what does it matter about his soul? The way so many lords speak about each other, about their servants, about humans, I'd stand by Lord Kwan without a soul over anyone else with their soul every time."

Despite my outburst, Urekkato didn't look surprised or even mildly annoyed. I'd done my best to keep from yelling, to hold back all the things I wanted to say and make a more general statement.

He kept his curious stare, looking me over one last time. "You know, you and Kwan are the only ones to openly challenge me. Everyone either tip-toes around it, or uses their rank to enforce their perspective. I think I'm starting to understand why he's so fond of you."

He leaned in.

I leaned back. But with the well against me, with nowhere to run, I was trapped.

"So, I'll give you a gift," said Urekkato, his voice now warm with a hint of mischief. "I want to see where this goes with you and Kwan, so how about an exchange? I'll bring you luck, and you let me borrow your eyes once in a while."

"My eyes?" I wanted to run then and there, or throw myself into the well. My hands instinctively pushing back against his chest, though my arms lacked the strength to make any difference. How was taking out my eyes supposed to sound like a gift? I would be practically useless without my eyes; and all the effort I put to learn to read, to write, to improve on any of my skills would've been for nothing. I'd be forever in the dark, more susceptible to bears and boars and other wild things—a burden to my family worrying after me.

"Not like that," said Urekkato, half with a laugh and yet half groaning. "I mean to see through your eyes."

I stayed still, staring. I didn't know what he meant, though I was sure it wasn't anything good.

"It's an easy enough spell for me to cast. I've done it hundreds of times. I want to see my old friend the way you see him, and watch how your friendship progresses. What the two of you do to make your bond."

Like eavesdropping? Spying? I shook my head. "No. That's creepy."

"Eh? But you haven't heard what you'll get out of it."

I shut my eyes and turning my face as far as my neck would allow.

"I'll give you a part of my essence," whispered Urekkato.

I winced.

"I can make it so you have a little more luck. Whether you need to find something, convince someone of something else, hide or escape—whatever you might need. No human could want a more valuable gift."

"I won't," I said, still shaking my head to emphasize my total rejection. "I don't want to be your spy for Lord Kwan."

"It's not spying," said Urekkato, levity in his tone. "And if it's too much of a personal moment, I won't look. Just close your eyes for four seconds, and it ends anything I can see from you. For a time."

"How would I know that's even true?"

He laughed. "Well, you're naïve, but you're not stupid. I'll grant you that."

Shy, I slowly allowed myself to look back at him.

"What could I swear on to convince you I'm not lying?"

He backed slightly, giving me a breath of space. Enough to think. "Swear on your princess. On her life and yours."

He chuckled. "You drive a hard bargain." He removed himself, freeing me from my trapped position. My relief was short lived as he unfastened his shirt and the layers beneath to expose his chest. Of course, on seeing my alarm, he wasted no time in teasing me. "Have you never seen a man's torso? Or do you find me handsome?"

Both of those were true to an extent. I'd never seen a man's bare body—it was different when we were all children and all looked relatively the same, but the rules changed when girls came into their womanhood and boys into their manhood. And I did think he was handsome—but all the Juneun were beautiful compared to humans.

His body was toned, strong without a gross excess of muscle, and not a single scar on him. Something that made me think of agility and power perfectly balanced as one.

With his claw-like finger nail, he cut a crossed slash over his heart. "I swear, on my life and on Eumeh's life, close your eyes for four seconds, and the spell will end for a time. It's under your control." The cut drew out a deep red from beneath the surface, then subsided quickly, healing over itself without so much as a blemish.

I didn't know what that was supposed to prove, though it seemed like something official. Then again, any sort of magic could look impressive if you didn't know what it was for.

"Now do you trust me?"

"No."

"It could help you, you know? If there's danger and I happen to see it at the time, I can send aide or come myself to resolve whatever is happening."

I immediately thought about the times Lord Kwan came home and was not himself, and of his injuries. Gumiho was gone, but what if there was some retaliation? What if he did need help? I didn't have magic or any impressive skill. In knowing how weak I was by compare, and how much I wanted to protect him the way he protected me, the decision felt impossible to make. It was too much like I'd be betraying Lord Kwan, allowing Urekkato to spy. Though, I could end it myself and prevent him from seeing much of anything. If he saw Lord Kwan needed help because of me, wouldn't that be a good thing? But, there wasn't the guarantee of Urekkato seeing it, and I didn't know how I'd make him see it.

"Well?" He'd started to put himself back together at a casual pace.

I looked between him and the house, deciding. "Will it hurt?"

"No," said Urekkato with a shrug. "It tingles and itches a little for about a day, until the spell fully sets. That's about it."

I still hesitated. "What would I have to do?"

He gave a kind smile, though I didn't trust the sincerity of it. "I just need your consent to cast the spell. It's a fickle piece of magic."

"Consent?"

"Your permission."

Why didn't he just use that word instead? It felt like I was leagues behind in my understanding of words, and trying to catch up the best I could since coming here.

I thought a while longer, and nodded.

"I need you to actually say it for the spell to work." He walked up, invading my space all over again.

Like before, my palms went to hold him back. And like before, my arms lacked the strength to achieve that. I stared into his cat-eyes, swallowing hard. "You have my permission to cast the spell. But only that spell."

His smile morphed, "Close your eyes."

My mind fast retrieved when Lord Kwan gave that command while standing so close to me. "Are you going to kiss me?"

"Did you want me to?"

I shook my head.

He chuckled. "No, I'm not going to kiss you. I'm casting a sight spell."

As expressive as he allowed himself to be, I found I couldn't read him any better than I could Lord Kwan. I took a breath, and silently prayed for strength, then closed my eyes. The touch of his nails brushing down my face caused me to flinch, and my fingers wrapped around his shirt. I didn't catch the uttering of his spell. It ended almost as soon as he'd started.

"And that's it," said Urekkato.

I opened my eyes. Nothing looked different, though they did tingle and itch as though there was just a little extra pollen in the air. Exactly as he'd said.

"For luck, however, that's a little bit different. You need to be undressed for that one."

"What?"

"I'm just messing with you." He snickered, seeming to ignore my scowl. His nails dug into his palm, causing the tiniest hints or blood to surface, and placed it atop my head. "And that should be all there is to it. You can let go of my shirt now."

I recoiled myself in realizing, a gasp escaping me.

Chapter 30
The Bead

I thought I was being clever, sneaking away the first chance I got while the guests were distracted by the theater performance. Not a word spoken by any of the actors, and their faces hidden behind masks, it was left to their dramatic and mesmerizing movements to tell the story, and for all else to imagine the rest. We'd done similar in the village, but lacked in the costume design and masks. But we all knew the stories well enough.

Blanket and clothes secure in my arms, I dashed to the kennels where quiet sleep surely awaited.

The thick, woven matt I'd made was still there, and the nights were not so cold. I felt some excitement in me as I laid down on it. I was too far from the rooms of the house to hear anything intimate, and no one would think to intrude over here. With luck, sleep soon found me.

That luck ended when I woke to the sound of something crashing. Night, and still very much dark, I couldn't see what caused the noise, or where it'd come from. What I did find was a coat over my blanket, and not one that I recognized. The air was significantly cooler than when I first hid away here.

Wrapping myself in the jacket and curling under my blanket, I tried to reclaim sleep from my racing heartbeat. Sudden memories came back. A part of me wondered if it was still there. I sat up, about to reach for it when my itching eyes reminded me. I shut them tight, counting. One, two, three, four. And opened to lift up the loose stone.

The soft glow deep within invited me to take it and play with it to help sooth me into another drowsy state. I slid the pieces still able to move, hardly noticing what each tile was until—click. Another piece stuck. They were jumbled pieces of characters, trying to say something. Curious, and with everything else quiet, I played with it more, seeing if luck would help me solve it.

Click.

It was weird, like the pieces deliberately weren't meant to match.

Click.

I kept trying, now invested in wanting to read the message, wanting to look inside. With every new click, it seemed like it shouldn't match, but somehow started to make sense.

A heart without pride, a hand without greed. Feet not idle, tongue not hateful. With eyes that see through stone.

It didn't make sense. Maybe it wasn't meant to. A riddle or a poem or a spell. Spell! Before I opened the box, I shut my eyes and counted again. Even if Urekkato was likely asleep, it made me uncomfortable. I knew I wasn't supposed to have this, and I didn't want him to see it.

Inside the box was a bead of light, glowing like soft starlight. Staring at it, I felt a sense of comfort and safety. It looked, odd as it sounded in my thoughts, like it was breathing. Like it had a heartbeat of its own.

I marveled at it until I heard heavy foot fall. A guardsman probably. But in my panic, I closed the box and hid it under my clothes as I fast pulled my blanket over me. A warmth coaxed me back into sleep.

I woke up before dawn, without anyone needing to wake me, and felt more refreshed than I had the day before. Quickly, I put the puzzle box back and closed up its hiding place, straightening out the mat and folding the jacket and blanket to sit neatly on top. The clothes I'd need to change into safe in my arms, I planned to get a thank you note written and set it on the coat in case the owner returned.

In Lin's room, I shut my eyes and counted, a part of me horrified with the thought that Urekkato might use me to peek at the women of the house. It wasn't something I thought about when I'd made the deal, and now I regretted it. He'd said that closing my eyes would stop the spell for a while. But how long was *a while*?

Lin scolded one of the other girls, coming into the room late and dragging her feet, hair in disarray and a hurried yawn slowing her down. She'd been accused of going to Syaoran for the night, only for her to snap back that she'd gone to one of Lord Kwan's brothers and that she couldn't be blamed for taking the opportunity for a more comfortable life.

Complaints circled, about needing to pick up on her slack if she was too tired to keep up, and that her ambitions were too high. One woman started to rumor that the girl might get too much of an ego now.

I tried to ignore it. The way they talked about each other sometimes, it made me uncomfortable, and reminded me of the rumors about myself that spread through my village.

The celadon dishware set out every evening during court fascinated me. I'd never seen such elegant bowls or ewers or teapots. The green glaze and low relief images on them were detailed, from the largest subject to the tiny flowers along the edges. One pitcher sported the image of a bird with grand plumage over a meadow. Monochrome, its glaze caught the light and made it look like something from a dream. Another was shaped like a lotus bud, two toned to distinguish itself. A wine vase flaunted its decorative vines and flowers etched in it, and a crane swooping through them. The gray-green color gave the flat image the illusion of depth, as though at any moment they'd come to life and flourish in color.

Then there was the white porcelain reserved for the honored couple. Standing out against the various shades of gray-green and brown tints, the porcelain's brilliance was ten-fold.

Iridescent, dark pieces were reserved for Lord Kwan and his brothers, distinguishing them without stealing from the fineness of the newly betrothed princess and her intended. Each of those pieces lacked any elaborate decoration etched in them. A single image for the initial aesthetic, but the real beauty seen in how it caught the light.

It must've taken someone half their lifetime to master the craft and create such things. And here it was, used as dining wear for special occasions, rather than as pieces of art to be admired every day. Like so much about holding court, it was something I couldn't understand.

As I set up the tables with two other women, Yua came in searching for Syaoran—who seemed to disappear some time ago, since no one had seen him after yesterday morning.

A scream tore our attention, cuing us to rush in the direction. Nothing terrible, except that the pomegranate wine was spilled and the vases broken. Several of the men complained about the waste of good wine. Meanwhile I was heartbroken at the smashed pottery, the loss of the art.

Yua sighed, sending me to fetch replacements.

It was easy enough, though I'd decided to take one at a time to avoid accidentally dropping or spilling any of it. The storeroom unlocked, its door ajar, I walked in on a scene: Lin and Kwang in the midst of a passionate undressing. Smiles and chuckles and hands everywhere. I'd clapped my hand over my mouth and closed the door. However, I still needed to bring the wines before the start of the feast.

They hadn't noticed my intrusion as I hurried to grab what I needed and get out. Dreading that I'd have to go back in repeatedly, I grabbed ewer after ewer to place outside and out of the way. Closing the door, I sighed my relief. Though, I went rigid again when I heard something fall from within, and breathless declarations from Lin.

I shuffled off, my stride restricted by my dress. Still, not wanting to spill, I kept to my plan of bringing one at a time. A lengthy walk, and the feasting underway, I tried to remain unnoticed. With several smooth returns, I pushed myself to bring the final two in one last transit. They were a little heavy, but I was sure I could do it.

I turned, and in my hurried steps I failed to see Juro right behind me. My worst fear of the night came to fruition. I'd spilled a generous amount on both of us and lost my hold on one of the ewers. It shattered on the pebbled path atop one of the large stepping stones, the wine fast escaping beneath the rock. At least I hadn't fallen and smashed the other or cut myself up. Juro caught me.

"Lord Juro, I'm sorry. I'm sorry," I made my frantic apology, getting back on my feet as my mind rushed to find some useful words. "Your robes. I, I'll clean them. I'm so sorry."

He held up a palm and shook his head. For a moment I feared. There was an effort put to my behalf over the smallest insult with words towards Urekkato. This was twice that I'd insulted Juro in some capacity. What was the punishment for that? And would there be anything to save me from it?

"I'm quite alright," said Juro. "The pomegranate wine will make it look as though I've murdered someone, but I've honestly looked worse. And you'll never get the stains out without magic. Don't fret. Besides all that, I saw you going back and forth and came to see if I could be of service to you."

"Service to me?" When I'd said the words, I realized his meaning.

"I should have announced myself," said Juro. "But I didn't think you were in that much of a hurry."

"You mustn't trouble yourself, my lord," I said in response, trying to say it the way I thought the other women might. "You are a guest. I am a servant."

"For now, yes," said Juro, taking a deep inhale. "But maybe not after your service to Lord Kwan is up. If, by then, you've grown an affection for me, you will not be a servant. If an affection has blossomed with my every visit, you might become my wife."

"Lord Juro, you know I can't—"

"Yes, yes, not while you are under a sentence of debt. I understand. Why I can't be allowed to pay the debt against you is beyond me, but," he took my hands, still holding the pitcher, "when it is just the two of us, call me *Juro*. Not *Lord Juro*."

I shook my head. "I can't." And I didn't want to.

He looked crestfallen, forcing a gentle smile. "I hope, in time."

I pulled away, turning and taking hasty steps. I should have learned my lesson the first time. My neck reared to look back. I should have been looking ahead. I collided with a redressed Kwang, spilling on him as well. Mentally I scolded myself, verbally I gave a profuse apology.

"You must forgive her Lord Kwang," said Juro, coming to my defense. "Holding court is an exhausting task, especially for an understaffed house."

Kwang gave an annoyed look.

"What were you doing in the wine stores, anyway?" pried Juro.

Kwang's expression changed, to the sort that I recognized meant his brain was grasping for an adequate answer.

"Lord Kwang was already assisting me, Lord Juro," I said. "He is my master's brother, so I couldn't refuse when he insisted."

Juro twisted his face, suspicious of the answer I'd given.

"It's been a long day for me as well," said Kwang, building on the lie I'd made for him. "If that's all that's needed, I'll see myself to my room and change."

I nodded and gave a slight bow, trying my best to play off the scene. Kwang didn't get more than a few steps away when Beom walked up. He froze at the sight of his brother. Meanwhile, I tried to appear as if I didn't notice and sneak past. He stopped me.

"Somehow, I knew you'd be in some far corner playing with one of our brother's servant girls."

Kwang held back his tongue, looking away.

"You're a mess." His cold gaze moved to Juro, then to me. "I suppose you're going to tell me this was somehow self-inflicted?"

"It's not what it looks like," said Kwang, but instead of the jovial and confident voice I'd known him for, he sounded like a boy. Not a warrior.

Beom scoffed. "You and Kwan are hellbent on making a mockery of our family."

I looked up at him then, at the squareness of all his features. He hardly looked anything like his brothers, with a more set brow and narrower, green eyes. As much as he appeared more a mountain of a man by compare, what intimidated me most was the sudden meekness of Kwang.

"Since this one insists on contemptuous behavior, action is needed to make her aware of her place."

"It was an accident, Beom," snapped Kwang, though it came out more whimper than it did fierce.

"It's an accident to splash wine on two guests of the house, on a Juneun lord, and to destroy the stock already set at the house?"

"The house?" I repeated.

"Are you so stupid to not remember your carelessness that caused the wines to topple? The entire reason you were sent to bring more, and did so in the laziest manner? Or do you think acting coyly will spare you?"

"But, I didn't do that, my lord," I said, now terrified. This brother, I knew wouldn't be lenient with me. "I didn't. I swear."

He ripped the jug from my hands, glaring at me as he set it aside and gestured to his brother. "Hold out your arm, girl."

I retreated my arms to my chest, as though I could somehow hide them, and shook my head. My knees trembled beneath me.

"Hold out your arm," said Beom, his scowl deepening into a snarl.

"Beom, stop," said Kwang. "This is not our house."

Juro was at my side, taking my shoulders to try and spirit me off. Beom grabbed, preventing my quiet escape.

"Someone needs to put discipline into them. Since Kwan will not." He yanked me from Juro.

"You overstep, Lord Beom," said Juro. "I have already forgiven any trespass on my pride."

Scared, I tried to make a run for it on my own. To hide in my room, or be anywhere else. Beom grabbed a fist full of my hair, standing me back in place. A horrible growl left him, the kind that came from a beast about to leap at its hunter. Both Kwang and Juro stepped back, unwilling to challenge. I didn't know it—I was too focused on the pain and the sound of my own shrieks to hear—but I'd ruined my chance to let Juro and Kwang wear him down with words. There was nothing they could do. I wasn't from their house, and Beom was the elder, a more powerful and higher ranked spirit.

He let go, leaving me to tremble and whimper in place. "Hold out your arm. If I repeat myself again, I will have you properly whipped rather than Kwang's hand."

On the brink of tears, I reached out as far as my muscled and good sense would allow. He grabbed my wrist, pulling to extend the full on my arm. At his gesture, a bamboo stick broke itself from the decorative dressing around the storehouse, and flew to him.

He offered it first to Kwang, as the offended family member, who shook his head in refusal. Undeterred, and more irritated, Beom smacked down on my arm with such force I was sure he'd broken it.

I screamed out, sharp, and recoiled as I fell to my knees. There was no holding back my crying now. I wept freely, holding my limb as it throbbed and stung with pain.

"Get up girl," commanded Beom. "Forty strikes. I knew it was a lie from the start."

Juro stepped between us. "Punishment has been dealt. You will cease this."

"Out of my way, Kurai," growled Beom.

I didn't look to see what sort of expression Juro had, but his tone grew sharp and cold as he leveled his voice. "I am a lord. And a guest. But strike her again, and I will have it as your declaration of war."

"Do you really think you could hope to win that war, toad?"

"Better to die with integrity than live in fear of a man's shadow."

"Then fetch your sword."

Juro stormed off. My only champion gone.

Kwang stepped in. "Brother, you are taking this too far. Do you even hear yourself? You're willing to declare war immediately after an announcement of peace? Over one servant girl?"

"I will beat out your defiance next, little brother, if you get in my way."

Kwang held his position.

"Step aside."

I'd only seen the feet, but knew that stumble from Kwang meant his brother had shoved him. I braced, waiting for the rod to come down. Worse, he pulled me back on me feet, holding me there until my knees didn't immediately collapse, and yanked my arm out again. It felt like an earthquake in my body, having to watch as he raised the bamboo to strike me again. The moment he started to bring it down, I flinched.

The strike never landed.

My eyes flashed open at the sound of two growling tigers. Lord Kwan held his brother's wrist, preventing the strike. Both of their jaws locked in place as they leered each other down, anger visible in each of their eyes.

"If there is a problem with my servant," said Lord Kwan, "I will handle it."

Beom scoffed. "Your lax attitude is why your servants cause problems. It's a blatant affront to the family, allowing them to do as they like without consequence."

Lord Kwan threw aside his brother's arm, never looking away.

Juro had returned with him, and came to me to comfort. One arm around me, and I was too frozen with fright to register it. "Were you in my house, I would never allow a single strike to you. Not for any reason." His other hand took in my arm, drawing back the sleeve to reveal a welt and a generous amount of red and swelling surrounding it. "Does it hurt to move it?"

I didn't comprehend a word of what he was saying or trying to do. I turned my head to look at him, and my face fell to cry.

"You've caused enough of a scene at my house," said Lord Kwan. "The girl is mine to deal with. Until her debt is labored off, she is mine. Not yours. You will address your anger at me with *me*. Not take it out on my staff."

"If I'd done so sooner," said Beom. "When you declared your love for a demon, our sisters would still be alive."

Lord Kwan said nothing, standing his ground until Beom gave in and walked away first.

"Hisa," called Lord Kwan, soft in his tone but with a lingering anger. "You will come with me. Lord Juro, Lord Kwang, you are missing the feast."

"Lord Kwan," said Juro, "surely you..." his words faded. When I looked up, I understood why. Lord Kwan's gaze, from over his shoulder, was a warning.

Kwang walked to him, meek in his attempt to apologize and met with the same icy look. He silenced and stepped back.

"Hisa," called Lord Kwan, keeping his voice low.

I got myself steady on my feet, taking small steps to follow behind.

"Clean up your face," said Lord Kwan. Without thought or hesitation, I obeyed, and concentrated on my breathing to keep from further weeping.

He led me around the house, far from the sight of the guests, and into his room. I cradled my injured arm, trying to protect it against invisible threats; he closed the doors behind me.

"Let me see," said Lord Kwan, his voice becoming softer.

I looked at him, for any hint of rage. When I saw only sadness, I held it up to him. One hand took my wrist, the other sliding down my sleeve and brushing over my skin. I winced at the touch, cool as it felt against my hot injury.

"I'm sorry he did this to you," said Lord Kwan, sounding like a broken man. "It should never have happened."

I was still in shock, and said nothing. Even as he used his magic to heal me, I just stared. My mind was blank.

After his spell ended, he cast another to banish the stains and smell from me. Then he stumbled, catching himself on the table. With a gasp, went to him.

"I'm alright." His words were quiet. A part of my gut knew he was lying, though the rest of me wasn't able to comprehend.

I wanted to say something, to be some kind of useful. But I didn't have anything intelligent to say. "I'm," I tried anyway. "I'm glad. That you're the Juneun who lives on this mountain."

He shifted his gaze to me, his face puzzled.

"I'm not sure we'd all survive, us villagers, if it was someone else here." Thoughtless, I hugged him. As I'd hugged my brothers, hugged Fumei—a deep embrace for comfort.

He returned it, lightly.

We stayed like that a moment, taking in each other's comfort.

"I'm sorry I'm such a troublesome prisoner."

"You make up for it."

We let go of each other, leaving me to look up and wonder.

"How?"

That hint of a smile was back. "Being an honest friend."

I shied. "Even though I keep messing up your fancy party thing?"

"With or without you, mistakes would be made. And Beom has made affronts on several of my house since he arrived. Given that, I can't even be annoyed at Syaoran's disappearance."

There were a hundred things I wanted to ask. I wanted to ask why Beom acted so hostile while Kwang more pleasant, and why the brothers didn't get along. Why was Eumeh engaged to Urekkato after we'd all thought it was his own engagement we were preparing for? I wanted to know about Gumiho, if she really was gone—she seemed like a force that was always there and always would be. Then there was what Beom said about Kwan's love for a demon, and what that'd meant. About what was so import with holding court, and why there were so many rules, and so many other things.

It didn't feel right in the moment to ask any of it, especially not after what just happened.

"You moved yourself back to the kennels," said Lord Kwan, breaking the quiet that took up the room. "You dislike your room?"

"It's not that, my lord. I'm just not," I tried to think of how to explain. "It's a lot noisier with so many guests. I'm not used to it."

"Noisier? That's an understatement."

I tucked my head into my shoulders, watching that hint of a smile grow. "The feast," I realized. "I dragged you away from it."

"I'm sure excuses have been made for me. It will start and end at Urekkato's discretion at any rate."

Despite what he'd said, I still felt guilty. There were probably more interesting people to talk to at a banquet than a village girl.

We sat there, side by side, saying nothing at all. And I liked it.

Late into the night, as the guests retired to their rooms and the household cleaned up, I crept back to the kennels for sleep. The note I'd left was gone, but the jacket remained, sitting atop my blanket, both still perfectly folded. Another thing about the strangeness of this summer I didn't understand.

I was too tired to think much of it. But laying down, my mind wouldn't let me sleep. A part of me was still too afraid. That somehow another lord or servant of would spring from a shadow to further torment me. Only mild relief came in remembering that court wouldn't last forever. Just a few days more.

Then came the temptation of taking out that puzzle box. I shut my eyes, counting, and took it from its hiding place once I opened them again. Sliding the tiles back to their cryptic phrase, I carefully opened it beneath my covers. The glow of the bead soothed me.

Picking it up, it felt warm. A comforting kind. The sort when a parent took your hand as a small child, or when a friend embraced you with love. It felt happy at my touch. I wasn't sure how I knew that, but it seemed that way. Feeling flowed into me, as though the bead of light knew me.

While I basked in the glow and the comfort of it, I closed my eyes to count, frequently. When I did grow tired enough, I put it away.

Chapter 31
What Everyone Else Thinks

In the following morning, word had spread about Beom, with the women in Lin's room in an upset.

"Someone lying to save their own skin. You and I were together the entire afternoon."

"It's no one in this room, that's for sure."

"Watch it turn out that it was one of Lord Beom's own staff, and they had the nerve to blame us for the wine mess at the house. Like we'd do that after having to work so hard to make it in the first place."

"Damned coward is what they are."

And while they went back and forth, in my heart I wanted to believe it was all truthful. That none of the women in Lord Kwan's service would put the blame on me. But if they were faced with an angry lord, maybe they would.

"I noticed Lin was gone for the entire evening," teased one woman. "Run off with Syaoran?"

"Since it seems like none of us are making any progress with the lords here, I wouldn't be surprised."

I saw Lin's face heat up. And of course, I'd known where she was. But a part of me wanted to prove myself an ally, and the words left me without consideration. "I passed Lin as I was getting the replacement wine, and she wasn't well. So, I said she could take a rest in my room where it was quieter and that I'd pick up her tasks for her."

A couple of the girls sported stunned expressions, looking to Lin as they asked for confirmation. She nodded, sheepish, building on what I'd said with the excuse of being in the sun for too long and taking on the extra work in the last few days; she closed with dismissal, saying that all she needed was extra rest.

After breakfast, however, Lin took me aside to fetch water for the kitchens. It wouldn't take the two of us, though it made the process a lot faster.

"Hey, thanks for sticking up for me."

"Hm?" I blinked at her, already exhausted.

"I was with Lord Kwang. Something tells me you knew that, though."

My brow bunched together and my eyes looked away. I remembered then about Urekkato's spell and shut them to the count of four. There didn't seem like a correct way to say that I'd accidentally walked in on them, and I didn't want Urekkato spying through me.

"I'm sorry I didn't get to you when you needed help last night. But I don't think I'd make things any better if I sprung out of the storeroom half naked."

"It's fine," I said, wanting to avoid any recollection.

"Lord Juro seems really fond of you though. I saw how tenderly he was holding you."

I shook my head, looking away from her teasing grin.

"If he does really like you, you should go for it. It's better than staying stuck as a maid, I'll tell you that much."

"He keeps implying a proposal, but I just want to finish out my sentence and go home to my village," I said. "I don't know if I could handle more events like this."

"A proposal? That's better than any of us have gotten. You should take it! Juro might not be much to look at and have smaller lands and a smaller house, but you'd probably never have to work another day in your life. The higher lords hold court, so you wouldn't have to worry about that either. The benefit to him is that he can keep his lands forever in spring or summer if he wants to. No more pickled fruit."

"I don't mind it pickled."

"The worst you might have to deal with is stomaching him. And if you've already managed to do that, then it's probably only a matter of getting used to it."

"Getting used to what?"

"Sex. You've already given him a taste, right?"

I went rigid, nearly tripping, and my face pinked up at how direct Lin was. "I haven't. Not with anyone."

She quirked a brow at me. "Never?"

I shook my head. "He said he wanted eight or nine children, but that seems like a lot. And I don't know that I'd want to marry him. He keeps smelling me, and it's a creepy."

"They've all got their vices," said Lin with a laugh. We paused our conversation until we were away from others again. "Men. They're obsessed with being fathers, warriors, and kings. If they obsessed about being good husbands and giving us ordinary girls a look, it'd be a better world. But we don't have money or land or titles for a dowry."

"A dowry?"

"Something the men get from the girl's family. It's sort of a way the family bribes him to marrying their daughter. Humans don't do that?"

"Not in the village. A boy usually picks a girl because he likes her. And she learns household skills from her mother."

"Makes things easier. But you'd still have to work all the time."

"I don't mind it."

"You wouldn't want to just do whatever you felt like and have someone else take care of everything?"

I did, once. "It actually makes me feel weird when someone does something for me. I've taken care of my family since I was nine."

"Is that long for a human?"

"I wasn't yet a woman. Not for another three years. And most girls in the villages don't marry until they reach nineteen or twenty."

"If there's no dowry, what do you do?"

"The men all help to make them a small house. Sometimes, if one of them is the youngest child, they move into that family's house. And their parents help to raise the babies. That's how it was with my father. My mother was from a different village. But everyone gets together for a celebration, and the bride and groom are gifted things from friends to help start their life together. Things for the kitchen and tools for future repairs usually."

"Not nearly as exciting."

"I used to dream about the day I'd get married."

"Not anymore?"

I stopped, reaching for my cheek. "After everything that's happened, I don't think there's any village boy who likes me enough."

Lin sighed, studying me with hands on her hips. "All the more reason you should take Lord Juro's offer. Show the village boys they missed out."

"Besides, it still feels weird living here. I don't think I'd fit in."

"You wouldn't have to. Just keep him happy in bed once in a while and give him a child, if that's even possible with humans. It's about all they want."

I cringed. "I only want to marry for love."

"Wouldn't we all? But how often does a chance like this happen? You could teach yourself to love him as you get used to him though."

I thought a lot about what Lin said the rest of the day. Was I stupid for wanting love, even if it meant a tiny home in a poor village? Everyone else seemed to think so. I went about my duties, lost in thought, acting on the cues I noticed rather than being attentive. The wine gone from my pitcher, I left to refill it.

Inside the store room, Urekkato was waiting. I blinked, needing a moment to register the scene.

"How's your arm?" asked Urekkato. He stepped forward, not giving me the chance to answer or ask how he knew. With one hand, he peeled my fingers from the ewer, with his other he slid back my sleeve to inspect. "Lucky you have Kwan as a friend. I saw Beom marching around and wanted to see what he was up to. I saw up until that first strike through your eyes. After that, the spell ended."

He let go of me, seeming more tender than any other time we'd met. Maybe there was something charming about him. Or maybe the spell I allowed made me see him in a better light than there was.

"He's that upset, huh?"

"I've been trying to avoid both of Lord Kwan's brothers since."

"What? No, not about that. He's angry that I'm the one marrying Eumeh."

I scrunched my brow at him.

"Every family sent a son they thought would best charm our king and the princess. Beom is too much of a brute and Kwang is too much of an idiot. That alone probably irritated him. To him, it seems unfair that he didn't have the chance to make Eumeh his. It's no secret that Kwan avoided being picked. Odds are, Beom might have seen to making sure every girl in Kwan's house was deflowered if he had been picked."

The revelation alarmed me. "Why would he do that? Wouldn't it have been a good thing if Lord Kwan was chosen?"

"He'd have done it out of spite. Might have already tried," said Urekkato, unconcerned. "Kwan practically handed Eumeh over to me, letting me take credit for Gumiho's demise. Don't misunderstand, I'm not complaining." He laughed, ignoring my discomfort. "To Beom, he probably sees it that he was held back from any of the glory. After all, Kwan is the younger brother and has more fame than he does. If you believe the rumors, Kwan is just as, if not more powerful."

I sighed, wanting no more of this. Urekkato seemed to be talking more to himself than me at that point, and I set myself to my task. There were things I wanted to ask, but at the same time I didn't want to accidentally expose some weakness to Lord Kwan. He took my arm as I went to leave the storeroom.

"But your friend is right. Take Juro's offer."

I became still, my blood cold. And I refused to meet his eye.

"He likes you without having you. You're in a rare position to make him do things the way you like."

My skin crawled, and I winced. "I don't want any part of those games."

"It's not a game this time. I think you should." He let go, smiling at me as he led the way out. "And if you're so unhappy in married life, I can visit you."

"That's kind of you, my lord," I said, choosing my words carefully. "But I don't think that'll be necessary. I plan to go home."

He shrugged. "Plans change all the time."

I knew he was teasing, trying to make me uncomfortable. He was a little like Syaoran in that way. Entertained by my squirming under implications rather than saying anything out of a desire. I may have come to Lord Kwan's house naïve, but I refused to stay that way.

Whether or not I was at home, I had to grow up.

The event of the final day of court was a dance. After all the politics and social calls and everything else that went beyond my comprehension, evening came. Feasting and dancing, with the newly engaged couple leading the procession and taking the first dance. The house had been open to all guests on the final day, so that Lord Kwan's personal gardens could be admired.

As it was the hottest day so far, the men had taken the paper paned doors and wall panels of the common spaces out to hang from the ceiling over the veranda. A better viewing of the house interior was given this way as well. Every lantern was alight as soon as the sun started to set, giving a beautiful glow to the house, the courtyard, and the gardens. Special lanterns were brought out to place on the koi pond; extra food was given to them before hand, so that they'd leave the delicate floating lights alone.

Likewise, the guests moved elegantly in their clothes, and the music carried over them like a breeze. I recognized one dance as the group performance that Feng and Syaoran taught me. Several others were done as a collective, though I didn't know the steps to those.

I wanted to be a part of it, to be bold enough to grab someone and take them into the routine as my partner. But it wasn't my place, or any of our places. Stealing glances to the other girls, several kept looking to whatever lord they'd been trying to attract, hoping beyond hope to be asked to dance and have some official statement made—a promise that their effort wasn't wasted.

So, I kept to the back of it all, unnoticed.

Lord Kwan didn't dance with anyone, though his brother Kwang delighted in a new partner every time. Beom was nowhere to be found, and I didn't know if I should've felt relief or concern by it. Urekkato took few dances, half of them with his bride-to-be, and the other half with ladies he took interest enough to ask. Even Juro found two ladies to accept a dance with him.

I could count the hours now. By morning, all the guests would be leaving, and wouldn't come back the rest of the year. We would get up and dress courtly one last time, only to see them off.

With most of everyone accounted for, I took the opportunity to sneak off to the kennels to move my things back into my room. I made sure to stay aware of my surroundings, not wanting to run into Beom or a servant of a different household that'd taken liberties with wine consumption.

In collecting my things, I couldn't help think about the puzzle box. It'd been abandoned since before I'd arrived. Forgotten. But, with hands full, I didn't want to risk taking it as well.

For the best, since my room held an unexpected sight: Syaoran, sleeping on my bed.

Walking up, I kept as quiet as I could. He looked so still and peaceful that I didn't want to wake him. A queer thought came, suggesting he might be hurt or sick. With my things set, I looked over him, assessing without touching him. He woke anyway. For all I knew, it was because I breathed too loudly.

In an instant, he grabbed me, claws ready. Then stopped once he recognized me, either from my face or the pathetic squeak of surprise.

"It's just you," said Syaoran, sighing his relief.

"Who else would it be?" I reclaimed myself and stood straight.

"You were sneaking up on me."

"You weren't moving when I came in. I thought you were dead." That wasn't entirely true, but it was the best I could come up with to tease at him.

He grumbled and laid back down.

"Have you been hiding here the entire time?"

"Not the entire time." As soon as he'd said it, he looked as if he'd spilled some secret. "Lord Beom isn't particularly fond of my presence. With his moods, I didn't want to give him a reason to come after me."

For that, I couldn't fault him. Instead, I took a seat beside him.

"I'm sorry," said Syaoran after a long spell of silence. "About, with Lord Juro. It was unbecoming of a Juneun to play on the emotions of others."

I looked at him, meeting his eye and seeing the sincerity of his bent brow as he apologized. "I forgive you. Everyone else wants to push me to accept a proposal from him. But even if I did like him, I don't think I'd be able to handle becoming a Juneun's wife. Not with how overwhelming holding court feels."

He sat up. "Have you entertained the idea at all?"

I shook my head, fixing my eyes to my lap. "Every time I even try to think about it, I can't. It feels too weird."

"Weird how?"

"I don't know," I said, shifting in place. "Whenever I imagined being married and having a family, it was always to an ordinary man. A human, in the village. But a Juneun is different. Humans age, grow old, and die. Spirits are immortal, aren't they?"

"To an extent, yes. I don't know if any of us have ever died of old age. It's never been peaceful that long." He moved, placing himself to sit in line with me. "There's other benefits to accepting Juro than a comfortable life, you know."

"What do you mean?"

"Some girls have a dowry. But if you don't, you can convince your father to refuse unless there's a high bride-price."

"Bride-price?"

"If a man wants a woman badly enough, sometimes a family will take her dowry and institute a price for her instead. Sometimes it's land and livestock, but usually it's gold. Something that convinces the family that even if he's not the sort of ally they want, he has enough wealth to help influence their political stakes and will take care of their daughter."

"That sounds just as bad as a dowry. Does anyone marry for love when it comes to lords and spirits?"

He shrugged. "Love comes and goes if you live long enough."

I sighed. "Thankfully they're all leaving tomorrow."

We sat there, letting the echo of music fill the space around us.

"Dance with me," said Syaoran.

"Out there? In front of everyone?"

"Heaven, no. We can dance here in your room. There's almost enough space."

I cringed. "No thank you. People already say enough things about me."

"There's a lot they say about me. What does it matter?"

"I just don't want to make more trouble for myself."

He stood up, offering his hand. "Then what about outside? In this part of the house, away from everyone. Just the two of us outcasts?"

I eyed him, wary.

"Be a shame to forget how to dance after Feng and I went through the trouble to teach you."

"I guess so," I said, still not convinced but taking his hand anyway.

"Consider it your way of thanking me for loaning you my jacket."

"It was you?"

"I don't usually go in the kennels because it always smells of dog. Kwan's brothers usually have a couple every time they come. But lately, everywhere smells like dog. Maybe it's one of the guests or their personal staff, I'm not sure—either way it puts me on edge."

"That's why you're hiding in my room?"

"Well, if you weren't going to use it..." he broke into laughter, leading me out the door and off the veranda to the small yard beyond for a dance.

I stumbled more often than I got it right. Even so, I smiled the entire time.

For a little while, I was just a normal girl.

Chapter 32
Broken Things

The morning of guests departing, the entirety of Lord Kwan's household stood to see them off with practiced farewells. Though I didn't know them, I kept quiet and imitated the rest.

"Hisa," Juro brought his horse close. A pretty roan mare with a black and white mane. "If there's ever anything you want that Lord Kwan refuses to give to you, you may write me."

Try as I might, my brow still furrowed and bent in my discomfort. "You're very thoughtful, my lord, but I think I'll be fine."

"I might also send things without prompting. Is there anything of particular interest to you, Hisa?"

A thousand things. "I couldn't ask anything."

He laughed. I'd accidentally made his pursuit more enticing and I didn't know how to avoid any of it. "Humor me with one request."

I hurried to think, looking to the moon gate and the waiting doors, the line of horses awaiting their riders—that was it! I looked back, smiling and dipping my head down politely. "Only for your safe return home, my lord."

He grumbled and sighed. "I will miss your sweet aroma. Until next time. And of course, to you as well, my friend."

"Until next time," said Lord Kwan.

Juro took off in a fast trot. His personal servants with him.

Urekkato called for me next, though gestured that I go to him. I looked to Lord Kwan for what to do. I'd been told to stay in line with the others until we were dismissed, and say nothing unless addressed first and to keep all answers brief.

Lord Kwan gave the slightest indication with his chin, eyes flicking from me to Urekkato for confirmation. I still hesitated, taking small steps.

The Cat Clan prince brought me close. I flinched. "Try not to end my spell so frequently. Otherwise, how will I know to send Kwan to you the next time you're in danger?"

"You did?" I looked at him, into his cat-like eyes, astonished.

"I'll be too busy after my wedding to look through your eyes too often anyway."

He climbed on his horse, a gray stallion whose mane was cut, and dismissed me.

I was more confused now about him than ever before. Sometimes he was kind, sometimes he was cruel, but always he was unpredictable (except that he delighted in my discomfort). At my place among the staff, I fidgeted, and couldn't help notice the odd glances turned in my direction.

Carriages were hauled away, all of us in unison to bid farewell, with Urekkato taking off afterwards.

Lord Kwan gestured for me to come to his side. Whatever the trouble, I genuinely didn't know. I kept an eye on the Cat Clan lord as he showed off while he still had onlookers.

"It was Urekkato that told me about my brother's behavior," said Lord Kwan, low. His eyes stayed fixed on the moon gates, turning only when another lord said their goodbye to him. "Juro was on his way to get his sword. A guest killing the host's brother, or a brother killing the host's guest. Which one is worse?"

I said nothing. They were both a terrible thing to me.

"What did he want?"

I looked from the gates to Lord Kwan, trying to think of how to best explain it. I didn't want him to think badly of me, agreeing to that spell. I'd done it with the best of intentions and forgetting all the possible problems it might cause. Now, my friendship with Lord Kwan was on the line, and I didn't know if he'd understand why I would allow it in the first place. "He's tried to get another rise from me, my lord. I've restrained myself from it. I don't want to put you in another position like before."

Another lord gave his goodbye, commenting on the deliciousness of the food, and rode off at a leisurely pace.

I stayed where I was, waiting to be dismissed.

"Good girl," said Lord Kwan. Something that annoyed me, as though I were a pet and not a person. Glancing to him, he looked just as tired as the rest of us. That made it easier to suggest it was carelessly said and meaning to compliment, but I still felt irritated by it.

The last of the guests left, and the gates began a slow closing, ceremony in their lack of speed.

It wasn't lost on anyone that Lord Kwan's brothers weren't among the lords that left. Syaoran and I exchanged glances, a shared unease in that realization. We were all dismissed, happily tidying up at our leisure and hanging the paper paned doors to let in the summer breeze.

Afterwards, I headed to my room, eager to change out of restrictive layers and into the clothes Fumei had brought me.

That same suggestion stopped me at my door. The feeling of being called back. It pulled at me, stronger than my loathing of my court dress. Only a look. But I would leave it right where it was.

On my way, I'd spotted Lord Kwan speaking with Yua, falling to her knees in a weep. He stayed in place, stone, but a somber expression seemed to want to come forward. I recalled vaguely that Urekkato said something on it, the morning I attended Lord Kwan. In either case, it wasn't my place to go, to pry. I wanted to be of comfort, but I didn't want to intrude on what looked like a very personal matter.

In the kennels, with no one around, I plucked out the puzzle box and peered inside. Soft warmth, like a greeting. It made me sad to think of putting it back, locked away and alone in the dark. I knew I couldn't take it with me. It wasn't mine. And guilt ran through me that I'd even taken it out and looked.

A crash sounded from the house.

Frantic, I couldn't get the loose stone up to replace the puzzle box. In my panic, I shoved it under all the layers of my dress and hurried towards the sound. The last thing I wanted was to get blamed for whatever happened.

Hardly out of the kennels, Lin found me.

"There you are!"

My insides trembled.

"I've been looking everywhere for you. Lord Kwan wants a word with us."

"The crash?"

"Let someone else deal with that. Probably a tired cook and a loose grip. Now come on."

I followed, wondering how likely Lin's dismissal was. As we passed the kitchens, one of the men growled about having seen a trickster demon bolt out. Syaoran, however, didn't seem convinced, waving his hand in front of his nose.

In Lord Kwan's room, the doors remained open. Both Lin and I stood, waiting for the reason he called on us.

"Yua will be taking some time away," said Lord Kwan at last.

Lin and I exchanged a look, fasting returning our attention.

"So, her responsibilities will be shared between the two of you."

"My lord?" started Lin. When his eyes went to her, studying, she became stiff. "Shouldn't the position be shared with a more permanent staff?"

He stared, his face unreadable.

"Hisa is a hard worker, but she doesn't know—"

"She will take Yua's place in attending whatever I need personally. You will take Yua's place in running the household. Is that too much?"

Lin beamed, shaking her head. "I will handle it, my lord."

He kept his watch fixed on Lin, measuring. "We may have need to hold court again next year." He looked away, towards the open doors as unknown thoughts occupied his attention.

"Again?" asked Lin. "My lord, then, would it be..." Lin's voice trailed, but he didn't look at her. "If you plan to make it more regular, we need a larger staff."

Finally, his eyes turned back to her. "That would be your domain."

A new excitement took hold of Lin.

"Choose wisely."

She bowed in a show of gratitude. "And, my new position entails anything else?"

For a long while he said nothing, rooting out Lin's meaning. "Your pay will also increase. Talk to Syaoran on the matter, and plan a budget for new additions wherever they're needed."

"Yes, my lord," said Lin, bowing again and looking at me to do the same.

I did, and we were dismissed.

While Lin was ecstatic about the news, I felt only dread. I hated court. I hated the suffocating layers and the unwanted advances of lords and the chide remarks of ladies. I didn't want to do it again!

"Are you okay?"

I broke from my anxious thoughts to look at Lin. "What?"

"I've been talking and you haven't answered."

"Oh," I said, looking out to the courtyard as we walked. "Sorry."

"I was saying that you'll have to get to his room to attend before breakfast. And don't worry about any gossip. I'll handle it for you."

"Gossip about what?" It struck me as soon as I'd said the words. I'd be in Lord Kwan's room more often, while he was under dressed, and likely with the doors closed.

"You covered for me. And I know nothing will happen between you two. Everyone knows that, but it doesn't stop someone's jealousy spreading rumors. So, I'll put an end to anything that comes up. You can barely admit you're a virgin without getting flustered, anything more might cause you to explode."

That was true enough. I felt glad to have Lin on my side, a friend to stop accusations about me. She didn't waste time with it when Syaoran tried to tease me. There was a hefty bit of paperwork to be done simply to acknowledge a promotion in rank and count coin for hiring new staff. I didn't understand half of it, though I tried my best to keep up.

On our walk out, something kept bothering me. Between Syaoran's tease, Lin's pointing out my discomfort, and Urekkato's mocking me, I couldn't stand it.

"Lin?" I didn't really have anyone else to ask. "What does it mean *to teach a man what you like*?"

She held in laughter as we walked. "Where'd you hear that? Wait... Are you actually thinking of seducing—?"

I took her arm, shaking my head furiously. "No! I'm just tired of having conversations go over my head. And if Lord Kwan does want court to be held regularly, I don't want to be kept ignorant about these things. Especially with..." I trailed, remembering to shut my eyes and count before going on.

"That's true. Next thing you know, a more perverted personal staff of one of the guests will try to take advantage. It's probably not a good idea for any of us girls to be naïve. I'd probably have been better off if I knew what to expect the first time."

"The first time?"

"I didn't always work for Lord Kwan. My family sent me to work for a richer lord first. I was about your age, maybe a little older. That's how he liked it, being the first to deflower a girl."

I shuddered.

"Some men are worse than others," said Lin, dismissive. "At least here there's less chance of being forced into a situation. Lord Kwan doesn't take much of an interest, and Syaoran enjoys more that a girl comes to him. The rest of them are opportunistic, don't get me wrong, they're just less brash about it."

My mind went back to Sen.

"Come with me to send out this missive. We'll go to your room after, since I should be instructing you on new duties anyway."

I reiterated about what I already knew. Rudimentary things—the basics, as Lin put it. Though the rest was overwhelming. So many phrases to mean the same lewd thing, and description of different ways and the things before made me space out from time to time. My mind actively rejecting while also curious and trying to understand.

"Mostly," said Lin, "men want to think they have the power to please a woman. They treat it more like a game than anything. Smiles and giggles leading up to it—are you alright?"

"I'm fine," I said.

"Your face is almost scarlet. Are you sure?"

"I'm just—I've never had this conversation before."

She quirked a brow, a concerned expression growing as she decided on something. "We can stop now and pick it up again later if you want."

I did want that. Except, to also never talk about it again. When I imagined my future life, being with a husband, it was never such a vivid imagining. Taking in a deep breath, I tried to force myself not to blush. "Let's get it over with."

She pursed her lips, weighing my choice against her own judgement. "There's not a lot more to say. I mentioned about not letting them know exactly how often you've been with a man, since they dislike a higher count. But it might do you some good to not mention you've never been with one either. Some men get excited to try and be the first."

"It sounds so strange, since they're more bashful about having a lower count with women or that it's their first, like you said."

"Men are strange creatures," said Lin with a sigh. "But there's not much else. As far as getting him to do what you want rather than what he wants, well, you have to figure out what it is you like. Convincing him to it is the trick. I'm not sure how to do that one though."

I was better informed, though it hardly seemed helpful. Maybe in the sense that I could better avoid things now, but as for what Urekkato alluded to, I still didn't know. Maybe this was part of his game, to lead me to have this complicated conversation.

"Figure it out," I muttered. But the idea caused me to shudder. I wanted it to only be with a man who I was in love with, and who loved me in return. The way it was explained sounded more manipulative than affectionate. I fidgeted. "Were you scared? The first time?"

Her expression changed, brow furrowing and jaw setting. "The first few times, I was. For a while, I didn't know it could be my choice as well. I put up with it because I held onto a promise he made. That'd I'd be his fifth mistress."

"Fifth?" I was shocked. When Juro tried to propose and mentioned keeping a single mistress, my body went cold. The more I learned about noble life, the less romanticized I found myself thinking about it.

"Just sleeping with a lord isn't exactly a worthy act. But becoming a mistress means you have privileges and some sway with him. Then you can pull your family into a little bit better of a position. It's the most we common girls can hope for."

"Sure, but I don't like that idea," I said, shying my tone to hide disgust. "I've always thought it was enough to have a wife. Why would he need anyone else?"

"*Need* might be a strong word," said Lin, reclining back. "In rare cases, a wife can't give him a son or any children, so the lord tries to make a natural heir some other way rather than see everything he's built go to someone else or be split between contenders."

"Why wouldn't it just go to his wife?"

"If we ran things, we'd make more sensible decisions like that. My guess is that they'll be too scared that they'd have to treat their wife as an equal or get smothered in their sleep."

Of all the things this conversation brought, that made me cringe hardest and tuck into myself.

"I think that's about it," said Lin. "I might be forgetting some things, but they're probably not important."

I'd been left alone not long after, looking for where to stash the puzzle box I'd taken. Everywhere seemed like too much of a suspicious place. Finally, I decided on the bottom of my stationery.

Out of court attire and back in my rough-spun clothes, I breathed a long sigh of relief. No more tight, rigid waistlines. No more restricted breaths. No more tiny strides to get to anywhere. I was free to move around as I pleased, to sprint if I wanted to. Yua explained why the set up was necessary, but the red lines marking where every piece sat didn't fill me with confidence in what she'd said.

Barefooted, I walked the veranda, enjoying the quiet of it. A quiet that came to a sudden halt when Beom drew his sword. Hot words flew from him, though I didn't have the context to make sense of them. His opponent: Lord Kwan.

Whatever the reason, the brothers stood to face off. Beom assumed an aggressive stance, Lord Kwan a relaxed one. With a roar, Beom charged, deflected and side stepped by Lord Kwan.

Another set of rapid attacks. One, two, three, four, five. Each one parried as Lord Kwan gave ground and moved himself out of line to some other part of the courtyard. Irritated, Beom knocked down a heavy planter to cut off access to one side.

"You continue to humiliate the family," growled Beom as he swung.

Lord Kwan leapt back, deflecting and climbing to the veranda.

Beom pursued, smashing whatever got in his way. "You abuse your position, and you forget your place!"

Still silent, Lord Kwan knocked down whatever he had in reach to create a barrier and give space.

"You keep that fox-bastard, allowing him to parade around as one of us!" He swung again, breaking a paper paned window. "You put a title on the toad!" Kicking aside debris, Beom ripped off one of the doors from its hanging spot to throw at his brother.

Lord Kwan dodged, side stepping and advancing with his brother now distracted and loose on his grip. One, two, three, the fourth strike cutting Beom's upper arm, five, six, seven, Lord Kwan didn't relent.

Beom pushed back, using raw strength over elegant swiftness to deflect with his sword. One hand released, rising fast to hit Lord Kwan on the side of his face. Lord Kwan stumbled, now having difficulty in deflecting his brother's swipes. The barrage stopped only after a risky move by Lord Kwan, going down and forward to catch his brother's wrist to stop the strike entirely.

I saw the start of transformation from both of them then. Hands becoming larger, clawed, the tiger pattern pronounced from their skin. Snarls from both of them, their eyes turning wild, and teeth shifting from a man's to a beast's.

The staff that'd come to see the ruckus got out of the way, though no one left. There was worry plastered on all of us, from both households.

"And then there's your little human whore."

Enraged, Lord Kwan pushed off, matching his brother's ferocity as claws and steel were exchanged. It happed quick, faster than I could see, and twice I had to get out of the way of their brawl.

"Is that why you gave up Eumeh so easily?" demanded Beom in a roar. "Does it make you happy to shame our parents?"

Lord Kwan lunged, knocking Beom to the ground to grapple. Beom tumbled back, kicking off his brother with enough force to send him crashing into the clay and wood wall. A snapping, shattering sound echoed through the air, as did the clattering of his sword away from its wielder. The final brother, making his appearance with a stark expression at the scene, panted from his run.

"You delayed vengeance for our sisters," growled Beom. "Protecting that devil was more important to you than honoring your family." He marched on Lord Kwan, who seemed torn between releasing his power to be a man again, and surrendering to the monster.

Beom was going to kill him, I could feel it.

I didn't pray for courage this time. I acted without it. Running to him, I tried to help Lord Kwan to his feet, to get him out of there! My intentions were over ambitious. He was too heavy for me to lift. No matter what words I used to encourage his own action, he was too stunned from the impact to respond.

With Beom almost over us, the sensible side of me screamed for me to run. The rest of me refused, needing to protect my friend. I crouched over, on all fours to try shielding him with my body.

"Step aside girl," commanded Beom.

I shook my head, unable to do anything else.

"This isn't the honorable death of a servant defending their master. If you do not move, I will cut you down as well."

I stayed where I was, looking him straight in the eye as I trembled.

"This is your final chance, girl." He took his sword in both hands, a warning.

I refused to move.

A growl sounded behind my other ear. The sort of growl that turned my blood cold. The kind that came from a predator about to make meat out of a man. I could feel in my bones that Lord Kwan was losing himself. I shifted my focus from Beom, throwing the full of myself onto Lord Kwan, as if somehow that alone would prevent him from becoming a monster.

"No," I whispered. "Don't go. I'm staying with you, Lord Kwan." I spoke my whisper as loudly as I dared into his ear.

The sound of colliding steel behind me. I looked over my shoulder, seeing Kwang intercept his brother's blow.

"For someone complaining about bringing shame to our family name," growled Kwang, though she stayed very much a man in his appearance. "You would use your sword on an unarmed woman? And while she is not on her feet? What honor is that?" He tangled the blades, pressing his brother back two steps. Taking his own stance, he awaited Beom's decision. Through it, I could see a kind of fear tugging at him.

Beom resumed his posture, raising his sword without hesitation. "Are you sure you want to do this, little brother?"

Kwang took a breath. "I will do what I believe is right."

Wary, Beom tapped the tip of his sword against Kwang's, testing, goading. Kwang launched. The clashing of steel fast, I couldn't count. Not that I could be bothered to count. Lord Kwan was fighting against himself and needed help.

I didn't know what I could do to prevent him from losing himself. The best I could come up with was to remind him of the happiest times I had in his company, about the peach grove and the brilliant lake at the top of the mountain, about the quiet, muggy afternoon sharing in art and tea.

Another crash as Kwang was thrown aside without grace. The fight didn't last long at all, and the youngest brother lay in a heap with a broken paper-paned door over him. A hissing growl in every breath came from Beom, and I was too afraid to look. I buried my face against Lord Kwan, and begged not to lose the kind and stoic Juneun that I called my friend.

His arm clung to me, and the sound of metal intercepting metal rang from behind. Lord Kwan held tight to me, his sword recalled to his hand and holding off his brother. He was wild, but still himself. His foot kicked out at Beom's shin, gaining a vital second to toss aside the pointed steel and get to his feet with me. My hands became a vice on his shirt in the sudden movement.

The rest of the staff continued to stay out of the way. Unwritten rules were broken, and they gave an abundance of space between themselves and the brawl.

Beom rushed in, roars as frequent as beaths came from both of them. One handed, refusing to let me go, Lord Kwan shoved off Beom's advancing strikes. I was dragged along, my feet barely touching ground. Lord Kwan took a cut to his neck, red sliding down the tiger pattern of his skin beside my face. I shrieked, not meaning to, and his grip on me tightened.

Another strike was landed on Lord Kwan, distracted by my terror, nicking his arm. His outraged expression fled, and the stony one I came to know reclaimed its place on him. He moved in on Beom, bashing his elbow into his brother's face.

Beom stumbled back, clapping a hand over his nose. All of which allowed Lord Kwan space enough to release me safely. He charged in, hitting the sides and thighs of his older brother with the blunt of his blade. Beom fell to a knee, compromising his every position, but saved from bleeding. Before he could climb back onto his feet, Lord Kwan's sword caused him to pause, the very tip pointed at Beom's throat.

Unlike his older brother, Lord Kwan gave restraint to his aggression.

The brothers leered each other down. The sound of groaning, and I realized Kwang had come to again, needing help. As I rushed to the youngest brother, Syaoran hurried to Lord Kwan.

Whatever words were exchanged, Lord Kwan held his expression, weighing his choice. "I will not run my brother through. But he is no longer welcome in my home."

He started to bring away his sword when Beom grabbed hold of it, glaring. "I have no brother who lives here." A slow start of blood dripped from his hand.

Kwang, on his knees, and realizing the exchanged, spoke up. "Then you have no brother in my home either!"

Beom's eyes shifted over to us, rage bright within them. He scoffed, watching Kwang get to his feet.

"You seem to be running out of family," said Lord Kwan. He yanked his sword free of Beom's grip. His other arm outstretched, its sheath came as he cleaned off the blade against his hanbok. Both pieces in hand, he put them back as one and walked away.

The beastly qualities of both brothers receded, leaving them looking like men once more.

"Syaoran, get this place cleaned up," commanded Lord Kwan, assuming his station once again.

Syaoran bowed, quick to obey.

"Hisa, you will attend me."

I hesitated, looking at Kwang for direction, since the rest of the staff was occupied trying to correct the damage done.

"You shouldn't have intervened," whispered Kwang. "Go to him."

With no more delay, I picked up pace to follow, shutting my eyes and counting.

His steps were weak. Out of sight from the others, he seemed more labored in his breath and struggling in his stride. I went to try and shoulder him. He didn't pull away. In his room, he nearly collapsed.

"Lord Kwan," I said, a little too loud, needing to rein in my voice. "What's wrong?"

"I over exerted myself," said Lord Kwan, weak in his tone. "Always with my brothers..."

"I'm sorry," I said. The realization came to me, coupled with what Kwang mentioned. "You used more magic protecting me again. I thought he meant to kill you and I was trying to protect you. Instead, I made things worse, didn't I?"

We made it to his bed. He laid down, brow beaded in sweat.

"In some ways, yes," said Lord Kwan. "But you prevented me from losing control. I heard your voice, and that was enough." His hint of a smile returned, eyes meeting mine. "Only Kwang knows about it. The rest of my family does not."

"Only Lord Kwang, and us here?" I asked. In his silence, my mind put together missing pieces. "That's part of why there's so few in your household, isn't there? So it's less chance of the wrong person finding out."

His hand took mine, cool to the touch, approving of my conclusion.

"What I still don't understand is why brothers would be fighting at all."

"Do you not with yours?"

"We argue, but," I thought back, to every instance I still had in my memory. "We rarely fight. And it's never that heated. In the end, we're family, and we look after each other."

I scooted to sit beside him, keeping him company until he regained more strength, enough to brush some of my hair behind my ear, revealing my scar. I looked away from him, self-conscious all over again. He'd seen it a hundred times before. Since my hair had grown long enough to conceal it, however, I felt secure in hiding behind it. Hiding more and more of myself from pitying stares.

"We're both a little damaged," said Lord Kwan. "But we're still here in spite of it."

My eyes stole a look back at him, curious, and saw a gentleness in his features. It was hard to imagine a Juneun as broken. They weren't like humans. But his words put me at ease.

Chapter 33
Swings & Saddles

Midsummer, and Lord Kwan was away. In my first day as his attendant, I embarrassed myself. Trying to be dutiful, I'd gotten up before breakfast to go to his room. When he didn't answer, I worried and peeked. He was still in bed then, rolling over with a groggy expression and calling me in. He didn't actually need me. It was more for the show and to keep others out of his room. He didn't put it past Lin to try and exploit the position; something I thought seemed out of character for her, though I only knew her two years and Lord Kwan for some decades.

Though, it still haunted me how everyone talked about each other. How the women talked about Lord Kwan, or any lord as a *prize*. It felt gross in my mouth to think about it—and worse to think if someone said that about me, making it seem like I should be so honored. I wasn't beautiful, or the most gifted, but I wasn't the worst at most things—I wasn't useless! Even if I made a mess of things during court, and I wasn't a proper lady or an adept servant for a noble Juneun... Was I worse off than I thought?

Things resumed, more or less, to normal. I picked up my riding lessons again not long after court ended, thinking that I may as well get used to it if I did decide to accept Juro's proposal. That's what everyone else said I should do, even if I didn't want it.

Why was I so spineless about this? Because I didn't have better prospects at home, now that rumors piled onto my lack of beauty and skill? I'd learned more in Lord Kwan's service than I could have ever hoped for at home. And if I asked, maybe the kitchen staff would teach me a bit. They didn't appear to dislike me, and I didn't mind fetching things and getting messy. In Yua's absence, I could use my temporary position to pressure an agreement.

Something in my gut burned with delight. I hated myself for considering anything less than love. What did it matter what everyone else thought? It wasn't their life! I couldn't back talk or be blunt as a servant girl. But I wouldn't be a servant forever. I could outright refuse anything I wanted then. My father and brothers wouldn't allow it, not after my having been gone for five years, I was sure of it.

Saburo picked up on my mood. His ears swiveled this way and that, his tail swishing, and he snorted in his breathing. Our pace picked up without my notice until an unpleasant and speedy trot made me feel as though I would fall. Then he broke into a canter. The noise around me faded away. There was only the air whipping past my ear. At the same time, I didn't feel that we were going fast at all. We'd smoothed out and my balance reset. It was as close to flying as I could imagine, and I smiled. I wanted to go faster, to leave behind every thought that my mind ever used against me, if only we could go just a little faster. I felt free. We ran that same length over and over, but I felt freer than I had since I was nine years old. It was me and Saburo and the wind, and nothing else.

When at last I felt calm again, I pulled back on the reins gently and cooed to signal my desire to slow to a stop. Saburo obliged. I knew then that I loved riding. Not because someone wanted me to, but because of that experience of freedom and oneness. I breathed deep, holding it for a moment before I let go. My smile stayed.

Syaoran clapped from the side, having filled in as my instructor. "That was beautiful! Good job. But don't keep Saburo stopped, let him walk a while to cool down his muscles."

I relaxed my hold, letting Saburo wander as I kept my head high. I wouldn't let rumors or teases bother me anymore, not without a fight. I'd go home so well skilled that it would be impossible for me to think it was ever foolish to wish for love. If no romance awaited me in my own village, I could ride to others. I would make it so that I could be limitless. That's what it felt like in that moment.

When I came out of my daydreaming, I saw Lord Kwan standing beside Syaoran in light conversation. He was home again, and I nudged Saburo to trot over softly to greet him. I dismounted with dignity, keeping my smile as I welcomed my friend.

"Is Saburo taking care of you?" asked Lord Kwan.

Before I could answer, start some small conversation, Gi came up with a request from Lin wanting to see me.

"She's wasted no time getting settled in her new station," said Lord Kwan, that hint of a smile on his face.

Syaoran crossed his arms. "She doesn't give anyone an inch to challenge her. I think she's holding the position well. I can see it stresses her, but she's not the sort to let anyone walk on her."

Lord Kwan nodded, looking to me. "I'll take Saburo, so you can go directly."

I handed off the reins, my smile struggling to stay strong. As I walked, I could hear part of their continued conversation.

"So you approve of my choice?"

"I do, my lord."

Going to a common space, Lin had three other women I'd never seen before. They sat with perfect manners and not the slightest slouch. All of their eyes went to me as I walked in and tried to make a good presentation of myself, even though I was coated in dust and sweat in my riding clothes.

I stood politely, moving only when Lin waved me over.

"Take this to the guardhouse at the outer gate. The faster, the better." She handed me a rolled paper, tied with twine.

There were a handful of questions I had. Why send for me and not have Gi walk it down? What made this urgent, and was it wise to have me be the one to carry it, especially in front of strangers? I ignored the questions, not wanting to embarrass her, and did as she asked.

I was barely out of the first gate and headed for the endless stairs when Lord Kwan called for me.

"What do you have there?"

I looked from Lord Kwan, standing in front of me, to the length of stairs that led into a decorative bamboo forest. "Lin wanted me to carry this to the gatekeepers below, my lord."

He held out a palm, a wordless command. And I obeyed. Watching him open it, I began to fidget. When he raised a brow, allowing his hint of a smile to strengthen, I squinted at his expression.

"Clever." He handed it off to me.

There was nothing important written on it. Times. And a simple phrase asking what they heard. "My lord?"

When he understood my confusion, he summed up the ploy. "She wanted to see their reaction, and listening to comments made about you."

"Me? But, why?"

"If I had to guess, I'd say it's to sift out anyone likely to cause problems and spread distasteful gossip. Who better to bait them than my human prisoner, now attendant?"

It'd been so long since I'd heard the word prisoner that I'd nearly forgotten. Outside these walls, the rest of the world surely remembered that fact.

"Yua used to call in Syaoran for similar reasons. Lin is astute, I'll grant her that."

"I was being sent on a fool's errand?" the words made my jaw want to lock up.

"And likely will again if she's not content with any of the lot so far. Though, it seems like a less calculated thought sending you all the way down to the outer gate. Unless she wanted them to run into you again."

I rubbed at my arms in new discomfort. "I don't like that."

"I imagine not," said Lord Kwan. "Syaoran can just as easily be let in on her scheme and create an illusion. If she panicked, it may have slipped her memory."

I sighed, about to part ways to head for my room where I could wash and change.

"Come with me, Hisa."

Blinking, I thought I misunderstood for a second. He didn't walk back through the inner gate to go to his room. Rather, he walked in the direction of my preferred spot between the walls. I followed, of course, and tried to guess at what he wanted.

"Are you confident enough to ride outside the walls?" asked Lord Kwan, though he didn't look at me or stop his stride.

Again, I didn't understand where this was all going. "Yes, my lord."

"We'll be going up the mountain in a few days. You'll take your own horse this time."

My smile returned, remembering the lake and the honey-sweet peaches. I didn't mind the rest of the walk going on in silence. My imagination kept preoccupied with thoughts on how to show off my horsemanship skill.

We stopped under the shade of the trees in my favorite spot, though he said nothing. I broke from my thoughts, looking at Lord Kwan and then to the surrounding area. I almost didn't spot it. A swing.

"You have these in your village, do you not?"

I rose on my toes, my smile widening. "I haven't gone on one in a long time. Not since I was little. But they were a bit different in the village."

"Oh? How so?"

I went over to it. "We weave the ropes ourselves. But they're brittle. And the bottom piece is usually whatever fallen branch that seems thick enough to hold a bit of weight for a while. One part or the other always breaks after a month or so." I admired the thick braided rope, and the wood seat carved specifically for this purpose, wide enough for two people to be on it.

"Climb on," said Lord Kwan.

I looked back at him, hesitating a moment. It was so fine a thing, and I still wasn't used to being allowed to use something like it at my own discretion. He waited, expectant, and I happily placed my feet on it. What I didn't expect was for him to push at the ropes and give me a gentle start.

I'd forgotten the rush of joy swaying higher and higher, with the wind pushing my hair forward and back in tandem with every rise and fall.

Then, he climbed on behind me, his feet to either side of my own, and his hands a little higher than mine.

"I used to spend all my idle time as a boy on one of these."

I looked behind me, past my hair to see his face as he reminisced. While I probably looked half-wild, his own hair, long and obsidian, kept a kind of dignity about itself. Very little broke from its neatly set place and whipped about his neck and face.

When he looked down at me, I smiled. His own smile grew a little too. We enjoyed each other's company a while, between the sun and the shade. A short time when I was not a servant and he was not a lord. We were simply friends. Absent minded, I hummed, stopping when I remembered myself.

"Why did you stop in the middle of the tune?"

I felt embarrassed, shrugging my shoulders. "I missed a part."

Quiet.

"I liked it anyway," said Lord Kwan. Whether or not he meant it didn't matter. It was the effort to comfort that restored my feeling of content.

Building up my courage, I started again, trying to get every note perfect.

"Relax, Hisa. It's just us."

I paused again, shying for a moment at the softness of his voice, and went on at my own pace. When I realized I missed a part of the melody, I redid it and continued after. Far from perfect, but an expression of how I felt.

We slowed, allowing the swing to stop at its own leisure. He stepped down with dignity, I hopped off without thought, and we walked back.

Along the way, I did a double take at something very unusual. Some ambitious creature had dug a wide hole, abandoning it to leave a mess.

"Hisa?"

I turned my head, seeing how far I'd fallen behind and catching up. It was probably nothing. Anything dangerous would've been noticed by a Juneun.

In our walking, as I relived recent events, a new question came. I hadn't asked my daily allowance since Lord Kwan left. "My lord?"

"Hm?"

"Why did you put up the swing?"

He looked over his shoulder, past his glossy hair, slowing his stride but never stopping. "I thought you might enjoy it."

"I do," I said. "But, why?"

He looked away, to the path ahead.

I was determined. We were just friends here, alone and away from the house. "I've been wondering why you do these things, since everyone else thinks it's unusual."

"Never mind what everyone else thinks."

"But I want to know the reason why, my lord. Not that I'm ungrateful—it means the world that I've learned so much. I just don't understand why you go out of your way."

"Did you not for your brother?"

"I did. But that was my brother, and I was terrified and desperate. You don't have any reason to be terrified or desperate about anything."

He stopped, abrupt, and I nearly walked into him. A swift turn, a severe look, and I felt I'd overstepped (though I didn't see how).

"That's your misguided faith in me," said Lord Kwan. "When... The night you stayed locked with me, I was in the same state as you. Terrified of myself. What I might have done to an innocent, or to someone I cared for. Desperate to get home where I could exhaust myself and end the nightmare. There were seconds when I regained myself, and saw you. I was horrified in thinking there was even the slightest chance I'd break free and that side of me would tear you apart."

I stared into his eyes, seeing a genuine fear I couldn't recall ever seeing before. "I know," I said. "But that's why I came out of my hiding and stayed with you. I was scared of you that night. But I thought, how much more frightened would I be if it was happening to me."

We held our gaze, sharing a new understanding of each other.

"You were kinder to me at my worst, than I was to you when you arrived. I'm ashamed to remember how cold I treated you." He sighed, looking away.

"I've already forgiven you," I said. "I'm not permitting you to act that way again. It's just that, I now see you had so much weight on your shoulders, and I complicated things."

He looked back at me, brow bent and soft smile returning. "Every time you pull me out of that darkness, I feel that I owe you."

I shook my head. "You protect the villages around the mountain, and none of us even know who you are really. And even if you won't say it, I know it was you who cured my village of the pox. There's nothing owed." I took his hand, firm for comfort.

He grunted, light and unbothered. "The duties of a Juneun. I don't see that as the same."

"Maybe not. I think I see them equally, though."

His hand gave a gentle squeeze to mine. "Were it completely up to me, I'd set you free now. I'm bound by oaths place among my station to see through any sentencing unless new evidence is brought to change the circumstance."

I didn't fully comprehend, but I thought of some way to ease the burden of his heart. "That's alright. I'd be less trusting of a Juneun or a lord who changed their mind on a whim."

It rained the afternoon of Lord Kwan's return. And the following day. I started to worry the ground wouldn't be solid enough for our trek to the groves. Thankfully, my silent prayers and hopes were answered as the deluge stopped soon after.

Anxious, I was up early that day. Dressed to ride, and waiting, fidgeting, too much to bide out the time with practicing drawing or writing, I took out the puzzle box. The bead inside always calmed me, centered me. It seemed sleeping, living, every time I opened the box, and gently waking at my touch.

The sound of footsteps, bringing breakfast, stole my peace. In a frantic motion, I put the glowing bead back and scrambled up the riddle before hiding it back under my stationery.

I was eager to be at the stables, arriving there early and watching as the stablemaster tacked up the horses. An arduous process, but I tried to learn through observation and not bother him. At times, it seemed a feat of strength to fit the belts snug on the animal and keep the saddle from sliding. Through it all, every horse stood patiently.

"You will ride Susa today," said Lord Kwan. The escorting guards taking their own mounts, and Syaoran with his preferred horse, Saburo neighed. "She will be fine on Susa. Did you not say yourself that she was competent?"

Saburo pinned his ears a moment, nickering. Try as I might, I couldn't guess at the other half of the conversation.

"I think I am no longer your favorite, Saburo," said Lord Kwan, teasing.

In response, Saburo's ears perked back up and his tail swished. A snort was given, and the shake of his neck.

"I'll be fine," I assured. "But thank you, Saburo. You're a good friend."

The stallion dropped his head, picking it back up as he pawed the ground.

"He's very fond of you," said Lord Kwan.

"I am too," I said. "Of him, I mean. He's the most beautiful horse I've ever seen."

"Oh? Maybe that is why he is so fond. Spoiled by compliments and the attention of a young woman."

I smiled and shrugged, approaching Susa delicately as Gi helped me up to the saddle. It felt weird. I'd grown used to how Saburo moved and carried us. Somehow, it was different on Susa. Not completely alien, but something in the line of having to adjust and understand her.

Saburo nickered at Susa as Lord Kwan mounted. Susa, in response, swiveled her ears and swished her tail.

"I have every faith that Susa will take care with Hisa in the saddle," cooed Lord Kwan, patting the stallion's neck.

I wished then that I could understand, and say something to give comfort to my friend.

The trek up was muggy, long, and disconcerting at times. I was still sore at the end, unaccustomed to riding for so long. And I wasn't any good at pretending otherwise. Before settling in for lunch, Lord Kwan used his healing magic on me.

No one seemed bothered by it. And it wasn't until setting up the picknick that I realized I was the only girl. I had no one to turn to for cues if some awkward situation came up, making me disquiet. Though it went unnoticed as we shared in dumplings stuffed with cooked duck and sekihan rice balls seasoned with ginger. A plum wine was passed around, tart in its taste, which Syaoran complained was because it was too young of a wine. Several salacious comments were made after his grumbling, all of which I stayed out of.

Both Lord Kwan and I reached for the last baozi dumpling, the knuckles of our fingers colliding. We locked eyes after, brows bent and insisting the other take it. He did take it, carefully tearing it in two and giving me the bigger half.

I realized in the last bites that I'd been over ambitious in my hunger. With my stomach feeling as though it'd burst, I started to doze off. Between that, the warm sun, the cool breeze, the soft grass, and the quiet of the scenery, it was difficult not to nod off. I found myself yawning, and pinching my arms to combat the sleepiness. It wasn't working as well as I'd hoped. I didn't doze off for long, not by the angle of the sun.

Syaoran shook me, the picknick already tidied up, and we walked to the grove with baskets in hand. Rather than eat a peach when the guardsmen took the full cargo back, I held it to admire. The colors, the softness of the skin, and the smell of it. I kept it in hand as we went further into the mountain, to where the stone tiger stood on its dais.

I still needed a bit of support when crossing the uneven ground, but handled it better now that I knew what to expect. The kudzu remained, looking thicker and wilder than I remembered. After a year, it continued to resist Syaoran's magic. Like before, we'd have to cross the top of it or wade through. And, like before, Lord Kwan carried me over. I still felt embarrassed, though to a lesser extent. We were friends now, good friends, and the awkwardness of it wasn't half as intense.

The same ceremony was carried out, and a one-sided conversation that was almost as disagreeable as before ensued. During which, I noticed the end of a reptilian tail and the corner hem of beautiful silk. I said nothing. If she was hiding, then she clearly wasn't ready for any of us.

Instead, I waited until the ritual of it all ended, staying still as Lord Kwan and Syaoran walked back with some conversation. Their backs turned, I hurried to the other side of the large, stone dais. Feng looked startled to see me, but I kept quiet, handing her the peach I'd kept.

"You really love him, don't you?" I whispered.

She looked between me and the fruit in her hands.

I wrapped my arms around her. "Then don't give up." I released her quickly, joining the others before any questions were raised.

Saddled and ready to head back down the mountain, Lord Kwan delayed, staring back at the lake.

"My lord?" asked Gi.

He turned his gaze, the hint of a smile on his face and the ends of his unbound hair catching the breeze. "Syaoran will lead you down. I will stay a while longer."

A curious look spread through the men, brows quirked. Mine too, though to a lesser degree.

"Care to join me, Hisa? Or are you eager to go back?"

I looked between him and the path back to the estate. "For a while, I suppose. There's still plenty of daylight left."

"Are you sure?" whispered Gi. "It might be a long ride."

"I can manage, I think," I said, giving a smile to reassure him.

Reluctant, they carried on, leaving me and Susa alone with Lord Kwan and Saburo.

We rode at leisure, until a wide meadow lay before us. Lord Kwan cued Saburo to pick up pace into a trot. I cued Susa to do the same to keep up. They went a little faster, and so did we, until I realized it was a silent challenge. His soft smile and knowing look goading me to push myself. And, keen to rise to the occasion, I kicked my heel into the side of my mare and cued her to canter. We passed them, a steady speed putting some distance between riders.

I could hear Saburo snort, picking up speed to catch up to us. As they did, Lord Kwan reached out, touching my upper arm before breaking off from beside me. A game, I realized. I held fast with my legs, pressing in my heels and giving more of the reins to Susa. We went faster, giving chase. I came close to touching him a few times, but always I worried about losing my balance. When I did finally touch back, I suspected he let me, or maybe Saburo did.

He pursued as we broke away in the game. I aimed for a copse of trees, planning to make the chase more difficult in weaving through before turning around. I'd need to slow a little, but I felt confident in the idea while the thrill coursed through my body.

It worked. They got close at times, but I was able to keep just enough space in the new terrain to stay in the lead. The ground began to slope, forcing me to pick a spot to run round and head back for the meadow.

I should have chosen better. Smooth rock lay hidden beneath the foliage, angled steep a short distance from a drop off some ten feet or so. Susa slipped, throwing me from her back. I landed hard on the ground, the momentum sending me into a tumble.

My worst fear came to fruition.

"Hisa!"

Chapter 34
Fever Touch

I scrambled to grab something, rag-dolled as I was, but my fingers found nothing. I was falling, sent down by my own hubris. My eyes shut, as though that would prevent my crash below.

I did land, or, rather, I was caught. Opening my eyes, breath trembling, Lord Kwan held me, protective. Tucked between him, the cliff-face, and the ground, it took me a moment to orientate myself and understand the scene. His breathing was also labored, eyes filled with worry. My body shook, and my voice refused to come. So we stared at each other, shaken from the event.

"Are you alright?" asked Lord Kwan in a near whisper.

I tried to speak, my voice in refusal, and nodded. Immediately after, with the facts of what happened solidifying in my mind, I clung to him in tears. A swell of emotion. Fear, certainly, but also the frustration at myself, the anger at the landscape, and how much I now hated riding. I needed a moment to let out my feelings and calm enough to collect myself.

The arm he'd kept braced against the rock fell away to wrap around me, tight to tell me I was safe. Even in such an awkward position for each of us, the feeling seeped into me. I let go of the torrent of emotions, forcing myself to take steady breaths.

Lifting my face up, I opened my mouth to thank him, to assure him. The shadow of something stole the opportunity from me. It's fur black, its teeth large, and its claws sharp. An enormous bear, bigger than any our hunters had chased off.

Swift, Lord Kwan threw his palm back, his spell blasting the very air to send the irritated beast tumbling. There was no ensuing brawl. It wasn't a stupid animal, roaring its complaints as it left. I understood then how much trouble I would've been in, had I not been caught by Lord Kwan. Left to crash and become broken, I would've made for a tasty morsel.

I struggled to my feet, trying to help up my friend. His breath still labored, and face slathered in sweat, my brain pieced together the expenditure of magic he'd done for the day. Then I looked down. A part of a branch sunk deep into his leg.

"You're hurt!"

He prevented me with a raised palm from touching it, and yanked it out himself. Red, flowing freely as a river. He used more magic to close up the wound.

"I'm sorry," I said, repeating the phrase to punish myself.

He shook his head. "An accident. I'll be alright. I just need some rest."

"Then rest," I insisted. "This is my fault. If I wasn't trying to show off, I wouldn't have fell and you wouldn't have spent so much of your magic."

He furrowed his brow, the start of a smile on him. "I shouldn't have pressed so hard. You've only ridden a year. And you don't know the mountain that well."

I couldn't return his expression. "I knew my limit. And I pushed anyway."

His smile faded. "Hisa..."

I shut my eyes, shaking my head. As I felt him try to pull me in for another embrace, I resisted. I wanted to hate myself in the moment. He pulled me in anyway. Wordless.

So, we sat there, waiting for Saburo and Susa to find a way to us. I sometimes forgot they were magic too, and not ordinary steeds. In waiting, Lord Kwan shuddered with pain.

"What is it?"

He shook his head.

Frowning, I took the initiative and pulled aside his clothes to look at his leg. He scolded, grabbing at my wrists to prevent me, but I could already see it. The wound was closed, but there was swelling and a hot redness. There was an injury deeper than what we'd seen, what he healed. A broken bone maybe, or a fracture.

Guilt drove me to leave him a short distance, searching for anything helpful. To my surprise, I'd found a bit of yarrow struggling to grow, and a marshmallow plant taking up the soggiest patch of earth. I didn't think I'd find those plants this high on the mountain, but I was glad of it.

I quickly cleaned off the root of the marshmallow plant, finding a stone I could use to grind it into a paste. The yarrow I separated leaf from flower from stem, each of them having a purpose. I could feel Lord Kwan watching me with curiosity, choosing to ignore it and focus on adding the stems to the paste. When I did get back to him, I instructed him to swallow the flowers of the yarrow, to help combat the swelling from the inside.

He gave me a queer look. The sort that suggested he was impressed and skeptical at the same time. But he did as I'd said.

Gentle, I applied my salve to where the swelling accumulated most fiercely, and placed the leaves over it in a protective layer. Next was to remove one of the extra pieces of my riding clothes to tear and make bandage wraps out of. It wasn't ideal, but it was the best I had. As much as it pained me to destroy the fabric, it was more important to do something to help my friend recover.

Saburo did finally get to us, with Susa limping behind, though the sun had long since set.

Lord Kwan made to stand, and, worried, I put my weight to make him stay seated. We needed to get back, but I feared the ride might do more damage to both Lord Kwan and poor Susa. It was dark, and the terrain uneven. I said all I could think to convince him to stay put until he relented.

"So Hisa is also a afraid of the dark?" teased Lord Kwan.

I blinked, my rattled senses taking longer to understand the joke. "A little," I admitted. "And there was a bear not too long ago, remember?"

"A bear right in this spot. And now it's dark. And you want to stay put."

His tone was light, and his words slow, but hearing them did make me feel silly. "Well, what happens if a boar charges us while we're wandering in the night? You already used too much magic."

"My own fault," said Lord Kwan. "I hadn't fully recovered since coming home."

I looked at him then. He didn't appear at all weak when he returned.

Catching my stare, he explained. "I have to appear strong. Stronger than however I feel. For the sake of others."

"You shouldn't push yourself so far," I scolded. "You're a lord. Couldn't you delay and make the excuse that things in your house happen when you say, or something?"

He smiled, soft, and something of amusement was in his eyes. "Are you going to scold and command me any time I'm slightly unwell now?"

"If it'll help," I teased. "I just wish you'd tell me why you do things like this."

He stared at me a while. I could almost hear him ask if that was my question for the day with how he looked at me. "For the same reason you ran up the mountain that night."

A complicated answer. One that didn't give any direct reason. But I felt I understood it, regardless.

As chill set in, so high in the mountain, I unfastened the saddles from the horses, taking the blankets from under to make a spot where warmth wouldn't be pulled from my friend by damp earth. I placed myself over him, awkward as it was, protecting him from cold while we rested. I didn't have any other useful trick to help.

Fireflies still glowed up here, no pattern to how they lit the dark, but a comfort all the same. They wouldn't be here if there was something disturbing, and would fast disperse if the tranquility was interrupted. Frogs sang out as well, few as they were compared to the villa. Distant echoes telling me that all was well.

I couldn't fall asleep. Lord Kwan nodded off, peaceful in his near silent slumber. With the rise and fall of his chest under me, I wondered if I was too heavy on him, though I didn't dare move and risk waking him.

The horses too, took turns in laying down for rest and standing guard.

I watched the fireflies, and the shadows made when the moon revealed itself from behind passing clouds, waiting to fall asleep. Even as I got comfortable acting as Lord Kwan's blanket, the feel of his heartbeat and breathing, I couldn't relax enough to sleep.

The rustle of foliage put me on alert, whipping my head in that direction. A white stag with a beautiful crown of antlers, the same one from my dream, walked through. It stopped, turning its head to meet my eye. He was beautiful.

"One of the sacred animals of this mountain," whispered Lord Kwan. "He's a gentle one. So you don't need to worry."

I looked from his face, back to the stag, watching it come closer.

"He was her mate, wasn't he?" I whispered back.

"Yes."

I remembered my dream, understanding the sadness I felt. "He's alone now."

Lord Kwan said nothing in return. Both of us watching the stag's approach.

It sniffed at us, breathing in my hair and blowing it back in a hot burst. Then he looked to Lord Kwan, recognition, and to his leg.

"I will be fine, my friend," said Lord Kwan, low and soothing. Though the stag didn't acknowledge the words. "Hisa is taking care of me."

The stag continued inspection, slow to leave once satisfied.

I'm not sure when I fell asleep, but when morning came, Lord Kwan shook me awake with a gentle grip. I rubbed the tiredness from my eyes, confused to find a thick blanket over us. One that hadn't been among any of our things the day before.

"Can you stand?" asked Lord Kwan.

I got to my feet, straightening myself the best I could. Likewise, he stood, assuring me that he regained enough strength to cast another healing spell for himself. He walked to Susa afterwards, using his magic on her leg. Releasing some other spell, the blanket we'd slept under turned back into leaves. Even as I fretted, he insisted he had enough strength, and tacked up the horses again. I tried to help, messing up the ties and lacking the strength to keep the saddles snug.

When it came to mounting up, I froze. Some piece of me held back my muscles, warning me of danger.

"Hisa?"

"I'll walk. I don't want to weigh Susa down with her leg as it is."

He stared, slow blinking. "Her leg is fine. And it's a long way back to walk."

I looked from him, to the saddle, to the mountainous ground, to my shoes, trying to come up with another excuse. My mind occupied, I didn't see him walk up to me. His hands about to lift me up, I pulled away in a panic. Realizing, I tried to meet his eye and measure his reaction.

For seconds, there was silence. "You're afraid."

I fidgeted, looking away.

"You won't fall again," cooed Lord Kwan, taking my hands. "We'll go slow. Saburo and I will lead." His free hand brushed back my hair, wordlessly asking me to meet his gaze. "Don't let your fear control you. The girl who ran up the mountain in the night—fearless."

It was a comfort, but I was still afraid. He lifted me onto Susa's saddle, and my hands gripped tight. I needed to convince myself to relax into a proper posture and keep a gentle hold on the reins. Through it all, Lord Kwan stayed beside me.

We'd made it back by the afternoon, Syaoran informing with concern that a search was being assembled. Lord Kwan dismissed, keeping a light tone to tease. Even so, I could feel the strange looks several other staff members gave us. From the new men and women of the house in particular. We'd been gone all night and half the day, alone, and returned with some of our clothing tattered or ripped completely. I knew exactly how it looked from their perspective.

Intrusive thoughts kept my attention, missing when I was cued to dismount. Syaoran took me off the saddle, and my reaction coupled with my squeak did me no favors.

On the ground, realizing what'd happened, I looked into Syaoran's eyes, shaded by his ginger hair and bent brow.

"Are you alright?"

"I'm fine," I said, matching his quiet volume.

"You're not hurt?"

I shook my head. "It's Lord Kwan who was hurt."

He gave a quizzical look, as though his every thought was now derailed. "So, you—he didn't..."

It suddenly dawned on me what he was asking. "No!" I whispered. "It was nothing like that. I fell from the saddle, going too fast to handle."

He sighed.

"I know how it looks," I said. "But that didn't happen, and that's the truth."

Taking me by the shoulder, we walked away, towards the house. "He's changed over the last seventy years. So, any assumption made is..."

"Was he like that before?" I asked, though part of me didn't want to know the answer.

"No," said Syaoran. "I just didn't know if he'd become like that since then."

I wanted to scold him, to defend the reputation of my friend, but I understood his concern, and I was grateful for it. Better, I thought, to have a friend that was concerned when nothing happened, than someone who didn't care at all if it did.

It was a few days after, when Lin asked me about getting new riding clothes. I'd said I didn't need any replacement, since what I had was still effective but now wasn't as sightly. She convinced me anyway, luring the idea of taking my old ones apart to make something new out of it during the days Lord Kwan was away. I'd chosen a deep blue with a hummingbird print at its ends. In the conversation, I felt dizzy and hot in the face.

Not from what we were talking about, I'd felt a little off that entire morning. It was more that the intensity of it began, making me nauseous. Lin took note, though I dismissed it as having been in the sun for too long in the past few days and only needed to lay down to rest a while.

In my sleep, a fever came over me.

I sweated through my night gown, wishing I had the comfort of my father and brothers to look after me. The warm, muggy nights didn't help. I tossed and turned, drinking water with an insatiable thirst through the hours, until my pitcher was emptied. I longed for home, my throat tight and itchy, my saliva thick.

Morning, and I stayed where I was rather than get up. My body shivered, despite the heat. Hair clung to my face and neck. Thirst drove me to get up, to put something on just for the sake of covering me, and fetch water from the well before hurrying back. I needed rest, hoping beyond hope that I could sleep it off.

My ears clogged, muffling sound and hearing things I knew couldn't be there. Next, the light teamed with my fever, playing tricks on my eyes. For a moment, I thought I saw Fumei, heard Fumei, waving for me to go outside. Humming drifted to me. I thought it was my mother's voice, telling me to be strong, that my father would be there any moment, and that she loved me. And I whispered back how much I missed her. She'd mentioned that I cut my hair, and I muttered about the lice outbreak. Then she talked about how lovely I've grown, and I argued that I wasn't. When she told me to look at the butterflies, I saw them fluttering about the room in the moonlight. Just in the corner of my eye, I swore I saw her sitting there, drawing them.

We were interrupted. My door opened, and the white stag walked in. My vision blurred further, sleep taking me.

I started to rouse when I felt crisp air over my skin, my entire body. And again, when I felt a hand on my forehead, my cheek, my neck, cool to the touch. A cold cloth was placed on my forehead, another over my neck, and several over my torso, under my pits, all of it pulling out the boiling fever from my blood.

Someone was speaking, a deep and gentle voice. I didn't catch what they'd said, and my bleary eyes didn't recognize much as I willed them to open. Long, black hair. It could be anyone. A silken, white night robe—the sleeve of one anyway, and a cool hand at its end.

I was helped to sit up, my eyes searching for what made me shift to this position. A cup of something handed to me. In my great thirst, I drank down the bitter contents.

Cool fingers rested against my skin.

"Lin, did you find Feng?"

"She's getting the herbs now, my lord."

I fell back asleep.

In the morning, I felt better, though not recovered. My delirium broken, I could make sense of my surroundings now. I still felt hot and my throat dry, and my ears were still a little clogged, but I had the strength to get up.

Syaoran came into my room, ears perking upright at the sight of me. "How are you feeling?"

"Not great," I said. "But better than I did yesterday."

"That fever really got you. The last two days were delicate."

"Two?" I repeated. "I only started feeling unwell day before yesterday when Lin asked me about sending an order for new riding clothes."

He bore a bewildered expression. "That was four days ago."

"Four?"

"You don't remember? Not even when any of us helped you to drink down a broth?"

"I... I remember a cup of something bitter. But nothing else." I looked down, realizing the night gown I wore wasn't my original one.

"Lin changed out your clothes twice. They were soaked with sweat. Just about any water you drank came out with the fever instantly."

I gave him a look of horror. "And, Lord Kwan?"

"He's resting." Syaoran walked up to me, placing a hand to check the heat of my skin. "Are you hungry?"

"A little," I admitted. "My stomach feels a bit sour."

He gave a warm smile. "You haven't had anything except force fed broths, medicinal teas, and water. I'll get something for you from the kitchens. You need to rest and regain your strength as well."

"Thank you, Syaoran."

"Hisa, I have to ask. When you were gone with Lord Kwan, did you run into anyone? Anyone at all?"

I shook my head.

"That makes it more difficult."

"Makes what more difficult?"

He swapped his warm expression for one of apology. "A fever sickness should've been something easy for Lord Kwan to heal. With so much trouble, he suspects it was magic induced."

"Magic? Someone put a spell on me?"

"It might have been meant for Kwan and hit you by accident. Either way, it's not good. If someone is blatantly targeting Kwan or his household, and on his lands, that's boldness. With Gumiho gone, it's hard to think who's behind it."

"Is Lord Kwan in trouble?"

Syaoran laughed. "That's not how I'd phrase it. There might be Kurai trying to retaliate in petty ways. But, I don't think he'll be in actual danger."

He left, coming back with a small bowl of rice.

I ate as much as my stomach would allow, and laid back down to sleep. My window open, threads of sunlight poured in, and felt good on my face. It lulled me into a quick slumber.

I woke again to the touch of cool fingers, my eyes fluttering open.

"How do you feel?" asked Lord Kwan, cooing.

I struggled to sit up, stopped by a gentle hand. "Unwell, but better than I did before, my lord. Thank you."

The start of a smile appeared on his face. "Good. What will they say about me if my prisoner was pardoned from death, only to be put in the grave half way through her sentencing?"

"What does it matter what they say?" I asked, teasing. A little too bold, though it was only the two of us and our voices quiet.

He studied me, his stone expression hinting at his impressed thoughts on my response. "And if I'd lost my friend?"

"I'm human, my lord," I said, taking his hand. "But I hope it will be a long time before you have to think about that."

His smile grew a little.

"What of you, my lord? You didn't push too far, did you?"

"I had Feng's help."

"Feng?"

"The Sho family are masters in medicine. Some years ago, she took pity on a human pleading for help, and sent him back with wild herbs to make a salve."

It was enough to make me pause for thought.

"It was the Sho that originally taught humans about medicinal herbs. Which ones to combat fevers, draw out poisons, and what ought to be made into a tea or a balm." His gaze drifted from me. "Over time, both sides have forgotten their history with each other."

"My lord?"

He looked at me again with a sadness. "I will be away some time come autumn. Summoned to a royal wedding. See if you can help Lin keep Feng and Syaoran busy or entertained and out of trouble while I'm gone."

I blinked, bewildered by the shift in topic, though I nodded all the same.

"Good girl," said Lord Kwan (which still annoyed me). He placed a kiss to the top of my forehead, leaving in a swift motion.

Again, I was stunned. Autumn was still weeks away, and I didn't understand the hurry. At the same time… my hand reached for the place his cool lips touch ever so briefly. It wasn't a romantic gesture; I'd done the same to friends and children and received it back. This time felt strange, like an accident somehow. At the same time—it bothered me. Was the gesture as a whole meant to treat me like a friend? A pet? Something, something else? It bothered me. So why was I thinking so much about it?

Chapter 35
Lord Kwan VIII

Kwan watched as the Cat Clan prince rode off through the moon gate, showboating from his saddle. Finally. He'd begun to exhaust himself, spending energy to make up for his small household. Had it not been the demand of the crown, he wouldn't have held court at all. A means to insult. After all, it was Urekkato who presented Gumiho's head. Not himself.

He was glad to see it end. Now, he needed rest.

"He's tried to get another rise from me, my lord. I've restrained myself from it. I don't want to put you in another position like before."

What was the Cat prince up to? Harassment of the staff was a staple of nearly every lord, though this one appeared more pointed.

There was also the irritation of the princess, intruding on his room twice after with more carefully worded commands to get what she wanted. Taken for the sport of spite. She lacked the cunning of lesser ladies; unnecessary when your station allowed an abuse of power, unmediated.

Realizing his longer than intended silence, he answered. "Good girl." Immediate regret followed. He could have said anything, or nothing, more elegantly. She said not a word about it. However, she was not in a position to speak her mind too freely. There was the question in her brown eyes that he couldn't bring himself to answer, to admit his mistake. She'd accepted it with more dignity that any lord or lady in court would've.

He recalled hearing of her outburst, and the surprise it triggered in himself. Given what he knew, it seemed better handled than if she had a title on her. Unrefined, but honest. Perhaps that gave rise to Urekkato's fascination.

Tired, he walked his gardens. Alone and at rest. Not for long, however.

Beom found his room is disarray upon returning to it mid-morning, throwing accusations at Kwan's staff, as he'd done with every slight and mess and accident since court opened.

Kwan broke it apart, dismissing his servant for retreat and ignoring his ill-tempered brother. On he walked, trying to maintain the façade of unbothered power. He couldn't show that he'd tried to make up for the lacking in his staff to accommodate so many guests, or that previous confrontation drained him further. Tempered disinterest would be his best bluff.

It came to not when Beom drew his sword. Kwan, cautious, waited until there was no doubt his brother meant to use his blade, and brought up his own. He didn't have the strength to match his brother, not as he was. Quick to think, his best strategy would be giving up ground and letting Beom tire himself out in his aggression.

Deflecting, side stepping, creating unfavorable terrain with things knocked to create obstacles and bide time. If he wanted to outlast Beom, he needed as much distraction as possible. Insult after insult slung, Kwan waited for opportunity to give his brother cause to back off.

Beom came in with more ferocity, pressing Kwan back and feigning one tactic in favor of a riskier one. Stunned, Kwan struggled to maintain his original plan, and parry the barrage of blows from his brother. He set himself to a perilous move, going down and forward to catch his brother's wrist to stop the strike entirely.

Unable to avoid it, their primal power came forth, answering their fury.

"And then there's your little human whore."

Primal power came flooding, indignant at his brother's uncouth antics. With new energy, Kwan went on the offensive, matching his brother.

"Is that why you gave up Eumeh so easily?" demanded Beom in a roar. "Does it make you happy to shame our parents?"

Kwan ignored him, abandoning caution in favor of fervent aggression. Blinded by fury, he lost his advantage, sent flying back.

Darkness began to consume his senses once more. An instinct to survive.

Don't go...

A voice, small and sincere, pleading. Just enough to remind him of the light, though he struggled for it. Through whimpering breaths and the sound of battle, he felt himself succumbing to the primal dark. The whispering of a gentle voice, speaking with compassion continued. If he lost himself...

He'd lose that compassion.

Stubborn, he fought on for control.

Senses returning, he found Hisa clinging to him and Beom's bloodlust approach. Without a second to spare, he called his sword to him, and held fast to her. A dance of steel like silver lightning. He couldn't find an opening to set her aside, not without collateral damage due. As blades sang against each other, the safest place for her was also the most dangerous place—made painfully obvious when his brother's metal graced against his neck, and a stream of red caused her to shriek.

Kwan tightened his grip as Beom's sword sailed to bite at his arm next. He couldn't act with total abandon, not if he wanted to keep her safe. He emptied his mind of his rage, allowing reflex to guide his next move until he could think what next to do. The muscle memory brought him down and close, lending him the idea of bashing his elbow into his brother's face.

Beom stumbled back, clapping a hand over his nose. At last allowing some reprieve to set Hisa safely away. Not a second later, Kwan charged in, determined to end this before another found themselves trapped in the brothers' brawl.

The dust settled with the very tip of his sword pointed at Beom's throat. "I will not run my brother through. But he is no longer welcome in my home."

Home, Kwan smiled in seeing Hisa's joy on Saburo. The stallion, too, looked proud. Such a small thing. Though he wanted to see how many small things brough that expression out. A memory from his childhood, when he was barely a man, intruded on him. When he'd shown a young girl the swing, and her fear of falling from it. The smile afterwards, watching her demand to go higher and higher. Bittersweet in his chest. Most memories now had streaks of scarlet with that girl.

Hisa didn't hesitate when shown the same trinket. Sheer delight. Quiet moments, when he was free from the ghosts of his past, and they could be themselves. Though, it couldn't be for long, not at the house. Always, someone would be looking for him with some trivial matter and occasionally one of importance.

What endeared him more was that she wasn't empty headed. She didn't accept anything for flattery or feel entitled to it. She searched for some equal exchange, wanting to give. Uncouth, and different from all else. He would miss her.

Saburo too, would be crestfallen, judging by his displeasure at Kwan's choice of steed to Hisa. The stallion was taken by her rough charm, making several complaints and questions of concern during their ride up the mountain.

A genuine sweetness, as Juro put it several times. And it showed when she surrendered her peach to Feng. He said nothing of knowing her hiding place, quietly observing how freely his human prisoner loved. If she knew, truly knew, Feng's perspective and sorted opinion... No, she'd have acted like this anyway. With nothing to gain.

A sudden thought halted Kwan's departure. How long had he gone without games? Gentle games, where cunning didn't play a factor in the pursuit. He longed for it, now that it dawned on him. The thrill of the wind whipping by, of knowing your surroundings and planning each move knowing it was likely to be countered. A wordless dance of riders, testing each other through laughter and bravery.

His heart picked up when she agreed. Syaoran was a fine opponent, but always too competitive. As he led on, seeing if she'd pick up, excitement followed. He wondered if he'd need to explain it, and relished in finding he didn't.

A worthy rival, and human! Were she on Saburo, he was sure he might never catch her.

When she fell, the musing turned to alarm.

He did catch her, feeling the assault of the wilderness punishing him for hasty action. He needed magic to save them, sending a little too much in his impatience.

"You're hurt!"

Anxious to get it over with, the tone of his companion didn't sink in until after. Concern, lacking greed or apprehension. "An accident. I'll be alright. I just need some rest." He could have pushed on, used the reserves of his magic to spirit them home. Though some piece of him stayed the notion, enjoying the strangeness of the moment.

"This is my fault. If I wasn't trying to show off, I wouldn't have fell and you wouldn't have spent so much of your magic."

A surge of shame coursed through Kwan, a needle in his chest. And he had to correct it in some way, be the source of comfort to her as she'd been to him. Though, nothing stopped her from assuming the role of caretaker. He watched her work away at the task she appointed herself, admiring her make-do attitude, and knowing that she'd feel the full soreness once the shock wore off. She wouldn't allow herself to be inconvenienced. Opposite to so many women he'd known in his life.

He found himself delighting in how she fretted over him, his heart beating slow with waves of warmth. Teasing, and being teased in turn, he felt comfortable in the absurd circumstance. "Are you going to scold and command me any time I'm slightly unwell now?"

"If it'll help!"

Kwan reveled in her tone, sobering when levity began to leave her words.

"I just wish you'd tell me why you do things like this."

He had a hundred excuses ready. All of them suited for various opponents of court and within his family. Hisa was neither. "For the same reason you ran up the mountain that night."

In slumber, she was a comfort to him. And at her slightest shiver, Kwan gestured his spells to manifest a blanket to cover her entirely, shielding her from the chill of night. She was such a small thing, yet made the biggest effort in whatever she put her mind to. A contradictory human. Unmoving, he sent his energy to loosen her muscles, lest fatigue wake her or cause too much pain in the morning.

The first kunai flew past his ear, sinking deep into the rock. The rest, his magic stopped midflight. Assassin's needles, darts, the smaller and more difficult to catch, magic or not. His gaze fixed on them, he kept still and burned them to dust.

Gumiho cackled somewhere in the shadow, her scent unmistakable on the breeze. "You always were too fast. In so many aspects."

He said nothing, eyes sifting through the dark. Saburo and Susa stood, pawing at the ground with ears pinned back. A warning.

"Who do you have there, hiding? Is it the snake, winning you over at last?"

Kwan said nothing.

"I'd bet her soul is sweet too. Just like the rest."

Again, he remained placid, tempering the racing rage of his beating heart.

"They all had such faith in you—that you would save them!" The glow of violet eyes, and gleaming, white teeth in a grin revealed her. "I used to feel the same. Just like you promised me."

"Before I knew the truth of you."

She vanished from one shadow, her voice traveling from the new one she hid in. "You knew. You always knew. You just didn't care at the time. Not when it meant you could have something all for yourself."

He caught a glimpse of her before she vanished again.

"I wonder how the new couple would react if I came to their wedding."

"You're welcome to try it."

"You never used to be so cold. But, then again, you used to be whole," she stepped out of her hiding place, presenting the tiniest shard of something glowing.

He knew what it was, and the flaunting of it caused his blood to boil.

"Come and claim it, if you can." She'd allowed this. Allowed them all to believe she was dead, waiting it out to see if he'd let his guard down.

She was testing, baiting to see if she could send him into a fury. This close to his home, that would spell the end to the very people he'd sworn to safeguard. He thought carefully, needing some display to bolster his bluff. A deep breath, and he allowed his magic to flow freely from him. The air crackled with electricity.

It was enough to give her cause to worry. "No matter. I'll sift out the rest soon enough. After I have all of it, I'll let you watch as I make things even. How many sisters do you have left? Suitors? Lovers?"

He allowed his magic to intensify.

She vanished.

Chapter 36
Lord Kwan IX

Home, Kwan debated with himself. Perhaps it was best left a secret. Something to stay his hand from turning on his kin, and lure her out on his terms. The same thought beckoned his caution: would secrecy leave them vulnerable? She had the audacity to trek on his lands, so close to his personal home.

Without the doe...

He needed insight. From someone who had nothing to gain, nor anything to lose. He'd sent for Hisa, only to be informed of her condition. It dawned on him then, how odd it was to have not seen her all day when she was usually about on some self-appointed duty. Finding her in such a state, the need to act fell over him. Lin informed him of her last interaction with the girl. It shouldn't have progressed that quickly, human or spirit.

It'd been days since his encounter. Why now?

His fondness extended beyond a master and a servant. Maybe that proved enough to make her a target to hurt him. And he didn't doubt that she wouldn't understand it if he started to distance himself from her. To have so few friends, only for one to isolate you. Like isolating the moon from the stars.

Saburo and Susa also seemed unwell, forcing his hand. He'd sent his house of guards to get Feng from the groves and bring her to his home. Somewhere he could protect her as well. Whatever she thought of his summons didn't matter, so long as it kept an innocent from becoming a pawn to Gumiho.

He thought it over and over. Feng was unaffected, though Gumiho seemed aware she was hiding on the mountain. Magic was at play, but not from her. It left his own household to cast the spell, or introduce it by other means. The obvious suspect was Syaoran. Anyone else who knew about the event outside of his home would accuse him first. What good did that serve Gumiho?

Then again, what did it serve to plague those individuals specifically, days after the encounter?

With word of some recovery, despite his exhaustion, Kwan went to her. He had to see for himself. And the sight brought relief. The realization of it solidified that he truly was too fond of her as his servant, as his friend. Silence became a discomfort as the notion rooted itself deeper, and he tried any other topic to help ignore it.

He rambled, seeing questions on her face. Questions he wasn't ready to answer. "I will be away some time come autumn. Summoned to a royal wedding. See if you can help Lin keep Feng and Syaoran busy or entertained and out of trouble while I'm gone."

More unspoken question came over her face as she blinked at him. And there was the thought of being away, of leaving his home, and everyone in it, unprotected for a time. If she fell ill again?

The words rang in his ear: *I'm only human, my lord. But I hope it will be a long time before you have to think about that.*

Too relaxed with himself around her, and too tired to realize the action, Kwan laid a kiss to her forehead. "Good girl." He didn't give himself time for the mistake to settle, leaving promptly and without a second glance.

It was days after, when full health was restored in his house, and he allowed himself to halt his magic, that he ordered a bath drawn. The ginseng restored some of himself, delaying the drain of his power, but it felt not enough this time.

Absent minded, he'd walked the veranda in waiting, aimed for the bath when he saw steam escaping it. Though, he was unaware that she'd had the same idea in her recovery. He saw her shoulders and back, still browned from a lifetime in the fields, through the start of opening the door. He'd closed it, standing there in confusion. Why should he, a lord, wait? And what difference was there when he'd seen more than a dozen naked women, lovelier and pale?

It was different from that. She wasn't a lover, or a spiteful princess, or an ambitious servant. She was a friend. Perhaps not for long if he'd gone in and ordered her out after having stripped down. Hand on the door, he hesitated. He couldn't do it. The value of her opinion of him outweighed the immediate pleasure of a hot soak.

One piece of himself damned the view of justice, advising him to send her away. Another piece refused to abolish his total sense of law. And a quiet piece harbored the feeling of comfort in every memory.

In three years, he would miss her.

Kwan watched the dancers during the wedding feast. The dazzling red, white, and pink colors of their silks moving in harmony, breaking only to form a new pattern that delighted the eye. A perfection that annoyed him.

He looked to the bride and groom, further irritated by the initial circumstance of it all. The insistence of his holding court first. Lacking a larger household, his energy was spent in making up for it, allowing the guests to enjoy themselves and pretend to be pleasant without hinderance. Only the mildest inconveniences escaped him. Whereas now, the decadence spanned an entire palace.

He shifted his gaze.

The bride, clad in shades of red, sat placid. A pond without wind above or fish below. Her features a perfect reflection of her status, painted to conceal anything else. Not a hair out of place.

And the groom in brilliant cerulean, with his family crest proudly displayed on his chest. Contrary to Eumeh, he grinned, relishing in his achievement and indulging anyone with high enough praise in conversation.

All of them blissfully unaware. From perfectly practice smiles and rehearsed conversation, to hungry eyes looking at a stranger they hadn't seen in well over fifty years. A stranger from a high family, and still unmarried.

The performance ended, applause given, and Kwan dismissed himself.

Outside, away from the chatter and the music and the stench of decadence, Kwan breathed in the night air. Humid, and fast becoming crisp and cold. He walked the grounds in the moonlight, acknowledged politely by patrolling guards.

Wandering, aimless, memories flooded back—of sentimental things, things once bittersweet now forever soured. He'd brought her to places like this when he was a much younger man, when he didn't care for power and laughed and delighted in court. He'd put peach blossoms in her hair in spring. Orchids in summer. Forget-me-nots in autumn. He was happier then, absconding out of their trappings and into fields of sunflowers, some as tall as they were, or taller. The memory of how they would hide their love for each other there burned him, causing a scowl to form. Memories now streaked with scarlet.

It was over now. All of it in the past, and better to be forgotten. There were no more moonlit escapades.

His lungs took in air, soothing away the intrusion on his heart.

"Kwan!" His brother's voice broke him from the thought. Kwang walked over, a pleasant expression on his face. "Isolating yourself again? You know at least eight girls have had their eye on you all night."

He looked away from his brother, slow and in full control of the movement. "You seemed to have them well entertained."

"What's wrong with that?" asked Kwang with a laugh. "Beautiful women want to give me their attention. Why not entertain it?"

Kwan grunted. "You sound like Juro. He's well aware of the social climbing, and takes full advantage as far as he can reach."

"Does that include your human servant?" teased Kwang.

Kwan said nothing, refusing to indulge in the gossip.

"You act like Gumiho is still around. The entire reason this wedding is even happening is because she's dead. Things can go back to the way they were."

"We can never go back to the way things were. Before Jiana."

The younger brother sighed. "You can't keep blaming yourself for that. You have to move on, let it go."

"But I let her get close," growled Kwan.

"It was centuries ago," groaned Kwang. "Are you going to blame yourself for Huan and Seung, too? They took up the chase, long before Jiana died. Our family has a reputation for acting rashly, and for our stubbornness. And we're not even the most reckless family of note! The Samjos have us beat there."

Kwan remained wordless.

"What about the rest of your judgement?" asked Kwang. "Borsi was loyal. If not for his soul getting stolen from him. Juro as well, even if his power doesn't measure up to any of us. Kaoru, Xan, Yanmei... Grandfather set an example. It can't be helped that we try to follow in his footsteps. People still talk about him. A harbinger of peace. A healer. Warrior. Every title except king."

Kwan sighed, slow and quiet.

"Do you wish you were more like Beom and Seong?"

Kwan pause at his brother's question. "Sometimes I wonder, if I was, could so much tragedy be avoided?"

Kwang shook his head. "What good does it do to think like that? I didn't know our eldest brothers the way you did. But everyone compares them to our grandfather. I don't think they'd want us to waste our lives regretting mistakes of the past."

Kwan looked to his youngest brother, the start of a smile on his face. "And our father thinks you're the one lacking the most wisdom."

Kwang shrugged. "Anyone can say something that sounds profound and call it wisdom. What we're in sore need of is compassion."

"Genuine compassion," corrected Kwan. "Not the mere appearance of it." He said the words, immediately regretting it. Was it compassion that drove him before, or ambition? A need to prove something, to be compared to his family patriarch? Or was it sincerely from the heart? He was young then, and perhaps he couldn't distinguish one from the other.

The younger brother mulled it over, looking to the stars.

Kwan too, looked to the heavens. Clouds dragged over, hiding precious light for spells of time.

"I'm going inside," said Kwang, "before I catch a cold. Imagine that being what I take with me from a wedding."

Chapter 37
Dog Days

After I'd recovered, and with Lord Kwan gone, I spent more time on the swing, wondering about things I shouldn't have even bothered with. Feng had her room made, and it was assumed she'd be there some time. I'd been entrusted with keeping order to some extent. And, the kiss. Even at the start of a crisp autumn, I felt my cheeks warm at the memory, and my imagination betrayed me in bringing up the feeling over and over in a variety of scenarios.

I was no longer safe in my daydreams.

"Did you put this up?" asked Feng.

I looked up, stupefied. "Lord Kwan did."

"Are you sure you should be on it?" She came closer, elegant, in spite of having the lower half of a snake.

With a nod, I explained. "He said I could use it any time I wanted."

"Generous, my fiancée. You know he sent for me? He wanted me to come back to his house."

I smiled. "I told you not to give up."

"Even so, you won't stay as my servant? He's fond of you, as far as humans go. It'd make him happy if you agreed to stay on as my attendant."

I shook my head. "Three more years of serving, then I go home to my family."

She sighed, frowning and keeping a distance from the swing, even though it didn't move except by how I shifted in standing. "A bigger room?"

I shook my head, smiling. "I don't think I'm cut out to live in a noble's house. When he held court, people kept... staring at me."

"That's one of the reasons I want you to stay," said Feng in a tone of complaint. "When we hold court, they'll be too busy looking at a human to be bothered with what I'm doing."

I didn't ask. Bunching my brow, I offered a look of apology.

"I suppose this can stay too," said Feng, eyeing the swing with suspicion. "Since you like it so much. I don't really see the point."

"You don't like it?"

She scoffed.

"Have you ever tried?"

That garnered a look of quiet outrage. "All it does is go back and forth until you fall off."

"You won't fall," I said the words, hearing them echo as Lord Kwan's in my ear.

She eyed me, deciding whether or not she believed what I said.

I stepped off, extending my hand to help her up. Reluctant, she accepted. There was steadying needed, with her tail trying to balance and wrap tight.

"I'll hang onto you the whole time," I assured. Slow and gentle, I walked back and forth with her.

Her hands clung to the ropes in a vice, her posture stiff. After several smooth passes, she relaxed. I took an extra step in either direction, allowing a slightly greater rise and fall. Her silken hair gracefully swayed with her. At one point, I spotted a soft smile on her face.

"What do you think?"

"Utterly ridiculous," said Feng, though her smile remained.

Once off, she brushed her fingers over her silken dress, ridding any wrinkle from it. A tremor from the ground, the mountain complaining, had us grab each other to keep from falling. It lasted only a few seconds, but in that time, I worried for my village.

"I suppose we ought to check in with the house," said Feng, calm as autumn leaves.

"Do you think the villages are okay?"

She gave me an odd look. "Probably. Humans are a resourceful lot. Even if something happened, there's nothing we can do."

"Not even magic?"

Feng raised a brow, a slight gnawing to her bottom lip and a finger held to her chin as she decided how to answer. "It's a different kind of magic. Maybe Juro could do something if he were here. Kwan, most definitely. But the rest of us have talents elsewhere."

I couldn't help my feelings, nor that my hands yanked at the ends of my sleeves. "Should we go to check?"

"They'll be fine," dismissed Feng. "Now come, we'll see to the house first."

I wanted to defy her, to run home and make sure my family was alright. But I was still a servant, and she was my master's intended. Wasn't she?

It was days after, and no word. I'd asked Gi, though he'd heard nothing of it.

As far as I knew, there was no serious damage anywhere on the mountain. Though what that meant to a Juneun might not be the same to a human. Syaoran complained more than ever that there was the smell of dogs in the air, making him cranky. Everyone brushed off what he'd said, myself included.

Then Feng screamed.

I was already between the walls, wandering, and rushed to see what happened. She was beside the swing, being harried by a playful thing coated in fur and mud and grass and leaves and more. It barked at her, cutting off wherever she tried to dart to, and wagged its tail. In my rough-spun cloths, I hurried to calm the situation, cooing to the dog.

"Get that thing out of here!" demanded Feng.

"The dog?" I patted him, stealing his attention and holding off a barrage of licks to my face.

"It's covered in mud! It's destroying everything."

I laughed. "He's still a bit of a pup. He just needs a bath."

"Just needs a bath? He ruined my dress!"

"I can clean it and fix it," I said, giggling with the dog's sniffing and inspection of me.

"How are you laughing when you're practically under its paws? It could bite."

"Humans say the same thing about snakes and biting, remember?" I reminded. "I wonder if this is why Syaoran kept saying he smelled a dog all summer." My hand found splotches of sticky fur, smelling faintly of pomegranate wine. "Maybe."

"Syaoran?"

"There's been weird things happening, and food would go missing. I bet he's also been the one digging holes and turning over the garden."

"Foxes hate dogs."

"I don't see a collar, or anything. He's probably not trained and doesn't know better."

"It sounds like you're planning on keeping it."

I looked to her, smiling. "He's not a bad dog, see?" I held the scruff of his neck, my other hand guiding him to sit and calm himself. "He reminds me a lot of Chocho, the dog in my village. And Lord Kwan has kennels."

"The dogs left not long after Syaoran came into Kwan's service. They kept barking at him."

"I could teach him not to do that. He's still really young."

"You'll never get Syaoran to let you keep him. Even if you somehow managed that, my future husband would tell you to send him away."

"Lord Kwan will be gone a while. But maybe if I get him cleaned up and trained a bit, he can stay. It's good luck to have a dog around."

"You might be wasting your time."

"I wonder where he came from. It's not likely that there's a bunch of dogs just running around the mountain. Did you get separated from a merchant, boy?"

"Syaoran hates dogs."

"Maybe I can keep him secret, just until I can show that he's not a bad dog."

A troubling silence came from Feng as I sat there, petting him and thinking of a name.

"I'll allow it," said Feng. "Get him clean—and I mean clean—and I'll help to mask his scent. It'll drive Syaoran crazy."

I laughed. "I'm not trying to drive anyone crazy. But just look at this little guy. Look at how cute he is. And he's all alone and hungry."

"You have a weird sense of what's cute," said Feng in a tone of disgust.

It was effort to get him clean. I'd borrowed buckets, brushes, and a length of rope from the stables. Most of the afternoon gone, he looked a lot better, and his energy had run out. His fur was thick and brindle in coloring. I recognized him as a kochi-ken dog, the same sort that a fur-trapper had when he passed through our village some years ago. He'd boasted the breeding lines of his dogs, asking if there was an interest in a pup; there was, though none of us could afford it. Chocho came from an accidental litter, unwanted, when Lan and Renzo had gone to the nearest city to replace tools that couldn't wait for a merchant (and if he didn't have the particular tools, the waiting would've been for nothing).

How such a fine dog came to be alone and stealing scraps was beyond me. Surely no one would dismiss or didn't want a hunting animal like a kochi-ken.

That's when it came to me. Koji. I would call him Koji. He was certainly small, for now, but his paws showed there was more growing for him to do. Lots more.

Koji enjoyed the brushing out of his fur, keeping still and perfectly posed. He wasn't a bad dog at all, and I was sure that I could train him. It would just take time.

Sneaking him in was another matter. He didn't pull on the rope, his front paws clumsily trotting as he looked up to see me rather than watch the path ahead.

For the first few nights, I slept in the kennel with him, worried he'd get lonely and howl. And I shared my meals with him, using the food as an incentive for training. Some days were better than others. I never quit though.

My time was spent between the walls as I'd snuck Koji out, playing with him and teaching him how to be a hunting dog; or, trying to. I didn't know how to teach him that. My best guess was to use a stick we'd played with, and teach him to wait until my command to get it. Sometimes I would tie him to a tree while I hid it, and then have him snuff it out.

On occasion, Feng would find me and watch as I tried my best to train Koji. Often, he was distracted with someone else watching and would look over at her rather than pay attention to what I wanted him to do.

As suspected, Syaoran complained more about the smell of dog (which gave Feng pleasure as she told him he was delusional). I just needed a little more time before I could show Koji and demonstrate that he was well trained.

Autumn grew crisper and crisper, keeping most of the household inside for cozy warmth with little else to do. Except on a particular day when Syaoran called for me. In a panic, I tied a length of rope between Koji and one of the trees, shushing him and hoping whatever problem wouldn't keep me too long.

I ran, trying to put as much distance as possible behind me to keep Koji a secret.

"There you are," said Syaoran. His tone kept an annoyance, as it had since I brought Koji in. "Juro is asking for you."

"Lord Juro is here?"

"That's what I said."

"And Lord Kwan?"

He sighed, waving his hand in front of his nose. "He hasn't come home yet. Juro brough the ginseng tea, but he's early—do you smell that?"

"Smell what?"

He gave me a crooked look, narrowing his eyes. "Never mind."

I waited for him to lead, not wanting to chance he'd find Koji yet.

Juro waited in the far back, under the shelter of the shrine. Secluded. Discomfort rose in me, not just from the setting and what I anticipated to happen, but because it meant I was further from Koji and couldn't hurry back to him.

Syaoran dismissed himself once I was delivered. My fidgeting began.

"I heard you fell ill in my absence," said Juro, once we were alone. "I'm glad to see you're feeling much better."

"I owe my health to Lord Kwan and Lady Feng." Again, I did my best to imitate how the other servants spoke when formally addressed.

"I should have been sent for," said Juro, taking my hand. It was then that I noticed no mud emerged from anywhere, unlike before. "You can imagine my distress."

I realized he waited for an answer. "I'm sorry if my ailment caused you to worry, my lord."

He looked me over, sighing. "Will you refer to me as *Juro*, at least when we are alone?"

I hesitated.

"You smell different."

"Different, my lord?" I saw the displeasure in his face at my address.

He let go of my hand. "I came to repair the earth. I'd heard there was a quake and that you had concerns about the villages."

Admittedly, I found myself surprised. "You're very generous for that, my lord."

"*Juro.*"

He waited, and I couldn't shake the discomfort in my mouth. Unable to keep my eyes on him and try to address him the way he wanted, I looked down. "Juro."

"You must know, Hisa, that I came swift. For you."

"Me?" my eyes flicked up again, for a moment.

He stepped closer. "Does undoing the damage of earth please you?"

I didn't know how to answer. It brought relief, but I also felt like there was the implication that I should be indebted to him.

"Help me to make you happy, my love."

A chill spread through my back. "I... it does, my lor—Juro. I worry about my friends and family at the mountain's base."

The tips of his fingers brushed against mine where they sat politely in front of me. "I've also brought a good stock of medicines with my usual delivery of tea. And, for you, Hisa," he brought out something wrapped in blue silk, "A gift."

"You didn't need—"

"For your birthday." He unwrapped it, revealing a hairpin from carved from nacre.

"My lor—Juro. You're very thoughtful, but my birthday isn't until mid-winter."

"So that's when," said Juro. I stopped myself, meeting his gaze as I realized I'd been tricked into revealing something. "Before, or after the solstice?"

I shook my head. "You can't be giving me this, L—Juro. I don't have anything to give in return."

He ignored me, pinning up my short hair. My eyes darted down, and my hand instinctively went to hide my scar. His own pried it off.

"A kiss," said Juro. "As my reward."

I hated this. I hated being put to feel like I owed that to him. "It's not appropriate, my—Juro." My voice came out as a whimper.

"Servant girls have done more for half as fine of a trinket," said Juro, hinting at agitation. "And I had the rest of my gifts brought to your room."

"Rest?" I looked up, feeling more cornered and confused than ever.

"So that you might get used to wearing nice things, and think of me when you wear them. A sample of what our life together might be like."

I blinked in disbelief, shaking my head.

"Let it be my one reward for all of my effort."

"I just, I don—I've never," I stuttered, trying to come up with some excuse that would allow me to avoid this and leave.

He pulled me, holding the small of my back as our bodies pressed against each other. I looked at him, brow bent and eyes pleading as my voice stayed stuck in my throat.

"One kiss," said Juro, "is all I'm asking for."

I started to shake, unable to run, unable to speak. My heart pounded, and my breath labored. His free hand glided up my side, fingers brushing my cheek and lifting my chin. He leaned in, and I shut my eyes, bracing myself.

Barking, and the weight of paws putting us off balance as Koji bounced on us.

"What? What is this?" demanded Juro.

"Koji!" I scolded. Though, in reality, I was happy for his rough intrusion. His paws coated in mud, I made profuse apologies as I settled him. "Lord Juro, I'm sorry. Your clothes—I'll take him to the kennels, now."

"That's," he seemed at a loss for words. "Yes. Please do that."

I didn't wait for conformation, letting my full discomfort show.

In the kennels, I breathed out some relief. Koji licked at my face. I put a stop to it, smiling with sad thoughts. He wasn't pristine in his coat anymore, and the ordeal that saved me wouldn't look good in the case to keep him.

"How did you get free?" I asked, futile as I knew it was. It didn't look like he chewed through, leaving me to suspect he'd wiggled out of the rope.

I stayed beside him a while, stroking through his fur. At any moment, someone would tell Syaoran about the event. With what time I had, I did what I could to make him presentable.

Enraged, Syaoran called me to the courtyard. I kept Koji with me, hoping beyond hope that I could prove his good demeanor and win over Syaoran's approval. Lin marveled as he walked beside me, though I doubted that'd be enough support to convince Syaoran's decision, as the acting master, to favor my side.

"I knew I smelled dogs!" growled Syaoran.

Feng watched from the veranda, amused by the whole thing.

"You kept this from me—made me think I was going insane!"

"Not on purpose," I whispered. "I just, I, I hoped that if I could train him, then you wouldn't make him leave—"

"That's not to mention the insult to Lord Juro."

"I'm sorry." I kept my head down, unable to look Syaoran in the eye while he was fuming.

"Send it away."

"But I—"

"Now."

"He's not a bad dog, though. He's not even barking or growling at you, see? He's sitting calm—"

"Hisa," scolded Syaoran. "Do not argue."

I tried anyway, meek as I sounded. "Can he stay just a little while? Like a trial period?"

"Hisa," his voice grew cold. "Now."

Desperate, I looked to Feng for help. She stayed unmoving.

"Gi," called Syaoran, irritated with me. "Take that animal and get rid of it."

"No," I begged, falling to my knees and wrapping my arms around Koji.

Gi walked up, discomfort on his face. "Sorry, Hisa."

I held tighter to Koji, met with a playful complaint from him. My eyes looked from Gi to Syaoran to Feng and to the dog in my arms, disregarding Juro's approach.

"Let go, Hisa," cooed Juro. "When we are wed, you may have a dog. Something a bit smaller and more manageable."

I kept my hold, a wordless request for Juro to do something, even if I knew it was useless. I'd denied him what he wanted, and couldn't expect he'd take my side now. Gi reached down, taking the rope from my grip and cuing Koji to come with him.

"I don't remember ordering a household gathering," said Lord Kwan. I looked up to see him walking through the moon gate, headed towards us. "Juro, you're here early this year. We were remised that you left the wedding celebrations."

"I," hesitated Juro, "had it on good authority that I was needed here to mend the earth after a tremor."

My brain compared what I'd been told, and what he'd now said to Lord Kwan. Urekkato. He'd looked through my eyes, and perhaps sent Juro away with the news for some game.

"Did you?" said Lord Kwan, steady in his voice, calm. "And the assembly here?"

"Lord Kwan," I said, before anyone else could get their word in first. I got to my feet, determined not to be ignored. "Please don't make me send away Koji. He's a good boy, and I'm working on training him to be better behaved. I promise he won't cause trouble. He's just young still, and—"

Lord Kwan held up a palm. "Who is Koji?"

"My," I hesitated. "My dog."

"Your dog?"

"I found him, my lord. He was half starved. That's why he was stealing scraps. But he's cleaned now, and I've been sharing my meals with him, so he won't—"

Again, Lord Kwan stopped my babbling. He gestured for everyone to disperse, eyes studying each of us. Gi walked back to Syaoran's side, letting go of the rope leash. Juro, as well, stepped out of the way, trying to pull me with him. I stayed put. Koji sat, perfectly still until a sneeze broke his composure.

Lord Kwan stared at the dog. Not with the same intense irritation that he did upon meeting me for the first time, but studying all the same.

"What should be done?" asked Gi.

Syaoran fussed with his face, resisting the temptation to pinch his nose from the smell.

Lord Kwan said nothing, taking his time. Then, he looked to me. "He stays in the kennels until you take him out on a leash."

"What?" said Syaoran. Disbelief consumed him, his head whipping between me and Koji to Lord Kwan.

"You will feed him yourself," continued Lord Kwan. "You will bathe him yourself."

"So," I started, my mind slow to comprehend, "he can stay?"

With a flick of his hand, he pushed back his long, black hair.

"You're not serious, my lord," said Syaoran. "Are you?"

Walking to his room, Lord Kwan answered, "I like dogs."

I smiled, beaming, and hugged my arms around Koji.

"Hisa," said Lord Kwan, still walking away. "The one from your village this time. After you've changed."

I looked down at my grubby clothes, a mess from Koji's interruption and my attempt to clean him after. It took longer than it should have for me to remember my task of attending him. "Y-yes, my lord." I took hold of Koji's leash, fast bringing him back to the kennels.

In my room, I hurried to undress and clean myself up. I couldn't tell if I still smelled like dog the way Syaoran complained, but I made the extra effort anyway so that it wouldn't come off on the dress Lord Kwan had given me. It didn't slip my notice that several new things were on my table, including a stack of persimmons. The bojagi silk wrapping, with its lattice knot and piece of decorative floral tucked in, looked expensive, never mind whatever it held.

That guilt and discomfort strangled my gut once more. True, I'd probably have nothing so elegant gifted to me again, but I didn't want to be obligated to return an affection I didn't feel. Already, my mind tried to come up with some polite way to refuse.

I tied on my undershorts, and placed on my bouses, one perfectly over the other, allowing the colors of both to show. The underskirt next, to hold the bouses in place. I'd started to tie it off when I heard my door slide. Juro came into my room.

"I'm underdressed, Lord Juro!" I held my arms and hands tight against my torso, bending forward as though it'd somehow conceal me better.

He closed my door, continuing his approach. "You didn't look at the one I brought you."

I understood the ire in his tone, however subtle. "Not while I'm serving. It'd be a shame if I'd accidentally damaged so fine a thing."

"You didn't look." His hot breath grazed the back of my neck. Hands gliding over my hips and around my stomach, his arms pulling me close against him. He inhaled my smell as I stood frozen. We stayed that way a moment, my mind unable to come up with how to escape. "I want to look at you." In a controlled movement, his hand reached and unbound the knot I'd made on the underskirt.

"Lord Juro!" I gasped. "Stop."

Mud began to pool around my feet, the cold touch causing further panic.

"I only want to look." He pulled the skirt free of my grip in a single yank.

"I'm scared, Juro!"

He paused. By luck, or because I'd addressed him the way he wanted in my panic, I didn't know. "Look at me, Hisa."

I shook my head, putting my entire will power into not crumbling to my knees.

He turned me to face him. My arms still braced against me. His finger lifted my chin, making me meet his eye. "I love you, Hisa. And you love that dog more than you love me."

"I do not know you!" I was shaking, fearful and angry.

Blinking, he mulled over the words I'd hoarsely said. "I forget. You're not the typical servant girl. We know little about each other. But I do love you, Hisa."

"Then why do you treat me like this?" I growled, trying to sound menacing in spite of my feelings. "You expect my affection and agreement, but you don't listen to my discomfort. I'm treated like I'm already your property and not a person. That is not love. And I will not marry without it, not even to the richest or most powerful Juneun."

He stared at me, saying nothing for a while. "That is what I want as well. But you have closed off your heart from me."

"I haven't—" I caught myself beginning to argue, walking myself into a trick of words. "I don't know how to speak with you, let alone anything else, Juro." It felt awkward and forced, not addressing him by title. I wanted to avoid his wrath in whatever form that might take, and so I complied with his original request.

Holding my face in his hands, he leaned in. "Understand, Hisa, that I'm used to certain things. What I am not used to, is fear. Or love. Contempt, I am used to. Reluctance, and loathing, among other things, yes. But I will make every effort, if you will allow me an eternity of affection."

Something I could try to work with, as my head stopped spinning. "I'm only human. I can't give an eternity of anything. And I am teased for it regularly. I fought to keep Koji because he's like me. Mortal. Limited in life with time."

Juro looked into my eyes with a tender sadness. "Then let us not waste more of it."

Again, I froze, blinking as I tried to figure out where I'd messed up my defense. The cold of the mud, and the trapping of my fallen underskirt distracting me.

"Kiss me, Hisa. Just once."

"I," I couldn't come up with an excuse. I didn't have to. His lips were already on mine. My top lip fell between his, wet and strange. It wasn't the soft, brush of a touch that Lord Kwan had given me in winter. It was a deeper kiss, meant to have feeling—a feeling I didn't have in return for him.

He pulled away, opening his eyes to look into mine. "I will..." his words trailed. A pensive sigh left him, and he walked out of my room.

Finally, I crumpled to my knees, my breath catching up to me and my ears ringing.

Chapter 38
Beautifully Tragic Life

I'd been left without option. Cleaning myself up again, I didn't have time to wash my dress. Reluctant, I went to Juro's gift. Soft orange and pale, yellow shades, with serval layers in a more mature design. The bouses were longer, thicker in their material, meant to cross over my chest like a snug robe. The sleeves too, were longer, wider, pretty. The skirt of it was one piece rather than two, thick at its upper hem, meant to sinch around my waist rather than just beneath my armpits. It felt a great deal heavier than what Lord Kwan had given me, and there was some sense of false safety in that.

Looking to the part of my room piled with mud, my gut soured. I wanted to take this off, to get back into my dingy, rough-spun clothes. The desire to throw it off increased when noticing frogs subtly embroidered along the thick hems. Soft to the touch, yet every piece made me feel like wearing it meant I agreed to him—that he'd marked me as his territory.

A crunch underfoot, and the prickle of something sharp. The hairpin. And I had nothing to fix it with. I started to panic. What if he asked about it? I could lie, but if he found out? He came into my room unhindered before.

Lord Kwan was waiting. Even as I brewed the tea and brought it, I couldn't think of how to keep it a secret and stave off Juro's anger. But perhaps Lord Kwan would have a solution if I explained things.

The hope was dashed when I saw Juro sitting with Lord Kwan, casual, as though he hadn't assaulted me less than an hour before.

"That's a lovely thing," said Lord Kwan, sounding content and caught up in pleasant conversation.

I tried to ignore it; and tried more to not look at Juro. My fear came to fruition somewhere in conversation when a lull allowed Juro to ask about the hairpin.

"I," I couldn't think of how to build on lies if he asked more questions. Lord Kwan had even said I was a lousy liar. "It fell out. Earlier. And broke."

"I'll fix it," said Lord Kwan, having taken his time, but speaking before Juro. "Is that why you've been so quiet?"

I shied my gaze, not wanting to admit or reveal anything.

In the night, as I went to check on Koji, I had to pass Juro's room. His door closed, I could still hear him with a woman. One of the new girls, presumably. And the same for the following two nights that he stayed. His attention towards me was softer, but no less uncomfortable, and I no longer could guess at what was safe to say.

"Hisa?"

"Yes?" I glanced around, figuring out how I should address him, "Juro?" Admittedly, my mind wandered, leaving me only physically trapped.

He looked me over, sighing. "If it's—about that day, I," he fought with his words. "I am sorry. My temper got my better."

I stayed quiet.

"I hate to see you so genuinely bothered. Tell me what I can do to have your forgiveness, and convince you to smile."

"I don't know," I looked away, searching the garden for something more to say.

"I will be gentle to you. You know that, don't you?"

I nodded, even though I didn't believe it.

"Kwan mentioned you have a love for riding now."

"Not anymore," I said, absently. My body tensed when I realized it, and he waited for further explanation. "I fell."

"My beloved," he took my hand, "I had told Kwan to protect you. Were you hurt?"

"Please, don't trouble yourself, Juro."

The conversation ended with his asking me to try and learn to love him, and the promise of more things to come until I forgave his beastly affront. I couldn't agree to any of it, not while my head was still spinning and my thoughts were fogged. I needed time to understand how I felt, and how to move past it.

Not that it halted gossip.

In my rough-spun clothes, I'd taken to restocking the tinder for the furnaces of the house before the weather became too cold. I didn't think of myself as too quiet, carrying out this small chore, though I went largely unnoticed.

"Don't misunderstand, Juro isn't exactly a prize to behold. But you saw that dress and pin. And she has the audacity to be miserable while the rest of us would kill to have that level of attention from a lord."

"Lord Kwan let her keep the dog because she was about to cry. She has to be sucking him at the very least, regardless of what Lin says."

"It's more than that, if you ask me. She spends most of her time with him while the rest of us are slaving away. Attendant, but I wouldn't be surprise if she attends to *all* his needs."

"And when she's not spending all her time with Lord Kwan, she spends it with Lord Juro, grasping at whatever straw she can get."

"Vulgar village rat."

"She's not even pretty."

"You don't need to be to bend over for a man."

"I heard she looked like a staved little boy when she arrived here, but I guess some men are into that."

"And I've been entertaining Lord Juro with nothing to show for it yet. The mud—and the smell when he's done!"

"Maybe she stomachs it enough that she deserves a reward."

"I'd stomach it happily if there was a guarantee of becoming mistress."

I held still, wanting to hide. My muscles had other ideas, shaking, turning hot—hotter than my ears. I shot up to my feet, scowling. Three startled faces stopped in their tracks.

"Or maybe I put in the best effort even though I'm human. And I don't expect rewards or to become a wife or mistress with sex while at the same time trying to shame someone else for the same thing. Maybe it's because I don't treat people like prizes that I can have something for myself. And maybe it's because I'm not so caught up in my appearance and comparing myself, so I'm not half as annoying."

Like with Syaoran and Urekkato, the moment angry words started to fly from my mouth, I couldn't stop them. At the same time, I didn't want to stop. It felt good to get these things off my chest, to not become a victim to someone else's poor opinion of me, to stand up for myself and not need to be rescued.

"If you're jealous of me, that's not my fault! If I do end up marrying Lord Juro, it's not because I threw myself at him in desperation. It'll be for love. Maybe if all of you were less selfish and started being honest, you wouldn't be so miserable."

I started feeling breathless, so angry that I swore I was at the brink of growing claws and fangs to lash out.

"I'm not trying to seduce Lord Juro, or Syaoran, or Lord Kwan. I'm happy enough to have them as friends. And I'll be happier when I can go home. Then I can come and go whenever I like, and I won't ever have to hear disgusting rumors about me from girls like you again."

They all looked past me, their expressions shifting from startled to annoyed to horrified. Setting their things down, they each put on a perfect bow. For a moment, I thought they were mocking me. Until I felt a hand on my shoulder.

"I don't think I've ever seen you this worked up," said Syaoran, warm in his tone.

I turned, feeling flushed. Juro was with him, bearing a happy expression. How much had he heard? Caught off guard, I fumbled, and put myself into a bow as well.

Juro took my hands. "So, you *will* consider?"

I went rigid. He'd heard at least that much.

"As for the rest, I could never take a mistress who thought so meanly of my bride."

It was all I could do to resist wincing. I'd dug my own grave at that point in my outrage, and there was no way I could think to politely retract.

"Ah, but she hasn't said yes to you, Lord Juro," teased Syaoran. "And maybe I want a mistress who's feisty."

"Syaoran!" I scolded, forgetting my place for the smallest half-second.

"Be careful, fox," said Juro, unamused with the prospect.

"You mean Hisa wouldn't pick me? She did say once that she'd never kiss me, so maybe you're right."

"I said I only wanted to kiss the man I'm in love with!" I realized too late that I fell into his baiting. "And I'm not in love with anyone, yet."

"Yet," repeated Juro, savoring the word.

Again, I felt uncomfortable and out of place.

"In any case, you can go back to your work," said Syaoran, waving off the women. "We came for Hisa, so you can go back to being jealous as well."

I wished he hadn't added that, and frowned at him. He ignored it.

Winter, and the house was restless. Preparations for hosting court in summer were already underway. I stayed out of it, taking apart my old riding clothes and outgrown house clothes to practice my stitch work while it was too cold to take Koji out for long. He didn't mind the cold, but I worried for his health. And though Lord Kwan specified to keep him in the kennels unless I took him out on a leash, I bent his command more than a little. Koji stayed on the mat I wove, content on the heated floor of my room, and on a leash. I kept my bunny out of his reach, making toys for him myself.

"Does Lord Kwan know you have Koji in here?" asked Lin, opening my door.

I waved her in. "He stays quiet."

The door now wide open, she brought in several packages. I stopped my needle work, setting it aside to help her.

"What's all this for?"

"Well, since your new station, you'll be color coded differently from last year when Lord Kwan holds court."

My brow bent at the mere thought of wearing that constrictive dress and all its wraps again.

"New riding clothes as well. The custom order took time, and there's a spare set. And a few things from Juro for your birthday. He sent a barrel of persimmons and apricots, and I helped myself to a couple. Do you mind?"

I shook my head. I'd shared out the persimmons he'd brought on his visit, not wanting them but also not wanting them to rot.

"That's one thing if you do decide to marry him. Summer fruits picked fresh, even in the deepest winter."

"They won't last long here though. It's too cold."

"Well, when they start, ask Xin to turn them into breads or pastries."

"Out of persimmons and apricots?"

"They make nice cookies. The last house I worked for used the abundance to bake them by the basket load before holding court. It'd probably make Juro happy to see that."

I sighed, setting things down. Packages, notes, I didn't want to look at any of it.

Koji shook out, waking up and wagging his tail. He looked over, waiting for me to say if he should stay or get up.

"Koji," cooed Lin, going over to pet him. "Who's a good boy?"

Good boy. Then I thought of what Lord Kwan had said at the end of court, and again when my fever became manageable. "Why did he say that?" I muttered.

"What?" said Lin.

I thought fast. "I was thinking, how I wish he wouldn't send anything else. It makes me uncomfortable. Like I'm supposed to feel indebted, and have to accept him."

"You can still enjoy that a man is doting on you, while it lasts." She stopped to ponder, squinting at me to better read my expression. "You're still hung up on that day?"

I'd told Lin after the fact, when light teasing pushed me too far. "I thought he was going to force himself on me." Then I began to wonder. "Would a man force himself on his wife?"

Lin shrugged. "Maybe. He could've come back while you were asleep. You wouldn't have known until he was on you."

Another reason I wanted to keep Koji in my room.

"Did you tell Lord Kwan?"

"I didn't want to bother him."

"You should. It's one thing if a guest has a willing girl, and something else completely if he violates her. It shows a severe lack of respect to the host; and Lord Kwan likes you enough to take it more personally. He certainly did with Yua."

"With Yua?"

"It was about seventy, maybe eighty years ago. One of the older sons of the Samjo clan."

"I never knew."

"Now, will you stop moping and tell him? I want to see that girl who chewed off the heads of three gossiping bitches. Syaoran said it was spectacular, but you're so quiet I have a hard time trying to picture it. If I'd caught them talking about me, I would've done more than some blunt words."

I chuckled.

"So, what do you want to do for your birthday?"

I shook my head.

"Oh, come on. Everyone who matters in the house likes you enough to want to do something. Last year, Yua and Syaoran had us stop what we were doing to put something together. It was hectic!" She laughed.

"That's exactly why I don't want anything. I'm not used to anyone making a fuss over me." Though, the imagination of Yua conducting a birthday surprise for me made me smile. She'd always seemed distant and straight to the point.

Lin groaned, putting her attention back on Koji.

"When is your birthday, Lin?"

"Yesterday."

I dropped my jaw. "Why didn't you say anything?"

"Why? What were you going to do about it?"

She had a point. I didn't have great enough skill to make something, or money to buy anything.

"Besides, I'll take some of your apricots as gift enough."

"I don't mind sharing that, but a gift should be something from the heart."

"Too sentimental. Most of us like gifts that are practical. It's why we put together that deel for you."

"In a single day?"

"It went a lot faster with everyone working on it, and a bit of magic. Most of it was alterations, since we had your measurements already."

Lin waved away the gesture, making it sound trivial, but I adored my winterwear. It was weird to think something that meaningful to me was miniscule to the person who'd given it. What was there that I could do that could measure to expectations?

"Lord Kwan is allowing solstice celebrations too. You should see this place when all the lanterns are lit up. It's beautiful."

"I didn't think spirits celebrated."

"It depends on the mood of the lord. But we typically have all sorts of cakes and egg custard and hold a house banquet. And a few games. It's not as exciting as court or other summer festivities, but it boosts morale."

"Women did all the cooking in the village."

"Oh, yeah?"

"And the men would hang bamboo ropes with bits of red ribbons tied on them. We'd all eat in the same house and try to stay up to see the sunrise."

Lin laughed. "Most of us are passed out from all the food and wine before sunrise. But I like the idea with the bamboo ropes. Could be something else to hang more lanterns. We still have a few days."

I walked to the shrine on my birthday, Koji in tow—though he complained, having to stay beside me on a leash rather than play.

The solstice passed, and the memory of how the lights looked, how warm everything felt because of it, stayed with me. Rowdy as it became, I didn't mind. One of the men acted too liberal after a heavy consumption of wine, with Lin prying him off of her and the house giving him a tease to remind him of his behavior.

I didn't understand the rules of the games, though it was fun to sit back and watch. The fruits Juro sent were shared out, making for greater delight and keeping some of the more devious taunts from being aimed at me. Lin warned that going too far might make me change my mind about generosity later on.

Things quieted since then, the most excitement being my asking Xin to teach me to make treats out of whatever fresh fruits were left from Juro, and to make a heavy, honeyed cake. It wasn't as difficult as I first supposed, though I still managed to make a mess of myself. Not that I minded, repeating the process verbally until I could write it down so that I could take it with me when I leave.

I still hadn't opened any of the packages or notes in my room, even with Lin's prodding. There was still a sense of dread. Even Syaoran's warm curiosity, setting aside his irritation for the day and handing me a silver coin, wouldn't sway me. I didn't want others to see, to talk about it, to convince me of anything.

So, I decided to go to the shrine for prayer.

To my surprise, Lord Kwan was already at the shrine, hands steepled, chin down, and eyes closed. I didn't know he prayed, for what or why, I couldn't guess. I hadn't thought that a Juneun, a powerful one, would need prayer for anything.

I tried not to disturb him, waiting as long as my anxiousness would allow before putting in the coin Syaoran gave me that morning and assume the same pose. I stayed in prayer a long time, ignoring Koji's whine and waiting for Lord Kwan to leave.

It seemed like an eternity, waiting, and I couldn't help but feel like I was being watched. Daring to open my eyes again, I peeked over to see that he'd finished his prayers and waited for me.

"What did you wish for this year?"

My mind went blank. I knew what I'd prayed for: continued strength, courage, good health, for time to go quickly so that I could be home once more, and to never be alone with Juro again. But I couldn't put it to words.

He smiled, soft. "Something I can give to you, hopefully."

It helped, but I fidgeted as I struggled to think how to outwit him. "Love's kiss. So, I can't ask it of someone who doesn't love me."

Brow cocked, I saw a second of mischief in his eyes. "Was mine not satisfactory?"

I felt myself starting to flush, needing to reel in my feelings and form sensible words. "It, it was, but," I gulped, needing a precious pause to gather myself. "This kind is different."

He slow blinked, assessing my nervousness. "From Juro?"

"No!" I said, a little too quickly. My eyes darted away and back, searching for how to reclaim some ounce of dignity. "It's—I know Lord Juro is your friend, but," I hesitated with my next set of words. But Lin was right. "He tried to force himself on me the last time he was here."

"He violated you?"

"Not, well, he stopped, but..." It was hard to meet Lord Kwan's eye as I tried to explain myself.

His stare took me in, smile faded. "What prevented you from saying this before?"

I looked down. His tone was gentle, patient, though I wished there'd have been some seething anger. "I didn't want to be the cause of any further trouble."

"Hisa, you are a part of my house. If I am troubled to protect you, that is my failing as a lord." He lifted my chin, coaxing me to meet his gaze again. "And you are a treasured friend. Are you not?"

"Yes, my lord," I whispered. A feeling of comfort wrapped around me. The kindness of his voice acting as reassurance.

He dropped his hand, leaving me to myself again. "I will better occupy him when next he visits, to keep the two of you separate. And keep in mind that you're under no obligation of secrecy. Come to me, as your friend, with any troubles you might have in the future."

As much as I would have rathered that Juro not return at all, I knew that was asking too much. There was business between the two, and it was unfair of me to demand a complete end to it.

"And you're certain there is nothing I can give to you today? Or, at least send for?"

I shook my head, smiling with some relief. "I don't need anything else."

His eyes studied me, deciding on something. "Close your eyes."

At that moment, I'd forgotten what I'd said before. "Lord Kwan, don't tease me like that. I've said before that a kiss shouldn't be coerced. And love's kiss especially."

He took a step forward, closing the distance between us, and lifted my chin again, a little higher, fingers brushing over my jaw and cheek. "Close your eyes." That hint of a smile returned.

For a long time, I didn't. I could pull away. I knew he wouldn't stop me. Or I could refuse it all together. But I didn't want to refuse it, and did eventually obey.

His lips fell gentle on my own, parting them to play with. The hand that held my chin slid back, behind my ear, and the other came to cup my face. All of it cool to the touch, all of it bringing a strange joy. My fingers found their way to his robes, taking hold high on his chest. Then he opened my mouth with his, and his tongue went to explore. I tried to do the same, inexperienced and clumsy as I was. It was weird and wet and gross and wonderful, stealing the breath from me and I didn't care. My heart raced, I became dough in his hands, nothing else existed, and I wanted it to never end.

When he pulled away, and I was able to suck in my breath again, I opened my eyes. My fingers loosened, reluctant to let go until a thread of drool between us broke. I cupped my face in embarrassment. Lord Kwan paid it no heed, keeping a soft smile.

"And that?"

I batted my eyes, my head in a fog.

"Was I no good?"

Shaking my head, I scrambled for words. "It was. It was... I liked it. A lot."

"That's good. I'd hate to learn now, after all this time, that my kiss was frightening." His fingers slid under my hand, thumbing away the last thread of spit from my lip and chin. Without a following word, he turned to go back to the house.

I stood there, shocked. Koji leaned on me, rubbing his face against my thigh, but I stayed in my unblinking stupor. I no longer felt a friendship between us. How could I? The kiss replayed in my head, over and over, faster and faster. My life had become beautifully tragic. Because I realized then that I was in love with Lord Kwan.

Chapter 39
Without Saying it

I tried to ignore the kiss, tried to ignore the feeling bursting through my chest and my head. Anything else! A distraction. I wasn't supposed to be in love with him. I couldn't be. He was my master—I was his servant! He was my jailor. A Juneun. An immortal spirit who would stay timeless, while I was only human.

My mind fixated on every instance of kindness, every time he protected me, saved me, every gesture of friendship and gratitude, and every time we'd ever been close. Most of all, on every kiss. It'd started like Juro's, only kinder, tender. Why did I think about it so much? I didn't want to, but I couldn't stop.

With constant replays in my head, I'd accidentally pricked myself in my needlework, more than once.

Frustration built up in me, threatening to make me explode into a thousand tiny pieces. I grabbed my pillow, plunging my face into it, and screamed. It helped to make me feel a little bit better. But only a little.

It was useless. I was in love—hopelessly in love—with Lord Kwan.

Going through my packages, I started with what I knew were the riding clothes Lin sent for. More practical shoes came with them. Better for mountainous rides, since I lacked the balance and elegance of a Juneun. I mused to myself that soon I would have a complete and glamorous wardrobe. Though I likely wasn't allowed to take any of it home.

Juro had sent more dresses in the same, more mature style. One of deep reds and greens, decorate with lotus and crane images. Another a soft, pastel coloring; lavender, peach, white, and pink, a print running down the skirt of it like a river. Always, I found the image of frogs somewhere in each piece. They were lovely things, but having them still felt like I'd agreed to become his property.

I looked from those, to the one—the only one—Lord Kwan had given me. He'd done so in seeing my shabby, outgrown appearance, and there wasn't a detail in it of a tiger. The shreds of the riding clothes he'd given me lay in a basket, waiting for me to decide their new use. Was it so different? It felt that way. One for the utility and practicality, and the other a wordless demand for me to accept.

I looked to the note that came with the dresses. Thinking I could make myself fall out of love by reading them.

To Hisa

One for winter, one for spring, both to wear as you will, my fragrant flower.

Do not shy from sending for me, or request anything you need.

I will send more apricots to you again soon, so that you are never without.

Until the day we are reunited, and our lips together again.

Let these gifts serve in my place to comfort and keep you from missing me too much.

Your love,

Juro

It didn't work. I felt a melancholic sort of guilt for Juro, and that was all that changed. Perhaps, if I read it again, tried to imagine him as someone I could fall in love with, I could erase my feelings for Lord Kwan. After several rereads, my feels were unchanged.

Frustrated, I moved on to the next, trying to distract myself.

Candied nuts and tangerines were sent from Urekkato, I thought it strange. How would he know when my birthday was? Through my eyes, of course. Didn't he have better things to do, now that he was married to a princess? The note with it, however, made me furious.

Hisa

I've never been more entertained. I think I will look through more human eyes from now on.

Should your beloved Juro come to your room again, take my advice: Let him.

I have no interest in spying on him. But please enjoy the gifts to help come your wedding night.

And, congratulations on your victory over Syaoran. Koji seems like a loyal creature.

However, do not expect that a man will be as obedient to you as he is.

He signed it with his collection of titles, some of which I'd never seen and didn't know how to say. Regardless of it all, I frowned. I could feel my brow turn sharp and my ears heat up. Let him? Let him? Let a man I didn't love take me when I wasn't ready for such a thing? What right did he have to suggest that? And how dare he make implications of my wedding night, or any time before or after! Then to tease me! Of course I didn't want a man to act like a dog. Of course I didn't expect obedience—nor did I expect to always obey. I wanted a love where we could hold each other up, not whatever selfish imitation Urekkato imagined.

Standing, I went to my stationery and took a piece of charcoal. I hoped he was watching now, that he would see through my eyes what I was about to do. I wanted him to have a message from me, clear and without confusion.

On Urrekkato's note, I wrote boldly: *I hate you*. My sloppier penmanship destroying the elegance of his own.

It distracted me from thinking about Lord Kwan's kiss (just not in the way I wanted). I paced around, fuming, with Koji watching me curiously. Again, I grabbed my pillow and again I screamed into it, until all the air was out of my lungs. In my upset, Koji barked, low and questioning. When I had the strength to look up from the cushion, I saw him wagging his tail, a low growl waiting to unleash another bark.

"Shh!"

He barked. And again. Thinking it was a game. The more I tried to hush him, the more excited he got.

"Lord Kwan and Syaoran can't know I brought you to my room, Koji!" I scolded in a whisper. "You need to be quiet."

I'd been scolded by Lord Kwan anyway. He insisted that Koji stay in the kennels and wouldn't be persuaded otherwise. Had I not taken apart my old deel, I could have put it on him. While Koji didn't seem to mind the snow when I took him out, it was colder at night.

After that first night, when I went to check on him, I found him cozy in a pile of blankets over the woven mat I'd made. While I didn't know who brought them out, I had my suspicion—later confirmed when I went to take him for a walk; Lord Kwan asked if I was happier with the situation, enough to ease my worries.

And the feelings I had for the Juneun flourished, warming my chest. Bold, I prompted myself to ask, "Lord Kwan?"

He stopped in walking away, controlled movements turning his head over his shoulder and the rest of him following suite.

"About... My question for today."

That hint of a smile grew on him. "Yes?"

"Have," I struggled to come up with the right words. "Have you ever been in love before?"

"How else would I know what you meant with that kiss?" He teased, and I frowned. Seeing it wasn't the answer I was looking for, he tilted his head to one side, measuring my irritation. "Yes." He walked on, saying nothing more.

It was a better answer, but still not the one I wanted to hear. I wanted to know if the feeling I had, the feeling he'd given me, if it was with him as well, now. Was he in love with me? I silently chastised myself for not wording it that way, for turning my inquiry in a safer direction.

Wandering, I passed the tea house, with Feng inside, an image of beauty and dignity.

"Sit with me, Hisa."

"I'm not supposed to bring Koji—"

She waved off my concerns. "Sit with me Koji." She gave the command, and Koji complied, happy to get his paws onto heated floors. "I'm glad I don't have to make you carry out chores well into the night."

"What do you mean?" I said, removing my boots.

"I overheard one of the new girls talking about how they planned to go to my fiancée's room. So, I've made sure she's too tired to try and seduce him."

I remembered my manners and bowed politely before taking a seat where she'd pointed. "I don't think he'd take her, regardless."

"Of course he wouldn't," said Feng. "It's the principle. That she would even try it. I'm glad you understand. Because you're human, I suppose. He dotes on you like a child."

The conversation quickly became uncomfortable. Lord Kwan had sent for Feng, made her a room here, and, short of a formal announcement, they were intended for each other. Did he really think of me as some child? His kiss suggested otherwise. Guilt ran through me. I'd fallen in love with someone who was intended for someone else, to be together for an eternity. Delusional, that's what I was.

"Are you listening?"

I hadn't been. "Yes," I said, smiling.

Feng looked at me with a frown. "In any case, I expect he'll make the announcement when he holds court." She offered me a cup.

Happily, greedily, I helped myself to the red tea, savoring the warmth flowing into my gut. It was then that I noticed the left-over honey cake and the persimmon cookies there as well. At the very least, my birthday food hadn't gone to waste; enjoyed even by Feng, despite her high standards.

Koji put his nose close against the table's ledge, his tail wagging and eyes wide at the treats. I allowed him some, watching him eat as though he hadn't already had breakfast.

"He's come a long way since stealing scraps," said Feng. "Syaoran still complains though."

I ignored her snickering.

"I'm actually surprised Juro didn't come here for the solstice, or after for your birthday. Must be the cold."

"Why would that matter? He's a Juneun."

"He's a toad," said Feng, as though it explained everything.

"And you're a snake."

"And the heated floors are what helps. I wouldn't be able to make the trek in or out of here during winter."

"For all Juneun?"

Feng threw a sarcastic expression at me. "Of course not. Do you think my soon-to-be husband would be stopped by trivial snow?"

"I've honestly never thought about it. All I really know about Juneun are the stories and from being here."

She sighed. "Oh, you poor, naïve, country girl."

Before she'd finished her words, a flurry of wind and ice kicked up. We both looked to the outside, searching for the cause. Powder white lingered in the air, a mist in its wake, though no sound of violence drifted to us. I returned my gaze to the table, my eyes going wide as I realized Koji stole more treats while I was distracted. Sharp, I scolded him, but he looked smug—as much as a dog could—in his successful theft.

Lord Kwan had left. Kurai had gone to harass one of the villages, one that was close to my own. Gumiho was gone. But other Kurai were still around to cause trouble. Though, Syaoran admitted how strange it was that any would choose deep winter to act, and so close to his home.

I found myself praying for his safe return, alongside the protection of my family. What surprised me wasn't that I prayed for Lord Kwan, but the desperate feeling I had in doing so.

My prayer was answered in the early hours of the following morning. Lord Kwan returned, somewhat feral, but mostly a man, causing everyone to hesitate. Was he enough himself to not need restraint? Or was he still too much of a danger? I'd hurried out, pulling on my deel but forgetting the sash to tie it together—though I remembered to close my eyes and count as I left my room. He stood in the courtyard, still and at war with himself, clothes in disarray, hair unbound, and sword sheathed in his hand.

I chanced it.

Walking to him, plodding a new path in the snow, his eyes shifted to me. A snarl formed, though the rest of him unmoving. Syaoran, and a few others, called after me in a whisper, a late attempt to stop me. In front of him, I smiled and bowed. I disliked seeing him chained up like a monster, and was happy enough to think he wouldn't need to be this time.

"Welcome home, Lord Kwan."

He bent his face down to look at me, snarl intact.

Braving it, I took a chance, remembering the fight against Beom. I leapt to wrap my arms around him, burying my face as he growled. I felt his arms raise, and the rigidness of his muscles.

"I'm glad you're safe," I said, calm as I could. "Please come back. You're not a monster. You're my friend."

I felt the tips of claws pressing into my back. I refused to move, and firmed my embrace on him.

"Aren't you?"

The claws glided over, a rigid wrapping of his arms around me in its stead. Slow, his hug became stronger and more natural, gentle. "Hisa..."

"I'm here, Lord Kwan."

He repeated my name. We stayed like that a while, and I ignored the cold climbing over any exposed part of me and biting through my night gown.

I wanted to say it then, confess my feelings. But my jaw kept shut and my voice stuck fast in my throat. A reminder sounded in my head: he intended to marry Feng.

He said my name once more. My face against him, I could hear his heartbeat, softening and becoming rhythmic as he reclaimed himself. He rested his forehead atop my hair.

"Brave as the day you arrived," whispered Lord Kwan. "You're lucky that worked. Instead of a far worse scenario."

"I knew it would," I whispered back.

He stayed wordless a moment, mulling over my claim. "Did you now?"

I nodded, slow to release him.

"Your village is safe. I promise."

I smiled up, offering a silent thanks before fetching tea as my task required.

Chapter 40
Lord Kwan X

What was he doing?

As Kwan entered his room, that became a repeated thought. He was fond of her, enough to make allowances, but he knew he took his teasing too far today. She looked like a frightened doe after he kissed her. Did she think less of him now? She'd closed her eyes, accepted the kiss—embraced it. Though he reminded himself that she was not in a position to speak too freely; did she feel obligated to the kiss?

He could have stopped at playing with her lips. He didn't need to go further. Some whisper in his mind coaxing him to do it, *like a lover*. And that he could jest after, antagonize a playful response. The concept fled when he'd opened his eyes.

His hand went to his mouth, nails and knuckles pressed on his lips. The taste was...

He shoved away the thought, irritated by it.

Sighing, his mind churned up the memory over and over. It seemed innocent at the start. A taunt between friends. Kwan chastised himself for it. She'd confessed the year prior of never having been kissed before. Of course he took it too far. He should've ignored the wish *for love's kiss*. Any gift might've sufficed. A cake. A shawl. Some bit of jewelry. No... That was the usual list for a typical lady of the courts. Was there nothing else he could've done?

Every conversation ran through his mind, looking for some clue, some way to make it up. He'd gone too far with his teasing.

Putting color to a picture, bringing it a little more to life.

Winter. Even if he demanded its immediate delivery, it wouldn't come until the thaw. Though, it was the best he could come up with. He sat himself at his table, the wave of his fingers bringing everything he needed from his stationery, and started drawing up the request. A simple enough thing. Canvas and paint were a pittance in cost, despite her claims. Which caused him to pause. Was it too lavished a thing? An insult to her perhaps? He recalled her discomfort in Juro's doting, even without the new context to it; perhaps the notion would be perceived in the same way. The attempt was for comfort, not to put her in a position feeling she needed to oblige him or reciprocate in some way. Was this no different from his more forward associate?

Kwan crumpled up the half complete letter, letting it burn to nothingness in his hand. He needed something better. Something to repair the friendship. The very thought of having lost her good opinion—why did it matter? Except that it did matter to him, with or without his understanding of the reasons.

Surely, centuries could grant him insight on a better solution. War, it seemed, was easier to navigate than unfeigned feelings.

He thought to the things she adored that he presented previously. Though, she'd now become aware they were out of a place of guilt on his behalf. Would she accept another gesture after the source of his shame was at her expense? She was too gentle, and likely would out of a sense of duty.

Staring at a blank paper and waiting inkwell, his mind continued to conjure suggestions only to retract them. He sighed, heavy. A whisper went silently through him, suggesting that he'd erased any further smiles and laughter from her.

Barking interrupted him. Haughty in the moment of his vexation, he stood, marching out. He knew the source, and had his suspicion of why.

Unable to calm himself, he gave harsh words, few as they were, ordering her to take her dog back to the kennels. When her sad expression kept, in lieu of fright, his heart weighed. He could've been more eased in his tone and phrasing—he should've been. He felt sure now that he'd jeopardized the friendship. She'd plead about the cold of the night. Something he knew to be true, and was the reason why any dogs he kept were grouped in threes to keep warm. Koji was alone.

Syaoran's foul mood, even without anything said, began to rub off. He'd taken his frustration out on the pup. Though, to go back now would lead to undermining him, perhaps force his hand. It wouldn't be the first time, and he'd hoped never to need to do so again. He didn't want rulership through fear. Kwang was right. Compassion was needed, and needed in such a way as to still come off the stronger.

He tore his sleeve, fixing magic to it and carry out his will in the kennels. Blankets, thick and plenty and warm. She smiled again the following morning, a quiet thanks. And his heart lightened with some relief. He didn't lose her complete good opinion, her friendship.

"About... My question for today."

The words gave Kwan certainty that their friendship held. "Yes?"

"Have you ever been in love before?"

He couldn't resist. His light mood encouraging the tease. Her expression changed, and he felt then that he'd overestimated. Again, walking to his room, it weighed on him. He'd overstepped. Him, a lord. Something that made him want to take it all back, to reverse what he'd done. And again, he couldn't think what that might be which didn't put her into a state of obligation.

"Lord Kwan!" A scout, gasping for breath, damp from ice and sweat, ran to him. A swift bow, and a grim expression, he gave his report. "The north village. A fox spirit—"

Kwan extended his arm, his sword flying to him. Without a following word from the scout, he made to leave. "Say nothing of it being a fox." His magic surged, answering his call for speed.

He'd charged in heedlessly, hoping swiftness would lend him some element of surprise in spite of the obvious trap. She'd waited him out, testing her lure.

The clash of magic and clamoring of steel rang out over the fires and terrified screams.

Kwan managed to press his assault and push Gumiho away from the village, away from increasing casualties in a feud they knew nothing about. He gave no quarter, not even to prevent injury to himself. When at last he found an opening, however risky, he took it. Feigning a swipe of his blade, he released one hand to grab at her throat. Alarm, fear, consumed her face. She grabbed at his wrist and fingers, claws digging in, and kicked out, every squirm to try and break free.

Kwan held his grip.

"You will return them all, and I will end your existence swiftly. It's the last mercy I will offer you."

She chuckled, strained as she was for breath. "All of what?"

He firmed his fingers. "Do not play with me, demon."

She smiled, cold. "I don't have them."

Furious, he took to slamming Gumiho into the ice. "Do not suppose that I will hesitate to make your last moment the worst you've ever known."

She coughed out a laugh. "It's true. When they died, their souls faded. There's nothing you can do." A toothy grin spread across her face. "You failed."

Another fit of rage, Kwan raised her to slam down again. This couldn't be the end. For Borsi, for Jiana, for the others unfortunate enough to succumb to her theft of their souls. He refused it!

She used his distress against him, slipping free and clawing at his face. He swiped back, loosing a roar and letting claws of his own show. His rage taking him, she chuckled. A small cue, causing him to pause in an attempt to reel some of himself back in. She moved in, taking her advantage. More and more, she became the fox queen, shedding off the appearance of a sultry woman.

She was baiting him, trying to throw him into a blind fury this close to his home. He realized the game, steadying himself—refusing to be her weapon.

"You don't have it in you," taunted Gumiho. A desperate move.

It helped him to settle his rage. She had no more army, no more devotees, and this was her attempt to use him against himself. Lies and goading.

Gathered, he inhaled deep, holding his blade upright and placing his palm against the back of it,. Eyes closed, he allowed his other senses to investigate, to test his assumption. No unfamiliar smell of magic, no sound of anything outside themselves. He began his spell, drawing from the mountain. The crackle of lightning building a charge. Gumiho moved in, understanding she'd overplayed her hand and hoping to force his fury.

He opened his eyes, cast his spell.

Darkness.

"Welcome back, Lord Kwan."

He felt still, the familiar voice recalling him to his senses.

"You're not a monster. You're my friend."

His heart gladdened, rallying strength to pull him free. He was tired. Tired enough to truly not remember Gumiho's fate. Something pressed on him, wrapped around him, something warm. The shadow's instinct started to take over, fighting against his heart's knowing.

"Aren't you?"

Yes. A thousand yeses. There wasn't a need for outrage anymore. Not with her. Not when it was...

"Hisa..."

"I'm here, Lord Kwan."

He strengthened his embrace, protecting her from whatever might be just outside themselves, the darkness subdued. Again, he could breathe, free from his own trapping. She brought him out of it. What was it about her? Regardless, he needed to do something, say something, to serve as a thank you.

"Brave as the day you arrived."

"I knew it would work."

He was tired. Even so, he extended his sight with a spell, looking to the villages that called Mount Tora their home. "Did you now?"

The wreckage of one would need to wait, if they could, for him to claim a small measure of recovery. Others were caught in Gumiho's lashing, though to a lesser extent. He would go to them, making a wordless prayer that they could hold out until he had the strength to set things right.

"Your village is safe. I promise."

Her expression wasn't what he'd assumed. Nothing noting the dramatic intensity of a courting lady, nor the look of expectancy he'd grown accustomed to. There was the pleasure and the relief of the news, but the joy stayed the same as it had when he was again himself.

He sent her off, making to retreat into his room as he always had on any other return. Feng insisted on her company, quickly dismissed when he remarked how he only required his attendant. Tired, and precise with his words, he didn't look to see how she reacted.

Waiting. He shed off his clothes, donning a fresh set, free of ice and wetness. Near the end, he'd heard his door close, though looking over his shoulder, he saw no one.

"Hisa," called Kwan, gentle, tired, as he fixed the last piece to himself.

"I didn't want to intrude, my lord," said Hisa, fingers fidgeting.

"You are my attendant in Yua's absence. Therefore, there is no intrusion."

She shut the door again, keeping out the biting cold. "It still doesn't feel right to come in at any time."

"Would you say that if it were your husband?"

Her cheeks and ears went pink, a tint of it on her neck. "That's different."

A new tease came swift to his mind, stayed from his tongue. "You needn't worry yourself. You are my attendant and my friend. There wasn't a hesitation to embrace me in front of others only minutes before."

"I, that—I mean, because I knew that would stop you from being chained up. And you weren't underdressed and isolated."

"So, Hisa would hesitate if my feral return was naked?"

"I didn't say that—but, there's, you..."

He smiled, taking a seat and opening the teapot. She'd realized the joke, and sighed. Her bent brow expression endeared him. She was not at all the trembling girl that arrived. There was a comfort, a familiarity between them now.

As she poured out the kettle, the contents in a steady flow, Kwan thought again of how he would miss her. Pieces of him debated whether or not to entrust the news of Gumiho. Would it be safer to make her aware, or to shield her from it?

When he decided, guilt spoiled his gut. She was only human, after all. The reminder ushering a bittersweet sadness. An idea came with the feeling. Something to make up for past behavior, and to keep with himself.

He sent her to fetch his stationery. Adding to his delight, she didn't hoover over him, allowing it to remain secret. His seal on it, and twine expertly wrapped, he'd send for it tomorrow.

Chapter 41
Riddles

Midspring. And the house was a buzz with preparations. The snow thawed, and new grass grew thick, we had weeks before court. I hated the idea. Even with a larger staff, I dreaded the thought.

A note had come for me. Several, in fact. Urekkato's was the easiest to find, and my ears heated at the mere sight. I read them as I walked Koji between the walls. More unwanted advice, and apology that he would not be at court, seeing to his marital duty. Good, I thought, better that I never spoke with him again.

I handed that note to Koji, letting him chew and tear it as his leisure. He wagged his tail at the sound of the paper tearing while his tongue worked to spit out pieces. I closed my eyes and counted after there was nothing left of the letter.

A note from Juro expressed his eagerness to arrive, and that he may come early. The end of it asked me to write him with whatever I desired him to bring. Again, I felt stuck. To not respond might come as an offense, enough to agitate him into indiscreet, entitled behavior. At the same time, making a request would suggest I considered—accepted—his advances. How I could outwit, and choose neither, was the complicated bit. I thought to say something akin to when he'd left court. But asking for a safe arrival or that he only be met with good weather sounded like I made an advance myself.

I was trapped.

I didn't want to accept this as my fate, but I didn't know where to turn. Lin and Syaoran would impress that I follow through and ask for something. Feng perhaps the same, now seeming eager to be rid of me since winter rather than to keep me on as her personal servant. I didn't know what caused the sour change, though I'd hoped that warmer weather would usher in a better mood from her.

Others might press that, if I wanted nothing, to bid he bring me something for someone else's delight. That, I was sure, would lead to Juro's ire. What I needed was a friend who had nothing to gain, nor anything to lose in helping my decision. Though, Fumei was at the base of the mountain, and my brothers there with her. My mind made the obvious answer of writing to them, though fast remembered that no one in the village could read. It was a skill I'd only recently acquired myself because of Lord Kwan.

Lord Kwan… of course! He'd said as much himself that he would keep Juro and myself separate.

With that in mind, I went to search for him. Easily done, as he was beside the inner gate where a host of things were being delivered. Though, on my arrival, announcing myself, he swiftly took my shoulder to turn me around. I didn't have a moment to understand when he commanded that I put Koji in the kennels and come to the swing with one of my night robes.

I was still his servant before I was his friend until my sentencing was up, so I obeyed. Though, I dressed over my sleepwear.

He didn't argue or protest when I showed up. Instead, he took my hand and lead me to the wall where butterflies gathered. I couldn't figure it out. He seemed eager and secretive and sure, though it made no sense to me. Even at the base of the wall, I couldn't clue it together: a gentle smile on his face and an expanse of paints at his feet.

"How confident are you in your art skill?" asked Lord Kwan. When I didn't answer, he jutted his chin to the wall in front of us. "It makes for a great canvas, don't you agree?"

Still, as I looked between him and the paints and the wall, my mind was slow to comprehend. "To paint here?"

He nodded.

"It wouldn't look good enough, my lord. I'm still learning."

"I think you've improved in the time you've been here," said Lord Kwan, answering quicker than usual and with a softness to his tone. He took up a brush, dipping it in the barrel of black color. "Paint with me."

My jaw fell open. "It definitely won't look good beside yours."

He kept his expression, studying me. "What does it matter? I want to see what you come up with."

Admittedly, the temptation was hard to resist. I found my hand reaching for a brush, my eyes kept going to vibrant yellows and pale blues and all the shades of green. With a last shy protest, he insisted again, saying to let it be wild and imperfect. That he was tired of perfect art as it was.

My excitement wouldn't stay contained. In the same second that my hand took another brush, admiring its perfect and soft bristles, I was bringing broad strokes of paint against the wall.

"Hisa," called Lord Kwan, low in his voice.

I looked over, seeing that he was in crisp white, and remembered what he'd asked of me. I rushed to the shade of the boughs and shimmied out of my top layers. It'd be a shame to tarnish my dress, the one he'd given me. I'd yet to dawn the ones Juro had sent, nor did I want to.

Matching him, now, I dragged my brush with absolute abandon. Color speckled my face and clothes. I didn't mind my effort being a little sloppy, or care that my tongue stuck out. It started to come together, little by little. I'd even forgotten, for a moment, that Lord Kwan was painting beside me, until I side stepped to reach higher on the wall and collided with him. Arms, hands, sides, thighs bumping in a single, clumsy motion.

My head whipped around, my eyes wide with surprise and embarrassment. His own expression held a question, soft and slow blinking. I made a meek apology, and his gentle smile returned. Nothing was said, continuing on unhindered.

I stopped again at the feel of fingers tapping my shoulder, jumping slightly and turning around. Lord Kwan, with that same smile, offered me a drink of water. It was then that I realized I'd been painting for hours. We took a break, eating a sampling of cakes under the shade of the trees with their new and budding leaves. Looking at the wall, our canvas, the difference in skill was stark.

"Let's switch sides," said Lord Kwan, unconcerned.

"I don't want to mess up your work," I said.

"Mess what up?" He gave a knowing look, a tease at me. "I want to see what you do with it."

I tried not to cross over the work Lord Kwan did, but after the fifth time I'd given up on being cautious. We'd gone from side to side, up and down, crossing paths. The whole time, Lord Kwan kept his placid expression and that smile on his face.

The sun hung low, illuminating our effort in a strange and pleasing way. We'd put together a scene captured in time. A lake, flowers and trees, small animals, a couple of men and a lady walking through—simplicity in the imagery rather than anything lifelike. He'd made it look so obvious—of course it would be positioned and colored that way, to show vibrancy in the flat portrait.

As I looked over the beautiful mess, I noticed how Lord Kwan didn't bother to correct any mistake I'd made, letting it simply be there on all sides. A pin needle of guilt poked my insides, glancing at how I'd accidentally gone over what he'd painted several times. He said nothing about it, staying in silent admiration.

"Should we continue tomorrow?"

I looked at him, unable to read his face, and back to the wall where so much still remained blank. Smiling, I nodded. Poor Koji would stay in the kennels, but only for a single day more.

By the end of the second day, my once crisp-white night robe was sloppily spattered and smudged in color. Compared to Lord Kwan, whose messiness was minimal, I looked utterly wild and may as well have no bit of the white color to show. But I liked it. And if it was too much hassle to clean, perhaps I would be allowed to keep this piece when I leave.

The thought saddened me. When I leave. I would miss my friend. Even though I had his permission to visit whenever I liked, I would find myself busy more often than not in trying to take care of my father and brothers, to keep up with the demands of the house and my village. And though I knew it was wrong, I was still in love with Lord Kwan.

I'd told him about my dilemma regarding Juro's letter. He'd suggested answering with a riddle. Something that seemed like a fool's errand, but had a simplistic answer at its core. I wasn't good with riddles, and my muttering of it earned me several suggestions.

The bird that can carry both rainbows and shadows.

The glow of the moon in the daylight.

A tooth from an animal that never chews with it.

The gem that is only found in mouths of the ocean.

A stone that contains starlight.

The polished breath of a fire sleeping inside its mountain.

I mulled them all over, unable to figure out any of them. Not until he explained it all. Then it seemed obvious. In trying to recall every detail I knew of Juro, I thought carefully about which one to choose.

"What do you think?" asked Lord Kwan.

I craned my neck this way and that. We'd added mountains to the picture, and a river. Butterflies of all colors and shapes were put in, some more elegant than others, always in pairs or groups and never alone. Lord Kwan had painted a family of hares, hidden away from the people, and a bird with brilliant feathers soaring over the lake. A dog was added to the visiting group of people, though it looked awkward and disjointed as a flat image trying to look up at something. Owls were painted against a tree, with a frog tucked away in the grass below. And a pair of deer at the far end of the painting, where the people had not yet come through.

It was, to me, a beautiful scene that offered a dozen stories. A little messy, not at all true to life, but like something out of a dream.

I spent too long admiring it, and didn't notice when Lord Kwan came to my side until his fingers combed through my hair. I sucked in a surprised gasp, looking up at him looking down at me. He paused only a moment, continuing to divide my hair and weaving it into two short braids, tying them off with the soft twine at the end of his sleeve.

Before I could ask, he took my hand to demonstrate how much paint was on my palms and fingers. "You keep brushing your hair behind your ears."

Awkward, I smiled. Even with my scar exposed. Only on remembering, I reached to cover it behind my fingers.

He wrapped his own around mine, lifting them away. "Does it hurt?"

I shook my head. "It's ugly."

Mulling over my words, he watched me a while. Silent, he walked to the mural, taking a brush from a sheer brown color. Delicate, he painted scars on the people in the picture. Not quite as unsightly as mine; though when I mentioned it, he insisted it was about the same. And still, they were beautiful.

In my room, I decided on asking for the glow of the moon. Composing my letter, I thought it sounded well enough. Though, that was before my eyes caught the edge of Urekkato's previous letter. The one I'd written over and looked at almost daily.

I remembered then that I still had a spell on me, and that he may have known about every riddle Lord Kwan had told me and which one I chose. Shutting my eyes, I crumpled up my letter, furious with myself. It was Urekkato last time who sent Juro. Of course he'd expose which one I chose and what the answer was.

But what else did I have? What trick or bit of wit could I use to prevent offense and refuse him at once?

I remembered: the puzzle box had a riddle.

A heart without pride, a hand without greed. Feet not idle, tongue not hateful. With eyes that see through stone.

Even I didn't know the answer to that, but I copied it down all the same. It did sound like I was genuinely asking for something while also not asking for anything. Midway through, I shut my eyes again, and once more when I'd finished. I didn't know how long *a while* was in ending the spell, but I wanted to keep this secret secure from Urekkato's meddling.

Let him.

The mere memory of the phrase on that letter made my blood burn. Would he have been so casual if he were a servant? A human?

If I hadn't only just kept the spell gone, I'd have stared at where I scribbled over his note. Again, I wished I'd never agreed to that spell. Even if Lord Kwan were in danger and in need of help, there was no guarantee of Urekkato seeing it.

My one comfort was that my eyes had always been closed when Lord Kwan... When Lord Kwan kissed me. I tried to shake off that longing, that memory. When I couldn't, and my emotions threatened to burst through me, I took my pillow to scream into it again. He was my friend, my master, and intended for someone else—someone he'd sent for, and who'd loved him for years.

How could I, when I would've been distraught to hear Kyu married someone else? The boy I'd secretly held feeling for, even knowing it was unlikely he'd felt the same way. Would it have been just as bad?

Ridiculous. That was one of the first exchanges we had when I began to labor. And I felt more that way than ever before: ridiculous.

Chapter 42
The Elk Lord

Summer, and guests already began to arrive for court. Several guard houses along the outer wall had been converted into small apartments; rooms for visiting Juneun to retire to. This year would be better accommodated. I'd wondered why there hadn't been this sort of thing available before, until I was reminded that Gumiho was once a threat in these parts, and Lord Kwan didn't hold court unless made to.

She was really gone. It felt strange to think about. So many stories told of her terrible deeds. Now they were just that: stories.

Juro was among the first to arrive. Lord Kwan had granted me permission before hand to keep Koji in my room during the night to help deter unwanted visits. I was walking him to my room that night when I heard Feng arguing. Having taken the long route to let him get some energy out, we walked the gardens outside of Lord Kwan's room.

"...But a servant girl is invited into your room? You sent for *me*. And you won't make any announcement of our engagement? Do you expect me to pine after you for centuries more until you can make up your mind?"

I didn't know what the argument was about, except that it sounded like Lord Kwan was not intended to become Feng's groom. Through winter and spring, I was so sure that was it. After all, he did ask her to come to the villa and made a room ready for her to stay a long while. It made sense that marrying her was his plan. Regardless, I didn't want to get caught up, or give Urekkato the chance to look through my eyes and tease my friends. So, I hurried on.

"What I expect," said Lord Kwan. Though, I tried not to listen in. "Is that you will put your affections towards someone who will receive them. In trying to shame me for your own feelings, you are wasting your breath."

"But why? What aren't you telling me?"

Poor Feng.

Though, I didn't have time to pity her as Koji broke through his leash. I called after him, unable to run in my courtly dress. Strangely, I couldn't recall seeing it was that fragile. A little tattered, since he did chew it, but not so much that it should snap.

I did find him. Juro held what remained of his leash just outside of the door to his room. Dread filled me. Court hadn't quite started yet, and already I'd put myself alone with him. I made my apologies as I went to collect my dog, with Juro giving reassurances but holding fast to Koji's leash.

"I did think of that," said Juro. "I couldn't quite understand in your letter what you wanted me to bring, though I suspect you meant acts of service to prove my love." He opened his door, leading Koji in, though he complained about being brought into a strange room. "Come, Hisa."

"Lor—Juro, it's not appropriate. Lord Kwan will get mad at me." I spoke like the other women, putting to use everything I'd learned the best that I could.

"We will leave the door open," said Juro. "So that it will be seen more innocently."

I tried to think my way out, to use what little I knew about Juneun society against his insistence. But as I noted the start of agitation on his face, I stepped in, my arms retreated as though they could somehow hide me.

He smiled, and fetched a thickly woven leash to replace the one I'd made. "This will be a little more secure. Can't have him running off to a guest who's unfamiliar with him." Only then did he hand over Koji to me.

"That was thoughtful, Juro," I said, quiet in my anxiousness. I still hated addressing him informally, feeling made to accept his advance. I turned to leave, stopped when he took my hand.

He breathed in my scent, and I shuddered. "Little more than two years now. And I will be free to formally propose. And you to accept."

I wanted to scold him, to refuse him outright. But I was in a dangerous spot, fearing his ire. "But, suppose your affection turns to a lady of the court? Someone who *could* spend an eternity of love with you?"

"Don't despair," said Juro. "It's doubtful I would find one with a scent even half as comparable."

"But if there is," I argued, quiet and desperate. "She would already be accustomed to the way of things. To wearing lovely clothes and jewelry. And if you want children... I don't know that a human could give you one, let alone more."

"Is that your concern? That you would be unable to repay my gifts?"

"Your gifts are too much, my l—Juro." He came a little closer, and I worried for a moment I'd provoked him.

"I will send more. So that you are used to them."

As usual, what I said went largely ignored. His other arm came around, holding a pendant. Opaque, cloudy white that seemed to hold a false glow of blue and purple and hint of yellow. A dream world trapped within it. And cut to the shape of a flower I was unfamiliar with.

"Moonstone," said Juro, soft.

My ears heated, no longer distracted by the beauty of the stone. It was the answer to the riddle I'd originally written.

"It's also called the lover's stone." He placed it beneath the wraps of fabric that held me straight. To keep myself from lashing with anger, I held still. "For love, fertility, sensuality—"

"Juro!" my scold came out as a whisper, shocked by the forward implication. He pulled me against him, breathing in my smell, and I fought to keep from shuddering.

"—and protection." He hadn't noticed my quiet outburst, or otherwise ignored it. "I put a blessing on it for you."

"A blessing?" I mentally scolded myself for letting the words fall out. I didn't want to know. I wanted to be rid of it.

"To protect you. I won't have another incident like your master's brother happen to my bride."

My eyes kept looking to the open door. "Urekkato told you to bring that, didn't he?"

Juro stayed quiet. His rhythmic breaths changed pace.

"And he sent you before. That's why you left the wedding celebrations early."

"A powerful friend."

"He's not. He's toying with us. If you knew the letters he's sent me—" I stopped, my mind quickly putting together a plan.

"Letters?"

"A lord tried to assault me. And Urekkato said I ought to have let him. That I ought to have been honored. I was so disgusted, Juro."

I could feel his breath intensifying, an anger attiring.

"Is that all I am? Some game to be passed around and have rumors made about me? I'm a person. And none of the high lords see me that way. Not even your powerful friend, a prince."

His hold on me tightened, becoming gentle only after I'd winced and made a hushed complaint of pain.

Koji barked, breaking the thick tension smothering us.

"I have to go," I whispered, feigning hurt feelings.

"Keep my pendant with you," said Juro. "And the hairpin I gave on my last visit."

My mind hurried for some way out of his request. "I'll be out of uniform from the other women. Lord Kwan wouldn't allow it." And I didn't want him to. I didn't want to parade around his gifts, to showcase I'd been marked as his territory.

"Hisa," he took my chin, turning it up to face him. "For me."

Before I could object, his lips were on me. An attempt at tenderness, though I felt sick. I pulled away the first chance I got. "I have to go."

I left as quickly as my dress would allow, Koji beside me.

Now what? How was I going to get away with disregarding what Juro wanted without getting myself into trouble? I'd already been unable to stay far from him.

In the following morning, with no excuse yet, I placed in the hairpin. Though, I hid away the pendent. Unlike last year, when staffing was short, every woman in the house stood an exact few steps behind Lord Kwan, and to the side in perfect display. As the guests who would stay in the house arrived, one of the women would escort them and return.

"Hisa," beckoned Lord Kwan.

I walked to his side, obedient in spite of my discomfort and distraction. He looked me over, fixing his eyes to the delicate bun that claimed most of my hair, and the pin nestled in it. Some of my hair had been allowed to stay down and forward, half hiding my scars. I answered his wordless question in a whisper, explaining my mistake from the night before.

He blinked, slow, and composed himself. "That is a predicament." For a long while, he said nothing more.

Another guest arrived with a small entourage of personal staff. Mei was instructed to escort him. Not yet dismissed, I stayed at Lord Kwan's side.

"There's a particular guest that has an interest in meeting you," said Lord Kwan.

The words reminded me of how Syaoran described Juro, and my fingers began to fidget, pinching at the suffocating layers of my dress.

"When he arrives, escort him to Feng's old room. She will not be joining court this time."

I looked up at him, quizzical. Though, she did have a tendency to run off when she was upset, from what I recalled.

"He's a gentle spirit," continued Lord Kwan at his own pace. "And he hasn't been in court almost for as long as I have."

I tilted my head, questions washing over me, but it seemed too rude to ask any of them.

"He's a shy spirit," said Lord Kwan, perhaps having guessed at my expression. "And not one for the ceremony of things. I want you to tend to him."

"His attendant, my lord?" my voice quivered as I asked, fearing for a moment that I'd be put into a compromising position. Though, with Lord Kwan, that didn't match to what I knew of my friend.

"Not in that sense, no. I ask that you be attentive to him while he's about in court. He's often overlooked for how reserved he is."

That beckoned more questions. I'd always seen Lord Kwan as someone very reserved, yet no one ignored him at all.

A man, taller than Lord Kwan approached the inner gate, a heavy sack slung over his shoulder, and his horse walking beside him. Long locks of brown hair stopped where his breast and shoulder blade ended, striking green eyes, and antlers that stuck out more to either side than they did upward or back. Unlike the other guests, dressed so elegantly to impress, he wore a simple hanbok set; something a man in the village might wear for a special occasion, but ordinary by compare to court. Even the coloring was subdued, in dull green and earthen tones.

I spent so long staring at the unusual sight that I failed to notice the two boys with him, neither older than myself by the look. Though, they lacked any trait resembling the man leading them. Likewise, they were not dressed to impress. No color coordinated uniform to indicate where they belonged. Their clothing was light and casual and perfect for warm, summer weather

"Lord Genji," greeted Lord Kwan.

Genji returned the greeting, so quiet I almost didn't hear him say anything at all. "My... horse lost a shoe." He struggled to make eye contact, his head hanging low, as though it were all the energy he had to be here. "Didn't seem right to keep riding after."

"My stable master will see to it," said Lord Kwan, cueing the boys to take the mare.

They may have looked humble in the way they dressed, but their manners remained perfect. A kind of discipline unmatched.

Genji's eyes fell on me, curious, and a whiff of an inhale to confirm his inquiry.

"Hisa will escort you to your room. I'll have Syaoran bring up your things."

"There's," started Genji, "no need. For the extra trouble, Lord Kwan." He shifted the sack to a more comfortable position, a silent demonstration of his capability and assurance.

I bowed, ignoring the continued stare from Genji as I led the way. He stayed quiet, until we were away from the commotion.

"You're..."

I didn't stop to look back.

"Human?"

"I am, my lord."

He became wordless once more, seeming to consider. On the second floor, I presented his room to him, imitating what I'd seen another woman do, and bowed again.

"Would you stay a moment?" asked Genji, slow in his words. His shyness unmistakable in his tone and demeanor, I offered a look of apology. "I have... questions."

"I'm not supposed to go into a guest's room, even invited."

He slid open the door, stepping inside. "It can stay open. There's too many people coming and going."

He was right, but I couldn't shake off how similar it was to Juro's proposition. Lord Kwan asked me to tend to him, though I didn't know how far that extended or what to expect; I only knew he wouldn't have asked me to do this if Genji was someone untrustworthy in certain regards. With a nod and bent brow, I followed.

He set his sack down in the far corner, asking me to sit at the small table provided. I wouldn't be able to do so comfortably, but obliged anyway.

"You're human?" asked Genji when taking a seat.

I nodded. "As I said, my lord."

"Yes," said Genji, hushed and in thought. "And you're... how did you come here?"

"The stairs, my lord."

He blinked, watching me through his perfect, shaggy hair, and grew a soft smile of amusement. "Into Kwan's service?"

"A debt owed, my lord." I tried to keep it vague without being dishonest.

"So, you... you're... he's... Lord Kwan is..." he seemed lost for words, eyes looking away and head lowering.

"He is a good master," I said, hoping to detract from his stumble. "And a good friend."

Genji looked at me, a gentleness in his eyes, kind and curious and shy. So green that it almost seemed as if the entirety of a forest stared back at me with interest. He appeared less like a lord and more like a strange boy, but I felt I'd found a kindred soul with him.

"My... My wife is—was. She was..." he hesitated. "She was like you."

Was.

"I'm sorry for your loss."

He nodded. "I loved her for almost fifty-eight years. The other Juneun lords thought I'd lost my senses."

I sat there in the silence that followed, trying to think of what to say or do. "What was she like?"

He gave a sheepish smile to me. "Her name was Isaden. And she was like the wind."

I kept quiet, encouraging him with a smile of my own, and letting him continue at his own pace.

"She could never keep still. It made for an interesting marriage. And, she was bold. Finding beauty and pleasure in everything. Even in coming to court. The others... didn't like when I brought her."

"I think that's their folly. She sounded like an interesting person."

His smile grew, though his head tucked slightly into his shoulders. "I... haven't come to court since... since she passed. As the last living member of the Elk Clan... I suppose it looked like I was throwing my family legacy away when I married Isa."

Without thought, I took his hand. "Never mind what anyone else thinks. What good is a marriage if there wasn't love in it?"

He became a little more confident, wrapping his long, squared fingers around mine. "That's true."

"Everyone says I'm foolish for wanting to marry only for love, even if he's the poorest man in the world. But there seems to be so much unhappiness in trying to marry for riches, that I don't think love is the foolish choice."

He watched me as I spoke, a bright smile on my face, and a quieter version on his own. "I think... If I had had a daughter. I think she might have been like you." My expression became quizzical, and he shied once more. "Isa and I never had children. We wanted, but... it was not fated to happen."

I kept a firm hold on him, placing my other hand atop for added comfort in the new quiet. I tried to come up with something to say, something useful. That he'd have been a wonderful father, or something like it. But nothing felt right. So, we stayed in continued wordlessness, letting the stilled touch of hands speak for us.

When his own servants came, we let go, a quiet dismissal allowing me to leave.

Chapter 43
Marry for Love

It wasn't until well into the night, when the first feast began, that Lord Kwan approached and gently removed the hairpin, bidding that I keep personal things to my room. I obeyed, of course, puzzled as to why he waited until then to say anything. It wasn't until I was in my room that I realized: a public display, so that Juro would see it was his command. It diverted any displeasure from myself.

Likewise, I wondered if Lord Kwan asked me to tend to Genji because his late wife was human. And I didn't know if it was meant as a taunt or as an act of compassion, a given familiarity. In my heart, I didn't want to believe he'd command it from spite.

During court, I did notice what was meant with Genji being overlooked. He stayed so still and quiet, his cup would empty without refill, and conversation would go around him rather than involve him. Often, it seemed he didn't want to trouble anyone with asking for something. So, I made sure to pass by frequently, and offer him any of the treats from a tray or if I could fetch something for him.

When he did try to hold shy conversation, I stopped to listen. Which, in turn, gave reason for others to chime in and allow my dismissal. I was Lord Kwan's human servant, and drew attention wherever I went and when I halted entirely.

Beom was absent, unwelcome since the year prior, but Lord Kwan's other brothers attended. The eldest two shared some similarities to him; though not like Kwang whose differences were so minor that he may as well have been a reflection of Lord Kwan. They didn't behave as brutish as Beom, but there was a coldness to them. Perhaps it was how they were expected to act as the eldest sons. I avoided them regardless.

At times, Kwang, as the more charismatic of them, caught on to my attending, he drew attention by striking up conversation or taking Genji into his company. Though, as expected, he hadn't noticed the Elk Clan patriarch except when watching me going about my work.

Twice, Genji was in the company of Juro. Though, he didn't seem to care for the former Kurai's boasting.

In another instance, a lady had caught him alone to make her advance. Mentions of how he must be wanting for a wife again, and to further his family line or else let his ancestral home fall into the hands of strangers. Poor Genji looked so uncomfortable with the subject and the attention, something I knew all too well with recent experience. I'd set aside the wine vase, out of sight, and went to fetch him, making up that his presence was requested and revealing it only after the fact.

It wasn't until the night before the final day that I was alone with Lord Kwan, serving a white tea as the feast turned down and guests went to their rooms.

"Lord Kwan?"

He grunted, sipping from his cup.

Wanting to keep Urekkato out of my eyes, I shut them often, counting. "Did you ask me to tend to Lord Genji because I'm a human?"

He took his time, mulling over my tone as well as the phrasing. "Being human is perhaps a detriment to his already shy nature. No, I did not."

I thought it over, staring into the steam of my tea. Before I could ask anything more, hardly a sound allowed to leave my lips, he went on.

"I chose you, out of my entire household, because you allow yourself to love others freely."

Blinking, my face twisted into more questions. I wasn't sure I liked the way he'd phrased it, though his usual level tone didn't indicate any sort of teasing.

"You have a natural compassion."

That sounded better, though I wasn't sure I understood.

"I knew you wouldn't try to press him for anything. You may have noticed some ladies in the court, and more than a few servants, eyeing him. Opposite them, you're more willing to give and comfort without the thought of reward."

The way he spoke, it reminded me of the gossip between the women in trying to become a mistress or wife to a lord, using whatever tactic they had to achieve it. "I know my place, my lord."

That hint of a smile dashed onto his stoic expression. "It's less that you know your place, and more that you truly do not. It allows you to act in the best interest of others. It endears Kwang to you. So, I knew Genji would feel comfortable rather than isolated."

"Do you, now?" I said, narrowing my eyes and smirking.

He paused before his next sip, looking at me and letting his smile grow slightly. Quiet lingered as we sipped at leisure. Cups refilled, he finally spoke again. "How do you like him?"

"I like him very much," I said, thoughtless. "He's a gentle and quiet sort of person. Neither of us really fit in. At the same time, we're doing our best to make the effort."

"Then you like him more than Juro?"

I stopped, turning my gaze from my drink to his face. Despite his placid expression, a look of mischief peeked through his eyes. "Lord Kwan—"

"More than Syaoran? Or me?"

I grumbled, nearly growling in displeasure. "You're teasing me."

"Juro wants you as his bride. Syaoran attracts many women with his essence as a fox spirit. And I'm the only one you've kissed."

"Lord Kwan!" I scolded. A bit too loud, I realized, with guests everywhere.

He kept his expression as he watched me. "Has anyone made an unwanted advance?"

I shook my head. True to his word, Lord Kwan had kept me busy and away from Juro. There had only been a single instance of Juro trying to get me alone again, intruded on by Lord Kwan asking if I'd completed my tasks, and bidding I get back to it so as to not keep guests waiting. Likewise, Koji would growl at any shadow lingering in front of my paper-paned door, made on edge by all the unfamiliar sounds and smells. Though, in fairness, I also still found it difficult to be at ease with the noise.

A little more than two years, and I'd never have to be in court for any reason ever again.

On the day guests began to depart, the entirety of the house stood lined up and bidding farewell accordingly, despite the rain. Lin, Syaoran, and myself stood nearest to Lord Kwan, befitting our positions in the house, with Syaoran's magic repelling the light shower from us.

When Genji rode up, his bay mare re-shoed, his gaze still shied from everyone. The rain didn't seem to bother him. Rather, it looked more as though the drops rolled off him without dampening any part of him or his horse, and some droplets avoided them all together.

"I... Um... I thought," frustration crinkled his face. "I put in my bid. To host Mokryon."

"I look forward to it, my friend," said Lord Kwan.

Genji glanced to Lin, Syaoran, and myself before darting his eyes to the ground and turning back to lord Kwan. "You will bring your attendants?"

"One or two, perhaps," said Lord Kwan. "I don't see the need to usher an entire household to Tetsuden."

Genji nodded, slight and slow, taking a last half glance in our direction. "She's... Thank you, my friend."

Lord Kwan dipped his head in respect, a wordless pride.

"I will stock the floral wines again. And... I will send the first of the lotus wine to your house directly."

"It was Lady Isaden's favorite. Or was it the lavender she preferred?"

A gentle smile came on Genji. "She had a love for both. Yours is a keen mind for memory. I think she enjoyed lavender more."

"I look forward to it, my friend. And your invitation."

With nothing more to say, a bow of the head was given, and Genji trotted off, slow to pick up speed. His boy attendants, horseless, transformed into magpies to fly at the side of their lord. I gawked at the magic, and Syaoran took his finger under my chin to close my mouth. He smirked as he did, though I knew his expression meant to reminded me of good manners while there were still guests.

Another lord, with his wife, rode up. And another, alone. A lady, and an intended couple, and more slowly went through with last bits of commentary and a polite goodbye.

Juro rode up, mentioning disappointment in my being kept so busy. A passive scold was issued to Lord Kwan, and a partial demand that I should be less worked so as to cultivate a stronger affection.

"You cannot keep her all for yourself forever," said Juro.

I worked hard to keep still, to not tuck into myself or turn red with emotion.

"Nor do I intend to," said Lord Kwan, pleasant and stoic in his tone. "There is simply too much to be done when hosting court. Otherwise, Hisa is perfectly capable of making her decisions and keeping her own company."

Even over the rain, I swore I heard at least one of the staff further back stifle a snort of a laugh.

Juro huffed a sigh, dissatisfied with the answer, and looked to me. "Tell me, one thing I can send to you. Apricots, I know. But something lovely for yourself, my bride, tell me."

I shook my head. "My needs and wants are met. But I thank you for your attentiveness, Lord Juro. You're very kind." I practiced my answer all morning, anticipating the question and wanting to present like a respectable member of the house.

"Hisa..." His face became crest fallen. Though I didn't want his advances and disliked his intent to claim me, I wanted to comfort and heal the hurt he showed. But I didn't know how without also making it seem as though I accepted his affection.

"I'm not used to being spoiled with gifts, my lord," I said, quiet, trying to think of how to remedy the situation. "I feel too guilty to ask."

His expression softened. "I will send when I have found something suitable. And, in time, you will grow used it, my beloved."

I didn't know what to make of that, dreading it already, even as he rode off. One comfort I had was in making myself believe he wouldn't listen to Urekkato anymore. The memory of my exposure and the kiss he forced on me still soured my gut and made my togue taste bitter.

At the end of it all, Lord Kwan gave his dismissal, and we all shared a resounding sigh of relief. The anticipation of being out of court-attire coursing through us, no one wasted time in going to their rooms.

"Hisa," said Lord Kwan. "When you're more comfortable, bring the cider to my room. The one with the yellow brim."

"Yellow brim," I repeated, committing the idea to memory as I nodded and hurried off as quick as my dress would allow.

Syaoran and Lin stayed beside me, walking to the veranda.

"So, the Mokryon," said Lin, sly. "Are you excited?"

"Excited? Why?"

Syaoran held in a laugh at my question.

"You can't tell us you missed it," continued Lin, quirking a brow at my blank expression. "Lord Genji was asking Lord Kwan to bring you!"

"Me? He said—"

"I think we keep forgetting that Hisa isn't used to the way lords speak to each other," said Syaoran. "But yes, Lord Genji was asking Lord Kwan to bring you."

"Taken with him?" teased Lin. "What are you going to tell Lord Juro."

"It's not like that," I complained. In my mind, I replayed every instance I had with Genji, trying to spot something other than innocent encounters.

"I don't think it's that way," said Syaoran. "His late wife was human, but I don't think that's enough for him to pursue another."

"She was?" said Lin.

"You didn't know?" I asked.

"I knew he was widowed, but not that his wife was human. No one ever really talked about her, so I assumed she was probably the daughter to a lesser lord."

"He told me the high lords didn't like that he fell in love with a human," I said.

"That's putting it mildly," said Syaoran. "From what I recall, I think she was the daughter of a poor merchant. Or was it a potter? Either way, they'd lost everything in a flood and Genji spotted her hauling tall stalks of bamboo and offered to help. Then offered the family hospitality while they rebuilt their home."

"That's when they got to know each other?" I asked.

Syaoran shrugged. "Probably. He financed it as well. I don't remember if it was before they were well off or after, but he'd asked her father's blessing. From what I've heard they were very happy together."

"I got that impression too."

"So, he has an appetite for human girls?" teased Lin.

Syaoran laughed. I frowned.

"I don't know if I'd phrase it that way," said Syaoran.

"It makes sense though," insisted Lin. "Maybe that's why Lord Kwan is fond of Hisa. Like master, like student."

"Master and student?" I echoed. "So, he was like a teacher to Lord Kwan?"

Shrugging, Syaoran summed things up. "Most sons of any lord spend some part of their life in their first century in the house of another lord. It helps to foster friendships and alliances. And, if you're lucky, a future marriage if the lord happens to also have a daughter. But the main purpose is to get the boy used to being away from family and finish up his schooling and swordsmanship."

"Did you have to?" I asked without thinking.

His ears drooped, going flat to either side. "It was... different, for the fox clan."

I regretted my asking.

"I happened to notice you didn't run off this time," said Lin, breaking tension. "Good thing of it. Regardless of Lord Kwan's brothers, we need all the help we can get with court."

"I figured they'd behave with Genji here. He's not shy if he needs to draw his sword."

"Don't you dare think about hiding now," scolded Lin, interrupting any thought Syaoran might have. "Or I'll get Koji to help me sniff you out."

As reluctant as I was, I donned the summer dress Juro had brought, needing a breathing fabric in the thick, rainy, hot air, and wanting to look presentable. The blouses colored plum and soft blue, the skirt a pale-peach, and a crimson ribbon to tie at the waste and secure all the pieces.

I kept silent around Lord Kwan's brothers, a mere servant girl unnerved by the presence. Only the youngest of the brothers acknowledged me. Yuz remarked that the staff ought to be uniformed, only for Lord Kwan to say he didn't see the point when it was only himself. Seong coldly reminded him that it was not only himself, though the words made no impression.

It wasn't until Seong snatched my wrist and yanked me after refilling his cup did Lord Kwan acknowledge his brother with a warning look. I shrieked from the surprise of it. His grip wasn't a painful one. He examined the hem of my sleeve, the floral print of it cut off.

"Toads."

I blinked, looking down to see the tiny animals embroidered in. And he released.

"You spend too much time around humans and Kurai."

"Do I?" said Lord Kwan in response, more to take up the empty air and hint at his irritation than a genuine question.

"Will you attend court elsewhere?" asked Kwang, trying to divert the conversation.

"I have no plans to take up court."

"You should consider," said Yuz. "Lady Asuka expressed an interest. You ought to speak with her brother on the matter, since her care fell to him after the passing of their lord father."

"It'd be one less thing our father could harp on you about," said Kwang. "It's a good match. And her lord brother is naïve enough to put more into her dowry."

Lord Kwan said nothing, hardly acknowledging either brother. "Seong. You are wed. What do you think?"

"You know my obvious thoughts," said Seong. "As far as Asuka, she's young and as naïve as her new lord brother. It's an advantageous match, if you can tolerate stupidity."

Lord Kwan rested his cheek in his palm, fingers folded. "Do you say that of your wife?"

An annoyed look spread on Seong. They stared at each other, measuring the insult and circumstance.

"Hisa," said Lord Kwan.

"Y-yes, my lord?"

"What do you think?"

The brothers turned to face me with crooked expressions, and I couldn't stop myself from trying to tuck in and make myself smaller. "I... I don't know enough to say, my lord."

"You have heard that she would have a high dowry, that she is stupid, and that the union would elevate my status. The marriage would bring in more to my lands, militant, and income. What do you think?"

My brow pressed as I looked at him. He spoke so forward and matter-of-fact, that he felt distant. "It seems cold." I realized, after, that I said the words in too free a state. "M-my lord. All I've heard is a transaction, but nothing really about the lady herself. Or about love. It sounds..." I managed to stop myself this time.

Lord Kwan blinked, slow and expectant. "Go on."

I hesitated, gnawing my lip and pulling my arms closer as though it'd make me invisible. "Hollow, my lord."

The start of a smile came on him, answering me with a grunt. "How is it that my human attendant speaks more sense than my brothers?"

Seong and Yuz gave sharp looks to Lord Kwan, though he continued with his drink, pretending not to notice. It was something that made me uncomfortable, being used to make a statement.

"Maybe she has a point," said Kwang, again trying to defuse tension. "Centuries of wedlock without an ounce of love does seem hollow."

"You can forge love, given centuries or more," said Seong, fast becoming stoic.

"Humans cease before seeing a century of life," said Yuz, dismissive. "All they care about is whatever happens in the moment. Fussing over love."

"Like a dog or some other pet," said Seong.

"Asuka's pretty enough. Perhaps I ought to take her up," said Yuz.

Listening to the men, lords of a noble house, speaking as calculative as the servant women, it made me want to scream. But I didn't want to disrespect Lord Kwan. I still held those same feelings since winter. And hearing his brothers speak about me, about humans and how trivial time was to a Juneun, all of it pained my heart.

Had Genji's romance been a fluke? Was Juro playing just as much of a game as Urekkato? I loved Lord Kwan. I loved that he wasn't boastful, that he was kind and tended to the needs of people who didn't even know his name. I loved that he was tender and protective and strong. And even though I was still afraid when he would come back more beast than man, and I would get frustrated with not understanding him sometimes, I loved that we could be ourselves with each other. I was hopelessly in love with someone I knew couldn't, perhaps wouldn't, ever return my feelings.

I both wanted to stay in his house forever, and never come back again.

What did it matter? Was it simply because he'd been my first kiss, and my first passionate kiss? Juro had forced his lips on me, and I felt not a thing. I had to be rid of my feelings. One way or another. I had to get rid of this childish hope.

Dismissed, I set to find Syaoran. I didn't know who else to turn to, and who would keep it secret. I only knew I needed to find some way to think less about my feelings.

I'd found him taking the shade by the restored well. Though, it seemed too public a place.

"I need your help with something." I grabbed his hand, making to drag him behind me.

He remained unmoved. And I stumbled back a step.

"Help with what?"

I shook my head. "Not here." Already, I was getting frustrated with myself, and wanted to back out.

He studied me, his fox ears turning slightly at some other sound. "You need to tell me something, or I'll stay right here."

My mind reeled, looking for any way to describe my plight without being so obvious. "When I first came here, only you knew I was a girl. And you sent help to me. You were the only one compassionate to me in those first few days. And between all the teasing and advances made and…" I could feel my frustration pushing me to tears, and swallowed hard to prevent them from falling. "You're the only one I can confide in for this."

He blinked, letting quiet hang as he weighed what I'd said. Then he stood. "The door then."

We walked, hand in hand. While his skin was still hot, I didn't find myself as fascinated by it. I prayed for courage, for this to work. In remembering, I closed my eyes to keep Urekkato from watching and finding the hidden door.

On the other side of the wall, I stopped, breathing in deep and struggling to gather words. "What is it?"

"I," already, I felt as though I'd messed up. "I want you to kiss me."

His warm expression turned blank. "Hisa. There's something you should know. About my essence as a fox spirit—"

"I just—!" I locked my jaw, upset at how quickly I would lose what I wanted to say. "When Juro made me kiss him. It's not always like that, right?"

"You want to compare me to Juro? That hardly seems fair. I—"

I grabbed him, fearing he'd talk me out of it. My problem wasn't that I didn't like kissing Juro, though it was a problem. My problem was how stupidly in love I was with Lord Kwan, and how desperately I wanted to be rid of those feelings. So, I pulled on his shirt, standing as high as I could on my toes.

Syaoran caught me, though pushed away. "Hisa!" his scolding came as a whisper.

"Help me," I plead. "I don't know what else to do with my feelings. I thought… if I kissed someone else, maybe…"

He relaxed himself, granting a sorrowful look. "I know how important a kiss is to you. It's part of why I suppress my essence more when you're near."

I dismissed what he'd said. After all, he didn't have the full context, and I couldn't bring myself to explain it. "Help me," I begged.

Staring down at me, eyes locked, he sighed. For several seconds, I thought he wouldn't do it. Then his eyes began to close as he leaned in. I closed mine, and our lips met more tenderly. It was warm and soft and wet, but not as exploratory as Lord Kwan had done. I liked it more than Juro's. I liked having it on my terms. But it wasn't the same. And those feelings I wanted to chase away held firm in my heart.

We parted, eyes slowly opening to look at each other again. It didn't help. And I was more confused than before. I dropped my forehead against his chest, sucking in breath to prevent any crying.

He kept his arms around me. "Hisa," whispered Syaoran. "This didn't make things better, did it?"

I shook my head once, still hiding my face in his shirt.

"Stand up for yourself. Even to Juro. And if you can't, I'll try to stand for you."

I gathered enough of myself to look him in the eye. "Lord Kwan's brothers say it's worthless for a Juneun to love a human."

"Do you believe that?" His soft expression and warm tone returned to him.

I mulled it over. Four words with the weight of a mountain. "I don't want to believe that any two people who know their mind, and who love each other could be called worthless. Regardless of if they're humans, or spirits, or both."

"Then don't," said Syaoran, lightness in his voice. "Whether you love a spirit or a human, keep believing that love has value."

I smiled, weak as it was, and put my head back down to soak in the comfort of his words. "Do you think I should marry Juro?"

"No," said Syaoran. "I think you should marry for love. Just like you said." He let silence hang over us, finishing with something that surprised me. "I think I will too."

Chapter 44
By the Lake

Hardly a week after the closing of court, the horses were brought out. It'd taken time, but I'd overcome that fear, practicing with Susa and learning her cues and movements as I had Saburo's. Though, I'd missed the stallion and often stayed in the stable to comb out his mane or pat him.

Koji didn't like being brought into the stables at first. If the horses were large to me, they must've seemed massive to a dog. In time, he'd learned they wouldn't hurt him, and would watch me as I practiced. On a rare occasion, he would get up and trot alongside us, giving some distance while looking at me and Susa with a curiousness to him. I was glad of it, since I'd hoped to have him along when riding up the mountain.

Not this time, however.

Lord Kwan's brothers had remained, and would be joining us. The eldest brothers made no secret of their dislike of Syaoran coming along. I didn't blame my friend for staying behind with that in mind. After all, he'd hid away several times before when Lord Kwan's brothers visited.

Though, when they mentioned a complaint about my coming, I ignored them. I liked going to see the lake, and to pick from the peach grove. And unless Lord Kwan commanded my stay, I wouldn't allow their snobbery to keep me from coming. I was determined to prove their low opinion of me didn't hold any actual power. My silent defiance.

Between the escorting guards Lord Kwan brought, and those of his brothers, it was a suffocating ordeal. Likewise, I was expected to be more restrained, and take my luncheon separate from the lords. Through it, Gi was a comfort, awkward as he was in trying to help me understand the rigid cues.

While the brothers disliked my picking the fruit, no one stopped me from doing so. Though, I wasn't allowed to eat any, not in front of the lords. There was too much ceremony, though I swore never to reveal my frustration. When I was bid to stay behind while the heirs of the Tiger Clan went to speak with the Dareun statue, I calmed. With no one around, and still a little hungry, I devoured a peach. And then a second.

It was a lonely journey. Though, before Lord Kwan had gone to the tiger statue, he asked me a queer favor. When bidding me to stay, he'd also said that I should pick a time to ride off a short distance and aim for the lake. It didn't make sense to me, but I didn't have the chance to ask any questions. Still, I was curious enough to see it through.

There were questions by the guards on where I was going, to which I simply replied: *the lake*. I didn't mention that it was Lord Kwan's instruction. If he'd made it so secretive, then exposing that wouldn't help.

I didn't ride fast, keeping to a soft trot and slowing when I didn't feel confident in the path I'd chosen. Susa nickered, like a question for me asked in a language I didn't know. Once far enough away, I explained, and her ears pointed up again. I didn't need to direct her after. Her confidence renewed, she took initiative in making a new route through the undergrowth.

It allowed me to look around, and take in the view. We came to a stop, listening to bird songs, and breathing in the thick air. Being away, with only Susa, bettered my mood. The calming sounds of the forest, a running stream, the wind rustling the leaves soothed me.

"Hisa."

My spine went cold, and my body locked up, pulling on the reins and irritating Susa. My head whipped to the source of the whisper. I should've guessed, even if I didn't hear Saburo walking up. Lord Kwan's start of a smile sat on his face, and a softness in his eyes. He looked relaxed at last, and my tension melted from me.

"You wandered off. I had to come looking for you."

I blinked, twisting my brow at him until I understood: that was the excuse he'd made.

"Since we're this far anyway, do you want to see the lake?"

"Isn't that far, though?"

"You already stayed the night with me in the wilds once."

"Lord Kwan!" I scolded his tease, my cheeks heating up instantly. In that same second, my imagination betrayed me again, digging up the memory and quickly assembling a fantasy of it being deliberate and without injury.

"It's a spell, for Saburo and Susa," said Lord Kwan. "It won't feel like we're going fast at all, but we'll be at the lakeshore before the hour is up."

"I," hesitation took me. "I do want to see it. But I'm scared that something will happen again. I don't want you to get hurt because of something I did."

His smile grew a little. "Do you trust me?"

I sighed, trying to read the hint of mischief on his otherwise stoic expression. I couldn't. But I nodded anyway.

With that, he led the way. "Besides, I like that you fuss over me."

I scolded him again. He ignored it.

"As though I weren't my titles and prestige but someone more ordinary. Anyone else would typically bombard me with questions and reports."

I sighed, holding in my grumbling words for more sensible ones. "I know you're a powerful Juneun. But you're my friend. And I don't think I'll ever *not* worry when my friend is hurt, no matter how powerful they might be."

"Might be?"

"Are," I corrected, brow furrowed.

He thought about it a while as we walked on. "I liked your fussing anyway."

"Didn't you also fuss over me when I was unwell?"

"Of course," he looked over his shoulder to me, "you're my friend."

The sentiment both warmed and hurt my heart. We went on, sometimes talking, but mostly riding in the comfortable quiet of each other's company. At the end of the hour, the edge of the forest came into view, and the lake beyond.

The gentle splash of its small waves, like it breathed the same as we did. I nearly leapt off my saddle to see if it was real. The water spanned so far, it looked just how I imagined the ocean. My head turned me, seeing how high the mountain reached from where we were. It might've easily been a day's ride with no clear trail to follow.

"The mountain is a cradle," said Lord Kwan, looking across the lake. "The sky, a loving parent. Watching the children of trees and animals basking below." The wind picked up, tussling his long hair wilder than I could remember. His clothes, too, danced, defiant in his stillness.

There was a weight to his words, even if I didn't quite understand why.

He looked at me, half turning, and with that gentle smile on him. "What do you think of the poem?"

Awkward, and feeling a little foolish, I answered. "I didn't know it was a poem. It felt... The words were pretty, but it felt unbalanced somehow."

A grunt, and he stared a moment. "Perhaps you're right. I may have lost my touch with creating poems."

"I didn't know you made poems."

"It's been decades since I've composed one properly. It's one of the few ways to express myself in my station."

I smiled, against the prickling cold of the wind, and pushed my hair out of my face as I went to stand beside him. It was only the two of us now; Saburo and Susa grazed a short distance away, bucking on occasion in proud displays of strength and endless energy. I decided then, that I would tell him how I felt. Even knowing there was hardly any chance of my feelings being returned, I would tell him rather than stay trapped by them.

Taking his hand, I prayed for strength. I'd kiss him, like he'd kissed me before, and he would know that it wasn't teasing. We stood there, side by side in front of the lake, watching the sunlight shimmer off the ripples. All I had to do was turn his face and pull myself up. The same way I did with Syaoran.

So why was it so difficult this time? When I tried to get rid of my feelings, I didn't hesitate. But, maybe, because the kiss would mean something this time—something honest, rather than desperation. At the slightest attempt to go through with it, I froze. I was at war with myself. The desire and the plaguing fear battling for what action I should take.

What was stopping me? We'd kissed before. Twice! A third kiss should be nothing. So why couldn't I do it?

Just grab him. Move fast, faster than I could stop myself. That's all I had to do. And I couldn't.

Maybe if I said it first. Once the words left me, there'd be no backing out. And if he thought I was joking, then I'd kiss him to prove I wasn't.

My jaw locked up. Say *I love you*, I told myself. I'd said those three words to my brothers, to my father, to Fumei and the children in my village countless times. But this was different. I knew that.

Another prayer for courage, I tried again, managing to take a breath and open my mouth before my voice abruptly stopped.

This was getting ridiculous. Three words. Even if I said them quickly, I just had to get them out.

"Lord Kwan?"

He looked at me, a gentleness to his usual stone-expression. Before I could choke out what I wanted to say, the wind picked up, muffling sound and ushering in a biting cold. I recoiled my hand from his, tucking into myself against the sudden sting. It was summer, and the wind rejected all warmth.

"This high up, the air is colder," said Lord Kwan. "It cools off more cascading down the forest, and chills across the lake." He turned, walking a short distance and gesturing for Saburo.

The stallion shook out, in no great hurry to obey his master. As a spirit, Saburo had a will and an intelligence of his own, stronger than a normal horse, and watching him always made me smile. From under the saddle pack, Lord Kwan produced a jacket. Green in color, with a pair of hares printed at one corner. It wasn't as long or as thick as my winter deel, though I was sure it'd offer plenty of warmth, regardless.

Wrapped in it, I offered a quiet smile of thanks as I hurried to get my arms into the sleeves and hold it snug against me.

"Better?"

I nodded. "Did you plan on this?"

He said nothing, flashing a knowing look in place of words.

"And what would you have done if I didn't agree?" I said, sly.

"I would have felt foolish," said Lord Kwan. "When you leave for home, I'll have to invent new ways of coming here. Where I can be without other matters vying for my attention, or pressured to return."

"You can't just leave whenever you want?"

"Not without an uproar in my stead. I dislike feeling watched, or that I'm expected to return in a set amount of time."

I looked away, back up the mountain. "I know the feeling."

"Oh?" said Lord Kwan, which I knew by now meant he'd come up with some tease. "So Hisa is also—"

"I'm the woman of the house at home," I interrupted, grinning as I did. "All the cooking and cleaning and sewing and laundry... And no matter how I plan and prioritize, something always disrupts it. It feels like, even on the longest days, I never have time to get everything done. It happens so rarely that, when I have nothing more to work on, I don't know what to do with myself."

"You draw," said Lord Kwan, hinting at a cheeky tone.

"That's after I stand around mentally running through all my chores for a long time." I laughed. It made my heart glad that we did know each other well enough for conversations like these. While I could still speak, I wanted to get my feelings out.

"I think I'll miss your running around and fussing," said Lord Kwan. "I've gotten used to it."

For whatever reason, that stole my voice from me. I wondered what he meant. If he shared my feelings, or if it was the friendship and the company.

"Syaoran has become very fond of you as well. Despite bringing in Koji and not telling him."

A hand fidgeted with my ear at the mere memory. I'd never seen Syaoran so angry. On the day I shoved him out of my own fuming, he didn't retaliate or yell, but he hated dogs so much that it couldn't be helped when I snuck one into the villa.

"We've become close friends," I said. "Since we're both outsiders when it comes to court and that sort of thing."

Quiet. Lord Kwan shifted his gaze elsewhere, considering it. "Perhaps I'm to blame. I thought the best method of protecting him would be to shut away everything. Instead, if he were brought into society more, maybe a tolerance would be made."

It was my turn to think on it. "When Lord Genji visited, he said that the other lords never accepted his wife as a human among them. I think you made the better choice. Syaoran might've felt like he was being paraded around. But in the house, he's made a place and everyone knew him over time."

"That's true."

For a long while after, we said nothing. Walking the brim of the lake, pausing now and again, but all of it in wonderful, wordless company.

Through it, I kept pushing myself to speak about my feelings. When would I get this chance again, being completely alone with no one else to know?

"I," my voice stuck fast behind my tongue.

"Genji is fond of you as well in such a short time," said Lord Kwan, distracting from my awkwardness. Or, perhaps never hearing me. "Soon Hisa will have too many Juneun suitors to pick from."

"Don't say things like that," I grumbled. A small piece of my heart delighted in the idea, after having spent so much of my life thinking I'd never have a single man's affection let alone more.

"Many more might line up after learning about Genji's favoritism to you."

"And what about yourself, my lord?" I said, in as smug a tone as I could muster. "We all thought you meant to announce your engagement twice in two years."

His stone expression broke, becoming awkward on him.

"So why did you send for Feng? Did you know that she was hiding away on the mountain?"

"I did," said Lord Kwan. "Very little trespasses through without my finding out eventually."

"But if you didn't intend to engage her, why did you host her all winter?"

He regained himself, a knowing look taking hold. "Why did you give her your peach?"

That caught me off guard. "I..." It was hard to describe. I still thought of her as a friend, and wanted her to be happy, but there was a little more to it than that. I wanted to be a source of comfort, to give hope. I wanted to be to her what I wished someone was to me. "I wanted to protect her."

"As did I," said Lord Kwan, taking his time. "Gumiho isn't the only threat. Even if she was gone, there are others who will want to rise up and challenge any Juneun they come across. Often, they'll start with the most vulnerable, and antagonize a full assault."

I blinked. "But Gumiho is gone. You said it yourself."

His eyes widened for less than a second, and he nearly stumbled in his next step. "True."

Chapter 45
Lord Kwan XI

Kwan found himself simply holding the brush more often than painting, distracted by the sheer joy on her face. She went back and forth, her tongue making its ungraceful appearance. A smile started on his face. He didn't have any plan, allowing her to take the lead, and fell into usual habits.

During their break, the difference was undeniable. One side all structure and the other side all feeling. Curiosity pressed him to make the suggestion.

The end result being strange, unrefined in so many ways, but delighting him. "What do you think?"

She stared, narrowing her eye at the painting with too much thought. Still, it amused him. In the quiet of it, he noticed a speckling of paint in her hair. She brushed it back, revealing smudges under it and on her ear. She didn't realize it. What a clumsy thing.

In steady, controlled movements, Kwan pulled the satin twine from his sleeve, breaking it in two. She shifted awkwardly as he finished, her hand quick to go to her face. He'd forgotten about the scar on her cheek.

"Does it hurt?"

"It's ugly."

The defeat in her tone stirred up feeling. As adamant as Hisa was about not caring for the handsomeness of someone, she became meek with her own imperfections exposed. He hadn't thought of it as ugly or beautiful. It was simply: Hisa. And it was strange that she didn't see herself in that same way.

Her renewed meekness prompted action. He couldn't think of why he decided this method, only that he wanted to give the kind of comfort he received from her. In the briefness of it, nothing else existed.

In the night, as everything settled in his mind, new trepidation emerged. Juro had been a trusted friend, someone who knew about his condition and provided blessed tea as a way to assist. If Juro wanted Hisa, why help to avoid it? But Hisa was also someone he treasured. If she didn't want to marry, he'd protect her from an unwanted suitor. Though, even he knew there was a favoritism between the two.

Was he not doing the same thing with Feng? Avoiding the unwanted affection, and quietly refusing a marriage the other insisted on?

It was a revelation that prompted him into another action, and drew up a letter to send to his former master. Genji was level headed enough that a long conversation, the plight woven in, could be resolved. Perhaps he was too much like his old mentor. Then again, that didn't sound like a bad thing, considering.

As court approached, Feng pressured more. He'd realized then that there wasn't much of a difference between his own situation, and Hisa's. Despite anything from an outside perspective, it was the same in a personal regard. He'd need to end it—decidedly end it—before court opened.

As expected, Feng was smug in her joy at his invite. Not a second was wasted to insist on his making an announcement of something he had no intention of doing.

"I will be making no announcement," said Kwan. "Not this year, or the next, or any after."

"What?" Feng's inquiry came as a gasp.

"Since I am such an embarrassment to my clan, I have chosen celibacy." He set down his tea, hardly a sound between the cup and table.

"You don't mean that," begged Feng.

"I will have no woman in my bed, in my room, in any relations."

She slammed her palms on the table, her own cup tipping over and spilling out. "You insist on it. And you won't acknowledge my own feelings?"

"I assure you that your feelings have been acknowledged. What I am unwilling to do is reciprocate them. I do not want you."

"You," she began to hiss, "You would discard me so easily?"

Kwan said nothing, deciding to allow Feng the opportunity to tire herself out.

"You don't care for the sacrifices I've made. Is it that I'm not titled enough? Wealthy? Beautiful enough?"

He kept silent, putting more interest in his tea than in her fit.

"And you have the audacity to pretend I don't know that a lord takes the women of his house into his room? The declaration of celibacy is insulting!"

Kwan looked to his window, showing nothing outside of his disinterest.

"You'll sit there to pretend that I'm insufficient, but a servant girl is invited into your room? You sent for *me*. And you won't make any announcement of our engagement? Do you expect me to pine after you for centuries more until you can make up your mind?"

"What I expect, is that you will put your affections towards someone who will receive them. In trying to shame me for your own feelings, you are wasting your breath."

"But why? What aren't you telling me?"

He returned his gaze to her with apathy. There were a number of things he kept from her, from most everyone. More, he needed her to hurt enough to leave Mount Tora, to be in the safety of her own home. "You may find better luck with Kwang. He's fool enough to believe your sudden feeling and tolerate your tantrums, if you're set on tying your family's name to mine."

"This isn't about names and titles!" screamed Feng. "I love you!"

"And I do not love you."

She froze, as though the life fled her with the cold of his tone. He regretted the words, honest as they were, but held to his stone expression. She needed to be away where she was safe, where she was free.

"You sent for me..." whispered Feng, a quiver in her voice.

He stared her down, reminding himself that tears were the most frequent weapon used by a woman in pursuit of a man. He would need to believe that. And believe his next set of words. "I no longer need you."

It plagued him, long after she'd left. While all else was abuzz with last minute preparations, his mind was, for a change, silent. Inward and out, he was wordless. Face in one hand, and pomegranate wine in the other, he breathed heavy and slow, staring at nothing.

"My lord?"

Kwan broke from his vacancy, slow to look over at Syaoran.

"Just to inform you that Lord Juro is settled in. As have Lady Asuka and Lord Fumito. And your brothers have just arrived."

Inhaling deep and loosing a sigh, Kwan nodded.

"Shall we prepare to serve the peach wine?"

Kwan shifted his gaze away. "Do. And prepare Feng's room for a new guest."

"New guest?"

He didn't bother to explain, wanting to get it over with.

Though, even sleep eluded him for several nights.

The opening day of court, an anxiousness came, knowing his former mentor would soon arrive. While Kwan couldn't explain it, he wanted to justify his favoritism with Genji's good opinion. But that assumed he would give his good opinion. The Elk Clan, down to the last, were never ones to be made to agree on anything if they didn't find it genuine.

It was a last-minute decision, but he called her to his side. He looked her over. She'd grown since arriving. Taller, yes. Her face more filled out, and hair long enough to twist into a bun. But that wasn't the point. It was when they were alone that he noticed it more, when she was free to be herself, and he himself as well.

When she began her muttering, he missed the start of it. Though, she seemed to wait for an answer. "That is a predicament."

He gave his instruction, and a brief explanation. Cautious, he kept to the bare minimum of it, fearing it would manipulate the result. He knew Hisa wasn't the sort with cunning to weaponize anything he said, but centuries of experience otherwise created a habit when he wasn't relaxed.

The sight of his master, arriving in odd fashion, was exactly how Kwan remembered him. The introductory conversation reminded him of one undeniable truth, the reason Kwan respected him—revered him in some ways: Genji was a man who preferred speaking direct over the formality.

It wasn't until an hour before the feast that they had a moment alone, with Kwan asking for a private conversation. There, discussion came about their last half century, both of them reclused and grieving in different ways.

"It's not your fault," said Genji. "About your brother and sisters. You are very much like your grandfather. I remember him fondly, as my former master."

"If I wasn't blinded by my own arrogance, I could've prevented it."

"There is no sense in thinking of what could or could not have happened. It simply exists now."

He listened to his mentor's choice of words and quiet tone, unsure of how to counter it. "I wonder if I am still too self-righteous."

"I suppose that's up to you. If you have tempered yourself better, then you needn't worry. If you have not, then begin doing so."

Kwan scoffed. "You make it sound eloquent. Easy."

"I've not been one for flowering up my words. I'm speaking to you as your teacher, and as your friend. A man in love will do foolish things, and will convince himself they are the right choices."

"More the reason to avoid it."

Genji shook his head, refilling his cup with red tea. "Men avoid love, making all other rational decisions, and call themselves enlightened. But you'll notice they do not call themselves happy.

A life without love is a lonely one. And a life with great love carries the risk of great loss. The question is not whether a man should avoid or embrace it, but if a man accepts it."

"Are they not one in the same? Embracing and accepting?"

Genji breathed out a grunt, considering. "If a man is told his destiny, it is common that he will do whatever he can to deny it, or he will go to seek it out. Both are miserable for it. I would not consider that acceptance. Rather, it is the man who knows his destiny and changes nothing about his plans. He knows seeking will not bring him closer, and that denial will not change it."

As Kwan mulled over the lecture, his heart and mind warred with each other. Could he really be expected to do nothing if he knew a calamity would come?

"About..." started Genji, shying from his direct approach. "The human in your household."

"Hisa," said Kwan, cuing his friend to speak his mind.

"What is the debt against her?"

"What has she told you?"

"I am asking you."

Kwan watched, understanding that his reflex to answer by questioning had made insult. "In lieu of her brother's crime. He'd shot down the white doe."

Genji sighed. "Hmm. There was a curious feeling when I entered your lands. An echo remains."

"In my distress, I'd ordered execution. Then she arrived, and the sentencing was delayed. And then Gumiho. The delay was too long, I decided to change the sentencing. It would be cruel otherwise."

"That is sensible."

"You agree?"

"I do. A sword that hangs by a single thread of spider silk over one's bed, gives no rest until it falls, and little of it then."

Kwan quirked a brow and shook his head. "You never were good with metaphor. But I think I understand you."

Genji sipped at his tea, the urge to say something written on his face. So, Kwan waited, patient in the quiet.

"She's your attendant?"

Kwan nodded.

"That is a high rank from arriving as a debtor. And she thinks of you fondly."

"Does she?" asked Kwan, more to encourage than to inquire.

"Someone of feeling. Without prompting. She speaks to the heart, with a complete disregard for decorum."

Kwan smiled from behind his cup.

"But I do have to ask. Did you ask her... because of Isa?"

Slow, Kwan's smile faded, and he set down his cup. "I wanted my master's opinion. Too many say I'm too lenient. From my perspective, an effort of genuine kindness should be rewarded."

"As opposed to the insincere kindness?"

A lengthy back and forth went on with regards to Feng. At times, Kwan dreaded he may have earned a hint of disappointment from his former mentor. The end of it interrupted with the start of the feast.

His staff in order, and some relief granted in his thoughts, Kwan noticed for the first time that Hisa sported Juro's gift to her. Knowing her feelings on it, his head quickly assembled the missing pieces from what she'd said earlier. There seemed no better a time than when most of his household and guests were there to witness. A discipline, and a protection. He'd need to stay vigilant.

"Did you ask me to tend to Lord Genji because I'm a human?"

The closing of court was near, reprieve from the rigidity of his class within reach. Genji had given his happy opinion when they spoke earlier that day. A good mind to her, and a warm heart. His master's approval stirred a pride in Kwan. "Being human is perhaps a detriment to his already shy nature. No, I did not."

Their conversation went in the usual, pleasant pace. There was more that Kwan wanted to say, to expose, and needed to practice his restraint over his tongue.

"He's a gentle and quiet sort of person. Neither of us really fit in. At the same time, we're doing our best to make the effort."

"Then you like him more than Juro?" His mind harkened back to an earlier topic. There was the implication from Genji, asking if Kwan attempted some match making, which amused him.

Kwan carried on with his soft teasing, entertained by Hisa's flustered state and willingness to play along without a hidden purpose. Her scowl was nothing near the severity of what a lady of breeding would offer. There was still a lightness to her, endearing him.

A whisper of a reminder came to him. "Has anyone made an unwanted advance?"

Her answer given, a kindly smile returned to her face.

He would miss her. In little more than two years from then, he would miss her.

With his master's final opinion given, awkward in the formality, Kwan's felt a greater sense pride. Though, he wondered if Tetsuden Castle might be an overwhelming experience.

His mentor trotting off, Kwan looked to his own little magpie.

No.

Not his.

In friendship, perhaps. But nothing more. He would miss her.

"You cannot keep her all for yourself forever," said Juro, breaking Kwan from distracting thoughts. He'd missed whatever else his former Kurai friend said before then.

"Nor do I intend to," said Kwan, following with a measure to sooth his friend.

He started to wonder if his own interference was unwise. There were other matters to consider. If he should have told Genji that Gumiho was still alive. Surely, his master would have given council. They could seek her out and end it, quiet the ordeal; she had no army, and against the two of them... His oath wouldn't allow it. His former tutor already having said that denial and embrace of a thing result in misery. In trying to chase out the fox queen, had he invited disquiet into his life?

Kwan glanced again to the magpie at his side. Someone who ought to have been a frustrating chore to deal with, or unnoticed at best. He would miss her.

Before the end of the farewells, he regained enough sense to remember he still hosted his brothers. For how long, he didn't know, nor what it was they hoped to gain if they decided to stay more than a day.

While he didn't care for how it annoyed his brothers to have Hisa attend them, his own silent grievance came with the news they planned to stay a few days after the peach gathering. Though, he suspected they wouldn't linger too long after that. Two of them were still unwed, and court provided the best place outside of an arrangement to navigate into a strategic alliance.

Genji's words echoed then, about love. They almost mirrored what she'd said only a year ago. It seemed so obvious then. Of course his old teacher would hold a good opinion of her.

Seong's sudden move stole away the happy thought. Kwan kept in place, needing his will to stave from reacting.

"You spend too much time around humans and Kurai."

It was a feat in of itself to keep from scowling, to keep from lashing at his brother's antagonizing. "Do I?"

As expected, his younger brother broke tension, steering the topic. When they were beside each other, the youngest sons of the clan could hold against the oldest. Apart, he'd come to realize, they relived their earliest years. War had ended, and certain hungers were not sated for some.

Conversation went down a predictable path, with sly insinuation woven in, and insults uttered without taste. Kwan ignored it, thinking instead how best to irritate his brothers enough to cause their leave.

"Seong. You are wed. What do you think?"

His answer came as no surprise. A reiteration of things already known.

Kwan pressed on anyway. And when he understood that the eldest among them wouldn't fall into the usual trap of this sort of talk, Kwan looked for a different avenue.

A human's perspective. And if there was argument, he could use Genji's good opinion of her. Regardless of what any of them thought, no one dared to openly speak ill of the Elk lord. He was, still, formidable, and followed the old ceremony of handling slander.

"All I've heard is a transaction, but nothing really about the lady herself. Or about love. It sounds…"

"Go on."

"Hollow, my lord."

Kwan could feel the indignation pouring from his eldest brothers. He didn't waste the opportunity. "How is it that my human attendant speaks more sense than my brothers?"

The pressure of magic directed at him, and he delighted in it. Waiting, his tongue and sword arm only needed the slightest retaliation to act.

As though on cue, and more dignified, the youngest brother spoke up, echoing Genji's and Hisa's words, and bringing in a lordly levity to them.

Unsurprising, Seong answered with pragmatism. And Yuz with insult.

In spite of the discontent, his brothers were determined to stay until they could speak with Dareun. Try as he may, the stubbornness of any tiger, once their mind is set, wouldn't allow for distraction.

Since he could not convince their leave, he plotted his own. If only for a short time. It hinged on agreement, though he was confident of it.

The rigid ceremony of what had become an annual reprieve grated his nerve. His brothers insisting that Syaoran's presence was an insult to their ways pressured his friend into abstaining from the ride.

Hisa, thankfully, was defiant. Ignoring commentary, she got into her saddle with dignity.

The exchange with the Dareun went on longer than he'd anticipated, addressing each of them rather than Kwan alone. It didn't matter. Whatever omen, whatever glad news, he'd decided to take up Genji's advice and accept it rather than to fight it or seek it out. Come what may, a popular human slogan.

The minutes ticked on in his thoughts, anxious to get back and see if she faithfully waited, or took on his intrigue and rode out.

Happily, the latter—though his face stayed stone, feigning a vexation on the matter.

She was easy enough to find. Saburo always knew what direction any of his mares went, no matter their speed. On the flat of a boulder, in a picturesque state. Her smile content, sunlight dancing through the trees on her.

A magpie indeed.

"Hisa." His smile returned at her jump. While he didn't mean to startle her, it was a humorous sight, endearing. "You wandered off. I had to come looking for you."

He was glad that she didn't barrage him with questions or chastise his scheme, and gladder still when she got riled up in their banter.

"I know you're a powerful Juneun. But you're my friend. And I don't think I'll ever *not* worry when my friend is hurt, no matter how powerful they might be."

Regardless of all else, he looked back with a fondness at the memory. Anyone else would wait around or insist they push on, a silent demand of action. She was different, pleading that he stay still. The reminiscing brought the echo of a feeling, of her small frame trying to shield him from the elements; the softness of her breathing and warmth of her cheek.

He realized how long he lingered on the thought, shaking it away.

Other conversation took place, distracting him.

"Have you decided to accept Juro's proposal?"

"Hm?"

"You've been wearing the dresses he's sent."

"Oh..."

Something in her defeated tone grabbed him, causing him to look over at her. His hand loosed its hold on the reins, wandering to her. When he realized it, he stopped, resuming his posture.

"It was muggier, and that one breathed a little more and was easier to move around it so I can attend you, my lord. Not, not that I dislike the one you gave me—it's my favorite one. But it's not really suited for working. And I don't want to damage it."

"And you don't mind if the ones Juro sent are damaged?" She looked away with discomfort, gnawing her bottom lip. Paused for thought, he redirected. "If you were to have another, what would you want it to look like?"

She blinked at him, squinting her eyes to read him. Kwan kept what smile he had, tilting his head expectantly.

"I don't know."

Brow cocked, he realized she figured out the implication. A discomfort lingered in it. "What if you were to make one?"

"I'm not that good at it, my lord," laughed Hisa. "But I have been practicing."

"Supposing you were well practiced. What would you make?"

That did the trick. Her face scrunched with thought. He didn't need to read her mind to follow; the unladylike contortions told him everything.

"I do like how comfortable the mature fashioned ones are. But I also like how pretty the ones like you gave me are. Either way, neither is very good for being a servant. I'm always afraid that if I move too quickly, they'll tear, or if I zone out then some part will get caught or get stained. If I were to make something, I think I'd want to make it like your hanboks, my lord. They're more practical."

"The pants?"

"I do really like the dresses, but as I said: they're not the best for being a servant or for work in the village. And if I were skilled enough, I could sew in something decorative. An animal or flowers, maybe."

A plan began to form in his mind. "And what color would this hanbok be? If you could pick any in the world, and it so happened to be laying around, which?"

A coy and childish look consumed her face, her head tucking into her shoulders. "Pink. Or maybe lavender. But I know an earthen color wouldn't show as much dirt or stains, and I'm messy enough as it is."

"It's poor form for a servant moping the floor to be messy as well, don't you think?"

"I do try my best. But I guess I get so caught up in trying to make everything else tidy that I forget about my own appearance." She smiled, wide and laughing.

"Would you keep the jacket of it pleated, or straight?"

"It depends on the season, my lord. I like the pleated look, but it might not be the best for this time of year."

"And the sleeves?"

"The closer fitted style. The wide sleeves do look handsome on you, my lord; but if I wore that sort, I'd probably get them snagged and ripped."

"I see. A very practical style."

"And if I were very skilled, I'd pattern it with peony flowers."

"Peonies?"

"They're my favorite. They come in soft colors, and they have so many pretty petals, and the smell—so fragrant!"

"I would have thought hibiscus was your favorite."

"Hm? Why that one, my lord?"

"Hibiscus means *to be gentle*. Peonies' popular meaning is *wealth and prosperity*."

"I didn't know that. Maybe I ought to collect the seeds if I can, and try to grow them in the village, so we can all share in it."

"It used to be the flower for bravery, but the magnolia is more popular for that meaning now. As well as beauty."

She didn't notice his closing words, lost in her own planning.

"Hisa. When we're alone, you don't have to refer to me as a lord, if you don't want to."

Brought out of her daydream, she blinked at him, quizzical.

"A friend shouldn't have to be so formal, especially when no one else is around."

"I suppose," said Hisa, a shy giddiness to her tone.

Quiet.

Bird songs, and the breath of the wind taking up the wordlessness in a distant, beautiful choir.

"But I think wisteria suits you more."

"Wisteria? Why's that?"

"Wisteria flowers mean *someone who is welcoming and steadfast.*"

Hisa laughed. "Lord Kwan has a high opinion of me."

Kwan shifted his gaze down and to the side.

"Which flower means the person has a big imagination?"

He looked back to her, taking in her eager expression. "Lupines, I think."

"Then, when I'm skilled enough, I'll make one with peonies, and one with lupine."

"Ambitious."

"What about you, my—?" He quirked a brow at her stumble. "My friend. Do you have a favorite flower?"

Kwan grunted his amusement. "I never thought about it."

"In all your centuries, you never thought about a favorite animal or a favorite flower?"

Kwan quietly reveled in her teasing. There was an innocence to it, in lieu of the facetiousness common elsewhere. "Sunflowers."

Hisa stopped her words before a single one sounded, mouth open and eyes darting into a different direction as her expression faltered.

"Were you going to say something?"

"I was thinking, then I'll make one for you with sunflowers. But, men don't usually wear something with flowers on it."

"Oh? You think I would refuse a thoughtful gift from my friend after she worked so hard on it?"

A shy and mischievous smile replaced her previous expression.

Quiet.

"What do sunflowers mean?"

Kwan looked back at her, soaking in her curious stare. "They can mean a lot of things. Radiance, recovery, hope, respect... a passionate love..." He slowed his words, watching her face twist with imagination. "Happiness, cheer, loyalty, adoration, and longevity. To name a few."

"That sounded like a lot more than a few."

"Warmth, strength, appreciation."

Hisa laughed.

"Thankfulness, peace, good fortune, and luck."

"Are there anymore?" teased Hisa.

"Most likely, but I don't know them."

Her smile grew, losing its mischief and turning up her cheeks. "It's so strange to think how one thing could have so many meanings. In the village, one of the elders would say things like *a cloud with a curly end means a big storm is coming*. Or that if birds are quiet, it's an omen of ill fortune—or that death is waiting for someone. But it's usually one or two meanings."

"It keeps things simple. Great houses enjoy complexity, and sometimes it can get overwhelming to try understanding what something means. A lot of miscommunication happens that way."

Chapter 46
Lord Kwan XII

His brothers left the morning after the ride up the mountain.

When you leave for home, I'll have to invent new ways of coming here. Where I can be without other matters vying for my attention, or pressured to return.

It'd been weeks since he'd said it, summer now ending. In less than two years, it'd be true. The thought kept distracting him, well into the night. Mokryon was a half year away, yet preparations needed to begin and missives sent before the snows came to slow everything. Tax and tribute needed collecting, payments needed distributing, reports on the welfare of his lands—it all piled up.

He'd been too ambitious in agreeing to court, and too lax in the half century prior. So much so, that he'd forgotten the nightmare that it was. Likewise, it'd been even longer since he'd brought a household as a guest. It was easier to go alone, and made for a show of strength.

With the belief that Gumiho died, the display wasn't needed. He still fretted. What was she up to? The last assault razed her army—no Kurai, sensible or not, would ally with her—or did it only appear that way? Between silky words, vexing beauty, and potent essence, she'd amassed a militia loyal to her; fox magic to that degree could easily manipulate an incautious mind to mistake illusions for something whole.

She'd noticed a waning in protection since the death of the doe, and her trespass could've spelled his death. Why hadn't she? For sheer sport?

Before, he went out of his way to sift her out or lure her in. Doing so again was reckless, pointless even.

Focus.

He already decided to accept whatever awaits, and temper himself with the result. There was his master's hosting to consider, to look forward to.

While he explained it to Hisa, Kwan still worried she couldn't fully grasp it. She would be his attendant, yes, but also a guest of Genji. There was the rest of his house to consider, and who else to bring.

Hisa's head bobbed, fighting sleep and reminding him of the hour. "You should go to your room, and rest."

"I can stay a while longer if you need me to."

"I plan to turn in after this last missive," said Kwan, cooing. His ink brush dried with how distracted he'd been. It was all he could think to convince her to take his dismissal.

Vigilant, despite the long spells of silence and boring subject matter. He would miss her. And the thought brought an ache. There was the cuteness of her getting flustered, amplified more when it was matters in the kitchen and something had made a mess of her clothes, face, and hair. She was more a magpie than a hare in those instances.

More, when her imagination did get the better of her and give her an idea, the oversimplicity of it held charm. She'd taken a tea bowl a few days ago, filling it with peach nectar and waiting patiently beside the swing. When asked what she was doing, she merely replied that she was trying to tame them. The butterflies. A fool's effort, but one he indulged, and sat beside her. If they were tame, she'd said, they'd come close and hold still longer to draw.

Always, compassion was her most prominent feature. He'd caught her on several occasions helping some small thing, victim to hubris. A spider, about to be swatted, was rescued with a vase and page of drawing paper, released to the garden far from the house. In another instance, she patiently untangled a mantis from the silk of an abandoned web, ignoring that it battled against her effort. Any moth or bee trapped in a fountain was scooped out by her. And despite her fear of snakes, she'd trapped one in a jug to take away from the chickens and release outside the wall.

Though the most fascinating was how she supposed she could train Koji to hunt without knowing how to properly do it. In showing her, she hung on his every word. And when things didn't go as intended, she grew frustrated with herself rather than her pet or her teacher. There was never an excuse made on her part.

He would miss these odd little diversions. He would miss her. From each huff to every laugh, he would miss her.

She'd forgiven his coldness on her arrival, though the memory haunted him with a sense of shame. In any instance that she hid away in the kennels or stable, he felt that he'd somehow failed her, knowing full well that wasn't true.

What was it about this odd village girl, a human, that he found such fellow feeling?

One of his staff claimed to have sprained her wrist, and it was Hisa who took up her chores without prompting, and checked in. Not a complaint was muttered from the human.

There was all winter before Mokryon. And he'd sent out his request, receiving several answers. Someone to teach her better than he might be able to explain. Of the options, Kwan tried to think of who would be kindest. The obvious choice was from the humblest family.

Though, they had a reputation of reckless ambition. The most noteworthy family might see themselves too highly.

Sight bleary, and head aching, he decided to leave the matter for tomorrow and take Syaoran into council in place of Yua.

Yua.

How was she? Had grief consumed her? Had she accepted it? It was too intrusive to write. He'd known it was wrong to prompt Eumeh into marriage so quick after Borsi. There was nothing he could do on that matter. A mutual romance, kept apart by circumstance and kin, only for a tragic end. A princess, and the lowest daughter of a lesser lord. Were they so different?

Questions for another time.

He disrobed, settling into his bed, and blew out the last candle.

Morning brought progress, slow as it was. Syaoran gave his opinion, though he was no substitute for Yua. They didn't know the applicants as well as she might, and would need to hope for the best with a guess.

"Syaoran," said Kwan. "Keep a pair of horses ready to leave. When Juro comes, I want you to take Hisa from here for a few days."

"Meddling again, my lord?" teased Syaoran.

"She's expressed her discomfort. Juro ignores it. And she's not in a position to be blunt."

Syaoran worked his jaw, considering. "Why me?"

"Is there anyone else I can trust? You did spend several days before looking after her, if I recall."

"That's an odd way of phrasing it. Trusting someone with Hisa. Does Lord Kwan think someone will harm or abandon his favorite servant?"

Kwan stopped in the midst of a brushstroke, ink slowly bleeding onto the paper. His heart took a sudden, hard beat, birthing a rage that died in the same instant.

"Or, is the master in love with his human girl?"

In controlled movements, Kwan raised his gaze to his fox friend, watching Syaoran's ears fall flat and his brow bunch.

"Forgive me. It's the plum wine, my lord. We've been at this since morning and it's after lunch."

Kwan stared, a slow and wordless blink as he studied Syaoran's posture.

"I may need a walk, clear out my head, my lord." He stood, giving a deep bow.

"Syaoran," called Kwan, stopping him at the door. "Have horses ready. And keep Hisa safe."

Syaoran turned back, blinking, and gave a guilty look. "Yes, Lord Kwan."

It was a still a while after the door closed before Kwan looked at the ink blot. Sighing, he set down the brush, crumpling the paper to burn in his hand. He'd need to start over on that one.

Too much required his attention. Yet, Syaoran's teasing distracted him more than it ought to. His favoritism didn't go without warrant—the same as when Syaoran and Yua had come into his service. How was this any different? Rumors had spread about him when Yua came into his house, and a few with Syaoran.

With or without the fox's jibe, gossip would spread, and likely would amplify when he brings her to Tetsuden Castle. He decided then to bring Syaoran as well for punishment, and to observe the evolution of the rumors. Though, that left the matter of his house. Lin proved capable and fierce, but had someone more experienced in tandem. Could she handle the pressure, and keep order? The temptation of trying undermine her by her sex would still linger, even if it didn't present so potently now.

He shook away the roaming thoughts, returning his attention to the task of narrowing down the applicants. At least to a manageable number where he could send for them and pick one in person.

Minutes after he'd finished, a servant knocked and announced themselves, carrying parcels. Maybe he did spoil her. As he had with every favorite servant since he was a boy. It was the way of things. Rewarding their attentiveness. This was no different.

"Is the courier still here?" Before he finished his words, his brush went to work. Syaoran would need something as well, befitting his position.

"Yes, my lord. He brought quiet the delivery."

Kwan tied off the letter in simple twine, handing it to his manservant and dismissing him promptly.

A week after Syaoran's teasing, and it still bothered him. Six girls stood in the courtyard, each dressed the best their families could afford, keen to impress the summons of a high lord and earn the position.

"And your name?"

"Niwa, my lord. It means garden."

He didn't ask the meaning, though it would help to speed things along.

"So, it does," said Kwan, mulling it over. It would sound auspicious, a garden for his magpie. No, not his. And the musing wouldn't guarantee sincerity in practice. "And yours?"

"Sujo, my lord. I don't know that my name has any deep meaning behind it."

Kwan stared from his shaded place on the veranda, Hisa's voice echoing as she called for Koji. "It might be bad luck to choose someone whose name has no meaning."

"But I am competent, my lord! I served as Lady Toyo's personal attendant for forty-three years. But... her new husband insisted on a fresh staff."

"I see." His eyes moved to the next girl. Round in the face, though with pretty blue eyes and a pair of brown cat ears.

"Tsuya, my lord. I believe you are a friend of my cousin, Lord Urekkato, the new prince."

"A cousin?"

"Distantly related, my lord," said Tsuya, the pride in her tone fast fading.

"Why do you not serve in his house?"

"I... made myself foolish in front of him, my lord. Ten years to the day as of yesterday."

A name that meant beauty, though Hisa was already a handful in her common upbringing. He needed someone level minded and tempered, and foolish usually involved gossip and haughtiness.

His gaze moved to the next.

She seemed late to realize his expectation, unnerved, no doubt. "Uno, my lord. It means—"

"Rabbit," said Kwan.

She nodded.

"Your sister is not with you?"

Uno fidgeted. "Mata was more afraid than I to come, my lord."

"Why is that?"

"We—um, it's," she rolled her bottom lip into her mouth. "It's always been the two of us, my lord. All we had were brothers. And all but one died in battle. She was afraid of your fierce reputation, and being away from the only family we have left."

"But you were not so afraid?"

"I admit that I am, my lord." She kept the gaze of her cattish, orange-brown eyes down more often than she looked up at him.

Kwan considered. She'd certainly have a lot in common with Hisa, and could better sympathize. But her lack of experience and nervous manner would only serve as a hinderance.

"Toku, my lord," answered the next girl when his eye went to her. "It means virtue. So, you'll not need to worry about the safety and preciousness of the lady."

"I did not know I needed to worry on that account," said Kwan.

Toku's beaming expression faded, her eyes looking about in sync with her thoughts.

Kwan looked to the last girl.

"Iseko, my lord." She spoke confidently, and smiled, despite being the youngest. It was a show to gain favor, commonly done to make up for any shortcomings. "For where the river meets the sea. It's good luck to have a water name in a house, so that it won't burn down."

Rehearsed lines.

He went through more questions, silently narrowing his choice in the assessment. An idea came when Syaoran approached, giving a curious look over them. They were all well aware that he kept a fox spirit in his household; but it was one thing to be aware and another to confront. Asking Syaoran's opinion, he watched for any body language cues from the women. Hostility to an established member, and a spirit, would naturally lead upset in learning they were to wait on a human.

Uno and Tsuya locked eyes with him, seeming bewitched. Iseko squirmed. And the others kept as straight as their experience allowed.

His friend, on the other hand, appeared distracted by them, stumbling over responses. All of it was interrupted at Juro's sudden arrival. While Kwan thought his toadish friend might arrive early, this was ludicrously soon. His eyes went to Syaoran, a silent cue for the fox to dismiss himself and carryout his order.

Still, concern filled Kwan's gut. He'd expected some notice before Juro's arrival, allowing time for Syaoran to abscond with Hisa. It would be a little more difficult now, but not at all impossible. So why did he feel so much dread? About the escape, and about their being away?

"Juro, you're just in time my friend," called Kwan.

"I see that," said Juro, a lust in his gaze. "What is this business about?"

"Selecting a personal attendant for a special guest."

Intrigued, he dismounted from his horse, giving instruction to the staff rushing to meeting him.

"My household will see to your things," said Kwan, calm but trying to coax his friend away. "I'll have your usual room prepared. Come, help me in deciding."

"An important matter, is it?" said Juro, walking to join Kwan on the veranda.

Time drew out, eventually moving the lot to wait on Kwan and Juro personally. A test, he excused. At least, keeping Juro in his room, spacious enough for the ceremony of things, he could while out the time and allow for Syaroan and Hisa to flee. During which, the thought distracted him, and Juro's conversation demanded the rest of his attention. He forgot more often than not to consider the actions of each girl.

"Of course, I would pick on the natural perfume more," said Juro. "But since they are a lovely lot, maybe it's best to choose by who they will be attending."

"A lady," said Kwan.

"A lady. And someone important to Lord Kwan."

Kwan said nothing, sipping at the tea and letting Juro's mind make conclusions.

"What is the occasion?"

"Mokryon."

"Ah, I see. That does narrow things down. I'm guessing it's your sister. Now that Gumiho is dead, she'll be allowed to attend such events again. Or, is it one of your nieces?"

"It will be her first attending," said Kwan, aiming to distract. "Of many, I hope."

"May we all! But, as you know, I will soon be going with Hisa as my wife if it satisfies her."

Kwan stared, his stomach tightening for a mere moment as he took his time in responding. "And if it does not?"

"It will be different when she is a guest and not a servant," insisted Juro, waving off any other possibility as he drank from his cup.

"That's true. It will be different for her," said Kwan. "What if she doesn't like going?"

"Of course she will like it! And, if she doesn't, then I will only bring her to one or two events per year, and allow her to stay home the rest of the time while I attend. I may still be in search of a mistress then."

Kwan listened, watching Juro behave so assuredly. It shouldn't have bothered him. It never had before. But it did now.

"Speaking of which, I should see to my beloved," said Juro, standing. "I have brought her the polished breath of fire, and had it fashioned into beads to make for a lovely bracelet. She's sent me a list, you see, to win her heart. If I can present her with the answer to every riddle."

"I admire your fortitude," said Kwan. "But Hisa is not here."

Juro quirked a brow, his smile fast forming a frown. "She is your ward two years more, no?"

"Yes," said Kwan. "But she is away. I sent her to gather ingredients."

"Ingr—? For what? What could you need that could not have been brought to you and stored away?"

"I thought her Lord Juro should taste her cooking, and prepare a few favorite meals from her village to sample. Naturally, I wouldn't have every wild thing. Particularly if it is a seasonal ingredient."

"But it is getting late, as you can see. And, surely, she will return soon."

"I think not. I'd instructed that she take as much time as needed to make certain she had everything. It could be a few days."

"Days?"

"We did not expect your arrival for another two weeks. I'd sent her only this morning. Less than an hour before your sudden arrival."

That seemed to do the trick. Juro grumbled and complained; though being told that she would want to surprise him, and that he should arrive timely next year to receive it, convinced him to stay in the villa, and only for as long as he originally planned.

The girls were dismissed the following morning. One, however, stayed behind. Not from Kwan's choice. She plead to be chosen, a desperation in her voice.

It came to a halt when a guard knocked on his door, urgent by the sound. The man couldn't have known that Kwan was well aware of Hisa having gone missing. He answered his guard in his typical casual manner. What was troubling was how he came to the news: Susa was in the stable, with the stable master answering to Juro on inquiry. The horse had run home without her rider.

Syaoran was perfectly capable, but alarm still coursed through Kwan's insides. He inhaled deep, slow to release. "Assemble a search party. Do not involve Lord Juro, lest he lose his way on the mountain."

She wouldn't be in actual danger. Whatever happened, Syaoran and Hisa were close—he would keep her safe. And that bothered him as well.

An urge prodded at him to leave, or to use his sight if only to ensure nothing tragic had happened. An instinct that was difficult to resist.

Chapter 47

Stolen

"Koji!" I scolded. He'd bolted after a squirrel and pulled the leash right from me. "You need to stay beside me when you're on a leash. We'll play as soon as we go between the walls where you can run."

"Hisa!" called Syaoran in a hushed tone. I barely turned my head and he was there with a grim look about him.

"What's wrong? If it's because Ko—"

"We have to leave. Now." He dragged me along, before I could resecure Koji's leash.

I didn't have time to ask questions. He'd pulled me right off my feet with his unnatural speed. We stopped abruptly, with Syaoran peering around the corner to look across the court yard. Blinking, I followed his gaze. Juro's horse was being led away to the stables.

"He's here even earlier," I said.

Syaoran shushed me. Looking at him, his ears moved to listen. "They're walking away. Let's go!"

Again, the ground fled from my feet as he hurried us to the stables.

"Are the horses ready?"

"Yes, Master Syaoran," answered the stable master. "I began tacking as soon—"

"Wait!" I yanked my arm back. "I'm not dressed to ride, and I have to put Koji back in the kennels—"

"There isn't time, Hisa! Get on!"

I scowled. "No. Not until you tell me why."

He didn't. Instead, he grabbed me by the waist and hoisted me onto his black stallion with him.

"Put me down! Syaoran!"

We were already trotting out the stables, and galloping through the gates. He put a hand over my mouth. A sudden fear took hold. Was Syaoran kidnapping me? Why? What value could I possibly be? I struggled to break free—to scream.

"Hold still! Or you'll fall!" scolded Syaoran, sounding more animal than I'd ever heard him.

The coward in me obeyed. The rebel in me fought that part and resumed my struggle. I was slung across his lap like a prize, kicking my heels against his shin and punching his arm to escape. I wouldn't be stolen quietly or without a fight. Not like before, when I was desperate and had nothing else to trade for my brother's life.

"Stop! Hisa!"

The forest rushed by us. Syaoran's horse snorted for breath with every stride.

"Let go!"

He dropped his arm around my midsection, holding me tight against him. The strength of his forearm, fingers digging into my side, and the muscles of his torso, all binding me. I struggled harder, kicking and screaming and clawing.

I was getting nowhere. An idea sprung out of my fighting, and I kicked my heel into his stallion's side, forcing him in a direction contrary to Syaoran's will. His grip slackened as he corrected. Then I bit him. Not knowing what else to do in a fight for my life, I sank in my teeth. Reflexively, he yelped, and the arm around me loosened. Enough that I could wiggle out of his hold and try to push him off.

Instead, I slid.

"Hisa!" He caught my arm, leaning back and not realizing he pulled on his horse's reigns too far as he did.

The stallion reared up, whinnying his complaint, and we were both thrown off, landing hard on the ground. In the tumble, I felt disorientated, and a sudden, sharp pain shot through my arm. The ground look to teeter left and right, but I tried to crawl away regardless and find somewhere to hide. Syaoran was on top of me—grabbing at me! I kicked and tried to smack, despite my dizziness and bleary vision.

He held me down. Pinned me.

"Listen to me!"

His knee landed between my thighs. I tried to continue kicking, flailing, anything to escape.

"Let me go!"

"Hisa!"

My vision began to correct, and I saw him clearly for the first time. Sunlight poured from the treetops, outlining him in an ethereal glow. He was handsome. I'd always known that, but it was like I'd only just realized how terribly handsome he was. I was pinned beneath him. We were so close. He was on top of me, panting. I was panting too. And I could taste his breath.

Thoughts of what he might do, what he could do, what I wanted him to do—sometimes all of them.

"Are you even listening?"

"Huh?" I realized then he'd been talking some time. But I couldn't hear him over his breath, my breath, and the racing drumbeat of my heart.

He sighed. "Too much at once."

Something changed then, though I didn't know how. He started becoming a little more like his ordinary self, though nothing about him actually changed. I noticed a flick of something then, behind him—a tail, a fox tail.

"Syaoran..." I whispered.

He gave an odd look then. "Still too much."

Again, he looked a little more like the Syaoran I'd known. Nothing about him physically changed, nor did he move to some new angle.

"I think I preferred when you were quiet and obedient."

To that, I scowled. It seemed enough of a cue for him to repeat what he'd said previously.

"Lord Kwan ordered me to get you away from the house when Juro arrived. I saw to the stablemaster first, but I didn't have the chance to tell you about it before he rode in."

I softened my expression, but held my frown. "Why didn't you say something in the stables?"

"You kept arguing and hitting me," groaned Syaoran. He sat up, letting go of my wrists but still straddling me. "I still can't believe you bit me. That timid girl from three years ago is just a memory now."

I laid there, the shock still in control of my body as my brain tried to piece things together.

"If you'd stayed still and stopped screaming, I would have explained it to you once we were far enough away."

"I thought you were kidnapping me."

"In the middle of the day?"

"I didn't know!" I struggled to sit up, that sharp pain now throbbing in my elbow. "Ow!"

"What?"

I went to hold the joint, only for pain to warn me away, and I found I had little movement.

Syaoran heaved a heavy sigh and grumbled. "He's going to chew my head off for that. I'm supposed to be keeping you safe."

"We can just go back," I said. As his hand reached for me, my own grabbed to try stopping him.

"I'm supposed to keep you away for a few days. Or do you want Juro staying longer because his precious Hisa is hurt?"

A chill ran up my spine, and I shook my head.

"It might just be dislocated, not broken. But it's still not good. I can roll it back into place, but you'll have to let it heal and keep from using it a while."

The pain already made so much of me feel hot, I didn't dream of moving it. "Will it hurt?"

"A lot," said Syaoran, his brow furrowed. "Try to relax as much as you can."

Easier said than done. I screamed as it popped back into place, and tears poured out of me.

He tore off a sleeve, ripping it to workable ribbons to make a sling. "I don't have magic to heal something like this."

"I'm sorry," I whimpered, the full weight of it all crashing down on me.

He offered a look of apology. "No sense dwelling on it. Just have a little more trust in me from now on."

My eyes looked into his, my body trembling. "Are you hurt?"

"I'm a Juneun. So, I'm hardier than humans."

That didn't answer my question. And when he ignored my stare, I asked again.

"No. I'm not hurt," said Syaoran, tempering his voice and forcing on a smile. "Can you stand?"

"I think so," I said. I didn't feel any pain in my legs or feet.

He helped me up anyway.

"Ow ow ow!" I'd lost my sandals, and hadn't noticed that the bottom of my left sock was heavy with blood.

Carefully, Syaoran scooped me up to take to a boulder to sit. Kneeling in front of me, my eyes fixated on his three tails.

"It doesn't look too bad. I'll put a wrap on it to stop any more bleeding."

"You have... tails."

He looked up, puzzled, and glanced behind with a scowl. A wave of his arm and they disappeared. "I relaxed too much of my control to calm you down."

"Control of what?"

"My essence." He took what remained of his torn sleeve, wrapping it snug around my foot. "How does that feel?"

"Tight."

He unfurled it, trying again. "Better?"

"It's still really snug."

"I don't want it to slip. The wound is in an odd place. Can you tolerate it?"

I nodded. Compared to the pain in my arm, the discomfort was negligible.

His horse walked up not long after, having found us. Like before, Syaoran scooped me up as though I weighed less than a leaf. And, like before, he sat me across his lap once in the saddle. Unlike before, I held to him rather than squirm.

"If you can hide your tails," I said. It was rude of me, I knew, but I wanted to break the new, awkward silence that fell over us. "Why do your ears still show?"

He shrugged. "I can't hide everything. Even if I could, the Juneun would know."

"But, you're also a Juneun. Aren't you?"

"Most would see that I'm still Kurai, first and foremost. Like they do with Juro."

"But he's a Lord. Why would they treat him any differently?"

"It's..." his voice trailed, and he sighed. "It's complicated."

That quieted me for a while. But only a while. "Where are we going?"

"There's a pagoda up this way. Kwan used to go there to get away from the house now and again. But it's been over a few decades. I'm not sure what to expect there, since I usually stay behind."

"Oh..." As we went on, my elbow and foot throbbed with heat, but the rest of me felt cold. I pressed against Syaoran, soaking in his warmth.

"Hisa?"

I looked up to him, his brow furrowed.

"From now on, promise that you'll trust me. And I promise I won't let anyone harm you."

"Where is this coming from?"

"I..." His ears went flat. "Since that time, when you were so ill. I don't want to see you suffer like that again. So, I'll protect you from magic like that."

"I know," I said. "We're friends. And friends look after each other."

He chuckled. "That's right."

Quiet.

When I couldn't take it, I started again, trying to steer a conversation without revealing too much of myself. "Do many Juneun, or any other spirits make friends with humans?"

He thought on it, his horse walking at a comfortable pace. "Can't say that I know of many. Who knows? But there's a sadness to humans. You're only here for a short while. So maybe we used to go out of our way to avoid friendships. Now it's second nature to not even think about it."

I mulled it over, and carefully selected my next words. "Genji married a human. Have there been others that did the same? Fell in love with a human?"

"Reconsidering Juro's offer?" teased Syaoran. "Or is it me?"

I frowned at him. "Never mind."

When the silence became too uncomfortable, I looked for any distraction.

"Did you ever find that thing you were looking for?"

He went rigid for a moment, looking at me with a start, and relaxed with a heavy sigh. "No. I think I might've lost it forever."

Barking echoed, causing Syaoran to tighten the reins and bring us to a stop. His ears swiveled this way and that, searching for the source.

"Wolves?" I asked.

"I don't think so. I haven't smelled wolves on this mountain in quite a while."

His stallion pawed at the ground, anxious. The undergrowth shifted. Something bolting towards us. And Syaoran readied himself for a fight.

Koji sprung out, tail wagging and happily announcing that he'd found me. He bounded around Syaoran's horse, ignoring how its ears pinned back and tail swished.

"I hate dogs!" growled Syaoran.

I chuckled. "I didn't put him in the kennels. He must have followed us."

"How?" asked Syaoran, skeptical.

"I've been teaching him how to track and hunt. But, it's mostly been under Lord Kwan's instruction."

He narrowed his eyes at me, ears wary of wherever Koji went. "I don't think you understand how fast we were riding. And it could've been a lot faster if you didn't thrash around the whole time."

"We stopped a long while. He must've caught up in that time."

Syaoran grumbled, unsatisfied with the answer.

"We can't take him back now. You said it yourself."

"Fine. But get him to stop making such a racket. I can't think."

I hushed Koji, giving a word and quick gesture to cue what I wanted him to do. He quieted to a playful growl, and quieted more when I repeated, keeping a proud look the entire way.

The pagoda wasn't too big. Seeming like a taller, fancy cottage more than anything like what I'd seen in pictures. The doors had stuck from lack of use. Much of the paper panes needing replacement. The inside was just as wild as the forest, coated in dust and leaves, and several signs that animals had come in for shelter. Syaoran helped me down and inside, using his magic to tidy up as he went through the building.

"I'll gather a bit of firewood and light the furnace. Hopefully nothing decided to nest in there and it's in good enough condition. Will you be okay here?"

I nodded from my seat. "I have Koji to keep me safe."

He opened his mouth to argue or tease, deciding against it before the first word spilled from him.

Alone, I wandered where I dared, backing off if the creak of a particular floorboard sounded too ominous. Everything was eerily still, except for Koji and myself. When I came across a storage pantry, I muttered my complaint. Some critter had broken in and made a mess of things. A cellar, however, was still locked.

"You shouldn't wander off," said Syaoran.

"I stayed inside," I said. "And I wanted to learn the place if we're going to stay here a while. But..."

"What is it?"

"I was just thinking. Why didn't we come here when Lord Kwan's brothers came suddenly?"

"Oh..." His brow bent, and his posture shied. "I didn't want to look suspicious fleeing the house. And the truth is that it's safer near those walls where guest laws apply."

I didn't know what a guest law was, but it sounded complicated. So, I nodded, pretending to understand. "Too bad we don't have a key. There might be something in the cellar we could eat."

Syaoran chuckled, flicking a finger. At his command, the lock opened.

It was cleaner in the cellar, though several spiders still called it home. The first steps were wet, though the rest of it kept fairly dry. Pickled things, past their use, were investigated. So much color lost from them that it was hard to know what they were at first glance. Cracked jars spoiled the rice and grains kept within them. But some things survived in the far back. Smaller jars of noodles and wild rice, honey and coarse salt, and a kind of legumes that I didn't recognize.

"Is there a pot and good water?" I asked.

"There's a seasonal spring and running stream. It's early into autumn, so they should still be there. And there's probably pots in the kitchen somewhere."

"It's a start," I said, smiling through my pain. It felt stronger now, weighing on me since I'd calmed. "We can have rice for dinner today. And noodles tomorrow."

Koji jumped then, putting his front paws on Syaoran and causing the Juneun to raise up his arm and scowl. "I don't understand why you wanted this when you had a perfectly good bird for a pet before, and you let that one go."

"Bird? You mean Tori?"

Syaoran grumbled, pushing Koji off.

"Tori was wild. And he wanted to be wild. But Koji is a dog."

"So what?"

"Dogs aren't wild."

Syaoran put a palm up, preventing Koji from jumping again. "You sure about that?"

Bickering aside, he did fetch what I asked for, and helped to get the stove in order. While we waited, we went through what we could salvage to sleep on. Most of the futons were chewed through by rodents, and coated in dust. But we made do.

The pain in my elbow grew, making it hard to focus on anything else. I tried distracting myself, looking out the doors and windows often and taking in the tranquility offered.

It seemed a shame that the place had fallen to this state. A large pond, almost grand enough to be a lake, must've once been a beautiful thing to behold. I tried to imagine lotus flowers and lilies everywhere. Then I thought about where a windchime might be; one made of glass would make a pretty sound for a pretty scene.

"Here," said Syaoran, handing me a cloth, cold with water. "For your elbow."

"Thank you." I felt stupid then. Of course Syaoran wasn't trying to kidnap me. It was my imagination wild with stories I'd heard as a child; they were cautionary tales, mostly. Still, looking at him churned up a memory. Something Urekkato once said. "Does Lord Kwan really put so much effort to get me out of trouble?"

Syaoran chewed, looking up from his bowl. "Of course he does. You're small, and weak."

"You make me sound completely helpless," I grumbled.

"It's because you're a human. Your trespasses can't be dealt with like it would if it was me. I'd get one hundred strikes for yelling at Urekkato or any newly appointed prince. I don't think you could handle five."

Much as I wanted to argue, he was right. A cold pain stuck like needles into my other arm at the mere memory of Beom's bamboo stick.

"It has some perks," said Syaoran, his tone jovial. "I can be a little lazy for a few days while I hide you here."

I blinked at him, scrunching my face.

"Don't let him know I told you, but Kwan is really nervous about taking you to Genji's Mokryon. So, he's taken on more to help you and make sure you have fun. Which means I also have more work to do."

"What's Lord Kwan nervous about?"

"Just call him *Kwan*. He's not here, and there's no need for formality when it's only you and me."

I shuddered, and my jaw locked.

"You don't call me *Master* Syaoran."

My eyes went wide. Was I supposed to be addressing him that way?

He laughed. "Calm down. No one calls me that unless they're particularly mad at me. If you start calling me it, I'm going to get uncomfortable."

"But *why* is he nervous?"

"He's taking a clumsy human to the ancestral home of his master where there'll be four times as many guests than when he holds court. Tetsuden Castle may as well be a city during that time. There's plenty to get nervous about. Losing you chief among them, since you like to wander off."

"Lose me? Is his castle that enormous?"

"I haven't been. But Yua has, and used to talk about how it's easy to get turned around. The buildings, the gardens, they're all grand. And the seven walls alone can make anyone lose their sense of direction. And Juro will be there."

He went back to eating, leaving me in cosmic dread. How could there even be that many noble family members, or any single place so large?

"And you won't be going so much as a servant as you will a personal attendant," said Syaoran, likely reading the many questions on my face as I nibbled quietly.

Koji knocked over his own bowl, making a playful whine.

"You'll probably share a room with him."

"Share—I, what? Is that expected of a personal attendant?"

"Not usually. But I think he'd be upset if his household walked into someone else's room. It'd be embarrassing to his reputation. And you are the most likely to have that accident. On the other hand, what happens if someone else stumbles into your room? It's safer just to keep you close by. Besides, the rumors are already out there, so this wouldn't be surprising to—"

"But those rumors are lies!"

"I know. They were spread around about me as well. That the reason Kwan stopped showing an interest in women, and I was suddenly around more. But those died off quick. The ones about Yua still circulate the gossipers."

"People thought you were his lover? But, you're..."

Syaoran raised a brow, mischief consuming his features. "You don't think I could seduce a lord?"

I went rigid. "It's just—in the village we, I mean, there's not—"

"It's not common," said Syaoran, rescuing me from myself. "The Samjos are more notorious for it."

"Notorious?"

"Well known, but not for good reason."

There was a comfort in knowing I wasn't alone in disgusting rumors. At the same time, I couldn't fathom why anyone would think Yua or Syaoran would be Lord Kwan's lovers. They were friends with him, and that was plain to see. But something closer, more intimate—I could feel my face contorting as I tried to figure out how anyone would make those conclusions.

"Don't worry yourself over it," said Syaoran, scooting a honey jar over to me. "People say stupid things to others when they're jealous. Take a wick of this, it helps."

"Why would anyone be jealous of me?" I asked, thoughtless.

"People are petty. They might've been jealous that he so much as wished you a good morning one time."

"That makes no sense," I said, dipping in a honey stick. "I say good morning to everyone every day, right Koji?"

His tail wagged slow, eyes watching me and head tilted with curiousness.

Syaoran shrugged. "That's just how jealousy is."

I couldn't dismiss the notion as easily as Syaoran. No one had ever been jealous of me over anything. Why would they? What would they envy? Having lost a mother, and taking up so many chores at a young age that I didn't have time to finish out childhood?

No one was ever jealous of me.

Except... Except for Fumei, once. She'd confessed she wished she'd had a sister like me who would brave some demand from the spirits. It was an odd thought as I sucked on the honey. For so long, I'd been the one jealous of her. And in Lord Kwan's house, I did envy how elegant and beautiful and educated everyone around me was. I could barely hope to keep up, let alone be equal. The inverse was an alien concept to me.

Lost in thought, I repeated the motions to devour more sweet honey. My gaze fixed on nothing in the vast beyond of the door.

"I'm convinced bees are directly made from heaven. Honey will cure anything. Any time you feel hurt or sick or you want better health, just have a spoonful every morning and night."

I chuckled. The wind rustled some of the foliage, gleaming my attention. "Yams."

Syaoran repeated, looking out the door.

"Do you see those hear shaped leaves?"

"Yeah?"

"You can follow the stalk and find wild yams buried there."

He grimaced. "I'm not a fan of yams."

"Really? I like them candied with ginger."

"Actually, that does sound pretty good."

"All we'd need is ginger and I could make it. The cooks in Lord Kwan's house have been helping me improve, and that's one of the first things I devoted myself to learning. It's simple, but it's really good."

Chapter 48
Atonement

We did happen to find one ginger plant that was in decent enough condition for cooking. I counted myself lucky for it. Then I remembered: luck. I could've kicked myself. How much had Urekkato seen through my eyes? I never should've agreed to the spell, even if it could help Lord Kwan.

It was only too bad I needed more than luck to speed up my recovery.

The morning after, I did feel a lot better. The pain in my elbow greatly subsided. It was as though a cool hand was gently placed there, easing it to be more tolerable. That was the same day Syaoran and Koji came back with a wild duck. And, for the first time, Syaoran gave Koji a word of praise. Syaoran's magic had shot it down, but it was Koji bolting to retrieve it without breaking its skin or anything else.

It was that night, in my deepest slumber, I was plagued by dreams. I dreamt about Lord Kwan's kiss, only for it to become Syaoran, and for him to be both more playful and more aggressive with it. I dreamt we were running and laughing, and that he caught me, showing me with kisses. Warm lips on my neck, my body pressed against his, feeling his toned chest and stomach, and his hand gliding against my thigh.

I woke panting. Syaoran stared into my eyes with a smirk.

"Good morning."

Panicked, I pushed away and slapped him. Realizing immediately after that it was all a dream and I was now awake.

"What was that for?" demanded Syaoran, launching into a sitting position and scooting away.

"I'm sorry!" I squeaked. "I was having a nightmare—and suddenly you were there! I'm sorry."

Koji barked, excited by the sudden action and riled voices.

"Sounded like the opposite of a nightmare," said Syaoran, rubbing his cheek. More from the shock and to make a point than from any chance I'd actually hurt him, but I still felt guilty.

During that first night, with the floors still cold, we figured something clogged the chimney, and shared all the bedding to keep warm.

"What was your nightmare about?"

My face started heating up.

"Was it about me?" teased Syaoran.

"I dreamt I was actually being kidnapped," I said, grasping at anything to redirect. "By Lord Juro."

"That is a nightmare," agreed Syaoran. "Are you scared we'll get back too early and he'll just ride off with you?"

I avoided his eye. "Something like that."

"I wouldn't let that happen," said Syaoran, on his feet and patting the top of my head. "As much as I like Juro, I don't want to see you miserable with him. Even if you bite me again."

"It was one time!" I shouted.

Koji barked.

"And it was when I thought you were kidnapping me."

"I still can't believe you did it though."

We went on, whiling away the time. Before midday, Gi found us, having spotted Syaoran's horse. Dismounting from his own horse and sweating, he rushed inside, calling for me. Both Syaoran and I looked up from our tea, puzzled. Likewise, he appeared bewildered by our casualness.

He explained himself, and the ghastly story that Juro saw Susa in the stables, and the accompanying story that the mare had run home riderless only moments before the discovery. A search party was formed, each genuinely believing Syaoran and I were in some sort of trouble. Gi found my sandal in his search and feared the worst, pushing himself and his horse until he came to the pagoda; it seemed a reasonable place to take shelter, assuming we'd made it here.

Syaoran laughed, teasing that the only trouble wasn't packing things to eat and taking a nasty fall on the way over.

"But since you're here," said Syaoran, "have a seat."

Gi argued the matter, wanting us to go back. Syaoran, half ignoring him as he poured a third cup, explained the situation.

"A few more days. Hopefully Lord Kwan won't be too severe when he sees Hisa's arm."

"It's recovering quickly," I argued. "I can move it a bit."

"Keep it still," said Syaoran, giving me a sharp look. "Let it heal."

"It'd be better to have Lord Kwan look at it right away," said Gi, caught between things.

"It would be better," agreed Syaoran. "But I was told to keep her away from the house while Juro is there."

"Sneak her in," insisted Gi.

"I'm fine," I said. I wasn't, and the pain of it exhausted me, but I wanted to make a stand of my own. I didn't want to be thought of as a helpless, human, girl.

"See? She's fine. She said so herself." Syaoran rushed the words out, hinting his worry.

Gi looked between us, finally calmed from his fierce search. "If it doesn't heal right, there'll be permanent damage."

"Really," I insisted. "I've been keeping it still and putting a cold cloth on it for the swelling. I can manage."

"If you're not staying," said Syaoran, "tell Lord Kwan you didn't find us, and ride back when Juro leaves."

"You want me to go back empty handed?" Gi's eyes narrowed, his tone indignant.

As he looked across the open space, he noted the bedding piled in one place, giving Syaoran a raised brow. In return, Syaoran smirked. I frowned. He never put the bedding away, complaining that he'd have to bring it out by nightfall anyway. Now it gave implications.

"Stop that!" I scolded. "Nothing is going on between us." My face heated up, the memory of Fumei telling me about the rumors resurfaced.

"That's not exactly true," teased Syaoran. "You did kiss me. And you bit me only a few days ago. Can't keep your lips to yourself."

"Syaoran!"

Gi rested his face atop his finger tips, groaning.

"So, are you staying or not?"

"I was commanded to find you both and bring you back."

"And I was commanded to keep her safe and away. You found us, so bring back the news that we're fine."

"Both of you stop it," I said, as firm as I could. "You're acting like children arguing over chores."

They didn't listen to me, but that didn't matter. At the very least I wouldn't be sitting there meekly. When Gi left, with the promise to bring word to Lord Kwan, and our word of returning in two days, I breathed some relief. A compromise.

"So," said Syaoran, sliding his hand around my waist. "Where were we?"

I scowled at his teasing, pushing myself away. "Stop that."

He laughed. "If nothing, it'll shift the rumors away from Kwan. Less to burden him with come Mokryon."

I shifted my weight, hand fussing with my dress.

"What?" asked Syaoran. "Are you that upset when I tease you? You know I don't mean anything by it."

I didn't look at him. Frustrated, for reasons that shouldn't have bothered me to begin with, I tried to think how to explain.

"Is it because I told Gi about the kiss? I don't think he even believes me, if that makes it any better."

It did, to an extent. I just didn't know how to deal with my pent-up emotion and exhausting pain all at the same time. I dropped to a huddled position, and concentrated on my breathing. Was I that much of a burden to Lord Kwan? Would my feelings make it worse?

"Hisa?" Syaoran bent down, one hand on my shoulder, the other at my side to avoid my injury.

"I don't want to be a burden on him."

He paused, considering. "Prisoners are kind of a burden. But all things considered, I'd say you're more a help than a burden. You help remind him to be himself. He even smiles now!"

I shook my head.

Again, a thoughtful quiet fell. "Did you want to leave today?"

I couldn't think. Everything crashing down, I couldn't think. Bringing my head up, I nodded. "But Juro is still there."

He looked at me, similar to how Lord Kwan would when deciding what to do. "I said you should stand up for yourself, even to Juro. And, if you can't, then I will for you. Selfishly, I kept us out when I knew we should have gone back, because I hoped you'd heal completely and wouldn't tell Kwan. Now, you're miserable and still in a lot of pain."

This was true, but I wanted to say something to comfort him, anything. If only this growing headache would go away.

Syaoran tidied up—as much as would allow, and tacked up his stallion. I wasn't looking forward to the rough terrain, muttering the complaint. I was sure it'd gone unnoticed until he offered a spell. One to put me to sleep for the ride.

I refused it.

Somewhere along the trek, going at a walk, I didn't need magic to fall asleep.

I woke as we came to the inner gate, an uproar in the making and the sun fast setting. Rubbing my eyes, my bleary vision worked to make sense of colors and shapes. My ears, however, refused to make sensible words amongst the chatter.

Someone took me to slide off Syaoran's thighs and gently touch the ground. He'd said something about it, though I didn't quite catch it in my tired state.

Juro pushed through, making complaints to Syaoran. I yelped as he tried to lead me away by the arm.

"Look at you, my beloved," said Juro. "I should have ridden out for you."

I couldn't pull away, not without hurting myself.

Syaoran stepped in. "Give her space, Lord Juro. It's been a long journey, and Hisa is—"

Quiet quickly fell as Lord Kwan made his wordless approach. He stood in front of us, and I'd forgotten to bow as I struggled to fully wake. When my senses caught up, I tried to compensate with having only one good arm.

Through it, Juro continued his complaints.

Lord Kwan ignored him, looking me over. "You're hurt."

I remembered then, and hurried to speak up. "It's my own fault. I was being stubborn and ignored when Syaoran tried to warn me, and I, well, I fell."

Koji barked his own complaint then. I shushed him the second time. Lord Kwan said nothing. He stared, stoic and regal.

Continuing to ignore Juro's complaints, Lord Kwan took my free wrist to lead away, bidding Lin to take Koji back to the kennels. Murmurs started up.

In his room, he closed the doors and guided me to sit on his bed. An uncomfortable feeling took hold. I hadn't known him to be so quiet in a long time. He looked me over again, a line creasing his brow.

"I should have done more," said Lord Kwan. He kneeled then, using his healing magic on my elbow. "Hisa..." His forehead rested against mine. "I'm sorry."

I shook my head. "You couldn't have known. Although, we left so suddenly, I did think I was getting kidnapped at first. Tell me what you're planning next time. I'll be more careful, and less stubborn." I tried to meet his gaze, finding that he'd shut his eyes. "So, don't be upset. Please?"

He scoffed, letting that hint of a smile to make its appearance.

Determined to get him to say something, I angled my face, pressing my nose against his and blowing sharp to tickle and tease. He simply allowed that smile to grow a little more, and rubbed his nose back and forth against mine, tickling me instead.

"How's your foot?"

"How did you know about that?"

He opened his eyes, meeting my stare. "I can smell the old blood."

"Oh," I said, blinking in rapid succession as my brain processed the information. "Sometimes I forget you're a Juneun."

"Do you?"

"When I look at you, all I see is... Well, you."

He blinked, in total control of the movement, and slowly lifted his head away to cast his healing magic to the underside of my foot. "How can I make up for my mistakes?"

I chuckled. "I've already forgiven you."

"I haven't forgiven me," said Lord Kwan, taking a more serious tone. "I was too laxed in how I went about things. As a result, you were hurt. Tell me something I can do to make it up to you."

Try as I might, I didn't know how to outthink him. Not when he looked at me with so much sorrow. I dropped my gaze, seeing how mistreated my dress was. "I should be the one to apologize. I've ruined your gift to me."

"Hisa," scolded Lord Kwan in a coo. "I wanted to get you a new one anyway, if you'd let me."

I laughed. "I don't think you need the permission of a servant girl for much of anything."

"But you dislike when Juro does so without your knowing."

"That's true," I admitted. "But it's different with you. I know that you're not trying to buy my affection." Because he already had it. Whether or not he knew it, he already had my heart. And I saddened at the thought.

He lifted my chin with the edge of a finger. "Hisa. Name one thing I can do. One thing I can give. So that my conscience is clear." Again, he rested his forehead on mine, brushing the tips of our noses with every gentle swivel.

A wave of guilt washed over me. This close to him, there was something I wanted. Something I wanted badly. "A kiss," I whispered, meek.

"A kiss?" echoed Lord Kwan, pulling away slightly and looking me in the eye.

I looked down and away, my nerves getting the better of me and my sensibility scolding me for having said it. "It's alright if you don't want to. I'll think of something else. Mayb—"

Our lips collided, tender and playful. I closed my eyes in an instant, following his lead and playing back. My hands went to his shirt, holding tight to keep him close. It wasn't the same exploratory kiss as before. It was the sort that Juro had forced on me, that I'd asked Syaoran for—yet it was different. Not just because of the cool of his skin, but something else I didn't have words for. The love in my heart flared, making me smile.

When we parted, there was no embarrassing string of drool between us. It was clean, and it felt like time itself had stopped to let us enjoy these few precious seconds.

"I will kiss you anytime you ask, Hisa," said Lord Kwan. "That will be my atonement."

I opened my mouth to argue, to say that I didn't want kissing to be his punishment. His finger went back under my chin, his thumb sliding across my lips to stop me.

"I want to," said Lord Kwan.

My face warmed. As did my heart.

And yet, my voice wouldn't come to say three simple words.

Chapter 49
Lord Kwan XIII

"How can you stay so calm when my Hisa is out there?" demanded Juro.

Kwan blew gently over his cup of tea.

"I should be out with the search."

"Syaoran is with her," said Kwan, feeling he'd made Juro wait too long for a response this time. "I'm sure there's no real danger."

Juro growled. "He's going to get his fox smell all over my Hisa."

Again, Kwan let a long silence sit over them. "Your Hisa?"

"Have you not been listening? My bride is in the wilds with a man known for—"

"I was simply wondering when she became *your* Hisa." Kwan sipped at his tea, making Juro wait and consider. "She cannot agree to become your bride while under sentencing."

Juro scoffed. "A formality!"

Kwan stared, as he typically did, concealing his own distress. "If they are somehow separated or in need, my house guard will find them. I have every faith."

Juro grumbled. "More men rubbing their scent on her. That best be the only thing—how do we know one of your house guards won't take advantage of her state? Rob me of my wedding rite..."

Breathing in, slow and controlled, Kwan watched the irritation consumed his friend. "Are you saying my selected household would wrong you? Or that I have by sending them?"

Juro scoffed, waving away the notion as Kwan refilled their cups. "I should be out there."

"What are we to do if Hisa returns and you are lost in the mountain?"

"You give me little credit. But I see your point."

"You do," said Kwan.

The same couldn't be said of himself. His own concern consumed him.

In the night, he cast his spell of sight, searching the mountain. Where was she? Not beside the villages. Nor the peach grove, or the lake. Where? His fingers fidgeted tapped on his table, his other hand half folded and holding up his chin. Where was she? If he couldn't spot her, how did he expect anyone else to find her.

"Syaoran," growled Kwan, low and impatient.

He'd never taken this long with the spell. If need be, he'd search every inch of the mountain. A hint of something caught his attention. Feint, but he saw the silhouette of Syaoran's stallion laying down to rest.

It was a start. His sword came to his palm at a gesture. Door opened, he used his spell for speed to leave unnoticed—as much as he could, leaving a wind in the wake of his initial step.

At the pagoda, he caught the smell of fire from the furnace, burning low. When his bare feet touched the cold floor of the pagoda, he raised a brow. Considering the neglect of the place, it wasn't too surprising, though it caused some anxiety to him. The door slid, whispering a complaint. It didn't take long for him to spot the bedding piled high. The fire-pit stove, still lit, illuminated the space in orange and yellow.

He would only look. Just to see that she was alright. And he would go home.

Koji looked up, wagging his tail but remaining silent.

Spotting Syaoran cuddled with her, his brow turned sharp. He wanted to tear off the covers, to be furious with his friend. In catching his thoughts, he stopped before he could reach. Likewise, he stopped his lungs from drawing too deep a breath too quickly, lest he wake them. It was cold. Of course they would share a bed. But it didn't prevent the suggestion of something more between them.

He stared. It shouldn't bother him. Some of the women in his staff often snuck into Syaoran's room. What difference did this make? Because she was human? Because she was his friend? That he was fond of her...? Too fond perhaps. But if she loved him, was it right for him to stay *too fond*? The hare and the fox were better suited than a hare with a tiger.

He shut his eyes, ridding himself of the thought, opening again when he heard Hisa's whimper.

Her brow was damp. He placed his fingertips on her forehead, light. A fever, and shivers. He noticed then that Syaoran's sleeve was missing. What'd happened? His fingers traced down, searching for the source. Her elbow. At once, he began his spell, stopping before completing. Was it wise? It'd give away that he was here. And if there was something more than friendship between her and Syaoran, would this ruin their privacy to it?

His hand started to pull away, stopped by the insistence of his heart. He couldn't ignore it. Only enough to lessen the pain, and avoid permanent damage. Even so, she winced slightly. Her toes stuck out. Something he thought odd. With the cold of an autumn night in the mountain, why would her feet be bare? He made to gently slid it back under the covers, touching fabric. Curious, he peeked.

Syaoran!

He was supposed to protect her. What happened? Again, he reined himself from his anger. The intensity of it was unbefitting. Still, he couldn't bear to do nothing about it. Her words rang back into his mind.

Didn't you also fuss over me when I was unwell?

He did fuss. And he couldn't explain why. His spell helped hasten the healing, but left enough alone to not appear obvious. A part of him wanted to wake her, to carry her home.

He stood, stepping away in silence. The grounds around the pagoda, once lovely and tranquil, now deteriorating. He walked the perimeter of it, lost in memories. Stopping, he breathed, looking past the tree tops to the stars. A glance back inside gave bittersweet thoughts. He'd restore this place for her, if she liked it, where she could be with the man she loves in peace.

And he would miss her.

When he heard of their arrival at the gates, it took restraint to not rush to her. She would still be hurt, and likely hungry. Upon seeing her tattered state—arm in a sling, sandals missing, hair unruly, and dress dirty and pinched with snags—he wanted to sweep her up, to make everything right.

But if she loved someone else, it wouldn't be appropriate. Regardless of Juro's presence, he wouldn't insult Syaoran if she loved him.

It wasn't until she bowed that he realized he'd been standing there a while, and noticed most of his household out with them.

The awkwardness in himself didn't vanish once they were in his room either. Not until her sharp, little breath tickled at his face. On her own accord, she brought him out of his melancholy. A gladness prickled in his heart. Pain, but a good kind of pain. He brushed his face against hers, reveling in the touch.

Warm. And a little cold from autumn's air. Their lips only a hair apart, it took his full restraint. He'd already made a mistake in mentioning her other injury.

"How did you know about that?"

His mind fast fetched an answer.

"Sometimes I forget you're a Juneun."

The notion amused him. "Do you?"

"When I look at you, all I see is... Well, you."

He began to understand, when she'd said it, that he didn't want her to become someone else's little rabbit, someone else's magpie in their garden, someone else's Hisa. But what could he do? He couldn't force the situation—not happily.

Their banter went on, with Kwan amused and hurt by it.

"But it's different with you. I know that you're not trying to buy my affection."

There was truth in that. And he was proud to know she understood why Juro behaved as such. She wasn't empty headed to believe there was no motive. But he wanted some way to make himself useful to her, or give her something to please her. "Hisa. Name one thing I can do. One thing I can give. So that my conscience is clear."

"A kiss," whispered Hisa.

His mind went blank, his heart missing its rhythm. He stared into her dark-brown eyes, and the thick, black lashes that surrounded them. "A kiss?"

Whatever she rambled about after, he didn't hear. The whole of the world fell deaf. Lips warm, nose cold, breath sweet. He'd lived long enough to kiss a number of women; some he did through affection, and others for the sheer pleasure. And few had enticed him to want to overstep. The sides of himself competed for what he ought to do, and restraint was needed.

He delighted in her playing back, letting him chase her in a blind and wordless game. He never needed to explain to her. She picked up on his cues, and was curious enough to follow through. Sparks ran through him. Not the sort for warfare. They celebrated in his touch of joy, in the softness she dealt, and in the clumsiness that reminded him she wasn't a courtly lady. She was Hisa. His perfectly imperfect, human, Hisa.

The thought caused him to stop.

Not his. Not unless she wanted. Confusion coursed through him. What he'd assumed before, and now, when she wanted for a kiss—what were her feelings?

They stared into each other's eyes. For how long, he didn't know. He used the time, waiting for her response, to come up with something himself.

"I will kiss you anytime you ask, Hisa," said Kwan. "That will be my atonement." The words were noble, but not what he wanted to say.

Hisa's face changed. Her eyes narrowing only just, and her brow pressed. She was about to object to something he'd said. Perhaps to say not to, or to accuse him of teasing. No matter the reason, he found a way to stop it. He remembered then what she's told him nearly more than two years prior. That a kiss shouldn't be coerced. And her previous rambling caught up to him as well.

"I want to."

He dragged the tops of his fingernails along her jaw, light in his touch, gliding to her cheek to stroke his thumb against her skin. She shied away.

Kwan quirked a brow, remembering then that that cheek held her scar.

"Hisa," whispered Kwan, stopping himself. It would only make things complicated for her if he spoke on newly realized feelings. "Look at me."

She swallowed, eyes flicking upward while her chin stayed tucked.

"Don't feel ashamed." He brushed her hair off her face, gently placing it behind her ear.

They stared into each other a while. Until a hint of awkwardness prodded her to drop her gaze and break the stillness.

"I'm sorry I ruined the dress you gave me."

He flashed a small smile, amused by her repeated apology. "I have something for that." He stood, walking the short distance to fetch the few items. "Do you remember, when we rode to the lake, how you described what sort of things you'd sew when you improved your skill?"

She tensed, her cheeks pinking. "Did you ask about it to trick me?"

Kwan shrugged. "If you don't like it, you don't need to keep it."

He handed them over, a stack on her lap and nervousness on her face—which twisted into confusion, and quickly shifted into recognition. Kwan tilted his head, awaiting her verdict.

"I can't repay this."

He scoffed, humored, and raised a hand to stop anymore objections. "Consider it an advanced payment. So, when your skill improves, you will sew up a sunflower one for me."

She raised a brow, flashing a sly smile. "You'd wear one patterned in flowers?"

"If you made it."

She smiled, hiding her bottom lip in her mouth and turning her gaze while her head slowly tucked itself into her shoulders.

"How did you like the pagoda?"

He realized his mistake when she answered with a quizzical look. "How did you know about the pagoda?"

He kept himself still, mind searching for an excuse.

"Gi told you?"

Wordless, Kwan allowed the assumption to hang. "Did you like it?"

"It was…"

His own expression faltered. She didn't like it.

"I think it must've been beautiful. But abandoned and in autumn, it seemed sad. I would've liked to have seen what it looked like before."

His smile started to reform.

"Why did you abandon it?"

To that, Kwan dropped his gaze. "I got obsessed in other pursuits, and too busy with the rest."

"Because of Gumiho?"

"Among other things."

She rocked side to side, her mind actively at work on how to word something. "Do you think you'll go there again, now that she's gone?"

He watched her expression. She wanted to see it restored. "Perhaps."

"Would you take me to see it? I did say I'd visit after I was free to go home."

"If it's convenient."

He ordered her rest. Juro insisted on being with her, complaining when Kwan prevented him.

"There is no need for you to linger," said Kwan. "I will attend her personally. You may return home to your lands as planned. Before winter sets in."

Juro complained, though Kwan didn't listen. Instead, he stared, stone faced and unblinking. Keeping still, he waited for the silence to pressure Juro's compliance.

"I suppose there is still Mokryon. Lord Genji did specify to bring your attendants, if I recall."

There was a separate worry. He had winter to figure it out. And he had winter to plan a renovation. A project to bring out that beaming smile from her.

Laying in bed, Kwan stared at the ceiling. Sleep eluded him. Too many thoughts of what he needed to do plagued him. It wouldn't be a restful winter. More, in his anxiousness, he'd neglected to choose which girl would act as tutor and attendant.

It didn't matter so much about family ties or beauty or the usuals. What mattered is that Hisa wouldn't need to feel so insecure and hide away. Genji wanted that. And, he, himself, wanted that.

Two days after, he saw Juro off. In relaying that Syaoran would be his personal attendant for Mokryon, both former Kurai looked shocked. Protests began, amusing Kwan. He said nothing more of it. There wasn't a need to expose Hisa as his second attendant. In this way, he could bide time until coming up with a better strategy to ensure her safety and happiness.

However, should Syaoran learn the truth, it might make him and Hisa happy. Then came the decision of how the sleeping arrangements ought to be made. He'd already put her in a predicament before, and it'd be a lie to say his own jealousy didn't play a part in thinking about it.

He pondered on it over the week following his friend's departure. Still having no pick for the task, and winter fast approaching, he'd need to send a missive. Thinking back on each of them, measuring their reactions to Juro and Syaoran, and their actions taken in the night they stayed, he might be better off starting over.

In the morning, he told himself. Maybe it was impractical. But he'd take the chance.

In his room, pouring a cup of peach wine that evening, he hoped to put the troubles of the last few days behind him.

Barking.

Kwan sighed. She'd brought Koji into her room again. Whatever the reason, it didn't matter. As master of the house, he'd need to correct the issue.

He'd taken his time, rather than rush in to scold as his brothers might do. She burdened herself enough with stern words in a leveled tone. There wasn't a need to escalate.

The calm of him fled when he opened her door, unannounced. He'd barely gotten a word out when he saw the puzzle box in her hands. Weighted heartbeats echoed in his chest.

"Where did you get that?" demanded Kwan, aghast.

"I—" started Hisa, disrupted by her dog.

Kwan went to her, swift in his step, and took it from her grasp. "Do you know what you could have done?"

She retreated into herself, hiding behind her arms and hands, eyes wide.

"This is not a toy!"

"It was just abandoned in the kennels," blurted Hisa. "I didn't think—"

His arm shot out, palm hitting the wall behind her as he leaned in, brow sharp and voice sharper. "You could have put the entire mountain in danger! You could've put everyone in danger! If this fell into the wrong hands—"

"I didn't know!" cried Hisa.

She trembled, eyes tightly closed. A pitiful sight, reminiscent of the morning she arrived. He realized then how close he was, towering over her, and that his voice had taken on a tiger's growl. He tried to temper himself.

"Why did you take this?"

"I just," she shook violently, forcing herself to look at him with tear-filled eyes. "I like looking at the bead inside. That's all—"

"You opened it?" the growl in his tone returned. "Stupid girl! You don't realize how—"

She ran. Bolting out the door as quick as her legs would carry her.

Kwan took a step to pursue, stopping when the haunting image of her fearful face kept flashing in his sight. Breathing labored, he continued his restraint. Of course she didn't know. How could she? Any time his brothers arrived unannounced, hounds in tow, he allowed it for one reason: the kennels. He could think of no better place, where the smell would deter a sensitive fox nose, should Gumiho ever be bold enough to sneak in. Syaoran, a lesser fox, always confirmed the stench lingered with his every complaint.

What he didn't take into account was ever having a human prisoner, and the chance they'd be placed in that particular kennel.

If she ran all the way to her village, he wouldn't blame her. He'd come close to striking at her, and didn't have the good sense to not be in control of himself as an excuse. No. No excuses. His heart felt a dozen needles pressing in at the thought. If he'd hurt her...

For now, they both needed the separation, to regain themselves. He stared down at the puzzle box. He could feel it in there.

Hours passed, and no sign of Hisa in the estate. Maybe she did run back to her village. Kwan walked the veranda, the puzzle box tucked safely under his shirt layers. His breath still calming, he couldn't clear his head of things. Most of all, the guilt pressing down on him. What would he do, if his palm touched her, rather than the wall?

There were things to explain. He at least owed her that much. Justified or not, his anger shouldn't have ruled his actions, as it had too often.

"Syaoran," called Kwan.

Syaoran stopped in the midst of closing his door.

"When Hisa turns up, bring her to my room." He continued his own stride, never pausing.

"I'll let her know," said Syaoran.

"Syaoran. Bring her. Right away."

Once in his room, Kwan sat at his table, facing the doors, and waited.

He'd nodded off at some point, staying perfectly seated, and woke to the sound of birds welcoming the dawn.

Eyes slow to open, his vision blurred and cleared over several seconds.

She didn't come back.

The slow flick of something grabbed his attention. A butterfly, this late into the year, sat on the brim of his tea cup. Alone, thought Kwan. He watched it, detecting a second one after a long while, and waited for it to reveal itself from behind the cup. A pair. He watched them, unable to nod off again as hours crept by.

"Lord Kwan?" Syaoran's voice. Likely to say that Hisa was still missing, and convince him of a search party.

Don't bother, he thought. Let her go.

His doors opened, showing only Syaoran in the frame.

"You are up," said Syaoran.

Kwan said nothing, staring right ahead.

"I couldn't sleep so, I thought..." Syaoran's words trailed. "Hisa wasn't on the estate."

Of course not.

"So, I had an idea, and let Koji out. He led me straight to her."

Kwan shifted his silent gaze, looking at Syaoran.

"Well, not straight to her," said Syaoran. "He chased a lot of things in the dark, and picked a fight with a young boar. Then he barked down a bear hole before—"

"She's here?"

Syaoran blinked, weary, and tried to read Kwan's face. "Yes, my lord."

Kwan sat there, exhausted, and anxious, saying nothing for a while. "Send her in."

A troubled look marred Syaoran's face. Perhaps he did love her. The irony of it—a fox spirit, and an ordinary human. "Yes, my lord." His words were quiet, hesitation in them.

Hisa came into frame, appearing cold and tired. The hanbok he'd given her coated in wilderness, and her newly grown out hair in disarray.

"Close the doors," said Kwan, low and even. When she obeyed, and made to close the inner doors, he brough out the puzzle box. Setting it on the table, he thought how he ought to begin.

Chapter 50
Soul

As confused as I was, I felt happy. I'd been tricked, but also given tenderness. Mostly, I was frustrated with myself. I had so many chances after the kiss to say how I felt, and I backed out every time.

But, he'd also said he wanted to kiss me. What did that mean? Of course, my imagination spun it to mean Lord Kwan was also in love with me. But, wouldn't he have said as much? Or was it because any time I asked for a gift, it was always the same thing, and this was more to humor me?

Even after several days, I still couldn't understand it. Lord Kwan said nothing about it in all that time, asking after my injuries and mentioning nothing more about the night of my return. But why was he so tender? I liked it, but I needed to understand what drove his gentle actions.

He'd said the new clothes were a preemptive payment, and I devoted hours into my practice to repay the token. It felt strange. I remembered then that I'd put so much practice into new skills, I neglected maintaining older ones. I'd be back to weaving sandals and blankets when I returned to the village, and hated to think I grew sloppy or slow after being spoiled in the luxury of the villa.

I'd written down every new recipe, with my penmanship much improved (though still not as prettily made as Lord Kwan's). My skills in art and sewing also got better; not masterful, but enough to suffice or look a little appealing. I still sometimes imagined that I was not a servant, but a student at a school, and thought about how proud I would make my family when showing off my new talents.

I did worry about Koji. Whether I'd have to leave him, or if he'd come with me. I didn't want him and Chocho to fight at first meeting, and I didn't know if I'd be strong enough to keep him beside me. So, I decided that the next few days would be dedicated to refreshing my straw weaving skills and putting more discipline into Koji. He'd be such a well-behaved dog by the time I returned that I was sure he'd impress the village.

Autumn was passing quietly, though Lord Kwan kept busy with some great agenda. Often, I would check on him in the evening, and find him at the brink of nodding off.

I decided on this day to surprise him with a treat. Something to keep his energy up. With the cooks' permission, I set to work on making adangi cakes. Feeling confident, I tried to make designs on them to look especially pretty. Nothing complicated, just a simple leaf pattern, but they still got messed up in the process of cooking. I'd spent most of the afternoon on it, realizing afterwards that I hadn't taken poor Koji out at all that day.

Even though the ground was cold with an early frost, it didn't feel right to leave him in there all day. I decided then that I'd take him to my room first, so I could make a pretty display of the cakes and leave them in Lord Kwan's room. Then I could take Koji on a long walk under the light of the full moon. And if we wandered a little far, I could stop to stargaze a while.

There wasn't much I had to make a presentation with. I thought about the wrapping paper I'd saved, though I worried the cakes would leave unsavory marks and ruin the aesthetic. Maybe a pretty piece of the dress he'd given me those years back. My tumble from Syaoran's horse, and the events that followed, had ruined it; so, I took it apart, determined to make something new of it. Though maybe this worked better. I still had a ribbon of fabric left from my old riding clothes. It'd make for a nice display if I was careful, and I could attach a note.

Regardless, I wanted to keep my planning private, and closed my eyes to count as frequently as I dared.

In trying to put it together, I should've paid more heed to Koji. There came a point where he was too quiet. Looking over, I saw why: he was chewing on my rabbit. I scolded him, leaping to my feet. In my rush to snatch it back, I'd accidentally knocked over my stationery.

He went for the cakes next, barking when I swooped to take them out of his reach. He'd hidden his head under the table, complaining, and I thought that was the end of it. I was wrong. Completing my delicate packaging, and in the midst of cleaning up the stationery, I panicked. The puzzle box was missing.

My gut shrank at the sound of a crunch coming from beneath my table. Again, I scolded Koji, but he stayed half hidden and wagged his tail. Diving under, I wrestled it from him, causing a mess in the process. It'd been opened, and the glowing bead out. Quickly, I stole it away before anything could happen, and replaced it in the box, shutting it.

Lord Kwan entered then. My shoulders tense, readying to explain that I didn't intend to keep Koji in here, and it was only for a short task before taking him out. But the words never left me. His expression was one of pale horror.

"Where did you get that?"

I followed his gaze, looking at the puzzle box in my hands. Through instinct, I understood a few things all at once. The puzzle box was his. He'd hidden it. It was something dangerous. The last part conflicted with what I'd known it for: comfort.

"I—" Koji leapt on me then, bouncing his front paws off my hip and begging me to play.

"Do you know what you could have done?"

I felt the box ripped from my hands, and new instinct brough them retreating to hide me from the roaring anger in his voice. My legs also acted on their own, backing me away blindly. I'd never seen nor heard him so angry. Not on the morning I arrived, or on the times he returned and was not himself. This was a different anger, one that terrified me.

"This is not a toy!"

"It was just abandoned in the kennels," I said in a hurry, my voice high pitched and panicked. "I didn't think—" His hand flew at me. I squeaked as I flinched, my body going rigid at the loud thud emanating from the wall.

"You could have put the entire mountain in danger! You could've put everyone in danger! If this fell into the wrong hands—"

I couldn't take it. I needed to defend myself in some way, even if just through words. "I didn't know!"

I could hear his panting, and the growls tangled with them. I didn't dare to open my eyes, hoping beyond hope that he'd calm enough to listen to me, and know it was an honest mistake.

"Why did you take this?"

A reasonable question. His tone reined in, I prayed for courage enough to look him in the eye and explain myself. I'd said so often before how I wouldn't touch what wasn't mine. Perhaps he thought me brazen for contradicting myself this one time.

"I like looking at the bead inside. That's all—"

"You opened it?" the growl in his tone returned. "Stupid girl! You don't realize how—"

The roar in his voice returned, his face fast forming a snarl, and tiger stripes began to appear. Instinct took over me. I ran. Out my door and in any direction, I ran.

My feet carried me without sandals across the cold ground, to the hidden door. I didn't close it behind me. My mind solely focused on getting away, with my heart outpacing my legs. Out the second secret door, I headed into the dark of the forest. The trees blocking out much of the light from the moon and stars. Too cold for snakes. The river was near. And it wasn't too deep. I could cross it. Cross it and run home.

The moment my foot plunged into the freezing water, I regained myself, coming to a complete stop before the water reached half way up my shins. My first immediate decision as myself was to get out of the river.

I stood on the bank, staring at the rushing, black water and beyond. I was too afraid to go back. But I couldn't go home either. I was stuck. And, not knowing what to do, I curled up into a ball, until I could calm and think up something.

He'd still be angry and in an uproar if I went back, especially because I'd been rude, and that I'd run. I'd forgotten my place. Spoiled by his gentleness, I'd forgotten I was his servant. I was stupid. A stupid girl, playing with things she shouldn't have touched at all, and believing myself in love with a high lord—a Juneun high lord. And stupid for ever imagining he would fall in love with me. He'd said it himself once, that it was precisely because I didn't know my place. I was a novelty. Nothing more.

Cold, but I couldn't bear to go back and face him. Not yet.

So, I sought shelter with one of the tiger statues that marked my way, and tucked myself against it. I'd leave once I felt I could face him and accept my punishment.

Barking. Koji found me right as dawn broke. To my surprise, Syaoran was with him, following.

I was to be brought before Lord Kwan. An apprehensive expression marred Syaoran's face as he relayed to me his recollection of last seeing Lord Kwan, and not knowing what was going on presently.

"Syaoran," I whispered. "You said you would stand up for me, even to Juro... Would you still do that, even if it was Lord Kwan?"

He blinked, brow crooked. "What do you mean? You're Kwan's favorite member of the household."

"But, if there was ever a time, would you?" I knew it was petty of me, asking Syaoran to pick me and my cowardice over someone who'd protected him and acted as his friend.

In quiet confusion, we walked back to the house, hand in hand. I squeezed, asking for comfort. In response, his warm hand held firm, thumb gliding in uneven circles over my knuckles.

I tried to keep on my feet in front of Lord Kwan's door. Every confidence I had of his leniency fled from me, recalling his fury. I shut my eyes to count, wanting this to stay as much a private matter as possible.

Alone and in his room, doors closed, I prayed for strength. A wave of something went past me, quieting the surroundings. A spell, I supposed. Then I turned to face him. Whatever bit of courage was granted to me left when I saw the puzzle box newly set on the table.

"Sit here," commanded Lord Kwan, gesturing to the corner nearest himself.

I obeyed, taking small steps, and sitting properly, despite my state.

For minutes, he said nothing. Nor did he look at me. My eyes went back and forth, staring at the box and then to him in search of some clue to tell me what to do.

"Where did you find it?" asked Lord Kwan, low.

I pinched at the long jacket of my hanbok clothing. "In the kennels," I whispered.

"Where?"

It took me a moment to understand he wanted more detail. "The one I was kept in, my lord. I wove a mat from the straw, and saw a slight glow from beneath a stone that was previously hidden under the stack."

He took a deep inhale, saying nothing more.

I waited, trying to bear the pressure of the silence.

"You opened it?"

My head instinctively tucked into my shoulders. "Yes," I said, hardly able to hear myself.

"Why?"

I didn't have an answer, not a good one. His face remained stone, giving me no cues of what to do. "I wanted to see what was inside, my lord."

He kept his gaze straight ahead, away from me.

I knew how bad it must've sounded, and searched for some way to explain. "The glow was a comfort in my first days here. I wanted to—"

"You should not have."

I stopped completely, looking at him in a silent plea. He didn't move. "I'm sorry..."

Another deep inhale, and a slow release, he shifted his watch to the puzzle box. "You're human. I expect you don't know what it is."

I shook my head in slow, tight swivels.

"It's not something that should be in human hands. Or the hands of any. And is the reason I put the warding spell on it."

I leaned slightly, trying to make some sort of eye contact, anything to help me understand.

"Undoubtedly, in the time you've been here, you've heard at least one rumor about me."

"My lord?"

Finally, he moved his gaze to meet me. I shied. His stare didn't harbor the same intensity as it had before. Instead, there was a sadness and a guilt to the way he looked at me.

"You're not an idiot. Not by nature. Naïve, at times, but not empty headed."

I kept wordless, unsure of where this conversation led to.

"Decades ago—longer, perhaps—I fought against Gumiho. Determined to make it a last confrontation, I was reckless. In doing so, I unwittingly left myself open. She ripped out my soul, attempting to claim it, and all my power, as hers. I managed to take it back before her spell was complete. But she stole a fragment of it."

As he explained, Urekkato's words came back to haunt me: *he doesn't have a soul.* Remembering, I shut my eyes again and counted in silence.

"To safeguard against her claiming the rest, I pulled it out myself to hide away. Any time my brothers came, hungry for war, they brought hounds with them."

It struck me then. "Syaoran hates the smell of dogs. Because he's a fox spirit."

The slightest hint of softness returned to his features. Approval, I thought.

"His isn't the strongest nose. Any time he complained about the stink of hounds, I felt secure that Gumiho wouldn't send another fox to sift it out."

"Because they wouldn't linger too long in the kennels," I concluded. "Let alone turn over every stone of the floor."

He recited the warding spell: *A heart without pride, a hand without greed. Feet not idle, tongue not hateful. With eyes that see through stone.*

"Outside of myself, as the one who casted the ward, it would be a very particular person who could open it without suffering the effects of the spell. I never imagined a village girl would fit the description. I don't receive many visitors as it is. And fewer who are human." That hint of a smile returned to him.

With it, I felt myself relax a little. So far, I'd not been punished or sternly spoken to. It was his soul. Were our places swapped, I'd be in a rage myself—especially now knowing the context. If there was a thief working for Gumiho, and they found it in my room... I'd put Lord Kwan in danger, unwittingly or not, I made him vulnerable.

I spent so much time realizing my folly, mentally chastising myself, that I didn't notice when he leaned in or that his hand rose to touch my cheek. I flinched in that second, eyes blinking rapidly to catch up my senses as I looked at him.

"I'm sorry," said Lord Kwan. "You couldn't have known."

I shied and shook my head. "I shouldn't have touched it to begin with. It's not mine."

There was silence. Then, the unexpected. He'd pulled me in slowly for an embrace. I didn't put up a fight, wanting more than anything to heal our relationship. Against his chest, even through his layers of clothing, I could hear the slow, rhythmic beat of his heart. The sound comforted me, and I wrapped my arms around his midsection, and closed my eyes.

"Will you look after it for me?"

I moved my head to look up at him. "But Gumiho is gone."

His soft features turned sad. "No."

To that, I blinked.

"I haven't said, because I don't want to stir up war."

"But, isn't it dangerous to keep that a secret?"

He shifted his gaze. "Yes. But better to come up with a plan carrying minimal risks, than to charge in and cause a high casualty and death count. Like what happened when our dragon king ordered a full assault." His eyes looked back to me, brow bending. "I'm trusting you with both this secret, and with my soul."

"But," my voice cut out, requiring me to gulp and try again. "What can I do to keep your soul safe from a powerful Kurai?"

"Syaoran complains that you always smell like Koji, regardless."

I groaned, sighing.

"And because I have faith in my friend." He placed a kiss on top of my hair, resting his forehead there afterwards.

There was a comfort in his words. But I worried now, more than ever, that Urekkato might see some part. I didn't want to tell Lord Kwan, to break the trust he had in me, and pledged to be vigilant in keeping both of these things a secret from the Cat prince.

Chapter 51
Servant Girl

It was the following day when I started feeling a little feverish. No surprise, considering that I'd spent a cold night out doors with soaked feet. I kept to my room the day after, unable to shake it off. Worse, my blood had come in and compounded my sickness. Compared to last time, however, it felt far more manageable.

Still, Syaoran fretted when he heard I was unwell. And Lord Kwan, on hearing, came to see me. I'd asked him not to spend his magic on me, now that I knew threats like Gumiho were still present, though he insisted on doing so anyway. I suppose, given the last time I fell ill enough to keep in my room, the concern was warranted.

It made me happy, knowing that he would still fuss over me. Maybe he wouldn't fall in love with me in return, but this might also be as close as I could have to love. My village thought I was ruined by him anyway; given five years, perhaps every village around the mountain would hear the same rumor. And I wouldn't be treated like his personal territory, unlike Juro. The closeness of our friendship would have to suffice in place of a romance.

I was well again in a few days, happily taking up chores and being out of my room. I stashed away the puzzle box, and decided that I might let Koji sleep in my room now and again to help keep his smell around. So long as he was quiet, no one would find out.

Before all that, I still needed to clean up my clothes. My plans fled from my mind when I entered my room to fetch them. My rabbit was in the wrong place. And it didn't look as tattered. Rather, it looked fresh. New.

In my work to improve my sewing, the one thing I never did was mend any part of the toy. It felt too much like destroying the last thing I had of my mother.

I rushed to it, picking it up to inspect with a tightly furrowed brow.

"My lady?"

I jumped at the sound of a stranger's voice, turning on my heel to look. A girl stood in my doorway, holding a closed basket. Black hair, styled prettily, framed her face and cascaded down her back. Brown-orange, cattish eyes stared at me with questions.

"I didn't mean to startle you," said the girl. "Are you Lady Hisa?"

I shook my head, twisting my expression as I dissected what she'd said. "I mean, I'm Hisa, but I'm not a lady."

She blinked, equally as confused as I was. "Lord Kwan hired me to attend and tutor a special guest of his. He said I would be attending *Hisa*."

I stared, clutching my rabbit.

Seeing it, she put on a sheepish smile. "I fixed it for you, my lady. Are you expecting?"

"Expecting what?" I said, thoughtlessly.

He expression faltered. "Is... That's a child's toy. Are you not...?"

I stared. My mind knew the implication, but denied it.

"Are you not expecting a child?"

"No!" I said, shaking my head furiously.

She stared, brow bunching. "Then... You're not his mistress?"

At the very word, I glared.

Without hesitation, she bowed with her apology. "Forgive me. I've only just arrived, and with all the talk, I assumed."

I stood, stupefied and not knowing what to do.

"If I may ask, my lady, since you're not his mistress. What is your relation to Lord Kwan?"

"His servant," I answered.

She looked between me and the veranda, back and forth with her mouth agape. "I don't understand."

"Neither do I," I said, taking brisk steps out to look for Lord Kwan myself.

I found him almost right away, tending to something in his room. He looked at me with a quirked brow, since I'd forgotten manners and didn't announce myself.

"Hisa?"

"Who is she?" I asked, accidentally rough in my tone.

He stared, silent.

It was his usual self, but something about it infuriated me today. "And why does she think I'm pregnant with your child?" I demanded.

He gave an amused look. "Does she?"

"It's not funny!"

He walked over, placing a hand on my head. "I was about to come find you. Uno is here to prepare you for Mokryon."

I swatted him away. "Why couldn't Lin or one of the girls here help me? What so sp—?"

His fingers went under my chin, thumb zipping my lips. "Hisa."

"Lord Kwan." I scowled.

His hint of a smile came on his face. "I wanted you to feel comfortable as a guest in Genji's home. Uno is here to help in that regard. Things are different away from the house. And it'll be seen as disrespect if you hide yourself away the entire time. Especially since Genji invited you himself. He expects to see you."

"See me?" I said, becoming sheepish with what that might imply.

"As he does with all his guests."

"But what's so different that I need an attendant?"

He looked at me, amused by my frustration, and brought his hand up. His fingers glided over my cheek and combed into my hair. "To style yourself, for a start. Syaoran would be happy."

"What does it matter if he's happy with my hair?"

He stared at me, blank. His hint of a smile fleeing, he blinked.

"What is Mokryon that I would need to know all this anyway?"

His previous expression resumed. "It's also called *Maiden's Day*, celebrating the legend of a famous Juneun who went into the fray against fallen gods in the earliest years of the world. She sacrificed her immortality, and became human. The day is to honor her memory. It's special to spirits."

Maiden's Day? I'd never heard of it, or the story that accompanied it.

"I wouldn't be surprised if four or five hundred guests arrived."

"Hundred?" I repeated with dread.

His smile grew a little, kindness glinting in his eyes. "Now you see why I want to make sure you're prepared? That's not including how overwhelmed I think you'll be with twenty miles of castle."

"Twenty miles?" I echoed, higher pitched than before. How could any one place be so large?

He quirked a brow at my horror. "Kwang's estate is short of eight miles. My ancestral home is fifteen. I like to keep things simple and smaller."

I'd always assumed Lord Kwan's home was large, or at least average of a Juneun lord.

"The royal palace is around fifty-two miles. I used to get turned around in there whenever I visited as a boy."

I was jaw dropped. Compared to the royal ground, Genji's home sounded humble, and Lord Kwan's miniscule.

"Best to know how to conduct yourself," said Lord Kwan. "You'll be free to wander the grounds, save for certain times in the day. Namely the early morning, and before and after the banquet. The rest of the day is yours to enjoy the castle, unless I send for something."

"Couldn't I just stay beside you or Syaoran?" I begged.

"You could," said Lord Kwan. "Though there may be times I need to send Syaoran for something. And I expect I'll be called to private conferences throughout the celebrations."

"I couldn't attend them with you?"

He gave one, slow shake of his head. "It wouldn't be a good look for you to cling to Genji's side either. He has his own duties as host."

I was doomed.

"I don't think I want to go..."

"Refusing Genji's invite would be seen as rude to both him and myself."

New guilt bit into my gut.

"If you really insist," said Lord Kwan. "I won't make you go. Genji will be disappointed. He's fond of you."

It was strange to have someone combing out my hair and tying it up. After a decade of dealing with it myself, I couldn't shake the initial discomfort. Uno stayed diligent, walking me step by step as she performed the task to help me remember it. I practiced it myself, of course. There was also the matter of etiquette. Feng had given me a good start, though in everything else I was still clumsy. The attendants of visiting lords and ladies would be dining together, and my table manners were a mess. My own ignorance of it would reflect badly on Lord Kwan and Genji both, making me determined to improve in the few months I had.

Uno didn't just help me to improve for Mokryon. Since she spent so much time around me, and with the cold of winter keeping us indoors, she also assisted with domestic skills. However, I couldn't have her and Koji in the same room. She expressed a fright of dogs ever since a couple had chased and bit her as a little girl.

The solstice right around the corner, she asked a question that burned in her since our first meeting, though she'd abstained from repeating. "So, you're not a lover to Lord Kwan?"

I shook my head. "I'm his prisoner, working off a debt. But we've become good friends since."

She scrunched her face, eyes looking off to nothing as she mulled it over. "He is strange. Not in a disrespectful way. Just that his decisions aren't what I expected."

I continued my needlework. "What do you mean?"

"You're his personal attendant. But he doesn't require you to go to his room for dressing or the usual expectations. You're his prisoner, but free to roam the estate. He's the enemy of Gumiho, but keeps a fox spirit in his company and highly ranked in the house. He called me back, despite almost everyone else having more experience and might be better to assist in preparing you. And you're the special guest I was appointed to wait on, but you're his servant and not a romantic interest. It's odd, don't you think?"

I chuckled. "Everything has been odd since I arrived. So, I guess I don't notice when it's particularly strange. Except sometimes."

"You mean me?"

I smiled at her.

She smiled back, demonstrating the next steps in a pattern. "If it's alright to ask, is it because you're intended for Lord Juro? Or Master Syaoran?"

"He doesn't like to be called master," I said, thoughtless. I realized again how laxed my manners were, understanding what Uno meant in my tutelage. "But, no. I'm not. For either."

She shrugged, offering a look of apology. "It's just, so much of the staff talks about how Lord Juro sends you lavished gifts, and says you're his bride."

I scoffed. "I wish I could give them away. But the truth is, I'm afraid of him."

"Because he's a Kurai?"

"Because he's intruded on me when I've tried to refuse him before. I don't want to invite his ire. Otherwise, I'd be blunt. For now, I'm still a servant. I can't be so bold."

"I understand," said Uno, stopping a laugh. "But, if you're not so attached to Lord Kwan, or he to you, why do you object?"

"I..." it was a question that'd come up so many times. And it never got easier to answer. I suppose it did look silly from an outside perspective—but if they knew, if they went through it, they'd understand. "He treats me like property rather than a person. I could never marry anyone who did that, no matter how handsome or wealthy."

She gave me a queer look. "That's fiercely independent of you. In other houses, a servant girl or boy is treated more like property than an individual. So, I guess most of us are used to it and wouldn't care."

It was my turn to reflect her expression. I hadn't noticed that in Lord Kwan's home. It wouldn't surprise me if his older brothers acted that way, but for it to be the majority? "Did your previous lord do that?"

She shook her head, shying. "The truth? He took us in. Me, and my sister, that is. We worked for him as low maids, but he fell in love with my sister and married her. Something she couldn't refuse. Though, it brought me up to learn all the things I'm showing you now. Comparatively, I'm far better off now as the attendant to a lord's special guest."

It always fascinated and horrified me to listen how the other servants saw themselves and their masters. Talks of status, competition, comparing themselves, planning, what they treated so casually and what was considered a great insult.

"But what about Master Syaoran? There's talk as well about how close the two of you are. And he is handsome. Certainly, he could afford for his wife to live comfortably—maybe not lavishly, but comfortable."

"We're just friends," I said with a laugh. "I did have a small crush when I first arrived. He was the only one who was openly kind and warm towards me. But I'm not the sort of woman he's attracted to. In any case, it'd be weird for a human and a Juneun to elope, wouldn't it?" I looked to read her expression, not only to her response, but to see if I'd used *elope* correctly in conversation.

"You refer to him as a Juneun?"

I nodded. "I don't see him or Lord Juro as Kurai. Neither does Lord Kwan or anyone here."

She took a moment to consider it. "I suppose. But, if Master Syaoran did change his mind, and confessed his feelings, would you refuse him?"

I chuckled. "I don't think that's likely to happen. But I never thought about it."

A pause took place.

"But would you?" prodded Uno, attempting a shy tease.

I shrugged, smiling. "Maybe. I could never take him seriously. He jokes too much."

Chapter 52
Match Making

The solstice came into full celebration. I dedicated time to help in the kitchen, and went long into the night making small cakes to hand out. I put the most effort into the ones for Lin, Syaoran, and Lord Kwan—as a thank you for their friendship. With exactly 1 left over, I gave it to Koji.

Games and feasting held, I couldn't help notice the quiet looks shared between Syaoran and Uno. It made me think about earlier conversations. Did Uno like Syaoran? And wanted to make sure she wasn't intruding on a relationship? From what I could gleam from stolen glances alone, the feeling was mutual.

I devised a plan. Inelegant as I was at my attempt, disguising it as practice for small talk, I thought I wasn't too suspicious in my questions and occasional return comment on Syaoran.

He wanted a girl who loved rice wine. Uno was fickle about what sorts of wines she liked, and only on occasion. He liked racing on horseback. Uno knew how to ride adeptly, though didn't enjoy it enough for sporting. With every new bit of information, it seemed like she barely met what he liked by half. When I asked what sort of man she liked, I became too suspicious.

"Why do you ask?"

Quick, I came up with some excuse. "There's always gossip about marriage. Shouldn't I expect more like it at Tetsuden?"

She pondered it, and for a moment I worried she didn't believe me. "I don't think as much. Mokryon is when men are more open to the gossip away from women, and apt to take action in staking a claim."

I cringed at the idea of being claimed. I knew Uno meant it more innocently, but it reminded me too much of Juro's behavior for me to not go a little rigid in my spine. "Is that how your sister and her lord...?"

Uno became sheepish. "No. But, it's a private matter, miss, please."

I made my apology, having to accept the new awkwardness I'd created.

When the morning of my birthday came, the air was particularly cold. I kept inside a long while, not bothering to dress and keeping my blankets wrapped around me as I stared out the window to a snow-covered garden. I became sleepy, dreamlike, staring at the beautiful white silence and the shadows panting shapes upon it.

Koji kept asleep, enjoying that I'd snuck him into my room for the night. He gave a yawn and a stretch, looking around before deciding that another nap was in order. I'd told Uno to take the day for herself, since I wanted to do things when I felt like and not work on remembering so many rules for only today.

I started to nod off again, lazy and comfortably kept between cold air and warm floors. Movement caught my eye. A white doe stepped delicately and slow, not making a sound as she foraged for food. I couldn't look away, transfixed on how elegant she moved. Every step or turn of her head, all of it like how a lady—a princess—might conduct herself.

"Hisa?"

I whipped my head to look over my shoulder. Lord Kwan stood peering through my door partially opened. I pulled my blankets closer around me. He'd seen me in my nightrobes before, but that didn't make me comfortable with it. I was still his servant, after all, even if I did want more.

"What are you looking at?" asked Lord Kwan, gentle.

"There's a—" I stopped when I looked back. The doe was gone, and not a trace was left to indicate she'd ever been there.

"Are you not going to the shrine this year?"

I shifted my gaze back to him, nodding. "I just wanted to stay warm a little while longer."

That hint of a smile came on his face. "I'll wait for you." He closed my door.

Wait for me? I looked over at Koji, who didn't stir in the least. Lord Kwan was waiting for me? What for? I hurried to dress, noticing how my deel's sleeves didn't reach over my palms as they'd done when I first got it. I'd grown more. Not surprising, I'd been here three-and-a-half years.

I still wasn't shapely or very feminine looking, except for my waist. I'd filled out in my time here, no longer too skinny, but neither was I plump. I suppose all my running about and keeping busy didn't allow for that. I would miss the cakes and other treats when I did return home, but I knew better than to dwell on a selfish thought.

Putting Koji on his leash, he sluggishly obeyed my command to get up and come with me.

Except for Juro, there wasn't a big to-do with my birthday, since I'd already had just about everything I needed. And I'd made the effort to know everyone else's birthdays, and think of what to make for them. I wasn't very good at guessing what most of the household liked or needed though. The best I could manage was sharing out the fruits Juro sent; being out of season, and ripe on their arrival, that was more pleasing than anything I came up with on my own. But at least that much made them happy. So much was sent, that they'd often become pastries to prevent them from spoiling, bringing further delight.

Lin complained that once I left, Juro would stop sending these kinds of gifts. *What are we going to do then?* Which made me laugh.

Outside my door, Lord Kwan stood, looking out over the glittering snow. I'd assumed he meant that he'd wait for me at the shrine. A battle ensued within me, trying to keep my cheeks from pinking.

When he turned to me, he said nothing about Koji. He pushed back his long hair behind his shoulder with the flick of his wrist, keeping a pleasant expression. "Shall we?"

I nodded, shallow and quick.

Koji yawned a high-pitched complaint.

"Good morning to you as well, Koji," said Lord Kwan. His gaze went back to me. "I'll allow it today."

We walked wordlessly. Syaoran waited at the edge of the path leading to the shrine, eager to give me his usual token. I smiled, thinking again of how to matchmake him and Uno. They did seem to like each other, and might make small compromises to be with each other. Uno didn't have a love of rice wine, but she didn't hate it either. And a pleasant ride could be just as nice as a thrilling race if it was with the right person.

At the shrine, I thought I saw Lord Kwan's happy expression quiet somewhat. For what reason, I didn't know. Perhaps because Gumiho was still out there. That helped me to decide what to pray for, and I wouldn't have to try outwitting him this time.

As much as I wanted to ask for him to someday return my feelings, it felt too much of an ask, and I'd already decided that our close friendship would suffice in lieu of a romance. Greedy, I'd also prayed for the welfare of my family and village.

When I opened my eyes, I answered him before he could ask. "For you to always come home safely. That's what I prayed for this year."

His brow became crooked, amused. "Hisa doubts my ability?"

I shook my head, smiling. "I hate when you come home and need to be chained. So, I prayed you'd come home safe and not need to go through that."

"But nothing for yourself?"

I shied, with Koji pressing his head against me in a silent beg to play.

Lord Kwan watched me. "You're eighteen now."

"Nineteen," I corrected.

He eyed me, as though I was the one who counted wrong. "Should I pledge to hold your wedding? Or does Syaoran have a place in mind?"

I laughed at his tease. "I don't think I'll be getting married any time soon."

He studied me, mulling over my words. "No request for paint? Or cakes?"

I shook my head, keeping my sheepish smile.

"Not a kiss?"

I chuckled. "But you already said I could have one at any time for your atonement."

"I did," agreed Lord Kwan. "But I've gotten used to that being your wish."

To that, I blinked.

"Will Syaoran get jealous?"

"Jealous of what?"

"If I kissed you again. And that's why you didn't want for it?"

I laughed. Since coming back, that'd been the center of gossip surrounding me in the house. Though I hadn't expected him to tease me so often. "We're only friends."

He kept his watch on me, bearing a gentle smile, and leaned in. "Nineteen."

I twisted my brow, looking into his eyes.

"Nineteen kisses this time."

There was no hiding my blushing. It came on too quick to battle back.

He leaned closer, closing his eyes. I did likewise, my heart throwing away any suggestion of resistance. A soft placement of his cool lips on mine, like how he'd kissed me the first time.

"One."

Then he kissed my forehead. I kept my eyes closed.

"Two."

On my nose. My cheek. A slightly deeper kiss on my lips. Back and forth between innocent and what I thought of as passionate kisses. His hand cupped my jaw at some point, and I held fast to his jacket. His fingers edged into my hair, his other hand going to the small of my back and coaxing me closer to him. With each exploratory kiss, I tried to keep up, anxious to do so again when our lips parted. How long I stood there in blind bliss, I didn't know. I savored the slow count and touch of each.

"Nineteen."

I could sense he was about to let me go and step back. I didn't let him. My hands firming their hold, I rested my head against his chest. Silent, I hoped—prayed—he'd say three words to me. Three words I somehow managed to shy away from when it counted.

He hesitated, eventually embracing me as I stayed put.

However, our moment was interrupted by an insistent Koji, openly whining that he was made to be still so long.

My birthday felt too short, leaving me to reminisce about what'd happened in the seclusion of the shrine. My mind and my heart continued to insist there was something more there, though I knew better. He was handsome and rich and powerful, and a Juneun, with beautiful ladies and pretty servant girls vying for his attention. I couldn't measure up. No matter how fond he was. The reminder of which, saddened me.

I tried to take my mind off it, and finally go through the things that had been sent for my birthday before the snows became too much.

Juro, unsurprisingly, sent more gowns. Undoubtedly, he meant for me to wear them during Mokryon. Then I remembered. I had no dress. I'd ruined the one Lord Kwan gave me, and I doubted that anything with pants wouldn't be well received at a noble gathering.

Dread filled me, now having to come to terms with an inescapable truth: I would need Juro's gifts. I would need to wear the very thing that made me feel like property. Even if I started now and didn't stop, I'm not sure I'd be able to sew up a decent one. If I'd had the sense, I would've asked Lord Kwan to send for one or two, rather than nineteen... no. It would've been wrong either way to be demanding fine clothes.

I looked at the deep periwinkle color of the skirt, and the hems of the blouses. The embroidered frogs on the blouse, overshadowed by the pattern of koi fish, were easily missed. The red ribbon that tied the pieces together helped to distract.

Another comprised of several white blouses, hemmed by either a pale orange or teal color, meant to be worn in a particular order. The skirt of it a washed green, with a simple floral pattern running down from the waist.

The final one seemed the most mature fashion. Soft, peach colored blouses and a powdered-blue skirt that faded to white towards the bottom. What made it seem the most mature were the sheer jackets, colored in white and rose. It'd taken me a moment to realize they were meant to stay over rather than be tucked under the skirt. Spread out, the end of the jacket stopped below my knees, and the wide sleeves did likewise. Beautiful things, but so much wasted fabric. And I was certain I'd somehow get them caught on something.

What other choice did I have? I didn't want to embarrass Genji, or Syaoran, or Lord Kwan.

Slippers were also sent, and the note which read more like Juro congratulated himself on having, more or less, made me into his doll to dress up. Included was his expressed desire to see me in them. I shuddered.

There was a note from Urekkato as well. I didn't want to look at it, but I also wanted a distraction from the storm of thoughts competing with each other.

I was better off ignoring it.

Hisa

What a strange thing you are. If I didn't know better, I'd think you tried to seduce Genji.

If that was your intent, I think you did an exceptional job of it.

Though, he was always soft for human girls.

And then to get so involved with Syaoran. To that, I'm not surprised.

Now, it seems you're spoiled for choice on a husband.

I'm interested to see where this goes, since I will not attend Mokryon this year.

I saw your reply to my last writing, which made me burst laughing with how obsessively you looked at it.

Your aching heart will have to bear not seeing me at least another year complete.

More to my interest is how you outwitted Juro in your last confrontation with him.

But you wound me with how you misled him about my character.

It's been a fun game with you. Though, I wish you would forget about ending the spell so often.

As I've said, I do have an interest in Kwan's relationship towards you, and I hardly see much.

If your desire really is to claim the fox for yourself, don't hesitate to ask for my help.

I can see it'd make for an entertaining relationship. More so than Kwan.

I suppose I'll help if your plan was for the Elk prince, if only to make more princelings.

Though, it'd make for less amusement in the long run.

And if none of your suitors can satisfy you, I may consider bringing you as one of mine.

Your scorn and squirming make for good sport when I'm bored.

I loathed him. I hated having made that deal with him, and now having to suffer his intrusion and his teasing. Couldn't I get even a little peace from him? It was hard enough sorting my feelings without humiliation from a Juneun prince. Is that all anyone thought? That I must be after a man because of a close friendship or in finding a kindred soul?

I took to my stationery. Writing my response in the corner. He saw through my eyes, but would he persist if he knew my feelings? I knew it was useless, but I could only hope.

Stop

Please

My vision began to blur with tears. It didn't seem to matter how angry I got if all he did was laugh at me for it. So, I stared at it, letting silent tears fall onto the paper. I didn't know when or how often he saw through my eyes. All I could do was hope he did see it, and would relent.

Chapter 53
A Beautiful Dress

Spring came swift, and with it came deliveries for our departure to Tetsuden. Among them, were cosmetics, with Uno showing me how to apply them so that my scars weren't so apparent. I practice religiously, hardly recognizing myself in the mirror at times. A small application of soft red on my lips, and my hair styled like a lady, I was staring at a stranger's reflection. Is that how I would've looked if I wasn't so accident prone? I saw parts of my mother in my reflection. Our eyes and chin were the same. But my nose and cheek bones were my father's.

I wasn't a beauty, but the girl in the mirror did look pretty enough to turn a boy's gaze. Though, maybe not enough to overcome the horrible rumors that were spread about me.

I couldn't believe how different I looked. Maybe enough to not be recognized by Juro. I relished the thought. Urekkato surely wouldn't recognize—except, if he'd looked through my eyes, he would know. My sole relief was in knowing he wouldn't go to Tetsuden Castle.

A special dress was also brought in, for the dances that would take place. Attendant or not, it was expected that I'd take part in at least one dance during Mokryon.

They were beautiful layers of soft reds, pink, white, and lavender, accented by bold streaks of slate blue at the hems. Simple, geometric patterns were embroidered into the blue, and floral designs were placed thoughtfully on the blouses and jacket of it—the more elaborate florals taking up the bottom half of the skirt, and included the occasional pair of butterflies or a hummingbird hidden amidst the threads.

The sleeves were absurdly wide, which I was told was for pockets as well as visual appeal. Ribbons for tying off were also unnecessarily long, and it took practice to get them evenly set so that their colors could be admired. And a soft twine rope, bearing Lord Kwan's colors, was fastened over my waist to show that I was there as his attendant.

It was a long ordeal to dress and undress, and I began to worry. Social rules in the noble class were more suffocating than my court attire. How did anyone get anything done?

Syaoran tapped on my door, announcing himself and asking after me. Panic set in. I didn't know how to explain that I'd been practicing getting into that dress, putting on the cosmetics and styling my hair for time. It already sounded silly and shallow in my head.

But when I didn't answer and accidentally knocked over a collection of things from the vanity, it caused enough worry for him to open the door.

I must've looked like a frightened fawn, rigid and awkward, blinking as I watched his face go from concerned to intrigued. A sly grin consumed his expression.

"Were you waiting for me?"

I frowned. "I wanted to make sure I could do this without taking hours at Tetsuden."

He stayed quiet, looking me over. "For me?"

"Stop that!"

He laughed. "I came to tell you that we'll be sharing a room at Tetsuden."

"What? Why?"

"Kwan wants company while he sleeps? I don't know."

I scrunched my brow at him. "All three of us in a room?"

"That's what I said. The others will be lodged in the common space. I'm guessing keeping you in his room is more to protect you, and keeping me there is to deter gossip. Well, lessen it at least."

"Maybe it's to keep *you* safe," I taunted.

He snickered at the idea. "Maybe." When we calmed, he stared.

"What?"

He shrugged. "You look nice."

I shied. I'd always wanted to hear things like that, to hear them genuinely said. And now, I didn't know what to do with it.

"We should show Kwan." Before I could object, horrified by the though, Syaoran grabbed my wrist and tugged me along. "He's going to see you like this during Mokryon anyway. May as well give him a first look."

"You already saw! Can't you just tell him?"

"Nope."

"Syaoran! It's not funny."

"It's not supposed to be."

Towed along, more than one house member did a double take at us, squinting. At the tea house, Kwan instructed Lin on another matter, leaving her as acting mistress while we were away. Looking at us, he gave his usual, stoic, stare. But I couldn't meet his eye, feeling exposed and tucking into myself.

"You look really nice," said Lin. "Is that what you're wearing for the dances?"

I nodded once, not daring to move my gaze from the floor.

"Reminds me of the one I wore to my first Mokryon. I might've been a little shorter than you back then."

"Wait," said Syaoran. "Then why didn't you just loan yours to Hisa?"

"If I still had it," said Lin. "Wasn't any point when I was between houses and needed the money. Not every lord takes care of their staff. You'd know that if you worked outside of Lord Kwan's house."

I stayed out of it, waiting for some cue that would allow me to hide in my room.

Lord Kwan stepped forward, lifting my chin to look at him. His eyes searched—for my scars, I realized—though he said nothing about it. "What do you think, Syaoran?"

"The same as Lin," said Syaoran, taking a casual posture.

"I'll have Uno take Koji on his walks then," said Lin, picking up previous conversation and taking notes.

I broke from Lord Kwan's touch, shaking my head. "She's afraid of dogs."

Lin stopped, giving me a quizzical look.

"Have Uno help to manage the stores and kitchen," said Lord Kwan after a pause. "Did you have someone in mind to oversee the restorations?"

Lin's brow furrowed. "I though Gi would be a good pick. Unless you planned to bring him to Tetsuden, my lord."

Lord Kwan shook his head in a single, smooth motion. "If he's better use here, that's settled."

"Lord Kwan is worried Gi will act impulsively?" teased Syaoran.

Nothing was said in response.

I was allowed to leave moments after, and didn't hesitate my retreat. A closing comment was given, reminding me to hone my confidence and not turn shy when strangers looked at me. They were right, but I hated hearing it.

I couldn't wait to get out of that dress, to take off the cosmetic, and to be my regular self again.

The day came to leave, with my things carefully packed and sinched to the saddle. Uno saw me off, fretting. My good impression during Mokryon would be a direct reflection on how she did in service to me. Another bit of pressure. A smaller pack was tied onto my saddle, since I was traveling the lightest—a gift for our host.

We set off in a trot, picking up a little speed once outside the gates and headed into the forest. There wasn't a trail that I could see, but the grasses and foliage appeared to bend out of the way for us. The air turned strangely cold, reminiscent of when I stepped through the lacquered gate. Having spent enough time in Lord Kwan's service, I recognized it as magic.

I started feeling nauseous. Not to an intolerable level, but enough to give me a headache. I loosened my grip on the reins, letting Susa take full control of our pace and direction. One of her ears swiveled back to check in on me.

Syaoran, too, reached to take my shoulder and give a shake. "Are you feeling okay?"

"I'll be fine," I mumbled.

"The spell is over," said Syaoran. "So you should be feeling better in a bit."

I nodded.

"Otherwise, it'd take until the end of summer to get into Lord Genji's lands."

"Huh?" I slowly looked around, realizing how different the forest seemed, and that we were headed towards a cleared road. When a similar spell took us to the lake, I didn't feel a thing. Maybe the dizziness was because of distance?

The trees were not the same, taking on a reddish hue in place of the usual brown of the wood. Their branches were high, and they stood further apart from each other, looking wide enough to house an entire family. There was something ancient about them, as though they'd always been there and would continue to always be there. I thought to ask if they were spirits. Surely, if the horses we rode were also spirits, couldn't a forest be made of spirits as well?

"They're beautiful, aren't they?" asked Syaoran, probably knowing my questioning expression. "The trees are why Lord Genji's ancestors chose this place to be their home. And anytime a Juneun was born in the forest, another tree would grow. The trees aren't spirits, before you ask, but there is something like magic to them. They sit at the top of this mountain, watching the centuries go by."

It sounded romantic and tragic all at once, and I found myself more mystified by the ancient place. "Is—"

"And no, Tetsuden isn't in a tree. It's a castle."

I made a quiet groan, my questions being so obvious to him.

After two hours of riding, we stopped for a break. Something I was glad for. There was a long ride still waiting, and I didn't want my arrival to be one met with stiffness and pain. Packed lunches were brought out, and wine shared, while the horses grazed.

Lord Kwan called me away, as all else let their meal settle. We walked a short distance, admiring the view.

"How do you feel?" asked Lord Kwan.

"I was a little unwell during that spell, but I'm better now."

That hint of a smile was on his face. "The spell only works in my lands, but it brought us to the boarder of Genji's territory. Can you handle a long ride?"

"I think so," I said, trying to measure the implication.

He nodded, allowing quiet to fall as we walked a little farther. "Saburo hasn't stopped complaining to me. He insists he ought to be the one to carry you, since learning you fell from another again."

I chuckled. "It wouldn't look appropriate for a servant to ride the lead stallion."

His smile widened only just. "Are you nervous?"

"A little. I'm more worried that I'll get lost the entire time."

"When we arrive, you'll see the staff uniform for Tetsuden. Genji keeps a full house, so it shouldn't be difficult to spot one of his servants to help orientate you."

I offered a sheepish smile in return.

"You'll be the one to present our gift," said Lord Kwan. "Since the rest of my company is men, it looks better that the lady in my entourage does it. It's bound up, so the key thing is to not drop it on reveal, and keep your eyes and head low when you offer it."

"Doesn't sound too difficult," I said. "Is it heavy?"

He shook his head. "Since Genji outranks me in society, it's appropriate that I bring something to show gratitude. If it were Kwang hosting, no gift would be necessary."

More rules to noble society. I wasn't sure I'd remember it all. Though, once I went home, I supposed I wouldn't have to. It was unlikely that I'd attend anything formal after my release.

Riding on, I understood his concern. It was late into the afternoon when we came to the first gates of Tetsuden. And while it'd been a downhill ride on a gentle sloping path, I still began to stiffen.

It looked like a city at the base of the actual castle, pressed against a sheer mountain face. White, stone walls and yellow, wood rooves marked out the castle, as well as being the tallest structure. The same scheme was applied to buildings of some importance, while more subdued architecture made the rest.

It seemed more town-like once in the first gate. Storehouses and livestock holds and craft stations sat tangled among thoughtfully placed stone and trees. Bamboo water catchers kept track of the time, none situated too closely lest their sounds overlap. Servants shuffled about their tasks, with some guests mixed in. We were escorted to the next gate, passing by a pretty park tucked out of the way of the main path.

Beyond the second wall, it appeared less crowded in terms of buildings, and more parks and gardens were visible. A lake was also there, with cozy looking accommodations for more notable guests. From there, we were led to the innermost wall, where a smaller lake was placed and there was no true distinction of where the gardens ended and parks began.

At the very base of the castle, Genji waited, presenting more regal than when he'd arrived at Lord Kwan's home. Dismounting, we made our polite greeting. I kept still while brief conversation was held between the two lords, until I was cued to present our gift. I tried not to let my eyes go wide. It was a blanket of the softest fur. I'd only ever seen sable fur once, a swatch that a passing merchant boasted, but I never forgot it. If the merchant was honest, and that small bit was priced so high, then a blanket was a rich gift indeed.

A servant took the offering from me, ceremony in his every movement.

Guests were expected to still arrive into the following day, which brough a small comfort. At least I wouldn't be bombarded with so many new faces right from the start. As our horses were taken, and we were guided to our room, I kept looking over my shoulder and back, trying to quickly memorize my way. We'd be staying on the third floor of the castle, in a spacious apartment (though they still called it a room).

Servants carried our things, keeping step behind us. It really was more elaborate than court at Lord Kwan's villa. For all his land, Lord Kwan kept his house small. I couldn't imagine if I'd come into Genji's service. Five years or twenty, I would probably never find my way.

Not that I had much time to ponder, as we were expected to change out of our riding attire and ready ourselves for the first banquet. A sheer divide provided me with some privacy in the room, but I still peered behind me now and again to make sure I was alone. I knew Lord Kwan wouldn't allow Syaoran to so much as tease about it, but the nervousness I felt in sharing a room with the two of them caused me to constantly check.

Chapter 54
Tetsuden

The evening went off smoothly.

It was the following morning that alarmed me.

"Hisa," whispered Syaoran, shaking me.

I groaned, swatting away his gentle interruption. Only to wake when I felt hot lips against my cheek. I jumped. He chuckled.

"Good. You're awake," said Syaoran, still in his night robe. "We're supposed to be attending Lord Kwan, remember?"

I was about to kick off my blankets when my hand sensibly clung on.

Again, he chuckled, quiet. "Hurry up. We can get breakfast afterwards."

He left me to my side of the sheer, ignoring my annoyed expression.

I didn't bother with fixing up my hair or hiding my scars, hurrying to get dressed. I needed to assist Syaoran in the morning grooming routine of Lord Kwan, more for presentation than anything. I remembered most of it from the last time I acted, truly acted, as his attendant, and from Uno's tutoring; though, her instruction was more focused on a lady's routine rather than a man's. I still forgot what order the combs were used.

Breakfast and after left Syaoran and I alone to do with as we pleased. I'd selected the winter dress Juro sent, hoping he wouldn't recognize me if I avoided the ones he wanted me to wear. That, and it was brisk this early into spring and so high in the mountains. A warmer dress felt more comfortable. I applied my cosmetic and styled my hair while Syaoran unpacked. He insisted he didn't need my help, and I'd brought so little that putting things away took no time at all.

"Enjoy the castle. It's only a matter of time before Kwan or Genji will want to speak with you. And Juro won't dare show up early since he's not a personal friend to the host."

"You don't need me to do anything?"

He shook his head. "I'll stock the room and head out myself."

"Stock the room?"

"We typically don't at home, but in a big place like Tetsuden, attending servants stock their lord's room with things like fruits or incense so he can retire from the day early if he wants."

"I could help out, so you don't have to go back and forth so much."

He grinned, making me feel uncomfortable. "Hisa is looking for excuses to be alone with me."

"I am not!"

"Are you planning to take advantage of me? I'm too tired from the journey to fight back. Be gentle on me."

"You're not funny."

He laughed. "You're blushing."

"Will you stop? I was trying to help."

He waved me off, still snickering. And I didn't hesitate to leave.

On my way out, I went slow, trying to make sure I could find my way back. Though I hardly started to walk the nearest park when my luck ran out.

Grabbed, a hand over my mouth, and pulled around a corner, fear and frustration competed in me. I wiggled, trying to dig in my nails, and trying to bite, as my legs kicked.

"You're feistier now," said Urekkato, hot breath in my ear.

I struggled harder.

"Calm down, and I'll let go."

Huffing, and unable to do much to break free, I held still. The moment he started to release me, I pushed away.

He chuckled. "You're almost cute when you're mad. Maybe that's why Kwan brought you."

"You said you weren't coming."

"I lied."

I turned, walking away, and stumbled to a halt when he took hold of my wrist.

"Aren't you going to greet me?"

"Maybe if you didn't grab me and gag me," I snapped. Only after did I remember that he was still a prince and I was a servant, and my face paled from the angry red state it'd become.

"Would you speak to me if you saw me coming? Answer honestly."

I furrowed my brow, dropping my gaze to where he held me and to the ground after. "No."

"I did see your response."

I looked to meet his eye.

"I'm not going to stop, I just want you to know I saw your reply."

I tried to pull away, my anger building back up. He laughed.

"You know, most people beg my forgiveness when they've offended me."

"Why would I beg forgiveness from someone who enjoys tormenting me?"

He smiled, sly. "You might need a favor from me later."

"I doubt it," I said, working in vain to pry off his fingers.

"And if you're against Juro, why are you wearing that?"

"I didn't have anything else!"

"Nothing?" He let go. "Guess that settles a few assumptions. If Kwan isn't dressing you to mark his territory, then intimacy probably isn't there. But what about the fox?"

I ignored him, eager to get away. I was fuming, searching for anywhere else to be as I walked, somewhere open where I couldn't get snatched up. Looking ahead again, I nearly collided with Urekkato.

"You and Kwan are the only ones who will do that," said Urekkato with a grin. "Everyone else can't wait to get my attention and grovel."

"I don't want your attention," I said, keeping my tone low and side stepping to continue on my way.

"So, it *is* the fox?"

I kept walking.

"Or is it Genji?"

I kept my pace.

Wandering, I found a place open and empty beside the larger of the lakes, which turned out to be several bisected. The ground had been dug out and filled with water to create the vast ponds and give the illusion of the walkways and buildings floating atop it all. It was pretty to explore. Bamboo and carefully selected trees gave the illusion of walking through a forest, and the guest rooms or other accommodations acted as a pseudo village that was tucked away. I must've walked it for an hour or more, admiring the dark wood and black roof tiles against the gravel pathways.

As long as the main road was in sight, I could find my way back.

A bridge, with a shelter built over the middle third of it, offered the most splendid view. Looking over the glittering water, with greenery and parts of the guest houses backed up to it, I felt enchanted. It really did seem like one of those dream-like water paintings.

Other guests walked by, or stopped to appreciate the scene. One stood a short distance away, enjoying the tranquility almost as long as I had. A woman, tall and still in her riding clothes, with a cherry-colored blotch of skin on her lower left eye that spilled onto her cheek. When she did take notice that someone stood there for a similar time, she looked over, gleaming my attention.

"A human?"

I said nothing, instead giving a polite bow in acknowledgement.

"Oh, you must be Kwan's human," said the woman. "I'd heard you might be here. Not very pretty though. With all the chatter I thought you'd be some great beauty, but you're rather ordinary."

I regretted being polite, needing to silently remind myself that my manners were a reflection of Lord Kwan and Genji.

"So how do you like it here? Tetsuden, I mean."

My brow bent, realizing I had to come up with an answer and not babble about it. "It's a lot to take in."

She laughed, leaning against the rail. "I can imagine! I haven't been to Kwan's estate, but I've heard it's small. He's never been one for showing off. Direct, to the point, the necessities. It's what made him fun to spar with."

"Spar with?" I cocked a brow. "But you're..." before I could accidentally cause insult, I let my words hang unfinished.

"A woman. But we Samjos have never been the sort to follow every convention if it doesn't suit us. Because of that, we get labeled things like *rowdy* or *undisciplined*."

"Even as a Juneun?"

She smirked. "If we conformed like everyone else, we wouldn't have come into as a high a station. So the labels don't bother us."

I smiled, looking back to the pond and the numerous carp swimming through in a dazzling display of variety.

"You don't say much."

I gave a sheepish expression. "I'm not used to nobles talking to me, my lady."

"Well, you're polite. And it's Towa."

I gave a bow for recognition. "Hisa."

"Hm. We have similar names then."

I didn't see how, but that hardly mattered when I spotted Juro in the distance. I made a respectful goodbye, with the excuse that I'd lingered too long and needed to attend my lord. Walking towards the main road, I prayed he didn't notice me.

Catching his reflection, my prayers were for not. He'd started following me. I picked up my pace, trying not to seem panicked. What I needed was somewhere to hide, but I'd only just arrived and didn't know of anywhere. My next hope was that one of Genji's servants would hurry to me and fetch me for Lord Kwan or some other matter, but it also seemed unlikely.

He wasn't supposed to be here this early. That's what I'd been told.

I walked to the castle entrance, pretending not to notice his following, or that he'd also picked up pace. My saving grace was that he kept to good manners himself and wasn't shouting for me.

Maybe I could lose him in going back to my room, or find Syaoran and make up some excuse. As I turned a corner, I caught a glimpse of how much he'd closed the distance between us. I didn't have time to come up with something clever. Nor would I be able to always avoid him if he recognized me already.

A new plan formed in my head, out of desperation. But it hinged on either Syaoran or Lord Kwan being in the room. So, I prayed, wordless and frequent, that Syaoran wasn't finished yet with stocking the room and would be there. If ever I needed luck, it was now.

Turning another corner, Juro was catching up—almost in range to call respectfully.

Up the last flight of stairs, I hurried more to get to our hostel. Opening the door, I found Syaoran setting up the last fixings of a fruit plate.

"Hisa?" He cocked a brow at my expression.

"I need you to kiss me. Right now!" I said, low.

I didn't give him time to object or ask questions, nor did I close the door. Putting my hands on his face, I pulled him in to kiss, straddling him. I tried to imitate the exploratory kiss Lord Kwan did. He caught on, wrapping his arms around me, and pressing me against him as he took charge.

His hands grabbed at my blouse, tugging it loose. One moving down to find my hip and glide behind, fingertips barring into my skin. He shifted to get more comfortable, accidentally dropping me and knocking over the display of fruits. I squeaked in surprise. But he didn't relent, keeping himself between my thighs. One hand held himself up from crushing me, the other sliding from my back to wander elsewhere, tugging at my dress to allow himself beneath. Likewise, his lips moved from my mouth to my neck.

I realized he took my plea to mean something else. In a new fit of panic, I pushed against his chest, trying to gain his attention in a whisper. "Syaoran!"

He chuckled. "Wait," said Syaoran, playful as he sat up. "The door is still open. Let me—"

I stopped as well, both of us panting, and followed his gaze. Juro stood in the door way with a horrified expression, walking away in a defeated manner. I calmed in the moment, taking the opportunity to scoot away and sit up. Syaoran gave me a quizzical expression, getting up and taking measured strides to the door.

My hair fell out of its style partway, and my clothes needed readjustment. The red from my lips had smudged off on him, making us both look a little absurd. I gathered myself, bracing for what I might need to do next.

The door closed, and Syaoran looked back at me, but I didn't dare break the silence first.

"You know, you could've told me that you planned to use me."

"I didn't have time," I whispered. "He was right behind me."

A look of mischief consumed him, and he walked to Lord Kwan's bed, laying half on it. "So, do we pick up where we left off?"

I was about to argue, stopping as I started to notice just how handsome he was. My irritation fast fading, I reached for him, fingers trailing over his cheek and into his hair. He was warm. He was always warm.

"You bit me," said Syaoran.

"I'm sorry," I said, transfixed.

"Do you want to bite me again?"

I withdrew my hand, but only a moment. It felt like I remembered something and forgot it in the same second. "No..."

"What do you want to do?"

"I..." I knew what I wanted to say. What I wanted him to do. But there was something in the way—a feeling wrestling with my fascination. "I want..." My eyes wandered away, looking to my hand and questioning why I was stroking his cheek.

"Are you in love with me?"

"Yes," I said, realizing that wasn't right. I blinked, breaking my gaze and recoiling my hand. "No."

Then it started to subside, the way I'd seen him, going back to how he'd always been. It dawned on me then that he'd taunted me and used his fox essence.

"Will you stop that?" I demanded, my fury returning.

He chuckled. "Just admit you have a crush on me. You beg me to kiss you, then you bite me, then you beg me to kiss you. I'm getting mixed signals. Just admit it so we can move on."

"There's nothing for me to admit to you," I said, firm.

"Why?"

I said nothing, headed for the door.

Syaoran continued to toy with me, getting up to follow and carrying a laugh in his voice. "Why won't you just admit you want me?"

"Because I'm in love with Kwan!" I cupped my hands over my mouth. My spine went cold, my eyes wide, and my knees shook as I looked at Syaoran's face.

He blinked, his expression blank. I could tell he was trying to see if I was being truthful, if he should make fun of me. For a while, we just stared at each other, one of us horrified and the other perplexed.

"You're serious?"

I dropped my hands, looking down to the floor and instinctively hiding behind my arms.

"I was only joking when I said you were..."

I kept still, scared and humiliated.

"But, then... why did you want me to...?"

Shaking my head, I summoned the courage to face him. "I know he doesn't feel the same way. I don't want to be in love, but I am. When I first asked you to..."

He raised a brow, keeping my eye. "It's because of something his brothers, or someone else said. But, you know that Genji's wife was—"

"Maybe it was a fluke," I said. "One romance between a Juneun and a human. But it didn't last. I'm not like Feng or Eumeh or—"

Syaoran took me into a protective embrace. "Stop that."

"It's true! Even his brothers think Genji's romance was ridiculous."

"Who cares what Kwan's brothers think? Have you seen how miserable those shits are? And you're going to listen to them?"

I laughed, the best I could manage in my state.

"What if he *does* feel the same?"

I shook my head. "I don't want him to be like Genji. The way he misses Isaden."

Syaoran gave space, looking down at me. "For as long as I've known Kwan, he's been a lonely person. He's already like Genji."

I knew he meant to cheer me up. But, how could I explain that more than just Lord Kwan's brothers didn't think he felt a love for me? Or that I didn't want to complicate more in his life? My forehead dropped into his chest, and I sighed with frustration.

"Isn't it better to have a little bit of happiness, than centuries of isolation. He already smiles more when you're around."

I said nothing.

"And if there's no romantic feelings with Kwan, you always have Juro."

I laughed. "Don't say that."

Chapter 55
Jilted Love

We'd been called to the top of the castle. A dispute made from Juro. It was already an awkward situation; now it involved Genji's mediation. At a wide table, Syaoran and I sat to one side, Genji opposite us, leaving Lord Kwan and Juro to sit to either remaining end. We were all far from each other. The table could easily accommodate a dozen or more men comfortably.

Before a word was said on the matter, Urekkato intruded, bearing a smug look. Claiming that the table was imbalanced, and in need of an impartial party to be fair to Juro. He lorded his title as prince to push through polite objection.

When Genji looked to me, I shook my head in a shallow and rapid motion. He sighed, and I realized my mistake. Urekkato now sat beside him, waiting to partake in the meeting.

"I have been wronged by your servant, Lord Kwan," said Juro. "First, it is your brother who beats on my bride, and now Syaoran has fornicated with her and robbed me of my wedding rite. And I suspect this is not the first time he's violated her."

"That is a serious accusation," said Urekkato. "With a serious punishment."

Genji looked from Lord Kwan, to Juro, to me, and back to Juro, in no great rush. "You are betrothed?"

"Not officially," said Urekkato, interrupting Juro's start. "A proposal has been made. But I do not recall that there was any answer given. Or, has that now changed?"

"There is a planned announcement of it the summer following this," said Juro, dismissive.

Lord Kwan kept silent and stoic, watching Juro the entire time.

"Hisa and I are fated for each other," continued Juro. "Lord Genji, surely you can sympathize with my position and my distress."

Shy, but needing to weigh, Genji answered. "I suppose."

"Hisa," said Urekkato. "Has an answer been given?"

I shook my head, my hands holding tight to the skirt of my dress.

"Speak up," said Urekkato.

"No," I said, timid under the pressure.

Urekkato tilted his head, resting it in the palm of his hand.

"I haven't accepted," I continued, quelling any implication of a delay in my agreement. This was likely my only chance to be candid about it, and avoid further unwanted advances. "Nor do I plan to."

"Hisa!" called Juro in alarm.

Syaoran put a hand up to his mouth, forming a loose fist to press on his lips and prevent laughter.

"I did try to express this before."

"But, you said—" started Juro.

"As a servant," interrupted Lord Kwan, "and in a sentence of debt owed, Hisa is not in a position to speak with bluntness. That is a liberty enjoyed by those above her station."

"A case of miscommunication," said Urekkato, relishing in the awkwardness.

"Hisa," said Juro, half begging and half scolding. "Reconsider, my love."

"It's well known in our master's household that Hisa has no feelings towards Lord Juro," said Syaoran. "Attempts were made to persuade her of the benefits, but she is adamant on her indifference."

"Indifference?" roared Juro.

While things went in the direction I wanted, I weighed in again, doing my best to sound like a respectable serf or lady, and not like a village girl. "I apologize, Lord Juro, if I was unclear. I never meant to lead you into the belief of otherwise. And the truth is that I will only marry for love, and not for any benefits."

"Hisa," said Juro, looking directly at me. "Reconsider. The life of a servant is uncertain, when your lord might turn you out on a whim and poverty is prevailed onto you. As wife to a lord with lands and capital, there is no such fear. Especially if there is a son between us—then you are secured. You cannot tell me you prefer Syaoran over myself, knowing that."

"It's been well established in my house," said Lord Kwan, "that Hisa and Syaoran share a deep affection. Are you really so surprised?"

In hearing that, my neck started to sink into my shoulders. Syaoran, however, crinkled his nose in the fight to keep from laughter.

"But what can he do for her?" demanded Juro. "He has no home, no titles, nothing to give her."

"That does complicate the decision," said Urekkato. "I suppose the final decision falls to her father, or whoever heads her family."

I needed to restrain myself from glaring. Prince or not, he said it to deliberately reverse what progress was made.

"I've said that I would only agree to marry for love," I said, determined to reclaim control. "Even if he was the poorest man in the world."

"I wonder if a father shares the same sentiment," said Urekkato.

Lord Kwan shifted his gaze to the Cat prince.

"If there is no formal union," said Genji, after a time, "what is the offense?"

"There is no strict ruling on a servant laying with another servant," said Lord Kwan. "Unless the lord of the house establishes otherwise, which I have not."

"Then, there is no offense?" asked Genji.

"Only in pride," said Urekkato. "Typically, this would be sorted out with a duel. First blood drawn ending the match."

"Is that not excessive?" asked Genji.

"Surely, during Mokryon, we can overlook the matter," said Lord Kwan.

"I've invested in the engagement," said Juro. "Now I'm to accept refusal on all sides?"

"Unless Syaoran is willing to take up a sword," said Urekkato, smug in his expression.

"No," I said, a little too loudly. All eyes on me, I thought fast on how to pacify the situation. "My Lord Juro, if it's a matter of expense, I'll return your gifts. But don't let blood spill on my account, please."

Juro glowered. "Then do so now."

I froze.

"My every gift to you," demanded Juro.

Urekkato snickered. "Lord Juro demands that Hisa undress this instant?"

Syaoran took a turn to glare at the Cat prince, about to argue when Lord Kwan spoke.

"That is an affront to me. Hisa is my attendant. I will not have my servants humiliated and made to strip publicly."

Between the words spoken, and the lowered tone, Juro reined in his scowl. "Very well."

"No blood, no stripping, it is a dull revenge for a jilted lover," said Urekkato, trying to rile up Juro again.

"Out of respect for my friendship with Lord Kwan, I will retract my last demand," said Juro, level.

"It's only a shame you don't hold that same respect for the woman you desire as your wife," said Syaoran.

I paled; certain his comment would undo the dying tension.

"My Lord Genji," continued Syaoran. "For your late wife, Lady Isaden, would you have behaved this way? Or you, my prince?"

Urekkato quirked a brow with interest, his tails flicking behind him. Genji, breathed in, maintaining himself as he considered. I understood Syaoran's outburst then: an appeal to their own egos, trying to turn it to my favor.

Silence. And I didn't know if that was a good sign, or a bad one.

"I will recoup your losses, Lord Juro," said Lord Kwan. "Since it has been invested into my household."

"It's not about the cost," growled Juro. "The investment into a bride is more than material things."

"Perhaps I've misheard," said Urekkato, "but to who do you refer? This assembly has confirmed that Hisa was not engaged to Lord Juro, and therefore cannot be the bride to which he invested in."

"That is true," said Genji, thoughtful.

"And there is no law to support retribution on jealous love without a break in contract. Since no contract, verbal or otherwise exists, there is no crime," continued Urekkato, delighting in his role. "Unless there is evidence not yet brought up, we may dismiss and continue on with festivities as planned." He smiled, giving me a knowing look.

Grumbling, Juro stood, being the first to leave.

The rest of us remained where we were in silence.

Lord Kwan stood next, and Syaoran cued me to follow suit. He gave a polite bow and apology to Genji, and we did the same. Even though, to my knowing, neither Lord Kwan, nor Syaoran or myself did anything to warrant an apology. Juro instigated the fuss. All I could think is that it was for the sake of manners in high society; something that needed to happen regardless of whether or not I agreed with it.

We left, following Lord Kwan wordlessly.

Before descending the stairs, I couldn't bear it anymore, and spoke up. "I'm sorry, my lord." While I couldn't tell what Lord Kwan was feeling in that moment, I didn't want him to be upset with me, quietly or otherwise.

He stopped. And so did we.

Breathing deep, he looked back at me, seeming weary. "It is to Lord Genji who you ought to say that. And to thank him."

I nodded, dropping my gaze. It was my first (and probably only) Mokryon, and I'd caused such a commotion through circumstance. "Are you angry?"

He resumed his stride. "No."

"At least let us better explain to you, my lord," said Syaoran, in a gesture to remove some of the pressure from me.

Lord Kwan said nothing.

I stole a glance to Syaoran, seeing his ears flatten.

Chapter 56
Lord Kwan XIV

*A*nd why does she think I'm pregnant with your child?

When Kwan's mind began to worry too much, leaving Lin, as inexperience as she was, in charge of the house, that memory climbed to the forefront of his thoughts. It replayed in his mind, offering more details with how annoyed she felt. There was something endearing about it. Not that he wanted to upset her, but there was the way she argued and challenged him that he found sweet. The absurdity of it summoned a quiet smile on him every time he glanced to check in on her.

Watching her in awe of the woods as they rode, he adored her. Every expression sincere. His own turning solemn when seeing warm conversation between her and Syaoran.

She'd repeatedly stated the innocents of their relationship. But the day Syaoran presented her in the tea house suggested otherwise. There was a kind of pride on the fox. It was a subject Kwan couldn't comprehend. Was it platonic or intimate?

In delivering every kiss, he couldn't deny his feelings. It was a genuine emotion he hadn't kept in his heart in centuries. Not since he was a younger Juneun, foolhardy and playing at being a man as he made careless oaths. But if her heart was reserved for Syaoran, or that she didn't fully understand her feelings, revealing his own was sure to complicate things.

Whatever her feelings, for whomever, Kwan didn't want to stand in the way of her happiness.

There was an awkwardness in tandem with exhaustion that first night, reminding Kwan of just how innocent Hisa truly was. He wanted to safeguard her, be with her, and felt a guilt for it. That he was somehow in her way.

It got the better of him somewhere in the night. After a full day's ride, she'd likely feel the repercussions of it, being unaccustomed to lengthy travel. Stepping soundlessly, he went to her futon, seeing her clutch her covers. Far from a picture of elegance, but genuine. She muttered her dreams, her expression changing slightly. He smiled, performing his healing spells to allow a more restful sleep.

Syaoran, more experienced, picked up the bulk of morning duties the following day. However, it couldn't be overlooked of how well they worked together. Kwan decided then to allow them the first day for each other. In stocking the room, they'd undoubtedly keep in each other's company to speed things along, and would find themselves finished before long. Whatever they decided on after wasn't his business.

Still, his mind was cruel in putting together the scenarios of what he'd do in Syaoran's position. Which parks and ponds to visit, and what she might like to view or try. It wasn't his place.

In his own wandering, his former master called on him, summoning him to the castle's top floor apartment.

"I've already drawn up the documents. Tetsuden and all adjoining lands are your inheritance."

Kwan stopped his sip of lotus wine, blinking.

"I... You know that I have no heirs," said Genji. "I must either name my successor, or allow my lands to fall to the crown to handle."

"Are you sure this is wise?" asked Kwan, setting down his cup.

"I had twenty-five pupils in my long life. Of twenty-five, seventeen survive. Of twenty-five, four sincerely respected Isa. Of the four, three survive. The wisdom is in choosing a successor most like myself."

"Because of Hisa?"

Genji remained silent for thought. "I have contemplated it this last decade. For most of it, I thought your obsession would put you into the grave. In finding you retain a gentle compassion, I reconsidered." He drank from his cup, letting quiet linger while he thought of how better to explain. "She's a gentle soul. And she's fond of you. I admit I was curious when the rumor came to me, though it wasn't until you openly held court that I knew something had changed in you."

Kwan breathed out a sigh, not having the heart to tell his old master that it was a façade to hide his secret. "It seemed the natural course of action. Lord Zhen held court in the same space of time, and likely to greater success."

"Success?" echoed Genji. "What is the success of a social gathering except to an unmarried man and an unmarried woman? But which of them knows the state of the people in their territory? I came to see if you'd taken an interest in those who relied on you. Hisa is an honest person, from what I can tell. Through her, I learned that you carry out your duties to the people without the need for recognition. Is it any wonder why so few achievements are tallied on you when you refuse basic acknowledgement."

Kwan stared. In a twist of fate, his delay in justice resulted in a different sentencing to a girl who would become the catalyst for his inheritance. By chance, when she'd been locked with him and chose to show compassion rather than give in to fear, and he in turn felt obligated to repay her, they'd confided in each other. He grew fonder of her, and she of him, all leading to this moment. An unlikely friendship, resulting from inconvenient circumstance, would make him the wealthiest in his family—heir to an ancient house.

"Do you accept it?"

Kwan bowed from his seat. "It is an honor."

Genji nodded, raising his cup and waiting for Kwan to do likewise before they drank. "Will you move your household when it is yours?"

Kwan paused. Overwhelmed by the prestige of it—something that would make pressure from his family cease—he didn't think of the logistics of it all. "No. They're comfortable in their stations there. I'll need to appoint a steward, assuming these lands require the bulk of my attention, and check in when I can."

He knew it was only a half-truth. He settled Mount Tora to press back Gumiho, and she was still out there. Any serious consideration to reside in Tetsuden would need to wait.

"It makes a better place to hold court."

Kwan half scoffed, bemused. "I suppose it would be expected of me, regardless of any lacking in enthusiasm."

"And the girl?"

Kwan's mind and movement stumbled at the question. He accented himself, clearing his voice of any melancholy and maintaining dignity. "When her sentence ends, she is free to choose her own way. I will not insist on her."

"It does you good to keep humans in your household, to know the people."

"So I've come to learn." He held out his cup, quickly refilled by a servant.

A spell of silence passed. Genji stood, gesturing for Kwan to do the same.

They walked the private grounds, keeping in conversation of things to come. In a short time, they came into the parks and parted ways. Genji to his role in welcoming guests, and Kwan to take in what he'd been told.

Lord of Tetsuden.

If things were different, if they really were as he allowed them to appear, and if Hisa liked it well enough... He scoffed, chastising himself and chalking it up to having seen his old master again. The mere idea was ridiculous.

So why did he hate himself for thinking that?

It wasn't such a ridiculous idea for his master. His heart was cold. Filled with the shame and expectations that burdened him since his last act of arrogance—a proclamation of love, of fury—and the tragedies that followed. Was he doomed to repeat his mistakes? Or was it simply wanting to live up to the legacy of Genji?

Further philosophizing stopped when he was summoned back to Genji's apartment.

Juro, in searching for Kwan to spill his plight, exposed it to Genji.

The accusation confirmed what he'd known: her heart already held Syaoran. It wasn't surprising, but the finality pained him. Needles in his chest, pinning muscle and pricking at his lungs and heart. Though he'd sworn not to get in the way of her happiness, and would've willingly handled it alone if Juro had found him first.

Now involving their host, that the offense was given by an invited guest under his roof, Kwan couldn't quietly aside it. However, Genji's affection couldn't be so apparent; not voided all together, which would make the case go quickly in his favor.

The issue became all the more complicated when Urekkato found them out. As much as he wanted to signal to Hisa and Syaoran, they were too far for him to do so discretely. Hisa's nervous action solidified the Cat prince's claim. Unaccustomed to politics, she couldn't have known to hold completely still and give no indication to her opinion of him; allowing time to courteously decline.

Predictably, Urekkato antagonized both ends, pulling at Hisa's naivety and Juro's pride. There wasn't much Kwan could do tactfully. Distracted by his own petty distress, he needed to restrain himself until clear opportunity allowed him to act.

"As a servant," interrupted Kwan, "and in a sentence of debt owed, Hisa is not in a position to speak with bluntness. That is a liberty enjoyed by those above her station."

Counter after counter, Kwan resisted his urge to make heated demands of his own, for the sake of not seeing her so miserable. Then, she surprised him. Weighing in herself, and taking a modest approach, Kwan's annoyance subsided. Impressed, he quietly conceded to himself another reality: that she was not helpless, and had courage.

"I apologize, Lord Juro, if I was unclear. I never meant to lead you into the belief of otherwise. And the truth is that I will only marry for love, and not for any benefits."

Juro's expression became severe in return. "Reconsider. The life of a servant is uncertain, when your lord might turn you out on a whim and poverty is prevailed onto you. As wife to a lord with lands and capital, there is no such fear. Especially if there is a son between us—then you are secured. You cannot tell me you prefer Syaoran over myself, knowing that."

There was truth to that, though Kwan wouldn't sit idle with a soft defamation of his own character. Before Hisa lost face, before Urekkato toyed with the circumstance, he spoke again. "It's been well established in my house that Hisa and Syaoran share a deep affection. Are you really so surprised?"

"But what can he do for her?" demanded Juro. "He has no home, no titles, nothing to give her."

Kwan felt a flare of indignation, needing to temper himself from haughty words. If need be, he would name Syaoran steward, regardless of principle or perception, so long as it served to nullify Juro's point.

"That does complicate the decision," said Urekkato, causing Kwan to hold his tongue a while longer. "I suppose the final decision falls to her father, or whoever heads her family."

Again, Hisa surprised him, speaking up to maintain her adamant stance in an even tone. She was determined to fight her battle with dignity, rather than fly into a rage or cower, and he admired her for it.

All appreciation ceased with Urekkato's next underhanded remark. Kwan gave a warning look, largely ignored, as his mind raced to find some new solution. He did, though at the cost of verbally admitting to the truth of the matter: that Hisa loved Syaoran.

"There is no strict ruling on a servant laying with another servant," said Kwan. "Unless the lord of the house establishes otherwise, which I have not."

"Then, there is no offense?" asked Genji.

"Only in pride," said Urekkato. "Typically, this would be sorted out with a duel. First blood drawn ending the match."

Kwan leered.

"Is that not excessive?" asked Genji.

"Surely, during Mokryon, we can overlook the matter," said Kwan.

"I've invested in the engagement," said Juro. "Now I'm to accept refusal on all sides?"

"Unless Syaoran is willing to take up a sword," said Urekkato, smug in his expression.

Again, Kwan needed to quiet his temper. Outrage would only drive the situation into needless action to satisfy honor. It was interrupted with Hisa's nervous outburst, forcing Kwan to reel his mind and search for what next to do to protect both her and Syaoran.

"Then do so now. My every gift to you," demanded Juro.

Urekkato snickered. "Lord Juro demands that Hisa undress this instant?"

Kwan didn't miss the glare from Syaoran. Of course he would want to shield her, but in this matter his speaking out might be met with steel. For both their sakes, he needed to speak first and with authority to halt haughty statements from Syaoran.

"That is an affront to me. Hisa is my attendant. I will not have my servants humiliated and made to strip publicly."

It was enough to get Juro to reconsider. Urekkato was another matter, unyielding to Kwan's own position. He thought his effort fast undone when Syaoran edged in.

"It's only a shame you don't hold that same respect for the woman you desire as your wife."

Fool, thought Kwan. Though he couldn't blame his friend. He was in love, and love made men heedless. It only made sense that he saw the mere suggestion as an injustice. His next words, however, further impressed Kwan.

"My Lord Genji, for your late wife, Lady Isaden, would you have behaved this way? Or you, my prince?"

Perhaps they were well suited for each other. In many ways, they were similar, and now took cues from the other in times of distress. And Kwan had to concede another truth: Syaoran loved Hisa.

"I will recoup your losses, Lord Juro," said Kwan, keeping a stoic tone so as not to give himself away. "Since it has been invested into my household."

"It's not about the cost," growled Juro. "The investment into a bride is more than material things."

Kwan held back a wince, thinking how to work around the matter and back into his favor, despite his own weariness. Thankfully, he didn't need to. Urekkato was bored with the ordeal.

"Perhaps I've misheard, but to who do you refer? This assembly has confirmed that Hisa was not engaged to Lord Juro, and therefore cannot be the bride to which he invested in."

In the silence that followed Juro's departure, Kwan digested all that transpired. And he came to terms that his feelings would not be returned. They belonged to another. With a heavy heart, he forced himself to accept that fact, convincing himself that love was too much of a distraction.

While he had the strength, he stood to make his formal apology for the inconvenience.

Walking, he shoved out fanciful and hurtful thoughts. Relegating himself to be as he was before.

"I'm sorry, my lord."

Caught off guard, he stopped. His heart pained at how she sounded. Perhaps she felt she'd disgraced him, or that he ought to have fought harder for her. Regardless of reasons, he couldn't bear to think he'd disappointed her. But he couldn't go to her as he pleased. It wouldn't be appropriate. Especially in the presence of her own beloved. He needed to give some distance, and allow the event to settle.

Breathing in, Kwan steadied himself, and looked back at her. "It is to Lord Genji who you ought to say that. And to thank him."

"Are you angry?"

He couldn't. He couldn't face her when she appeared so defeated. "No." It was not his place to comfort her.

Syaoran said something in return. Kwan, wrapped up in his own pity and having missed it, continued on.

Chapter 57
Duel

That eve and the following day held more awkward tension. In staying true to my word, I'd dressed in my riding clothes so I could return everything else I'd brought to Juro. Finding where his room was, and delivering it without putting myself in a horrible situation, however, I didn't know how to do.

Alone in the room, I listened to the indistinguishable chatter of the crowds outside. While I wanted to walk the grounds and take in the scenery, I didn't want to further embarrass Lord Kwan, Genji, or Syaoran. It was still expected that I would join one dance; and disrespectful if I rejected every one.

A servant came to my door, saying that the high lord requested my company. I remembered that I needed to make my own apology to him, and to thank him for not pressuring me into anything, dismissing the complaint. Following, I thought it odd that I wasn't taken to the top floor like before, instead stopping one short and down a corridor. Not that it mattered, since I knew Genji wasn't the sort to compromise me.

Which is why I was surprised to see I'd been led to Urekkato's room. My spine went rigid and my legs stiff. I felt the life drain from me, knowing that I needed to find a way to escape while also knowing I couldn't outrun him or hide well enough to avoid it. As the servant left, I didn't know how to show my distrust and convince him to escort me away.

"Hisa," greeted Urekkato, too familiar in his tone and flashing a sly smile. "Come in."

My legs obeyed with leaden reluctance.

A flick of his finger, and the door closed. "What are you wearing?"

I stopped near to him, trying to avoid eye contact. "My riding clothes."

He snickered, "Planning to run away?"

As much as I didn't want to, I knew I also had to thank Urekkato for putting yesterday's ordeal in my favor. In slow and controlled movements, I went to my knees to bow; the same bow I'd given almost two years before in Lord Kwan's room. "Thank you, my prince, for dismissing the accusations against me."

Silent. And I didn't look up to see his expression.

"Did Kwan put you up to this?"

I rose only just, half sitting on my legs but never removing my gaze from the floor, and shook my head. "No, my prince."

He shifted his weight to one leg, tapping his other foot. "You're not much fun like this. Now stop it and get up."

I wanted to refuse, to stubbornly stay in a lowered position just to irritate him with little consequence, but my feet were smoothly under me. In what quiet disobedience I could manage, I kept my head down.

"Stop looking so sullen," scolded Urekkato. "You won against Juro. Admittedly, in the most anticlimactic fashion, but a victory nonetheless. Now come."

I didn't understand what he meant by *anticlimactic*, even as I followed. Not that his opinion of the quality mattered. We stopped at one of his wardrobes, where a dress in simple green and white colors sat.

"What do you think?"

Confused, I looked up at him.

"I saw you packing away the others. So, I took this from one of my maids close enough to your size."

"What? No," I said, frowning. All humility fleeing. "You can't take things from someone and give them away!"

"She's my maid. And she has others. I've often taken them from her." A wry grin spread on his face with his insinuation.

A shiver shot up my spine.

"Unless you really do want to walk Tetsuden naked."

I huffed, not wanting any part of his game. Damning my manners, I turned to leave.

He laughed, catching my wrist and yanking me back. "That's better. I thought that would make you the most upset."

No matter how I looked at Urekkato, I could never read him. Did he fabricate having taken it from one of his servants? I didn't believe he had the compassion or foresight to have it made for me. His interest was in making me uncomfortable rather than in friendship or kindness.

"Genji asked me to give it to you."

I didn't believe that either. It didn't make sense to have Urekkato deliver it rather than summon me himself, as a start.

"It was his late wife's. You've noticed how tender he is in remembering her. Naturally, he held on to them for the sentimentality. And, naturally, he couldn't fathom handing them off."

"Lady Isaden's?" I asked, thoughtless and blinking. I looked back to it, remembering the fond conversations shared. Then I shook my head free of it. "I can't."

"Hm? Refusing a gift from your host is bad manners."

"If it hurts him to part with it, wouldn't it hurt him to see someone else wear it? And that's assuming you're telling the truth."

He chuckled. In an instant, he closed any remaining distance between us, reenacting how he'd pinned me against the well. This time, however, I glowered, trying to push back and hold my ground.

"Normally, a servant thanks their prince when given a gift. Not question its origins or sincerity."

"I'm not accepting anything you want to give me. I regret making that deal with you before, and I won't make myself indebted to you in any other way."

He tilted his head, smiling. "What is it about you that these other lords make such a fuss? No wealth or beauty or much else to offer. Is it in a *special* act of service? And of all them, you gave it to the fox?"

I felt my face, my neck, my ears turn hot, boiling. My scowl deepened, my heart pounded like a war drum, and ringing drowned out all other sound. I was tired of this. The same insinuations, the same taunts, threats—endless! It wasn't that I couldn't stop myself. Rather, I wanted to. I hit him. Hard as my open hand could, I hit him.

His face bore shock, though it didn't move despite the force. My anger fled, remembering. I'd just slapped a Juneun. Worse, a prince. I felt myself paling, knowing I had nothing to fight back with.

He scoffed, a slow laugh following. In a blink, he pinned my hands high, and I was bent back uncomfortably. Out of instinct, I kicked and squirmed, unwilling to submit.

"Hold still."

My legs started to still, while the fire in my veins kept them from complying completely.

Leaning in, he whispered his hot breath into my ear. "If I actually wanted to, do you think a slap would change my mind?"

I still tried to wriggle free, knowing full well it wouldn't do anything. It was the principle of the matter. That I would fight to the end. Lin said as much. That it was one thing for a willing girl, and another thing entirely if he forced himself. But did that still apply to a prince? He'd pushed himself into a private meeting before, using his title.

"I'm not actually interested," said Urekkato, regaining a playfulness to his tone. "It's entertaining to watch you. Any other servant wouldn't dare raise a finger. But you look more like a mouse or a juvenal rabbit caught by a cat. Is this how you and the fox get on?"

"Get off!" I demanded. I didn't have anything to make him do as I say, but I'd resolved myself to not stay quiet in this harassment.

"I would, but I'm supposed to be distracting you while Syaoran and Juro have their duel."

I stilled and my eyes went wide.

"He didn't tell you? Of course not. Otherwise, he wouldn't need me to keep you busy." He smirked, loosening enough of his hold to let me up.

Without hesitation, I leapt to my feet, my mind now frenzied in the fear that Juro meant to kill Syaoran. If he was still wrathful enough to insist on a duel, what stopped him from going further than first blood, or to make first blood in piercing Syaoran's heart?

"Where are they?"

Urekkato stayed silent, smirking.

I shoved, unable to move him at all in my desperation. "Tell me where they are!"

"What will you give me for it?"

I wanted to hit him again, stopped only in the realization that I was wasting time. So, I ran.

"Good luck," called Urekkato.

As much as I wanted to refuse the idea, I would need it. I needed luck to help me think where they would be holding a duel that both Genji and Lord Kwan were against. And I would need luck to guide me there.

It would have to be far from the main road, and away from any accommodations to stay private. Somewhere with space and level ground—perhaps shaded this early in the day, making it undesirable for guests to want to go to. It would also need something to obscure it, shrubs or trees or something else. Something other than a storehouse or some other structure that was likely to be sought out by the castle staff. Maybe a park or some other garden in the backside of the castle, northwest.

My wood sandals on, I hurried while trying not to draw attention. While it would be justified to expose Juro's hotheadedness, I didn't want to tangle Syaoran and Lord Kwan in it. I didn't want to humiliate Genji.

I muttered my prayers, that I wasn't too late, that I could find them soon, that I could somehow stop it. Gravel crunched under my sandals. With every step, it echoed as I went further from any gathering, my feet somehow knowing the way. For a short stretch, there was only the sound of my footsteps, my racing heartbeat, and sighing bird songs. Then, there was the sound of metal colliding on metal.

I walked faster. Jogging. Sprinting. As fast as the ground would allow me. How I wished for woven sandals. Wished for something to allow me better balance so I could run with complete abandon.

A park, right where I'd suspected, with Juro and Syaoran facing off. I panted, my heart going faster to push me on. To my eyes, they didn't fly at each other so much, but my ears heard more than what I could see.

At the edge of the grass, my legs froze, and I couldn't will myself to be hurled into the fray. What use was I? I had no sword, no skill to fight. Even if I had both, I wouldn't be a match for a Juneun—let alone one with centuries of experience!

While I could only catch the sight of one or two clashes, I heard at least four slaps of steel. In one instance, they'd moved clear across the park, and I didn't see how. The empty swings of a blade in the wake of it.

I'd found them. But what could I do?

At last, they slowed, enough for my eyes to keep up, both looking worn. A standoff, sizing each other up.

Unable to help myself, and not knowing if I'd get another chance to get through, I called out. A fatal mistake. I didn't see how it happened, catching only part of it and the end result. Juro cut into Syaoran's upper arm. Powerful or not, I feared too much that Juro would kill him, and bolted in.

In my race to him, I slipped on the grass, crashing down on myself. Frantic, my palms pushed me up to look as my feet struggled to get back under me.

Syaoran was on the ground, disarmed, and bore a new cut on his upper cheek. Juro held his sword pointed, ready to deliver a last blow.

"Juro, stop!" I begged. Seeing him move for an attack, I flinched. Nothing came. And the silence prodded me to look up.

Lord Kwan caught Juro's arm, keeping him from striking Syaoran. They leered at each other, indignant at the actions of each. A wordless conversation. Something I recognized when there was bad blood between two men as they tried to hold themselves together in the presence of others. Though, in the village, the matter was solved before month's end. I didn't know if that held true to a Juneun or someone of the noble class.

"You have already drawn first blood, Lord Juro," said Lord Kwan, hinting his displeasure.

Someone stood beside me, offering a hand to help me up. At the sight of white, pointed nails, I refused, choosing to steady myself and slowly stand rather than accept Urekkato's gesture.

Whatever exchange took place between Juro and Lord Kwan in that time, I missed. I only managed to catch that Juro's sword was sheathed, and that he held his head high as he walked to pass me.

"Lord—"

He cut off my attempt. "Do not presume to know me, Hisa. We are strangers now."

A bitterness swept through me. While I'd wanted Juro to leave me alone, I didn't do anything to be treated so cold, or for Syaoran to be roughed. I'd grown too strong willed and passionate in my upset, and angry words leapt from me without looking at him.

"You wrote to me, once, asking what it is you could give me. Do you remember my reply?"

I heard the halt of his footfall.

"*A heart without pride, a hand without greed. Feet not idle, tongue not hateful. With eyes that see through stone.* What I wanted was for you to become a better man. Someone I thought you were capable of being, so that I could love you. But you chose pride and possessions and fury over what I'd wanted. What you promised to give."

I didn't face him, taking that he was still there from the watch of Syaoran and Lord Kwan, and the lack of gravel crunching.

"I didn't care for trinkets or handsomeness. What I care for is compassion. To be treated as an equal, not with jealous contempt."

Judging from the continued watch and silence, I'd perhaps gone too far in my self-righteousness, and needed something to reset the course.

"I can understand your anger at me, your frustration. And I forgive you for it. But I will not forgive an attempt to brutalize another to spite me." I tried to keep my words eloquent as I battled a monsoon of emotion. "If I was ever unsure before about whether or not I could love you, I know now that it is impossible. I could never give my heart to someone whose jealousy would drive them to this, callus to the misery it would create."

The sound of grass bending underfoot indicated Juro's leave. I stood as I was, drawing in deep, shaky breaths. In that moment, I remembered how stupid I was to think I could survive five years without tear-shed, without breaking. It seemed I did that more often than I kept strong for nearly four years.

At last, Urekkato spoke with levity. "I think that's the most I've ever heard you speak since meeting you."

I didn't care to banter with him, realizing that Syaoran was still hurt and on the ground. Snatched from my thoughts, I went to him. The wound on his bicep wasn't as deep as I imagined, bleeding but not in danger of losing the arm. And the cut to his face was shallow, brazed by the edge of Juro's sword, though worryingly close to his eye.

"You shouldn't have agreed to this duel," I scolded, keeping my voice soft. "He could've killed you."

"I had him right where I wanted him," joked Syaoran.

"This is serious," I said, looking him in the eye. "You didn't have to accept the fight. Not for my sake."

"I didn't," said Syaoran, matching my tone. "I did it for him."

I blinked, twisting my face with a question as I studied him.

"I didn't want it to seem like I was letting him win, even if that was the plan. He for sure would've tried to kill me if he thought I wasn't trying to match him."

"Then, it was…" I trailed my words, my mind piecing it together and finding it too odd.

"To restore his pride and sense of worth. From his perspective, you chose me over him, and he needed something to assure him of his quality."

I scoffed. "That's one of the dumbest things I've ever heard."

Urekkato laughed. "It's hard for a woman to understand a man's mind."

Syaoran bent his brow at the Cat prince. "It's... a complicated thing to explain."

Lord Kwan moved away from us then, baring a strange look of pity. Something about him seemed, somehow, melancholic, heartbroken in a way. I felt then that I'd disappointed him, shamed him even, and I didn't understand how or why. In his slow stride back to society, a quiet cue was given for Urekkato to join him, which the Cat prince obliged.

I didn't have the time to assess what it meant, or why my heart hurt from it. Syaoran's wound needed tending.

"There's salts and herbs in our room, right? Or any salves?"

"Not for this," said Syaoran. "But I can send one of Genji's servants to get what I'd need, and tell them it was from an accident."

"We should still try to cover it, and try to prevent infection before a more thorough cleaning."

"And keep some discretion," added Syaoran.

I dismissed it, taking the ribbon from my hair to wrap around it.

"Have you told Kwan about what really happened? Or how you feel?"

I shook my head. "I haven't had the chance. And I don't want to bother him after causing such a fuss."

"It'd probably help."

"But what if I only make things worse?"

He sighed. "Worse for him?"

I understood the implication. The problem was that I didn't want to admit it. That I was afraid to hear my own feelings being rejected. It was shameful, I knew, since Juro had freely expressed his intention and I'd rejected him. Now I feared facing the same answer.

"I wouldn't know how to make him understand," I said. "Everyone else thinks I'm an idiot for not wanting Juro, or for not allowing him to indulge in me."

Syaroan took my hand, stopping my work. "Not everyone. Don't forget, Kwan does try to keep you away from him, and vice versa, because of your discomfort. Out of everyone, he'd be the most understanding. The two of you are very close."

I smiled, a chuckle leaving me. "He said the same thing about you and I."

He shrugged, growing a mischievous smile. "Maybe Kwan is secretly in love with Hisa."

"Don't joke like that," I scolded. "It's bad enough that half the house and now a chunk of everyone here thinks you and I are in a secret love affair. I don't need you making fun of me as well."

Chapter 59
Lord Kwan XV

Urekkato made his happy announcement at the start of the first official banquet. The reason he'd come. Eumeh birthed a child in the winter—a princess, favoring her Cat heritage over the dragon line of the Mireu. Which also explained her absence.

Applause and congratulations were given as though some great achievement was made, rather than an expected inevitability.

Kwan excused himself early, leaving the hall and going out into the cold night air. He wandered, taking in the lantern displays and the warm glow as they hung from branches and ropes. It was only a matter of time before the space was once again filled with guests coming to awe at them. His brothers and sister included.

Genji's own household worked meticulously to get the look of it all, tireless in the effort. Kwan wondered if they looked at their tasks with excitement, pride, or saw it merely as duty. No, not merely, but duty nonetheless.

Dutiful.

It finalized in his head that his feelings were misplaced. Comparing the concern she had for him when they'd fallen years prior, and the concern she had for Syaoran earlier that day, was there an obvious difference? Of course there was. As for what she said about the kind of man she could never love, he knew himself. A jealous hatred claimed his heart from the day of Jiana's death, and he'd become callus in his pursuit. His arrogance had led to the tragedy.

Folly. To love a mortal. Then again, he hadn't thought so when it was Genji's relationship or Juro's affection.

"I heard you brought the fox and the human," said Sara.

Kwan stopped in his stride, putting little effort into acknowledging his sister.

"If father knew your choice beforehand, I might still be locked in our house."

"Congratulations on your escape," said Kwan, flat.

"As long as no one causes too much of a scene, I expect I'll be allowed to court as well."

Kwan said nothing, watching his sister's even approach in her elegant attire; dressed according to her rank in society, and patterned by pink magnolias for the occasion.

"Seong escorted me," continued Sara without prompting. "His eldest daughter will be attending these events soon enough."

"The courts will be richer for it," said Urekkato, sauntering up.

Both Sara and Kwan made their polite bow, acknowledging his station.

Urekkato smirked, allowing them up. "I suppose how soon she arrives depends on how good a chaperone he makes for you. And you've already wandered off alone."

Sara soured her expression. "I am in the company of my brother."

"You were. And in a few seconds, you will be alone. I have business to speak on with Kwan. You needn't involve your sweet self."

To that, Sara gave up all pretense of pleasantness.

"I advise you stay vigilant, Lady Sara. Lord Juro is newly available again, and Zhen is in search of a rich woman himself."

"Arrogance," spat Sara in a low mutter.

"What was that?" said Urekkato, a slyness painted on his face.

Sara merely bowed; more from obligation than respect.

Holding his smirk, Urekkato led on. "Come this way, Lord Kwan. I believe the lanterns by the lakes are better viewed in this direction."

Reluctant, Kwan followed. As much as he'd look for a way to disengage with his sister, he resented being pulled away by an equally unwanted companion.

"You seem glum," said Urekkato, amused. "Well, you've been glum the last century, but more so than usual." He chuckled to himself.

Kwan watched from the corner of his eye, giving no reply.

"I suppose the events of the day dampened your mood."

Continuing his silence, Kwan guessed at what Urekkato's game was. He'd played both sides in the assembly—how he knew of it was another matter, since there was no question that he didn't honestly stumble upon it. Then, to play informant to the duel taking place, and Hisa's rush to intervein; if it'd been a secretive matter, he couldn't happen to know any of it, yet informed with absolute surety.

"She slapped me this morning. Hisa, that is."

That, Kwan couldn't ignore, and gave his attention to the Cat prince as they walked.

"I assure you, I had it coming."

"What was the provocation?"

Urekkato grinned. "Seeing how easily she could be seduced."

It was an effort for Kwan to keep himself stone.

"Lord Genji requested her presence, and Lord Kwan is fond enough of her to bring her. Then there's our former Kurai friends willing to shed blood over her. Such a fuss over a mere mortal. I thought she sported well enough to garner the attention."

Kwan said nothing, letting Urekkato go on to expose himself.

"She's gotten feistier since my last meeting her. I suppose it can't be helped when living with a tiger. More so if she sports with one. I might visit her tonight while the fox is away."

On impulse, and out of view, Kwan acted. His forearm against Urekkato's chest, he pinned the prince to a stone retention wall. "I made you a prince. If you force your advance on any in my house, I will unmake you."

Urekkato chuckled. "Would it be a force? She gave herself to the toad and the fox."

Kwan didn't relent, leaning into his hold. "I don't care for insinuation."

Urekkato grinned. "I'm beginning to think Lord Kwan is in love. Perhaps that accounts for his defense against Juro. But then, why prevent the sword from the fox?"

"Because a lesser man would allow it." His word in, Kwan released the Cat prince.

"You follow Genji too closely," said Urekkato, impulsively checking himself for any tenderness. "It does make sense for her though. Syaoran has a handsome face. And if the maids are to be believed, he's a more versatile lover. That's where the benefit ends, I'm afraid. She should've insisted Juro change his face to look more handsome, and enjoy the luxury of a higher status. It might not be long before she realizes her mistake."

"Perhaps Prince Urekkato is in love," said Kwan. "You seem well informed on her whereabouts and her intensions."

Urekkato laughed. "It's entertaining to watch her try and navigate the world. That's where any interest ends. If she did want to be my mistress, I wouldn't have her. It'd be less amusing. And she's not a pretty thing to look at."

"I hadn't noticed," said Kwan.

"It's difficult not to notice," said Urekkato.

Kwan restrained himself from saying anymore. If he were blind and she were beautiful, he'd love her. But he was not, nor was she, and he loved her. His feeling grew from the things unseen.

"She sent her things to Juro," said Urekkato. "He won't have anything to do with them. It's quite some luck, don't you think?"

"How so?"

"She won't walk Tetsuden underdressed."

They parted ways not long after, leaving Kwan to ponder while Urekkato took to the first dance of Mokryon.

He shouldn't have bothered with dwelling on it at all. It was as good as decided. He'd reside in Tetsuden and appoint Syaoran as steward to Mount Tora. The house was modest and near enough to her family. She'd live just as well as a titled lady, and already had a love of looking after the area.

"The way everyone talked about Kwan's human, I thought she'd be a little more to look at."

A feminine voice broke him from his thoughts. He'd wound up back in the castle, his feet moving while his mind was absent. Stopping, he didn't find the source; likely, from around one corner of the dim lit hall.

"You'd think a lord of his caliber would prefer a beauty for an attendant."

"She's not very tall or shapely either."

"I heard she was having an affair with the Kurai guests."

A pair of female serfs turned the corner, a candle in hand to better light their path, in time for Kwan to catch a grimace on both of them. He'd kept still, and they didn't notice until it was too late to make the turn seem like a stumble. Now aghast, they stared at him.

Calm, he approached, watching the concern grow on their expressions. He stopped in front of them, deciding what to do. An idea came, inspired by Urekkato.

With swift momentum, he stole off the one carrying the candle. The nearest door flying open, he brought her in. It shut. Pinning her, seeing the surprise and the labored breath, he allowed her mind to piece things together and calm.

"I would prefer a beauty," said Kwan.

His fingers pushed the stray hairs from her face, and he leaned in. Her body moved to accommodate him. Stopping short of her lips, he moved to whisper to her.

"It's a shame there isn't an enticing enough woman in Tetsuden." At a casual pace, he let go and righted himself. His steps sounded in a leisurely rhythm, the door sliding open with a sigh to reveal the startled servant on the other side. He walked past, paying no mind.

Was vanity still the topmost piece of gossip?

Thinking back, he didn't realize she was a girl on first meeting. Now, when better dressed and her hair grown out, she was easily seen as a woman. A little hare indeed.

Walking further, he intended to retire to his room, only to stop when he saw it lit and heard Hisa's voice. No. He wasn't ready yet.

Shifting his direction, he went to the courtyards, where bonfires and music and dances continued.

They more or less all looked the same. The ladies, their dresses, and the robed suitors partnering with them. Smiles and painted faces, jewels and gold shining against the flames, and rehearsed laughter. Did it never change?

"There you are!" called Towa, swatting his back. "You shut yourself away for so long, I started to think I wouldn't recognize you."

Kwan gave the start of a smile. "You haven't changed."

She spun, showing off the dazzling layers of purples and blues, lined in black. "Don't you think?"

He kept his expression, resuming his watch on the dances. "Do you expect me to ask you?"

"To dance?" laughed Towa. "I never could manage it. Give me a sword, and I can match most in the arena. Give me a nice dress and a partner, and I may as well have been born a fish."

He grunted his acknowledgement, saying nothing more.

"I met your human the other day."

"Did you?" said Kwan after some time

"She's a sweet thing. A little shy."

"Overwhelmed, I expect. She'd never left her village until coming to my household."

"That makes sense then. I thought she seemed more sincere with manners, if not a little clumsy."

"You hold no issue?"

"Should I? Juro was looking for her that same day. Honestly, I was surprised to see him here, given his reputation."

"He pursued her."

Towa laughed. "He has odd taste, I'll grant him that. How does she like him?"

"The feeling is not reciprocated." Kwan folded his arms, putting off the women making wordless pleas for him to go to them.

"Hm. Even with all the benefit? It's quite the leap from a common village girl to the Lady of Shigeru House. Have you counseled on it?"

Kwan watched a group of perturbed women, dissatisfied with standing without a partner for so long. "She's old enough to know her own mind."

Towa drew in a long breath. "My own family is determined to match me with Haru. He's kindly enough, and his family name well rooted, but he's also an idiot. I don't know that I could love a stupid man, but I may not have much choice. His family's wealth and lands are comparable to my family's, so it's not so far of a stretch. It's the name that matters, and I'll likely have no say unless I can humiliate him just enough to make refusal more enticing than saving face."

"Calculated."

Towa stretched. "Such is the life of a noble's daughter. Except that most are more complacent than I'm willing to be."

"Willing?"

"I don't mind making compromises if, in the long run, it suited me."

Kwan thought then to something said repeatedly: that she would only marry for love. As independent as Towa appeared, she played the same game as all ladies.

She wrapped her arm around his, leaning on him. "Come with me."

Kwan ignored her.

"I know you find this as dull as I do," whispered Towa. "Come with me. Like we used to do."

Kwan inhaled deep, considering. He wanted for a distraction, but he wanted a temporary solitude. At the same time, he didn't want to go back, to find her there—him there. Better, he thought, to allow them their victory and a secluded night.

He relented, allowing Towa to lead him away.

To the lakeside apartments, and into her room, he allowed her lead until a jealousy rose in him. In a slow passion of kisses, he embraced her, hands leisurely finding the ties of her dress and tugging them free.

She chuckled, expertly finding his own fastenings and undoing them. It wasn't impatience, but convenience, allowing him to shoulder off his own clothing and reveal her in his own time.

He sat her on a counter, tossing aside her top layers with his own, and trailed his kisses behind her ear, down her neck, and to her collar. Her hands trailed up his arms, tracing over his muscles. Working his way down at his own pace, he sampled his lips against her breasts, letting his hands explore her taut sides and back. Then, he slid off her skirtings, parting her thighs to indulge, pulling her close for his reach. Her toes pawed at his hips, inching off what remained of his clothes.

In a fit of passion, he yanked her back to her feet, turning her to bend over and pin as he slid into her. She reached to hold him close in his rhythm, managing to only grab hair.

He was not her first lover, nor she his, and this was not their first intimate session. But those days were long ago, when he sought refuge from his frustrations, and she only to rebel against conformity.

In that regard, nothing had changed.

Chapter 60
A Secret Garden

Morning, and Syaoran and I exchanged a worried look. Lord Kwan didn't come back for the night. We'd kept a light sleep, waiting to wake at his return. It never happened. I swelled with guilt, despite Syaoran's assurances.

Halfway dressed, Lord Kwan entered the room. Syaoran greeted him, causing me to panic and hurry up to attend him. His hair unbound and clothes disheveled, he looked tired. I wasn't so stupid as to not guess. I'd caught men and women sneaking out of rooms that were not their own, and had an extensive talk with Lin to rid myself of some ignorance. In knowing all that, it pained my heart, confirming that his affection would be withheld from me.

Syaoran must've suspected my heartache, trying words of comfort to potentially deny the reason Lord Kwan was kept away. I held in my tears. It was a silly thing for me to get upset over. I wasn't entitled to his affection, and hadn't the courage to express my own feelings. I shouldn't be surprised that he would find himself with another woman, a Juneun. I was just his human servant.

Yet, the reminder of it all only cut deeper into my heart.

I took solace on the far side of the smaller pond nearest the castle, hiding myself behind the water lilies and lotus flowers not yet in bloom. It still looked large enough to be called a lake, though the wooden walkways crossing parts of it detracted from the thought.

I'd taken a bowl of rice and a bread bun with me for breakfast, in no mood for company and with little appetite. Between the heartbreak and the feeling of having disappointed the spirits I adored, my stomach soured. Unable to make myself eat, I'd tossed a pinch of rice far into the water, watching the koi discover it and go into a frenzy.

Absent minded, I tossed another pinch slightly closer. And again after they'd finished that, until I could see their many colors swimming as close as they dared. The pond still retained a dropped edge, preventing any of the fish from accidentally beaching themselves. Before half my bowl was emptied, they'd come right against the ledge, keeping me company as I pinched off more of my breakfast for them.

"They only come up to someone who's gentle," said Genji.

I'd been so lost in my own fog that I didn't notice when he approached, and scrambled to get to my feet for good manners. He waved aside the bow, gesturing for me to resume my place, and sat near to me.

"There's always been a few who come to Tetsuden, and try to lure the koi close. But the ones in this pond have a particular nak for only coming to someone they know is a gentle person." He kept his shy tone and slow words, bringing a comfort with them.

I watched him, looking as timeless and regal as the giant trees just outside of his castle's walls. "How can they tell?"

He shrugged. "They can tell."

"Are they spirits too, my lord?"

He showed a soft smile, shaking his head. "They've always been ordinary koi, since I was a child. These aren't the originals, but they've learned how to pick up on someone's compassion and another's trickery."

I stuck the tips of my fingers below the water's surface, feeling them glide by or against my skin. "I like them."

For a while, we sat in comfortable quiet. I could breathe in that time, able to better suppress all the events of my first days here. Genji didn't mention any of it, simply being there as a friend.

"The castle is so big," I said at last, awkward and feeling I needed to. "I keep worrying that I'll get lost."

He took his time to look over at me. "I... tend to forget. Most of my life has been on these grounds."

"My village could fit in here a hundred times over, or more. It makes me not want to touch anything, afraid it'll break."

"Don't be," said Genji, carrying a chuckle in his deep voice. "Afraid, that is. Rowdy guests are... Three doors and a window have been replaced this morning alone. You're not... You're different. From that. The koi know it."

It was a silly conversation, but it made me feel better. My stomach still too sour, I finished giving the rest of my breakfast to the carp. "Did Lord Kwan get lost when he lived here?"

"Not often," said Genji. "Isa did. And demanded a map... if she was going to stay. She still got lost."

I chuckled. "It must've been a different world for her. Did she like living here?"

Genji shied. "Once she... she liked it more when she knew her way. Sometimes, she tried to lose her way on purpose. I would have to find her."

"And you always did?"

He gave a slight nod, smiling.

Another spell of quiet fell over us. I dipped my fingers back into the water, letting the fish come up to investigate. "I'm sorry for causing so much trouble, Lord Genji."

He held still a long time, uncomfortable, and I regretted saying every word. "Love... makes us act rashly."

I shook my head, withdrawing my hand. "Syaoran isn't in love with me. And I'm not in love with him."

Genji replied with a sheepish look. "I didn't say anything about Syaoran."

I blinked at him. "Lord Juro?"

He shifted.

I sighed, unable to comprehend the cue. "Lord Genji, I think of you as a kindred soul."

He tucked in his head slightly, smile strengthening. "I'm glad."

"If," I hesitated. "If I were in love, with a Juneun, and he didn't feel the same way, what do you think I should do?"

Studying me, he pondered the question a moment. "I think you're sensible enough to know."

"You said yourself, my lord, that love makes people act rashly."

He shied, putting his gaze back on the water. "So I did." Another bout of silence as he mulled it over. "I knew my heart without knowing Isa's. With love comes the risk of heartbreak. But, there is also the greatest reward from it. If... If both are willing to work on it."

"It seems love is a complicated thing," I said, putting on a smile for him. "And I don't think I'll ever understand it."

"Why?"

It took a few seconds, mustering up the courage to say it to someone outside of myself. "I know that I'm not very pretty, and that I'm not good at a lot of things. I'm trying to get better, but... I don't think I'll be good enough at any particular skill that someone would fall in love with me. Genuinely fall in love. Not the jealous or possessive sort, but a sincere and kindly love."

His expression filled with reminiscence again. "Isa was the most beautiful creature in the world to me. All any of the Juneun... all they could say was... how she was a beauty for a human. I liked her cooking. It... wasn't to a banquet standard. But, I liked it. People will look for any reason to separate themselves, ego, mostly... from someone they envy."

I listened, wrapping my arms around my legs, and resting my head on my knees.

"Don't think so little of yourself. Isa... Isa was beautiful. But, if I were blind and didn't know it... that she was beautiful... I would have loved her all the same. There are things more precious that others can't see. They don't take the time to look closely. Patience, determination, compassion... The most beautiful traits come from within."

I smiled. "You are a romantic, my lord. I can see how you won the love of the woman you wanted."

He blinked, giving me a puzzled look. "I... wouldn't say I *won* her heart. Love is not a prize. It's... It takes conviction." He returned his watch to the pond, the sun rising enough to wake the flowers. "I think every good heart is worthy of love. To people who value forgiveness over resentment."

"It would be hard to love a resentful person," I agreed. "Or for them to love. I wonder if they'd change, knowing that." I sighed, looking back to the pond and feeling pity at the thought.

If a person isolated themselves, obsessed with a vengeance that turned them cold, would they even recognize love? Would they change, and let go, in the pursuit of it?

From the corner of my eye, I saw someone approach. Lord Kwan, stoic faced but somehow softer than he'd looked these past few days.

"Am I interrupting?" asked Lord Kwan.

I stood, nearly forgetting my manners, and greeted him with a polite bow.

"You interrupt nothing," said Genji. "Will you join us for the view?"

Lord Kwan gave a single shake of his head, a slow and smooth gesture. "If you'll permit me to take my attendant, I'll be on my way."

Genji nodded, cuing Kwan to take his leave and for me to follow. In doing so, I kept glancing over my shoulder to Genji, looking for any clue on what to expect. I found none, becoming sheepish myself. Lord Kwan seemed more distant and cold only this morning, leading me to believe he'd decided to terminate our friendship and would perhaps now reprimand me the way other lords did with their servants.

We walked through a side entrance of the castle, down several halls to the other end. I bunched my brow, realizing that we'd come through the only way to get to this part of the grounds. A canal had been cut, dividing the walk way and allowing for a gentle flow of water to hum peacefully. The branches of magnolias umbrellaed over us from either side, their blossoms in full bloom for the occasion.

Lord Kwan continued a few strides more, the wooden walk way silent under every step. "It's the private garden. Guests typically won't come here unless given permission by the master of Tetsuden."

I stiffened at the knowledge. "Then... are we...?"

Lord Kwan turned to look at me, a start of a smile on his face. "I have full range of any part of the grounds. And so do you." He reached his hand out.

Desperate to reclaim how we'd been before, I accepted. Afraid that there was change to it, I did so slowly.

"You didn't put on your cosmetics today," said Lord Kwan.

I blinked, having forgotten. "I didn't want to be around others today. I know it's rude, but I didn't want to bring any more trouble to you."

He breathed out a quick sigh. "Hisa, trouble will happen whether or not you're within a mile of it."

It gave me a small comfort, knowing he wasn't so upset with me, and we walked on hand-in-hand. The cool touch of his strong fingers, wrapped around my callused ones, put me at ease.

"I want to show you something special," said Lord Kwan.

I felt my cheeks pink, thankful he looked at the path ahead, and made a quiet agreement.

"Each generation of the Elk Clan has added to the garden. The canal was made by Genji's grandparents. And the magnolias were planted by his great grandparents."

I awed a little more at the beautiful path. The color above and the patterns of shadows below, and the scent of it all pleasantly hanging in between. "What did Lord Genji add?" I asked, absently.

"It's what I want to show you."

I smiled, needing to contain new excitement.

Several paths branched from our main route, with curiosity causing me to squint as we walked by to see what enchanting secret they led to.

Sunlight poured down on the other side of the magnolias. The canal tapering into a pond, we crossed the closely lain stepping stones. The trees on the opposite side leaned over, shading the second half of the pond. While it looked again like a forest, I admired how the light trickled through the leaves, creating a pallet of green over us, and painted the ground in soft shadows.

The path had become stone here, leading to creeping wisteria. Another pond, and a bridge made from the woven, living vines waited for us.

"This part used to be cleared and ordinary," said Kwan. "Genji planted a single wisteria tree as a boy, and over time it grew enough to spread out and make this."

"With magic?"

"A little. There was a bridge before, and the wisteria wrapped around it. So much was eventually consumed, he removed it entirely and let this take its place."

"It's beautiful," I said, awing.

Lord Kwan stopped, looking at me with a gentler expression. "It is."

I tucked in my head, keeping my sheepish smile. He led on, and I let my expression grow. The flowers were waking from their winter slumber. Half were still new buds, the others in various stages of bloom, and all of it wonderful as they hung above. Without thinking, my free hand reached up, grazing the lowest hanging bunches of flowers, soft and tickling against my skin.

Sunlight flashed through pinpoint breaks in the wisteria. A glitter of light as I walked.

On the other side, the ancient tree stood with its great canopy. The stout, gnarled trunk and thick branches held up a ceiling of flowers and leaves; beautiful shades of purple, speckled by pale green. Its dark wood cemented itself into the ground where bulbous roots peered out near its base. Some of the roots reached out, claiming the wide, earthen mound surrounded by water. A stele stood sentry in front of the tree, standing tall and proud in defiance of any weathering. Some of the roots there vined up to hold It in place.

It was a sight unlike anything I could ever imagine, and I pinched at myself to make sure it wasn't a dream. "This is all one tree?"

Lord Kwan nodded. "Do you like it?"

"I do."

He watched me a moment as I wandered, facing as high as my head would go and on my toes. "Lord Genji proposed to his late wife here. And held their wedding the following year."

"It must've been ideal. I don't think anyone could refuse a proposal under this tree."

"No?" said Lord Kwan. In that instant, I knew he was about to tease me, and braced myself. "Shall I fetch Syaoran?"

"Lord Kwan!" I scolded. He kept his expression with a soft smile, and I huffed out a sigh. "Syaoran and I... We're not—"

"I know," said Lord Kwan, placing a twig of wisteria in my hair. The flowers hung elegantly from what I could tell; it wasn't a clumsy attempt. "He sought me out this morning, determined to explain the details of it."

"He did?" I asked in alarm, backing away. "W-what did he tell you?"

Lord Kwan quirked a brow. "That the scene Juro happened on was a rouse. And that there's no intimate attachment between the two of you."

I retreated into myself somewhat. I was glad that Lord Kwan understood the particulars, and that Syaoran left out the confession of my feelings. But a lingering guilt wouldn't leave. "Are you angry, my lord? That we allowed a lie?"

He turned his attention upward, to the fanfare of violet. "No. I would've liked to know the rouse beforehand so that I could better defend you both, rather than be caught unaware. But there wasn't the time to understand it." His gaze returned to me. "If I led you to think you displeased me, I'm sorry."

I shook my head. "I'm just glad it's sorted out now."

He mulled the words over, walking to me. "What do you think about a wedding in this spot?"

I twisted my face, letting it slack when I remembered how he came back to our shared room this morning. "It'd make for a beautiful place," I said, trying to keep out as much sadness as possible.

"Hmm," said Lord Kwan, taking in breath and studying the area. "What side would you hold it?"

I gave a sorry look. "I think that's something better discussed with the bride-to-be, my lord."

He looked at me with a raised brow. For a long while, he stayed like that, and I avoided meeting his eye. Again, he offered his hand to me. "Do you want to see why they built the castle here?"

Curious, but also wanting to move away from the previous topic, I accepted. On the other side of the wisteria island, more stepping stones lead away. I remembered, as we rounded the tree, to close my eyes and count. The stones led into a cave. Water trickled in small streams from the cliff-face, curtaining the entrance. I raised my arm in what I knew was a miserable attempt to keep dry. Lord Kwan held his sleeve over me, shielding me more effectively.

A brook slithered through the cave, its voice echoing in the dark space. The sound of distant drips, of a waterfall, joined its chorus.

Worried I might slip, my steps became shorter and slower. Lord Kwan held me against him, his arm hugging my waist as he whispered that he wouldn't let me fall. Words that reminded me of every time I ventured into something new, and he kept close.

Light illuminated the area a short distance in. A narrow waterfall, no taller than Lord Kwan's house, threw mist into the brilliant touch of sun while the rest crashed on the rock tiers leading down.

He led me around it, showing that a fire flickered behind the fall, nestled in its own alcove. In spite of dampness, it danced without care.

"It's called the *Qilin Plume*," said Lord Kwan.

"A qilin?" I echoed. I'd seen a few depictions from merchants, and in parts of the castle, with none of them looking very much alike, though I didn't know much about the creature except that they were gentle despite their fierce appearance.

"Genji's family are the descendants of the qilin," said Lord Kwan. "The flame was named for that reason."

"The water doesn't put it out?"

"It hasn't since it's discovery."

"Is it magic?"

He shrugged. "It might be. No one outside the family has ever touched it."

Hearing that, I closed my eyes again to count, making every effort to keep Urekkato from looking. "Is there a flame like this in your ancestral home?" I asked, eager. Looking at him, and seeing that slight discomforted, I regretted my words.

"No," said Lord Kwan. In seeing me shrink away, he went on. "But there is a sacred place there. Called the *Well of Oaths*. The cave it sits in stays in eternal spring, even in the deepest winter."

I smiled again. "It sounds like a romantic place."

He gave a humored scoff. "I thought so too." Catching himself, his face gave a half-second of shock, as though revealing something personal, and looked away.

"I'm sorry," I said.

Bent brow, he met my eye. "You have nothing to apologize for. I've been unfairly cold."

I echoed his last words, contemplating. "Is that why you brought me to see this place?"

"It's one reason," said Lord Kwan. "You can come back any time you like when you're here."

I nodded, taking his hand. But in our first steps, a spell of melancholy consumed me. For whatever reason, I had the distinct feel things were going to change.

"What's wrong?" asked Lord Kwan, concern marring his usual stony expression.

"I..." I didn't know how to explain it. And maybe it was laughable for me to brood. "Kiss me?"

He blinked, perplexed at the odd timing. His hint of a smile returned, and he retook my hands. I took in a small, sharp breath. Then he raised up my hands in his, laying his lips on my knuckles. It was my turn to flash confusion. In seeing my expression, his smile grew slightly, and he took a step closer. He leaned in and I closed my eyes. His lips didn't land on mine, however. Instead, he planted the kiss at my hairline.

Chapter 61
Dancing

Out of the cavern, I saw the slightest movement at the water's edge. A lizard tried to climb out, determined to stick to a sheer spot rather than move to a shallower point. Without thinking, I let go of Lord Kwan's hand, walking the short distance to scoop it out. For my effort it bit down on my thumb. I flinched, nearly dropping it—not from any hurt, there wasn't any, but the surprise of it. On the ground, it scuttled off without so much as a look back.

"Here," said Lord Kwan, taking my hand.

I realized he was about to cast his healing magic, and recoiled. "It's alright. It didn't really break any skin, see?" I turned my palm over, revealing on a slight abrasion outlining where it bit down. "You don't need to waste magic on that. It's hardly visible, and it doesn't hurt."

Keeping his gentle smile, he wrapped both his hands around the one I presented. "Anyone else would've shrieked and thrown it."

I chuckled. "It's my fault. I probably scared it. And it doesn't know I was only trying to help. If I was stuck and desperate to get out, and some strange, giant creature plucked me up, I'd bite too." I could almost hear Syaoran's teasing as soon as I'd said it.

Lord Kwan watched me, considering. With a nod, he gestured for us to continue.

Under the wisteria, whether because it was such a romantic setting, or because I was jealous in the thought that he'd want to marry someone else there, or from my own selfishness, I stopped. Building the courage, and remembering to end Urekkato's spell, just in case, I made myself meet his eye. Again, he bore a confused expression.

"Kiss me?"

His face softened again, sighing. After his first step, I shrank into myself, putting all my courage to be more specific.

"A real kiss."

He quirked a brow. "The others were not?"

It was a weird way of putting things, but I'd already said them. "I meant—not..." I lost how to explain as soon as I got the first word out.

Not that I needed to say more. His thumb and fingers held up my chin for him, and he leaned in to kiss my lips. A gentle parting of mine into his, enough only to taste. My face heated up, and my eyes lulled closed. It was brief, but I found myself happier with it.

He led on with me in tow.

On the other side of the wisteria bridge, he stopped, and looked at me expectantly.

"What?" I said.

"Are you going to ask for another kiss?"

My eyes went wide. "Lord Kwan!"

"Lady Hisa."

I quieted. The only person to call me *lady* was Uno, and I felt a discomfort with it. Shying, I whispered. "Don't call me that…"

He tilted his head. "If you do marry a Juneun, you would be a lady."

Brow bent, I reminded him. "I did say I'll only marry for love. And I don't think any spirit, especially a noble, will want me for a wife. Not one that could genuinely love me."

"What makes you think that?"

"I hear how they talk about me," I confessed. "And they're right. But it's the one thing I swore not to yield on."

He observed me only a moment more, relenting and resuming our trek.

In the evening, I dawned the dress especially made for the dances, and tried to push out the memory of the last time I wore it. I'd even taken a little longer, just to wait out Syaoran. Looking over, I sighed at the other dresses. Juro refused to take them back. At the same time, it felt too odd to wear them. Though, it was better expected.

Outside the room, I nearly leapt out of my skin. Syaoran was waiting for me.

"Are you ready to go?" asked Syaoran with a smile.

"I thought you already left," I said, a hand over my chest to still my racing heart.

His fox ears twitched. "It'd look weird if I left you behind. We're supposed to be a couple now."

I flashed a pathetic look. "But Lord Kwan and Lord Genji already know that's not true."

"Lord Juro doesn't."

I'd forgotten. It did make things awkward, but Syaoran kept steadfast for my sake. The least I could do was try not to appear uncomfortable walking out to the dances with him.

"I'll take the first dance with you," said Syaoran, already planning. "And two more somewhere down the line, so it looks like I'm favoring you."

I whispered my thanks, and he lifted some restraint on his essence. It was already difficult enough to keep track of all the rules and customs I'd barely heard about this past winter, never mind adding a ploy to keep Juro away in polite society. For that, I was glad to have Syaoran looking out for me.

It was a long walk, with plenty of gaps between anyone being around, and leaving Syaoran to pester me about confessing my feelings. Not that it mattered. I explained to him that Lord Kwan thought about holding a wedding under the wisteria tree. Since his affection for me was in friendship, what good did it do to try and compete with a Juneun lady? It was already selfish of me to still expect a kiss from Lord Kwan whenever I wanted, but I kept that from Syaoran.

We watched a few dances first, waiting until one I knew the steps to came up. In various parts of the spectators, and among the dancers, I spotted Lord Kwan's brothers, and clung to Syaoran.

"They won't take so much liberty," whispered Syaoran. "Not in Lord Genji's home. But it's still best not to find yourself alone with any of them. If you do, say that Genji himself summoned you and you can't make him wait."

I nodded, committing that small lie to memory and praying I wouldn't need to use it. "Did it take you a long to learn all this?"

Syaoran chuckled. "Years."

It brought comfort, though I still fidgeted.

When finally we danced, I was far from elegant, but I hadn't missed more than two steps, which Syaoran made up for. Other dances went on, with Syaoran staying beside me until he felt adequate time had passed. Juro, on noticing we were there, danced with a different girl at every turn, becoming more prominent in his gestures when Syaoran and I joined, and again when Syaoran took another girl for a dance.

"Kwan's human, Hisa," called Towa, catching my attention. I gave a polite bow at her approach. "I told you we had similar names. Did you think I'd forget?"

"Not at all, Lady Towa," I said. It was a lie, since I didn't expect anyone new to know my name. Even Lord Kwan's brothers still referred to me as *Kwan's human*.

"Who was the man you were dancing with?"

"Syaoran? He's..."

"A fox? Must be Kwan's other attendant."

I returned my watch, saying nothing.

"He's handsome," said Towa. "Are the two of you close?"

I shied, starting to fidget. "Yes."

A pause ensued before her reply. "Good for you. Kurai or not, he's nice to look at, and he has the favor of someone from a powerful family. A servant girl could do worse."

Renewed discomfort washed over me.

Another dance passed. And another. Towa moved on before long, socializing amongst her peers. Syaoran took measured rests, coming back to me later to ask for another dance. Before I could accept, Urekkato intercepted, using his titles to push his way in.

I refused.

"It'll look rude," said Urekkato. "Or are you really determined to embarrass Lord Kwan and Lord Genji both by refusing a prince and honored guest?"

I stiffened, looking to Syaoran for some cue. Brow bent, he jutted his chin for me to accept.

"I'll take care not to tire her out and bring her back to you," said Urekkato.

Syaoran gave a slight frown at the comment, and I made no effort to conceal my own displeasure.

"Why do you even want to dance with me?" I whispered.

"Because I know you don't want to," said Urekkato. "It's fun watching you try to wiggle out of things. Doesn't the fox think so?"

"About?"

"Watching you *wiggle out of things*?" He smirked, holding me closer than needed at every opportunity.

"Is that all you can do? Threaten with sex and swords?"

"When one stops being affective, the other tends to suffice," answered Urekkato without missing a beat.

"Don't you have better things to do than harass me?" I missed several steps in the routine. Not deliberately.

"*Better* is subjective." He put his hands on my waist, lifting me higher than necessary in a pirouette, and plopped me back onto my feet in sync with the other dancers. "Or, I could tell Juro you're not really laying with the fox."

I paled, stumbling even more. Something which Urekkato took advantage of in keeping me against him. Wincing, my mind told me to pretend not to care. Perhaps, if I didn't show discomfort, he'd get bored with me. That was the whole reason for what he did, having admitted as much. An easy thing to plan, and a hard thing to do.

When the dance ended, I made a polite bow, turning on my heel to leave. He caught my arm. Using all my will, I didn't react.

"You remember the way to my room?" asked Urekkato in a low whisper. "In case you get lonely."

I kept silent, making myself stay still.

"Oh? Hisa is considering it. Remember that it's two floors above your own."

"You know that I won't," I said, trying to sound stony. "If I were a great beauty and could have any man in the world, you wouldn't be in my consideration."

He laughed. While I couldn't tell which part of it warranted his amusement, I also wished I'd said nothing at all. In my wordlessness, he released me, and I wasted no time retreating to Syaoran's side.

We exchanged quiet glances, waiting for a dance that I knew. My hand grazed his in a silent plea, and his own gently took hold.

"He knows," I whispered.

Syaoran's fingers gave my own a soft squeeze, and his expression showed slight concern. A wordless understanding. Awkwardness played in when we danced again, both of us trying to hide it.

All I could think was how glad I would be to leave a place with so many people around. Since arriving, I got stares and harassment. I would be glad to leave, to work off one last year in Lord Kwan's villa, and to go home where I wouldn't... Except, would they stare at me? The girl who stayed with the Juneun for five years, with all the rumors about what I did there. Would I be so unwelcomed in my own village?

"Don't let him think he got to you," whispered Syaoran. "I'll handle it."

"How?" I asked, keeping our conversation quiet.

He took my hand, offering a kind smile. "I'll think of something."

Lord Kwan made his arrival alongside Genji, both appearing content about some unspoken matter. Maybe something to do with the conversation beneath the wisteria. My eyes started to scan the crowd, trying to think of which woman captured his heart enough for that kind of talk. Every Juneun woman was a beauty, which didn't help me decide. I'd even spotted Feng among the masses, almost not recognizing her without her serpent tail.

I spent so much time fixated on trying to guess, I didn't notice Lord Kwan approach.

"Are you engaged for the next dance?"

My shoulder's jumped high at his kind voice.

"No, my lord," answered Syaoran, giving a subtle push to my back.

Lord Kwan offered his hand, giving his full watch to me. "May I?"

Stiff, I nodded. "Except—I don't know this one."

He tilted his head. "The next one then."

The music ended, the dancers stopped, a familiar rhythm picked up, and I was led away. I don't know what possessed me, but I couldn't keep stupid words from spilling out of my mouth.

"Wouldn't you rather be dancing with the girl you're in love with?"

He looked at me, brow quirked. "Who would that be?"

I blinked, unable to answer right away as the dance started and required my full attention to not trip. Falling in rhythm, I spoke. "You were gone last night. And under the wisteria, I thought... Aren't you in love with one of the ladies here?"

His gentle smile stayed on him as a glint of amusement reflected in his eyes. "No."

I was more confused, and found that I couldn't form a follow up question and remember the steps at the same time. When a second dance I knew followed, I accepted Lord Kwan's offer to continue without hesitation, smiling as I did.

My heart felt light again, unburdened in knowing he didn't hold someone special in his own. In that dance, I'd only missed one step.

Breathless, and happy, I returned to the bystanders beside him. Syaoran was gone. When I didn't see him in the crowds or among the next dancers, I assumed he'd gone back to the room—something I thought odd, considering he'd said to take up at least one more dance with me to appear like we were a couple. Still, it seemed the most logical reason for his absence, and a good idea.

An even better idea when Urekkato started to make his way over.

"I'm sorry, my prince, but I was about to retire for the night, with Lord Kwan's permission."

"You won't grant me one more for the politeness?" insisted Urekkato in a sly tone.

"Perhaps another night, Prince Urekkato," said Lord Kwan, picking up my discomfort. "I am tired myself and require my attendant."

Urekkato eyed us, his gaze slowly trailing with suspicion while his expression held. "Another night."

I bowed, as did Lord Kwan before escorting me away.

"I don't mean to drag you away," I whispered. "If you wanted to stay."

"I don't usually enjoy dancing, or watching it go on," said Lord Kwan.

"Then...?" I trailed.

His stony expression softened a little more. "I wanted to dance with you."

I drew my eyes back to the path ahead, my neck tucking only just into my shoulders, and my cheeks happily pinking. "With me?"

"You should know by now that I prefer your company. And I wanted to make sure you indulged in some fun, considering the rough start."

It might've meant nothing more than friendship, but I let myself believe otherwise, mustering two quiet words. "Thank you."

Chapter 62
The Way Things are Done

Syaoran skulked in late into the night. I woke to the sound of the door slide open, quiet as it was compared to so much else. Groggy, my head turned just enough for my eyes to take blurry recognition before succumbing to sleep again.

In the morning, after attending Lord Kwan as usual, and still not fully awake, I entered into mindless inquiries.

"Where were you last night?"

"Lady Towa had me away," said Syaoran, quick and irritated.

I tidied up the vanity in the room. "Had you away? For what?"

He tensed, needing to breath in deep to calm himself. "For favors. She had my head between her thighs until she was satisfied."

I wasn't naïve enough to not understand, especially not after Lin explained things to me and made me more aware. Stupidly, however, my mouth continued on, confused about Syaoran's bitter tone. "You don't like her?"

"It's not about liking her!" snapped Syaoran. "It's about not being free to refuse. No, I don't like stuffing my face in a woman's thighs. But it's the fact that I'm pushed to either perform the favor or be punished with some conjured lie."

Stiff from the shock of his volume, as well as the relay, I blinked. "But, you're a man. And she's... it still happens?"

He scoffed. "I'm a servant. If not for being able to throw Kwan's name behind me as a shield, I'd be brutalized beyond more than—this."

"I'm sorry," I said, facing him and stopping my task to show every ounce of sincerity I had. "I didn't know that could still happen. The talks amongst the women in Lord Kwan's house, I thought it was something that only happened to a female servant. It never occurred to me that..." my words trailed, seeing his frustration. "I'm sorry." I now felt a guilt for having pressured him into kissing me, and my anger at his teases for it lessened by more than half.

In realizing the conversation, I shut my eyes, counting. I didn't want anything more, anything personal, to accidentally be shown, and scolded myself for not having done it sooner.

He shook his head. "It's fine. Men tend to keep it to themselves. How would it make us sound? *A woman forced herself onto me*, and everyone else will say something like *how tragic*, or *didn't you enjoy it?* The other end is, if something is said, there's always the chance she'll reverse it and claimed it was us who forced themselves on *her*."

It all sounded awful. To be a victim, to not be believed, teased and harassed—even punished for it. My heart weighed heavy for him. "Syaoran. If I ever... If you felt like I... With the kiss—I'm sorry."

He forced out a chuckle. "You acted out of desperation. I can forgive that. But if you still want more of me, remember to be gentle."

"Syaoran!" I scolded. With a huff, I reeled my temper back. "Regardless, it shouldn't have happened to you. And I'm sorry I wasn't beside you to deter her."

He scoffed, giving a forced smirk. "There's nothing you could've done. Whether it was Towa or Zhen or Beom, it wouldn't make a difference if you were locked on my arm or not."

"Beom?" I repeated. "But... he's also a man."

"So is Zhen. What's your point?" said Syaoran, continuing to put away our futons.

I stared, jaw dropped.

"At least Zhen has the good enough temper to allow an escape. He prefers when his boys come willingly."

"Beom made you..."

Syaoran stopped completely, looking at me with sorrow. "It was back when I first came into Kwan's service. And it's not something I like to talk about. Ever."

That explained it more. I'd always assumed Syaoran hid when Lord Kwan's brothers visited because they hated fox spirits. Now, the desperation of it became clearer. My own horrible memories concerning Beom resurfaced. "Why is he so hateful?" I muttered.

"Who knows," said Syaoran. "Who cares to know?"

"Did you say anything to Lord Kwan?"

"No. I never said anything. I shouldn't have even told you about it at all." He looked away, shaking with rage.

"Why? When I told him about Juro trying to—"

"Because it's humiliating, Hisa!" yelled Syaoran. "I don't want others to know. It'll only encourage more harassment than I get now for being a fox spirit."

I stayed in stunned silence. Gathering myself, I went to him, trying to lay an embrace for comfort. He pushed away. Not violently, but enough to reject the gesture. I settled for placing a hand on his shoulder.

"I just don't understand why they would do that. You're just as much as Juneun—"

He pulled from me. "Because we're still servants, and that's what they do." He stood, pacing out his frustration. "If I was titled, like Juro, it'd be significantly less, and I could openly refuse any of it."

I did wonder why Syaoran wasn't titled; assuming it was some complicated social rule.

"Kwan did try," said Syaoran. "He titled Juro, and granted lands. A couple others, but... Because Gumiho was..." He rested his face on the tips of his fingers on one hand, the other holding to his hip, letting out a rushed sigh. "It'll take a while."

"I'm sorry," I said, heartbroken for him. "I'm still a stupid, village, human girl. I don't understand all these things and why they're needlessly complicated."

"You're not stupid," said Syaoran, defeat in his tone. Dropping his arms, he dragged himself back to sit beside me. "Almost from the moment we met, you treated me as though I belonged in that house, without question."

I shrugged. "To me, it seemed obvious. Besides, you were the only one who tried to look after me when I first arrived."

He chortled. "Two outcasts. Kwan knows how to pick them."

Softly, I bounced my side off of him. "I'm glad I met you, Syaoran. Even if you do frustrate me a lot."

He chuckled. "I was going to say the same exact things, but I guess I should pick something different."

To that, I laughed.

The days following in the near week-long celebration went by more peaceably than when it started. Still, I never journeyed too far from the castle, fearing I'd lose my way or get pulled aside by a guest too liberal with wine. How anyone could learn their way around, I didn't know.

There was so much to do and see without the additional displays and kiosks. I'd learned that I could get one free treat from a cook stand simply for being part of Lord Kwan's house. The former student of our host, and still in close friendship, created an eagerness to appease. Kiosks with wares outside of food, however, weren't as relaxed with their policies. I was offered a discount, though I hadn't the money anyway, so I simply admired and didn't dare to touch any of the lovely things.

There'd come a day when Lord Kwan and Genji sat away from the events, engaged in a game of shogi. They'd invited me to play, but, in having never played before, I was content to watch them.

Wandering one of the water gardens, I almost lamented that we'd leave the day after tomorrow. It was the last day of Mokryon, and those in the castle were expected to stay one additional day to rest from the festivities.

Newly confident, I went to every dance in the nights following my first. Always, Lord Kwan would take at least one dance with me. Syaoran, of course, did likewise to continue our rouse—and I kept fiercely close to him when I could. Even Genji took my hand in two separate dances, though he didn't speak at all in that time. I didn't mind. It was better than when I was made to feel obliged to accepting Urekkato and try to keep stoic in all his talking.

Most days, I kept to Syaoran's side for hours, trying to act as a deterrent for him. He grew tired of my company somewhere in the day, separating with the assurance that he'd be fine. Often, Lord Kwan would find me and occupy my company.

When alone and walking any part of the grounds, I reveled in the quiet and the far-off chatter. There'd be stretches of time where my footsteps were the loudest thing in the area. On hearing raised voices, and not wanting to accidentally involve myself, I started to walk back the way I came. Until I recognized one voice as Beom's.

My curiosity caused me to stop. And while I knew it was for my own good to ignore it, I couldn't, and crept to the source of the sound. There were other voices, familiar, though I couldn't place how I knew them. Not until I heard Kwang's, sounding in a hurry for something. Careful, I slid the paper-paned door open only a sliver, using the strength of my finger in as slow a motion as possible.

Lord Kwan, and all of his brothers were inside, as was another man, older, who I guessed to be his father. A young woman, whom Syaoran mentioned was Lord Kwan's sister, sat poised to the side. It was a family assembly. And while I shouldn't have spied, I couldn't stop my curiosity in wanting to know what the other members to Lord Kwan's immediate family were like.

Severe, at first glance.

"And you have the nerve to willfully ignore Iseul in favor of your servant," lectured his father, seething.

"From the first day, she's caused a fuss," said Seong. "Involving the newly appointed prince, as well as our host."

"I will mind my own house," said Lord Kwan, disinterested in heated words. "As you undoubtedly mind yours, as well as others."

"Insolence!" spat his father, pacing.

"When Kwan doesn't parade himself with Kurai and humans, he's taken in the company of the Samjo girl," said Seong.

"It seems Kwan is more interested in making a mockery of our family than any duty to our traditions," said Beom. "He keeps himself willfully ignorant of how this also affects prospects for our sister, only just returning to society."

"You mistake me," said Lord Kwan. "The decision to lock Sara away was not mine. And any mockery of our family comes from onlookers, not myself."

His father struck at him then, and my hand gripped tight to the frame of the door.

Yuz and Kwang half rose from their seats, a gesture to plead leniency as they called for their father. For the small show that it was, I felt glad; not every member of Lord Kwan's family was against him, even if they didn't particularly like me or Syaoran.

"I will not suffer more of your arrogance!" roared his father.

Lord Kwan, opposite, kept himself restrained.

"If it is brought to me, by her family, you will marry Iseul," said his father. "After giving Eumeh away, this is the best opportunity you have to maintain our position in society and erase the folly of your past."

"If the arrangement is much desired, you have other sons," said Lord Kwan. And his father struck at him again. Rather than retaliate, or show any hint of discomfort—though I knew it must've caused great pain—Lord Kwan stayed stony.

"Unlike my youngest sons, the eldest remember the point for coming to Mokryon," said his father, a growl in his voice. "You've given away most of your lands to Kurai, abusing your position with titling them. Iseul's dowry alone makes up for your lacking. And it will position us better to match Sara. But only so long as you stop fraternizing with servants and take your prospects seriously!"

"That's what all this fuss is about?" asked Lord Kwan, sarcastic amusement in his voice.

"If you challenge this, boy, I will cut you from inheritance."

"Cut it," said Lord Kwan, quick to answer, and gaining a unanimous look of shock.

"You would disown your family?" asked Sara, speaking at last. "Are you so eager to create a greater rift between us—for Kwang will do the same, as always, when you behave heedlessly!"

Lord Kwan said nothing, eyes locked with his father's.

I couldn't understand it. Why a family would treat each other with such brutality, or pressure one member into marrying before he was ready—especially given they were seemingly immortal, and hardly affected by the passing of time. What I didn't understand most of all was why Lord Kwan allowed himself to be beaten and berated. Why didn't he fight back, or stand up for himself? He was one of the most powerful Juneun. Not a small and timid human.

When his father brough up that black bamboo rod again, my fury took over me, and I slid the door wide open without announcement or grace.

"That's enough!" I commanded, feeling my face turn hot. "A family is supposed to look after one another, not be at each other's throats."

"Hisa," warned Lord Kwan, low in his voice.

But I couldn't stop myself, not by choice. Rage consumed me beyond the point of reason. "Lord Kwan has done nothing to deserve this. If anything, Lord Genji and Prince Urekkato both speak very highly of him and what he's accomplished. They say nothing about the achievements of his brothers. I'd be surprised if the prince even remembered their names."

Lord Kwan stood then, marching towards me and taking me away from the stunned and scowling faces. In his rough motion, I saw the marks of the bamboo rod displayed on him, and only felt more righteous in my defiance, even as I was dragged off.

Away, Lord Kwan pulled me into a storeroom, bearing a severe expression, and slammed the door closed.

"You should have kept out of it," growled Lord Kwan.

"But, they were—"

"It's not your place!" Again, he looked at me with a rage.

I stiffened, but my own fury prevented petrification. "I couldn't just stand by like a scared mouse and let them do that to you!"

I saw him fight to retain himself, tempering his next words. "You don't know what you've done."

I held my gaze, realizing for the first time how heavy I was breathing. Silence. Both of us trying not to lash out at each other. "Why would you let them treat you like that?"

"He's my lord father," said Lord Kwan. "It's the way things are."

"That doesn't make it right!" I argued. "You've done nothing wrong. Whatever happened before you came to Mount Tora, I know you've made up for it."

"You know nothing."

"I know that whatever it was, you would try to make things right. That's who you are. You look after all of us. In the villages and your home and everywhere you go. Even the animals and the earth."

He tempered himself more, heaving a sigh. "You cannot go bursting into a private meeting, regardless of the reason."

"But—"

"Hisa! This isn't a game."

We leered at each other, and my bold impulse had me shove him. Or, I tried. He stayed unmoved, with only his expression becoming slightly bewildered by the intent.

"You always stand up for me. For all of us! And you won't stand up for yourself?"

Lock jawed, he worked to loosen his muscles enough to answer. "They're my family—"

"They're bullies! And no matter who it is, don't ask me to stand by and watch them hurt you. I won't do it. Even if it was my own father and brothers, I won't just sit there and let it happen!"

"Hisa, stop!"

I obeyed. Not out of fear, but from my own breathlessness.

"You have no idea what trouble you could've caused. Things are different here. And I've spoiled you too much for you to know that." He looked down and away.

My heart dropped. "Of course I don't know," I whispered, still seething. "There's a lot about the Juneun nobility I know nothing about. But, what I do know is that no one should have to suffer needless ire. Or be belittled for the mistakes they've made in the past and tried to atone for."

For a long time, he was silent. "I'm not sure I can atone for everything I've done. Whether or not you believe me, my father has every reason to still hold scorn against me. I don't expect you to understand it all."

"Maybe I don't want to understand!" I snapped. "Why would I want to give sympathy to someone so cruel to their own son?"

"Hisa," said Lord Kwan, meeting my eye with a tone of finality. "That is enough."

It was enough to make me shy from haughty words, but not dissuade me entirely. I dropped my gaze and quieted. "You took up a sword against your brother for me. If it was my father beating on me, and my brothers berating me, would you do nothing?"

"That's not the same, Hisa," said Lord Kwan with a lingering irritation.

"Then explain to me how it is different!" I shot my sight back on him, scowling. Not for long, however. His saddened expression tore at me. "Tell me why I can't fight for someone who's important to me."

He stared. "Hisa..."

I hugged my arms around myself, my heart heavy and my head throbbing, and I looked away.

He went on with a sigh. "You're still that girl who ran up the mountain."

I shook my head. "I want to be better than I was back then. To be able to do more than just sob and beg."

He lifted my chin in his hand, a single, swift motion that demanded my attention. "Hisa. You're fine just as you are."

"Then why do I feel so useless?" I countered, now punishing myself. "To the point where I try to protect you and end up needing you to save me."

His hint of a smile returned. "I appreciate that you want to fight for me. That's already more than most Juneun women are willing to do. Even with magic at their disposal."

I tried to smile back for him, failing. And I couldn't tell if he was angry and trying to put me at ease so that I would stop my arguing, or if he sincerely meant it. So, I stared into his eyes, searching for some clue to help me better understand him in that moment. When he started to leave, letting me go, I clung.

"What is it?"

I hesitated, but they'd said as much in all the arguing that he wasn't engaged. I shut my eyes, counting, and looked at him a last time while my courage was still present. "Kiss me?"

His perplexed expression returned; keeping still, he studied me, trying to read me.

I started to let go. Maybe I was wrong, and his decline of who his family preferred was because he'd found someone else that they disapproved of. "If you don't... don't want—you don't have to. It's fine."

His fingers slid under my chin again, turning my cheek, and he placed a kiss at the center of my forehead.

The perfect gesture. And I felt myself unburdened from my own upset.

Chapter 63
Lord Kwan XVI

K wan remembered it clearly. The morning Syaoran ran up to him, behaving not as himself, and demanded a private conversation. His mind had gone blank of everything else in hearing the most important part of the exchange: she hadn't given away her heart. Not yet. It'd been a rouse against Juro's continued advance.

It required all his will to not rush out to find her. No... That was too forward. A thundering tiger would only scare a magpie into flight. It was different with her. While a lady of court would be dazzled by a dramatic declaration, he couldn't expect her to accept the gesture simply because it came from himself and not Juro.

There was also to consider how she described the sort of man she would never give her heart to, and if she categorized him that way. He'd need more subtlety to see where her affection for him ended, and if it was only a fondness.

The wisteria tree made for an excellent excuse. He'd compared her to it before, and perhaps the memory would help him to make her understand his feelings. She liked the idea of it, or the imagery, at least. Though, there seemed a sadness and a sort of rejection when he asked her opinion. Any lady would have guessed he referred to herself with those sorts of questions and become giddy. Hisa dismissed it, placing the standing inquiry to a third party, or otherwise not counting herself as a possibility.

In an effort to repair any awkward feeling, he brought her to the flame behind the falls. The tension eased, distracting from previous conversation. Too much so. He'd been caught off guard by a more personal question. While he knew she meant it innocently, his instinct was to hold suspicion and cut off all inquiry.

But she was Hisa. Not Gumiho. Not a greedy woman sifting out what aesthetic would best compliment her or that she could use to her full advantage. Hisa satisfied herself with a vague description, asking nothing particular after; he'd slipped too much in his tongue.

Nor was she empty headed, understanding, to an extent, his meaning for delighting her in an impromptu excursion.

He comprehended better that she felt a friendship only with him. Or, so he thought.

"Kiss me?"

He stared, desperately wanting to understand. It didn't matter how she'd dressed or styled her hair, or whether she hid behind a cosmetic. Her dark-brown eyes, lined with thick lashes were always Hisa. He wanted to pull her in with animalistic fervor, to let the action be his expression.

No.

He would only frighten her as Juro had. Above all else, he didn't want to be the source of her fears, still hating himself for the night she bolted away. Were a thousand arrows pointed at her, he'd take them all. Even if she didn't love him in return.

Outside the cavern, he was reminded why he felt so strongly for her. Her tenderness towards the things that could never repay her. Unrivaled in genuine forgiveness and understanding—not in complex social orders, but at the core of things. A giver. Wholehearted and sincere.

He wanted to say it then and there, that he loved her, that it was her he wanted to take vows with beneath the old wisteria tree. But there was too much in the way. Not least of all that she saw herself as a servant first.

"A real kiss."

Despite his joke, his heart picked up.

She began to fumble, and he feared she would reconsider. Soft, warm, and perfectly imperfect Hisa. She reciprocated his gesture, emboldening him to mischief.

"Are you going to ask for another kiss?"

Her face twisted to surprised offense. But something about the stark expression endeared him. "Lord Kwan!"

"Lady Hisa." He tried the title onto her, wanting to know if she discerned his meaning.

The entirety of her changed as a result. "Don't call me that…"

A needle of guild pricked inside his chest. Desperate, he persisted. She chastised herself in response, and he was no better off in knowing her feelings.

Fondness. That's all it was.

In the second night of Mokryon, he'd decided on consoling himself with a dance. It wasn't so unusual for a master to take his favorite servant, or for friends to engage each other.

"Wouldn't you rather be dancing with the girl you're in love with?"

Again, he found himself surprised by her assumptions.

"You were gone last night. And under the wisteria, I thought… Aren't you in love with one of the ladies here?"

That was it. A distancing based on a misunderstanding. He felt a relief in knowing she didn't jealously hold on to her thoughts, and new hope swelled that he might be able to properly learn of her feelings.

In their escape from the crowds, and the following conversation, he tested.

"You should know by now that I prefer your company. And I wanted to make sure you indulged in some fun, considering the rough start."

For a while, she gave no response. Had he pressed too far? Made her uncomfortable? It was all the more difficult, given their stations to one another, but had he made it impossible?

"Thank you," said Hisa in a sweet tone, quiet as it was.

And Kwan didn't know his answer.

Nor would he in the days following. How much he wanted to indulge her with anything she admired, refraining for her own sake. He didn't want her to feel indebted to him. When entertainers took up a square and dazzled the masses, he couldn't look away from her. Her smile, her laugh, he wanted to do something to make her direct those at him. He wanted to take her hand, to pull her into his embrace, and not care who saw or what they said. But not at the cost of her good opinion of him.

There was frustratingly little else he could think of, even when summoned by his family. His attention only present when she was mentioned bitterly. They spoke as if she were a mange dog in the way of things, rather than a person of interest to their own superiors—willfully denying it through jealousy.

Kwan treaded the conversation, holding back from drawing his sword. Whole, he could best his brothers. In lacking his soul, he was uncertain of the outcome; regardless of it, he wouldn't dishonor Genji with provoked violence in his home. Nor would he reveal that Genji appointed him as the inheritor, lest it draw up more demands. Better to keep it secret, even from his youngest brother. The humiliation would be returned a hundred times over when the transition took place. Were it tomorrow or a century or more, it didn't matter.

His stoic reveling ceased with Hisa's outburst. Kwan had never seen her so furious. For the briefest moment, she was neither a timid hare or an awkward magpie, but a tigress. When his mind caught up, he warned with his tone. She didn't relent. The foolish girl was about to expose too much of herself, unwittingly about to walk into a position he couldn't protect her from.

In leaving, taking her with him, he showed disrespect. But better that than to see her suffer the consequence of a world she didn't understand. His frustration took hold of his tongue.

She didn't back down. Not right away. And not out of disrespect. He wanted to keep her safe, and to make her comprehend it in an instant. He just didn't know how. Through it all, her good opinion of him staved off an anger, but cultivated his frustration.

"Tell me why I can't fight for someone who's important to me."

Her words caused him to stumble. There was a lingering fire in her eyes, even as the rest of her began to submit to her emotions.

He'd already decided to endure whatever her punishment onto himself, knowing it would break her, deliberately. And he'd decided not to say a word about it, if only to protect her further. In looking at her now, he wanted to pull her close, to shield her from what she'd done.

But both emotions were still too hot for it to be understood.

"You're still that girl who ran up the mountain," said Kwan, admiration in his every word. It'd taken until recently to realize the amount of courage she mustered nearly four years ago. Now, it didn't seem so much like a pathetic groveling. Rather, an act of love.

He'd wanted nothing to do with her then. Things had changed, and now he wanted only for her to stay, knowing full well her desire to go home.

He would miss her.

Resolving himself in that feeling, he let go. She grabbed hold.

"What is it?"

Everything about her became calm, shy, reverting to the girl from years before. "Kiss me?"

Confused, Kwan watched her. She'd been fierce only minutes before, tempered shortly after, and the flame in her eyes started to dwindle. She was punishing herself, and the need to safeguard her from it took over.

He loved her.

As angry as Seong was on Kwan's return, next in line to become the family patriarch, he hesitated. Kwan declared that he would take the full punishment, and his eldest brother, usually hungry for war, couldn't bring himself to raise an arm against him. Yuz stoutly refused, defaulting it back to their father.

Not a one of them showed more than the slightest hint of a wince as Kwan endured every swing. Kwang was the one who fidgeted most, restraining himself in watching. One hundred strikes, and bruises in their wake.

It was left to Seong to further discipline his brothers, allowing their father to retire elsewhere. He dismissed Yuz and Beom, leaving them to escort Sara about the grounds. After a long, glowering stare, Seong relented and stepped behind his brother to kneel.

"You shouldn't have provoked him," said Seong. "Beom already gets father riled up. More easily now, with mother's health in decline."

Kwan said nothing, keeping still despite the agony across every inch of his back. He winced at the touch of his brother, a surge of pain from it.

"Why didn't you give up the girl? You suffered more because of it."

"Because it would break her," said Kwan after a long silence.

Seong sighed. "You spoil that child too much. Like you did with the fox."

"What use am I if I cannot protect my own household?"

"Take off your shirt," commanded Seong, softening his tone.

"Because of what grandfather said about the worth of a man?" asked Kwang.

Kwan obeyed, moving carefully to avoid as much pain as possible, needing Seong's help in the end. "It is not by how one treats their equals, but their inferiors that heaven judges us."

"Hold still," said Seong. "My healing isn't as potent."

"I have to give Hisa credit," said Kwang. "Despite being human, and a woman, she keeps putting herself in the fray to defend her master. That level of loyalty is rare to find."

"Seung was like that," said Seong. His voice threatened to choke in just speaking their late brother's name, forcing him to swallow to maintain his conviction. "It led him to an early grave. There's a line between a loyal act and a reckless one."

How different would things be, if Seung hadn't followed his older brother and chased after Seokga to retrieve their eldest sister? Their mother might not be as bereft, and their father less harsh. Seong might've been able to follow a gentler nature, and Beom better tempered. Perhaps the tragedy of Gumiho would never have occurred. If the three eldest had lived, what a different world this might've been.

Everything changed after their deaths, with their father prioritizing power and political strategy over all else.

"She should know her place," said Seong. "A servant does not interfere with the affairs of their master, or his associates."

Kwan winced, becoming lock jawed at the start of Seong's spell.

"Is Juro still set on having her?" asked Kwang.

"Do not engage with gossip of that level," warned Seong. "It's unbecoming."

Something in his older brother's sentiment made Kwan realize. His youngest brother was now without a mentor. Since Borsi, there was a hushed attempt to undo all association and place him into new guidance.

When he was dismissed, Kwan made for the castle to call on Genji. An arrangement was made, one his father couldn't readily refuse. If, in three years' time, a better option did not present itself, Kwang would be set here, able to maintain some of his jovial nature. It was Kwan's duty, after all, to look after those younger than himself. Only, he would do so in his own way.

He had no right to ask it of Genji, pleading his case to his for master's gentle soul. While reluctant, Genji sympathized with the circumstance, agreeing to take one last apprentice.

"It is unorthodox to take more than one pupil from a family," said Genji. "I suppose it does suit me to do so."

"If there is anything to repay this favor," said Kwan, "ask it of me."

A set of cups and small vase of jasmine wine were set before them, with the Elk prince gesturing to his servants to not wait on them so closely.

"You asked me why I wanted to name you heir," said Genji, pouring the wine. "I had always planned, when Isa was alive, that Tetsuden should go not to the most powerful of my pupils, but the kindest."

Kwan sipped, mulling over the information. "If you find Kwang to be more fitting of that description, I'm inclined to agree. I will not quarrel it."

Genji's gentle expression picked up a smile. "Isa supported the decision. A good woman isn't a perfect woman. It's her imperfection that can make a man feel powerful, and bring him to his knees at the same time."

Kwan studied his former mentor, looking for what he implied.

"I was too grieved when she died. If not for this past year to reintroduce me to all my surviving students, I feared I would not have a successor. And that her most treasured places would be ripped out by whomever the Mireu deemed worthy of Tetsuden."

Kwan allowed the start of a smile, catching Genji's meaning. "Should there be a lady of this castle, I will temper some decisions."

Genji nodded. "Your staff are enjoying the grounds?"

"Syaoran is dismayed with the crowds. But hiding away will do him no favors."

Genji lingered his gaze. "The rest?"

Kwan's smile inched up, "Hisa likes it. She's overwhelmed by the society, but I think she's fond of the flora. The trees in particular."

Content, Genji asked nothing more, allowing them to sip the wine in a spell of splendid silence.

In the final night of dancing, though he still ached, Kwan sought out Hisa, if only to be certain she didn't hold a disdain for him. They'd parted ways so awkwardly that day. In seeing a welcoming smile on her face, he relaxed himself.

"Dance with me?" asked Hisa.

It surprised him, since she'd never taken the initiative before. She'd grown used to him asking, he supposed, and they'd stayed in each other's company so long. A lingering pain and stiffness reminded him of his earlier beating. But how could he refuse her? She smiled at him, a light in her eyes.

He offered his hand, ignoring the warning looks of his brothers elsewhere and the curious brows of others. Any move too wide or too sudden caused a hot throb in his muscles, as did any point when the dance required that he lift her; she wasn't heavy by any means—simply the tension in his shoulders from lifting her caused pain.

"Are you alright?" asked Hisa towards the end of the dance.

"Shouldn't I be?"

She frowned with a huff. The music reached the end, and polite applause took up the air.

"It felt like you were distracted with something," said Hisa as they walked back to the sidelines.

"A long day," said Kwan.

She kept a concerned expression, reaching up for his face, to where she'd seen him struck. Not now, he realized, catching her hand. Not so publicly. He reminded himself then, that she was still his prisoner and servant. To confess his feelings would only pressure her acceptance—seeming to demand it. Until she was free to blatantly refuse him, he needed restraint.

Else, he was no better than Juro in his behavior.

The memory of it reminded him of another reason to prevent a desired touch. They still had to keep the rouse of her intimacy with Syaoran. The thought of it irritated him, soothed only by the knowledge that she didn't have anyone in her heart yet.

Wait for me, Hisa, he thought. Wait for me.

Chapter 64
Know Your Place

The last night of dances. I was glad to know things didn't stay awkward between myself and Lord Kwan. Silly as it was, knowing he'd never return my feelings, I still wanted him to think well of me and be open in our friendship.

We retired early, and probably for the best, avoiding Urekkato among others. My frets began in returning to our room, realizing I hadn't seen Syaoran in a while.

"What's wrong?" asked Lord Kwan.

"I'm a little worried for Syaoran," I said. "I know that there's a lot of Juneun who aren't the friendliest towards him."

"He will be fine," said Lord Kwan, trying to reassure. "Regardless of feelings towards fox spirits, he's a guest. Shutting him out of sight of everyone would only perpetuate unfavorable perceptions of him."

It sounded well and all, but Lord Kwan didn't know the extent of the harassment. Likewise, I didn't know how much I could say to justify my anxiousness. He'd kept it from Lord Kwan for his own reasons—the same way he kept from blurting out my feelings for Lord Kwan, I needed to refrain from speaking on his behalf.

To my relief, Syaoran entered little more than an hour later, seeming himself. At least, as far as I could tell. The one thing I thought odd was in his tending to Lord Kwan, helping him shed out of his formal clothing. His fox ears flattened a moment and he shut his eyes a few seconds before continuing—something I didn't recall him ever doing before. I ignored the strangeness of it. Since coming here, I'd been so overwhelmed by emotions and events that I undoubtedly missed a number of normal tics he had.

But there was something about this time that stuck out. I couldn't quite place why.

Instead, I kept myself happily occupied in thinking of how everyone not accommodated in the castle would be leaving, and how I could more freely walk the gardens without dread.

In the morning, I noticed Syaoran perform the same tic in attending Lord Kwan. When we were left to tidy the room, I couldn't help myself, much as I tried to resist.

"Why do you keep closing your eyes like that?"

His fox ears went pointed. "Like—? Oh. They're just a little itchy. Must be the extra pollen in the air."

It seemed like a reasonable explanation, given we were in spring and surrounded by blooms. My mind wouldn't relent. There was something about it that sounded familiar in an ominous way. And I didn't recall him doing this when we first arrived. Could it really be a delayed reaction?

The last things put away, I decided not to dwell on it. While Juro and Lord Kwan's family would be leaving, Urekkato was still in the castle and I would have to avoid him if possible.

That's when I realized.

"Are you leaving, Hisa?" asked Syaoran, opening the door.

"Not yet," I said, closing my eyes and counting. "Come here and help me with something."

He twisted his expression, closing the door and coming beside me. "With what?"

I stood in front of the vanity so I could watch his face. "I tripped yesterday and I think I injured my back. I'm the only girl in Lord Kwan's guest staff, and... would you take a look? If it's nothing, that's a relief, but if I hurt myself, I'll need to rest it before we ride home."

A nervousness crawled over his expression, and he folded his arms. He looked between me and the vanity while I pretended not to notice, his ears starting to flatten. "I guess."

While I didn't know how long Urekkato's sight spell could be ended for, it stood to reason that he wouldn't tell Syaoran either. He'd never get a look if we knew exactly. I unfastened the ties of my dress, holding to the skirt and waiting for Syaoran to slide down the bouses to look at my back.

As expected, he hesitated a second after his fingers touched the collar, his eyes noted the vanity mirror, and he shut them. I counted. One, two, three, four, and he opened them again. Frowning I spun on my heel.

"Urekkato put his sight spell on you!"

Syaoran jumped, surprised by my sudden shift and tone. "What?"

"You closed your eyes and counted."

"I wanted to give you privacy!"

"Then why did you open them again?" I demanded, fastening my ties in a hurried manner.

"To see—is that why you stood *right here*?"

"I needed to see your face to be sure. You closed your eyes and counted to four. That negates the spell for a while."

He frowned, face flushing red. "How do you even know about that?"

"Because he tried to make the same deal with me."

"Deal?" echoed Syaoran, blinking and perplexed.

I realized I was about to accidentally expose myself, scolding him for something that I'd also done, and looked away. "He offered me his essence of luck. I told him it was creepy and felt too much like spying." I didn't want to lie. That had happened, though with more details. "Why did you do it?"

"I—" Syaoran hesitated, darting his gaze and working his jaw. "He knew we weren't. And he threatened to tell Juro. I, I was trying to—"

"To protect me," I said, realizing.

We stared at each other, our emotions settling. I threw my arms around him an instant later, holding him in my own protective embrace. His arms fell around me in a gentle squeeze.

"You're my best friend," said Syaoran. "I love you."

"I love you too," I said. Why was it so hard to say that to Lord Kwan?

We let go of each other, slow and making sure the other was ready for the release.

Walking the grounds in the afternoon, I felt better able to breath, and certain that Urekkato wouldn't be watching through my eyes on a boring excursion. He'd said he casted his sight spell hundreds of times. Surely, someone else would be of interest, leaving me free to neglect ending the spell so frequently.

I waited out most of the bustle before entering the stables, even if the coming and going was more from servants than any lord or lady visiting. I felt bad for not having visited Saburo, and snuck over treats to share among the horses that'd brought us to the castle. In little more than a year, I wouldn't be able to see the stallion as often. And I lamented that.

Outside the stables, I'd spotted Genji being pressed upon by Lord Kwan's sister, stalling her host from seeing off other guests with suggestive language. Shy, and more accommodating than other Juneun, Genji kept averting his gaze with a rigid stance. In seeing his discomfort, and in wanting to snub someone unbothered by the abuse towards Lord Kwan, I straightened myself to make an appearance. In the short walk, my mind raced to find some excuse to pull him away. Syaoran had said to tell anyone trying to lure me with the excuse of Genji's summons. The question now was what excuse I could conjure to pull Genji himself from an uncomfortable situation. Any guest still in the castle didn't have the same sway as the host.

Except one.

"Lord Genji," I announced with a respectful bow. "The prince has requested you on an urgent matter."

Genji paused, perplexed. "Did... Did he say what the business...?"

"He did not, my lord," I said, thinking fast on how to persuade things. "It was not my place to ask."

Nodding, Genji excused himself and gestured for me to lead on. Far enough away, I revealed the rouse.

"You looked trapped, my lord," I explained. "And Lord Kwan did say to look after you when you came to court. He didn't specify when or if I should ever stop."

Genji chuckled, brushing back a stray hair from my face. "That was kind of you."

"If I did disturb something, my lord, I apologize."

He gave a single shake of his head. "You acted perfectly. I will be... taking your master's younger brother into my tutelage. Lady Sara... she wanted an excuse to be around more."

"I thought it looked that way," I said, relieved that my action didn't cause my friend any trouble. "She wants to be your wife, doesn't she? And if you have a place in your heart for more of the family, it makes sense she'd take the opportunity."

"Observant of you," said Genji with an approving smile.

I chuckled. "It's taken me up to now to get it. And I don't want to see my friend pressured into marriage—even if it is to Lord Kwan's sister."

He studied me a moment, bearing a warm expression. "Kwan hasn't been this lively in a century. And... I don't recall last seeing him dance with the same woman. Not every night."

"Never?"

"Or... in the same night."

I chuckled, cupping my mouth to better muffle it. "I know he said he doesn't usually like it, but maybe something changed his mind."

Genji lifted a brow at me, taking the lead and continuing our walk. "There's... there is not an attachment...? Between the two of you?"

"A friendship, my lord," I answered. "I don't think it goes any deeper than that."

Silence. He contemplated something as we entered the castle. "Kwan was my student for a long time. And... a friend longer since. He was more impulsive, when... when he was young. Eager for a legacy."

"That sounds a lot different than the Lord Kwan I know," I said. Though, I did remind myself just how much I'd changed in the last few years. Between my mother's death and coming up the mountain, I was different every year. Little by little.

"The things he experienced... surrounding Gumiho... it changed him."

"What was he like before?" I asked, hesitant.

Genji gave a sheepish smile. "More like his younger brother."

It made me smile as well. Kwang seemed the only brother Lord Kwan was fond of. The only one full of life and willing to humor.

"Hisa," called Lord Kwan, patient and pleasant. "Lord Genji, are you in need of my attendant?"

"Not at all," said Genji. "Simply enjoying her company."

Polite, I left Genji's side to follow Lord Kwan. In the silence I thought about what our host had said. We were fond of each other. How far that extended... More than friendship? I still doubted it after the menagerie of beauties making their appearances during the festival. He'd danced with at least one other woman aside from his sister, I was sure. I wasn't his only person of attention.

What Genji implied—if Lord Kwan did feel more, he would've said so, wouldn't he?

"Lord Kwan?"

He glanced to me.

Now came the hard part. "Are you in love with anyone?"

Something in his expression became cold. "Is that your question for the day?"

I felt my face slacken, taken aback. Throughout spring, I'd been more frivolous in my questions, and he indulged me. I'd thought the formality of the arrangement was gone. "Yes," I said, shying.

He looked ahead. "No."

My heart weighed heavy at the direct answer, and I kept silent the rest of the way.

We stopped in front of our shared room. I opened the door, as my duty to him, but he gestured for me to enter first. Since coming to Tetsuden, I didn't understand him. Sometimes I was his friend both publicly and privately. Other times I was merely his servant, even in private.

Inside, I found a dress on his bed. Not one of mine. And my heart hurt. Did he want me to see this? To know another woman was here with him, even after he'd said he wasn't in love? Then again, to the Juneun lords, love and sex were separate matters.

"It's the one you were admiring the other day," said Lord Kwan, casual and warm.

"What?" I broke from my despair, looking to him and back to the neatly lain garment. The pale teal and soft blue, styled opposite from the mature ones I brought. It was the same one I'd seen near the start of the celebrations.

"I had it altered for you." He stood at my side, placing his hand on the opposite shoulder. "Otherwise, it might've been yours the following day."

"Why are you doing this?" I asked, my voice going hoarse.

He shifted his gaze to me, a kindlier look in his eyes and that hint of a smile returning. "I wanted to do something to make you happy. After the incident with Juro, you looked so miserable. I should have prepared better for you, so it could be avoided all together. I got caught up in other matters, and I'd forgotten."

I stared into his eyes, trying to read his expression and frustrated with myself for finding I couldn't.

"Will you forgive my neglect?"

To that, I dropped my gaze, bringing my arms and folded hands against my chest. "A master doesn't need the forgiveness of a servant."

"No," agreed Lord Kwan. "But a friend does."

I slipped from his touch. "I don't understand."

His start of a smile faded, replaced with something akin to bewilderment.

"I thought I did a decent job guessing your feelings and moods. But lately they're in so many directions, and I don't know what you mean by any of it. I'm confused, and frustrated, and I don't know what you want..."

He brushed his fingers against my cheek, pushing stray hairs behind my ear, and brought me into a gentle embrace. All of it slow. His arms became snug, as though trying to protect me from myself.

"Our roles here are different, and more complicated by who our host is," said Lord Kwan, tender. "I shouldn't have expected you know every subtlety."

Listening, I clung to his shirt, burying my face in the soft, red fabric.

"I'm sorry. I never meant to cause you distress, Hisa. I care about you. Deeply."

I started to slide my arms around him to return the embrace, stopping when I realized my cosmetic was rubbing off. I pushed back, a shock of horror going through me.

He blinked, looking down at my expression. "I've overstepped?"

"N-no. Your shirt—I'm so sorry!"

He quirked a brow, inspecting. "It's alright."

I opened my mouth to say more, realizing what it probably looked like to anyone else.

"Hisa," interrupted Lord Kwan. With a stroke of his hand, the blemish was gone, reminding me again that this was a simple matter for many Juneun. "I only want for you to be happy."

I stared at the clean, bold coloring, slowly drawn to the koi fish embroidered at each shoulder. "I'm sorry," I said. "I've been overwhelmed, and I let it get to me."

He placed a hand atop my hair, fingers stroking through. "I would've been surprised if you didn't get overwhelmed at least once. Even without a rough beginning."

"I'm really not cut out for these sorts of things," I said, putting on a smile to battle off frustrated tears from forming. "I'm still just a village girl."

His free hand came to my face, thumb wiping aside a stray bead of water. "Not just," said Lord Kwan. For a mere second, I thought he meant to say more, but he left it at that.

Chapter 65
Fox Spirits

W e'd nearly reached the edge of Genji's lands where Lord Kwan could then cast his spell to spirit us home, when one of the magpie servant boys flew up to call for Lord Kwan. There was some matter to return to regarding his brother's apprenticeship. He'd ordered my dismount, lifting me onto Saburo and placing my sack with us.

"Saburo knows the spell," said Lord Kwan. "He will take you back. I will arrive shortly after. Tomorrow at the latest." Nothing more was explained as he sent us off, sharing awkward glances.

Dizziness took me before reaching the other side of the spell, as it had before. I bore it better, knowing now to expect it. However, recovery from it fast ended when we came through the inner gate.

"Where's Lord Kwan?" demanded Lin as we dismounted.

"He stayed behind with unfinished business," said Syaoran. "He'll be here tomorrow."

"We need him now," said Lin, impatient. "It's about the new girl, Uno."

"What about her?" I asked, unfastening my things from the saddle.

"She's a fox spirit spy," said Lin.

Syaoran and I both stopped to look at her.

"Just because she's a fox spirit, doesn't make her a spy," I said.

"Then why did she hide it from everyone?" snapped Lin. "Everyone knows about Syaoran being in Lord Kwan's household. If she didn't come to spy or work against us, she shouldn't need to hide her identity."

"How did you learn this?" asked Syaoran. His voice kept steadfast, though his ears flattened in submission.

"Koji got off his leash two days ago," said Lin. "She ran and took a tumble. Her hair fell out of place and her ears showed."

"That's not enough to say she came here to spy," I said, righteous anger brewing up in me.

"Hisa," commanded Syaoran, "calm yourself."

"But—"

"Put away your things," continued Syaoran. "This a matter for the master." He took my sack from me, a cue to follow.

Reluctant, I obeyed. At my door, he looked over his shoulder at me, closing his eyes as he breathed out a sigh. I realized his meaning, that he was ending the sight spell. When he turned away to open my door, I did likewise. Whether or not Urekkato told him I had a sight spell on me, or if he only suspected, he didn't mention.

"Uno's not a bad person," I plead once inside.

"I know," said Syaoran. "I already sifted that out."

My expression twisted.

"From the moment I saw her," explained Syaoran, "before Lord Kwan picked her. I knew she was a fox spirit."

"But—then, why didn't you—?"

"Because it wouldn't do any good," said Syaoran, half scolding me. "How does it look if one fox deems another has no ill intent without evidence, only her word?"

I couldn't argue that much, not after how much the nobles gossiped and what grief it brought on Lord Kwan. It'd look suspicious if Syaoran was the one to make the decision. Lin probably did all she could to show a level headedness, and not have her position challenged while not acting so hastily.

"Then let me at least stay beside her," I said. "She's my attendant, and my responsibility, right? So—"

"Absolutely not," said Syaoran. "Everyone knows Kwan has a bit of favoritism, even if he won't admit it. Regardless of whether it not it's true, it'll look that way. And it'll breed resentment in the house. You have to let this run its course."

"But she's good!" I argued. "Can't I do anything for her?"

He sighed, giving me an apologetic expression. "Not without evidence of her good character. Gumiho may be gone, but that doesn't absolve every fox spirit of wrong doing if they served under her. Who's to say Uno isn't loyal to a different Kurai? I know it sounds convoluted. And it is. But that is the argument they are making."

I started to understand more, feeling the sting of defeat before I could fight. "That's not fair."

"I know," said Syaoran, half matching my tone.

"Can't I at least see her?"

He stared a while, deep in thought. "Only for a short while. With someone supervising it—not me, a house guard. Whatever you want to do or say needs to be done in that time. No going back and forth. Doing that will only draw in more suspicion."

I nodded, taking my turn to think of every possible thing I could do or bring to be of comfort. Likely, she'd be in the kennels like I was. Where Koji was. The poor girl, as if things weren't bad enough for her. I didn't wait for Syaoran's approval, yanking off the covers of my bed and digging through to find a warmer dress to give. We weren't sized the same, but I thought it would help having a change of clothes and means to clean up—to not feel like an animal.

In remembering my earliest catastrophe, I fetched a cloth for that as well.

I'd asked the cooks for extra spring peas with her supper, knowing that was her favorite. They relented when I agreed to thresh the rice. Gi became my escort when I explained things, and we pretended not to notice the side eyed glances and grumblings.

Uno stayed curled in the far corner of the kennel opposite Koji. In seeing me, her eyes flooded with tears. "Lady Hisa!"

I cringed at the title. "They said I can't stay too long, but I tried to bring as much I could think to help."

Gi, keeping stoic, opening her cell and allowing me in with my armful of things.

"But, my lady, that's your bedding," said Uno, shying.

"It can get cold in here," I said. "And the floor is uncomfortable stone. You'll catch a cold, or worse." I set the things down, trying to appear dignified. Quiet, I couldn't help look at her black, fox ears. "Why didn't you say anything?"

She retreated into herself, and I saw the reflection of what I probably looked like four years ago. "I... I didn't want trouble. So, I would fashion my hair over my ears. My tail is easier concealed with my dress. I'm sorry. I wasn't looking to cause problems, I swear! I was only—"

I wrapped my arms around her. "I know. You have a kind soul. Lord Kwan will see that too."

"Will he make me go away?" asked Uno, timid. "If I go home, disgraced like this, I'll reveal my sister! After everything she's done to get us away, and my brother-in-law—"

I shook my head. "I know how you feel. And even if everyone says there's nothing I can do, I'm going to still try and fight for you."

She stared, lashes batting away water.

"Are you ashamed to be my attendant?"

"No, my lady."

"And I'm not ashamed to have you. You're a good person. I'll do everything to make Lord Kwan see that. He won't send you away."

"I'm afraid of him..." admitted Uno in a whimper. "He hates foxes."

"He might seem stony and cold, at first," I said. "But he's kind. He tries to be just, and he takes on more responsibility than any other person is willing. I promise, he doesn't hate you. Even after he learns you're a fox spirit, he won't hate you. And Syaoran agrees you're a sincere person."

She shifted her stance, dropping her gaze. "Will Lord Kwan listen to Master Syaoran?"

"He's a fiercely loyal friend," I said. "I think Lord Kwan will listen. Believe in him."

I stayed with her as long as I could, holding her, until Gi prompted me to leave. All I could do is promise that I wouldn't forsake her, and I meant it.

Sleep evaded me through the night, and the following morning stretched into forever, in no rush to pass by and bring Lord Kwan home.

He arrived in the late afternoon, dismissing any urgency from Lin and calling for my attending him with a red tea. As much as I wanted to ignore the request and get right to helping Uno, I knew I had a better chance if he was more rested from the journey first; and I could make the first case while attending him.

For a long time, we said nothing. He looked occupied with thoughts as he sipped at his tea, and I tried to conjure up the best way to plead on behalf of Uno.

"Hisa," said Lord Kwan, sounding distant.

"Yes?"

"If you had someone dear in your heart, would you tell me?"

I blinked. Where did that come from? He didn't look at me, making it harder to guess what he meant by it. "My lord?"

He turned his head enough to meet my eye. "Would you?"

I did have someone like that in my heart. I had him. But, even now, with the perfect opportunity to say it, I couldn't. Why were those three words so easy to say to Syaoran, but not to the man I was hopelessly in love with?

"I would," I said.

Why was I such a coward? Maybe from some deep part of me that already knew what his answer would be. Regardless of what anyone implied, he'd said himself that he wasn't in love with anyone, and it was childish to think my confession would change that—or that it would cause him to fall in love with me over any Juneun lady.

He stared at me a moment, making me think he wanted to say something more.

"And you, Lord Kwan?" I said, if only to break the silence. "Would you tell me if you had someone special in your heart?"

His hint of a smile made its appearance. "I would."

It should've made me happy. Instead, I forced on a smile. For now, I knew there was no one he was in love with, but I also dreaded the day when he would tell me there was. And I still couldn't make myself confess my feelings, much as I wanted to.

"Lord Kwan," I started, making myself brave. It didn't last more than a second. "I have a favor to ask. About Uno..."

His expression went from one of friendliness to intrigue to its usual stone-self as I explained. I'd hoped he would say something, rather than study me with a cold stare. When he stood, I sucked in a small gasp, feeling that I'd ruined any good chance of correcting the situation, and that I'd been too bold in my friendship with Lord Kwan.

He walked out without a word, leaving me stunned where I sat. When I regained myself, I bolted after him, only to be caught by Syaoran along the veranda.

"Don't," said Syaoran. "He's going to her now. You can't be seen interfering."

I looked at him, pleading.

He set a hand on top of my head. "I know. I'd be the same way if it was you. That's why we can't make it look like we pressured his decision, whatever it might be."

He was right. My going would only make things more difficult for Lord Kwan. Remembering the trouble I caused in Tetsuden, I relented.

An hour had passed. I kept beside Syaoran, pacing while he tried to seem unbothered with his own serving of floral tea. When Lord Kwan emerged from the kennels, Uno in tow with her hands folded and head low, I needed to resist rushing to them. Looking to Syaoran, I made a silent plea for what to do.

He gave me a sorry look, and nothing more. Something I took to mean I ought to stay put, but that there wasn't a certainty in that decision. When I couldn't bear it, I went after them at a brisk pace.

"Lord Kwan," I called. "If I—"

Again, Syaoran caught me, interrupting my beg and putting me into a bow. "We will wait here, my lord, if you require either of us." He put more pressure between my shoulders, coaxing me to sit in a deeper, humbling bow. "We await your decision."

Uncomfortable as it was, I knew he meant to shield me from my brash action. In this matter, we were his servants before his friends. So, I sat at the edge of the veranda in front of his door, proper, with Syaoran by my side. Not a sound came from the room. He'd likely cast his silence spell, as he'd done when explaining the puzzle box to me.

The sun now set, I stayed in place. My legs tingling and fast turning numb, I didn't move. Syaoran took my hand, firm for comfort, keeping perfectly still otherwise. Crickets began their songs, and we waited.

When the door at last opened, Syaoran cued me to take another humbled bow, waiting for Lord Kwan to speak.

"Collect your things from the kennels, Hisa," said Lord Kwan. "They are not needed there anymore."

I looked up, uneasy. Uno stood to one side, bashful and shamed. When I opened my mouth to say something, to ask, Syaoran again stopped me.

"If you don't require either of us, allow me to assist Hisa's retrieval."

Lord Kwan nodded, giving a last, wordless look to Uno, and stepped back to close his door.

Desperate, I looked from Uno to Syaoran and back until I had the cue to get up. Then I leapt to my feet to go to her.

She shied from me initially, like a child that'd been thoroughly scolded. "Do you require my assistance, my lady?" asked Uno in a whisper.

I blinked, taking it in. "Does that mean...?"

"I will stay one year longer," said Uno, sheepish. "Unless dismissed before that time, if you no longer require me."

"That's good news, isn't it?"

She struggled to meet my eye. "After I make my formal apology to the house... But it's likely I'm exposed beyond the estate, and jeopardized my sister."

I threw my arms around her. "We have a year to think about how to fix things. Don't worry." Somehow, the promise flew from me easily. My own reputation destroyed in my home, I didn't know how I would make this pledge hold.

Chapter 66
The Bath

The following day, when tensions relaxed, I took liberties for myself in arranging a hot bath. I'd won a victory, and wanted to sooth away the restlessness and exhaustion of the past week. Between Juro's hostility, Urekkato's relentless taunting, the demoralization of Lord Kwan's brothers, the overwhelming experience of Tetsuden and Mokryon, and then for poor Uno, I wanted to pamper myself.

Koji stuck by my side, having missed me. In starting the furnace to heat the tub, he brought me stick after stick to throw for him, and I happily obliged. In filling the tub, and knowing it would take some time, I played a little while longer with him, struggling to convince him to go back into his kennel for a short while.

That's when I started to worry. Lord Kwan allowed me to use the bath house at my leisure, but would surely be upset if I absently let it overflow. Finally getting my dog into his pen, I raced back. Just in time.

The water still flowing, it'd reached near the brim. Sliding off my wood sandals, I took brisk steps to the lever to stop anymore from spilling into the enormous tub.

Steam rose from the surface, filling the air with the oils of jasmine and sandalwood I'd added. I breathed in deep, savoring it, and began my undressing. I unfastened the ties holding the over-skirt to my blouses, letting the piece drop to the floor in a soft heap, and did the same with the underskirt. Stepping out of my under-trousers, I collected it all to fold quickly and set aside to prevent unsightly wrinkles. And the same with my blouses.

Steam filled the space. A warm mist that invited me to the source. At the edge of the tub, I dipped in my fingers, feeling the wonderful heat of the water, and slowly put my feet in.

Lord Kwan emerged from the bath, taking in a new breath of air as water rolled from him. Standing, he wiped aside the hair that glued itself to his face as the rest clung to his toned body.

I gasped, a shriek caught in my throat as I dunked myself in and turned away. My face became hot, my ears ringing, and I braced for angry commands.

"Hisa?"

"I'm sorry!" I blurted, speeding up my words to explain myself. "I was putting Koji back while the tub was filling. I didn't know you were already in here!"

Silence. Only our breathing and the drips rolling from him into the tub sounded.

"I ordered a bath drawn," said Lord Kwan.

Awkward, and shying, I echoed myself. "I didn't know."

Water churned. "I suppose it makes sense that we'd both have the same idea."

Unable to help it, I peeked over my shoulder. He'd resubmerged, leaving from his breast and above exposed.

"Could I ask you to turn around?" I managed to squeak out. "So I can dress?"

"You could ask," said Lord Kwan, teasing. "But you're already in the water. You may as well clean up."

I shifted uncomfortably, wondering how he could stay so casual while I clung to the edge of the tub and pressed my body against it to hide. "You're a man."

"Yes."

"We shouldn't be in the same bath."

"Why not?"

"It's not appropriate. And I'm still..." I struggled not to choke on my voice. "I'm still your servant."

"Oh? Hisa is going to take advantage of her master?"

My spine went rigid, and a shot a glare to him. "Lord Kwan! You shoul—"

"Lady Hisa."

I stopped, sinking myself to my chin.

"You don't trust me to respect you?"

"I do," I stumbled. "It's just, with how everyone already talks about me. And you—us. I..."

"That you are my whore?" he spoke slow and deliberate, less a question and more matter-of-fact.

I nodded.

"None of the other houses believe in that gossip. It's restricted to here."

I kept still. I knew he meant to comfort me, but all I could think was of the news of those rumors in my village. Water churned again. I could hear him coming closer, and pressed myself tighter against the tub.

"Hisa," cooed Lord Kwan. "Will you let jealous words dictate the rest of your life?"

I could almost feel him right behind me. Silently, I wanted him to reach out, to touch my bare skin, to turn me and pull me in for a kiss. I wanted to scream out that I was in love with him. And I hated myself for it. What a laugh Urekkato must be having right now. In my shock, I'd forgotten to close my eyes to end his spell.

"I'll keep to the opposite side," said Lord Kwan, starting to move away. "Whatever your decision."

Something about his words calmed me. In it, I reflected on the other Juneun men. How Juro wouldn't have given me space, how Urekkato would man-handle me. Syaoran might respect me enough not to touch, but he'd absolutely tease me without reprieve. I remembered our rouse, and how he'd taken me to be serious in passion. I remembered the fear in thinking I wouldn't be able to stop him, the anger when Urekkato tried it, and the helplessness with Juro.

Meanwhile, the man I loved relented his teasing, making no attempt to hold me against him. And I wanted him to.

I could go, and he would respect my private escape. Knowing that, now I wanted to stay. It didn't make sense to me. Nothing about my feelings and wants made sense when it came to him. But that was my decision.

What would staying do? Ignite rumors that already existed? Beautiful ladies during Mokryon did everything to get his attention, throwing themselves at him. Of course he wouldn't take me. What did I have by compare?

I let my shoulders resurface, forcing myself to be comfortable, and looked for the scrubs. By him, of course. And I didn't know how to claim any of it without abandoning more modesty.

"What is it?" asked Lord Kwan, pausing his own cleaning with a bent brow expression.

I realized I'd been staring as I thought, and needed to clear my voice. "The scrub," I said, meek.

He glanced over his shoulder, seeing that most everything was hoarded to his side. Without hesitation, he grabbed a wood tray and the things atop it to walk to me. Instinctive, I braced against the wall again.

"I won't look," said Lord Kwan, stretching out his arm and turning away his face and body.

I snatched the offered tray, meaning to taking it delicately and panicking all in one motion.

That start of a smile flicked on his face, and he returned to his place.

"You're not angry that I... saw you?"

"Should I be?" teased Lord Kwan. "There have been times in various states of undress, and in the bath, that a servant has come in urgently. This is the first time it's been accidental, or any sort of casual."

"I wouldn't say it's casual," I muttered, shy.

He shifted his gaze to me, causing me to sink down an inch. "I think I like the company."

"Don't tease like that," I said.

He kept his watch on me, his start of a smile holding firm.

"What?"

"I'm waiting for when Hisa asks me to kiss her."

My face flushed deeper, and my eyes went wide. "Lord Kwan!"

He remained as he was.

It reminded me. "Nineteen."

He didn't so much as flinch. "Hm?"

"On my last birthday. You gave me nineteen kisses, unprompted. I just wanted to know why. I keep thinking you have someone else in your heart, but it didn't feel that way when..."

"You never ask for anything. And I wanted to see you happy."

I studied him, trying to clean up without exposing myself. "That's all?"

"Does there need to be more?"

"I just... It never seemed right for a prisoner to be demanding gifts, no matter the reason."

He stopped and looked at me, a hint of a plea in his eye. "Hisa..."

I felt myself plunging into a new despair, and hurried to think of something to distract. "Why were you under water so long?"

He paused, likely confused by the sudden shift. "It clears my head."

I couldn't fault him for that, being guilty of having done the same.

Getting out was a whole other matter. Nervous, I kept peeking over my shoulder to make sure he refrained from looking at me. With how most others would've treated the situation, I suppose I was paranoid. I felt a great deal of relief when I at least got my under-trousers and blouses on. Fixing my underskirt, my trembling hands fussed with getting the ties to sit flat.

I didn't think I was at it too long, until Lord Kwan came up behind me with a comb. "Your hair has grown out."

I went still at the sound of his voice so close behind me, and with the tenderness in his tone. At his touch, my cheeks pinkened. He combed out the mess I'd made of it in the bath, gentle with every patient stroke. It wasn't so long in growth, barely coming to the ends of my shoulder blades. Most girls my age in the village had their hair at their waist—some to their hips. The same as Lord Kwan and his brothers, and of most Juneun noblemen. Juneun ladies' hair reached past their thighs or beyond.

"It looks good," said Lord Kwan.

My face warmed at the sentiment.

He began to braid it, and I found I didn't have it in me to leave his pleasant touch. I held still. A tree quietly basking as a breeze combed through its branches. When his fingers grazed the edge of my neck, goosebumps sprang up, tingling down my arms. My heart beat with the force of thunder, about to burst in its delight, and my breathing became shallow and slow, shy of fleeing altogether.

He tied it off with a piece of silken, red twine, laying the braid over my shoulder. It was all I could do to make my legs keep me upright. A hand to either shoulder, he laid a kiss atop my head. I closed my eyes, praying for the strength to keep me from falling into a heap.

Why was he behaving this way? So tender and perfect, and at the best worst time. I dared to believe there was a deeper affection, with my own thoughts berating me for it. He wasn't in love, and had said so himself.

"Ask me for something, Hisa."

"What?" I broke from my enchantment.

His slow breath tickled at me, wisps of it gliding from behind my ears and neck. "I haven't thought of you as a prisoner in a long time. Ask me for something. Anything."

I scoffed, or tried. "What right does a servant have to ask something of her lord?"

"When it pleases him to see her happy."

That took me by surprise. He didn't give his usual pause before answering. A whelmed feeling washed over me.

"Anything, Hisa. Name it."

Of course there were things I wanted. A thousand things. But it still felt greedy to ask. For so long, I'd been used to putting everyone else first, with the occasional surprise of some second hand or broken thing that I treasured. I was already spoiled here—I knew that.

"You already take care of me," I said. "I don't really need anything." Quiet. "And my favorite things were when you taught me to read. The swing, the mural, I liked these things the most because it was with you. It made me feel like we weren't so different."

"Hisa…"

"I've learned so much here. And I can take those skills home to help make life in the village a little easier. I never had the time or opportunity before you made me your servant."

His hands slid around, arms wrapping me in an embrace. I saw then that he hadn't fully dressed either. His torso was still bare.

"You brought me peace," said Lord Kwan. "Something I can never hope to repay you for. But let me try."

Chapter 67
Confession

B*ut let me try...*

 Those words followed me the rest of spring. I'd given in, asking for more art supplies to continue practicing while I knew I had the time to dedicate to the craft. Often, Lord Kwan would be beside me, silent, with that small smile on his face, composing poems. He never told me what they were unless I asked, to which he'd recite the one he was working on. The words had a flow and imagery to them, even if I didn't understand how.

Riding up the mountain for our mid-summer visit to the groves, my mind would bring up the feel of those last moments in the bath every time I looked at him in the quiet. I wanted so badly to believe that embrace meant something—something deep, something more. So many times, I wanted to tell him how I felt, until the fear of making things too awkward between us convinced me to stay quiet.

I still had little over a year to muster the courage.

I would tell him. Just, not yet.

Without his brothers attending, the picknick and gathering of peaches were a great deal more relaxing, even with a momentary drizzle. Court would be held nearer to the end of summer, when traveling and socializing between the nobles grew tiring and would likely mean less visitors. But I still dreaded that his brothers, and likely his sister, might come.

As soon as Lin was seniored into her position, she'd be given the option to join in the yearly trek—which gladdened me, so that I wouldn't be the only woman in the group. It didn't seem likely that Yua would return to the house any time soon (for a Juneun).

Likewise, Lord Kwan had sent for several new horses to bolster the stable, better assuming his status as a lord and continuing the pretense that Gumiho was gone.

I wondered if the kudzu was still there, since Feng had left the mountain. The peach picking half done, my mind wandered. So, I didn't see Lord Kwan run to pin me down.

The trees broke—smashed under some unearthly brute force. Fox fire burned hot and sickly, moaning over the shouts of the house guards that'd escorted us. I'd flinched in the suddenness of it, my eyes trying to slow things down to understand the scene, and I saw the snarl of Lord Kwan's face.

Eyes wild under his scowl, tiger patterns came onto his skin as he bared his teeth fast becoming long and pointed. His hands, too, seemed thicker; his nails turning sharp.

"If you won't come to me," taunted a woman's voice, "I figured it was time I came to you."

Lord Kwan leapt, his sword drawn. It happened too quickly for my human eyes to see.

"Syaoran!" I called, thinking of who could help him. But when I looked over, I saw my friend on all fours and petrified. Rushing to him, I shook with vigor, lacking the strength to budge him. "Syaoran? Syaoran snap out of it! Lord Kwan needs help!"

A broken bough of a tree moaned, creaking as it ripped away from the trunk to come crashing down over us. I clung to Syaoran, knowing I couldn't outrun this fate. His arm lassoed me, yanking me close as we rolled away.

More destruction, and half the escorting guards injured from the fray. The flames grew, howling against the wind on the mountain that spread it beyond the grove.

"Syaoran," commanded Lord Kwan. His fingers against the back of his blade, it took on a glow, crackling with magic. "Get them out!"

Syaoran didn't move, propped on his arm and staring with horror at the ground.

"Now, Syaoran," roared Lord Kwan, charging back at his foe.

Lightning speed, I couldn't see more than the whisp of a blur, and echo of what'd already happened when my human eyes caught it. There was an instant where I saw Lord Kwan appear more beastly, and streaks of red like rivers down his face.

He was in trouble. Whoever this was, they were matching him. I realized then who.

Gumiho.

In a moment of control from my terror, I climbed to my feet, struggling to help Syaoran to his. A cold sweat consumed his face, his eyes wide and vacant, and his body shaking almost violently.

I didn't know what to do. What could I do? I was human. I had no magic. No feat for battle. I had nothing to help him—to help Lord Kwan!

If there's danger and I happen to see it at the time, I can send aide or come myself...

That was it. Much as I hated to admit it, I was glad for Urekkato's spell in the moment. Letting go of Syaoran's arm and taking his face, I put my strength to make him look up at the disaster. I did the same.

"Syaoran. Look. Use Urekkato's spell. Make him see that Lord Kwan is in danger!"

He remained trembling and unblinking. I didn't know if Urekkato was watching, or how I'd make him. All I could do was pray.

"Please," I begged in a whisper. "Protect him from Gumiho."

The crash of another branch from elsewhere, shrieks of horror and pained groans. I whipped my head to see the source. Gi had deflected another large, burning bough from crushing another man. He was injured as well.

Sucking in a deep breath, I prayed for courage. "Syaoran. We need to get out of here."

He didn't hear me.

I slapped him, hard as I could. It didn't hurt him, but that wasn't the point. It was the shock of it, breaking him from his petrified stupor to look at me that I needed.

"Lord Kwan can't fight her and protect us at the same time," I said, working to keep my voice more akin to comfort and refrain from letting it quiver. "Help me get them out of here."

He nodded slightly. Enough to acknowledge what I'd said. I helped him up.

"Even if the horses ran, we need to get everyone away." I noticed the red on Syaoran's pant leg then, clinging to him and the source of the wet color. I didn't dare to look myself over, fearing it'd stop me if I saw anything.

We hobbled out, with myself leading to find the safest route in the debris to go through while the men supported each other in their injuries.

Thankfully, the horses were not gone, but nor would they come closer. They were spirits, and perhaps understood the severity of the situation, knowing we would need them.

I hesitated mounting up, staring back the way we'd come, silently begging for Urekkato to see, to help. The sound of the battle like the distant thunder of seven storms colliding, flashes of magic sporadic on the horizon. In one moment, it looked further, in the next, it'd come back near to where everything started.

Syaoran lifted me up into the saddle, ignoring my surprised gasp, and mounted up behind me.

"What are you—"

"Kwan said to keep you safe, so that's what I'm going to do."

Despite his words, taking a more steadfast tone, I could still hear a tremble in his voice. His hands, too, shook, as he reached for the reins. I snatched them up.

"You can better protect all of us if your hands are free," I said, allowing his statement to carry and give him some dignity. Looking over my shoulder at him, there seemed a relief to his eye. A silent understanding.

I kicked at his horse's side, taking lead in a gallop. I didn't have time to be afraid of falling. In that moment, all that mattered was getting us home. If the best I could do was lead a safe route, cuing when to slow and where to turn, that's what I'd do.

The gates in view, I breathed in relief. So often in that trek—that usually peaceful trek—did I hold my breath, uncertain, that my sides felt stiff.

In the courtyard, I dismounted first, calling for the others and helping to get Syaoran down. After the ride, he'd started to feel his wound. The entirety of the staff, after several shouts back and forth to rally, came out. Uno, shaken by the sight, was bid to fetch certain herbs and where to bring them.

I stayed by Syaoran's side, helping to carry him to his room. Having dealt with wounds before, accidents happened all the time in our village, I had a bit of knowledge. Though, I'd never tended such a large gash. When Lord Kwan had returned, bloodied, Yua had taken the lead in treating him. But there were still things I could do.

There were cuts to his torso as well. He sat for me, practically naked, as I cleaned the wounds, pouring generous amounts of the rice wine he always kept in his room after it. Now wasn't the time for modesty or to complain about spilled drinks.

Uno brought salves, making a startled squeak and closing the door at the scene, and only coming in when I commanded it immediately after. The largest of his injuries still bled, needing to be cauterized. She'd heated a knife, and helped to restrain Syaoran as he bit down on a thick, rolled cloth.

Other injuries required stitching, which he bared better. Additional effort went to cleaning the rest of him, preventing anything from interfering with the salves, and applying a clean wrap wherever possible. I repeated silent prayers during the process—for Syaoran to heal without complication, for Urekkato to have heard my plea, for Lord Kwan to come home safe.

Night fell, the sounds of Lord Kwan's battle were nowhere. Did he push Gumiho back? Away from the mountain? The image of his snarling face flashed in my mind, how different it was from his usual placid expression. He'd been angry with me, shouting. But this was different. She'd attacked his home—destroyed his sacred grove—and put the people he cared about in danger. Would he be reckless? Please, don't be reckless. Come back...

"Hisa," called Syaoran, weak with exhaustion. I'd done all I could, and a fever started in spite of my best effort. "Stay with me?"

I put a smile on for his sake. "I'm going to check on the others. I'll be right back, I promise."

I stood to leave, and he caught my wrist. "Stay...?"

It struck me as odd. I'd never seen Syaoran this way. A few times, he'd looked downtrodden, his pride in defeat, but never did he look scared and boy-like until now. The danger was gone, but his terror remained.

"I'll stay," I whispered, and resumed my place beside him.

He looked torn, a disbelief in his next set of word. "It was Gumiho."

"I think so."

He shook his head. "It was. She's still alive. I thought..."

"Whatever the reason," I said, forcing myself to sound firm. "I have faith in Lord Kwan. Even if Urekkato can't go to help him, I know he'll send her away and come back for us."

Syaoran stayed silent.

"Urekkato said that Lord Kwan was the one who killed her. And that he let everyone think Urekkato did. If the Cat prince wants to keep everyone believing that, he'll have no choice but to go to Lord Kwan's aide."

Syaoran forced on a smile. "That's not what I'm afraid of."

My face twisted with confusion.

"I know Kwan will come back," said Syaoran.

"Then what are you afraid of?" I asked in a coo.

"Do you remember when I told you about my sister?"

I nodded.

"Gumiho is the reason we were separated. Now that she's back, I'm afraid for my sister."

It dawned on me then. "That's why you were so panicked looking for that thing you lost."

His brow bent, furrowing into a plea, and he turned his face from me. "When Gumiho was gone, I thought, at the very least, my sister would be safe. Even if I never found her again."

My heart hurt for Syaoran in that moment. I saw so much of my own brothers in him. The weight of responsibility Kenta would take, the guilt Raeden showed when we last spoke, and the defeat of Hisato when I took his place.

"Let me help you," I said. "If you won't go to Lord Kwan for help, then let me—"

He turned to me again, shaking his head. "I don't want to see you get hurt."

I blinked, needing a moment to understand. "Is it that dangerous?"

"To a human, yes."

There was nothing I could do. And I hated myself for it. I couldn't help Syaoran any more than I could help Lord Kwan. I felt useless.

After a week had passed, my fears intensified. The summer monsoons had doused the fires, leaving a black scar on the mountain. Juro was sent for to see what could be done to heal the land from Gumiho's savaging.

In my own desperation, I wrote up a letter to send for Genji. As Lord Kwan's former master, surely he'd have the strength to help, to bring Lord Kwan home safely. I knew he wanted to keep Gumiho a secret, but, after her attack, would there be any hiding it? I had to try. What little I could do to help, I wouldn't be stopped.

Gi thought I'd lost my sense asking him to ride out and deliver the letter, and might've refused if I didn't threaten to go there myself. His horse galloped with lightning speed, the likes of which I hadn't seen in my riding. It dawned on me then that they'd slowed themselves to that of an ordinary steed for my benefit.

I wished now, more than ever, that I'd had some great gift—some magic or warrior's skill I could use to help. But I was merely human. An ordinary village girl with no special talent. Useless.

All I could do was pray. And it felt like that wasn't nearly enough.

When Gi returned, and Juro did arrive, I feared all the more for Lord Kwan's absence. I'd taken up tending to anyone who needed, and picking up the slack where I could, so much that I didn't have time to notice Juro's coldness towards me. Syaoran did his best to comfort, but I saw the worry in his eyes.

Uno had taken to sleeping in my room, unnerved by Juro. To my surprise, Syaoran kept Koji in his room, claiming the smell of dog would mask his own and ward off other fox spirits.

It was that night when something came crashing through the gates. I leapt from my bed in fright, as did Uno. Roaring like thunder shook my bones. It might've been any number of things, attacking while Syaoran was still recovering and Lord Kwan was away. My senses begged me to stay hidden. I ignored it with what courage I possessed.

Running out in my night robe, I gasped in horror. Lord Kwan, more beastly that I'd ever seen him, stood panting, searching. The men of the household, including those not yet fully recovered sprung into their roles. Chains in hand, they made to restrain him.

With a swipe of his massive paw, a sharp gale-wind blew them back—ripping off parts of the roof, tearing the paper-paned walls, and dislodging anything not rooted to the earth.

In the moment, I was afraid. He was in a blind rage, and so far gone from himself that he couldn't wrestle for his own restraint. His body large, shoulders shy of reaching the ceiling, and more tiger than man, I froze.

Syaoran made his appearance, wasting no time in casting spells to enchant any restraint and bind Lord Kwan in his state. Again, they were batted away, and he didn't recognize Syaoran as a friend—charging him with tooth and claw. A spell ready, Syaoran vanished an inch away from death.

In his blind fury, Lord Kwan lashed out at anything around him. Syaoran cast a spell of foxfire to lure him away. If he could tire Lord Kwan enough, or keep him distracted!

Juro took up the restraints, putting his own magic to it and managing to bind some of Lord Kwan's beastly back half. Not for long. A forceful yank freed the chains from Juro's grip, and he set for Syaoran again.

The fox used his same evasive spell, casting it too late this time. He reappeared not too far from me, slammed into the wall with new wounds. I called out, rushing to him, unaware that

Uno had clung to my side and stayed in tow like a child. Syaoran struggled for breath, and fought to keep his eyes open.

Again, Juro set to restrain Lord Kwan, managing to tangle up a front leg and some of his upper body. The men scrambled to grab hold, and free Juro to repeat the technique.

Lord Kwan's rampage hardly slowed. No matter what magic was cast or how many chains were thrown on him, he didn't still.

I didn't know what else to do, and bid Uno to stay with Syaoran while I made for Lord Kwan.

"Hisa!" called Syaoran, but I was already past his reach.

Juro caught my arm. "Don't."

"It's my duty to be by his side when he returns," I said, trying to make my voice sound more in control.

"Not like this," said Juro. "Not in this state."

"He would never hurt me."

"He won't recognize you!"

I breathed in deep, preventing my own anger. "You said yourself that we are strangers to each other now, Lord Juro."

His face slackened from its harshness. "Hisa…"

"Let me go to my master," I commanded, doing my best to keep from shaking.

Frowning, he released me. I took in another slow breath, steadying myself with a prayer.

You're still that girl who ran up the mountain… Fearless.

He'd said that to me more than once. If ever there was a time I needed to believe that, it was now. I took slow, soft steps to him, stopping when his attention fell on me. I smiled and bowed. Somewhere in there was still the Lord Kwan I knew—the man I'd come to love.

I made my greeting. And he roared back, yanking sharp and partially freeing himself. I don't know what came over me, but I'd run into him, throwing my arms around him.

"It's okay," I said, trying to coo and not sound so terrified. "I'm here. Always here, Lord Kwan."

His restrained paw made a clumsy step, landing on my foot. There was no fleeing now. Not from the thundering growls or blood curdling howls or ear shattering roars.

"I'm not leaving!"

I was pushed, losing my grip and scrambling to reclaim it. He bit down on my arm, teeth sinking deep.

I screamed from the pain, but I wouldn't let go. He needed saving. I didn't know how I would accomplish that, but I wasn't going to give up. So, I held fast and buried my face into his fur.

"It's okay," I whimpered. "I remember you. I remember that first night I saw you like this."

His teeth stayed where they were, and he growled low. Whatever fuss beyond us, I couldn't hear.

"You were scared, and all alone in that room. So, I stayed. I stayed beside you. And I always will. Because..." I could feel myself crying, the agony of my arm wanting me to scream endlessly, and my heart battling it to make me coo and comfort. A continued whimper would have to suffice. "I love you."

He didn't move.

"I love you, Kwan. For so long... Come back... Please come back..."

His growls lessened. And his mouth fell away from my arm. It hurt. It hurt so much. But I made myself embrace him. The only thing I had to try and protect him.

"I love you," I whispered again.

Chapter 68
Lord Kwan XVII

After a long ado of reassessing Uno, and tired from the week before, Kwan didn't detect a hint of dishonesty. Merely a desperation. He'd run her around, tiring her to see if there was any slip in her story. None. It wasn't rehearsed, but consistent all the same. She and her sister had fled from Gumiho, fearful of their queen and the warpath. The bond between them severed through sacrifice.

It'd been her sister to insist on her application, rather than take it up herself, hoping to bestow better protection as well as favor. Whether the intention was in seducing Kwan through innocence, or mere elevation by association with his name protecting her, or if her brother by law had a hand in the orchestration, remained unclear. Not that it mattered. A jibe at his past or the greed of his station was irrelevant at present. The girl's greatest fear was exposure. A lingering notion from Gumiho's reign—undoubtedly, her lord brother pressed her to go since hearing of the queen's downfall.

Some legalities still needed review the following morning. Though, with the headache of the past week, Kwan decided to ignore it and called for a bath to be drawn. He walked the veranda, using the mountain air to clear out his thoughts.

A small voice and a playful bark drew his attention. Watching, he stayed transfixed on how happy she looked. More at ease here, where she felt safe. A far cry from how she'd arrived. He started to smile as well, listening to the sound of her laughter.

A magpie indeed.

His pacing brought him to the bathhouse, where steam already seeped out. He thought it was quick, given how long ago he'd called for it. Or, perhaps his wandering had gone longer than he intended.

Inside, the tub half-filled, he breathed in the perfume and undressed. Head under the spout, he enjoyed the sensation of the water cascading down.

On a whim, he submerged, staying for as long as his lungs would allow. The crashing noise of the water stopped. He stayed longer, relishing in the weightless feeling. When he needed breath, he stood. A shriek instantly drawing his attention.

"Hisa?"

It took a while for his ears to process her rambling into something sensible. She was so close to him, bare and shy. No false modesty. No pale, porcelain flawlessness. She was real. And it took all his will not to reach out, to check that this was, in fact, real.

"Could I ask you to turn around?"

He found her endearing, and couldn't help tease. "You could ask."

The more frustrated she became, the more he felt besotted. Until she became saddened. His heart cooled with guilt. Before he realized, he was going to her, a want to comfort and protect her, and stopped when remembering their nakedness.

She was so close to him. And it tore at him to see her so distressed. His hand reached out, needing him to remind himself again of their circumstance. He didn't want her to feel obligated to him. So, he recoiled.

"Will you let jealous words dictate the rest of your life?"

It weighed his heart to think she would despise him for this. That she would reject him. She wasn't above it, having rejected Juro—something he was certain his entire female staff would've gladly taken.

Hisa wasn't like that. And he loved her for it.

"You're not angry that I... saw you?"

Amused, Kwan corrected. He'd thought it the other way around, even if all he'd caught were the backs of naked shoulders.

"On my last birthday. You gave me nineteen kisses, unprompted. I just wanted to know why. I keep thinking you have someone else in your heart, but it didn't feel that way when..."

Kwan steeled himself. He didn't want her to suspect, to think she was required to accept his advance. It hurt in his gut, swallowing words he longed to say. It hurt more hearing her refer to herself as a lowly prisoner. Not his Hisa... Except, that she wasn't his. There was every chance she'd never be his.

Out of the bath, having removed the stopper, he given his word to keep turned. A word that he broke. Sensibility gone with the two of them like this, he glanced over his shoulder. Her back bare, and lower legs exposed, as she fastened her under-trousers. After these past years, she still retained a farmer's complexion, and he'd found that he liked it. He liked her sun-kissed face, and the dark-brown eyes surrounded by thick lashes.

He was halfway to her when he snapped out of his thoughts. Now, needing an excuse, he grabbed a comb. "Your hair has grown out." He reached, needing to focus so that his hands wouldn't tremble. "It looks good."

It seemed such a silly matter. He'd combed her hair before, and she his. No, this was different. Intimate, in a way.

He broke off a piece of twine from his pants, using it to tie off her hair. He needed to maintain some level of distant dignity. But how could he? She was warm, and sweet, and there. And it pained him to hear the words echo in his mind, that she was only a prisoner, his servant, a mere village girl. She was none of those things. She was Hisa. Clumsy, excitable, compassionate Hisa.

He laid a kiss to the top of her head.

"Ask me for something, Hisa."

"What right does a servant have to ask something of her lord?"

When he is in love with her. "When it pleases him to see her happy." He couldn't think, except how much he wanted to expose his feelings, and to know hers.

"I've learned so much here. And I can take those skills home to help make life in the village a little easier. I never had the time or opportunity before you made me your servant."

That was it then, he thought. She desired for home. Of course. It was a selfish thought to imagine she'd want to stay.

He wanted to reject that as truth, wrapping her in an embrace. A silent plea. Stay...

"You brought me peace," said Kwan. "Something I can never hope to repay you for. But let me try." Circumstance prevented what he meant by it.

I love you.

Through summer, he'd neglected much of his usual duties for upcoming events. What did it matter? If she wanted to leave, then this short time was better spent in her company while she was still there.

Up to the groves, he wondered if she'd accept another private ride. It may be one of the last chances. He started a smile, watching her fingers stretch high as she balanced on her toes to reach at a particular peach.

He'd been so lost in his thoughts that he almost didn't catch what was about to happen.

Chapter 69
Lord Kwan XVIII

Kwan led Gumiho away. At least, he thought that was the case. He realized his habit of chasing her now betrayed him. He was away from his lands—any family lands—in pursuit. He wouldn't be able to draw from the mountain to help sustain his power.

A surprise came in his next confrontation with the fox queen. Urekkato intercepted, staving off a gruesome blow from Kwan's side. Gumiho, too, looked caught off guard, fleeing for more favorable ground. In this matter, distance was the enemy. He couldn't allow her the time to regroup and counter.

"What are you doing here?" growled Kwan.

"Saving you," said Urekkato, smirking. "Isn't it obvious?"

In their chase, Kwan only found himself more irritated.

"I'm a man of honor," continued Urekkato. "I was only able to marry Eumeh because you let everyone believe I was the one to slay Gumiho. If the fox queen lives, what will people think?"

"How did you learn of her return?"

"I already told you," said Urekkato, breaking away to seize opportunity. He cast his spell, cutting off Gumiho's retreat to strike. There, he harried her, searching for an opening as Kwan closed in.

Fox tails batted aside spell and steel alike, biding time enough for her to cast her own magic and vanish.

Kwan ignored the grin on the Cat prince's face, getting to the heart of the matter as his eyes searched out their quarry. "And how did you know to come here?"

Urekkato chuckled. "I'm lucky."

Rather than banter, Kwan dashed to where he saw the slightest movement in shadow. Their pursuit picked up.

"I would've come earlier, but I've been vigilant in my marital duties," said Urekkato.

Kwan barely humored him with a side glance.

"Eumeh is newly with child again."

Kwan said nothing, putting his every sense into their chase.

Colliding with Gumiho on open ground, she danced through their attacks. Something Kwan realized meant this wasn't the real one. It was her illusion. He broke away, eyes quickly scanning for her hiding place.

A shift in the thicket. He pursued with all abandon.

His blade met hers, eyes on her cold grin.

"How unlike you to send for help," taunted Gumiho. "Are you really that scared of me now?"

Kwan gave no response, pressing her back with every swing of his sword. She moved in on a miss, swiping her claws at him. Red slowly spilled from his cheek. In his fury, he released one hand from the hilt of his weapon, grabbing her wrist and yanking. Their heads collided. She gasped on impact, sharply pulling away.

He didn't relent. He couldn't.

He swung wide to force distance, signing his free hand to summon lighting. She evaded. Vanishing, she reappeared behind him, dagger firm in her grip.

Urekkato charged, managing to nick her thigh.

For a moment, Kwan's heart flared in rage, his stomach going tight. He'd made that oath. A foolish boy playing the part of a man to make such a promise. He hesitated. Enough For Gumiho to fall back.

Like with the grove, her tails laid waste, using the environment against them. They were separated then, unable to pin her. Foxfire burst, fast consuming the wood debris. By chance, he saw Urekkato's folly. Another illusion.

She was behind him, about to strike.

Kwan rushed to him, calling out a warning. Another illusion. Gumiho lured him into reckless action. Now off balance, he struggled against her. He began an outrage, the beast taking over. He could control it a little.

Until...

The illusion of Jiana. *Why didn't you save me...?*

He stumbled. His mind knew it was a trick. That Gumiho assumed his sister's face.

Little brother... The sound of Sueng's voice caused him to turn. *You were supposed to be better. He didn't learn from us...*

He didn't save us...

Too weak...

Enraged, Kwan roared out, freeing his magic to go wild. The aftermath of it cleared away the surrounding forest.

Panting, Kwan steadied himself. It wasn't real.

"Predictable," said Gumiho.

Kwan remained unmoving, allowing the façade that he'd not yet recovered himself.

She chuckled, low and sinical. He could hear her approach.

"Worn out already? You never did last long."

He stayed silent, needing her to come a little closer. He could hear her every step. Her breath. The slow beat of her heart. And he heard the knife she pulled from its sheath.

He spun on his heel, feigning a swing and taking her neck into his palm as she ducked, putting a firm squeeze—history repeating. Though, this time, he wouldn't succumb to the lies she'd given him. "Where is Jiana's soul, you rotten bitch?"

"Rotten?" repeated Gumiho, forcing a grin. "Flattery will get you nowhere."

He squeezed. "Return it. Now. And I will make your death clean."

She forced as much of a laugh as she could, clawing at his fingers to try and break free. "I don't have it."

Keeping his hold, he pointed the tip of his sword to her eye.

She smirked. "I'm telling the truth. When she died the soul vanished. Just as I said before. Why do you think I keep letting you go, *my beloved*?"

"Then I have no use for you—"

Her tails. One into his left calf, one into his right thigh, another boring into his side. She slipped from under him.

"Kwan!" called Urekkato.

He saw the start of her smirk, and his eyes went wide. Shadows lay beyond, shapeless and growling in the mists. "Urekkato! Stay—"

Darkness.

He woke, pinned by his own sword, his bleary vision struggling to focus.

"The Kurai sacrificed were worth it. Half of you couldn't tell an illusion from the real thing, as it was. A successful test. Your own lot was worn away, so it'll be easier now," said Gumiho, speaking to a pinned Urekkato. "Oh good, Kwan's awake."

"Your quarrel is with me," growled Kwan, struggling against the pain of his bindings.

"And what better weapon than one of your own?" said Gumiho.

Kwan paled at her cold smile, using what strength he had to try escaping. He wouldn't let Urekkato suffer the same fate as Borsi. Nor anyone else!

"It's time to make you mine, little kitten," cooed Gumiho. A tail pinning each of Urekkato's limbs, he writhed in a fruitless attempt at freedom.

"I am not the same as your Kurai pets," spat Urekkato. "I am a Juneun. I won't be some puppet to a shadow whore."

She placed her hand over his chest, still baring that cruel expression.

"I am a Juneun!"

She dug her nails in.

"I am a Juneun!"

She leaned in.

"I am a Juneun! I am a *Juneun*!"

Closer and closer, her smile spreading as he repeated his declaration with a growing panic. Kwan freed himself, stumbling in his step and cursing. Fast in thought, he put his healing magic to work. He couldn't save his kin like this. Hurrying, he called to Gumiho.

She ignored him.

"I am a JUNEUN!"

She placed a kiss over his mouth, stifling out the repeated phrase.

Urekkato's eyes went wide, his writhing violent.

When she parted from the kiss, a bead of light followed, leaving Urekkato in a breathless, petrified state. Delicate, she grabbed it in her other hand, and turned her gaze to Kwan. "I don't want you to die, my love."

Kwan stared with horror, his healing too slow for his demand.

"I want you to suffer. Just like I suffered." She licked her lips, placing Urekkato's soul upon them. "And you'll suffer at your own hand."

"Let him go," growled Kwan.

"No," said Gumiho. "I think not." Her tails released the Cat prince, his eyes wide, breathing erratic, and body perfectly in place. "Urekkato. Kill Kwan for me."

Obedient, Urekkato took rigid movements to reclaim his sword. There was no fighting it. He charged at Kwan, blade held high.

Kwan stretched out his hand, gripping his own sword. He parried, holding off Urekkato's downward thrust.

"What's it going to be, Kwan? Your life? Or his?"

Kwan said nothing, pushing off Urekkato and jumping to his feet.

"Kwan," said Urekkato, urgent, hushed, but still himself. "You have to kill me. Or take my eyes." He swung. His body compelled to obey Gumiho.

How cruel this was. When Borsi's soul was taken, ripped from him, he'd been rendered hollow. It made the necessary deed easier. But the soul of a Juneun, stolen so ritualistically, left him able to see their actions and unable to stop themselves. Kwan couldn't bring himself to think of the necessary deed. Not like this.

"I'm not blinding you, much less killing you," said Kwan, equally as low as he parried every swipe. "You're going back to your princess and child."

Urekkato continued an unwilling assault. Kwan, keeping his defense and giving ground, glared at Gumiho, despising her amused expression.

Kwan worked in a fury to overcome Urekkato's agility, to disarm him and subdue him somehow. But with every technique attempted, Urekkato countered. A well practice warrior, even against his will, took preservation in the fray. It wasn't a mindless charge.

Urekkato sent out a cutting gale. Kwan summoned the wood of tree roots to shield him. When Kwan sent lightning, Urekkato negated it with earth mounding up. Blind in the haze, they continued their deadly dance, colliding blades again.

"You don't understand," said Urekkato, still hushed and in a hurry. "My sight spell. If she finds out about it, there's no telling how she'll use it against you—against anyone!"

His fast whispered plea clicked the missing pieces in Kwan's mind. That's how he made his luck.

"Syaoran—Hisa—!"

Kwan's mind finished Urekkato's pleading explanation, pressing back with all force. Taking the turn for assault, he worked to put Urekkato off balance, moving with a fury while biding his patience for an opening. There came one, at the cost of Urekkato's sword cutting into Kwan's side. He took it anyway, crying out as his claws reached—swiping Urekkato's eyes.

The Cat prince screamed out, falling to his knees and clasping his face as blood spilled unhindered. Urekkato incapacitated, Kwan set his rage at Gumiho. He'd take back the soul and kill her, or die trying.

He charged.

Darkness.

Darkness...

He'd fallen too far into the shadowy absence, feeling nothing but a hatred.

"I'm not leaving!"

The voice gave him a start. Distant and muffled. Something was wrong.

Hisa?

Hisa!

Where was she? He'd never been this far gone. He could hear her. Hear her scream. Hear her whimper and cry. No... Not...

"...I stayed beside you. And I always will."

Hisa... I love you.

"I love you, Kwan..."

His anger settled. Whether or not it was real didn't matter. He loved her. *He* loved her. Hints of light returned to his vision.

"Come back... Please come back..."

Hisa...

That was the last thing he remembered before being confined.

Chapter 70
I Did This

I woke, not remembering when I'd fainted the night before. My arm was swollen and throbbing with pain. Everything else bore a stiff ache. I was in my room, bandaged and feverish.

Lord Kwan. Where was he?

I tried to get up, stopped by a hand.

"Stay still," said Syaoran in a near whisper. He looked exhausted, fairing no better than myself.

"You need your rest," said Uno.

Syaoran put a brave smile on for me, dragging his gaze to her. "Lord Kwan will be pleased that he kept your attendant on. She's worked tirelessly on both of us."

"But... I need to get to Lord Kwan. I made a promise—"

Syaoran placed a palm on my collar bone, pinning me down. "Not like this. You're in no condition to leave your room, much less try and tame him."

Tame him? "Is he still...?"

Grim, Syaoran nodded. "I've never seen him return like that. It'll take a week—days at the very least."

"But I said I would—"

"You're staying here," scolded Syaoran.

"We almost lost you last night," said Uno. "I was scared for you. Why would you do something like that?"

My brow furrowed as I looked from Uno to Syaoran. His expression softened, knowing the reason.

"And Master Syaoran stayed beside you to monitor your vitals and oncoming fever."

"You lost a lot of blood, Hisa," said Syaoran. "You forget that you're human. You're not as durable as a Juneun. I'm surprised your arm wasn't completely crushed."

"You suffered four broken toes," said Uno, helping to demonstrate the seriousness of my state. "Please, rest."

"What about you?" I asked.

Syaoran picked up his smile. "I can rest easier, now that I know you're awake."

"I can stay alert a little while—"

Uno's words were cut off by a deafening roar. Barking followed from some other part of the estate.

"Koji—"

"He's in my room," said Syaoran. "And I don't think you have to worry. Half the women in the house have been going in to check on him the moment Kwan was restrained. He's quite the ladies' dog."

"Stop," I said, weak with a chuckle.

"I think he makes them feel a little safer. With Gumiho... And he doesn't mind the treats they insist on sneaking over to him."

"I told you he was good," I teased.

"The whole of the house has been briefed. The new staff in particular," said Syaoran.

I didn't understand right away. Not until looking at Uno's discomfort. Lord Kwan's condition. It needed to remain secret.

"What about Urekkato's..." I trailed, having almost blurted out a different secret.

"I don't think there's anything to be done about it."

With a sigh, he sent away Uno, allowing us to try and come up with some solution in private. I had one idea. Admittedly, not a good one, and waited to be alone before I could try it. On a small strip of paper, I wrote my plea. Something I would stare at as often as I could until I got some kind of response.

I'll do whatever you want. Please don't tell his secret.

Four days after, I was still not recovered enough to go see Lord Kwan. It didn't seem to matter if I insisted on seeing him or being useful elsewhere in the house, Syaoran wouldn't hear of it. I still had too much of a fever.

That morning, Juro opened my door, but didn't come in or speak one word. Several seconds of silent staring, and he walked away. The roars and growls had subsided immensely, a good omen, but all I could think was how I'd failed to help him. I stared at that scrap of paper, hating myself more for not remembering to end Urekkato's spell.

It was more painfully obvious now how useless I actually was to Lord Kwan. Of course he wouldn't be in love with me. It was a childish notion. So, I made up my mind that I'd tell him and get my rejection over with. When court was over, I would tell him. If my last year as his servant was unspeakably awkward, it would make it easier to leave for home.

Alarm came in the following afternoon, when Lord Kwan stumbled into my room. Labored in breath, uneasy on his feet, and his face pale and damp, it was my instinct to go and catch him before he collapsed—calling his name. Until my ankle shot up pain to remind me how laughable that concept was. Even if I wasn't so injured, I didn't have the strength to carry him in any capacity.

In seeing my attempt and sudden stop with a quiet yelp of pain, he looked more concerned. Straightening himself, he took brisk, uneven steps to my bedside. He stared into my eyes, bearing a deep sadness. His fingers graced my cheek, moving my mess of hair out of the way. It seemed like he wanted something, but I couldn't tell what.

I swallowed hard, taking his other hand. "You should be resting."

He shook his head, closing his eyes and laying his forehead against mine. The tips of our noses rubbed, once, twice. Then he looked to my arm, lifting from me and assessing.

"I did this..." muttered Lord Kwan.

"You didn't know," I said. "You weren't yourself. You—"

"Hisa," scolded Lord Kwan, wincing and fast forming a scowl. "Do not make excuses for me. Let me, for once, feel the full burden of my actions."

I frowned, trying again. I was supposed to be there to comfort him, and he came to me instead. "You can't blame yourself."

"Then who will I blame?" He stopped, realizing the coldness of his tone and giving me a look of apology. "Regardless of the reason, it was my teeth that did this. I hurt you..."

I didn't know what to say or do. He was set on bearing the guilt upon his shoulders.

"You're the last person I ever want to see hurt," said Lord Kwan. "And I'm the one who did this to you."

"I forgive you," I said.

"Don't," snapped Lord Kwan, tempering himself. "Don't be so good to me, Hisa. Yell, curse me, but don't offer me that kindness."

"I already decided it," I said. It pained me to see him try to punish himself. "You wanted me to ask you for something, so this is what I'm asking. Accept that I've already forgiven you. And that you won't be so stupid and reckless." My voice began to crack, and tears fell from me. I didn't know how much I wanted to cry. Once I started, I couldn't stop. "I was afraid you wouldn't come back..."

He wrapped his arms around me, snug and gentle. "I heard you call for me. And I feared I would be too late to reclaim myself, and lose you."

I placed my uninjured arm around him, burying my face in his shirt as I sobbed.

"You're precious to me, Hisa."

I basked in the words. He was precious to me too. But in my weep, I couldn't make my voice say those three words.

Chapter 71

I Love You

Juro stayed until Lord Kwan's full recovery, sending for the annual ginseng tea rather than travel back and forth. Despite whatever trouble occurred because of me, he was dutiful to his friend. A trait that I did admire. So, I couldn't understand why he didn't act that way towards everyone else. Still, there was a lingering scorn, and we didn't speak to each other. I behaved as a servant, and he ignored me for the most part.

Whenever Lord Kwan had the strength, he tried to atone for his actions in healing others, delaying his own recovery. In serving Lord Kwan, I tried not to fuss too much and annoy him. With the repairs needed, court was canceled. I felt relief for that, though I wished it was under a different circumstance.

"I will not be returning in autumn," said Juro, mounted on his horse. "The year may be more difficult for harvests, but it is for the best. The earth needs to rest."

Lord Kwan nodded. "I am in your debt, my friend."

Despite his coldness, it didn't feel right for me to not say anything. He'd stepped in when we needed help. "Lord Juro," I called, quieter than I intended.

He stiffed a moment, looking down from atop his cheek.

I made my polite gestures and a deep bow. "Thank you."

There I stayed until cued otherwise.

"If," said Juro, "in one year, you have changed your mind, Hisa." He was slow to turn his head slightly to me. "Do not hesitate to send for me."

I kept still, not knowing what else to do. His tone remained distant, but the phrasing personal.

He kicked off, trotting out of the inner gate before going into a canter. Thunder groaned beyond, ushering another series of rains.

I'd forgotten. The anniversary of my arrival into Lord Kwan's service was today. Time was picking up, in a hurry to get to the next summer. I had to tell him. Before I never get another chance, I had to tell him how I felt.

Easy enough in theory, but I could never find the right moment. Another week had passed. Lord Kwan stayed up in the late hours sending formal apologies and cancellations. Tedious work. Through it, I stayed beside him with jasmine wine at the ready.

It was a hot and humid night, as always, when I noticed how quiet things became. The rain had stopped, long enough for crickets and other insects to start their night songs. Late, with everyone else in bed hours ago.

This was it. I could get my rejection and scurry to my room without being noticed. I closed my eyes and counted.

"Lord Kwan?"

He paused, his mind catching up. Since Juro's leaving, he seemed distracted, taking longer than it should to complete his written regrets. Gumiho probably weighed on his mind, and I regretted that I'd began. But, if I didn't, I might not have an opportunity like this later.

I swallowed, working to steady my voice. "I... only have one year left. After that, I'll be going back to my village."

He watched me.

"It feels like I've been here longer than four years. So much has happened." I was losing it, rambling when all I had to do was say three simple words. "I can't tell you how grateful I am to have learned so much." My voice quivered, and I started to feel frustrated with myself.

He stared, brow pressed and jaw loose, blinking slow and deliberate.

"I've... there's something I wanted to say. And—for a while now—I..." I could feel tears welling up. My body rebelling to prevent me from telling him. "I..."

He kept his gaze. I couldn't take it. I was losing this battle against myself, and started to look away. Started to. His hands caught my face, bringing me in for a deep kiss. It surprised me.

He stopped suddenly, pulling away and giving me a fearful look, as though I should scold him or slap him. Instead, I grabbed his shirt and brought him back to me with all the force I had. Imitating the kiss he'd given me years before, I pried open his lips with mine, becoming the exploratory one this time.

He wrapped his arms around me, pulling me against him. My hands left his shirt, gliding behind his neck to keep us together. His tongue took lead, I straddled his hips, his fingers fled from anchoring, feeling my sides and down to my thighs.

A rush of excitement, though I fumbled in my attempt to mimic. His hands went under my dress, sliding to the back side of my hips to grab and play. I squeaked in delight.

Things went faster, more than I could keep up with. He'd unfastened the ties of my dress, and removed my blouses. My trembling hands struggled to take off his layers as well, and he compensated by ridding himself of it for me. We were on his bed, bodies rolling against each other. I broke from his kiss, needing breath, and his lips fast found the side of my neck, causing my skin to tingle.

He'd undone his trousers, tossing them aside, and slid mine off with a gentle, firm grip. I could smell him and feel him and taste him and see him, our voices lost to panting breaths. Always I pulled him back to me, and always he obliged. My face was hot. My heart was racing. My lungs couldn't keep up. I was dreaming. But I was awake.

His fingers explored my body—from my breasts to the small of my back to my waist to my rear. Then between my thighs and up. I stopped, startled by the touch and pushing my hands against his chest. I noticed then that the lamplight was snuffed out. We were bathed in the glow of the starts and moon as the clouds departed the sky.

He stared at me, quizzical. As much as I'd ever seen him. "Do you want me to stop?"

I answered his whisper with a meek shake of my head. "No."

His finger went in, and we slowed all else down, falling into a rhythm. The cool of his skin felt good against the muggy, summer air. At this pace, I could enjoy every touch.

My thighs began to quiver, becoming slick with his playing.

"If it hurts," whispered Lord Kwan. "Tell me. I'll stop."

I was too lost in the haze of passion to fully grasp what he meant, but I nodded all the same. Shallow, rapid nods as my chest heaved from under him.

"Good girl," said Lord Kwan, going into me.

It hurt almost instantly, but I didn't want him to stop. A slow rhythm allowed me to get used to him. From some deep seeded instinct, my hands went under his arms to grip his back, and my heels anchored behind his thighs. Moans and sharp breath left me without warning. We were tangled in each other, and I didn't want it to stop.

He began a faster pace, chuffing, and I struggled to keep hold. Pinning my wrists, he continued, a playful smile on his face and a delighted growl in the back of his voice. My back arched, my involuntary noises turned sharper, coming more rapidly. I throbbed around him. My knees losing their will to cling to him. He spilled into me with a deep and labored groan, stopping a moment after.

Panting, we looked at each other, catching our breaths and smiling. He kissed me, and I kissed back.

"Hisa," cooed Kwan. "My Hisa."

I giggled at that, and the kiss he placed after.

"My sweet Hisa." He kissed at my neck. "My beautiful Hisa." He kissed at my shoulder.

I stopped. My hands pushed against his chest, suddenly aware of what'd happened—what we'd done and where I was. I became aware of my nakedness, of his, and that he was on top of me—that I was under him. That the window was wide open, as were the doors, and that his hair acted as a curtain between us and the world.

He paused in his residual passion, perplexed and staring.

"I'm not..." I whimpered, turning my face away to expose the scar on my cheek. "I'm not beautiful."

Our breathing doused, he softly pinched my chin, coaxing me to look at him. "You are to me."

I smiled, my heart warm and bounding. Words I thought would never be directed to me, and by the man so out of my league that I'd fallen in love with.

He kissed the top of my forehead, bringing my attention back to him. "No more tears."

I coughed out a chuckle and echoed his words.

"I love you, Hisa."

I couldn't believe it. It had to be a dream. But, touching his face, I knew it wasn't. It really was him. And he'd really said those words.

"If... If you don't feel the same. I understa—"

"I love you, Kwan."

We stayed in each other's arms, close, dealing out the occasional caress to be sure this was real. I'd fallen asleep to the sound of his breath and heartbeat.

Morning was a different story. I'd awoken with pain an hour before dawn, curling up and wincing.

"Hisa?" asked Kwan, groggy. "What's wrong?"

"Everything hurts," I whimpered.

He blinked, sleep heavy in his eyes before he understood. Placing his palm over my breastbone, he drew down past my belly and thighs, to my knees. I stayed tightly curled, and he repeated the motion. The pain lessened, enough for me to properly meet his eye with bent brows. His expression soft, waiting as a wordless question was asked. I shook my head, and he performed the gesture a third time. It wasn't gone, but a great deal more tolerable. He'd only just recovered, and I didn't want him to over exert himself with me.

I scooted closer against him, pressing into his toned, muscled body, and he wrapped his arm back around me in silent comfort, laying a kiss atop my hair. He fell back asleep before I did, keeping me in a protective embrace.

I'd expected some of it to hurt, as Lin had explained, over estimating what I could bear. I didn't like this part. At all. It made me think of how scared I'd been, in tandem with the excitement I lost myself in. I didn't know what I was doing, and tried to keep up in the passionate awkwardness. A hare trapped by a tiger.

What if he didn't like it? And his confession was habit or some sort of obligatory response?

I shut my eyes, forcing away the plaguing thoughts. He was my Kwan. I was his Hisa. Rumors about us being like this already existed in the house and in my village. So why did I feel so guilty that we gave into our emotions to make it true? If everyone else insisted it was true before, and made from greedy lust, what was wrong with now that it was born from sincere love?

Long past the rising hour, someone came to check in on Kwan, knocking. He denied them, nuzzling his face into my neck. It took everything in me not to giggle from the sensation. In moving too quickly, I winced again.

Kwan propped himself up on one arm, concern marring his expression. I shrank into myself, looking down to my legs. Following my gaze and back, he placed his palm on my breastbone. My own hands took it, preventing the spell, and my lips placed a soft kiss to his knuckles. He stared, taking a moment to understand.

"Can we just stay here? Like this?" I asked, whispering. "Just for today?"

His start of a smile returned, and he placed a kiss at my hairline. "If you want to." He brought me back into his embrace, the two of us enjoying the silence and the touch of one another.

It wouldn't be for half a day. Syaoran, concerned, came knocking, and refused to be dismissed.

With a sigh, Kwan got up, taking the cover sheet with him to wrap lazily around his lower half. A gesture of his hand and a fresh sheet flew from its storage cupboard to cover me. He slid open his inner door halfway, not revealing who he had in his room.

Syaoran's concerned tone vanished, replaced with a stark and stumbling set of words. I half rolled over, trying to listen in.

"Lin would know, or have it on record," said Kwan.

"But why to Hisa's room?" asked Syaoran.

Kwan said nothing more, closing the door in a slow, smooth motion. In his first steps back to me, Syaoran pieced it together.

"Hisa?"

"What did you tell him?" I asked, looking between Kwan and the door.

"I told him to bring a remedy for you." He sat on the edge of the bed, resting his forehead on mine.

"For the pain?"

"That as well."

It took me longer than it should've to realize what he meant. Bashful, I couldn't help my next question, dropping my gaze to see his fingers shyly laying against my own. "Did you like me?"

"I love you, Hisa."

"That's not what I..." I rolled my bottom lip between my teeth, holding it there as I though how to phrase it.

"The sex?"

I flinched at how direct he worded it.

"I did." He brushed my hair behind my shoulder, cupping my cheek after, and I held to it rather than the sheet. "It was with the woman I love."

I smiled, scoffing. "Why didn't you say you loved me before?"

"I never wanted you to think you had to agree," said Kwan. "Why didn't you say that you felt this way?"

"I did try," I confessed. "But it either seemed like you wanted someone else, or that I'd annoyed you too much. And when I learned that wasn't true, I would try to bring it up. But I was afraid you wouldn't feel the same. I worried that I'd only make our relationship too difficult."

"Sometimes," said Kwan, fondling my hair. "But not forever."

In my room, Uno waited with a kumquat sized herbal pill and persimmon wine. I was instructed to swallow it whole and not bite down, and that the wine was meant to chase out any residue of its taste—this method being preferable to a preventative tea. Even after downing the wine, my jaw locked up from the bitterness and I shuddered (my tongue making an ungraceful appearance at the end).

Lin came in, raising a brow at my ghastly expression. "That bad?"

"I've never had a piece of medicine like it," I said. "I didn't think it'd be that big, or dry, or bitter."

"Oh, that," said Lin, closing the door. "Never mind then. You get used to it. I was talking about *him*."

I echoed her last word, my face growing hot and my eyes going wide at the realization. "Can we not talk about that?"

"So, it was bad?"

I looked to Uno, hoping for some kind of help in escaping the inevitable conversation. She stayed seated, shifting uncomfortably, and kept her gaze down.

"It was..." I started. "It's one thing to have it explained. And another when..."

Lin laughed. "We've all been there. At least you didn't bleed—or, that's what I've heard. San changed out his bedding." She handed me a small jar of pea-sized pills. "For any leftover pain."

I shook my head. "It wasn't... the way you explained it—he took care with me."

Lin leaned back where she sat on the floor. "More than I can say about his brother."

"Lord Kwan's brothers frequent here?" asked Uno, timid.

"Not often," said Lin. "Don't get me wrong, Kwang is handsome, but he's a lousy lover."

Both Uno and I scolded in a hushed tone.

"What?" said Lin. "It's only us girls. All things considered, we're doing well for ourselves."

I echoed her last sentiment. A thought coming as my stomach churned with the medicines. "About... is it always like that?"

"Like what?" asked Lin.

"Painful?"

Again, Uno shifted uncomfortably. "I don't know, my lady."

"It depends on the man, I suppose," said Lin. "But I thought you said he took care of you. Only after?"

I shook my head. "No. He said that, if I said it hurt he'd stop. But..."

"He didn't?"

"I never said to."

"Do you think he means it?" asked Uno, unable to look either of us in the eye as the topic continued. "That he really would stop, if you said?"

I hadn't considered. And now it was a fear. I loved him—that much was still the same—but I didn't want to submit and endure pain every time he wanted to have sex.

"The way he doted on Hisa before," said Lin, "he probably would."

Chapter 72
Lord Kwan XIX

Kwan didn't have an inclination for the passage of time as he climbed out of darkness. He didn't know if Gumiho lived through his rampage. If Urekkato lived, blinded or not. In the shadow, he could still hear the Cat prince's scream of agony. Another layer of guilt he would have to carry with him.

I love you.

That small voice beckoned him back to the light.

Exhausted, his vision was slow to focus. His arms leaded, his legs numb, he didn't see her. The room was empty in a haze of burning incents. In the time between coming to, and someone checking in, he couldn't comprehend it.

"Where is Hisa…?"

The house guards unbound him, refraining from an answer until he repeated it. At their news, Kwan shoved away, stumbling and collapsing. It wasn't true. It couldn't be true. Not Hisa. Not her! He refused help, or any guidance to his room. Ignoring the cautioned words and the insisting of his rest, he supported himself along the walls. He had to see. Panic flooded through him, disbelief clouding his mind.

Somewhere in his trek, he passed out, waking in his room and in a fresh robe. He couldn't keep still. Leaping to his feet, he stumbled onto his knees, breath fast gone. He got up, ignoring Syaoran's concern and refusing his help. A silent prayer repeated in his thoughts with every uncertain step.

When he made it to her room, he felt some relief. In bed, and not too gravely hurt. Until she revealed the fullness of her injury. His heart sank into his gut. All at once, he remembered her shriek and the taste of blood. The monster that he was, flying into a rampage and thoughtless of the consequence.

"I did this…"

He'd hurt her. The woman he loved. He'd broken her arm, and her foot faired no better. He wanted her to scream at him, punish him in some way.

With her every attempt to comfort, his guilt piled. How could she continue such compassion?

"I was afraid you wouldn't come back..."

He looked at her face, to her beautiful, dark, brown eyes. Tears. It tore at him. How was he worthy of her tears after he'd savaged her? He was supposed to be the one protecting her. Not... He embraced her, a futile attempt to shield her from her own fear.

"You're precious to me, Hisa."

Precious, Kwan thought, because I'm in love with you.

In the days following, he took rest. Never able to stay still, he felt the need to atone wherever he could. His own house suffered in his beastly rampage. The very ones reliant on his protection. It was as Gumiho said. At his own hand. And by his own hand, he would work to heal it.

"You shouldn't exert yourself, my friend," said Juro, enjoying a thin pipe. "I can maintain things until you are well enough."

"My conscience will not allow idleness," said Kwan.

Juro watched him. "I tried to stop her."

Kwan looked to his toadish friend.

"Everyone describes her as an ordinary hare. When did you last see a hare confront a tiger?"

Kwan gave a hint of a smile. "She's too bold for her small stature."

"Something to admire," said Juro. "Her fox couldn't protect her, though he put on a show for it. I suppose staying here wouldn't require too much protecting."

"Jealousy diminishes your account of his skill. There was a time he always bested you, sometimes barely. Love is a distracting force."

Juro scoffed. "I admit, I still love her. Though not in the way she wants."

"Which is?"

Juro shrugged. "Half the younger ladies at Mokryon are dazzled by what I could provide for them. And not a single servant girl refused me. I needed a salve for the itch that followed. She's not taken by gifts or land that winter never touches. It may change, when she's no longer enchanted by handsomeness alone."

Kwan grunted, considering his own treatment and his feelings.

"You returned worse than I've ever known," said Juro, swapping topics. "I didn't know if there was enough persimmon wine to quench the beast. And the ginseng is running low as it is. I've sent for the annual case to be brought. You may need it more regularly than you like."

Kwan left what little smile he had, resting his face in one hand. Between the warmth of the summer air, and the cool of the deluge, he found a sort of refuge in the noise beyond his room. "I will cancel my hosting."

Juro snickered. "There will be quite a few perturbed hearts. I had it on good authority every family coming would bring all of their eligible daughters. There was vexation from being ignored at Mokryon."

Kwan said nothing, the tediousness of it already mounting in his thoughts.

"What did Gumiho do?" asked Juro. "To push you that far?"

Breathing, Kwan steadied himself, and looked to his friend. "I was too late for Jiana's soul."

Juro lingered his watch, a silent understanding. "A direct descendant of a god. Some say Gumiho might be impossible to kill."

"I saw how she did it," said Kwan. "The absolute terror as she sucked out the soul."

"You'd felt it once, as I recall," said Juro. "It's siphoning your own energy. The burden of an incomplete soul."

"I hid away the rest to prevent her theft." Kwan paused, remembering the taunts. "I wonder if she's only toyed with me this entire time. Knowing."

Now recovered, Juro had no reason to stay. Parting, the former Kurai gave his regards, and a word of omitting this year's blessing. Kwan didn't argue. He knew his friend had spent too much of himself as it was, and let him make the terms to maintain dignity.

His mind, while tired, went to work at how he would compensate for the sake of all who called his lands home. The villages and animals shouldn't be punished for his own lacking. There were also the missives to write up, informing of his cancelation. Repairs were ongoing, slowed by the summer rains, and the restoration of the pagoda needed checking. The groves were an additional matter. If at least one tree survived, he could use grafts to regenerate the rest.

Every thought ceased with Juro's word to Hisa.

"If, in one year, you have changed your mind, Hisa. Do not hesitate to send for me."

That's right.

They'd only a year left, and she would leave. Few would the moments be that he could see her again. And there would come a point when she did not visit anymore.

In one year, he could freely profess his feelings, and she would be able to give an honest answer. She'd refused Juro, who openly and aggressively doted on her. He wasn't fool enough to think a more restrained approach meant she approved him instead.

The thought demanded his attention, despite more important tasks. Through it, she'd stayed beside him, downtrodden. The quiet sadness in her posture bothered him with a hurt in his heart. He wanted to act on it, refraining in the knowledge that the unprompted gesture would put her into too awkward a position.

"Lord Kwan?"

It took a moment for her voice to reach his mind, clearing it to give his full recognition. As she spoke, fast becoming a ramble, her body trembled. He tried to understand, to think of something to help.

"I've... there's something I wanted to say. And—for a while now—I..."

Tears swelled in her eyes. And he couldn't take it. Not to see her so upset. Before he could stop himself, remember their circumstance and the need for restraint, he kissed her. Soft, warm, sweet, he moved to embrace her when his consciousness caught up to him.

He broke away, fearing he'd only made things worse.

When she took initiative, his chest felt tight and weightless. No more thought went into what they were doing. He'd given in to the desire, finding the places that tickled her or resulted in a sharp squeak that delighted him. She fumbled in trying to undress him, something he found cute, enticing him all the more.

He fell into his habits, basking in her touch while his fingers explored her. He grew stiff between his thighs, prompting him to go between hers.

She pushed against him, causing him to pause. In the silence, he though she meant to change her mind—that he'd been too aggressive in his performance.

She allowed him. And he tempered himself, wanting to guide her. He savored the gentleness, patient with her. Finally, she answered the plea of his fingers, and he felt his excitement pick up.

"Good girl."

Euphoric. Not a task or a distraction, but a passion. Enthralled by her noises, he took charge of positioning her. He wanted to look at her—at his Hisa.

His.

"My beautiful Hisa."

She turned from him. A full stop to her pleasure. Something he didn't understand. Had he said something wrong?

"I'm not beautiful."

It tore at him. The sadness on her face, the defeat of her tone. He didn't want to see her that way—easily surrendering to insecurity. He wanted her to see herself the way he did. For the compassion and openness. For the beauty that he fell in love with.

"You are to me."

Her smile returned. The smile he adored.

"I love you."

In saying the words, he realized their position. What had he done? Was it a mutual desire, or a feeling of obligation? He'd forgotten himself, forgotten why he withheld. As he tried to explain, her touch reassured him. As did her words.

"I love you, Kwan."

He stared at her most of the night, fingers lightly combing her hair and down her cheek. Warm skin, light breath, she was real. He didn't care what anyone would say. They could chastise for centuries to come that he chose her over a well-rehearsed lady. That he chose someone gentle over someone with a coy façade. She was imperfect, and ordinary, and human. And that made her precious.

Let them talk. What would they have left to say when he'd announce his inheritance of Tetsuden? How much would they tease him for having a human wife? It didn't bother Genji. Why should it bother him? In the notion, Kwan amused himself. He would take her there. Perhaps every spring to enjoy the grounds in private.

While he slept, he remained sensitive to her touch, waking when she stirred.

"Everything hurts..."

He'd forgotten that as well in his love-making. She'd never been with a man. He'd grown used to women having explored someone else before him. Hurried, he used his healing, not wanting to see her in the slightest discomfort from him.

"Can we just stay here? Like this?"

He smiled. She'd spoken his very thoughts. He wasn't ready to part from her yet, to return to being a lord.

The demands of the house, however, prevented their shared wish.

Syaoran's expression changed five times, at least, upon seeing Kwan. He ignored the stumble of words, issuing his own in lieu of any explanation. That the missives would be sent out tomorrow, and the progress for repairs and restoration would be checked in on. On a whim, he ordered for a third floor to be installed, making for a larger, private apartment. A final, though not least important direction was in sending for fresh sheets and for a woman's morning remedy to be brought to Hisa's room.

"But why to Hisa's room?"

Kwan didn't explain. It should've lent itself evident. That, and he found entertainment in the bewildered expression on Syaoran's face as he closed his doors.

Returning to her, he enjoyed how genuinely bashful she looked in the daylight. His Hisa.

"Did you like me?"

"I love you, Hisa."

She fumbled her words again, cheeks turning pink. His sight soaked in how adorable she was in the moment.

"The sex?" Again, he found it cute how shy she went about it. And how strange it felt that she thought she needed to compare to lovers in the past. There was a joy to be had in her inexperience—in being the one to learn how to please her. There was no demand on his end to get it right. Instead, it was something that could be managed with time, a new experience in every entanglement.

An honest confession of feelings followed. Kwan felt like a fool for not having picked up any sign of her true affection. Things that, now, seemed so obvious.

Upon her leaving his room, he continued his smile, carrying it as he freshened up and dressed.

Their usual quiet company in the days that followed brought a different kind of joy. They were not so shy with gentle touches. Not in a lustful way, but in such a manner to signal how they cherished each other. He did want her intimately, but knew better than to abuse the new passion between them.

With all important affairs seen to, he delighted in glimpsing her playing in the gardens with her dog. Rowdier than any proper lady would allow themselves, and he loved her for it. If not for the house requiring his attention, he'd stay for hours.

Chapter 73
Refusal

I'd thought that things would become awkward with me and the household, or between myself and Kwan. It was, in a way, but not to the intensity I'd dreaded. There were questions, though I didn't know what sort of answer I could give. A curiousness, more than anything, with regards to Kwan's usual stoic nature. So, it did seem odd that a village girl, a human, brought out a passion from him.

I couldn't rightly comprehend it either. How it all happened. I'd just fallen in love, and the man to whom my heart belonged fell in love with me.

Mostly, it was the odd expressions in my continued willingness to take part in any chore that needed seeing to.

The nights alone in his room were spent as usual. Added with our fingers intertwining and unprompted kisses to my forehead, among other gentle touches. Things I took a guilty pleasure in. I'd worried he'd demand regular intimacy, and I didn't know if I was fully prepared to handle it again. I loved him. And I did relish when we were tangled in each other. It was after that I was afraid of.

He kept busy during the day, laboring just as hard as the rest of the men on the repairs. Today, he'd left, going alone to the groves to see what could be saved and what needed to start over. I knew the place was important to him, even if I didn't fully understand why—only that it was sacred to him, and there was a ceremony in tending to it. Whether the peaches were a special breed, as my practicality told me, or if they had some divine aspect to it like the old folk tales would describe, I didn't know. I'd eaten the fruit and felt no different for it. No one had tried to stop me.

With no further chores, I took Koji between the walls to my favorite spot. Picking up a stick, we played for hours. While I began to tire, he had energy to spare. Before I could throw it again to fetch, Syaoran found us and snatched it away.

I'd fast given up on trying to take it back as he teased me, telling Koji to fetch it instead. Excited, he darted right at Syaoran, leaping up. The surprise of it caused my friend to stumble back and drop it. Grimacing at the paw prints, his magic cleared it away with the flick of the wrist.

"Thought you'd want to know that Kwan is back, Lady Hisa."

"Stop that," I said with a frown. "I told you not to call me that."

"As Lady Hisa commands," said Syaoran with a smirk.

I wrestled the stick away from Koji. "When did he get back?"

"A few minutes ago. He's checking in on the third-floor installment. Must be excited."

"Gives me a little time to bring his drink and change," I said, throwing the stick far in the direction of the gate. "I didn't think I'd get so muddy."

"You're not excited?"

"About what?"

"Sharing a suite with him," said Syaoran in his matter-of-fact tone, crossing his arms. "The third-floor. It'll be done by autumn if we can keep good pace."

I froze a moment. It was the natural course of things, I knew, but it still felt sudden.

"Are you not staying?"

"Yes—no. I mean, I did still plan to go back home for a little while to make sure my family is alright. But, now... I don't know. Until recently, I never thought to stay."

Koji returned with the stick, head held high.

"Then talk it out with him," said Syaoran, half-groaning while he smiled. He sent me off, kicking the back of my thigh with his ankle.

I repeated my throw, Koji running ahead. When he picked up the stick, however, he trotted right past me, ignoring my calls and scolding as he presented his find to Syaoran.

He laughed, pretending to struggle with taking it from the dog. "I'll take him back."

I scoffed with a smile of my own. "And you didn't like him at first." Running, I didn't give Syaoran the chance to retort.

I'd cleaned up quickly, putting on the lightest dress I had to combat the summer air, and fetched what survived of pomegranate wine. I neglected resetting my hair, eager to be beside him and tying it back with the red twine. In my haste, I forgot to knock and announce myself, walking in as he'd started undressing.

I closed the door with profuse apology, and shut my eyes to count.

Silence.

"Come in, Hisa," said Kwan, a hint of amusement in his voice.

It took longer than it should've to remember that this was a trivial matter. We'd already seen each other naked and been intimate. Embarrassed, I slowly opened the door to come inside.

He bore that gentle smile, continuing to shed off his shirt layers.

My cheeks flushed at the sight of his proud torso. I was his Hisa. And he was my Kwan. "I brought up the pomegranate wine."

"I didn't think there was any left," He folded his shirts over his arms in the laziest manner, tossing them onto the bed as he walked towards me.

"It's your favorite, right? When I was cleaning up, I found a couple of smaller bottles that were misplaced, so they managed to survive everything."

Standing before me, he took my chin to lift up, kissing my forehead before kissing my lips. I chuckled, hooking my hand behind his neck to bring him back for a second kiss on my lips. In response, his arms snaked around me, picking me up to twirl once in a fit of joy.

Back on my feet, he took the wine from me, setting it down elsewhere as we locked ourselves in another kiss. I broke from it first in a chuckle. Kwan answered with a flurry of his lips against my neck, his hands slowly exploring my arms and sides.

"I missed you," said Kwan.

"It was only for a day," I said. "But I missed you too."

I started to fetch the wine cups when he reeled me back in, a playful thud of my back against his chest. His teeth grazed my ear, making me flinch and giggle with the tickle of his breath. He continued playing with my ear, soft bites leading to kisses brushing against my neck. I'd gotten so enraptured with the touch that I didn't notice his hands freeing my blouses to expose my breasts.

"Kwan!"

"Hisa."

I whipped my head to frown at him.

"What?" His thumbs brushed up and down my lower ribs, hands stopped on my belly.

"We shouldn't."

"Why not?" The rest of his fingers dragged upward.

I didn't have an answer ready, my mind hurrying to find any excuse. "It's the middle of the afternoon."

He smiled, a hand cupping over each of my breasts. "Oh? Hisa only wants to make love after the sun sets?"

"N-no..." I stuttered. "But won't people know that we're...?"

"We weren't exactly quiet our first night," said Kwan. "I can use a spell to contain it, if you're concerned."

When I couldn't come up with how to phrase it, he proceeded in my silence, sliding off my blouses to deliver the touch of his breath and lips down my back. A pleasing touch, and distracting me from trying to come up with what I wanted to explain.

We moved, suddenly. Over to his table, where he bent me over, my chest against to cool, polished wood. More of his touch went along my spine, my hair tossed to one side, while his hands took their time going beneath the skirt of my dress to feel my thighs and hips. I froze. It wasn't until he'd unfastened my under-trousers, sliding them down that I found my voice again.

"Stop," I whimpered.

He went on. Fingers going around to my inner thigh and up. An echo of fire and pain springing forth.

"Stop!"

He did. And a puzzling silence hung in the air.

"Hisa?"

I shook my head, trembling.

"What's wrong?"

It took me a moment to gather my strength. Through it, he was patient, his hand gliding slowly against my back in comfort.

"I don't want to," I said, cowering. A part of me warned I was about to throw everything away, another telling me I was a fool since we'd already done it.

"Sex?"

I tucked into myself.

"Hisa," cooed Kwan, helping me upright and taking my chin in his fingertips to meet his eye. "I didn't confess my love in exchange for sex. I love you. And if the woman I love doesn't want to have sex, that is fine. As long as she still loves me."

I couldn't help a small bit of fear, something in my gut telling me this was a trick. "You're not mad?"

His soft smile returned, and he embraced me. "I'm not angry." He kissed into my hair. "A little sad. Was I that awful?"

I shook my head, pushing away slightly as a nervous laugh escaped me. "No, no. It's not—" I took a breath, steadying myself. "I'm scared of getting hurt. Like how I was last time."

He blinked at me, perplexed. His gentle smile slow to return. "I'd already confessed that I never want you to feel obligated to me."

I returned the expression, though shying and looking away. "Will you seek out a mistress in my stead?"

"I wasn't planning to," said Kwan. He brushed the wild hairs away from my face, tilting his head to meet my eye. "Hisa. I'd gone ninety-one years without it. Another thousand won't be the death of me, so long as I still have your heart."

I looked at him, giving a sheepish smile. "It wouldn't be a thousand."

He cupped his hand against my cheek. "You still think you are my servant. In love, it is I who am your servant."

"You, my servant?"

"Yes," whispered Kwan.

I shook my head, my smile broadening. "I would rather you were my equal."

"Am I not, already?"

"Are you?" I teased.

"I am a lord," said Kwan, stretching his neck to lay a light kiss on my lips. "You are my lady. Is that not equal?"

"I'm just a village girl," I said.

"Are you?" teased Kwan.

Chapter 74
Breaking Point

Autumn.

The rains had long stopped, and the ground left to dry. Even with my saying that I didn't want to have sex, Kwan didn't withhold his affection. It was in the way that I'd wanted. A slower, tender set of encounters. It surprised Lin. She'd teased, that he respected my desire not to lay with him, saying that every man had his breaking point.

The third floor complete, later than expected, Kwan offered if I wanted to join him in a room with a provided second bed, or stay where I was. My few belongings were carried up only days after I'd agreed.

Lin's words still bothered me. She was more experienced with men, but Kwan had spoken sincerely. I knew it was cruel of me, but I'd tested him now and again, climbing into his bed to see if he would press for it.

He didn't.

And I quickly found how much better I liked sleeping in his embrace rather than alone. At times, I would start a tirade of kisses and enjoy the return. Other touches were played with, though he refrained from going too far between my thighs. In other instances, I would go back to my own bed; he'd ask, but didn't try to prevent me.

Sometimes, I'd wanted it to go there. But I needed to know whether or not I really did have any say in this part of romance.

I became bold in my thinking that I had more control in this aspect, despite anyone casually insisting otherwise. However, doubts crept back when Syaoran repeated too similar of the things Lin had said. He was a man, and had known Kwan longer than I did. Much longer.

It came to a head when Uno questioned it. Uno, who'd staved from commenting much at all.

"He won't grow bored?"

I didn't quite understand until it was better explained. Rather than asserting myself, I might've hastened his disdain. I'd never had a boy like me, let alone a man be in love with me, and my naivety was obvious.

"Kwan?"

He grunted, half asleep.

I shifted in his embrace, the only sound outside of infrequent insect chirps. "The last time you wanted us to... You pinned me to the table."

Half of a smirk flashed on his face. "My preference in love making."

I held my bottom lip between my teeth a moment, thinking how to ask. "Do you get frustrated with me?"

Kwan opened his eyes, groggy, and propped himself up to look at me. "Where is this coming from?"

"Do I?"

He sucked in a tired breath. "Sometimes. What is this about?"

I shook my head, averting my gaze.

"Hisa," said Kwan, gentle. "Speak openly with me. Shouldn't I be allowed to know why the woman I love is distressed?"

I tried to look at him. A nervous swallow shut my voice.

"Whatever you fear about us, Hisa, it is false. I make no plans to take another woman when the one I love is here beside me. And, if she does not wish to engage in certain pleasures, then it is a false love for me to refuse that wish. Is it not?"

Shy, I nodded, understanding his attempt to comfort me in my doubt.

"Love demands that we ask things of each other, that we trust in each other. I will keep no more secrets from you. But I ask that you keep none from me as well."

I smiled. "My fear is in gossip. A false fear. I didn't mean to seem like I doubted your sincerity."

He resumed his embrace of me, and I scooted closer to him. As a reward, he placed a kiss at my hairline. "My brothers will be here at week's end."

"What for?" I asked in a sudden panic.

"Word spread of Gumiho's return. Naturally, they want to know what it is I plan on doing about it. I received the letter this afternoon."

My mind raced with cold thoughts. "I should move my things back."

"Why?"

"Because—what will they say?"

"They'll say what they like. But it is not theirs to decide. That power is ours alone."

"I don't want to cause you more trouble."

"Trouble seems to follow us both, whatever the circumstance. I am not ashamed of you."

His final sentiment echoed in my heart, easing my frets.

"Are you ashamed of me?"

I shook my head, smiling wide. "Of course not."

When his brothers did arrive, I didn't hold the same level of confidence. To his dismay, Beom was turned away. Kwan hadn't forgotten. And it led to immediate tension. They'd only stay a week at most, though it didn't seem like it'd be a friendly stay.

In the first night, when I returned to our room, his brothers flashed odd looks as I passed.

The majority of conversation revolved around a hunt for Gumiho, with Kwan dismissing the idea. He insisted that a hunt would only lead to disaster, as it'd done often before—notably under the crown's order. When they grew frustrated, they lashed out at the evidence of my being there; that he'd spoiled me too much, and I was only a novelty. He ignored it better than I could whenever I heard any part of it.

Was it true? That I was only something to pass the time, under the guise of being in love—of mere infatuation? An anger in me rejected the harsh words. They'd been the same, tired insults since before Kwan and I confessed our feelings. What I couldn't avoid was the thought of being a toy rather than an equal, as we'd promised each other.

Unable to ignore it, and while I knew it was unkind, I wanted to test that as well. I needed something to see if I was treated as his servant, or as his love. It was reckless, dangerous maybe, but I had an idea.

Midday, as the brothers held another conversation to pressure Kwan's cooperation, I climbed the stairs. My heart pounding, my legs telling me to turn back, I prayed for courage. More when I reached the doors.

"Urekkato claimed presenting her head for the princess's hand," said Kwan. "Let him chase her."

"The Cat Clan princeling hasn't been seen in over two months," said Seong, level in his tone. "Winter is almost here. The snows will make tracking and traveling difficult."

"It seems you've wasted a journey, then," said Kwan.

"You spend far too much time doting on your human," scolded Yuz. "Have you forgotten what Gum—"

"I forget nothing," said Kwan. "With every pursuit, it's led to grounds favorable to her. Her recent assault was to lure myself away, rather than chance an entire household on my land. She's alone now, and isolated confrontations are to her advantage. And if she's not alone, what better prize could she hope for than to wipe out our line with every son of our clan charging in?"

"You think she's hoping we'll hunt her together?" asked Kwang.

"Why do you think I deny the notion every time father sends you?"

It sounded like they'd settled, contemplating the logic. In a short matter of time, undoubtedly, they'd harass Kwan for being with me. While tempers were paused, I took my chance, sliding the doors open as far as my arms would reach.

They all turned to look at me.

"Get out," I said, quieter than I meant to. "All of you."

Seong was the first to anger. "Who are you to dictate orders?"

I steeled myself, repeating my command in a slower, steadier voice.

Yuz, with a sever expression, went to stand, stopped by Kwang.

"You are a human," said Seong. "We are Juneun. You should know your pla—"

"Get out," said Kwan.

Seong looked at his brother, muscles tensing.

"This is my home," said Kwan, stony. "You will leave us."

"I am the elder brother," said Seong.

Kwan stayed unmoved. "The eldest. And lacking respect to his host."

They silenced.

"Leave us," said Kwan. He'd supported my command without even knowing the reason.

Reluctant, they did, glaring at me as they walked out. I closed the doors, trying to maintain courage.

Kwan sighed, slow to stand. "Hisa, you can't simply walk into a meeting of lords and make demands—"

I ignored his words, walking brisk to him. Flinging my arms around him as I leapt, I stopped his concerns with a kiss.

His hands caught my sides, giving in briefly before breaking from me. "Hisa. Now is not—"

I didn't give him the chance to argue, pulling him back for a deeper, more exploratory kiss, careless of where my toes landed and if I'd stepped on his robes. He stumbled, relying on me for balance. When I guided him to sit, he didn't fight me. I straddled him next, breaking from our kiss as I moved him to lay back in the stack of cushions lain decoratively along the bedside.

He stared at me, brow pressed and mouth half open in wanting to say something while at a loss for words. I stared back, hurrying to think what to do next. If he did have a breaking point, or if he meant what he'd said.

I rolled my hips atop his, never looking away. His fingers dragged down my sides, leisurely finding the hem of my skirt to play with before sliding under. He held the backs of my lower thigh, his thumbs finding their way beneath my under-trousers to perform a metronome against my skin. I leaned over, placing myself against him as I stole another passionate kiss. His hands responded with a more assertive playing with my legs, making their way up to my rear.

I squeaked with how rough he'd grabbed, causing him to smile. When he tried to roll me over, I resisted, grabbing his arms to pin up, the way he'd done with me. A bewildered expression consumed him as he allowed my guidance. I gave a serious silence, catching my breath, and went back to my playing. His chest heaved, arms starting to come back. I dropped to pin him more forcefully. He blinked at me, looking me over in our wordless game.

I felt him rise beneath me, and played a while longer, watching his frustration in resisting. His breathing picked up with greater excitement in seeing me reach under my dress. My fingers brushed against him, teasing. Greater anticipation came when I'd unfastened my blouses, keeping my back straight as he wanted to move beneath me. I saw the struggle of his arms in wanting to come forward, wanting to grab and play with what was exposed.

The cushions slid from under his head, swallowing him in his fit, and I couldn't help but pause to laugh. He revealed his face, removing the cushions from around him as he lay flat with a smile.

I took his hands to hold my torso, leaning over as my hips continued their sway, and planting another kiss. My own body responded, dripping down my legs.

I stood up then, walking away.

He blinked, staring after me with the clear confusion, and propped himself up. "Hisa?"

I walked to the table, shimmying out of my under-trousers and assuming the position he'd wanted me in before. I only smiled in response, my eyes looking down and back with an invitation.

Kwan didn't understand, not right away. When he did, a slight smile took his expression, as did a hunger.

I trembled at his touch. My skin prickled with his fingers gliding down my back and breath on my ear. I hadn't realized how hot I'd become until the cool of his newly exposed body pressed gently on mine. His arm came around, both pinning me and keeping him balanced, lest he crush me. His other hand went to play between my thighs and up for his own satisfaction. When he slid himself in, I breathed a sharp, whimpering gasp. But I welcomed it.

He started slow. His hand pressing in as it rubbed on my thigh. In an instant his pace would change, often without warning or reason. He went straight, holding me as thick fingers dug into my skin. I couldn't do much, panting and moaning and fully focused on feeling how he moved.

When he grabbed a fistful of my hair and pulled, I yelped. He stopped, both of us panting while he gently released me.

"Are you alright, Hisa?"

I nodded, reaching to where he'd grabbed. "It just hurt."

He rested his forehead at the base of my neck. "I'm sorry."

"The wood hurts me too," I confessed.

Panting, he looked over my shoulder to the table. "Hang on." He walked away, leaving me to feel like jelly for a moment while he fetched a cushion to place under me. "Better?"

"I think so," I said.

He kissed at my neck, breathing in my scent. "Do you want me to stop?"

I shook my head. "I'm happy. Even if it does hurt a bit later."

"I'll try to stay gentle," said Kwan, hands exploring me again. "I don't want to hurt my Hisa."

Chapter 75
Well of Oaths

The winter solstice was almost here, and the house was in frenzied excitement for it, despite not having Juro's favor and gifts of fresh fruit. Uno appeared the happiest that I'd seen her, reminding me a little of Fumei.

It was a poorer celebration than last year, with all that'd happened, though it didn't dampen anyone's merriment. During which, Kwan brough up a flute to entertain with. While I was enchanted by it, Syaoran teased that he was out of practice with the instrument. He took the criticism in stride, admitting that it'd been some twenty years or more since he played it.

When I objected, and the attention went on to me, Kwan said I ought to sing. To that, I refused with a deep flushed face. He'd said I'd sang prettily, though all I could do was compare how other girls in my village had more beautiful voices. I did get persuaded to do it anyway, met with quiet applause and approval after—more for the politeness in my effort than from sincere enjoyment.

On my birthday, Syaoran waited for my usual trek to the shrine, presenting me with a small, gold coin. "I told you, gold is the last one given, since you're not a child anymore by human standards."

"Isn't there something you'd rather spend it on?" I asked.

He shrugged. "Not really. I don't go out into the world too often, and I don't have family that needs it."

I felt torn. I knew I should give the coin to prayer, thanking the gods for everything I'd been blessed with—things that, five years ago, I didn't think would be possible. But I also greedily wanted to keep it.

"What's wrong?" asked Syaoran.

"I was just thinking," I said. "But I wouldn't know where to send a missive to get things like new fabric and thread."

"Oh, just ask Kwan," said Syaoran. "I doubt he'll tell you no."

I shook my head. "I wanted it so that I could bring them back to my village to make things for my family. And for my friend who's looked after them in my stead. I don't want him to worry that I'm not coming back—I *am* coming back."

Syaoran grinned. "Hisa's being sneaky."

"It's not sneaky!"

He laughed. "The snow is too deep now to send for anything. I'll show you when things have thawed enough."

"You will?"

"If you're going to stay, you should know these things. Now go take your gold to the shrine, and don't worry about the rest."

"But won't I need—?"

He waved off. "I'll show you come spring."

I thanked him, sharing a hug and hurrying off to fetch Koji and go to the shrine. I knew exactly what to pray on. Not only to thank the heavens for how my life turned around so fast, but to wish for something important. I wanted a long and happy marriage. It would be the first time in years I wished for something purely for myself at a shrine.

Kwan was already there in prayer; part of me wondered what he'd wished, if it was something dire or something happy. He always looked so serious when praying.

He waited for me, though didn't ask this time what I'd wished for. Instead, we kept in company of each other, walking all the cleared paths around the villa. I'd let Koji loose, watching him bound through snow and half bury himself with excitement.

The hours went by. I'd hardly noticed the cold air.

Kwan laid his hands on my shoulders, stroking slowly down my arms as he kissed the back of my head and whispered. "Let's go inside."

Which I knew to mean he also wanted us to go into bed. It wasn't so regular a thing, and on the occasion that I refused, he didn't persist. Though, I'd only refused once. In a strange way, I knew him a little better, learning what it is he liked, and both of us making slow discoveries of what I liked.

In our room, he led me to my bed, eager. Not for undressing, but for something set atop. The reason he hadn't asked my wish. A dress, similarly styled to what Juro had insisted on me, in dark orange, soft gold, and deep peach colors. Printed along every hem were peonies, vibrantly colored to stand out. All of it heavy, and suited to hold warmth in deep winter. No tigers hidden in the threading, nor his house colors tied on it.

"But—"

He stopped my objection with a light kiss to my cheek. "Can I not spoil the woman I love, and who loves me in turn, with one gift?" He wrapped his arms around me, swaying us.

I shied. "It looks so expensive, I'm afraid to even touch it."

Slow, he took my hand to place on the garment, guiding my fingers over the soft material and grab.

"I don't have anything to give you," I said, losing my will to argue while a ball of guilt sat in my stomach.

"You don't have to."

"Kwan," I scolded.

"Hisa," said Kwan.

I huffed. "Then... let me make something for your birthday."

He smiled, a little wider than I'd yet seen. "Oh?"

"Then I can't feel guilty for accepting."

He studied me, holding his expression. "If you like."

My face grew a wide smile. "Your birthday is in early spring," I said, standing. I started to shed my deel in the warmer house, walking to change. "I remember there was a bolt of dark-blue cloth that'd look handsome. It's not much, but maybe I can—"

He swiped me up to drop on the bed. I squeaked in surprise. From there, he looked into my eyes, his expression still pleasant, as his fingers traced over my exposed torso. A way of asking. I shyly tucked in, still smiling, and shook my head. He responded with several kisses to the ticklish spot on my neck, seeing if I was sure.

I giggled uncontrollably. "Not yet!"

He stopped, meeting my gaze again. "I love you, Hisa."

"I love you." To think of how difficult those words were almost half a year before, and how easily they came now, it made me laugh.

He'd loved me for some time as well. If I'd confessed sooner, how much happier I'd have been. How much trouble and heartbreak I could've avoided if I were braver back then.

I did bring him to my bed later in the evening. Most of our time spent in gentle caresses and slow kisses. He was never in a rush, which gave me ample time to think of what I wanted to do to play back, or if I wanted to simply mirror his touches.

There came a point where he scooted back, propping himself up on his elbow, and pulled off the covers in a wordless watch. When he'd done nothing after, my nerves got the better of me. Enough to blurt out and shy away.

"What?"

"I'm just looking at you," said Kwan, soft. The backs of his fingers glided up and down my exposed side, both of us bathed in a contrast of cold moon light and warm lamplight.

The scars along my hands and arms, from various cuts and other injury of village life, seemed more prominent then, as did the pox scars that speckled my body. I was still embarrassed of them, how ugly they looked compared to the less worked hands of a Juneun woman, and tried to hide them without noticed.

He caught the attempt, stopping his rhythmic strokes to take one and place his lips in my palm, eyes looking into mine. A kiss to the back of my hand, another to my wrist, and down my arm, tender and slow. I saw the faint line of a scar across his cheekbone, my hand reaching to cup his face. There, my thumb stroked along its length. His body bore more, though all of them difficult to see unless you already knew, and even then.

"Do you think I'm ugly?" asked Kwan.

I shook my head with a laughing smile. "No."

He leaned over me. "Then stop trying to hide yourself."

I wasn't sore in the morning. A little numb, but nothing like I'd been afraid of since my first time. It felt all at once strange yet natural to wake up beside Kwan. Despite that, I still wasn't used to Uno coming to attend me, or the horrible morning remedy. I was glad for her help, since the remedy often made me nauseous, sometimes to the point of losing appetite, and slowed me down from any routine.

Her mood from the solstice carried over, making it impossible not to share a similar joy. Especially when she hummed a tune I wasn't familiar with.

"You've been humming more," I said, infected by her happy state.

She paused, flashing a sheepish smile before continuing with my hair. "I was able to write to my sister about my elevation."

"Elevation?"

"Mm-hm. Originally, I thought I would only be here one year to groom a relative of Lord Kwan for her debut. As an attendant for a special guest, my station was the same. Now, I'm staying on to attend Lord Kwan's consort."

"Consort?" I repeated again. I'd heard the word, but never in full context to understand.

"Concubine," said Uno.

I turned, still not comprehending. I knew the word from stories, but it didn't feel like it fit our relationship.

Uno stared, puzzled. "His mistress."

I paled, blinking at her.

She deepened her expression. "Is that not...?"

We stared at each other.

"I thought..." stumbled Uno. "You're not wed. And, you share the floor. And I bring you a morning remedy sometimes. I thought—is it not the case?"

I stared longer, in silent denial of the evidence. Uno gave a hasty bow, dismissing herself in the growing discomfort.

It wasn't true. It couldn't be true. But, if it wasn't so, then why hadn't Kwan made a proposal? I'd been so caught up in my feelings that I'd assumed the best outcome. What if that wasn't the case? Kwan never specified to anyone what our relationship was. He'd only said he was in love with me.

Before I knew it, I was walking the veranda in a haze. Mist clouded the ground this early in the day, and I'd walked off without my deel to keep warm. Not that I was bothered by the winter air, the haunting realization of things took all notice away from how cold it was outside. Other girls talked about how becoming a mistress was as high as they could hope for. But I wanted for more, even if he didn't have a bronze coin to his name, I wanted to be more than that.

My feet carried me to the shrine, ignoring the icy bite of the path.

How? Why? I'd given a gold piece for my wish. For the one thing I wanted purely for myself, I gave the richest thing I ever held. I stood there, lost in my despair. How was I supposed to explain to my father and brothers that I planned to return to take up as mistress—or say anything at all?

I didn't know how long I'd stood there, numb. Nor did I notice Kwan's approach until he laid his hands on my arms.

"Let's go inside," whispered Kwan, about to kiss behind my ear.

I tore myself away, putting distance between us and scowling. "Is that all I am?"

He said nothing, slow blinking and puzzled.

"Did you only want me to be your mistress?" I felt my throat tighten as my voice began to break.

He studied me with a sullen expression. "No."

"Then tell me what I am to you! If you won't marry me..." It took every ounce of my strength to look dignified and not cry.

Taking his time, he extended his hand in an offer for me to accept. A peace gesture. I refused it.

"There's something I need to show you, Hisa."

I stayed rooted where I was.

"I will explain everything there. And put every doubt you might have to rest."

I didn't move.

"I promise." He stayed put. Perfectly statuesque as the mist gave way to new, silent, snowfall.

There was a pleading in his eyes—that part of him that was locked away trying to reach out—which convinced me to accept.

"Your hands are cold," said Kwan, low and hinting concern. He unfastened his sash, slipping off his coat to drape over me. In doing so, he noticed my lack in shoes. "You'll catch your death at this rate." He gestured to the black pine, waving his hand at a branch hanging over us. The needles dropping and forming a pair of fine, green slippers.

I didn't realize how cold my feet were until I stepped in each shoe, feeling the softness and something resembling warmth.

"Come," coaxed Kwan, gently toting me along.

We went to the stables, and saddled Saburo. Kwan climbed on first, extending his arm and helping me to sit in the same fashion Syaoran had made me. I felt magic almost the moment we were out of the shelter. A flurry of wind and snow blinding me, I tried to keep my eyes open, to see how the spell worked as we left the gates, catching a glimpse of the same white doe, stopping in her tracks to look up. More magic turned my stomach over as we galloped.

When we slowed, and I felt the magic fade from around us, I opened my eyes. We were in a forest. One that appeared similar but different to what I'd known on Mount Tora. As I orientated myself better, I knew it had to be a different forest.

"Where are we?"

"My family's ancestral lands," said Kwan, patient in his tone.

I sucked in a sharp gasp. "Is it okay for us to be here?"

"Why wouldn't it be?"

"I just meant..." My voice trailed.

"Because we don't get along too well?" said Kwan. "It is still my birthright to return here as I please. My brothers might bar me from their lands, but my ties to here are not severed by disagreement."

Saburo plowed on through the deep snow, snorting with proud power in every stride. The trees held more crisp, white ice, like a tower of laundry baskets piled with cleaned linen. The world around us slumbered soundlessly. My breath steamed, catching sunlight. I pulled the coat closer around me, suddenly reminded.

"Aren't you cold?"

He showed a soft smile. "I will be fine."

That wasn't a real answer. Pressing against him, I put the coat to reach around both of us, the best I could manage, and held tight to the end of each sleeve. For the effort, his smile grew a little.

A cave waited ahead, untouched by winter. Moss lay at its entrance, and a warmth hung in the air.

"This is..."

Kwan dismounted, helping me down. "The entrance to the *Well of Oaths*." He took my hand, leading me inside.

Not far in, I heard the rhythmic dripping of water. While dark, I could still see a bit of the things around us. "Why did you want me here?"

He said nothing until we came to a large stone, its center carved out like a bowl where the drips collected. "I entrusted you with my soul."

At his words, I quickly closed my eyes and counted, making sure to keep Urekkato out.

"I wanted to explain to you my reasons for taking it out in the first place."

"So that Gumiho wouldn't steal it," I said.

He looked at me, forcing on his hint of a smile while his eyes seemed melancholic. "That's one reason." He breathed in, readying his next set of words. No more secrets. "I loved her. Once."

I froze, shocked by what he'd said. For as long as I'd known, Kwan and Gumiho were eternal enemies. They'd always hated each other. "I..."

"You're surprised," said Kwan. "Most of the lords among Juneun knew my attachment. The girl that is Gumiho was a different person to the fox queen now. We were wildly in love. Reckless. I used to sneak out of Tetsuden to be with her."

It broke my heart, hearing him speak so fondly. I knew he'd probably had lovers in the past, or maybe fallen for someone. But it still hurt to hear it from him.

"I ignored anyone who tried to tell me I couldn't be with her. That it was a dangerous thing. I tried to be too much like my grandfather, too much like my master. And when others tormented her, I brought her here to make a vow."

"A vow?" I held my breath. I didn't want to hear it. I didn't want to hear him say that he'd married her. That he couldn't marry me because of it. I wanted to run. But my feet stayed glued to this spot.

"The reason I allowed everyone to think that I, alone, had some power to go against her. I vowed that I would protect her from all of them. Not one would take a blade to her without mine intercepting it. And when she was no longer the girl I loved, I realized, to my horror, the mistake I'd made."

I blinked, unbelieving. "But, then—"

"In my vow, I said I would protect her from *them*. Not myself. I feared that I might be forced to turn my hand against my kin, and went after her on my own. It was the only way I could be sure not to add more in bloodshed. I don't know if she's dead after this last confrontation, or still out there."

"Kwan..." I breathed out his name, hardly able to bear the heartache in his voice.

He scooped some of the water in one hand. "Maybe I'm still reckless. Centuries later." He turned his eye to me. "In wanting to make a vow to the woman I now love with all my heart. Who carries my soul."

"You don't have to," I said, hastily.

He watched me a while. The water dripping on unhindered.

"I vow that I love you, Hisa. And, if you'll accept, I will make you my wife. Never a mistress. Or anything less." He drank what was in his palm before I could object, or say that this was proof enough.

I didn't know what sort of magic would bind him to that oath, or if there was any at all. It was the sheer audacity that he'd made such a big performance, so out of his character, that convinced me.

He held a soft, expecting smile. "Now, there's no reason to doubt again." In two short steps, he stood over me, cupping my chin and resting his forehead on mine, our noses brushing against each other. "No more tears."

I echoed the sentiment. "But, then, why haven't you made a proposal?"

He lifted his head from me, meeting my eye. "I cannot make a proper proposal until you are fully free to decline. By all accounts, I shouldn't have confessed my feelings to you yet, or taken you into my bed."

"But I'd felt the same way," I said. "And more than once I'd taken you into my bed. Isn't that enough to make both of us fully free?"

He gave a single shake of his head. "Not from a righteous stance."

I breathed in deep and sighed. Deciding how to argue.

"Will you accept this as an informal proposal?"

"Of course I will," I said, happily, and reached up to bring him into a kiss.

Holding me, I felt light enough to fly. Grounding again only when we ended the embrace.

"Do I need to make a vow?"

"No," said Kwan. "It is not required."

He started to lead us away, and I stopped. My thoughts and feelings tangled in each other. I wanted to make a gesture of my own. Some bold statement of my fidelity. So I stepped to the well. Scooping out a measly handful, I tried to temper the storm inside me to come up with what to promise.

"I vow that I will love you, Kwan. And that I will never again doubt your affection or your heart."

Chapter 76
Reassurance

We lingered at the well a while, enjoying the solitude and sharing a coat. Nothing was said between us in that time. It wasn't needed. When we did return, finding the house in an uproar over our absence and calming only after, we went to bed. Not to do anything. We laid beside each other, still dressed. Kwan would caress my face, slow to go to my hair to fondle and play with it. And I did likewise when I felt like it.

I wouldn't allow outside opinions to bring me low again. For the rest of winter, I kept my head high with confidence, and spent most of my idle time in sewing up something to present to Kwan in spring. The dark-blue color of the fabric, patterned with thin, silver lines, would look handsome in a number of ways. With so little of it, however, I was limited. I wasn't skilled enough to make a full outfit yet, but I had to think cautiously of what to make. A half-coat, I decided, where I could embroider in sunflowers at the bottom hem.

Uno helped me now and again. And sometimes, when I took to the veranda for a change in scenery, Syaoran checked in. I'd done my best to keep Kwan from seeing it, wanting to keep it as a surprise.

When spring arrived, I still wasn't finished, working carefully to make it worthwhile.

"Can I not see what you've been working on?" asked Kwan, teasing at me.

I'd been delayed with a thought. If any light from Kwan's soul shone through the puzzle box, the way I'd found it, who was to say it wouldn't happen again? Not that I thought anyone in the house would ever try to open it, let alone take it, but my anxiousness prompted me; I'd taken the scraps of that blue fabric to fashion a small pouch to better hide his soul.

Refusing became harder when he placed his arms around my mid-section, and rested his chin on my shoulder. I'd promised him it by his birthday, and so I relented. "It's not finished yet," I said.

He examined it, looking over the stitchwork. I winced when I saw any snag or mistake that escaped me before.

"I think I will be the luckiest lord," said Kwan. "Since I will have a wife so dedicated into making something this fine for me."

My cheeks pinked, and my heart swelled with pride. "A few days more, and it'll be ready."

He kissed at my jaw. "I like it."

"Really?" I asked, looking at him.

He nodded. "Kwang is hosting Mokryon."

I shied. "Can't we stay?"

"I have a few things to discuss with my brother. Mokryon is as good an excuse as any to call on him." He stood. "Come. So, you can pick out what it is you'd like made."

"Made?"

"Unless you want to wear what Juro sent you."

I understood his meaning, shaking my head and getting up to follow.

In the common space, Lin and Syaoran went over bits of paperwork, standing to bow and gesturing me to a spread on a separate table. Uno worked on adjustments to her court attire, standing to do the same as Lin and Syaoran. Out of habit, I'd started to do likewise and felt a little foolish for it. But it made the question more apparent: Would I still need to behave as Kwan's servant away from home, or during court?

"I intend to present you as my guest," said Kwan, perhaps knowing my question from how I'd fumbled in my actions.

The spread of papers and strips of cloth caused me to twist my brow. The pictures of elegantly dressed women a mystery until I read over what each page described. Colors and patterns and styles demonstrated so that I could send for my own. Though there was nothing mentioning costs, causing me to hesitate.

"I neglected you last year," said Kwan. "I won't make the same mistake."

A guilty excitement brewed up in me. "You already gave me one in Tetsuden, and another for my birthday."

"What if I want you to have a thousand more?"

I laughed.

"It'll be warmer at Bitgaram, since it's in the low lands rather than a mountain."

At the mention of his brother's castle, I wondered. "Does your estate have a name?"

"Hm?" He studied me a minute, taking his time to answer. "I've called it *Inori*."

I repeated the name, committing it to memory.

"Which ones do you like?"

I rolled my bottom lip between my teeth. "There's so many..."

"Take your time."

I'd selected a matured style dress that sinched at the waist—soft, pastel green for the blouses with wide sleeves, and a sky-blue for the skirt embroidered with small butterflies, tied off with a peach-pink sash. When prompted to pick another, I chose another waist cinched dress of a different style—muted blues and pinks making up the pieces, accented by deep burgundy. I wouldn't know what the finished result would look like for certain, but I thought I'd done a decent job in considering what would look appropriate without drawing attention.

At a third prompting, I refused. Kwan smiled, taking my written instruction to Lin.

"I'm going to the Iori pagoda," said Kwan, "to see what is still needed. If Hisa changes her mind on these, help her in my stead."

"Yes, my lord," said Lin and Syaoran.

With nothing more to say, he walked out the door and leapt, leaving a gust in his wake.

"Hisa must have a profound effect on our master," said Syaoran, hinting mischief. "He's been more lively these last few months than in the last fifty years."

"She's a sweet girl," said Lin in my defense. "Better than some pompous, perfumed, spoiled brat, if you ask me."

"Lin loves Hisa," teased Syaoran.

Lin hit his arm for it. "She's still willing to help around the house and share out things, even though she's not a servant anymore. I would've indulged in the luxury."

Syaoran snickered.

"I'm not used to being waited on," I said. "Even now, it feels strange. I don't think I'll ever get used to it. And I still don't know what a lady does in the day if not help out where help is needed."

"Don't you dare try to change her," scolded Lin, preemptively.

Syaoran laughed. "But if that's how village girls are, maybe Hisa can recruit a few to come back with her when she goes home."

"Goes home?" Lin looked at me.

"I'll come back," I assured. "But I want to make sure that my father and brothers will be set without me. And I need to repay the girls who've been looking after them in my stead."

"They're men," said Lin with a whine. "They'll be fine."

"Don't tell her that," said Syaoran. "What if I'm sick and no one will tend to me? Or, worse, one of the girls tries to take advantage—"

"Quit complaining," said Lin. "Were you like this around Yua?"

"She didn't understand my humor."

I sighed, holding in a laugh as I shook my head.

"Did you still want to go over what I promised in winter?" asked Syaoran.

I nodded, standing when he did.

"We'll fetch what we need out of the secretary room. This way."

Following him, giddy as I was to learn something new, I felt a pinch of guilt. The feeling intensified in the smaller room when I saw the costs of the fabrics. I was about to bold back and change everything I'd selected when Syaoran grabbed me.

"Stop. It'll only make him sad. He keeps wanting to dote on you, and he thought of how to do that without making you feel pressured. He actually looked a little excited watching you."

I sighed my complaint, but let it go. I knew he was right, and it wouldn't have bothered me this way if I was kept ignorant.

"It's actually a little funny, seeing Kwan try and figure out how to make you happy when you're so easily made awkward."

"That reminds me," I said, the memory coming from nothing in particular. "Did you ever find..." I didn't know how to word it, keeping it vague yet direct.

"N-no," said Syaoran. "I'm still looking."

I furrowed my brow. "I wish you'd just let me help you."

He shook his head. "I don't want you to get hurt by it." Stretching his arm across, he pulled his sleeve out of the way to direct my attention.

It wasn't a complicated matter, most of the difficulty was in my head. On seeing how it was done, it seemed obvious now. Syaoran fronted the cost, under the condition that I should make something for him as well: a pair of socks—the most beautiful pair in the world. I made no promises about the beauty, but did say that I would try.

"These things tend to go faster for Juneun who are either skilled after decades or more, or who can use magic. It'll be interesting to see a human take on it," said Syaoran as we put everything away.

While my selection was made into a rush order, it still only arrived the night before we left for Bitgaram. I was pleased with how it turned out, eager to show Kwan. He gave an approving nod. Everything packed, I had a hard time falling asleep. Kwan had tried to comfort my nerves, helping sooth me a little. I was terrified that I'd somehow embarrass him. I wasn't a lady, nor did I know how to act like one, and nothing would change that. At times, I was a difficult servant.

He assured me that I was over thinking it, and had less to worry about in predicting Juro's absence to lessen any awkwardness. Too close to the ocean. The news filled me with more excitement and dread. I'd never seen the ocean.

Before leaving, Uno sent me off with morning remedies and a flask of wine, in case I needed it. Discomfort came with the thought. I still wasn't ready for others outside the house to know. Past experience from holding court reminded me that discretion was hard to do, and my face heated.

As it had before, I felt nausea going through the spell. Bright sunlight caused me to squint and blink, missing when we'd rode into a vast, sloping meadow, bisected by a long river that emptied into an endless body of water. The air instantly sticky with salt and heavy with the smell of wildflowers, I ignored Kwang's castle for the first few seconds. Low mountains with a soft incline stood orderly from each other. Everything opposite of the dense forests and steepness of home; our rivers looked like twigs compared to the one slithering to the sea.

My stare broke when Kwan called my name, leading on to his brother's castle. It seemed a quaint, almost cottage version of Genji's home, situated between the tallest mountain and the valley. From here, there didn't seem too many walls and gates to pass through, which would make navigating a little easier. It was still a great deal larger than Kwan's house, but felt somehow more manageable to meander. I noticed then that each mountain peak was dotted with an outpost of some sort.

Several hours after, the sun hanging low (though I knew we hadn't ridden a whole day), we came to the outer gates. The guards stepped aside, allowing us free passage. No directions were needed, with every guard and servant letting us pass and giving a show of respect to their master's brother.

We dismounted nearer to the castle doors, having arrived a day early for Mokryon. Kwan embraced his brother, noting that their other relatives had recently arrived.

Unlike in Tetsuden, the household stayed one room down from Kwan rather than a collective place on a separate floor. I was given a room divided from Kwan by paper pane doors; becoming one room when fully open. Whichever way I preferred. Part of me, knowing he wanted us together, appreciated the option.

Awkwardness came when I didn't know where I ought to be for supper. Did I belong with the nobles, the guests? Or with the servants? Kwan, likely reading my anxious features led me away to dine beside him. I'd never felt more watched than I did during that meal. It took my complete will to not shake, and pretend not to notice anyone staring or whispering. My stomach shriveled, not allowing me to eat much despite being so hungry. I worked hard not to be clumsy, to make every movement smooth, to not breath too loud.

Realizing that there'd be more guests in that hall the following day and through Mokryon, a silent panic stirred in me. I tried looking for familiar, friendly faces without being obvious. None. To my relief, Beom, Juro, and Urekkato were notably absent. I'd hoped Genji would be there, shy as he was.

In the following day, I stayed beside Kwan in walking the grounds. He'd sported the half-coat I'd made, and kept a calm smile on his face. I felt bashful, and he responded in starting up soft conversations as we roamed the gardens. In particular, I liked the rose arches. As the day progressed, I began to feel a little at ease. It bothered me less and less when other guests walked by. Kwan treated our relationship as the most natural thing, continuing to comfort without saying so. On a whim, he plucked a rose and cleared it of thorns, placing it into my hair. Something that reminded me of how he behaved beneath the wisteria tree.

I'd made a passing comment about wanting to go into the meadows and the ocean, thinking nothing of it. Kwan promised we would before leaving, and I smiled bright at the prospect.

We didn't dance that first night. I was already tired from my nerves. Kwan didn't mind, laying beside me as we slept. He disliked dancing as it was.

In the second day, I was left to my own while he called on his host brother for something. There weren't many places I could retreat to for hiding—not like in Tetsuden—so I practiced keeping my chin up and back straight as I wandered the grounds and passed the kiosks. Kwan had given me a few bits of silver to spend as I liked, though it didn't feel right to do so. But I did when the smell from one kiosk was too much to ignore.

The urge struck again, passing a jeweler's stand. A small, jade pendant, carved into a phoenix drew my gaze. I'd never been able to surprise him with a gift, and this might be my only chance.

In the room, I'd undressed to clean up, washing away the salty air from my skin and recombing my hair. Even if Kwan didn't care, it was important to me to try and look more respectable for him. In the midst of dressing into the gown he sent for last Mokryon, he returned to the room. I'd jumped at first from the sudden sound of the door fast sliding open, and let out a nervous laugh in my recognition. He closed the door just as quickly, seeming pleased about something as he took brisk steps.

I smiled, trying to gather myself more quickly and express that I'd only need a minute more to be ready for the dance.

He didn't listen, pulling me in for a passionate kiss and pinning me between himself and the drawers. My blouses came loose, several pieces dropping and the ties falling away.

"Kwan!" I scolded in a whisper.

"Hisa," growled Kwan in response, moving to my neck.

In a swift movement, he lifted me to sit at the edge of the drawers, putting himself between my legs. I'd made quiet, half-hearted objections. All of them relinquished with the excitement of his forward behavior. His lips moved down to my chest. Out of instinct, I took hold in his hair for balance. Hurried, he moved the skirt of my dress out of the way, his hands moving from my hips and rear to my thighs. It was when he ripped my under-trousers that I genuinely scolded and pushed back.

"I'll get you another," said Kwan, undeterred as he went in for another kiss.

I broke from it, pushing back. He stopped, staring down at me with an eagerness as we caught our breaths.

"What is this about?"

That soft smile stayed on his face, a hand coming to stroke my cheek. "Happy news."

I blinked, rapid to try and understand.

"I want to celebrate."

I grabbed his other hand as he started again. "Won't you tell me what it's about first?"

"A surprise for you. And the reason I wanted to come to Bitgaram."

"That's not much of an answer."

"I promise it's not a lavished gift. But it means keeping my vow to you." He caressed my face, looking into my eyes.

It was strange to think how cold his own were on our first meeting. A combination of orange and yellow and brown that made him look fierce. Now, there was something happy in them, gentle.

"And a new pledge to you, so that you never need worry over me."

"Huh?"

"Regardless of whether or not Gumiho is still alive, I will not chase after her. Never again will I return beastly and not myself. Not now when I have something, someone, precious to lose."

I smiled wide, relief sweeping over me. "You mean it?"

He nodded. "I never want you to worry, or fear me. Nor do I want to see you hurt." Leaning in, he stopped short, and my heart pounded with anticipation. "To harm my gentle wife, I couldn't bear it."

I blushed at his sentiment. *My gentle wife*. Joy ran through me, wanting to come out in tears. I put a stop to them by pulling him into that undelivered kiss.

We didn't go to dance that night either.

Chapter 77
Lord Kwan XX

Kwan felt a burden lift from his shoulders, confiding in her beside the well. Not even Kwang knew the reason why he alone chased Gumiho. He half expected to be chastised or scolded for his folly. Instead, she'd shown compassion. In explaining his reasons for withholding a proposal, she made no gripe, accepting the circumstance.

More, he delighted in her sincere concern for him in the cold. She was kind. Something he cherished and wanted to remain that way.

Then, there was her own vow. One she didn't need to make.

They sat in comfortable quiet, huddled under his coat while he rested his chin and cheek atop her hair. He breathed her in, his Hisa. The memory of her savaged arm by his account—that he'd almost lost her—weighed in his heart. He needed to break the bond to Gumiho, to free himself of rushing in if she was still a threat.

There were few he could think of that might know how, and none of them savory. If it meant protecting her, he'd endure whatever humiliation came with it.

In presenting him with the half-coat, he marveled at the embroidery. She remembered. A conversation that most would've forgotten, the day they rode to the lake's edge. His wisteria girl. It made him all the more eager to see the pagoda restored. A place where they could be alone with each other, unbothered. She was human, and full of surprises. It wouldn't be a dull marriage; one he would, instead, treasure.

Watching her fret over what to choose for herself, it entertained Kwan with a thought: what would she do with a wife's income? He didn't know if humans were the same in their marriage, owing a portion of revenue to their wife. Then again, perhaps they never encountered so long a lifetime for quarrels and mistreatment to be brought to their rulers. Juneun typically stayed out of intervening too much with human affairs. Hisa would probably send most of her new income back to her village in gifts. The imagining of it amused him more. He only hoped her sweetness wouldn't be taken advantage of by former neighbors.

Again, the memory of her arm flashed in his mind. What if he couldn't break his bond to Gumiho? If he died, what would become of Hisa? It wasn't the first time he thought about this. The reason he wanted to go to his brother's hosting was that very concern.

On arriving to Kwang's home, he noted Hisa's enchantment with the river pouring into the sea, reminded then that she'd never seen it. He started to smile, endeared by the cuteness of her wide-eyed stare at the ocean. He supposed that, for some, there might be a fear of getting too close. And he didn't want her afraid.

So, at her mention of wanting to go up to the sea, to experience it, he felt relief. He reminded himself then that she was the girl who ran up the mountain in the night. Of course she wouldn't be afraid. She was Hisa.

When formalities on Kwang's behalf ended, Kwan called on him, trying not to draw attention.

"I'm actually surprised you came at all," said Kwang. "After what happened on your mountain, and canceling court, I would've thought you'd shut yourself in again." He gestured at a servant to set the table, and brought over a bottle of apricot wine. "I should've guessed. You want something. And you want to keep it secret from the rest of our family." With a boyish grin, he and Kwan took a seat.

"I did secure you a tutelage with Genji," said Kwan. "Or would you have one of our elder brothers suggest a mentor to father?"

Kwang snickered. "This must be something important if you're bring that up."

Kwan said nothing, taking his offered wine to drink. With a flick of the hand, his brother dismissed the servants, leaving them alone to speak.

"I'll keep your secrets."

Kwan took his time, measuring his words and his brother's reaction, casting his own spell to silence them from eavesdroppers. "Genji has named me heir to Tetsuden."

Kwang stopped mid-sip.

"Naturally, if I were to die, that inheritance falls to you. The next youngest son."

"O-okay," stuttered Kwang, overwhelmed with storming thoughts.

"I want you to waive your claim to it," said Kwan. "And sign it over to my widow."

"Widow?" repeated Kwang, twisting his brow and blinking. "But, you're not yet—"

"To Hisa."

Silence. Lasting longer than Kwan anticipated.

"To... Hisa—? You mean you—?"

Kwan said nothing, keeping his watch on his brother.

"Have you thought about this? Really thought about it?"

Kwan kept still.

At a loss for words, Kwang fidgeted, jaw dropped and eyes darting to other parts of his apartment room in search of something to say.

"My last return home, I nearly killed several of my household. Another confrontation may mean my end."

Kwang furrowed his brow, loosing a pensive sigh. "I see your concern. But... Hisa is human."

Kwan said nothing, sipping from his cup of wine.

"She's a sweet girl, I agree," said Kwang. "A mistress, I'd understand. But you're not serious about marrying her."

Kwan remained silent.

"She's human. I know Genji's wife was human, but it was a fluke. Aside from it, she doesn't have titles or a dowry, or anything to bring. And she has..." Kwang's voice trailed, his finger still pointing at his face.

Kwan continued his stoic stare, giving only a single, slow blink in response.

"You're serious? You know our father would never allow it."

Kwan remained statuesque. Watching.

"Say something!"

Kwan took his time before answering, tempering himself. "I will make a formal proposal to Hisa. If she accepts, I will marry her. And if I die, I want to know that I'd done all I could to make sure she's looked after."

"Think about what you're asking," said Kwang, reining himself in. "Inori, Tetsuden—and all its adjoining lands—to a human girl who likely won't have it more than sixty years. She wasn't brought up in this world, Kwan. How is she supposed to handle the finances and upkeep and staffing...?" He trailed with his brother's pointed gaze. "You want me... to..."

Kwan kept still and silent.

"You want me to handle it for her. Is that it?"

Kwan said nothing, leaving his brother to sigh in frustration.

"It would've been easier to just ask me to take her as a mistress if you—" he stopped, seeing a scowl begin on his brother's face. "I wouldn't have touched her! I'm only saying it'd be easier than what you're asking me now. Think about how this looks. You're choosing a human over your kin. Over your brother."

"Genji is fond of her," said Kwan. "If she chooses to stay on Mount Tora, you will assist with whatever she needs. If Genji and I are both gone—"

"I'll—" Kwang paused, breathing in to ease his emotion. "I'll handle it. It'll be a pain in the ass, but I'll handle it for her."

"If she wants to be—"

"If she wants to be involved, yes, I won't keep it from her." He swallowed whatever remained in his wine cup in a single gulp, refilling it for another swig.

Kwan waited. "You will sign off your claim." It wasn't a question.

"I will sign off my claim."

"You will look after her."

"I will look after her."

"As though she were your sister."

"As though," continued Kwang, speaking slower to emphasis his compliance, "she were my sister." He refilled their cups again.

From beneath his robes, Kwan produced the papers needed to legalize the inheritance transfer. His brother waved a hand, his stationery floating over. Patience was needed, waiting for one request to finish before presenting another.

Despite compliance, it wasn't an easy exchange. Questions and specifications and amendments were necessary. Prominent among them that, if there was not a child, the inheritance would fall back to Kwang; and if there were children between them, they would be brought up for proper inheritance and titles—which meant drawing up new documentation. More amendments would be needed depending on sex. Pending was noted, and would close if there was no child born or expected upon Kwan's death.

Tedious work. Hours of it. The final stroke of the ink-brush lending peace of mind.

"You're not planning on getting yourself killed anytime soon, are you?" teased Kwang, hiding his frustration.

Kwan gave a single shake of his head. "That is where I ask another favor."

His brother sighed, pouring the last of the wine between them. "After this demand, how bad can your next one be?"

"It depends," said Kwan. "Which members of the Lion Clan are here?"

Kwang raised a brow. "Why them in particular?"

"Theirs is the clan that forged *Bird Song*. A sword for kings."

Kwang leaned back on his palms, pursing his lips as his mind created a shortcut to answers. "You want them to forge a sword with a specific purpose? Or, one for slaying Gumiho?"

"One strong enough to cut a bond made in the water of our ancestral home."

Kwang quirked a brow. "Why not borrow *Bird Song*? Dae Jum's eldest grandson lost it in a contest to Zhen the last time I held Mokryon. Rumor has it, he's under house arrest by the crown prince for the next twenty more years. My first hosting as the new master of Bitgaram was lively."

Kwan didn't care for the gossip. The important part being that something which could possibly break his oath to Gumiho was nearer at hand.

"Who am I sending for?"

Zhen sat across from the brothers, grinning. It'd been a delicate conversation, needing to be sure the sword could be used the way Kwan needed before exposing anything. "And they say the Samjos are more foolhardy. To make such an incautious promise. Now, things make more sense."

The brothers said nothing, with the younger imitating the demeanor of the elder.

"You won't put me into submission with silence and rank," said Zhen. "I think I'm due a little more if you want *Bird Song*."

"The sword is a mere possibility," said Kwan.

"Don't give me that," said Zhen. "Don't pretend you have more options. It means revealing this unfortunate piece history. And the easy solution to all this would be to take Lord Kwan's head. Or, the Mireus would see it that way. And we can't ignore a king's order."

"What do you want?" asked Kwang, impatient.

Zhen's smug expression intensified. "Your sister."

"Out of the question—!" snapped Kwang, stopped by the gesture of his brother's arm.

"If Sara is betrothed to me, and Kwan to my sister Towa, I will break the oath for you."

"I can promise neither," said Kwan. "It is my father who can match my sister, if you cannot secure her acceptance. And I am recently promised to another."

"You cannot un-promise?" teased Zhen, testing the patience of the brothers.

"No," said Kwan, flat.

"Then what *can* you give me?" asked Zhen, sighing and feigning boredom.

Kwan kept still. While Sara did go out of her way to antagonize him, even in childhood, she was still his sister. A gilded cage, she'd called it. Despite everything, he couldn't bring himself to go through in trying to persuade her to accept Zhen.

He stood. "We will reconvene tomorrow."

It seemed the only way, for now, to bide time and come up with something tempting, was to leave. His family was right in their chastising. In a haste to build allies, he gifted lands and bestowed titles too liberally for there to be anything that might entice Zhen. Perhaps from his inheritance lands, though they weren't fully his to give.

"Uncle," called a sweet voice.

Kwan paused in his stride, looking over to Yeona as she trotted up. Her pace a mess in the battle against wanting to run over while maintaining ladylike dignity. He watched with an intrigue, now seeing her grown and struggling to contain girlish glee.

"May I walk with you?"

Kwan nodded to her request.

She took his arm, holding up her hand fan to her chest. "You look downtrodden, Uncle."

Kwan grunted.

"More than usual, I mean."

"Do I?"

"I thought you'd be happier to see me in my first outing."

Rather than debate or defend, he redirected the conversation. While Yeona presented sweetly, he hadn't seen her often to know her well. Better to avoid than accidentally give way to gossip. "How are you liking your first time away from your house?"

Yeona shrugged. "Mother says it's too dangerous for me to leave the castle unaccompanied. But she goes out unattended without thought. Father is here, grandfather is here, my uncles are here, my brothers are here, and it is my uncle's home. How much safer could I possibly be?"

Kwan didn't engage in her venting.

"Father left the raising of myself and my sisters to Mother. And she wouldn't explain most anything needed to navigate society. I was just supposed to already know somehow. And when I don't, I'm scolded for it. I hoped I would have a little freedom away from the house. But I'm watched every second of the day—I cannot breathe!"

He was reminded again of Sara, describing her gilded cage.

"I don't understand how the world could be so impossibly dangerous that I cannot step one foot out the gates of my own home, yet we hold court and festivals and parties. How Mother can go to visit a friend and be gone a week or more, unattended, yet my walking the arbors and not come inside as soon as the sun sets could spell my death. I've been kept naïve and made to feel afraid of anything beyond home, all while believing it is some fault of my own making rather than the neglect of my upbringing."

"The concern isn't without some warrant," said Kwan.

"Because of Aunt Jiana, who died when I was a baby. That was so many years ago. How could the world possibly be more dangerous? At times, I feel more like an inconvenient pet than a daughter. I'm praised when it suits my parents, and ignored when I am not useful. Which is why I've given myself a mission on my first outing."

Kwan merely grunted his acknowledgment.

"Before Mokryon ends, I will be married."

"Ambitious."

"And I'm recruiting you to help me in my efforts, Uncle Kwan."

"Are you?"

"Father says you lack all respect for family values."

"He's misinformed," said Kwan, tempered in his tone. "I have the greatest respect for family. We simply disagree on how where it ought to be upheld, and where it ought to be challenged."

Yeona smiled. "Which is why I'm recruiting you. You know the lords present, do you not? I would've asked Aunt Sara, since she knows my plight like hers. But she's set on getting her own way, and I would *only be a distraction*. Could you not sympathize with my perspective?"

"In what way?"

"Our family seems to like ostracizing whoever doesn't fit perfectly in their design. So, I'm relying on you to make introductions on my behalf and help me find a husband."

Kwan tilted his head down to better look at his niece.

"I know you want to tell me I'm young and impetuous," said Yeona, direct. "But as a wife, I might have a little freedom. I want some control of my life—even in just small matters. Mother wouldn't so much as allow me to pick out a dress."

"A husband, chosen in haste, might jail you still."

"But not if you make the introductions," plead Yeona. "If you help me to choose a husband who is not so suffocating. You and Uncle Kwang called on Lord Zhen not long ago."

Kwan said nothing, not wanting to slip into some baited game.

"Wouldn't he make for a good match? He has a list of achievement to make him a tempting prospect. And his lands are said to be beautiful and full of fragrance. That was the reason he was sent to the royal palace, was it not? To charm the youngest princess?"

"Lord Zhen has a reputation of many things," said Kwan, trying to dissuade hurried actions.

"I know. My own boy attendant made mention of his discomfort. But all that would mean for me is that I wouldn't be needed so often in his bed. Besides, I'm not fond of my boy and I don't think I will bring him into my household when I am wed. He parrots too much of Mother and feeds her need to exaggerate to anyone who will listen. Usually Father. Sometimes I think that rabbit you sent me has more freedom than I do."

Kwan watched her, trying to read into how much of what she said was sincere, and how much was a façade. If nothing else, she was direct. More than he'd come to expect from the usual ladies at court.

"You will make an introduction, won't you?" asked Yeona. "At least so I can see if I like him at all for myself. I'd hoped Lord Genji might come, and introductions made that way. If he did, Father couldn't object. And a gentler husband would mean I wouldn't be so confined. If not Lord Zhen, then Lord Haru—though I'd heard rumor that he's newly intended on a girl from the Masa family. However, if you think he is not too fond of her, perhaps you could introduce me still?"

Kwan found it almost amusing. His niece had the tactics of a vicious lady of court, though lacked the cunning to keep it nuanced.

"I am determined, Uncle," said Yeona when Kwan didn't respond. "If you don't help, and go to my father instead, I will behave more persistently and elope. Better that scandal than to be imprisoned by my own family."

Kwan led them away, to a more remote part of his brother's water garden. There, he spoke more freely while staying hushed. "If you are willing to be a pawn to another family, perhaps you are too naïve."

"At least it would be my own choosing," said Yeona, matching his volume.

"Do you know what you would be getting into?"

"No," admitted Yeona. "And the way things are, I still wouldn't know in three hundred years."

Kwan watched her, reading her expression, and heaved a sigh. While a part of him argued against the idea, he did (to some extent) sympathize with her. She needed an escape, and he needed something to temp Zhen's compliance. "Lord Zhen is housed opposite the ocean view."

Yeona blinked.

"I will make the introduction."

Chapter 78
Lord Kwan XXI

It'd gone better than Kwan could hope. While they'd found Zhen at the start of scandalous intimacy with a servant, it was quickly forgotten with Yeona's appearance. Enchanted by prettiness, amused by her forwardness, and intrigued by her dowry and sheltered upbringing, the high lord was hers before the end of a half-hour.

A formal announcement would take place the following night, after Zhen's part of the bargain was paid.

Relief in his heart, he went back to his room. He wanted to tell Hisa everything, to see her approve of his ordeal. His sensibility reminded him that her perspective of it might not align with how his society would see things. But he had to tell her something—to share some good news with her.

In their room, he was glad that he wouldn't need to search the grounds to find her. And, in seeing her, a forceful happiness compelled his actions.

She scolded his name.

He growled hers back.

She'd said something, though he didn't catch it, eager to share in this feeling of elation with her. He'd stopped thinking all together, acting on every impulse until he felt her push on him. Hardly noticeable, but enough to get his attention.

"What is this about?"

Kwan explained—or tried to. His mind occupied with a previous set of wants. When she objected to his advance, he gathered his thoughts, stringing together some semblance of sensible words to give her.

"I never want you to worry, or fear me. Nor do I want to see you hurt." He leaned in, stopping short and waiting for her cue. He could taste her breath, feel how close he was to her, smell the lingering salt in her hair, and stayed fixed on her dark-brown eyes thick with lashes. "To harm my gentle wife, I couldn't bear it."

Wife. He wanted to repeat the word, use it at every opportunity.

She pulled him in to kiss, fast working to undress him, and he resumed his playing and enjoyment of the moment. At times, she submitted. In other instances, she gave way to some playful impulse. All of it made him smile.

At her most rambunctious effort, he found himself amused and intrigued, rewarding her with a single phrase, "Good girl."

They ended in bed, where the chatter of the crowds outside the castle didn't seem to make it to their ears.

"I'd always hoped that, someday, I could thank the Juneun who healed my family. My village," said Hisa, dream-stated. "I never imagined I would fall in love with so great a man. Or that he would have a place in his heart for me."

Kwan listened, playing with rebellious locks of her hair.

"Some days, it doesn't feel real. I'm almost afraid to sleep."

He paused in his fiddling.

"What if I wake up, and it was all a dream?"

"It can never be a dream," said Kwan. "Not when it saved me from a life of nightmares."

"Saved you?" repeated Hisa with a laughing smile.

Kwan grunted, letting go of her hair to allow the back of his index finger to run up and down the length of her collar bone. "An ember from ashes. Or the grasslands when the river breaks free of a beaver's damn."

She mulled it over, her fingertips tracing his muscles.

"We'll go to the sea tomorrow," said Kwan.

Hisa looked up, a smile consuming her.

"And we'll go home the following day."

Her expression faltered. "So soon?"

Kwan shifted, reading her face. "You're disappointed?"

"I..." Her bottom lip half-hid itself. "I was hoping I could dance with you again while we're here for Mokryon."

He watched her turn sheepish, bringing his thumb to brush down the tip of her nose in a playful manner. "We'll dance tomorrow. And go to the sea the following day."

She smiled.

"Hisa is happy?"

She nodded with a quiet giggle.

"Magpie."

"Which reminds me!" Hisa flung herself out of the bed, grabbing the nearest thing to cover her nakedness.

One of his own robe layers from the day. She shuffled to the drawers, tying it to keep the article from falling off her smaller frame. It wasn't overwhelmingly large on her, and it presented a sort of cuteness. There was something about seeing the woman he loved sporting his clothes in the most disheveled way that endeared him.

She returned to him with a small pouch, hardly able to contain a proud expression. He took the offering, watching her climb back into the bed and hang over his shoulder with a shy hopefulness. She rested her chin on him, arms loosely slung around his midsection.

Kwan fished out the trinket. Nothing extraordinary in its craftmanship, nor a very pretty piece. But it was how proudly she thought of it that muddled his opinion of the thing.

"I always want to give something in return whenever you've done something for me. I don't have any particular talent or know what I could do to show how much it means. Nothing really feels like enough to express that I love you."

Hearing that meant more to him than the jade. A delight in his efforts receiving some appreciation, rather than be seen as expectation. "I like it."

"You do?" asked Hisa with renewed excitement.

Kwan turned his head to meet her eye, giving a single nod. Her hold became snug, and she buried her face between his neck and shoulder ticklishly. "In the future," said Kwan, waiting to regain her attention. "I like the jam dumplings you make."

"I always worry I've salted the dough too much, and the jam gets too tart."

"It pairs perfectly with floral wines."

She beamed. "Then I'll make some when we get back. As often as you want."

"What do I give in exchange for so many pleasant treats?"

Her face slackened, leaving Kwan to see her mind working to come up with an answer. "Say that you love me?"

"I will say that regardless," said Kwan. "Is there nothing else?"

She rested her head back on his shoulder. "I'll think of something."

A loud pop and flash of colored light spilled into their room, both of them looking to the window. Hisa scooted closer, flinching at first to the explosive sound, and in awe of the dazzling display after. He watched her a moment, taking in her image, and made his way to observe the event with her. More often, he looked to her face than the fireworks, seeing the glitter reflecting in her eyes and off the shine of her black hair.

He rested his cheek atop her head, savoring everything around them in as the finally began.

When it ended, she looked up at him, meeting his eye in a quiet stare, smiling. "Kiss me?"

He mirrored her expression, subdued, and placed a kiss at the base of her forehead.

Morning.

Kwan dressed before the first rays of light painted the sky in opaque splendor. He looked at Hisa, asleep and still wrapped in his robe, and placed a soft touch of his lips to her cheek. Once his oath to Gumiho was nullified, he could let go and begin anew with her. To be a better man than he was before.

Outside the walls, and between mountains, Kwan's swift speed carried him like a gale to the appointed spot. Zhen waited beside Kwang, *Bird Song* in hand, the medicine woman of the Lion Clan among them, and a young man with her. Human, with a horse-cleaving sword set before him. Kwan moved his watch, expectant.

"It takes more than a sword to break this kind of oath, Kwan," said Zhen.

"The boy?" asked Kwan, level in his tone.

"Lady Sue's ward."

"A prince," said Sue. Tall and fit, she still suited the part of a lady in her layers of soft colors. "At the request of his step-mother."

Kwang shifted his weight. The next silent question hung in the air.

"I said I'd bring *Bird Song*," said Zhen. "I never said *I* knew how to break your oath with it."

Kwan frowned, displeased with the idea of more knowing his shame. Though, there was no avoiding it now.

"Let's begin," said Zhen. "While the sun is both here and away."

"A pledge from your well," explained Sue, "cannot be unmade. It can, however, be transferred to another."

She slid her palm against the edge of *Bird Song* as Zhen presented. Two blades at the hilt, intertwining into one at its halfway point. The ethereal green of the metal waking with threads of sunlight dancing on it, Kwan marveled at the craftsmanship. Forged from a star that fell into the sea, the sword seemed somehow alive and aware.

Zhen nodded, gesturing for Kwan to bare a part of himself. "Which hand?"

Kwan kept his gaze on Zhen, measuring. "The right."

Zhen shrugged. "Your sword hand. An interesting pick." He gestured to a large, flat stone.

Kwang set up a soundless spell, keeping their meeting private from the world, while his brother lay his arm down upon the rock.

"I suppose it makes sense," said Zhen with a slyness to his voice. "You did say you were newly intended." He held the blade high, watching Sue's blood creep down its edge. A single drop fell from its tip, cuing Zhen to bring it down into Kwan's hand. The sound of the blade, a robin's mournful war cry, as it sliced the air.

Kwan held in roars of pain at the plunge. Growls and groans escaped through clenched teeth, his every instinct telling him to attack. Through will, he stayed on his knees, arm stretched out.

Sue's ward walked up, regal, and handed his enormous sword to Sue for safekeeping while he completed the transfer of the oath. Even in his pain, Kwan felt there was something off. He'd assumed Sue would be the one to take his oath. Though, perhaps in putting it to a person more easily subdued was the preferred method.

The boy's right arm on the stone, across and to the side of Kwan, he braced himself. Zhen removed the sword tip from Kwan's hand, blood fast pooling. Kwan fought the urge to recoil his hand, breathing his pain to keep still until the ordeal was through.

When Kwan's blood reached the princeling, Zhen repeated the motion, holding *Bird Song* high and waiting for a single drop to fall before bringing it down. It cut through the blood and into the princeling's hand. The boy wailed, his body arched with nowhere to retreat while his hand stayed pinned. He fought to regain himself, reclaiming some semblance of dignity for Zhen to finish.

Bird Song stayed in place, held there until the first rays of sunlight washed over the scene. Slow, Zhen removed the sword tip.

At once, the boy pulled away, trembling at the sight of his wound.

Kwang, ready, hurried to tend to his brother's injury.

"Let it heal naturally tigers," said Zhen. "Or a piece of that promise will stay with you. Even this won't be of help then."

Kwan held in his fury, allowing his brother to clean and dress the wound.

The boy, perhaps a little humiliated from crying out, took to trying to wrap his own hand in a hurried manner, and stand poised.

"Gumiho is now the ward of Prince Joben," said Sue. Swift as lightning, she took the horse-cutter to the boy, his body and head landing separately. "And that is treason."

Kwan looked on in horror. "What is the meaning of this?"

"The transfer of your oath required noble birth, *Lord Kwan*," said Sue. "The human king desired his natural son to inherit, and named him crown prince. His human queen sent the boy away. She disliked the idea of a child that wasn't hers claiming the throne. And my late husband kept him, if only to use later in mortal affairs."

"You said nothing about the death of an innocent," growled Kwan.

"A human," said Sue. "He was useless until now."

"He did nothing," said Kwan, a threat in his voice. "You slew him for the sins of others."

Sue threw a cold look. "Not every war is won through the might of sons. You'd know that if you had more sisters."

"A pleasure doing business," said Zhen, casual and disinterested. "It seems we're all paid up and happy. Sue is free of her obligations. Kwan is free of his impetuous oath. I'm set to wed

Yeona—and I expect the announcement to be carried out tonight. A public display supported by the host won't allow for her father to refuse."

Kwang spoke first. "It will be carried out. As promised."

Kwan turned his scowl from Zhen and Sue, to the corpse on the ground. Starting his life anew, in blood. No... "We're not done here, yet."

Chapter 79

Bitgaram

K wan was gone when I woke up. For the best, since the morning remedy often left me without appetite anyway. I kept thinking of how he phrased it. *My gentle wife*.

I held it in my heart, leaving to get something to eat in the afternoon. A variety of fish I'd never seen were the main course of the luncheon. There were clams, similar to what I sometimes found in the river; and while I didn't like clams, I took a couple to have something familiar.

"Try the seal meat."

I jumped at the new voice. Towa.

"Smart thinking to get in early. It's usually gone pretty quick."

"I missed breakfast," I admitted, wary.

"Try it," insisted Towa, placing a thin slice into my bowl. "A lot of this is exclusive to the coastlines. You won't get them staying on that mountain."

She waited, expectant. I couldn't shake how we'd last met, and what Syaoran had said. Restraining my expression, I tasted it. Fatty, and tender, the flavor wasn't bad, but unexpected.

"It was a shame Kwan canceled court. I was looking forward to it."

I kept quiet, unsure of how much was already known.

"I haven't seen him much here either. I started to think he'd gone back to being a shut-in. But if you're here, he has to be around."

"I'm not sure where he went," I said. "With Lord Kwang, I think." A part of me fell into old insecurities. Towa was a Junuen lady—pretty and bold and making no secret of her interest. Silently, I reminded myself of Kwan's oath to me. Even if it wasn't magic or binding, I trusted that gesture.

"My brother told me Kwan is recently engaged. But if there's not a formal announcement of it, he can't be serious about her."

I frowned, wanting to object—to shout. But we weren't ready. He'd explained it to me.

"You're his attendant," said Towa. "You must know who it is."

I paled, realizing our meeting wasn't coincidence. "I'm not supposed to say."

"You can tell me," said Towa, sweet in her tone. "It's not Feng. She'd have told everyone. So I'm guessing she's from a lesser house. Probably one too poor to make a proper dowry. But he's been known to lay with ladies of all ranks, and Kurai if they interest him, so it's not surprising if that's the case."

The words stung. I already knew Kwan had lovers before me, Gumiho among them, but it still hurt to be reminded, reigniting my hostile insecurity. "I can't say."

"You can trust me," said Towa.

A pinch in my gut disagreed.

"At least tell me if it's someone here."

I knew I shouldn't say anything. But a defiance burned in me, daring me to reveal everything. "Yes. She is."

"Narrows things down," said Towa, starting to scan through the guests.

My nerves gave way, and I left. I'd hardly eaten, and all appetite disappeared again. In my distress, I'd taken the wrong stairs to get back to my room. While Bitgaram was smaller than Tetsuden, the halls were uniform with little to distinguish where I'd gone.

I didn't realize I was at the wrong room until I'd walked in, closed the door, and noticed a set of lady's combs on the table. Puzzled, I stopped, taking in every difference in the smaller room. With a sharp gasp, I bolted out.

Lost.

I tried to retrace my steps and reorientate myself, but I couldn't remember which of the parallel halls I'd come from. In hearing voices, I panicked again—which, I realized was ridiculous of me after the fact—and hurried to some niche alcove to hide. An enormous, beautifully sculpted vase occupied the space, making the perfect place to disappear.

"I don't know why he totes around that girl," said a feminine voice. "A human is a novelty, but I heard she's a bit of a disaster. You've seen her face, right?"

"She uses a cosmetic to try and hide those things, but it's not well done," said another woman's voice. "Especially on her cheek."

The first verbally shuddered. "It was the talk last year when he brought the fox as well. I suppose he likes making a public spectacle when he's not recluse."

"I'd heard she and the fox are lovers, and it caused so much disruption that he's separated them this time."

"The fox? And the human? I feel sorry for him. Kurai or not, he's handsome enough that a prettier servant would be happy with him, despite having no title."

"Maybe it's between her legs and his that won him. That's all I can think of."

"Maybe that's why Kwan brought her and not him? Although, if he came to my room, I'm sure I could do better than a gold-digging human."

"From what I know, he doesn't have any intention of making her a mistress. She'll be back with the other humans soon."

"Do you think he's gotten bored? Only so long you can look at a face like hers, I suppose, no matter how good she is in other aspects."

"He still puts a lot of attention on her from what I've seen so far."

Their voices faded the further they went, and I could no longer make out the echo of their conversation. Gossip and vanity ruled over the women in gatherings like this; sex and violence ruled the men. It was endless scheming for power, and birthing rumors out of jealousy. I told myself that, trying to make myself believe it.

It didn't matter what they thought. It mattered what Kwan thought—what I thought! So why did I suddenly feel so exhausted?

Slow, I came out of my hiding place, and began finding my way back to my room.

No. No! I wouldn't let this be how I remembered Bitgaram.

Defiance roared in me, and I set myself to be more diligent in my cosmetic application for the dance. I'd spend the extra time making it flawless, and give them nothing else to try and hurt me with.

In my room, I dressed and styled my hair, making everything as precise as I could, and cleaned off my face to start afresh.

There was one problem. I couldn't find the cosmetic. I searched, frantic. I knew where I'd left it that morning, but it wasn't there. Did it fall and accidentally get cleaned out by a maid, or kicked out with me as I left? Was it deliberately taken? Perhaps I was mistaken and placed it somewhere else? It didn't matter. It was gone.

The sun began to set. Another night of dancing and festivity would soon start. Truly defeated, I unbound my hair, combing it for bed.

As I went to unfasten the ties of my dress, Kwan walked in.

"I was looking for you," said Kwan, kind in his voice.

I didn't have the heart to look at him. Afterall, he changed his plans because I'd wanted to dance. "I'm not feeling well."

From my peripheral, I saw him walk over, setting something down along the way. He laid his hand on my forehead, cool to the touch. I flinched and pulled away.

"Hisa?"

I stayed quiet, not looking at him. Gentle, his fingers took my chin, coaxing me to meet his eye.

"What's wrong?"

"I lost my cosmetic," I whispered, placing my own hand to hide my scars.

He pulled it away, slow and soft, revealing the full of my face again. "And? I like you as you are."

I tucked my neck into my shoulders. "They'll all stare. And talk. More than they already do."

Kwan rested his forehead on mine, brushing the tips of our noses together. "I'm not ashamed of you."

My gaze fell.

"Hisa," cooed Kwan. "I want you to be my wife. It doesn't matter what anyone else says. It is my decision, and yours. I will not hide you, or that I am in love with you, away."

Assured, I looked at him again, putting on a smile.

"They still gossip about my own faults and flaws," said Kwan, caressing my face. "Do not let jealous words rule you."

I nodded.

"I have something."

He stood before I could object or ask, fetching the wrapped thing he'd set down and returning. A hair pin, decorated with peonies in near lifelike appearance.

"Do you like it?"

I nodded, my smile growing.

"Allow me," said Kwan, taking my hair. He combed it, making a simple bun to set the hairpin in. I didn't argue it, basking in the tender touch and affection. When he finished, he set his hands on my upper arms, placing the bridge of his nose along my neck. "Will you dance with me?"

The squall in my mind stilled, and my heart warmed as it took a slow rhythm. "Okay," I whispered, allowing my smile to grow.

He helped me to my feet, leading us out. I stopped at the thresh of the door. He looked at me, head tilted.

"Kiss me?"

That hint of a smile returned to his face. A soft kiss to my lips, and another atop my forehead.

In the courtyard nearest the castle, an announcement was made by Kwang. A man with silver-blue eyes and sharp features, dressed in iridescent black robes stood, presented with a young woman in lavished pastels who bore a similarity to Kwan's eldest brother. The crowds clapped, muttering words of surprise and approval. An engagement, perhaps, since it looked similar to when Kwan hosted court to announce Urekkato and Eumeh.

Something caught my attention through the crowds. Seong, standing perfectly still with a woman beside him whose expression appeared severe in disapproval, and Sara fanning herself in a huff. I didn't understand the scene, since everyone else seemed happy enough for the new couple, and surely, they were aware.

I didn't have time to think too much on it, led away by Kwan to take the first dance with him. Across the space I noticed the new couple also taking to dance. At the very least, attention would be drawn away. Relieved by that, my smile held strong.

"The hair pin looks lovely on you," said Kwan not long into our dance.

I'd practiced more, not needing to place my focus on the steps, so I could look more to his face and into his eyes as we moved about in synchrony. Midway, my mind caught up to tell me something. Kwan's hand was wrapped. "You're injured," I said, quiet.

He said nothing, following my worried gaze. "To break my old oath," said Kwan, matching my volume.

"The dance won't strain you?"

He picked me up to carry a pirouette, placing me back on my feet in sync with the others. We broke away to turn in a single spin, and came back together.

"It'll heal," said Kwan. "You needn't worry."

I still did.

His hint of a smile spread slightly. "Hisa will worry over her Juneun husband's every cut?"

I chuckled, shaking my head. "I still forget sometimes. To me, you're just Kwan. The man I love."

"And you are Hisa. The woman who holds my heart and soul."

The music ended, allowing for new couples to shuffle in and others to leave. We stood amid other spectators, our hands linked around each other. It didn't matter if anyone looked or what they said. As long as Kwan was beside me, I felt safe from it.

Towa found us, elegantly dressed and more feminine, rather than her usual masculine attire. "And I thought you hated dancing."

"I'm more fond of it with Hisa as a partner," said Kwan.

"Is that so?" asked Towa, a slyness to her tone. "How does your intended feel about it?"

Kwan narrowed his eye at her, reading into the words. I held his hand a little more firmly, reassuring him. "She's shy. But enjoys a dance."

"And me?" asked Towa. "I'm not as coordinated. But maybe the right partner could teach a fish how to fly?"

Kwan studied a moment, deciding. "If Hisa has no objection."

I shook my head, tucking into my shoulders slightly. "Of course."

Slow, he let go of my hand to take Towa for a dance.

I did mind. It was the habit of obliging others that caused me to speak without thinking. Standing alone, fidgeting, I watched them. They didn't seem so off sync with each other, and some conversation was held between them. My eyes looked around, making sure Urekkato (among others) really wasn't around. In my scanning, a glint of something caught my attention. The pendent I'd given Kwan, tied around his belt.

My heart warmed, and my fidgeting lessened.

When he returned, Towa parted politely with a knowing look. I didn't ask. Part of me didn't want to know—feared it even.

On and off we danced. The evening winding down, that part of me surrendered. "What did you and Lady Towa talk about?"

Kwan took his time in answering. "She asked about my secret fiancé."

"Oh..."

"I told her that it's no secret. She's the only woman I enjoy dancing with."

My smile returned, growing wide and bright. In that same moment, fireworks took to the sky. Colors painted the ground, dancers, and onlookers. Now, truthfully, I didn't care who was watching us. Were we the only ones dancing and all the world looked our way, I didn't care.

It was the most perfect dance I'd had.

Chapter 80
Jealousy

We slept in, taking breakfast in our room rather than to make a social appearance. I didn't need a morning remedy, and ate with gusto. Never having seaweed before, I didn't know what to expect. There was a saltiness to it, but it wasn't terrible. Mostly, I stuck to whatever was most familiar to me.

Outside the gates, and dressed lightly, Kwan scooped me up to use his speed to get us to the beach. It was a more direct magic, but it still made my insides quiver, and I needed a moment for my feet to remember themselves. My hair kept in its braid, and nausea was notably absent.

It wasn't long before I took off my sandals, bettering my balance without them in the sand. Clumsy, I hurried to the water's edge, towing Kwan in hand. The texture of the sand changed where the ocean soaked it; in the seconds that I awed, a wave rolled over my ankles. I squeaked, laughing as I exclaimed how it felt ice cold. And, not wanting to ruin my dress, I gathered the hem of my skirt to hold with my shoes.

We walked along the shore, letting waves roll past us. Now and again I would find a vividly colored shell and pluck it up. Chipped, broken, worn with time, I liked them all the same, and started to build a small collection. Clam shells, snail shells, curious spiral shaped ones, and ones that were porous and spherical. I'd found the dried husk of something called a sea horse, and another of a different animal called a sea star that was missing two of its legs. When Kwan said nothing more, I added them to my keepsakes in my gathered skirt.

I had no sense of the time passing between the warm sun, cold ocean, wild breeze, and tempered sand. Spending the day with the man I loved made the hours irrelevant. Nor did I have any sense of how far we'd walked until we came across a fishing boat that'd beached with damage and a frustrated crew of men.

They'd waved us down, asking for help. Taking his usual time, Kwan offered to bring the vessel far enough where the tide wouldn't drag it out. They'd realized then that he was a Juneun and fell low to bow. Kwan gave no notice of the gesture, letting go of my hand to drag the cumbersome boat further on land. I held in my laugh, knowing I had to right—five years ago, I would've done the same thing.

The men stared in awe as Kwan pulled up their boat at a steady pace, unassisted.

"You must be guests of our own Lord Juneun," said one man, no older than twenty-five by the look of him. "We've been catching glimpses of the fireworks. Is there some sort of celebration at the castle?"

I nodded. "For Mokryon. It's an annual festival the Juneun hold in spring. But a different Juneun hosted it last year."

"You're a Juneun too, then?"

I shook my head with a chuckle. "No, I'm human, like you."

He looked confused, twisting his expression into a dozen questions.

"I'm—" I couldn't help it. I was dying to tell someone, to share my happy news. "I'm his intended."

"Then, you're a princess?"

Again, I shook my head. "It's not like that. Kwan and his brothers are high lords, but not princes."

"Oh, I meant, your father is some far off king, isn't he? For a human girl to be engaged to a spirit, you'd have to be a princess or something, right?"

I was about to explain when a larger wave crashed over, knocking me off balance. I dropped everything as I fell, caught by the young man. The force of the retreating wave began to pull me. Scared, I held fast and shrieked. In response, he put a more secure arm around me until the water returned to the sea.

"My sandals!" I realized.

"I got 'em," called another of the men, dashing into the ocean and wading quickly to snatch them back.

I breathed my relief. "Thank you."

"You've never been near the ocean, have you?" asked the young man.

I shook my head. "No, it's my first time." I took my shoes from the other man, a little older, judging by his belly. Forlorn, I set my gaze at the sea, having lost every little thing I'd picked up in one fell swoop. Looking back, I saw Kwan standing with a raised brow and small basket in his hand.

On his approach, he asked if he could buy the basket. The men insisted he take it and whatever else he liked as compensation, expressing their gratitude.

"The basket will do," said Kwan, offering it to me. "For my beloved."

The young man became straight backed as I took the basket, placing my shoes inside it. "Wait just a moment Master Juneun, Princess." He bolted to his boat before I could correct him.

I blinked, looking up at Kwan for a wordless exchange.

"I will inform your Lord Kwang about your distress, so that he can deal with it more appropriately."

The remaining two men stuttered, giving their thanks.

The younger returned in a sprint, holding something up. "Since you lost all yours, Miss Princess, take this as a thank you." He panted, handing me a round kind of shell with an odd flower shape in it. "It's a sand dollar. My little sister likes to collect them—but only perfectly intact ones like this."

"Shouldn't it go to her?" I asked, now feeling guilty.

He laughed. "She has dozens. Probably close to a hundred, right uncle?"

The eldest among them nodded. "No idea what she plans to do with them all."

"If there's anything more," said the other. "It's the least we can do to thank you."

With a nod, we left, continuing down the beach. All the while something felt off. Looking at Kwan's face, his stoic expression seemed somehow displeased.

After a while, he broke the stillness between us. "He liked you."

I blinked, not understanding.

"The boy who put his arm around you."

"I don't think so," I said with a laugh. "A wave knocked me over and tried to pull me in. He caught me, that's all."

Slow and silent, Kwan half rolled his eyes and shifted his gaze elsewhere.

Bewildered, my mind argued with itself over what his behavior meant. Was he...? No. Impossible. "What's wrong?"

Kwan said nothing, continuing an odd pout.

"You're... are you jealous?"

A slight scoff left him.

I laughed. "What for?" When he said nothing, I leaned against his arm, content. "I often feel jealous of the Juneun ladies. They've known you longer than I have. Sometimes I think I can't measure up, and that you'll realize you don't actually want me for a wife."

"Ridiculous," said Kwan. "If I wanted any of them, I'd have made some announcement long ago." His words seemed to surprise him. His eyes told it all. "There was a thought. That you'd want a simpler, less political life. A life with your kin."

I flexed my fingers in his hand, sighing my comfort as I stayed against his toned arm. "You don't need to worry about that. If there was the slightest chance he did like me, it's only because he thought I was a princess and I didn't get the chance to tell him that I'm not. I'm just an ordinary village girl. Nothing special."

"You could never be an ordinary village girl," said Kwan, causing me to look up and meet his eye. "Because you're Hisa. My Hisa."

I chuckled. "And you're my Kwan."

By mid-afternoon, we set ourselves to go back to the castle. Kwan carried me, using his speed again, and stopping beside the river to clean off excess sand and salt.

At the castle, a serf trotted up. Kwan's brother wanted to see him.

We parted, agreeing to meet again at supper. On my way to our room, I browsed through the finds I'd accumulated on our stroll. Despite having to start over, I was happy with my collection of broken keepsakes.

All pleasant thoughts fled when I opened the door to find Seong waiting. I blinked, my mind needing to catch up, attempting to make sense of why he was there.

"Kwan isn't—"

"*Lord* Kwan," said Seong. "And I am aware." With a flick of his finger, the doors closed behind me. "I know the stunt from last night is because of you."

I went stiff, but said nothing.

He stared. Not the sort of stoic, studying stare I'd grown used to from Kwan. His held a rage with it. A tiger's stare at cornered prey. "My brother has always been difficult. Now, he's openly oppugnant with family. What is it you hope to gain, girl?"

I didn't understand what he meant. While I knew Kwan didn't get along well with much of his family, he'd been only forthcoming since our arrival to Bitgaram. Hoarse, I started to squeak out my defense. "I don't—"

Faster than I could blink, he'd left his sitting place by the table and was standing over me. I retreated into myself, as though being smaller and wide-eyed would somehow protect me.

"Whatever he's promised or planned. End. It."

Defiance took over me, even as my voice whispered and quivered. "I won't."

His palm slammed into the wall, shy of my ear and nearly deafening it a few seconds. I sucked in a sharp, shaking gasp, frozen in place.

"You are his whore and his play-thing. He parades you around for now because you are human and a novelty. He will be bored soon, and in no shortage of lovers beautiful and comely. And you will be old and tossed out, such is your breed."

I steeled myself at his words, forming a scowl. It dawned on me what he was doing. He was trying to frighten me. He wanted me to surrender and obey, digging at insecurities I already made myself ignore. While he went on, I retrieved memories that proved otherwise. The pledge by the well, in a cave untouched by winter. The half coat I made him, and how he wore it openly. The jade pendent and the dancing, and his own moment of jealousy. Most of all, I held fast to every instance where he'd called me his wife. Short of beating me, I wasn't going to let Seong manipulate me.

"You're wrong," I managed to whisper, even as I trembled.

Seong watched me with seething displeasure. "I think not. There are things in his past you know nothing about."

"That he was in love with Gumiho, once," I said, a little stronger. "He already told me everything. And I've forgiven him—regardless of whether or not you have, I don't care. I trust what Kwan has told me over whatever you say to try and frighten me off."

His other palm slammed. My shoulders flinched, body shivering in instinctual fear, but my eyes stayed locked with his. "I know that promising my daughter to the Samjos without my consent has something to do with you. I wouldn't be surprised if Urekkato's disappearance had something to do with you either."

My expression loosened with confusion.

"You idiot girl," growled Seong.

Defiant, I forced my voice to carry on despite its quivering. "It's true that I'm not as educated as a Juneun lady. I don't even know what oppugnant means. But I'm not stupid. Everything since the door closed is meant to make me afraid of you. To obey and cower. Do you plan to beat me like Beom did to get what you want?"

"If that is what it takes," said Seong, evened in tone.

"Lord Genji wouldn't resort to that. Neither would Kwan. But perhaps you're not so great a Juneun as either of them."

"You address your master too informally," growled Seong.

I went on, as far as my fleeting bravery would allow. "He is not my master. He's the man I love with all my heart and soul, and I will not betray him no matter who demands that I do."

Seong glared, leaning in. For a moment, he seemed more tiger than man. "You're not special. Many servant girls once thought they were special to him. Kurai girls thought they were special to him. The occasional of your kin might've thought she was special. You will be forgotten like the rest of them. He is a Juneun. You are not."

"Genji didn't think so," I said in my hoarse whisper. "He loved Lady Isaden to her last day, and after."

Seong's expression went unchanged, his voice low, threatening, and his words slow. "You will be forgotten. It is my brother's nature."

"And I still love him," I said, using the last bit of courage I had as my knees shook. "More than I will ever fear you."

The door opened. Kwan stepped in, harboring a cold expression. For a while, no words were exchanged. A deafening silence hung thick in the air as the brothers leered each other.

"If you are angry with me," said Kwan, low and with the hint of a growl, "then take it out on me. Do not stoop to Beom's antics."

Seong straightened, speaking with venom. "I didn't strike at your precious whore."

Kwan's eyes narrowed.

"You should have let father lash her, rather than bear it yourself. Perhaps, then, she wouldn't be so obstinate."

I paled at his words, my scowl lifting and all remaining defiance extinguished. I hadn't known about that. Kwan never said a thing, and my mind raced to figure out when and why.

At Tetsuden.

"I believe your wife is looking for you, brother," said Kwan, level in his voice.

Seong's frown deepened. Wordlessness, suffocating the space between us with magic. As he made to leave, Kwan spoke again.

"You will address her as Lady Hisa the next time you are invited to my house."

Seong scoffed. "You really mean to go through with making this human your mistress?"

"No," said Kwan. "And you will address her as Lady Hisa when next you are invited to my home."

Seong stopped, meeting Kwan's eye as another bout of quiet consumed the room.

"Call her my whore," said Kwan, "and it will be met with steel."

"You would throw away everything, for a human? You were daft enough when it came to Gumiho. Have you no shame?"

"It appears not," said Kwan.

"You try too hard to emulate your teacher, little brother. But you forget that you lack the backing of Tetsuden and its adjoining lands."

Kwan said nothing else, allowing his brother to have the last word. Seong left, and Kwan calmly slid the door closed.

My knees gave way, and I slid down the wall I'd been back into.

"Hisa," cooed Kwan, coming to my side. "Are you alright?"

Trembling, I forced my voice back into my control, my breath erratic. "I'm not hurt. Only shaken."

He looked me over, and pulled me into a tender embrace.

I collected myself enough to recall pieces of horrible news. "He said Urekkato is missing." I looked up, pleading. I had to come clean about it. "I... Th-the first time you held court. He found me alone and-and I was persuaded into a deal with him."

As I fumbled with my words, trying to make them sensible enough to explain myself, Kwan kept a quiet watch on me.

"I, I let him put a sight spell on me. I didn't know what it was all about, and he made it sound harmless—I regretted it immediately, but he wouldn't take it back! And, then... the day in the groves..."

His face went unchanged, patient with me.

"I was afraid she was going to kill you. So, I wrote down, begging him to help, and I kept looking at it, praying for him to see it. I'm sorry. I'm so sorry!"

Kwan stayed stoic, observing.

"Is it my fault he's missing...?"

"No," said Kwan with a single shake of his head. "Urekkato never came to my aide."

As much as I hated the Cat prince, I felt relief at that.

"What else did Seong say?"

Chapter 81
Secrecy

I was glad to be back on the mountain, away from unwanted stares and hostile meetings. I didn't have to worry about false words and trickery to guilt me into anything here. My feelings stayed torn since Seong's tactics. On one hand, I was relieved that whatever happened to Urekkato had nothing to do with my begging his help. On the other hand, I was upset that he'd ignored my plea when it mattered most—the reason I'd agreed to the sight spell at all.

A giddiness nestled in my heart. Kwan's last words to his eldest brother rewarded the faith I'd held during my confrontation.

I wanted to celebrate that, and went to fetch a rice wine. While the household brought in our things, tidied up, and readied a lunch, I shuffled to one of the storehouses I knew still had stock. Unpacking could wait.

As I approached, I heard voices. Whether from the distraction of my small mission, or the weariness of travel, it didn't dawn on me that they came from inside the store room until I'd started opening the door.

They hushed, and my eyes fell on Syaoran and Uno in a somewhat compromising position. Embarrassed, I squealed out a quick word of apology and shut the door. Standing there, face flushed and hand over my mouth as I stared at the door, I concluded that I would never understand Syaoran. Uno was hardly how he described a perfect partner, and what I originally thought was a crush turned out to be suspicion, but now—what did it matter?

I turned to leave when the door slid open again.

"What did you want?" asked Syaoran, irritated.

I looked at him, a little confused by his tone, though I couldn't blame him. "Rice wine," I said. "We only just got back. I thought you were somewhere in the house with everyone else."

He let out a long sigh, reining in his expression. "What you saw—it's not—"

I held up a palm and shook my head. "You two don't have to explain yourselves to me."

He twisted his face, becoming quizzical before his fingers went to massage his forehead as he left. I turned to go in, almost colliding with Uno and the bottle of rice wine in her hands. She appeared sheepish and ashamed, flinching when I thanked her.

"It's alright," I whispered. "If you like him, it can't be helped. Even I liked him a little when I first came here."

She looked horrified. "It's not—" She stopped, shrinking into herself with a guilty expression, and nodded.

I thought nothing of the incident for days. Summer fast approached, and, slowly, everything was restocked. Things seemed on track to go back to normal.

However, the timing of my return from Mokryon weighed on Uno. On a day when Kwan left the house to check in elsewhere on the mountain, she couldn't stay silent any longer.

"My lady?" Her voice quiet, almost fearful caught me off guard. She stopped combing my hair, and I stopped mending socks.

"You don't need to call me that," I said.

"Y-yes. I, I just..."

I turned to look at her. "What's wrong?"

"Master Syaoran bid I say nothing. But it feels wrong to keep it a secret."

"Keep what a secret?"

"The," she hesitated. "The reason he brought me into the storehouse, that day. It wasn't for an affair. I accidentally walked in on him searching through Lord Kwan's apartment."

"Searching for what?"

"I, I don't know," said Uno, still quiet in tone. "He wouldn't say. But it looked suspicious. I thought you ought to know, perhaps bring it to Lord Kwan."

"Oh, that," I said. "He's told me. It was by accident, but he told me. It's something misplaced. And, with the new lay of the house and things moved about for the seasons and occasions, I guess it's better to check everywhere. Just in case."

"But... in the apartment?"

That did strike me as odd. "Syaoran has been a trusted part of the house for decades," I assured. Partly for Uno, and partly for myself. "And he's been a good friend to me, from the night I arrived to now. Whatever his reason..." I couldn't shake how strange it was.

Why did he search the third floor? While he'd said to me that his missing thing shouldn't be handled by a human, why demand secrecy from Uno who didn't know better? Shame? That he was in here while Kwan and I were away? Maybe. If so, why not brief Uno and stay vague? Surely, she'd understand.

"It's not my business," I said, sighing out my resolve. "I wish he'd let me help him. I think it's a matter of pride more than anything."

"If you're sure, my lady," said Uno, slow to resume. I did likewise. "I just thought you should know. After hiding my identity as a fox spirit, I don't want to keep anymore secrets or give rise to distrust. If I'm dismissed from the house, I'll never get a chance like this again. Not anywhere. Never mind as high a position."

"I'd never let that happen," I said. "You've been kind from the start. In the short time I've been here, I've had to learn that it doesn't matter what anyone thinks. Kwan doesn't care for appearance, and neither does Genji. They value character."

"I've only heard stories about the Elk prince," said Uno. "If he approved of my character, I might be able to convince my sister to stop hiding herself. I could see her if she and her husband came to court."

I was reminded then how long so many of the girls went without seeing their families. Something that made me feel a little selfish for grieving five short years. "Do you miss her?"

"Every day," said Uno. "I want to make her proud. She'd always looked after me, when it was only the two of us. She wanted me to make something of myself, and not end up as her husband's mistress."

"To her husband?" I echoed, twisting my brow.

"He's not a cruel man," said Uno, seeming to realize she's spoken too freely. "But it'd be a lie to say he didn't take advantage of how desperate we were."

I knew better than to ask, but the words came out anyway. "Who is your sister's husband?"

Uno paused, hesitating. I turned to look at her, seeing her eyes dart away and her black fox ears drooped. She seemed pained to say anything more. "The bastard son of Lord Seong. Lord Kwan's eldest brother."

I was mortified. "His son?"

"Born to his mistress," said Uno. "But not acknowledged."

Things made more sense and less sense at the same time. The secrecy and fright. I'd assumed her sister's marriage from desperation had to do with their poor circumstance, and then a little to do with their identity as fox spirits. It didn't dawn on me that there might've been a threat to refusal of this magnitude. Kwan's brothers—most of them—seemed to hate fox spirits, regardless of whether or not they had ties to Gumiho.

"We were a little fortunate," said Uno, picking up on my unease. "My brother by law has more opportunity and access than his bastard cousins."

"Cousins from who?" I asked, quick in my words. I was terrified of the answer, but I'd already said it.

"The now late lord brothers to Lord Kwan," said Uno, curious in tone. "Without their fathers, nearly everything was closed off to them. As it likely is for Lord Beom's child."

"Beom?"

Uno flinched, having spilled more in the last few minutes than she'd meant to ever reveal. "Born four summers past, my lady. No one seems to know anything, outside of the girl claiming he sired the child."

I tried not to fixate on that conversation and the strangeness of it all. Instead, I occupied my time with my usual things, and plan what to do when I get home to settle everything. Practicing my sketch work, and watching Koji prance around the pond to look at the koi inside, I reminded myself to come up with a way to repay Fumei for having taken care of my family and loaning me her clothing. Perhaps a lovely dress of her own. If Juro didn't want them back, there was no reason I couldn't give those ones away.

The last time I spoke with my friend, she'd pledged to remain unmarried until I made a good match first. It seemed like such a valiant thing, though I knew it must've been a hard and lonely promise to keep. And if she was determined to not engage with anyone who thought meanly of me in my absence, I could invite her up to help find her a good husband elsewhere.

My thoughts were disrupted when cool hands took hold of my shoulders, and a kiss touched my cheek. I smiled, looking over to meet Kwan's gaze.

"Let's go inside," whispered Kwan.

I shook my head, maintaining a soft, happiness on my face.

He tilted his head, kissing just below my ear, then to my neck.

"Not today," I whispered. When he paused to look at me, I explained. "I'm... my blood is in."

"So?"

I shook my head, half scoffing while my smile stayed. "I don't feel up to it."

Kwan relented, bringing me into a kind embrace. For a while, we stayed like that, enjoying each other's stillness.

"Do you need a tea?" asked Kwan, quiet and patient. "For pain?"

I chuckled, quick and soft. "I'm managing."

We remained in place, brought back to our surroundings when a splash sounded. Koji slipped into the pond, his front half submerged up to his neck. He looked around, confused, and struggled to get his paws back on dry ground. I laughed, watching him shake off the water and pretend nothing happened.

"When you're feeling up to it," said Kwan, "I want to take you somewhere, and show you something."

"Take me where?" I asked, meeting his eye again.

He said nothing. Staring a moment, his hint of a smile grew, and he walked from me.

While we didn't engage that night, I still went to his bed to be beside him.

As sleep started to take hold, I couldn't contain that question any longer. "If we had children, what would they be?"

Kwan looked at me, a curiousness to him. "A boy would be the young lord of Inori. A girl, the young lady of Inori."

"They'd have you name?"

"Naturally." He scooted, propping himself onto an arm. "What is this about?"

I squirmed a bit. "Uno said her sister was married to Seong's bastard son. And accidentally mentioned about the ones from your late brothers."

"You worry I will not acknowledge any child born from the woman I love? My wife?"

It sounded ridiculous when he put it that way.

He caressed my face, regaining my attention. "Half-human or not, they will be my children. Born from my wife. That is all."

I was put a little more at ease. Outside fears clawed at my insecurities to no avail. I shouldn't have doubted.

"You never mentioned your late brothers."

His cool embrace returned to me. "I hardly knew them. They died when I was a child. My two eldest sisters died before I was even born."

It shocked me. And I could now understand, a little, the frustration of his family. To have lost so many children took its toll, and must've made for a rigid upbringing on the rest. Not knowing what to say in response, I wrapped my arm around him, keeping close to provide whatever comfort I could. While I still had questions, it felt too invasive to ask any of them.

Chapter 82
The Pagoda

Summer brought an eagerness to Kwan's usual stoic demeanor. Rather than saddle any of the horses, he slung a sack over his shoulder and scooped me up. He kept secretive and mischievous about the ordeal. We'd be away for a few days, yet left Saburo and all others behind.

Unlike Bitgaram, I hardly felt anything in our trek, figuring it was due to the mountain being Kwan's domain.

We touched down at the front of a pagoda. One that looked vaguely familiar. Except, that it was pristine, and the gardens were thriving.

"This is..." My words trailed as I gawked, my mind unable to make the obvious connections.

"What do you think?"

I jumped, lost in thought. "It's... You restored it." I looked up at him, seeing him waiting for my approval. "For me?"

"You said you wanted to see how it looked before my neglect."

I smiled, taking his hand in mine. "It's wonderful."

He watched me a moment. "There's plenty of space to add things to the gardens if you like."

"Are there lotus flowers and lilies in the pond?" I asked, excitement piling on me.

"Some," said Kwan. "But we can add more."

I nodded. "I think it'd look pretty with lots of lily pads floating. And the flowers would make it fragrant."

He led us inside, giving a tour in his own way.

Despite how dark the interior was, shaded by the surrounding trees, it felt more welcoming than it did almost two years prior. Sparce of any furniture or decoration, Kwan asked what I'd like to have in there. It'd be a place where we could retreat to now and again, and get away from the demands of the house. It didn't matter to me how lavish or prettily it was made; the gift was that we could be in each other's company uninterrupted. I was happier still to find the kitchen restored and restocked—where I can test my new skills and do something for him in return.

"We should keep a vegetable garden here," I said. "Just a small one. But, someone would need to tend it... I guess that would make things complicated."

"I can show you the forage garden," said Kwan.

I echoed his words in a question.

"Things that would naturally grow wild. So, there's not a need for anyone to tend them." He watched me, measuring my smile. "But if you want a proper garden, I—"

"A forage garden is more than enough. Show me."

We walked out of the pagoda, around the pond to its far side.

"I had the pond stocked with perch, trout, and pike rather than koi," said Kwan. "During the restoration, I wanted to give you options. I remembered you like eel, but they don't do well outside of the lower river."

"Do you like fishing?"

"I used to. But I hadn't a reason to take it up in a while."

"Maybe we ought to see if you still like it tomorrow," I said with a laugh.

He nodded.

We came to a fenced off area, sturdy enough to deter a handful of common pests; though a bear or determined boar could still break in. Inside, I didn't notice at first glance. Everything blended in well enough to look like any other part of the forest. Squinting, I distinguished the wild radishes from the ginger and the yams. A fallen log, placed there deliberately, served as a spot for wild mushrooms to gather. The trees within were all fruit bearing—young, but able to produce a small yield.

"It's perfect!" I said, standing tip toed.

"If I planned better," said Kwan. "I would've told one of the cooks to meet us down here. A raw diet for a few days is fine with me—"

"I'll make something," I said, hurried in my excitement.

He looked at me, puzzled at first, relaxing into a mild amusement. "Take what you want."

I didn't waste time. In my father's house, I was limited in my skill, doing my best to keep up. In the last few years, I'd practiced and learned more. My plan was to go home so well skilled that I could ignore whatever rumors there were about me. Now, I would come back up the mountain, where rumors didn't matter. They'd never reach me.

As I took careful thought on what to harvest and what to leave, Kwan plucked off several tangerines.

Keeping supper simple, I wordlessly glanced at Kwan to get his opinion. Vegetable porridge, seasoned with a pinch of ginger and chili wasn't a very pretty meal—but beauty didn't indicate quality. It wasn't the sort of thing I'd normally see around the house, and I worried he wouldn't like it.

"It's good."

I smiled. "You don't mind that it's nothing fanciful?"

"I never cared for fanciful," said Kwan. "A lot of effort for the aesthetic and little to the flavor. I like this better." He took another bite, eating at his usual pace.

"Sorry I didn't make any dumplings this time."

He looked at me with a knowing smile. "You could let me help you, rather than lay about and wait."

I tucked in my head, raising my shoulders in shy refusal. "I want to be able to do this for you."

Amusement started to show on his face. "Hisa will spoil me, but will not let me spoil her?"

"You spoil me as it is," I argued.

"Let me spoil my future wife a little more."

It was harder to argue when he called me that. And I think he knew it.

"Ask me."

It took me a moment, but I thought I had a way to tease at him. "The bird that can carry both rainbows and shadows, the glow of the moon in the daylight, a tooth from an animal that never chews with it, the gem that is only found in mouths of the ocean, a stone that contains starlight, and the polished breath of a fire sleeping inside its mountain."

He watched me, amusement staying in his expression. "I will fetch them myself for you."

"Don't do that," I scolded.

Kwan merely tilted his head in response.

Under his gaze, I felt a little sheepish. "I like most when you're with me."

He waited, studying, and sat down his bowl. Scooting closer, he placed an arm around my waist, half-leaning against me and resting his cheek in my hair.

It rained in the night. Not that we needed a reason to keep in each other's embrace as we slept.

Breakfast was light: a simple bowl of rice. I'd left dough to rise while we went out fishing in good weather. Wild strawberries grew nearby, ripe and sweet to snack on as we waited. It was a long ordeal, and quiet half the time, but I whiled away any boredom taking in the beauty of the area, dipping my toes into the cool water, and absently mentioning something with Kwan entertaining whatever I'd said briefly.

He'd been the first to catch something on his pole. A small trout that he let go, since it was more trouble to make into a meal than to let it grow and hope to catch again. He'd caught another, though it got away before we knew what it was. When finally I caught something, my bamboo rod slipped from me. Kwan grabbed it in time, helping to pull in a catfish that would make for an excellent dinner.

At the pagoda, I saw to the dough again, deciding to turn it into strawberry-stuffed buns. I quickly fashioned a filling from the wild fruits we'd brought back, and some of the honey that'd been stored away.

After I'd left them to rise one last time, and lit the oven to heat up, I met Kwan on the veranda, taking in the view. It'd be a while before I needed to get back to the kitchen.

"I wish every day could be like this."

He moved his gaze to me, lounging in the humid, summer air. "Maybe not every day. But we can make an effort to come here often."

At that, I smiled, and found myself lost in daydreams. So much that I didn't register when Kwan got up to walk in front of me. Looking up, meeting his pleasant, stoic expression, I thought nothing of it. He leaned down, resting on his palms, and placed a light kiss to my lips. Then another, and another.

I let myself fall into it, one of his hands sliding to my back and pulling me closer. My knees straddled him, but my mind didn't figure out where this was going until his affection moved to my neck.

I pushed away, brow pressed with a giggling smile. "We're outside."

"We are," said Kwan, looking at me.

I blinked, remembering that we were alone out here. He kissed again, sliding up the skirt of my dress.

"My Hisa labors away to make me happy. I want to make her happy in return."

I broke from him in new realization. "I don't have a morning remedy."

He stared at me a moment. "Do you trust me?"

It was an odd question. Of course I did. Right now, however, it felt like it had a different meaning.

He pulled me to the edge of the veranda in a swift yank. I gave a squeak of surprise, causing his hint of a smile to grow, and quivered. But I didn't stop him. Kwan waited, and I didn't refuse. A cruel part of me was curious. He kissed, gentle until I relaxed, and he moved to my legs—kiss after kiss, working their way up. When his lips went between my thighs, I shuddered. It wasn't gross or unpleasant, just strange and new.

As he went on, introducing his tongue, I found myself starting to tremble around him. My mind couldn't keep up to guess what he was doing. It was a weird culmination of touches, licks, and sucking that made my spine want to go limp. During his indulgence, his arms wrapped around each of my thighs, holding me steady while my knees were too weak to anchor to him. It was an inconvenient combination of pleasure and frustration, and I didn't know what to make of it.

My chest heaved with breath as he continued, and I couldn't keep myself upright. When he finished, and I was jelly, he went to clean off his face, leaving me to reel from the experience and decide if I liked it or not. *That* wasn't in Lin's explanation. At least, not more than the briefest mention.

When he returned, he lay beside me, both of us looking into each other's eyes, wordless. He played with the seams of my blouse, occasionally brushing a finger at my chin. In turn, I fiddled with stray hairs near his face. I liked this part most.

Relaxed, I remembered the oven, sucking in a gasp and getting to my feet.

It rained the following two days, trying to limit what we could do. But with no one around and the air heavy with heat, I danced in it. Dressed bare, and my hair glued to me, it felt refreshing. There was something about the pelting droplets that calmed me and helped to clear my head.

When the clouds cleared the day after, I let myself take the afternoon to be lazy and enjoy the muggy brightness of the day. Comfortable in the solitude, I forwent the usual layers of dress in favor of a light night robe. The air stuck to my skin, bringing an oddly pleasant sensation when the breeze picked up.

Kwan shared the sentiment, dressing likewise as he leisurely peeled tangerines for us to share. I laid against him, soaking in the cool of his skin as I started to doze off. Like he had days before, he silently asked with kisses and caresses.

We were stripped, delighting in the touch of one another. His fingers between my thighs, I reminded him that I didn't bring a morning remedy.

"Trust me."

Slick, he slid in a whole peel, honey dabbed on its inside. It was a little uncomfortable, but it allowed him to follow and for us to tangle ourselves. It'd been a wait—since Bitgaram. A different thrill came with how exposed we were, sunlight and shadow playing on our skin as the breeze rustled the branches above.

Sticky and sweaty, warm and cool, we immersed ourselves in each other.

Finished, we stayed together, catching our breath. He delivered a light kiss to my neck. I giggled. Then to my breast. Calmed, he removed the peel and honey, his seed caught in it.

"The morning remedy is more effective," said Kwan, discarding the peel. "But if you prefer this..."

I smiled, sitting myself to lean on him.

"I've been told the taste is horrible. This way is more delicate, but manageable."

I echoed his last word with laughter lingering in my voice. "It's not very comfortable."

"No?"

I shook my head. "But the remedy does sour my stomach a lot. I don't know if either one is any better."

He took me into a gentle embrace. Our bare skin basked in the air and the sun and the shadow.

I wondered that night about other things. How Kwan had mentioned making the effort to come here together often in the future. Did he think about a future with me, the way I thought about a future with him? What did it look like from his perspective?

I remembered Genji in that moment, as we lay next to each other, with only the smallest threads of moonlight shining through the windows.

"Do you want children?" I asked.

Kwan stirred from his quiet thoughts, mulling over my question. "Is that Hisa's way of saying she wants to make a child right now?"

I chuckled. "No, I meant—" I paused, needing to think of how to phrase it. "Genji wanted children with Isa. Would you be upset if we couldn't...?"

He studied me, saying nothing for a long while. "I think I would be sad. More if you wanted children and none came. But I don't think I'd be miserable or always unhappy. As long as I still had your love, that is enough."

Playing with the ends of his hair, I began to daydream. "If we did have a child, would you want a boy or a girl?"

"If we had children, I'd want both."

"What if I was only able to give you girls?"

His hand stroked down my breastbone, lingering at the top of my stomach. "Then we will have daughters. And I would pray they're as ambitious in their passions as their mother. And they they're fond of riding the mountain with their father."

That made me smile. So often, families wanted for boys. Someone who could act as head of the family, labor and provide feats of strength. Kwan's casualness and delight in the thought of girls took a level of pressure from me. "And what if I gave you only boys?"

Kwan leaned over me, brushing his nose against mine and causing me to giggle. "Then we will have sons. And I would pray they're as brave as their mother. And that they're fond of hunting with their father."

I laughed. "What would we name our first child?"

He looked at me a long while, thinking. "Haneul, for a boy."

"Haneul?" I repeated the odd name.

"It means *heaven sent*."

I echoed the name again, becoming fond of it.

"Nabi, for a girl."

"Why Nabi?" It was a name I was familiar with. One of the families in the village had a tradition of naming their first-born daughter that.

"Because it means *butterfly*."

I gave a soft smile. "I always thought I wanted to be a mother. But I think I idealized how it'd be when I imagined it."

"What do you mean?"

"A friend of mine in the village was married the summer I ran up the mountain, and had her first child that winter. But the baby died that same winter, without any warning. Bringing a child into the world is scary enough. To lose one so shortly after..."

He rubbed my side, slow and rhythmic, for comfort. "You don't want any?"

"I'm just scared that I wouldn't know what to do if something happened."

"You would," said Kwan. "With every incident, I watch you working to try and make things right. To help. To heal. And I'll be there with you. With or without children, I'll be with you."

"Would you take a mistress?"

He shook his head, eyes staying on me.

I scooted closer, pressing against him. He kept his arm snug around me, giving a sense of security.

Chapter 83
Going Home

Coming back to the house after nearly a week away brought a bittersweetness with it. Koji bounded over, yanking free of one of the girls, the moment he saw me. I hugged him, muddy paws and all. Kwan was given no reprieve either, with Syaoran taking brisk steps to report in on several matters. It was hard to believe how much still demanded his attention when we weren't even away from the mountain and only a short time.

I fell into my old roll, going to fetch tea to bring to our room. He was already sitting among paperwork when I brought up the kettle, and didn't look away as I set everything and poured him a cup. Putting our things away, he stayed engrossed in looking over the papers and shuffling them in some meticulous order.

Even though his face was always stoic, it somehow looked more serious. Rather than take something to occupy my time, I moved to sit beside him.

"Is there anything I can help with?"

Several rapid blinks later, pulled from thoughts to understand what I'd said, he shifted his gaze to me.

"There has to be something I can do—rather than sit and idle myself with embroidery and tea."

He studied me a minute. "They're complicated matters. Most of them anyway."

"Shouldn't I learn these things so I can be useful to my husband?" I insisted.

His start of a smile appeared, seeming to approve. Sharing his work, he explained to me the matter of each issue and how he thought to resolve it. Taxes, the state of the lands in his domain, reports of failed harvests (or underperforming ones), cases of illnesses since the closing of last summer, possible blights, status of metallurgy, textiles, artisan crafts, and commerce were among the things needing attention annually.

If I came across an unfamiliar word in reading things over, Kwan relayed it and its meaning, and I worked to commit it to memory. He wasn't lying about the complexity of it all. On the rare occasion when I could provide some sort of insight, he took it into consideration. I didn't try to say more than I knew, lest it hurt Kwan and the villages around the mountain.

Through all the documentation, I gained a better idea of important matters for my family as well. Notably, I learned the usual routs of furriers and merchants. When I absently made mention of needing to remember to stock my brothers with pickling jars, Kwan stopped his work. A moment passed, his watch on me as he conducted a series of silent decisions. With a gesture, more from his stationery glided to him, and he started a separate note. Unable to help myself, I leaned over to look.

He was sending for the jars. I opened my mouth to argue.

"You said you wanted to be sure your family would be well taken care of, did you not?"

I heaved a sigh. It was the fault of lingering pride on my part, and I knew it. We'd always relied on fair exchanges in the village, and were naturally wary of outside help.

"I'd make for a careless son-in-law if I neglected my wife's family. And I doubt your father would approve of a careless man asking to marry his daughter."

My heart warmed, picking up its rhythm, and my smile spread.

"You'll take Saburo when you go down the mountain."

"Saburo? Why?"

"It would grieve me to see my Hisa having to carry so much, and the trek is long. What will I do if a missed step caused injury or worse?"

I knew he was partly teasing, but it did make sense.

"And I don't think Saburo would forgive me if I sent you on with anyone else. He's that fond of you."

"As I am of him," I said happily. "From the day I met him, he seemed like the most noble stallion."

"Do you say things like that to him?"

I nodded.

"Explains why he's endeared to you."

"Kwan is not endeared to me?"

He locked eyes with me, hinting amusement. "I will always be endeared to my wife."

"Yes, but are you not endeared to *me*?"

A slow blink, his expression held. "Always."

I rested my cheek on his shoulder, savoring my victory.

"I won't go down the mountain when you leave," said Kwan. "Whatever you need to attend, I won't interfere."

It made me sad, but I understood. "I'll try not be long," I promised, pressing myself closer against him.

"Is there anything else you want to take home?"

"There is, but he has to stay in his house on the mountain."

For that, I was shortly rewarded with a kiss to my hairline.

"I worry about how they'll fair in winter," I confessed. "I used to pickle as much as we had supplies for, and weave whatever I could manage, or exchange for something I wasn't skilled enough to make. I'd keep watch on dry stock, and firewood, but my brothers took the bulk of that labor."

He directed his ink brush with precision, jotting down more to list.

"Stop," I said, playfully reaching out. "Poor Saburo will be too weighed down."

As the day of my return home drew closer, I wished for summer to slow down. My favorite days became the rainiest ones, where there was nothing to do but listen to the symphony from the sky clattering, and keep in each other's company.

In three days, I would leave for my village.

Kwan teased that we shouldn't have sex until I returned, so that I would miss him all the more and want to return sooner. Undeterred, I took the initiative more than once. There was a sense of liberation when I did, and a look of intrigue in Kwan's expression. He reveled in the strength of my legs as I straddled him, and took a curiousness as I decided how to guide his hands. While I did enjoy making things go on my own terms, I still preferred when he led. I didn't feel nearly so clumsy when he assumed control; and, it allowed me to play in reversing our roles just to surprise him when I wanted.

"You'll forget me," said Kwan, playing with the ends of my hair.

"No, I won't. If anything, you'll get tired of waiting and forget about me."

"I could never forget you, Hisa," said Kwan. "It's impossible. I will miss you too much."

"I won't miss you much?"

He shrugged. "I still think you might remember a simpler life, and not want to return."

"I will return," I said, final. "You're my Kwan."

His arms embraced me as he took a deep, sleep-filled breath. "And you're my Hisa."

We stayed like that a while. Then, he seemed to get an idea, looking into my eyes with silent mischief.

Reaching over me, he grabbed at the red, silken lace he'd once tied my hair with. The one I often used when I braided my hair.

"Give me your hand."

My eyes looked between him and the thread, and my expression twisted as I held in an unceremonious giggle. Curious, I obeyed.

Kwan tied an end around one of my fingers, and the other to one of his own. "I dislike the idea of destiny. It implies things were inevitable, no matter what one does in life."

I started to catch on. "So, we take fate into our own hands?"

He nodded. "Fated or not, I choose you, Hisa. If I had to endure every sorrow all over again, to be with you, I would."

I brushed my nose against his, planting a quick and gentle touch of my lips to him.

"When you come back, I'll make a proper proposal, and go to ask your father for his blessing."

"You know my answer already," I said, smiling.

Slow, he brought me into another strong embrace. And I did likewise. We broke the thread, vowing to mend it on my return. To forge our fate, rather than leaving it to the stars and moon.

The morning of my leave, and part of me resisted. Saburo was saddled and anxious. He looked a bit silly, a kingly stallion now a pack-horse. Kwan helped me up, exchanging a few last words.

"Take this as well." Discrete, he handed me the puzzle box.

"Are you sure that's a good idea?" I whispered.

"You have my trust," said Kwan. "And, if you decide you'd rather not return, let Saburo bring it back. I will know your answer that way."

"I am coming back," I said, half laughing.

He looked into my eyes, gentle in his expression. "I love you, Hisa."

"I love you too, Kwan," I said, leaning down to kiss him. "With all my heart."

"With all my soul."

I hurried to tuck away the puzzle box, making sure it'd stay secure.

Lin brought over Koji, saying her own farewell to the dog. Likewise, Kwan patted the dog, bidding he look after me in his stead. There was something odd about it, amusing me, though I couldn't quite place what it was that made me think so. Kwan stood, and Lin handed off the leash.

"I will wait for you," said Kwan, fingers lightly fiddling with the ends of my sleeve.

"You won't wait long," I said, holding up the thread around my finger. "I promise."

We trotted off, the voices of everyone at the house fading as we went. Somehow, it felt a great deal longer of a journey than the night I ran up. Though that was five years ago now.

I was eager to see my family, to show off all that I'd learned, to tell them all my stories, but I dreaded it at the same time. It was hard to believe how much had changed.

Hours passed, and I thought it more impossible how I could've made such distance that night. When the red gate came into view, I sighed my relief. It was still early in the afternoon, and

I was almost home. Passing through, an odd feeling swept over me. Not magic, but something. I couldn't explain it.

As we entered the village, I smiled bright. It was exactly as I remembered it. Except for the men who stopped to gawk at me as we passed. Uncomfortable, I cued Saburo to hasten his pace, with Koji barking behind as he followed.

It wasn't quite evening when I reached my home, taking the conventional route, but the sun hung low in the sky. My father emerged from our house, perplexed at first as I dismounted. I felt awkward, realizing how I must've looked in my riding clothes and braided hair. When he recognized me, he hurried to come to me, dropping everything to put his arms wide. I did likewise, meeting him part way for a tight embrace.

"You're back. You're home," said father, over and over in a joyous weep.

"I'm home," I said in return, unable to stop my own tears. When we did let go of each other, father gave me a look over.

"So much like your mother. We missed you so much, Hisa."

"I missed you too, Baba," I said, bringing him in for another hug.

Parting, he noticed Saburo standing patiently. "What's all this?"

"Gifts," I said. "To help make life a little easier. Store jars, heavy bedding, and supplies so I can teach you all to read. We can better negotiate with merchants that way."

He didn't look impressed.

"By the end, I was more guest than prisoner to him."

My father turned to me then, assessing. "What they say in the village. I refuse it. I don't care what they want to believe."

"Fumei told me," I said. "Heaven only knows how or why that rumor was spread."

He hesitated before nodding, taking my hand for assurance.

"Help me bring this inside?"

Barking. Koji stumbled on a napping goose and took its threatening hiss to mean play. I laughed, explaining to my father that this was my dog and eagerly showed off his obedience. It took a moment to get his attention, but he became a disciplined creature once he realized I called for him.

It felt strange to walk in my family's house again, as though I didn't belong there anymore.

Not long into unpacking, Hisato came home from hunting, calling for father and asking about the horse grazing just outside. He stopped when he saw me, frozen and wide-eyed. I stood awkwardly, not knowing how to break the tension—if I should speak familiarly, pretending I'd never left, or if there was something important I should say. We seemed not to recognize each other at first. How different we looked after five years.

Hisato set down the fowl he'd caught, taking a hesitant step, then another, until his feet carried him brisk to me. His arms wrapped tight around me, and mine to him. My face hidden in his shirt, I heard my twin brother weep.

"I thought I'd lost you," said Hisato.

I shook my head.

"That I'd good as killed my sister."

"You didn't," I said, pushing away to look up at him. He was taller than me now, and not just by a little. But he was skinnier too.

"I never forgave myself for that day."

"There's nothing to forgive," I cooed. "Even if the outcome wasn't so happy, and I knew it, I'd still run up the mountain to protect my brother."

He brought me back into a snug embrace. "I'm glad you're home."

Into the eve, as I prepared supper, Raeden and Kenta came home from the fields. Like Hisato and father, they stopped, seeing a stranger—a ghost. Raeden was the first to drop his tools, abandoning all thought of removing his shoes as he ran up to take me into his arms. Kenta approached with more control, refraining from explosive gestures. So I hugged him first, at ease after he returned it; soft, slow, and powerful, he held me firm against him.

I didn't have much to work with come supper, already going into what Kwan had sent with me for spices and dried goods, but we ate heartily. Questions flooded in between bites, making me smile as I watched my brothers behave patiently while I answered one thing so they could ask for another helping. I could see my father wanting more, though he said not a word, and shared out with him. From his old habits, he tried to refuse it and give his refilled bowl to one of us. His children.

Koji, opposite, had no trouble making himself at home.

Chapter 84
My Friend

The following morning, I was up early to prepare breakfast. Hisato stayed near, not wanting me from sight. Occupying the space, and eager to say, I relayed my plans to him. That I would teach them to read and write and how to understand the phrasing of someone trying to speak over them. Anything that would be useful to make trading with the passing merchants more fair.

"What do we need to know that for if you're here?"

"I'm not staying forever," I said. "Kwan asked me to marry him. And when I go back, I will tell him yes."

"Who?"

"Lord Kwan," I explained. "The Juneun who protects the mountain."

Hisato's face paled in horror.

"He's not like what we thought," I went on. "I did start off as a prisoner. But became a servant, and a friend after. Then, we fell in love—"

"He was your jailor," scolded Hisato.

I blinked at him. "Yes. For a time."

"You can't go back."

Indignant, I frowned. "I can stay or leave when I like."

"He's—"

"Five years ago," I interrupted. "I had no prospects. And I tried to make myself believe I could be happy being the caretaker for everyone else who was chosen for love while I was left behind. I was lonely, and tried to convince myself that was okay—and my heart ached so much from it. So, you'll excuse me that I did find a good man who does love me, no matter how unlikely it seems."

Hisato's face morphed, heating up.

I interrupted him again. "If he wanted to whore me, why let me leave? And why me when there's a hundred beautiful women more than willing to take to his bed? He chose me, and I chose him."

My brother shied, from the directness of my language or my tone, or something else entirely, I didn't know.

"I came home to make sure all of you would be well without me," I said, softening my voice. "When things are settled, I will go back to accept his proposal. And he will ask father's approval for my hand." I continued my cooking. Unable to stand the somber tension, I sighed to say more. "Without those rumors about me, I knew none of the men here took a liking to me. Kyu liked Fumei. All the boys did. And how could I compare then? I was limited with what I could do, and I wasn't pretty enough to make up for it."

"Hisa..."

"It's true."

Silence.

"I had enough time on the mountain to learn a great deal. Even though I'll never be a beauty, or exceptionally talented, Kwan fell in love with me anyway."

There was no more said during breakfast, as the rest of my family ate up until their bowls were clean. In the morning light, I could better see that they all looked thinner than I remembered.

Newly alone, I finished my unpacking, and set everything in order of how I planned to use them. First on that list was to thank Fumei for caring for my family in my stead. The heavy winter dress from Juro was exceptionally pretty. And if it didn't quite fit, I knew now how to alter it.

Koji followed after me, though Saburo continued a lax grazing, looking up to keep me in sight as I walked. I realized he meant to guard me in his own way, just as I'd decided to keep the pouch with Kwan's soul tucked with me, lest the puzzle box get lost.

At Fumei's home, her mother came to the door with a sever look. "You've some nerve coming here."

I raised a brow, not really understanding. If my reputation was so bad, what did it matter? Whatever rumor about me couldn't transfer to someone else. "I came to see Fumei, so I could thank her for all she's done."

"You'll go home and not bother us again," scolded Fumei's mother. She closed the door without a following word, rudeness intended.

I wasn't dissuaded. If anything, I was angry, and pounded at the door incessantly. When she opened it again, I spoke with as much authority as I could imitate. "I am Lady Hisa of Inori house, bride to Lord Kwan of the Tiger Clan, and I've come to see Fumei." I tried to title myself and speak like Urekkato in the moment (being the most arrogant Juneun I knew). If he watched me now, he was probably laughing.

She looked taken aback, unsure what to do with my presentation.

"I've traveled a long way, and I will not be refused," I said, taking a step forward.

She took a step back, baffled, and I advanced to come inside, leaving my sandals politely by the door. I didn't need directions in finding her room, the one she shared with her sisters.

What I didn't expect was finding my friend in such a woeful state. She looked miserable and tired, seeming startled that I came in.

"Fumei? What's wrong?"

Fumei stared in disbelief. "She let you in?"

I hurried over, setting down my present and the borrowed clothes. "What happened?"

No sooner did I sit beside her, Fumei threw her arms over me in a weep. "I'm so sorry!"

"Sorry for what?"

It was a while before she calmed enough to explain. She'd used the excuse of foraging to go to the upper river to see me last summer, and crossed paths with a nobleman hunting on the mountain. He'd forced himself on her. Kenta found them, fighting off the man and carrying her back to the village. He'd snuck off from the fields with the same intention of trying to see me. Which made his return look suspicious, and gave rise to an alternate tale of things.

"But he didn't," said Fumei, still sobbing.

I held her, trying to be of comfort. I remembered then what my father had said, thinking at first, he meant about my reputation. He meant to protect me from a repugnant perspective of my eldest brother. I wouldn't have believed it anyway. The Kenta I knew always tried to behave like the best of men.

"He tried to save me. And was hurt. And he still carried me down those steep slopes." She lost the battle to hysterical sobbing.

I sat quietly, trying to show that I believed her.

"He offered to marry me," said Fumei when she regained herself. "But I'd made a promise not to get married until you had a good match first. They said refusing only proved he did it."

I waited for her to collect herself, thinking of what I could do. Absent, I fiddled with the red thread around my finger. An idea coming to me then. "I did find a good man. He loves me."

She looked at me, blinking her puffy, pink eyes.

"He's a Juneun lord, and I plan to accept his proposal after I've settled things at home. So you don't have to refuse another marriage."

She shook her head, her voice becoming hoarse. "I don't want to marry. Not after…"

I held her tighter, as though that would somehow protect her. "I'll be a lady to a great clan. I could help to find you—"

"No!"

I blinked at her, rapid in my confusion.

"I don't want another man to touch me—ever!" At her last word, she seemed startled by her own voice. "I don't want to marry. Even if I did, I'm locked in this house."

"But you didn't do anything wrong!" I said, surprised by my own volume. "They can't lock you away for something that's not your fault."

Fumei shook her head. "I fell pregnant from…"

It was my turn to be taken aback.

She sniffled, wiping her face. "It died before it was born."

"But that's not your fault either," I cooed.

"I wanted it to die," whispered Fumei. "I prayed that it would. But, by that time, everyone knew. Kenta kept offering marriage, but I can't."

"You owe me nothing," I said, failing in my attempts to comfort. "Kenta would leave you be if you explained it. I know he would."

"I don't want him to feel he has to. There's no point in him being this miserable as well. The other men stopped harassing him only recently. He put more effort into the fields than all of them. Something to prove. He's a good man, and he deserves a wife who will love him and lay with him. I can't."

"Then, come with me when I go back up the mountain," I said, out of ideas.

"What?"

"No one will bother you there. And you can decide what you want. Who's going to refuse you being a guest to the new lady of the mountain? I'd like to see them try."

Fumei cleaned her face, looking me over. "You've changed, Hisa."

"My hair grew out. And my clothes are different. That's all."

"No," said Fumei. "You're bold. You used to be so shy before."

I smiled with a sigh. "I had to learn to be truly brave. Everything else I learned, I did because I wanted to."

She stared with an awed look I never thought she'd give me. For most of our lives, it'd been the other way around.

"I brought you something," I said, trying to redirect the conversation. I brought over my present, placing it between us.

"It's beautiful."

"I wanted to do something to thank you for taking care of my family. I'm not skilled enough to make one like it, but I will be someday, with more practice."

"It must've cost a fortune. You're sure you want to give it to me?"

I stood. "Try it on. If it's too snug, I can fix it and bring it back."

"You know how?"

"It's something I learned while up the mountain."

Fumei forced on a smile. "I remember you could scarce lengthen sleeves."

Chapter 85
Brothers

The dress nearly fit Fumei, though was snug at her chest. It didn't take me more than a few days to correct it, and I was impressed with how much my skill improved to make it look almost seamless.

I'd insisted on teaching my brothers to read each night, reluctant as they were. I couldn't blame them after a day of laboring. But I wanted us to start so that it became more natural when winter arrived. There'd be less to do, leaving more time to keep inside where it was warm.

It took time for me to get used to village life again, reminding myself to go into the forest for fruits and other foraging finds. Koji shadowed my every move, perfectly happy in the goings on. If ever he spotted something, he'd stand with a raised paw and wagging tail, pointing as he waited for me to say whether or not to fetch it. Having him made meals heartier more often than not. He'd become a fine hunting dog, and a loyal friend.

Raeden grew particularly fond of him during a hunt. We'd crossed paths, and Koji chased out a goral in line for Raeden's arrow, barking at the downed animal. It was a stocky enough creature that we could cure a lot of the meat to hold through a good chunk of winter, and he rewarded the dog with pieces as he field dressed the beast. Not wanting to waste, I hurried to empty my basket into my shirt, and use it to carry any of the organs I knew how to cook. I kept careful so as to not crush the pouch containing Kwan's soul, or to ruin the thread around my finger.

While Raeden wanted to bring Koji with him, now that autumn was here, he didn't listen to my brother. Raeden was still more a stranger than anything to the dog.

We walked home together, Raeden carrying our prize on his shoulders while I took his bow and quiver in tandem with my basket. Walking up to the house, I was horrified. Juro was there, speaking with Kenta. My eldest brother stood tall, arms crossed, and I could only imagine the conversation.

"What's going on?" asked Raeden.

Juro looked over, watching us approach, and painted on a pleasant smile.

Before Kenta said a word to influence any thought, I spoke up. "Lord Juro is a Juneun. A friend to my intended, Lord Kwan."

Juro's smile fell.

Both Kenta and Raeden questioned.

"As I told Hisato, I plan to accept Kwan's proposal when I return to his house."

Clear confusion sprawled on Kenta's face. "Then... Why is he asking for father's approval of an engagement?"

"I don't know," I said, level and dignified. "He'd previously told me we ought to be strangers to each other unless I changed my mind in refusing him." I turned my gaze to Juro. "I have not."

A silent unease set over us. Revealing Kwan's soft proposal stole Juro's usual argument of what he could provide by compare.

"When was this proposal?" asked Juro.

I was about to expose Kwan's folly, stopping when I remembered what he'd said about my status. I couldn't say it was in winter, that he'd pledged himself by drinking from his family's sacred well. "The day of my return. When I would not be obligated to accept him and could deny him fully. He asked, and I agreed on the condition that I can make sure my family will be alright with my absence."

Juro pursed his lips, thinking. "Will your family approve an engagement to your jailor?"

An anger rose in me. Using an underhanded term to influence my family's opinion. I wanted to take something away from him, to lash out somehow that favored me—that I'd already lain with Kwan, and stolen any wedding rite. But I couldn't. It'd only vilify us both.

Before I could come up with a counter, my father walked up with Hisato, fishing poles in hand and a catch in their fish basket. Juro made his greeting with high respect, timing it before I could say my piece. He reiterated his reason for coming to my father, who looked between us and weighed what was said.

"Go inside, Hisa," said father.

"But, Baba—"

"Now, Hisa."

I obeyed, hearing the seriousness of his tone. Raeden joined me, only to set down his hunting prize. He too, bid me to stay inside, promising to handle things. But I couldn't help myself, coming as close as I dared to listen in.

A back and forth ensued, with my brothers expressing their distrust and Juro boasting about what he could provide, including a bride price. I held fast to the thread on my finger, praying. Hisato stepped to my defense, declaring that I was not something to be sold. Juro ignored him, keeping his attention to father, assuring him of all the splendor of things guaranteed to care for me.

Continuing his attempt to persuade my father (who'd yet to say a thing), he promised a high position in his house to Kenta, and schooling for either Raeden or Hisato, adding that he would send a maid here to look after my father and remaining brother.

Without seeing any of their faces, I could tell it was harder for my brothers to argue against the idea. A Juneun with wealth who could take care of me and all my wants, who could lift my family out of poverty almost overnight, and send a small annual tribute to keep my father's house stocked through winter. He made it sound so wonderful. A life of ease. And all it would cost is my father's consent to give me to him.

My gut sank and stung, fearing he'd made a superior impression than Kwan before I could explain things. Fingers folding into a fist, the thread dug into my skin as I prayed more desperately. Then, to my surprise, my father refused it.

"One Juneun took my daughter from us for five long years. I will not suffer another Juneun so entitled to take her from me forever."

Juro argued against my father's cold words, trying to appeal enough for him to reconsider. When that didn't work, he brought up the rumors about my reputation, and how he, unlike anyone else who knew them, held no prejudice. He promised my father that I would be treated kindly, lavishly, all the right things to say.

"Hisa will stay here, where she belongs," said father. "There's not a promise or price in all of heaven that will convince me to hand over my daughter while I still breathe."

Juro frowned, saying something in return. I missed it entirely, trying to shush Koji as he complained and pawed at me.

The following weeks were quiet between us. I kept busy in pickling and preserving and trying to teach my brothers. Absently, in praising Raeden's learning, I mentioned how it wouldn't be long before I returned up the mountain.

"No," said father.

I stopped, staring at him.

"You're not going back. You will stay here, with your family."

"I told Kwan that I would come back to accept his proposal."

He gave me a stern look. "No."

Stunned, the next words fell out of my mouth without thought. "But, why—?"

"That beast took you from us once. Never again."

"But he's already—"

"If you like a man from one of the villages, and he asks, maybe. Not a spirit. Juneun or otherwise."

"Baba, you don't understand," I pled. "Kwan's not a cruel person. He's protected us from Kurai, and makes sure the earth is fertile to hold harvests—he doesn't have control over droughts and floods, but he tries to look after all of us! He cured us of the pox that ravaged the villages. Remember how I'd said to you that I thought I saw someone come in our house and heal us? It was Kwan!"

My father slammed his palm down. "I'm not losing my daughter again. That's final!"

Hurt. In my heart, I understood his perspective, but to be so ignored... I left for my room, trying to hold back tears until I was alone. It wasn't the same as standing my ground against Fumei's mother, or Juro, or Seong. This was my father.

I didn't know how long I laid there on my pillow, sobbing and staring at the red thread on my finger. Long enough for the fervor to fade. Kenta crept into my room, taking a seat beside me.

"Hisa?"

Tired, I used what strength I had to clear up my face and look at him.

"You know father didn't say that to be cruel. He said it out of fear."

I nodded, unable to do much else, and dropped my gaze.

"During the last five years, we didn't know what was happening or if you were alright." He took my hand in his, giving a firm squeeze. "We thought he killed you. Then that maybe he brought you into his bed, put you through some kind of neglect. Father worried so much that he kept falling sick."

My eyes darted back to him, new concern running through my thoughts.

"The way he sees it—the way I still see it—he took you from us, and kept away any news. Raeden worried so much that he said he was going to steal you back. And Hisato was distraught that entire first year, even after. And I felt I'd failed. I couldn't protect my sister. My only sister. The one who looked after me when she was still a child herself. I failed..."

I couldn't bear to see my brother so upset, and threw my arms over his shoulders. "You didn't."

He held tight to me. "I didn't know that. I didn't know anything for those five years."

When we did let go of each other, a new understanding filled the space.

Kenta reached around himself, presenting me with a bundle. "I know you told Raeden that we should sell these things, but I couldn't bring myself to do it." It was my canvas and paintbrush, among other assorted art supplies. "I didn't want to get rid of it, in case it was all we'd have left."

I looked from the collection of second-hand things, to my brother, and back. While I was angry that he put himself into more hardship in holding on to these things, my heart was touched that he kept them.

"Do you really love him?" asked Kenta, stealing my attention. "That Juneun on the mountain?"

I looked to my finger first, then back, nodding. "Things in Juneun society are different, sometimes hard to understand. But Kwan is a kind person. He genuinely wants to help and be useful. He even tried to wait until the day I would leave before expressing his feelings for me. But, I didn't know and tried to express my own before then. It happened in a clumsy and wonderful way, but it happened. Both of us too afraid to say anything for a long time, and thinking the other wanted someone else, until it all came bursting forward."

"You like him that much? Even though he jailed you?"

"I know it sounds weird. It sounds like I'm stupid for falling for a man who sentenced me to be a servant. I think it was inconvenient for him. He doesn't have a prison or a dungeon, and I was in his way a lot that first year. Then I started to understand him, and why he did things the way he did. We started to become friends. He was the one who taught me all the things I'm teaching to you now."

"That seems like a leap."

"It didn't happen right away. Looking back, it seems fast, but it took the span of years before we fell in love."

"And you're sure that's how you feel?"

I nodded. "I am. I love him, Kenta."

"Then why didn't he come down like that other Juneun?"

"He didn't want to get in my way, or present like he was trying to bully father into approval. How would it look if he came down right as I was free to come home?"

"And if you decided to stay here instead?"

"He wouldn't come after me if I wanted to stay."

"How do you know?"

"Because I know him."

Kenta sighed, looking directly at me. "I know you used to think no one would want to marry you. I want to be sure you're not agreeing to this spirit out of desperation. I don't want you to be miserable, Hisa. You're my sister. I want to see you happy in life."

I shook my head. "Juro, the spirit that came here, had made proposals and advances. But I refused him. I couldn't stand to think about being trapped in a marriage with someone who assumed my obligations and ignored my discomfort."

Kenta blinked at me.

"What's that face for?"

"I've just never heard you speak like that."

"Like what?"

"Like... how I imagine a princess would speak."

I laughed.

"You're sure he'll make you happy?"

"I know that he'll try." It didn't seem enough to convince Kenta. "Would you have made Fumei happy?"

He went rigid, turning his gaze and shying into shame.

"You want me to be happy, meanwhile you were willing to marry a girl you didn't love to protect her."

"That's different."

"No, it's not. I know about the rumors while I was away. And I wasn't able to defend against them. Now there's the rumor about you and Fumei, and you wanted to make them go away at the cost of your own happiness. But Fumei refused. She didn't want you to be miserable either." Hearing myself say it all aloud, I realized. "It must've taken a lot of courage."

Uncomfortable, Kenta tried to explain his side. "I didn't think about how it looked. I was trying to do the right thing. And when I was accused, I tried to correct it. When I couldn't, I asked her to marry me, because everyone else thought so badly of us. Everyone said we should, to make things right."

"Everyone in Kwan's service said the same thing about me. That I ought to accept Juro's proposal and go along with whatever advance he wanted. A poor, ugly, naïve, village girl. How many opportunities would I get at a decent man, let alone a wealthy Juneun who can make the trees bear fruit year-round if he wished? I was ridiculed for refusing. Other maids talked about how they wouldn't hesitate to say yes, even though they didn't like him at all."

"They really tried to make you do that?"

"Well... a lot of them tried to convince me. But, in my heart, I couldn't. And sometimes I would feel guilty for my decision. Saying yes would've done so much for all of us, and saying no for my own happiness was selfish. It would eat away at me."

"And you fell in love after?"

"Long after. Kwan and I were newly friends when Juro started making his intentions known—going so far as to tell others we were already engaged, even though I'd either not given an answer, or refused him."

Kenta awed, taking the story in. "You and Fumei. Despite what everyone else says would be best, you made up your own minds. If Fumei saying no to me took courage, what did it take for you to make your own decision?"

Admittedly, I felt a wash of pride. "It wasn't easy."

"If you truly love this other Juneun, then let me speak with father when you're ready to go."

"Really?"

He nodded. "You've looked after us since you were nine. The women in the village used to chew us out when we complained. And we started to appreciate that you tried. When you were gone, we realized just how much you'd taken on. No amount of old paintbrushes and scratched canvases can repay all you've done."

"I always loved when you would bring me something, even if it was falling apart. Sometimes I felt so frustrated and lost, hopeless; having that small reward from you helped me to keep going, to keep trying."

Kenta smiled. "I suppose we'll have to learn how to fend for ourselves. Otherwise, you'll be stuck here."

Chapter 86
In the City

Through winter, Kenta took my instruction more seriously, encouraging Raeden and Hisato to do likewise. While they practiced, keeping near the firepit, I worked to put together new clothes for them and weave sandals, useful things.

Often, I'd look to the mountain, or to the red thread, wondering about Kwan. How was he spending the solstice? Did something come up to drag him away and into the cold? If he missed me always sitting beside him while he worked on some matter, or was he relieved? He had a household to look after him if he became too engrossed in something, but I still worried for that too.

Which is why I found myself happily surprised to discover a small, wrapped, gift with a tag bearing his handwriting.

For Hisa

I held that piece of paper close to my heart, the pouch containing his soul wedged in between. He remembered.

Inside, one of the shells I'd found on the beaches near Bitgaram. One of the few intact, a scallop with a pretty, pink hue to its outside, and shining nacre inside. He'd polished the nacre, making it more brilliant, and fastened a pearl to that side, petite and perfectly round. A thin, gold chain was strung through it. A necklace. It must've been costly, but I loved it. I loved that he thought to use a memory to make the gift—something I'd chosen for myself. Immediately, I put it on, promising to wear it every day and take care not to be clumsy enough that it broke by accident.

Through the rest of winter, I'd look at that necklace, and to the thread around my finger, staring out my window to the mountain before the dark of night made it impossible to see. More than once, I caught the shimmer of a white doe walking soundlessly through the snowfall, leaving as I cleared my eyes of the stinging, cold air.

In spring, when the ground thawed enough, my brothers spent more time away from the house to hunt and work the fields. I said nothing of my continued plan, not wanting to upset father and put him into a state. Coming home, Kenta continued to try learning, encouraging our other brothers to keep at it as well.

One method of practice, to keep my brothers' interest, was in relaying the prices of goods made new. And of more mechanical processes like fermentation of otherwise ordinary plants. Things like flower cultivation didn't hold their attention until I mentioned how high ladies spend small fortunes in redesigning their gardens.

Hisato liked the stories I'd brought to read, the one about a lone warrior with a code of honor in particular. Though none of my brothers cared for the poetry, it was something to help them improve the skill.

There was still the issue of who would take up as the woman of the house in my absence. I saw how my father and brothers tried to make do after the accusations on Kenta; no one would allow a girl to come to help keep the house, tend to laundry, mend clothes and blankets, weave sandals, or so much as cook a meal. The men of the village had strength enough to work the land and fend off dangers, but fell apart without someone to care for them at home.

I didn't know if silver would persuade change, or if it'd appear like I suggested buying out a member of their family. Given how unsavory so many spirits viewed attending a single human in their lord's home, that didn't seem like a viable option either

My best bet was to find someone in the city, similar to how Kwan hired the women in his household. It was a different way of life between villagers and big townsfolk. After explaining, there still might not be a girl wanting to take up the job at any wage. Regardless, there was only one way to find out.

Saburo saddled, and Koji wagging his tail in anticipation, I paused with Hisato insisting he come with me. I would've argued, though I reminded myself that I didn't have Kwan's protection this time in going to a foreign place. Mounted up, Saburo refused Hisato's cues and kicks, standing with his ears pinned back. While unorthodox, I took lead in the saddle, and we went off at a comfortable pace. I expected the trek to take most of the day, though we reached the edge of the city within the hour.

Saburo was a spirit as well, with magic of his own, I remembered, explaining it to Hisato. He didn't understand it well, but he also hadn't been as exposed to magic as I was.

Even with my experience in castles, maneuvering the town was overwhelming. I didn't know where to begin. Keeping Koji to a leash, he was just as out of place. Our saving grace was in being able to read the signs—things I'd have ignored before but now grabbed my attention instantly.

A tailor's store. Since I'd brought two of the other dresses Juro sent, figuring I might get a better price selling directly, it made for a point where we could orientate ourselves. Having seen the cost of fabrics, I had an idea of what the exchange should be. Fearing robbery, I left the rest behind; should times become dire, my brothers could sell them off—after today Hisato would know what a fair price would be. And I could better demonstrate a fiercer negotiation for it.

On entering, however, I was ignored. Despite that I'd been the one to introduce and present the pieces, the clerk spoke to Hisato. Even Juneun lords didn't try to pretend I was invisible to this extent.

When he gave his price, I took the pieces back, garnering a bewildered look on his face.

"That's less than half," I said.

"I assure you," said the clerk, to Hisato, of course, "this is a fair price."

"Not according to what you have posted right there," I said, pointing to a printed sign at the end of his workbench.

Astonished. But he still said nothing to me.

"This was a gift from the Juneun. Lord Juro. I only thought to sell it because I've since outgrown it."

His mouth slowly fell open, but he said nothing.

Hisato looked between us, starting to follow me out.

"Hold on," said the clerk. "How do I know it came from a Juneun?"

"Between us, my brother and I have been the most forthcoming," I said, irritated. "And since you treat me as lesser, I'll find another buyer."

He tried to call again, but I'd made up my mind.

"Are you sure, Hisa?" whispered Hisato.

"If he's that dishonest from the beginning," I said, "there's no point. I know there has to be more than one store who'd give a fair price. The city is too large for there to be only one tailor. We'll find a more honest clerk, and ask them for direction on where to look for a maid afterwards."

"A maid?"

I nodded. "Someone to take care of you all when I go back up the mountain."

"Hisa," snapped Hisato, stopping me from mounting up. "You can't go back."

Saburo pinned his ears.

"I can, and I will," I said. "When I'm sure my family will be well without me, I will go back to Inori and accept Kwan's proposal. Kenta supports me on this."

He looked shocked.

"I explained it to him."

"But that man jailed you, Hisa!" scolded Hisato, trying to keep his volume low. "He would've killed either of us over a deer."

I frowned. In the later stages of our friendship, after court was held, Kwan explained to me the significance of the doe and the stag. "It wasn't just a deer."

Hisato blinked, brow screwing at my calm tone.

"The white doe and stag were gifts to help protect the mountain. They were guardians—spirits."

His face paled. "I... I shot down..."

"Without her, it takes more effort and energy for him to protect the mountain and all the villages—even here! Lord Genji saw how much of a toll it was taking on Kwan, and gave him the pair."

"Gave?"

"Kwan used to be Genji's apprentice. And they still have a strong friendship. You'd like Genji. As powerful of a Juneun as he is, he's a very gentle person. And one of the few who didn't make me feel like such an outsider. I was even invited to his castle once. He's kind."

While my brother remained wordless, I climbed onto the saddle. Rather than mount with me, Hisato took the reins to lead us through the bustling streets. He looked after Koji and watched the surroundings. I searched for any sign that seemed promising.

Silk textiles.

It was an older building, with a balding man pausing his work to come over. I braced myself to be ignored, and I was at first. Looking past him, I saw women brushing in base dyes or committed to a detailed design with their stencils, and men using the might of their bodies to more precisely dye the cloth in a vat of color. When embroidering a piece, both worked diligently, not even bothering to acknowledge us.

Hisato introduced me, a cue to present the dresses. We weren't so naïve as to not become a little cunning in trying to conduct business. If I would be ignored, then Hisato would play the part of middle-ground. He faltered, however, in trying to recall the origin of the pieces, leaving me to repeat it.

"A Juneun artisan?" asked the clerk, looking more intrigued. "Explains the quality. The threading here is gold-leafed."

That was something even I didn't know, which made me feel all the more guilty and furious.

"Is there any way to prove it came from this Juneun specifically?"

"His crest is embroidered there," I said, pointing.

The clerk leaned in, squinting at the small toad details. "So it is."

Given previous experience, it surprised me that he listened and responded.

"Grandpa Chiso!" called a feminine voice. A girl, no older than seventeen or so, waddled in with trays stacked high in her arms. "I have lunch—"

Without hesitation, Hisato went to take the trays from the girl, freeing her from the cumbersome balance.

"Oh. Thank you." She gave a slight bow before reaching up to take the top trays and hand them out.

"Where is Ren?" asked the clerk, Chiso.

She shrugged.

Chiso threw up his hands, exacerbated. "And your sister?"

"At the potter's."

"Nine granddaughters... Only three of them work. Four grandsons, all of them missing when there's work to be done." He turned his attention back to us, sighing. "I know a client who might want them. They might need altering, though. But the best I can offer for one..." he penned something down, presenting it to us.

Hisato blinked, looking to me for confirmation. It was better than our previous offer, but not quite what I'd hoped. I shook my head.

"I really need a better price," I said. "I'm leaving to be married soon, and I need the money to pay a maid to care for my father and brothers in my stead."

Chiso stared, twisting his face. "Where did you say you were from?"

"The northmost village."

"That's quite the trek."

I started to fold up the fine things again, disappointed.

"I'm surprised the two of you are well read," said Chiso. "Half my sons can barely handle it."

"I learned while I stayed with a Juneun lord as his servant," I said. "And I've been teaching my brothers."

"How many brothers?"

"Three of us," said Hisato.

There was a look to Chiso that made me curious. "That's what I can do for one, but! If you'll let me bring this to my client, and humor me with a request, I can send fifteen percent of the profit." He tallied the math, writing a new offer beside the old. "That would be the total."

Hisato shifted, his eyes fixed on the amount.

"I don't know," I said, wary. It was closer to what I'd wanted, but the thought of not having it all up front brought discomfort.

"Twenty percent," said Chiso. "But, play along with something. My grandchildren need a good scare."

"I'd rather n—"

Before I could get the words out, Chiso called back. "Chyou! Tell your sister I found her a husband, working the farms in the farthest village. I'm tired of supporting idle hands."

I was mortified. So was Hisato by the look of him.

The entire assembly stopped to look at Chiso. "If you're all going to gawk, rather than work, I'll sell it all off and send all of you away. Live my last years like a prince instead of working myself to the grave."

They shuddered, hurrying with their meals.

Chiso turned back to us, speaking hushed. "My youngest daughter works at the noodle shop beside the lodgings further in town. I'll send her to be your maid. It'll whip the rest of them into behaving."

"Your daughter?"

"There's a man who stays at the lodgings most of summer and harasses her. If it gets her away—and your brother seems more trustworthy in five minutes than most men in the city do in their entire lives. They'd have let Chyou carry on without the thought to help. Rural folk have those traditional values, and it shows. He looks to your advice rather than bolster himself on decisions."

Shy, Hisato admitted, "She reads better than I do."

"Respecting your sister. That's a fine young man." Flattery now freely flowed from Chiso. "If you say she'll be safe, and reputation intact."

We both squirmed a bit at the implication.

"It'd make no difference in raising the percentage a little more, since it'll come back into the family anyway."

"That's true," I said.

"I can send one of my sons with the rest once I have it, and use the excuse it's to check in on his sister. He can collect the other with a similar bargain at that time."

"Won't that look suspicious?" asked Hisato. I'd been thinking the same, mulling over what was said.

Chiso scoffed. "I doubt it. They're oblivious. It's my fault for making their lives too comfortable and doing all the work myself."

"It does seem like an ideal arrangement," I said.

"Must be luck," said Hisato.

I remembered then that I still had Urekkato's essence, and sight spell, on me. My relief slowly replaced itself with irritation at the thought.

"I do still have things to take care of," I said. "Why not send your daughter with the percentage, and we can start then? And Hisato can ride back a while after with the other dress to make it seem more like how you implied, rather than her being a maid."

The deal was struck. As was the sale of other trinkets shortly after to another vendor. Leaving the rest of the day to find a breeder for hunting dogs, and a horse master for a good mare. I managed, but soured at the cost.

The amount I got from the nacre hair pin would pay for the mare, already bred—something that would make hunting and transit easier for my brothers. And a foal would ensure a second generation, prolonging the time they could use a beast of burden. Regardless, I consulted Saburo's opinion of which seemed best. A good thing of it, since he disliked the first mare presented to us. I suspected they wanted to take me for a fool, seeing how fine a stallion Saburo was and how humbly Hisato and I dressed (save for my necklace).

An unease was brought in explaining that he served to a Juneun lord and was on loan only until I had a steed of my liking. No more old nags or unbroken brood mares were presented. When Saburo didn't mind a selection, I picked from intuition. She wasn't the prettiest or tallest, but there was a kindness in her eyes.

Buying a pup, I needed to use the profit I got from selling the obsidian bracelet Juro brought—the polished breath of a fire. Kochi-ken dogs were as expensive as I remembered. But since Koji made a good hunting partner, despite not wanting to listen to Raeden, I thought to get a pup to train from scratch. Koji could help show what we wanted, and my brothers would have a loyal friend to help chase out game to bring home.

A female sat away from the rest, curiously tilting her head at her siblings making a fuss. She was big, compared to the rest, and quiet. I thought it a good idea; and if she became a good hunter, maybe having a litter from her would bring a second generation. If it was a big litter, some could be given or sold—Renzo might be happy to have a pup since Chocho had past the year prior. The important bit of it all was making her part of our poor family and helping my brothers. More dogs would deter boar from coming into the village.

I thought about selling the moonstone pendent—I intended to originally, anyway—but remembered what Juro said about it. He'd put a blessing on it, for protection. With that in mind, I had a better use for it.

We headed for home that evening. If not for Saburo's spell, we'd need to stay overnight, making me all the more relieved to have him.

From new habit, since coming home, I placed a hand over my chest to feel the pouch holding Kwan's soul. Summer was fast approaching, and I missed him more than I thought.

Chapter 87
Lord Kwan XXII

The night after her leaving, the room was still. Kwan lay in bed, no longer used to the complete silence. He looked across the space to where her bed lay tucked away, void of her silhouette and soft, rhythmic breathing. Sighing, he turned to his side, avoiding the vacancy. A string of red stared back at him from his finger. He closed his eyes, clearing out the distraction.

Court would be held at summer's end, keeping the façade of power. He'd heard nothing of Gumiho in the last year. Nor Urekkato. Had he done it? She'd tested herself in coming onto the mountain, leading to the assault after. She'd known protection was limited. The best front he could do, now, was hold regular assemblies where powerful Juneun gathered. If she was still out there.

He soured at the thought. So much life lost in haughty battle. And for what? Better if he'd been left to handle it alone, rather than an impatient command by the Mireu King, goaded by Urekkato and the others. There was also the uncertainty of how many Kurai were willing, and how many were subject to the will of Gumiho holding their souls.

Whether or not the oath breaking worked, caution was better than assumption. The image of the boy flashed in his mind. An innocent, caught in the scheming of high lords. Titles alone couldn't spare the human princeling. These were the games they played.

Maybe he was foolish for having made a new commitment. There was no guarantee of his end, but it was too enticing to refuse in exchange for *Bird Song*. If nothing more, it ensured added protection for her, for his Hisa. She might not see it the same way, and he'd have to confess the circumstance to explain it to her. Only girls, only boys, none at all, as long as she didn't hate him.

The guests buzzed with gossip during court, speaking of Uno's appearance and wondering who would make for a finer prospect for Kwan amongst themselves. Not that it mattered.

Hisa seemed to no longer exist to any of them once out of sight. No one questioned her absence that first day of court.

The second day, in his apartment, was another matter.

"Lord Kwan is secretive," said Zhen, sly. "Underhanded arrangements, which he doesn't tell his brothers, breaking oaths made from his ancestral well, and trying to cheat me out of a promise."

Kwan stared from across the table, setting down his cup of wine. "I have no intention of cheating you out of anything."

Zhen smirked, leaning on the sword where he sat. "Still pretending the games of society are beneath you while you play them? Were you planning to trade me half-bred brats in exchange for *Bird Song*?"

Kwan leered.

"You omitted to say whether they'd be bastards."

"I am promising you titled heirs. Is that not sufficient?"

Zhen looked him over, measuring. "Where is your human anyway? Your bed must be getting cold."

Kwan narrowed his gaze.

"You wouldn't be fool enough to try and title offspring from a human. Are you fool enough to make a human your wife? Poor and unsightly as she is?"

Kwan's palm slammed on the wood, shaking the whole of the table. Low and threatening growls left him.

Zhen quirked a brow. "You really mean to go through with it?"

Kwan stayed as he was.

"Why should I trade *Bird Song* for half-breeds?"

"Then don't," said Kwan, level in tone.

Zhen's expression changed, the bravado fleeting. "I don't believe you'd let *Bird Song* slip through your fingers for a human."

For a long while, Kwan stared, saying nothing, waiting for Zhen's fidgeting to gain aggression. "I've made my offer. If it is not to your liking, we have nothing more to discuss." He needed to rein in his temper to make the bluff work. A play to Zhen's ego, in wanting more ties to an older family name.

Scoffing, Zhen's smirk reappeared. "An alteration. Humans don't live more than eighty years at best. I've no doubt you'll marry again after. As will Genji." He relaxed himself, putting on a bluff of his own. "Arrange for my sister to visit your old master privately. Encourage an affection."

"You think I hold power over Genji's decisions?"

"I think you hold influence."

Kwan waited, weighing. "I guarantee nothing outside of their meeting."

"I suspect you said the same thing to your niece. And now..." A grin slowly spread across him.

Still, and unimpressed, Kwan said nothing.

In the night, he wrestled with sleep. Between his conscience and the emptiness of the apartment room, he fought to keep his eyes shut. When he did, he dreamed. She was back, climbing on him, sharing in a kiss, and another. An level of assertiveness he wasn't used to. He wrapped his arms around her, keeping her close. It felt real. And different. Enough to cause him to wake fully.

Black hair, and brown eyes, but it wasn't Hisa. He frowned. She blinked, leaning in again with pouting lips. At her touch to his own lips, he stopped her. His senses gathered, piecing together the reasons. She was a servant, though he didn't know from where or to whom. One of few who took note of Hisa's absence, and made an ambitious move. An attempt to elevate herself.

He sat up, wordless in his displeasure. She batted her eyes, unable to comprehend, and slid her night robe off. Taking her arm, Kwan pulled her out of bed with him in a rough movement, wrapping his sheet around her as he towed her to the door. Outside, he let go, seeing her bewildered expression as he stepped back in and closed his doors swift and with little grace.

Alone again, he massaged his temples and eyes. On a whim, he made for her bed rather than his own, breathing in whatever lingering scent remained when he collapsed in it. She'd left her rabbit, a treasured possession. Kwan stared a while, slowing his breath to take in her smell from it. His eyes trailed, finding that thread on his finger again. Soothed, he fell asleep.

Boldness, more aggressive than when he newly began holding court again. With every approach from a lady in want of an engagement, and every invite of a servant wanting a more comfortable life, he regretted his decision to host.

It couldn't be avoided, Kwan reminded himself. To gain *Bird Song*, to maintain a show of control, to safeguard the mountain. Gumiho knew now that she could confront his home with little resistance.

So why hadn't she?

Until he was certain, caution was key. Not for himself. For her.

In another restless night, he took a walk, fanning away the thick, summer air as he did. By sheer coincidence, he came across Uno, harassed by a drunken serf not his own. So intoxicated, he didn't notice Kwan walking towards them.

A bamboo rod flew to Kwan's gesture. Three swift strikes to the man's back. He turned, readying to fight, and paled when he saw the offended host.

"Who is your master?" asked Kwan, severe.

Falling into a pleading bow, he whimpered.

Kwan repeated his question, a low growl in his voice.

"Lord Bul Gae, of the Fire Dogs," answered the man in a quiver.

Kwan studied him over, deciding how to handle it. "Rise."

The serf obeyed.

"Deliver a message to your master."

He nodded, unaware to the depth of his insult. A strike to his face sent him stumbling.

"Deliver this message, for bringing a servant who cannot control his wine intake." With nothing more to say, Kwan snatched Uno's wrist, towing the trembling girl away.

While he expected some harassment, negligible and easy to dissuade as the host—since he'd been known to keep curious company—he didn't think any would wait until after the lights turned out to lure away the young fox spirit. It was too underhanded for any dignified person.

In his room, he released her and closed the doors. "You will stay here for the night."

Walking to his bed, an eerie feeling prickled his skin. Looking back, he saw the poor girl shaking as she tried to undo her layers of court attire. One piece fell away, and then another, and he couldn't make sense of the scene.

"What are you doing?"

She jumped at his collected tone, shuffling to him with a whimper. "I'm sorry. I've just never..."

Kwan blinked, slow and exhausted.

"I've never lain with anyone." Her hands trembled violently, trying to unfasten the next piece.

"I did not bring you here for me."

Ears flat, she looked up timidly with a question.

Kwan gestured to Hisa's bed. "While court is held, you may sleep here for your protection. Not for my entertainment."

Chapter 88
Lord Kwan XXIII

Tedious harassment came from Juro and his prying. Implying Hisa's fondness of Uno made her a contender for his mistress if she pleased.

Kwan thought nothing of it until autumn, when Juro returned unhappily.

"Lord Kwan!"

Kwan looked up from his tea, away from the drying gardens and across the courtyard. Though, he stayed seated on the veranda peaceably. "Lord Juro."

"What is this I hear of your engagement to Hisa?" demanded Juro, marching up.

"Since you are the one who heard it, relay it to me," said Kwan, unbothered and sipping his drink.

"I'm in no mood for your jests, my friend. Hisa herself declared it as fact when I went to ask her father's blessing."

"I take it things didn't go favorably for my friend." That did bother him, though he tempered his tone. "Tea?"

"Is it true?" demanded Juro.

"My engagement?" said Kwan, hinting a smile. "I have made a proposal to Hisa. And I'm waiting for her answer."

"You had no right," scolded Juro. "Knowing my stance, you had no right to go behind my back and make a proposal!"

"Behind your back?" echoed Kwan. He set down his tea cup, picking up a round pear to peel. "I initially tested to see if an affection could be encouraged towards my friend. When you declared yourself a stranger to her at Tetsuden, I felt free to express my own feelings when it was appropriate."

Juro's jaw locked. Righteousness fleeing.

Kwan poured a cup for Juro as he waited for a response, and refilled his own. "Hisa is capable of knowing her own mind. If she refuses me, there's nothing I can do."

Juro scoffed, taking a reluctant seat. "And why would she refuse you?"

"Did she not refuse you before my affections were known?"

For a while, Juro kept silent, sipping his drink as he mulled over the words. "What is it that drew a high lord to her?"

Kwan glanced over, reading into Juro's stoic expression and defeated, resentful tone. "She wasn't afraid to love what was unloved by others."

"And not for her own gain," added Juro after a moment's thought.

"The rest of my household tried to encourage her affection for you, my friend, giving their perspectives. Your favor was not unwanted in my home."

Juro flicked a smile at that, grunting.

"Lin was the most disappointed. She grew fond of the summer fruits you sent in winter."

"Lin is too ambitious."

"She guards her position fiercely. I will be aggrieved should she elope or take up with another lord."

Slowly, the tension dissipated between them.

"The half coat you're wearing...?" asked Juro, jutting his chin to the sunflower pattern.

"Hisa made it."

Juro's eyes narrowed.

"She promised to put her skill to work and make something for me, prior to knowing my affection."

Juro sighed, long and heavy. "I should've given her more of my time."

"Perhaps," said Kwan. "But your duties required you to be elsewhere."

"What is duty compared to the love of a woman?"

Kwan looked at his friend, studying his posture. "Meaningless."

"You've once loved and loss," said Juro. "Was it meaningless?"

Kwan dragged his gaze back to the drying garden, at the start of a long slumber. "Until I loved again."

Juro pondered the sentiment. "Did you always love her?"

"No," said Kwan, glancing to the thread on his finger. "But then I learned to."

Winter, and it became quieter still. She'd always been up to something, clumsy and unable to move about soundlessly. And when she was hushed, he'd find her working on some passion. Now, it was simply mute.

From new habit, as he looked over any missives or plans for the upcoming spring, he'd glance to his side where she'd sit. Absent, he thumbed the jade pendant she'd given him. While he'd hoped she'd return before the first snow, even sending for a trinket to present to her, he didn't want her to feel obliged to expedite whatever business she had. The intrusive thoughts and desire to go to her started anchoring themselves in him.

Was she well? Sick, injured, lonely, cold? Or perfectly content?

The solstice arrived with a buzz among his household, and he felt more the part of an observer without her shuffling about and displaying boisterous emotion. His usual anticipation later in the year stopped short. Knowing that, he went to the shrine the morning of the new year to pray.

The eve of his usual visit, now without her, he couldn't take it. The trinket placed delicately in a box, and prettily wrapped, he scribbled a dozen tags, discarding them one after another.

From Kwan. That seemed somehow too forward.

I love you. Too much pressure.

I miss you. Too dramatic.

He eventually settled on one he disliked the least: *For Hisa.*

No one noticed his departure.

At the base of the mountain, the snows were shallower. He'd no doubt that his footprints would be covered by morning. Finding her house was easy. All he needed to do was see Saburo. A shelter was built to the back of one house, near the furnace. A warm place, sturdy, and carefully lain out for the stallion's comfort.

With the start of a smile, Kwan placed his gift beneath the shelter, biding that Saburo make sure she received it. A few steps, about to leave, he felt pulled back. He'd never taken the time to observe the settlements under his protection, assuming them all to be more or less like those under his father's domain when he was a boy. Curious, he meandered. This late into the night, he didn't suppose anyone awake to bother him, and strode unhindered.

A familiar sense drew him. Stopping at a window, he carefully inched it open to peek inside. Hisa, bundled and warm, clung to the puzzle box in her sleep. Koji lay curled at her backside, guarding in his own slumber. The sight freed Kwan's heart of worry. As long as the dog was near his soul, his essence placed on the beast would act.

More wandering brought him similar sights in this village. In one home, he noticed a fine dress laying over a girl around Hisa's age. What the connection between them was, he didn't know, but it gave him something to ponder as he toured himself through the next village and the next.

Wherever he noticed ailment, he crept in soundlessly to asses and heal.

The towns and city were harder to go unseen; but he'd already gone through so much of his territory that he felt compelled, and curious enough, to view the rest and gain some awareness of the ongoings in his care. It felt more detailed than mere reports to observe things for himself, and he considered making his self-guided tours an annual ordeal.

In some ways, humans reflected Juneun, mimicking superficial behaviors and hierarchies. In other ways, they were completely alien. Class allowances were stricter, gatekeeping on education and artistry, and sex was something of a public commodity in the more urban areas—as opposed to being strategically used or convenient for a master and servant, or other members of a household.

It seemed everything in the human world had a price, strategic or not. Foreign as it was, he felt he understood them better—understood *her* a little better. Reminding him of a promise made long before.

Spring. Mokryon would come soon enough, though he had no intention of attending.

More concern rose about the missing prince, with Eumeh having birthed another girl and Urekkato nowhere to be found. Had he done it? By accident or otherwise? Guilt sharply tore through him. In that same instance, he remembered Hisa's confession of begging Urekkato's help on his behalf.

Maybe it was wrong that he withheld it from her.

No. He couldn't think of the torment it would cause her if she knew. She'd meant to help, and Urekkato's arrogance led him to answer what he could've easily dismissed. There was no news of a body, which both gave him hope and cause to worry. Better to avoid the talk all together.

After, and unexpectedly, however, Feng called on him, arriving with sincere irritation.

"There were rumors at Mokryon," said Feng, taking her tea with practiced grace. "That you did not make an appearance because you're recently engaged."

Kwan said nothing, hardly granting any acknowledgement with more than a glance.

Syaoran, however, found it hard to serve and maintain his composure. Feng glared in his direction, which did little, if anything.

"What I didn't hear was to whom Lord Kwan, who'd sworn his chastity when last I spoke to him, was engaged to."

"Seems an important detail to leave out in a rumor," said Kwan. "For what reason do you call, Lady Feng?"

"What reason?" echoed Feng with venom. "You refuse me for decades—centuries! And then to say you took an oath of chastity, only for this disgusting rumor to come up not three years later."

Kwan, unbothered by her rehearsed fits, studied her a moment. "What is it you want?"

"I want to know if these rumors hold truth!" demanded Feng. "And if so, which cunning wretch did you promise yourself to?"

After all this time, Kwan could no longer tell if this outburst was sincere, or scripted.

"Say something!"

Taking his time, and sipping from his cup, Kwan answered. "I made a proposal."

Uno announced herself, stepping in with pomegranate wine to serve. Feng eyed her and looked back to Kwan with an implied question. One he didn't care to answer. She didn't notice a prominent absence. Only that a pretty maid, resembling a previous love, was now there.

"A proposal to who?" asked Feng, seething.

At his own leisure, Kwan spoke. "To Hisa."

Feng's expression went blank. "Your human?"

Kwan ignored her, gesturing for Uno to fill his cup.

"A *human*?" reiterated Feng. "You ignore me for centuries, and have the audacity to propose to *her*? Some, some scrawny, unshapely, peasant?"

Kwan said nothing, allowing Feng to exhaust herself in her tirade.

"She didn't even have half-decent manners before I taught her!"

"It was not her manners I adored," said Kwan.

"Then, what?" snapped Feng. "Her face?"

Kwan lifted his gaze to her, sharp.

Feng's shoulders and chest visibly rose with her breathing. "Is that what you wanted? Someone to pity? No, no wealth, no title, no beauty—no breeding? She's a novelty. Fleeting. What could she give that I couldn't?"

Kwan set down his cup, looking directly at her. "Sincerity."

Her expression morphed, a deep scowl softening to a question.

"And compassion," said Kwan, resuming his casualness.

"Have I not been?" demanded Feng.

"Not without expecting reward."

She swatted the teapot from the table in her fury, spooking Uno and causing Syaoran to step aside. "Did I not endure the ridicule of your brothers without complaint? That I was so low at birth to have my title—my birthright—withheld from me for so long?"

Kwan sipped, as though she'd kept perfectly still. "The circumstance of birth and title never factored into my decision."

She threw the plates next. Kwan ignored it. In her rage, Feng lashed out in the apartment room, stopped only when her ire went to strike at Hisa's things. Syaoran and Uno kept to their station, unable to act or flee without permission.

Kwan stepped in, faster than a bewildered blink, taking Feng's arm to halt her tantrum. Calm, he gave his command. "Stop this."

Feng met his command and cold expression with tears.

Chapter 89
Village Life Again

Summer ushered in rain ruthlessly, and delivered several setbacks with it. During one storming day, I'd set to see Fumei again. It was her birthday, and I could think of no better time to bring her something to try and comfort her.

A basket of apricots, and the moonstone pendent with them, I made the muddy trek. While Saburo nickered, implying I ought to take him, I didn't want him to suffer the rain during my visit. An oilpaper umbrella sufficed if I was mindful and walked slow. In a moment of greed, I'd bought it from the first merchant that passed through the village. It wasn't so pretty, but I thought it would work to preserve my clothing if I needed to go into the rain.

I was quickly learning that my time away made me different from the village girls, more than before. I didn't quite fit in, nor could I hide myself so easily anymore. There was an expectation that I would return as timid and obedient as before, and accept how things were without trying to find some solution to make my family a little more comfortable. Even the merchant bore astonishment at my new comprehension of things in my negotiating. Everything I'd learned and memorized to become more useful at home now served to make me stand out in odd fashion.

I dwelled a little on it in my walk, coming to terms that I neither belonged in my village nor among Juneun. My life had become complicated in ways I couldn't imagine five years ago.

Fumei's mother didn't turn me away this time. Though, that didn't mean she welcomed me either. An awkwardness fell over us, but I was permitted in to see my friend.

"You were always better at finding fruit trees," said Fumei, seeming in slightly better spirits than she had the last time I saw her. A sadness lingered in her, both of us trying not to churn it up.

"I never had much choice," I said, smiling for her. "I had to come back with something when I went into the forest."

"That's true," said Fumei. "I had sisters helping me." Quiet hung, waiting for Fumei to say something evidently on her mind. "I'm sorry I didn't do more for you back then. You were just a child taking on so much."

I shook my head with a light laugh. "You were a child too. And your friendship was enough. It made me feel like I wasn't so strange or alone. Then..." my thoughts trailed into somberness. "When you needed me, I wasn't here."

"That's not your fault."

"It wasn't your fault either." Awkwardness thickened the air. "I brought something else for you." I fished out the moonstone pendent. "It was blessed by a Juneun with a spell of protection."

"It's beautiful," said Fumei, marveling. "Did your Juneun bless it?"

"No. But a close friend of his did. Not all the Juneun are kind, the same as humans. One of them was singling me out for his frustration, so I was given this. But I want you to have it."

"Me? But, what if..."

"Kwan wouldn't let it happen. And I'm not the same scared little girl I was back then."

Fumei stared at me, slowly bringing her gaze to admire the pendent again. "I wish I was as brave as you."

"You came up to try and see if I was alright. More than once. And Raeden told me how there were more boars that year on top of everything else. You are brave, Fumei."

She shook her head. "Not anymore."

I took her hand. "That's not true."

She looked at me.

"There were lots of times where I thought I wasn't brave at all. But I think it was that I just needed a break from being strong all the time."

She forced on a weak smile.

"You'll find your courage again. I know it."

A few days of sun, breaking the monsoons, I took the day to breathe and pause in my own working to settle things for my family. Set up on a soft slope, I took my charcoal and canvas to draw out something that I could later paint. After a long winter of weaving, I worried my hand might've forgotten how to sketch.

Raeden played with the pup, which he'd named *Satsu*, continuing to train her with high praise. Hisato disagreed on the name, but the pup decided to respond only to her favorite. Though, that might've been more to do with Raeden's voice than the name itself. He'd become immediately attached to her, devoting every hour he couldn't leave to hunt or labor the fields in training her, needing to be pressed into practicing his reading from Kenta.

When my back began to stiffen, I stopped my drawing, looking over my progress and grimacing at where I'd made too many mistakes. As much as I tried to correct them, they left unsightly scars on the canvas.

Calling for Koji—having chased at some wild thing—I waited and stretched, basking in the bright sun and muggy air. When I spotted him trotting over, he held a wild duck in his mouth, head held high with pride. The thing wasn't dead or badly hurt. Something we could maybe tame and keep at the house for eggs (and meat if times were dire). It took a bit of convincing with the poor thing quacking as I tried to coax Koji into giving me the duck, but he eventually let go.

It would be a while before I took my canvas out again. I needed paint, and would have to wait for the merchants. And probably for the best. The mare I'd purchased was in labor, with Saburo standing guard. It was still early into summer, and I hadn't expected the foal until closer to the solstice.

Hurried, I found a place to hold the duck, giving it radish leaves to occupy it while I went to the mare. An experienced mother, she didn't need any help, and produced a pretty filly, gray and dappled with white. Both of them catching their breath, she encouraged it to stand and take its first steps. I awed at how strong and capable the newborn was so soon into life.

Excited, I took off to tell Lan and get his thoughts on the baby's health. A good thing of it. He advised I bury the placenta and any afterbirth to discourage predators from the smell. Something I wouldn't have thought of. He'd said she needed a name to seal in the luck.

Looking at the black fuzz of hair she had for a mane and on her little tail, and the snow pattern on her gray coat, it seemed obvious what I ought to call her. Yuki.

While Lan said she looked in good health, as did the mare, I still worried about some wild beast coming, and slept outside with them that first night, Koji beside me. Not every night. Sharing my frets with my brothers, we formed a rotation of who would sleep out there on clear nights, since it was unlikely anything would be out if it rained.

It was little after a week when I heard a ruckus. The night started with a deluge, but must've cleared up sometime after. Koji roused, barking and racing me to the door. In the dark, I grabbed whatever my hand felt might help scare off the source of the noise, and I threw open the door. Koji wasted no time, like a bolt of lightning, he sped off. Catching up, I could make out that he wrestled with something. Something big.

With a shriek, I swung, the clang of it on the ground told me I'd grabbed a shovel, and that I'd missed completely. Then there was swearing. A man, I realized. A thief!

Saburo was on him as well, snorting and rearing up. A rope hung loose around the stallion's neck.

My brothers arrived, with axes and arrows, surrounding and chiding. Koji, however, wouldn't release the stranger's arm, wrestling him to the ground again as he cursed and swore. My father came out, quick as his joints would allow, bringing a lantern.

I recognized the man immediately. He'd sold me the mare in the city. Angry, I chewed him out in fierce tones. Though, we didn't quite know what else to do with him. Kenta bid me to go back inside with our father, promising he would handle it. While I didn't know what he was planning, he said it in the way that made me believe him—the way that meant he'd keep his promise to the fullest.

Raeden was the first to come inside an hour later, bursting into my room and looking pale. "It's not true, is it?"

"What?" I looked up from stroking through Koji's coat.

He marched over, grabbing my shoulders. "You're not really going back to marry that Juneun, are you?"

I blinked, tired and missing context.

"Kenta told the thief he was stealing a horse that belonged to the bride of the Juneun lord on the mountain. He was just saying that as a threat, right? You're not actually going back to the man that imprisoned you."

It took a moment, but my mind caught up, and my heart was touched. Kenta really would support my decision. With a soft smile, I answered. "I am."

"Hisa—"

"Don't you remember when you snuck in?" I said, keeping my voice hushed to avoid father hearing us. "I said he wasn't the sort to use and abuse me. And he never did. I served out the sentence for poaching, and was let go as soon as time was up. He's a good man, and I love him. And he loves me."

Raeden matched my volume. "If he loves you, why didn't he let you go sooner?"

I sighed. "He explained that we had to see the sentencing out once it was given. Otherwise, there'd be consequences by the other lords. It wasn't a matter of keeping me at a whim, but of showing he didn't hold justice only when it suited him." Reading his face, I tried to better explain. "It's difficult to understand how lords do things. And more so when they're Juneun. But there's an order and a logic to it. If the man who forced himself on Fumei was imprisoned, would you be happy that he was let go simply because the lord liked him?"

"That's—"

"If that thief had stolen Saburo and the other horses, would you be okay with relaxed justice? Or is it different only because I'm your sister?"

I could see he was lost for words, partly startled by my assertiveness in the matter.

"I know what it looks like from an outside perspective, but I do love him," I said, my tone gentle.

Koji leaned against me, yawning a high-pitched complaint.

"He's kind to me," I went on, stealing a look to the thread on my finger. "When we talk to each other, I don't feel inadequate or lesser. I'm just a person talking to a person. When I confessed that I couldn't read, he taught me. No judgement on my poor upbringing. He simply offered if I wanted to learn. If there was something I wanted to do, he didn't stop me. I improved so much in my skillset. And if I got stuck, he did his best to help me. And when other Juneun harassed me, looked down on me, he protected me. It's not a perfect romance, but we keep trying to be better for each other. That's all I can ask."

Raeden scoffed, turning away. "You belong here, with humans."

"To what end?" I asked. "I'm not a beauty, or clever. When those rumors spread about me, what chance did I have, really, to belong here?" I went on before he could speak. "I'm not marrying him out of desperation. If I went far enough away, as I am now, I might have a husband. But likely not one so patient and kind with me."

I understood his concern. It was the same with all of my family. All I could do was hope I'd explain things well enough to change their opinions.

Chapter 90
Lord Kwan XXIV

Absent minded, Kwan brushed his thumb over the carved relief of the jade pendent in a slow metronome. In trying to clear his head from the annual reports and fretting over the upcoming court, he walked the veranda, stopping where he'd once spent endless hours in her company as she doodled something of passion. Part of him suggested he rearrange the gardens to entertain the guests with new aesthetic. But he didn't have the conviction to make drastic changes while Hisa was away. The thought that it might sadden her, even a little, prevented his impulse.

Staring out, his mind adrift, he watched the butterflies conduct their dances over the flowers. None of them without a partner. He sat, making a gesture and waiting with an open palm for his flute to arrive. Not so much as a rumor of Gumiho. Maybe he'd done it.

Going through practices, trying to play from memory, he thought about what he'd do for leisure. If she was gone, he'd have more of it. Hisa, undoubtedly, would be scribbling away or putting something together, unable to stay idle. Refreshing old skills of his own wouldn't be such a bad idea, and would keep in her company.

He paused, thinking of what songs she'd like. Would she know which were love songs and which were referencing folklore? A lullaby, perhaps. In any case, he fast found that he no longer had them memorized, and would need the sheet notes.

Searching for it, he'd picked up a sketch book accidentally sorted into his things. One of Hisa's. Rather than continue his search, he browsed it. Noting the slow improvement as he progressed through the pages. It brought a hint of a smile to his face. Always, she tried to get better on whatever she set herself to do. How rare a trait that was.

Unable to help himself, he brought out her other sketch books to look through. Humans seemed to apprentice not for improvement on a passion, but set on an income. Juneun improved merely because it was expected of them in their long lives, and not for a love of it. At least, that'd been his experience.

"Does Hisa know you have those, my lord?" asked Syaoran, teasing at the thresh of the open door.

Kwan looked at him, stolen from his reminiscing. He'd come to the page where he'd shown her a simple technique, and her attempts to copy.

Syaoran held up a small note. "Your brother's seal."

Kwan stretched out his hand, letting the note glide to him. By the size and the seal, he'd guessed at the content of the letter. "Will you insist on hiding yourself away this time?"

"If it can be helped," said Syaoran.

The table flew past Kwan to smash against the wall behind him. Unbothered, he sipped at the peach wine in his hand.

"Of all the foolhardy things!" roared Seong. "Was it not humiliation enough to whore her and parade her around? You intend to marry that girl? A human?"

The discussion came to the climax after only twenty minutes. In an attempt to prevent his decision, Feng went to his brothers to reveal his intention. It seemed a pleasure for each of them to destroy his home in their fits.

"Humiliation to who?"

In a flash, Seong had him out of his seat and pinned to the wall. Kwan flinched upon impact, but otherwise kept stoic.

"It was my mistake before doing nothing when you declared yourself to that fox-devil. Now you mean to pledge yourself to a lowlier creature? To spite our family?"

"Since when is my intimacy the concern of my brothers?" said Kwan, deliberately avoiding Seong's meaning.

"Do I look entertained by your antics?" growled Seong.

Yuz stepped in, coaxing them to part. "Kwan surely knows his mistake and will correct it. I'd like to have all my brothers at my wedding and civil."

Seong shifted his gaze.

"I do not consider my proposal a mistake," said Kwan, defiant.

Seong pressing in, emphasizing his strength on his younger brother. "I won't endure this a second time."

"You are welcome to ignore," said Kwan.

"If you will not break off this ridiculous engagement," said Seong, giving a threatening growl, "I will ensure that she does."

In a flash, a scowl consumed Kwan's face. He pushed off, exchanging blows. Seong drew his sword, forcing Kwan to fall into defensive motions. Yuz, calling out, stepped between, giving one precious second needed for *Bird Song* to come to Kwan's hand for a counter. It caught the eldest off guard, perhaps not expecting such ferocity. Thrown aside, sword drawn, Yuz couldn't make a safe interception in the lightning of their spar.

The clashing of steel, and the war cry of thrush whistles cutting the air, echoed. The bones of his house shook with every collision—the speed of which might bring it down. Kwan didn't care, meeting his brother's equal abandon. When opportunity presented, he stalled with the casting of white thread and kicked at Seong's shin, bringing him to his back, *Bird Song* at his neck.

"If you touch her," growled Kwan, breath heavy, "I will not perceive you as my brother."

Yuz tried to remove his younger brother. Kwan shove him off.

"All of this," said Seong, matching Kwan's tone, "for a human beggar?"

"All of this," said Kwan, "for my wife."

Seong measured, but didn't relent his sneer. "For a Tiger to fall so low. It wasn't enough you spend your days fraternizing with Kurai and bedding humans. Now you pledge yourself to a common hare of a woman."

Yuz took his stance, readying to launch if needed.

"A magpie," countered Kwan. "Better a love and fleeting happiness, than an eon of dissatisfaction for the sake of convenience."

"You'll be lucky to count fifty-years of your fleeting happiness," snapped Seong.

"Think it through," said Yuz, attempting to reason. "Such a short life will cause instability to your house."

Taking his time, and reining himself in, Kwan answered. "A life alone has been a source of instability. At the very least, I will choose my downfall."

"You are choosing a human," snapped Seong, "over your own brothers. Your family. Your kin."

"I am choosing a sincere love," said Kwan, even. "Rather than jealousy."

The show of strength kept on until Yuz and Seong rode through the moon gate in the following day. More magic used, to maintain the façade, repairing the damages. At least, as much as could be through magical means. Tempers cooled, wounds healed, Kwan collapsed in his room.

"My lord!" Uno rushed to him, panicked and calling for Syaoran.

Absent, and feeling himself wane, Kwan asked for Hisa. To be at his side during his recovery, as she'd always been since discovering his secret.

"She's still with her family, my lord," said Uno.

Syaoran hurried to help lift him. "Uno, bring the ginseng tea up."

She nodded, acting without hesitation as Syaoran carried Kwan to his bed for rest.

"Where did you end up hiding?" asked Kwan in an attempt to tease.

"Between the walls," said Syaoran. "It's become a great deal more pleasant there in recent years. There's a mural now. And a swing. Things to while the time."

"Uno?"

"I'd lost track of her," admitted Syaoran. He stayed beside Kwan with the tea delivered, dismissing Uno to go as she pleased. "What was the cause for this visit?"

"An objection to Hisa," answered Kwan, casual. He stole a glance to the thread on his finger.

Syaoran gave a look of apology. "As much as I like Hisa, I can't say I blame them." He went on, ignoring Kwan's sharp watch. "Having a lady for so short a time, and to grieve the loss after, there'd be displacement among the staff. For her household. I know it's only Uno, for now, and Hisa likely wouldn't bring on more, but they don't know her like that. Looking at Lord Genji, after Lady Isa passed, the disorientation alone strengthened the prejudice. And to not have an heir brings more concerns. Even if he'd had only one daughter, it'd eased the tensions and uncertainty."

"Genji is perfectly capable of selecting an heir without natural born children," said Kwan.

"That's not the comfort you think it is," laughed Syaoran. "Unless he picks someone whose lands border his, it's a difficult balance. Maybe impossible. And choosing a neighbor may lead to a hoarding of power."

Kwan turned his head to his friend then. "I have no heirs. What should happen to Inori?"

Syaoran quirked a brow. "It'd go to your younger brother."

"If he fell with me?"

"I don't know," said Syaoran. "To Beom, probably."

"And if I chose Hisa as my heir?"

Syaoran snickered. "You jest. You'll long outlive her, my lord."

"There were times I almost didn't make it back," admitted Kwan.

Syaoran stopped, smile fading as he considered.

"Do you think she'd be capable?"

Realizing the question was serious, Syaoran fumbled. "I think she would try, my lord. It'd be easier if she had the support of even one of your brothers."

"Would she have your support?"

Syaoran blinked. "I don't think that matters. I have no title and no stake."

Kwan kept silent in his stoic stare.

Sighing, Syaoran answered. "I'd do my best."

Left alone in his room, an unease ebbed at Kwan. He'd spent much of his energy, but couldn't ignore the whisper of Seong's threat in his ear. His sight heightened, he looked through the mountain, to the village below, searching.

Where was she?

Between the slope of the forests, the fields stacked on one another, and the vastness between houses, he stretched his sight. When he found her, he frowned. Canvas and paints aside, her day of leisure was interrupted by an unexpected guest.

As she spoke with him, Yuz looked over his shoulder, likely feeling Kwan's spell.

Frowning, Kwan observed and resisted the urge to go down himself. Even if he'd the strength to confront his brother, he needed to trust Hisa. Trust that she'd stay steadfast as he did, and not waver under the threat or pressure of his older brother. If Yuz struck at her, however, he wasn't sure he could stay uninvolved. No. He was sure he couldn't.

Whatever the conversation, she kept herself composed and serious.

Chapter 91
Family Life

Nearer to the solstice, the weather warmed significantly, thickening the air. There wasn't much for idle time where I could paint. My days were occupied in foraging and tending the garden and ducks, or in weaving and sewing, and, of course, helping to train Statsu and Yuki. They'd make for fine hunting companions and protective friends.

More, a wedding was planned for a girl one year younger than myself to her beloved (a boy from a different village). I'd spent hours every evening working on something to give as a wedding gift. When a merchant had bolts of white fabric and a small collection of dyes, I had a plan. Not for courtly clothes, but for a beautiful blanket. I'd outlined what I wanted with thread, acting in place of a stencil, and took care so as not to smear the color once added.

With clear weather, I took full advantage to give the lengths of fabric their first rinse and rid them of excess dye. Setting them in the sun, I decided to work on my canvas while I waited for them to dry. It made for an excuse to let Koji run free.

I'd been engrossed in my art, and didn't notice someone approach until the last strides. After a moment, I recognized the man as Kwan's brother. Standing, I gave a polite bow and greeted, confused as I was.

"I'm told my foolhardy brother has engaged himself to you."

I looked up, blinking and not sure how to respond.

"You know the very idea is impossible."

This again. I dropped all politeness in my posture, standing straight with my feet firmly planted. "If the idea is impossible, why did you come to speak with me, my lord?"

He frowned. "Since Kwan is too hardheaded to understand the ramifications of the union, I assume you're sensible enough to comprehend."

It seemed a usual thing to try and talk over my head. So, I countered simply. "From what I understand, you, and Seong, and likely Beom—perhaps the whole family—dislike that I'm human, and that somehow makes me unworthy."

"Crudely put." He crossed his arms, a subtle display of his muscle beneath his clothing.

"So, you came here to try and put me in my place. You've wasted a journey. My place is by Kwan's side."

"Impudent girl," growled Yuz, baring a scowl.

"I love him," I said, a little louder to emphasis how I wouldn't crumble at his tone. "And if he wants me beside him, then that's where I will stay. I'd sworn repeatedly to only marry for love, and I've turned down other Juneun offers—even as everyone else told me I should accept. I will marry the man I love and stay with him all my days."

"That is precisely the problem." Yuz looked over his shoulder, as though something more interesting beckoned his gaze. "You are poor, of ill breeding, and short lived. Your presence will only bring hardship. And when you die, you will leave disorder in his house."

"Lord Genji didn't think so. And neither do I."

He looked at me, unamused. "You cannot weaponize Lord Genji's name with me, child."

"I don't plan to," I said, staying rooted. "Merely to show how a more powerful Juneun disagrees with your way of thinking. You can't threaten me with things like titles, or say that no one else would support our marrying."

"You know not the disorientation left in the wake of Genji's human wife—"

"Her name was Lady Isaden," I interrupted, for no other reason than to bully him back. "And she was like the wind."

He blinked at me, astonished at my boldness.

"Lord Genji and I are friends. He spoke to me about his late wife at length. There isn't much I don't know. And Kwan has a more manageable household that my own departure—"

"You are too presumptuous, girl."

"I suppose next you'll bring up Gumiho to try and scare me away," I countered. "But Kwan has already told me all of it."

He stared. A red color surfaced on his neck, and his breathing deepened.

"You're running out of things to threaten me with, Lord Yuz. I'm poor. I'm not pretty. I'm Human. And I'm better informed than you think about my friends and the man I love—the man I will marry."

"You would have him disowned by his family? For you?"

"From what I've seen, *family* is only a word to you," I snapped. "You treat each other with contempt. You may as well be soldiers—or strangers—clawing for power."

"Then you know nothing!" He stepped forward, looming over me.

Scared as I was, I wouldn't let my feet move, and silently commanded my body to ignore any desire to tremble. I couldn't let him see that I was frightened, even slightly.

"If you cannot understand the way of things as they are, then you do not understand the weight of what we've lost. My brother's ignorance nearly destroyed us once before, and he's set to repeat his past."

"You're wrong," I said, quieter than I intended. "Is that how you threaten him? Bringing up the past? Because, if that's all you can think of, maybe that's where you should live. But I've spent too much of my life already living in the past and wishing things were different. Not anymore. I don't have the luxury of a long life to waste in the past. So I will live in the present. And into the future, *with* my husband."

He leered at me, and I could tell he searched for something else to try and force my submission by the intensity of his brown-orange eyes.

"My brothers thought Kwan my jailor. Cold and callused. And they've accepted my decision. I'm more fortunate than him in that regard."

His expression slackened. Tension loose, he pulled away only just.

When he parted from me, I waited until he was out of sight before I collapsed and allowed myself to shake. Koji ran up, and I clung to my dog, my little protector, as I held off tears.

A year complete since I'd come home. Autumn seemed to want to come early, ridding the clouds from the sky and ushering in cooler nights. While there was an awkwardness to my coming to a wedding in the village, it morphed into a different kind at my gift. I stayed determined to show I had worth beyond rumors, and earn back my reputation. Something I could use to mend the reputation of my brother.

I wasn't sure how much good it did, except to bring curious looks and marvel at the thing. She'd packed it delicately, I heard, before leaving for the other village to begin her new life.

I wasn't naïve enough to think I'd get such a reception at my own wedding. But I preferred the idea of a smaller gathering. Perhaps held at Tetsuden, under the wisteria tree, like Kwan suggested. It did make for a pretty scene in my imagining.

After that event, Fumei braved coming over to see me, against her mother's wishes.

She'd brought over wild grapes, and we talked at length as we worked on some menial task in preparation for winter. All of it interrupted by a different visitor. Spotting him through the opened door, allowing a cross breeze, I went rigid. A rush of indignant anger coursed through me. I wouldn't be found cowering in my house, but meet my adversary head on. If I made myself go out to face him, maybe I could trick my body to think it shouldn't want to tremble or flee.

Stopping short, I made my polite greeting to Beom.

He stared a long while, looking past me to Fumei peeking out from the doorway and back in slow and controlled movements before speaking. "My brother Yuz is marrying this autumn."

I dipped my head in a slight bow. "Congratulations."

"Are you so naïve to think I came to bring this as news?"

I steeled myself. "I think you came to take your turn in trying to scare me out of my engagement."

His face grew colder, silver-green eyes boring into me. I kept still.

"You will end this absurd infatuation."

"I will not," I said, final.

He narrowed his gaze. "If you do not, I will—"

"Strike me?" I interrupted. "As you did before?"

From right behind me, a low growl. Koji was there, picking up on my mood.

"Mind your tongue, girl."

"I will mind my tongue as strictly as you mind your hand."

Beom breathed in deep, glancing over his shoulder and tempering himself. "You are a toy to him. And once you've aged beyond any usefulness or sport, you will be discarded for another. Whatever child you might produce will go untitled and ignored."

I couldn't stop my next set of words. "Speaking from experience?" He'd tried to get at me with tired tactics, things Kwan and I had already talked about and I knew weren't true coming from Beom. "At least your late brothers had the decency to acknowledge their children in their life. You're more brute than lord by compare."

His face became sever. In his offense, his hand went to his sword. "Speak of my late family again, and I will cut out your tongue."

Koji barked.

"Why am I such a threat?" I demanded, ignoring all else. "If I'm only temporary, why are all of you so worked up? Should I expect Kwang to visit next? Or another from Seong?"

"Because your association taints us!"

Koji lunged at Beom's roar, and I almost didn't catch him.

"You know nothing of Juneun society. Of what it is to act as a lord."

"Maybe I don't want to!" I snapped back, trembling. "It looks to me like a miserable kind of life in nice clothes, drowning in wine and hiding in castles!"

To my surprise, Fumei ran out, fearfully trying to pull me away for my own protection. But I wouldn't budge.

Beom scoffed at the sight, speaking low. "You'd have been better off with the toad."

"So would the woman who bore you a child," I said in equal volume. I knew I shouldn't have, but there was no stopping once my anger took control of me, anchoring me to finish the fight.

"I'm not afraid of you anymore, Beom. I know Kwan won't tolerate you striking me. I don't think Kwang would either. Nor would Lord Juro or Lord Genji or Prince Urekkato."

He raised a brow at how assuredly I named off prominent Juneun figures, appearing indignant. I wasn't so sure my list would actually come to my defense, but I held my bluff.

"While you were abusing servants, I was fortunate enough to earn friendships and make allies. Do you want these names on your list of enemies? I imagine it's already a long list, given your temper and lack of control."

"You speak too bold."

"Were I still a servant," I countered, soothing Koji (though he still growled). "Now I speak freely as your sister by law."

My self-proclaimed title did the trick. A final offense that stalled his words, forcing him to carefully choose his next action. Hand away from his sword, he vanished in a step, leaving a violent gust in his wake.

I'd done it. On my own, I'd stood against adversaries that five years ago would've had me whimpering on my knees. It solidified in me that I was no longer that scared girl dashing up the mountain in desperation. No longer Hisa of the little village. I could never be that girl again.

Now, I was Hisa of Inori.

Chapter 92
Lord Kwan XXV

At his brother's wedding, before the snows closed in, Kwan found dissatisfaction in the display. Not from hurt feelings, but the mask of it all. The pretense of romance when it was a measure of strategy, preying on the ignorance of Asuka's brother.

All I've heard is a transaction... It sounds hollow...

Regardless of how they viewed her, Hisa had more foresight and wisdom that most sitting at the banquet.

It'd been more than a year.

What he'd give to be home, beside her, watching the first snow of winter. He'd wanted to go to her, stopped only in the thought that his presence would seem to pressure her. Undoubtedly, his brothers made their visits to pressure her in the opposite. Was he wrong to stay away?

He'd sent down means of apology of it all. Now, he wondered if he should've given it in person, rather than a brief note to convey it.

In the night, he dreamed of her. Not of anything grand. He dreamed they were laying in the summer grass beneath the shade of a tree, and he listened to her laughter and watched how bright her dark-brown eyes became when she smiled. They played in his dream, rolling about, carefree, somehow ending up at Iori. The sun shining off the lake, lilies planted and in bloom, she'd playfully pinned him, and he let it. The touch of warm lips. Sweetness of breath.

He dreamt she straddled him, taking lead, and he smiled at her. As the dream became more carnal, more real, he woke.

Towa was on him.

Outraged, he threw her off. Her surprise caused her to grab him, yanking him with her. In their tumble, he wrestled her under control, now pinning her to the floor.

"What are you doing?" growled Kwan.

Towa chuckled. "You're lively."

Scoffing, he let go, getting up and fixing himself and his night robe. "I am pledged to another."

"The human?" asked Towa with obvious skepticism. She sat herself up, but made no effort to correct her appearance. "You're not serious about that."

Kwan said noting, glaring at her.

Amused, Towa rolled her eyes. "Leave it to you to pick the most unorthodox of partners. But I don't see why we can have one more night for old time's sake."

Kwan remained unchanged.

"You never refused before," said Towa, shrugging.

"I never had reason."

"Kwan. She's a novelty. Admit it."

He gave no reply.

"Don't think I don't know about your dealings with my brother. He's not head of the family yet, but he plays the game better than our father. I doubt I could entice Genji. If I did, all I'd need is a child from him and Tetsuden is as good as mine for my family. Predictably dull."

Kwan walked to his door, opening it, and saying nothing more.

The final day of celebration, his mother found him, disrupting his solitude. "You used to be such a happy child." She took a seat beside him, overlooking the courtyard.

Kwan kept still, giving no acknowledgement.

"What are you fighting with your brothers about now?"

He shifted his gaze to her, staying his head from moving.

She smiled, soft and comforting, gently stroking her hand through his hair. "Is it over a woman?"

To that, he turned his head to her, slight enough to give his attention.

"I was the one who suggested sending you to court Eumeh. You were always the romantic."

He leaned away from her touch. In response, she laid her hand on his.

"Is she worth this feud?"

Kwan tempered his tone before answering. "She is to me."

"She must be a beauty, having this affect on all my sons."

He tried to smile, repeating his answer.

"A Kurai girl? Or low born?"

"Human."

She paused. "A princess?"

"Penniless."

A long silence. "Does she make you happy?"

He turned his head to look at his mother, the eyes she'd passed on to him and the regal layers befitting her station. "I plan to marry her."

Her face became a question. "I'd strongly advise against it. But I know, once you're set, there's nothing I can say to change your mind."

He tried to read her expression for more meaning, the soft and sympathetic features of her porcelain skin keeping things unsaid.

"I won't say that I approve, or that I understand it. But I don't want to lose my son again, or see him so wounded."

Kwan blinked, taking in his mother's gentle tone.

"Your father is disciplining Beom after last night's scene. I know you don't understand—your father's never been one for long talks—but he lost you too that day. My suggesting you for Eumeh appealed to him over sending Yuz when I explained. Having a princess's dowry would bring a measure of security to his most audacious son."

"Power in place of protection," surmised Kwan.

His mother resumed her gentle play of his hair, keeping hold of his hand. "Before you were born, we'd lost two of your sisters. Then our two eldest sons. After Jiana, he became obsessed with trying to keep the rest of you safe the only way he knows how. And I want you to be happy, whatever path that might take."

Kwan looked away with a frown. "You excuse his behavior?"

"No," said his mother. "But I understand why. I am your mother. And I am also, still, Jia of Taiseigen." She placed her fingertips under his chin, coaxing him to look at her. It'd been some time since hearing his mother's maiden title, beckoning him to soften and return his attention. Jia slid her hand to cup Kwan's face. "Are you sure this woman will make you happy?"

Softly sighing, Kwan answered, a slight smile disrupting his stony expression. "I think she will try." He took his mother's hand, keeping the gentle touch where it lay.

"And you to her?"

"I will try."

Chapter 93
New Arrivals

Mid-autumn, and an arrival happened. The profit from selling the dress I'd taken to the city, Chiso's daughter, and her three-year-old son. She gave profuse apology at our confused faces, for the delay and for the circumstance of her arrival. It'd been timed to send her as the first snows fell. Too late to send her back in good conscience. Chiso had downplayed and embellished certain details woven in with the flattery.

It wasn't so much that a man harassed her. Rather, she'd been charmed by him, lain with him willingly, and became pregnant. But he wouldn't acknowledge his son, and had no intension of marrying her. He didn't mind, however, having her back in his bed when he passed through. She'd continued in the desperate hope of changing his mind. It'd been a strain on her family, dealing with the stigma that discouraged any new business.

She was my age, towing her toddler and vowing to work hard if we didn't send her away. Her son was growing, and it would be harder to conceal him. Being made to go back would expose her, and bring shame.

Had she come a month earlier, in fair weather, I still wouldn't have sent her away. There was a time, with Juro's aggressive advances, where I might've faced a similar position—that Fumei faced not long ago. It wasn't an exact match of situations, but what would that matter to an outside view?

When I assured her, she breathed her relief. Her son looked around, staring at nothing, with a finger high in his nose. She'd swatted it away, introducing herself as Osa, and her son as Osamu.

Right away, she wanted to get herself orientated and started on the job, to which I was thankful. It ridded the air of awkwardness. She didn't know how to do quite a bit. Skills that were commonplace in the villages seemed entirely lost on women in the city. Something I found odd, but patiently taught the best I could, giving encouragement. Osa had never woven sandals or blankets or straw coats before, nor did she know how to pickle any late harvest foraging. Things that were essential here but were commodities easily purchased in the city.

That in mind, I wouldn't return up the mountain until summer at the earliest.

My father had questions when he came home. Again, we argued, though I tried to temper myself so as not to put him into a state of ill health.

"I don't care what he sends to compensate," said my father, severe. "There's no price worth my daughter!"

"He's not trying to buy me from you," I argued, frustration taking its toll.

My father waved his hand, dismissive. "You will stay here. With your family. Where you belong. I don't care what he says. I don't care what he sends. I will not give my blessing."

Kenta spoke up for me first, true to his word, reminding father of my age and that I was not a stupid person. He stayed in control of his voice, using the same tone he would when he wanted to sound steadfast and respectable—the tone he used five years ago, promising to bring our brothers home.

After the initial shock, my father scolded him. Chastised him for taking my side and having no regard for his own appearances with rash action.

Anger grabbed hold of me. Not the kind that made me want to shout and fight, but made me hold still and level my voice. "With or without your blessing, I will marry Kwan."

He looked at me, astonished.

Unable to stop myself, wanting to take more away from any argument, I exposed the depth of truth. "I've already taken him into my bed. And I will go back up the mountain to take his offer of marriage come summer."

My brothers bore shocked expressions. Osa, not knowing what to do, kept out of sight during the spat. And my father said nothing the rest of that day and into the night.

He said nothing for a week.

We did speak again, as I went out to stock and store firewood with winter bearing down. He'd come to a similar idea, spending the morning after breakfast to chop wood. I'd stayed in to help clean up, and to start Osa on weaving, before venturing out.

"He..." began my father, catching me off guard. "Your Juneun. He treats you well?"

I nodded, brow bunched and unsure of where this conversation would lead.

"Makes you happy?"

Again, I nodded. "He does."

He fidgeted with the ax in his hand, keeping his eyes on the log he'd stood up to split. "The, uh... The girl. And her son."

My mind hurried with some lie to protect Osa's privacy. Something simple. "She's widowed."

He nodded, still unable to look at me and putting a lax hold on his ax. "She's... She works hard."

I put on a smile for him. "She's not used to this. But she wants a better life for her son."

"That's all any parent can do." He swung down his ax, splitting the log. Slow in his pace, he continued the work. "Try to make a better life for their child."

I knew what he was trying to tell me. Even without the exact words, I appreciated it. An ember of warmth sat in my heart.

"When you... You'll come back to visit?"

I nodded. "Yes."

"Good. Good, good." He tossed the small splits onto a pile, bringing up another log to go through the same motions. "You're my daughter. I, I wouldn't part with you for all the silver in the world. Let alone anyone who didn't make you happy. If you say this man is someone who will take care of my only daughter. Someone who will, who will make her happy. And that you love him..."

I dropped everything as I heard his voice beginning to break, and ran to embrace him. He hugged me back, holding tight as though I were a little girl again.

Winter progressed slowly, letting the snows silently blanket the ground early. Raeden and Hisato made a routine of checking traps in the forest, on the off chance that something stirred and got itself caught, often bringing Satsu with them. The growing pup complained, not nearly as fond of the snow as Koji was (who'd taken most mornings to destroy any neat patch before coming in to warm up by the cooking pit).

Osa made fine work of the fabrics I had, her skill surpassing mine. Kenta didn't mind playing with the baby to distract from temper tantrums. And a fondness began between Osa and Kenta. My father, on occasion, would also play with Osamu, and reminisce about when all of us were that age.

Clouds hung low against the mountain, graying the sky for days at a time. On one such morning, as I gathered tinder for the furnace, I felt the eerie sensation of being watched. Snowfall was sparce, and mist still lingered on the blankets of white. I didn't see her until she was only a few strides away. The doe. She approached with caution, sniffing at the air. This close, she seemed not quite there, though I saw her perfectly. She was soundless in her step, and the flakes actively drifted from her.

I held still, captivated.

Sniffing at me, her breath felt neither warm nor cool. I hardly noticed it at all. She lingered at my belly, moving up my torso to smell where Kwan's soul was tucked beneath my deel.

Her ears lifted, alert, at the echo of Raeden calling for me. I turned my head in response, looking back a second later to see she was gone, leaving no trace that she'd been there at all. With a sigh, I called back and hurried to restart the fire that brought warmth to the horses and the house.

Raeden stood at the entryway, Osamu in his arm. The toddler stared on, fingers in his mouth, at a man squatted down to pet Koji beside a stack of parcels.

"Gi?"

He turned with a bright smile, standing as he wished me a blessed birthday.

"What are you doing here?" I asked, returning his expression.

"Don't tell Lord Kwan, but I was supposed to bring this a lot earlier. Well, most of it."

"Why didn't you?" asked Raeden, thoughtless in tone.

I scolded him, giving a look of apology.

"There, um…" Gi shifted uncomfortably. "I'd already asked Syaoran to help me with a private errand."

I shook my head. "You don't have to explain—"

"What errand?" asked Raeden at the same time.

"I…" Gi became bashful in that moment. "I asked him to disguise me as a bird."

"That's a little weird," said Raeden.

I scolded my brother.

"It was for a selfish reason, Lady Hisa," said Gi, a tone of apology.

"It's fine," I said. "And you don't need to call me that."

"*Lady* Hisa?" echoed Raeden.

Gi gave a puzzled look. "Syaoran said I ought to, since—"

"Don't listen to Syaoran," I barked, not meaning to. "He knows I don't like it."

Gi insisted on carrying in his delivery. Part of me knew he was acting as he would for Kwan, but another part of me suspected he was curious to see my childhood home.

Kwan sent a new deel for the winter, and boots to match it. A warmer dress colored in earthen green and deep blues, heavy and decorated with butterflies while brown fur lined the hems. He'd sent a pair of slippers for summer, likely worrying I'd run through my others with how demanding I was of them.

A letter accompanied the gifts. An apology for the behavior of his brothers, closing with his understanding if I was dissuaded from accepting his proposal.

…Mine has never been an easy family. If a quieter life suits you more, or you perhaps dread the politics or further harassment, I would not hold it against you.

I will wait for you, Hisa, whatever your answer may be…

How I wished I could send a note back, assuring him that I would return soon. That I missed him. And to thank him for the thoughtfulness. I wanted to do something for him in turn—make something for him. But I didn't have his measurements.

Osa paused in sewing up a shirt for Hisato, and watched Gi with fascination. A thought came in that moment. Stalling, I asked Gi to stay for tea, so I can write up a response to send with him—something to assure Kwan I still had every intention of coming back in summer, that my brothers and father had started to warm to the idea and would give their blessing. After, sending Gi with my reply, I asked if he could bring me any record of Kwan's measurements. I wouldn't be done with it by the time I went back, but I'd at least get it started and work diligently on it through the rest of winter.

There were questions from Osa, of course. While she'd shied from the earlier argument with my father, there wasn't a clear mention of Kwan being a Juneun. Through the conversation, I noticed a quiet jealousy—something that, five years ago, I didn't think I'd ever witness from anyone about myself. Maybe it did seem unfair from her perspective. I was a village girl from a poor and remote area, lacking worldliness, wealth, connections, and beauty. Osa, opposite me, came from a place of culture and commerce, a family business that brought security in her position, and skin free of blemishes. Yet, the man she'd loved denied her a marriage, and left her with a child he wouldn't acknowledge. Now, she came to a remote community, away from family and comfort, watching as the man I loved sent things to ensure my own comfort as he patiently waited for me.

I worried the winter would now continue with tension, eased and growing when Fumei came with a heavy, honeyed bread and thick cream.

Before the sun got too low in the sky, I took a coin to the shrine at the base of the mountain. There, I prayed for my intended, that he would have a winter of ease, and that summer would come quickly so I could return.

Kyu had come to the shrine as well, steepling his hands for prayer but not giving a bronze coin in turn. I hardly recognized him with how long it'd been. "A few years back, Fumei said she won't accept a proposal unless you were married first."

I blinked, unsure what to say in return.

"I always liked her. And I still wanted to marry her, even after your brother forced—"

Before I realized, my hand struck him. And I didn't regret it. I wouldn't hear that lie repeated. His face turned from my slap, stunned and speechless. I tempered my tone, reining in my breath. "She made that promise in retaliation to the awful rumors that sprung up about me."

He stared at me, frowning and holding his cheek.

"And I won't let her be pressured into accepting anyone who scoffed at her promise. Or who believed any of those lies about me, and about Kenta."

I made to storm off, grabbed by Kyu. "So, you think you're better than us now? Nicer clothes and strange men coming to the village to see you, and everyone else is now beneath you?"

I glared. "I thought we were equals! Never once did I say I was better."

His expression morphed. Severe to quizzical.

I pulled away. "It's a good thing I stopped having a childhood crush on you."

"What?" asked Kyu, absent while his mind still reeled.

Refusing to entertain, I walked away.

"You were always jealous of her!" called Kyu.

Turning on my heel, I glowered.

"And I bet you were so smug when you tricked her into making that promise. You knew it'd mean she'd never get the kind of life you were so envious of."

"She's my friend!" I shouted back to argue. "And if this is the kind of person you are, I'm glad she made that promise. Fumei deserves better than someone so selfish."

"You're calling *me* selfish?" retorted Kyu.

Barking echoed, growing closer by the second. Koji, plowing through snow, came swift to my side, baring his teeth. How he slipped out of the house, I didn't know. Likely, he followed the sound of my raised voice, charging when he saw a stranger. Regardless, I was glad he came.

"All you've done in the only time you've talked to me is complain how Fumei doesn't want to marry you. What would be your excuse if she hadn't made me that promise and refused you anyway?"

He deepened his frown, looking between me and Koji in deciding what to do.

"I was away for years, and you didn't have the decency to simply say hello. That's about as snobby as many of the high lords."

"You made her take an impossible vow!"

I stood my ground. "Because you think no decent man would want me for a wife? Because I'm not pretty? Because I'm not exceptionally talented? Because of those lies that spread around? If you were stupid enough to believe things like that, then you're not decent yourself."

Koji growled, his hair on end. Even if he didn't understand why Kyu and I were yelling at each other, he'd grown from a playful pup to a loyal defender.

"And you *are* stupid for believing Fumei took an impossible vow." Again, I tried to rein in my voice to become civil, and waited for him to argue simply so I could interrupt. "I'm engaged to a Juneun. Someone with strong convictions and compassion. But now that I know exactly how you think of me, it's changed a lot about how I think of you."

I stomped off, not allowing a word to follow. The encounter solidified more just how much I'd changed in my time away. The old me would've shied, too meek to fight back, and probably cried that the boy I'd had a crush on for so long scolded me, or that he professed he didn't like me back—let alone both.

But I wasn't that Hisa anymore.

Chapter 94
Lord Kwan XXVI

Kwan didn't know whether to feel annoyed or happy when Syaoran returned with a letter from Hisa. He'd instructed that the delivery go unseen, as it had before. Undoubtedly, his servant's affection for Hisa stimulated a curiosity. Still, seeing she sent a reply filled him with pleasant, and dreaded, anticipation.

Summer... She'd made a definitive plan of return, adding relief that her family approved of him thus far. He'd fretted they'd hold anger—justifiably so. Engrossed in careful reexamination of the letter, making sure he understood it properly, Kwan missed Syaoran's asking of something, dismissing him to do as he liked.

It'd be half a year, and other things still needed his attention. In his wandering, he noted the neglect of some roads going into the more removed villages under his care. Sanitation in the southmost city also brought concerns, draining into the lower districts. He weighed whether he ought to intervene, or let the politics of the humans handle their own.

There was also the promise he'd made to Syaoran.

No news of Gumiho or Urekkato, though that didn't mean either were gone. If she was still out there, puppeteering the Cat prince, he'd need allies to protect his home.

Kwan frowned in remembering Zhen's implications. Though, he was running out of gambits, already regretting that one, but having nothing else to entice a proud Samjo. Given time, he could think of alternatives. For now, better to forge alliances until he was certain of things to come.

Promise me that you won't be so stupid and reckless.

He'd given his word on that. With or without a binding spell, she expected that much of him. And he wasn't sure he could keep it. If they were in danger, what constituted reckless? Would she think that in bargains struck from means of caution?

Any speaking of engagements wouldn't dissuade lower lords, insisting their daughter ought to become mistress if not a wife. Kwan supposed he could delay that sort of agreement—that if they'd not found a better prospect within a century... He wouldn't need to love or lay with any. And could call on their support meanwhile.

All I've heard is a transaction.

626

He inhaled deep, breathing out long and heavy. Again, Zhen's chide echoed in his thoughts. He was playing the same games as the other high lords, lost in his own self-righteousness. He wanted to protect his wife, his future with her, and began to understand how poorly equipped he was to do that.

In the week since receiving Hisa's letter, he'd drawn up several contracts in his lordly scheming. Staring at them now, he couldn't go through with any of them. Taking them in hand, Kwan let them burn into nothing within seconds.

He shifted his gaze outward, to the snowflakes performing a soundless dance as sunlight glinted off of them in their descent. The snow fell more frequently this year, deepening winter. Another thing to take into account for those under his domain.

He walked the veranda, mulling over decisions to come. At the shrine, he prayed; what that offered, remained to be seen. So often, it seemed like an empty gesture done out of habit rather than steadfast belief. The gods had been silent for centuries.

The afternoon dwindled. As Kwan wandered, lost in his thoughts, he realized it'd been too quiet of a day. Even with Hisa's absence, Syaoran would come up with some inquiry or report on some trivial matter.

Late into the morning, a curiosity crossed Kwan's mind. Finding Lin in the midst of preparation for spring duties, he noted the continued absence of the fox spirit.

"When did you last see Syaoran?"

"Syaoran?" echoed Lin, looking up from a spread of papers. "Not since... Yesterday morning? He was talking to Gi, I think."

Kwan blinked, slow and considering. "Gi took leave two days after the solstice for a private matter. He won't be back until the equinox."

In return, Lin gave a quizzical expression. Uno, beside her, looked between Kwan and Lin, sharing a similar puzzlement.

"Didn't Master Syaoran say he would be taking something to Lady Hisa again?"

"Not that I'm aware," said Lin. "He took down some measurements about a week ago because Hisa asked for them, but I think that was the last time."

Saying nothing more, Kwan walked on, thinking over the oddity with every controlled step. If Syaoran harbored a growing anxiety, Kwan couldn't fault him. For a time, Gumiho's supposed death lent a melancholy, only for a wrathful return to press harder and an unknown outcome still present. He wondered if he really could accomplish every pledge without playing the high lords' games.

The days following saw him revising propositions, only to discard them again. If he'd had more certainty on his adversary, the choices would become obvious. Likewise, he didn't want to risk a marriage of discontent in making rash decisions.

Uno announced herself, bringing tea that was not sent for. Meaning, some personal matter prompted the action.

"What is it you want?" asked Kwan, direct as she served the drink.

Uno flinched. "It's... Master Syaoran hasn't been himself these past two years, my lord. More so that Lady Hisa isn't here."

Kwan concealed an intrigue, though he hadn't noticed too much out of the ordinary with his friend. "Meaning?"

She shrank into herself, standing ready for a command. "I know I've only been here a short while, and it's not my place to question my superiors, my lord. I do understand my place. But when I first arrived, Master Syaoran seemed more relaxed and warm, kindly. It struck me as strange to see him become increasingly distant and nervous, my lord. I did bring up an instance to Lady Hisa, though she thought nothing of it, so I tried to ignore it as well."

Kwan watched her, measuring the weight of her words. Looking to the thread on his finger, he pondered. He'd known the closeness between Syaoran and Hisa, though not romantically; a change and distancing from his own love and intimacy with Hisa didn't appear likely. Perhaps it seemed like he'd forgotten his promise to the fox spirit. Or, that a guilt ran through Syaoran after agreeing to Urekkato's sight spell. Kwan hadn't pressed the matter on Syaoran—Hisa's own confession displayed a flood of regret.

Uno kept her feet still, fox ears flattening and eyes looking from him. The silence lasting longer than intended

Before he could give an answer, Syaoran announced himself. A wordlessness fell, allowing Uno to collect herself and Kwan to clear his thoughts before calling him in. Grim in his expression, the fox spirit held out a letter from Tetsuden. A letter with a black stamp.

"What was he doing that far south?" asked Kwan, a desperate demand in his tone.

The serf shook his head. "The summer before this past, he'd called up his arms. He didn't give a reason as to why then, my lord. All he'd said, on assembly, is that he was taking up the hunt for Gumiho."

"She took down his militant alone?" Kwan's realization brought a shock to his own understanding.

"Not alone, my lord," said the serf. "There was an account from a survivor that she still had a legion intact."

To that, Kwan frowned. Of course she'd hidden away part of her force. Gave life to illusions, allowing them to think their previous assault was enough. Heven's sake! He'd thought as much when positioning Urekkato to claim the credit. As he chastised himself, the memory of Gumiho pulling out Urekkato's soul, and the end of a conversation, returned to him.

He moved his gaze, dismissing the serf as the details anchored themselves in his mind, churning up questions. Walking, he thought on it. Why would he go after Gumiho? What prompted the chase? In pacing Genji's private apartment—half the size of the entirety of Kwan's own house—he searched for clues, something that beckoned further investigation.

All of it disrupted when Kwang burst into the room, panting. A letter with a black stamp in his hand. The brothers locked eyes, exchanging a silent understanding. He righted himself, wordlessly pleading to his elder brother.

Kwan kept perfectly still.

"Genji," stumbled Kwang. "Is he...?"

"He's alive," said Kwan. "His condition is delicate. A catatonic state. Young Lord Mireu has him in a slumber to help his recovery. The rest is in heaven's hands."

"There's nothing you can—"

Kwan shook his head in slow, precise movements. A part of him fearing his former master's soul might've fallen into Gumiho's claws. A debate went through his mind. Would it be dangerous to keep that possibility secret? In relaying what he knew, he chanced trusting his little brother with that knowledge. When questions followed, Kwan revealed his witnessing Urekkato, admitting his selfishness in withholding that until some certainty of Gumiho was known. Though, he said nothing of Hisa's confession, hoping to protect her involvement with the Cat prince.

"I still don't understand what spurred him to go after her," said Kwang, looking often to the doors that divided Genji's personal chamber from the rest of the apartment.

"I'd like to know that myself," said Kwan. Bothered, now to the point of needing answers, he dismissed the staff entirely from the floor, and searched with abandon.

"What are you doing?" asked Kwang, perplexed by the anxious change in his brother's action.

Kwan said nothing. In his silence, his brother followed suit, though at a more cautious pace.

He'd almost missed it, needing a second glance to recognize Hisa's handwriting. Kwan's heart sank. Unfolding the letter, a needle of pain went through him. A desperate plea from her, asking Genji to save him—begging secrecy. She was fond of Genji, and unwittingly sent him to his doom.

He read through it a second time, and a third, feeling the echo of her fear in each word. No. No more. He'd end it now. Letting the letter burn to nothing in his hand, he marched out.

"Where are you going?" asked Kwang, brow screwed as he tried to decipher his brother's severe expression.

"I'm hunting Gumiho. And putting an end to this."

"Alone?" protested Kwang.

Kwan stopped. He glanced to the scar on his hand, and the red thread tied on his finger. "No."

Kwang fell into wordlessness. Surprised by the answer.

"Send for Juro. Send for anyone who will willing take up arms."

"Didn't you say that's what she wanted—"

"At the peak of her power. I suspect she thinks I will rampage alone, bound to my oath."

"Then let me go with you!"

"No!" Kwan flashed a furious look. "Word will spread. Undoubtedly our brothers will want to take the hunt. Do not rob our mother and father of all their sons."

"Genji is my master now," argued Kwang. "I can't sit by and do nothing."

Kwan studied his brother. "This won't be like Borsi."

"Kwan," begged Kwang. "Let me avenge my friend. My masters. Not for glory, but for my own sake."

Kwan inhaled deep, choosing his next set of words. "You're not ready."

"To hell I'm not!" barked Kwang. "I won't send for anyone. Do it yourself." Wind churned with his every step, magic making to storm with him.

Kwan caught him by the shoulder. "It will take more than us to get to her. Urekkato is still her puppet." A stare down ensued. Relenting, he heaved a sigh. "We will both send for our vassals. And any friends we have. Give them direction and urgency. You and I will go ahead, to lay in wait, and see if it's enough to distract Gumiho."

Kwang blinked, taken aback by his brother's steadfast tone.

"Beom and Seong want to lead an assault. Let them. Genji's force might've taken her by surprise—enough to think this is a similar case. With luck, we can launch a successful ambush. Together."

Kwang nodded, newly certain of himself.

Chapter 95
Betrayal

Snow lingered into spring. Glittering ice clung to the ground, defying the turning of the season. I wasn't deterred, and kept to my planned schedule. To my relief, Fumei again braved coming to see me, and helped in explaining typical day-to-days of the season, despite the unusual cold.

Time wanted to slow the closer it came to summer. I found less to do, waiting until the new season to demonstrate all that remained, since I wasn't sure Fumei would come in my stead to help Osa. Not that I minded, since it meant working on what I planned to take up the mountain. When Gi returned with the measurements, I eagerly set out the fabrics and threads, thinking of where to start and what to make. Often, I tried to imagine Kwan looking a little surprised by it.

Gi teased, saying I could easily send for something. I ignored it. I didn't expect to sit around and let everything be done for me. As much as other girls in his house dreamed of plush comfort, I still enjoyed keeping busy; and there was always something new to try, to learn.

While I'd hoped my teaching would encourage one of my brothers to go to school, they kept hardheaded, saying it was impractical. Though part of me wondered if they feared such a drastic change after the chaos that fell in my absence.

I was older now, and wouldn't let fear decide my fate. I stayed determined to take charge of what I wanted rather than what everyone else expected, starting with love. Looking to the thread on my finger, I smiled. Several times, I worried I'd been too rough with it, and glad to see it remained whole. When I returned, I would tie my fate to Kwan's. Whether or not heaven intended for us to end up this way didn't matter. We chose to be together.

At times, I recited the spell on the puzzle box to myself. I'd been the one to open it and not suffer its retribution. He'd chosen me before he'd met me—or, that's what I sometimes imagined when looking at the box during restless nights. Though, now, I swore it looked a little different from how I'd found it those years ago. Perhaps the climate affected its aesthetic.

I hadn't a reason to open it, deciding to keep Kwan's soul in the pouch I'd sewn and have it on me at all times. Lest Satsu chew on the box, or Osamu play with it and lose it. Even if it was unlikely, the decision made me feel better.

Clouds hung in the sky, bidding winter's chill to stay. As I tended to my sewing, I still needed to stretch out my elbow now and again, feeling it grow stiff. Osa spoke about how raising a child was both easier and more difficult than anyone could prepare for. I'd been curious, thinking to ask rather than daydream or dread what may come. Though, we were interrupted with Uno's sudden arrival.

I heard her calling, and Koji barking. Fearing the worst, I dropped everything to go and catch the dog. To my surprise, however, Uno paused only a moment, patting Koji and hurrying to me, breathless.

"What's wrong?" I asked, a new fear growing in me.

Pale and panting, Uno gave me a pleading expression. "It's Lord Kwan."

My heart sank into my belly.

"He's holding off Gumiho. But he can't go much longer. He needs the puzzle box with his soul."

"Gumiho...?" I echoed, remembering how he last returned from battling the fox queen. Instinctively, my hand clasped over my chest where I kept his soul tucked away.

"He received word that Genji fought with her and was left for dead, and saddled Susa to go after her."

I felt all the warmth flee from me. Genji. I'd sent the letter begging his help. When Kwan returned, I thought nothing of it. He was a shy spirit, and Kwan had said himself that no one came to his aide.

"Kwan needs the puzzle box," repeated Uno.

I nodded my understanding, hurrying to fetch it without a second thought. "Where is he?"

"Far into Genji's lands, eastward," said Uno, following.

It took a matter of seconds for me to get the puzzle box, my head spinning with the news. "I'll saddle Saburo. His spell can take me right to where Kwan is—he'll always be able to find his mares. Kwan told me that years ago."

"I'll take it," said Uno. "I can use a little magic to stay safe."

I refused. "There's a spell on it. If you open it—"

"I won't," said Uno, urgent. "I'll take it to Kwan. I'm a much better rider. It'll be quick."

There was something that felt wrong in this, and I clung to the box. Shaking my head, I insisted. "Kwan entrusted this to me. And I'm to be his wife. I won't abandon him."

She sighed, looking from my eyes to the box. "Then let me come with you, Hisa. I can protect you. A little, at least."

I nodded, glad to have a loyal friend to brave the journey with me. As I saddled Saburo, hasty and needing expert hands to help, I'd forgotten to change out of my home-made clothing and into my riding attire. I didn't think about it, or let myself delay. I didn't need to look proper, and if my clothing snagged and tore in trying to save the man I loved, the I'd happily pay the price.

I went to mount up when Hisato caught my shoulder. "Hisa, what's all this about?"

"I have to go," I said in a hurry. "Kwan's in trouble." I did my best not to sound so distressed and worry my brother.

Even so, his face paled. "You can't go alone."

I opened my mouth to argue.

"If your Juneun is needs help, it's dangerous."

Breathing in, I tempered myself and chose my words carefully. "I'll be fine. Uno is coming with me. Her magic will help keep us hidden. I can handle it, I promise."

He hesitated.

"I *will* come back."

He let go, though I could see how much it pained him. As I mounted up, helping Uno, Hisato patted Saburo's neck. "You take care of her, horse lord. She's my only sister."

Saburo snorted, proud and assuring.

Secure in the saddle, I kicked off. "Find Susa and Kwan, Saburo," I whispered my command.

He moved smooth beneath me, picking up speed in a slow transition as he carried me off. Barking followed. Koji, like a bolt of lightning chased us.

"Go home Koji!" I scolded. "I'll be right back. Go home!"

Saburo picked up more speed, taking us into the forest. The waking greenery rushed by, a flurry of shadows pierced by light as Saburo galloped. Nausea churned in me, but I held fast and tried to ignore it.

We emerged between a town and a forest, both in ruin. Kwang lay against a broken tree, labored in breathing and in a dazed state. Without thought, I dismounted, ignoring Uno's call as I hurried to him. Likewise, I didn't heed Saburo's discomfort.

Shaking him, I tried to rouse Kwang, asking what happened. His eyes struggled to look at me, his voice hoarse and robbed of any complete words.

"There's nothing we can do right now," said Uno, placing a hand on my shoulder.

As much as it pained me, I knew she was right. But Kwang had always been the pleasant and obliging of Kwan's brothers. I couldn't just leave him. Without medicines or magic, what was there I could do?

Saburo snorted, and an idea sparked in me. Running to the stallion, I took his reins to make him meet my eye. "Go get help."

He nickered low in response.

"We'll be fine, but Lord Kwang needs to get out of here, and I can't tie him to the saddle—he'll fall. Find someone who can help and get them here."

Again, he nickered.

"As long as I can get to Kwan and give him back his soul, everything will be alright. Don't worry."

He stared, something of an understanding in his dark eyes.

"Now go—go!" I smacked his shoulder, urging him.

Without a whinny or neigh, he took off, free of carrying me. In turn, I made a silent prayer for him, and for Kwang. A promise that I'd do what I could to make things right.

"This way," said Uno, taking my arm. Her skin felt warm, though I was too distracted to realize the familiarity.

I clung to the puzzle box, and to the soul hidden under my clothes. Something didn't feel right. More than the desolation, something was wrong. In my fret to find Kwan, I ignored my souring gut, rationalizing that it was from Saburo's spell bringing us here. So, I ran to keep up, following Uno through the maze of embers and debris.

When we came to an opening, I saw Kwan and broke free to hurry to his side.

"Hisa! Run!"

I swore it was Kwan's voice, though the image of him was perfectly still until I touched it, revealing the illusion. Blinking, my mind took too long to comprehend.

"I'm sorry, Hisa," said Syaoran, snatching the puzzle box from me.

When I looked, Uno was no where in sight. Instead, it was something gruesome. A monstrous demon fox of deep red and black fur, easily the size of Kwan's house, standing in wait as several of her tails pinned Kwan, battered and bleeding, to the ground. Gumiho. Beside her was Urekkato, half bare and one of his eyes milky while the other pooled with red, a chain around his neck held taut in Gumiho's claw. Syaoran, with a sorry expression, went away from me, presenting the puzzle box to her.

"No," I breathed. A storm of questions and conclusions flooded me, freezing me in place.

"You're sure this time?" asked Gumiho, in full command. "I won't tolerate more games."

"I'm sure," said Syaoran in a desperate hurry. "I didn't know the last one was empty. But Kwan entrusted it with her, and she brought it here. I promise—please!"

I realized all too late what was happening. My feet picked up in a race to reclaim the box, forgetting. "You can't!"

"Stop her," said Gumiho, apathy in her tone.

Urekkato's chain fell away, and he carried out her order with a deep grimace. Holding me close, he prevented any further advance. "Hisa," whispered Urekkato. "Run. Get out of here. If you say you're running away, I might be able to let you go."

"What?" I said, stupefied as I looked at his pleading expression. It dawned on me then that this was against his will, more potent than whenever he'd made some magical command on me.

"She'll use you to hurt Kwan. You have to get away before she can think what to do."

Again, a torrent of conclusions rushed in my thoughts. Among them, I remembered the pouch hidden in my shirt. The pouch that held Kwan's soul. "I'm leaving. I won't intervene. I don't have anything to stop this." I spoke quickly, wiggling to get free.

The sound of wood crushed under immense force. I gleamed the sight of Gumiho breaking the box to splinters, displeasure sprawled on her face. As I tried to flee, my wrist was caught by Urekkato, muscles tense in futile resistance.

Gumiho held up a glowing fragment, looking from it to Syaoran to me.

Understanding, and ears flat in terrified submission, he rose and walked to me. "I'm sorry, Hisa." He felt around me, searching.

"You can't," I whispered back in a desperate plea, thrashing to prevent him from finding the soul. I could hear Kwan's pained groans, struggling against the weight of Gumiho. "You're good, Syaoran! You can't!"

"I don't have a choice," He growled, flinching at his own words. His hand fell over the pouch, causing a second of pause before he fished it out from beneath my shirt. Though I resisted, there wasn't much I could do. He left me, pouch in hand, with heavy steps.

Gumiho looked back to Kwan, reveling. "You entrusted a human? You're more foolish than I remember."

Kwan said nothing, leering at her.

"She must be important to you. Perhaps the first thing I'll make you do is hold perfectly still and watch me devour her, unblinking."

Syaoran stopped, ears pointed. "You promised you wouldn't hurt her if she came!"

Gumiho's attention turned, slow. "What's more important to you, kit? A human?" She lifted a massive paw, letting an image form. A young girl with ginger hair and fox ears, in deep slumber. "Or your sister?"

I could see the rigidness of Syaoran's posture, at war with himself, and whispering a last apology among curses.

Gumiho reached for Kwan's soul, and I struggled more to break away from Urekkato's hold.

"I can't let go," said Urekkato, hushed and in a panic.

Soul in hand, Gumiho let the other glowing fragment fuse with it.

"Let her go!" roared Kwan. "She has nothing to do with us. This is between you and me."

For a while, she said nothing. "I doubt that. You entrusted *her* with your soul." A cruel smile, like a snarl formed on her. "She's someone important to you. So, you can watch as I eat her, body and soul." Looking between us, a new thought shone in her eye. "Better yet, why don't you kill her and serve her to me?" She lifted her tails from him, and I watched with horror as he stood, taking up his sword.

"Hisa," whispered Urekkato. "You still have my essence. Use it."

While I didn't really know how to do that, always assuming luck acted on its own, I nodded, twisting and thrashing to slip from his grip.

"Gumiho," plead Syaoran. "My sister—you swore to release her if I brought you the soul."

The fox queen narrowed her eyes at him. "After I am sure. Lest you turn your sword immediately on me."

"Syaoran," called Kwan, pained in his voice as he walked towards me. "She won't return your sister. It's all she has to manipulate you for her own gain. Why would she let go of such a servant?"

Gumiho bark fierce over Kwan's reason. "Silence!"

Kwan's jaw locked shut.

Syaoran looked between us and Gumiho. A rage and a fear marring his every feature. "Where is Mui?"

Gumiho ignored him.

"Where is my sister?" demanded Syaoran, shaking. "Let me see her!"

Again, she ignored him, keeping her sights set on my flailing as Kwan approached with sword in hand. I didn't see when, but Syaoran drew up his own sword, making to charge for Gumiho and have his demand met. She shifted her watch, swatting him with force enough to send him crashing into the remains of a shop.

In that moment, I slipped from Urekkato's grip, a second before Kwan brought down his sword, and ran. I knew I couldn't outpace, but I bolted in primal fear. Aimed for the way I'd come from, threads of white pulled a support beam, causing the collapse to block my escape. My legs wouldn't stop, slipping halfway as I turned sharp. I rushed to another dilapidated building, fast searching for places I could squeeze into or use to create some barrier. Unable to slow, I collided with a plaster wall, panting as I turned. In horror, I screamed, racing away before the sword tip found me—sinking deep into the wall instead.

It was all for nothing when I found that my feet brought me back before Gumiho and with no where I could hide—not easily. Kwan came, steady in speed and brow pressed as he fought a futile battle with himself.

Barking.

Koji rushed to me. How he managed, I didn't know, I didn't care. Gumiho winced at the sound. Syaoran roused.

"Get rid of it," hissed Gumiho.

Urekkato, rigid, took up his blade to obey. As he sprinted in, Syaoran intercepted, calling for me to get away.

I was about to, when something Feng said echoed in my ear. Maybe it could work. When I'd said to fetch and pointed at Syaoran before, it didn't seem to matter what he had in his hand.

Taking hold of Koji's scruff, I redirected his attention. "Koji!" I pointed to the bead in Gumiho's claw.

Syaoran hates dogs.

Any time he complained about the stink of hounds, I felt secure that Gumiho wouldn't send another fox to sift it out.

"Fetch!"

With speed rivaling Kwan's, the dog took off. A show of alarm caused the fox queen to flinch and back up a pace. I didn't know how, though I didn't have the luxury of time to wonder. Kwan's sword came close, too close, to finding my flesh. I sucked in a sharp gasp and ran. Still, I dared to glance back, seeing Kojii navigate debris and avoid a devastating swat. The glint of steel reclaimed my attention, causing me to whirl in a desperate dodge.

The sound of Gumiho's yap brought me to a halt. Kwan dropped to his knees, plunging his blade into the ground. Looking over, Koji chased after the dropped soul, rolling quick towards a pile of rubble. I raced to it, fearing it'd be lost and back in her hands.

Growls. Koji snapped at Gumiho, trying to reclaim the soul. With a smack of her paw, he yelped and tumbled away. For a moment I hesitated, wanting to go to him, and needed to remind myself that it'd be useless if she took back the soul.

It bounced and detoured from its route. With luck, I scooped it up.

A screech like a finch, and the collision of metal, Kwan intercepted Gumiho's grab at me, the green of the blade reflecting the fires around us. In the same instance, my eyes caught Urekkato throwing Syaoran to the ground, bloodied but breathing.

"Hisa, run!" commanded Kwan. And I didn't need to hear it a second time.

The sound of battle behind me, I searched for an exit.

"Bring me the soul," shouted Gumiho.

In an instant, Urekkato caught me, wrestling my fingers for the soul with a grimace. "I'm sorry..."

Through luck, I slipped from his grip, turning on my heel to run. He grabbed my braid, yanking me back. I yelped, trying to stay on my feet. The sound of a heavy thud, and a pained howl from Kwan, I looked to see him knocked aside with Gumiho's clawed paw held high to slam onto him.

I called, a beg to stop, knowing there was nothing I could do.

Something flashed by me. Feng, swift as an arrow, wrapped around Gumiho's arm to bite down, hissing. In the same second, Urekkato released his grip to fend off a more immediate danger. Beom, already displaying a tiger pattern, crossed swords with the Cat prince.

In the moment of confusion, I stared and stumbled.

Kwang's voice caught me, urging me to flee and breaking my stupor. In a flash, he rushed by me. Gumiho tossed aside Feng with little effort, sending her flying to crash down. The youngest brother caught her, calling her name as he used his body to cushion their fall.

I didn't stay. As much as my feet wanted to take me to them, to make sure they were okay, to find Koji, I knew I had to get Kwan's soul out of the area—away from the fox queen. Taking the nearest rout, I looked for any direction that might lead me to safety.

Saburo whinnied, and I hurried to follow the sound. If I could get to him, ride out, everything would be fine. I didn't dare look back, unwilling to temp myself as I commanded my shaking legs to go faster. Catching sight of the stallion through a narrow break in the debris, I felt a moment of relief. I could make it!

That hope was quickly stolen. The ruined wood, unable to continue supporting the weight of the rubble, collapsed. Panicked, I looked to every direction, and paled when I turned around. Gumiho charged at me.

Cornered.

I don't know what possessed me, as I clutched Kwan's soul in my hands. Maybe the immediate memory of almost losing it to Urekkato, trying in vain to resist, or something else. Like a guilty child, I shoved his soul into my mouth, as though that might somehow prevent the theft.

Seeing my attempt, Gumiho slowed a single stride, bewildered. A second that spanned an eon allowed my eyes to catch other faces, battle worn, share the same confusion.

My folly didn't end there. The bead that was Kwan's soul rolled behind my tongue, forcing me to swallow it.

"Doesn't matter," said Gumiho with resigned apathy.

She sent a long claw to swipe on me. Shrieking, I flinched, raising up my arms. A burning heat surged through me, accompanied by a thundering roar. My muscles shook, my eyes opened. I was glowing, hot white crackling off me; a tiger, ethereal and opaque, took to my defense, white threads leading from it to my body, and to Kwan. Every part of me hurt. Sharp pain. Knives on every inch of me as the titan battle waged in rapid attacks and counters. I could feel my energy failing, my breath being stolen.

Not knowing what to do, afraid of what was happening, I dragged my feet to Kwan. He struggled to get up, limping to meet me, calling for me with a stark expression. I collapsed, caught in his arms, and begging for help as the pain surged again—lighting flaring from me. Kwan's eyes plead, and he placed a kiss on me, deep and open mouthed. I felt the soul rise, coaxed from me.

Darkness.

Chapter 96
Lord Kwan XXVII

Kwan paled, horrified as Gumiho's claw swiped down. He called for Hisa, blinded in the instant that his soul responded. It didn't put him at ease. Not in seeing Hisa in a new danger. A Juneun soul wasn't something a mortal body could contain. He struggled to stand, using *Bird Song* to carry his weight. He had to get to her. It was killing her—his soul, was killing her!

He caught her, acting desperately. Even in retrieving his soul, she fell limp, fast growing cold. Staring, he looked for any sign that she wasn't...

Fury churned in his gut, a scowl consuming his face. Kwan turned to Gumiho, the tiger dissipating and leaving her in a pant.

"How far you've fallen," mocked Gumiho. "All this, and for what? A human?"

He laid Hisa down, gentle, a silent promise.

"This was your champion?" continued Gumiho. "And you gave her your heart. How precious."

Kwan stood, wordless, taking *Bird Song* back in hand, and walked towards her. He ignored the battle between his brothers and Urekkato, keeping his sight fixed on his own enemy. The one who threatened the life of the woman he loved.

"Did you swear yourself to her as well? The same as you did to me?" a cold laugh left her gleaming teeth.

Now whole, his injuries mended effortlessly. His muscles thickened, tensed, and his pace picked up.

Gumiho growled, bluffing confidence.

Kwan charged, sword singing a sharp war cry as it cut the air. Leaping with abandon, he deflected her swipe, assuming his primal form to match her ferocity—claw for claw. He pressed his weight, meeting her every counter. A scratch to his face. A bite to her arm. Teeth to his cheek. Paw crushing down on her neck.

She slipped from him, reverting to her feminine form to better maneuver past his larger body. He matched her, steel against steel.

"You're awfully worked up over a mortal," taunted Gumiho. "A lover? Even by your standards, it's ridiculous."

Kwan said nothing, grounding his measure. A singular goal.

She vanished in a shadow, forcing him to pause and search her out. And ambush from behind, stopped by Seong's blade. Glancing, Kwan caught sight of Yuz carrying Hisa to safety, Kwang with Feng.

Outraged, Gumiho gave ground, creating distance and casting a spell to send spears of ice flying. Kwan swung a wide arc with *Bird Song*, shattering the creations as its metal sang out. A second glance, fretting over the safety of his family, he noted his father's presence, carrying off an unconscious Beom as he directed Juro, shouldering a limp Urekkato.

Calls, from one family member to the other, unintelligible to Kwan's ears.

A mist blanketed the area, bringing a sickly glow around the flames defiantly burning through it. Kwan stole Seong's attention, bidding he protect their family and the prince.

Seong didn't protest, heeding his brother's concern. "The Sho and Samjos have her legion held off."

"Keep Syaoran and Hisa safe," said Kwan, steadfast and final as he raised his sword.

Seong squared his jaw, relenting soon after. "I'll look after them."

With that, Kwan dashed into the haze.

Quiet.

The sound of his breath and the war drum of his heart breaking the stillness.

Fox fire sprang forth. He shielded with a spell, holding his hand in a steady gesture. Renewed silence. Assassin's needles flew at him, deflected by the swing of his blade. Noiselessness followed. Kwan centered himself, blade straight, ready.

She charged, again in her fox form. He countered with a spell of lightning. An illusion. Swift, he held *Bird Song* to parry behind him. The scratch of steel echoed.

"You loved me too," said Gumiho, frustrated and falling back into the mists. "And you didn't fight for me."

"I loved who I thought you were," said Kwan, collected. His eyes peered through the wisps of water, seeking out shadows.

"It was always going to be this way..." said Gumiho.

Kwan didn't answer.

"Fate brought us together. And gods drove us apart."

"Hatred drove us apart," said Kwan. "Yours. And mine."

Silence.

"Was there no part of you that could've loved me as I am?"

Kwan held up his sword, placing a palm to the back of it. "Was there no part of you?"

Quietude fell over. "Then there's truly nothing left of us. Only dreams and nightmares. Mist, and fury."

An echo of pain pricked at Kwan's heart. "Aera..." He said her name, the one he'd always known her by in times before hatred.

Black threads raced to tangle him, cut by *Bird Song*'s edge. She sprung from the haze, blade meeting blade, over and over. The bite of each sharp edge ringing in the desolate air. He caught only glimpses of her as they collided before falling back into shadow. Kwan bided time, his senses keen to distinguish her from illusions.

He left himself open, feigning a fault in his defense. Her blade found him; and his to her gut. His hand caught behind her neck, pulling her in for a kiss. The other released *Bird Song*, and pressed against her breast. In understanding his attempt, she thrashed, unable to break free from his strength.

At last, he pulled from her, and her soul followed in his breath. He snatched it and shoved himself away from her. *Bird Song* clattered to the ground. Gumiho stumbled, falling in a heap. In every detail, as the mists cleared, Kwan fixed his eye on her, prying her dagger from his side.

Bloodied, and her soul in hand, he walked to reclaim his sword. She scooted back, bleeding and fearful.

"Heel," commanded Kwan.

Gumiho stilled.

"My sister's soul," he picked up *Bird Song*, "return it."

"I already told you, twice," panted Gumiho.

Kwan looked down, standing over her. "You will tell me where Syaoran's sister is hidden."

Rigid and reluctant, her hand fished out a bead, glowing, from beneath her silk layers. At Kwan's gesture, it floated from Gumiho to his palm. He placed it carefully into his own layers, holding fast to Gumiho's soul.

"In the Hyeon Mountains. Under the Crane Stone. If you can open it," said Gumiho, giving a cruel smirk. A gambit. Something to bargain with.

"Urekkato's soul," said Kwan, ignoring her bluff, "return it."

Again, her resistance and sneering did nothing. Like before, she reached beneath her silks and produced the Cat prince's soul. Repeating his own gesture, Kwan tucked it safely into his shirt.

"I suppose your next demand is that I grovel," said Gumiho. "That I serve you as pay—"

Kwan cut the side of her neck, letting blood flow freely in rivers.

"The soul is useless to you if I die," barked Gumiho in a hurry, eyes pleading.

Kwan watched, stony. "Useless?" He held it up. "It will tell me you are dead."

Her expression faltered, the finality of it setting it. "Kwan... I love you..."

He said nothing.

Slow, she fell unconscious. The bead in his hand, like the end of a candle, began to fade soon after. Unhurried.

Chapter 97
No More Tears

I love you, Hisa...

Whispered to me in the nothingness. That's what I heard. I knew the voice from somewhere. Somewhere between promises and dreams.

Hisa...

Kwan... That's who. I remembered. But felt so tired, so weak. So cold...

I'm here, Hisa.

A warmth graced my face.

I'm here. Always here... Hisa...

I felt myself being called back. To where, or from what, I didn't know. The light touch of lips on mine, like a butterfly's kiss.

Sunlight danced on my skin. A breeze brought the scent of jasmine and peach blossoms. Melodies of birds, soft and distant, broke the silence. My eyes batted against the brightness, and the shadows of leaves as they swayed. A room. Familiar, yet I couldn't place it. Plush blankets over me, I lay on a soft bed. All of it somehow familiar.

It was my room. Kwan's room—our room. While I ached in my movements, I made my head turn to look around and orientate myself.

Long, black hair, draped over the still features of the man I loved. His face lain down, he'd fallen asleep at my side.

"Kwan," I whispered, and hardly that. I wanted to call out, to reach and pull him in.

His eyes were slow to open, and I repeated my quiet voice. He looked at me then, as if not believing I was awake. I smiled at him, the best I could. To my surprise, he smiled back, bright.

"Hisa," said Kwan, breathing out elation.

In that moment, he was someone unfamiliar to me. I'd never seen him so expressive.

"Thank the heavens. Hisa, you're awake."

Blinking, my worn mind tried to understand what I was seeing, hearing. "Kwan?"

"I'm here, Hisa." He took my hand, skin warm. "I thought I'd lost you."

It was all strange, taking me a while to piece things together.

"Gumiho is gone," said Kwan, firming his hold for reassurance. "For good this time."

"The soul…"

"I have it," said Kwan, keeping a gentle smile and pressed brow. "I owe its safekeeping, and its return, to you."

I began a new smile, remembering then and pausing. "Urekkato. He was—" I made to get up, stopped by a surge of pain.

Kwan supported my effort, expending some of his magic to ease my hurting body. "His soul is returned." He met my eye, seeing if I understood or believed him. "I'm sorry." He turned, reaching to bring me a cup of water.

I drank with a great thirst, giving my mind time to catch up. "I thought. You said he never—" again, he took my hands in his. That alien warmth soothing me.

"I didn't want you to blame yourself for his arrogance. I kept it from you, hoping to protect you. For that, I am sorry, Hisa."

"So," I stuttered. "H-he's not…?"

"He's not dead," assured Kwan. "He's recovering, like you. His eyes might never be as they were before, but he will live."

"Beom was there," I said, remembering more of the battle. "And Kwang—"

"My brothers are safe and well," cooed Kwan, easing my anxiousness. "As are Koji and Saburo."

I breathed my relief. "Feng?"

"She's at Bitgaram, hosted by Kwang."

I blinked.

"They've grown a closeness. After he protected her, she felt compelled to repay his actions and care for him in his recovery."

To that, I smiled.

"Syaoran and Uno are safe as well," said Kwan. "I left your side only once, to bring his sister here."

"Then, she's alright too?"

He nodded.

"I'm glad."

"You mustn't blame Syaoran's—"

I shook my head. "I ran up the mountain to beg my brother's life. I couldn't blame Syaoran from any part of my heart. Or you."

Gentle, he took me into an embrace, whispering my name. For a long while, we stayed that way, allowing me to revel in his scent, his heartbeat, the strength of his arms, everything that assured me this was the man I loved. This was Kwan. In my joy, tears fell from me.

"I thought I'd lost you," said Kwan.

I shook my head against his chest. "Never."

When he parted from our hug, his thumb wiped away the free rolling drops. "Hisa."

I looked up to meet his eyes. Eyes that now held so much light and expression.

"Will you marry me?"

My smile beamed as I nodded, unable to stop from crying. "Yes. Of course I will."

His fingers softly cleaned up my face. "No more tears."

"No," I started to repeat. "Except happy ones."

He placed a kiss to my forehead. I pulled him down to my lips.

Milton Keynes UK
Ingram Content Group UK Ltd.
UKHW051226050524
442175UK00007B/312